W9-DDJ-411

THE ANNOTATED

AMERICAN GODS

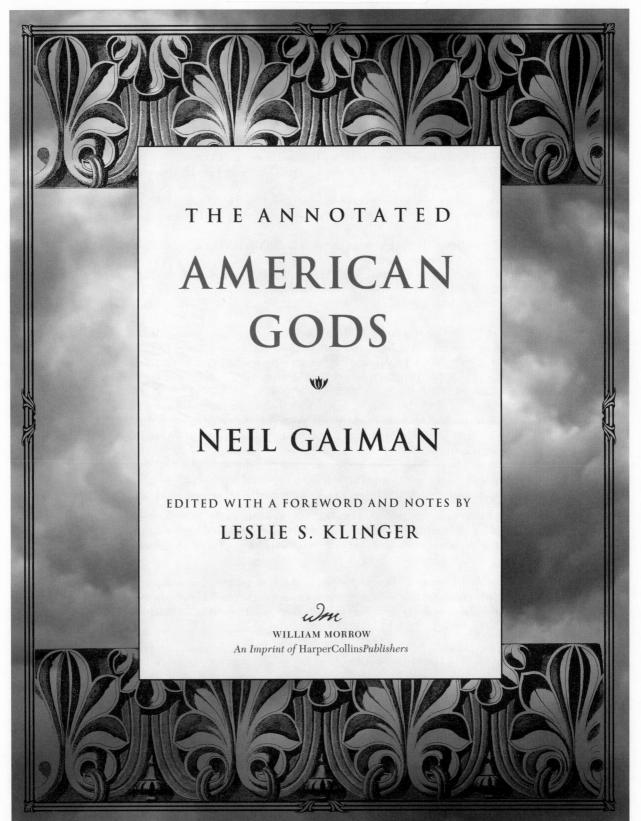

THE ANNOTATED

AMERICAN GODS

NEIL GAIMAN

EDITED WITH A FOREWORD AND NOTES BY

LESLIE S. KLINGER

WILLIAM MORROW

An Imprint of HarperCollinsPublishers

FIRST EDITION

Designed by Fritz Metsch

Frontispiece: Nineteenth century wood engraving by Kretzchman of the painting by William von Kaulbach. @Copyright Charles Walker/TopFoto/The Image Works

Library of Congress Cataloging-in-Publication Data has been applied for.

ISBN 978-0-06-289626-1

19 20 21 22 23   IMG   10 9 8 7 6 5 4 3 2 1

FOR THOSE WHO SEEK THE GODS—

past, present, and future

CONTENTS

AMERICAN GODS:
An Annotated Introduction°

WHEN I FINISHED writing *American Gods*, in early 2001, I gave the manuscript to my then-wife, Mary. She read it, and then told me that she wished that there had been footnotes all the way through, explaining who the various gods and suchlike were. The manuscript, she explained, was written as if she ought to know who these people were, and she didn't.[1]

When I first started dating my current wife, Amanda,[2] in 2009, she read *American Gods*, and told me on finishing that she wished she had known what I was alluding to and referring to in the book. She added that she didn't like the book because it made her feel stupid.[3]

This book, then, is for both of them, and for anyone like them, people who read *American Gods* and dreamed of a version with useful footnotes.[4] It's also for people like me, who just love annotated books.[5]

1. Mary Therese Gaiman (b. 24 September 1956). She asked if I had any books that could help her. I found an Encyclopedia of Gods and told her who to look up whenever she got stuck, and she enjoyed herself a lot more.

2. Amanda MacKinnon Gaiman Palmer (b. 30 April 1976). American singer-songwriter and author. She likes *The Ocean at the End of the Lane*, because it is filled with feelings. She thinks *American Gods* would be better if it had more feelings in it. I tell her they are there, just a long way below the permafrost surface.

3. She is not stupid.

° The notes to this Introduction are solely the work of the author. All other notes are the work of the editor.

I've written elsewhere about Les Klinger (he is by profession a lawyer, and by inclination an annotator and editor. Lawyering pays better[6]), and how I met him (he discovered and adopted me at an annual dinner of the Sherlock Holmes group The Baker Street Irregulars[7]), and how he wound up annotating *Sandman*[8] (I said no for many years, and eventually, worried I was forgetting things, said yes).

When it was suggested that we should annotate *American Gods*, I had the voices of all the loved ones who have ever told me it was undoubtedly very clever, but they wished it was annotated, in my head, and I embraced the idea with enthusiasm. It exists to help those who need no help as well as those who would like a few pointers in the right direction, especially because the Starz TV series of *American Gods*[9] sends more and more people to the book every year.

I allowed Les access to the original handwritten manuscripts of *American Gods*. This is something no author should do until they are safely dead, because the awkwardness and embarrassment of false starts and wrong names that preceded the finished versions of the plot and the characters are meant to be known to nobody but me while I'm alive, and I have done my best to forget about them. Les has taken huge pleasure in telling you about them.

The most dangerous thing about allowing Les to annotate anything you have

4. Technically, of course, annotated books don't have footnotes. They have marginal notes. These are footnotes because it's what my word processing program knows how to do.

5. I think the first I ever encountered was Martin Gardner's *The Annotated Alice* (1960). I loved discovering that there were originals of the Victorian poems that Lewis Carroll was parodying, things I had not known I needed.

6. This statement is guesswork on my part, based on years of knowing authors, although not annotators, given Les is the only member of the clan I know, and lawyers. Perhaps there is somewhere out there who lawyers for love and who annotates for money, but I have not met this person yet.

7. The following year I was invested into the Baker Street Irregulars, under the honorific title of The Devil's Foot. I love the Baker Street Irregulars dinners, which take place in New York in January, although I have missed too many, as Amanda normally arranges things so we are somewhere warm, which New York isn't, in January.

8. A comic I wrote, published by DC Comics between 1988 and 1996, and revisited several times since, that tells the story of Morpheus, also known as Dream of the Endless. It's at this point a 3,000-page story, that makes the 500-odd pages of *American Gods* look like somebody clearing their throat.

9. Created by Bryan Fuller and Michael Green and starring Ricky Whittle and Ian

written is his tendency to show people the places where you had no idea what you were talking about. Fortunately he delights in these moments and uses them to explain to the reader why you might actually have known what you were talking about, after all. He did it for Sir Arthur Conan Doyle,[10] he did it for Bram Stoker[11] and H. P. Lovecraft,[12] and, may all the gods in this book bless him, he did it for me as well.

I hope you learn many interesting things about America[13] and about Gods. And, of course, about Shadow.[14]

NEIL GAIMAN[15]
June 2019

McShane as Shadow and Wednesday, Emily Browning as Laura and Pablo Schreiber as Mad Sweeney. It takes the story in this book, turns it upside down, shakes it, reconfigures it, and makes it many things, including funnier, more televisual and broader in scope.

10. Sir Arthur Ignatius Conan Doyle (22 May 1859—7 July 1930). Writer and creator of Sherlock Holmes. Les Klinger's *New Annotated* edition of which is in three volumes, two for the short stories and one for the novels. They are a complete delight.

11. Abraham "Bram" Stoker (8 November 1847—20 April 1912). Irish author, best known for his novel *Dracula*. I wrote the introduction to Les's *New Annotated Dracula*, published in 2008.

12. Howard Phillips Lovecraft (20 August 1890–15 March 1937). American writer of horror and weird fiction. I discovered while checking dates on this footnote that while the first Les Klinger *New Annotated H. P. Lovecraft* volume, introduced by Alan Moore, came out in 2014, the second, *Beyond Arkham*, was published in September 2019.

13. A real place, very similar to the fictional place of the same name in this book.

14. A character named after a 1988 song by Elvis Costello and David Was called "Shadow and Jimmy," recorded by Was Not Was on the album *What Up, Dog?*

15. Neil Richard Mackinnon Gaiman (b. 10 November 1960). British-born writer and storyteller. Still has most of his hair.

THE GRIFFIN AT TEMPLE BAR.
BY C. B. BIRCH, A.R.A.

FOREWORD

YTHS ARE THE stories we tell ourselves about the world. These stories explain why things are the way they are, how things happen, and, occasionally, how they got that way. Myths are usually tales about *gods*, beings with powers or attributes that are supernatural. The histories of the gods, their wars, feuds, rivalries, births, deaths, marriages, and love affairs, and especially their interactions with mortals, populate the myths of every land and culture and every epoch. Myths engage, entertain, and enlighten listeners in the same manner as poetry, drama, or even philosophy. Carl Jung suggested that primitive myth-tellers *became* the poets, dramatists, and philosophers of societies.

The Greek poet Xenophanes, writing between 570 and 475 B.C.E., cautioned: "But mortals think gods are begotten, and have the clothing, voice, and body of mortals. Now if cattle, horses, or lions had hands and were able to draw with their hands and perform works like men, horses like horses and cattle like cattle would draw the forms of gods, and make their bodies just like the body each of them had. Africans say their gods are snub-nosed and black, Thracians blue-eyed and red-haired."[16] Myths, therefore, are fundamentally stories about humans, or exaggerated aspects of being human.

What was true in Greece and other parts of the ancient world remains true today. Gods are everywhere, and their plasticity—or, to put it differently, our ability to shape them as needed—makes them immortal. Yet, as has often been

---

16. Fragments 31–33, *The Texts of Early Greek Philosophy.* Edited and translated by Daniel W. Graham. Cambridge: Cambridge University Press (2010), pp. 109–111.

observed, *religion*—the worship of divine beings—seems to be less and less relevant, as scientific research and exploration reveals more and more about the details of the physical and material world. "This method of looking at the world has achieved great results," notes Karen Armstrong, in *A History of God* (1993). "One of its consequences, however, is that we have . . . edited out the sense of the 'spiritual' or 'holy' which pervades the lives of people in more traditional societies at every level and which was once an essential component of our human experience of the world."[17]

Armstrong's comment may be true with respect to "traditional" societies and traditional religions. Contemporary societies, however, experience a different kind of spirituality. Sigmund Freud argued that a sense of the spiritual is inescapable. "I believe that a large portion of the mythological conception of the world which reaches far into the most modern religions, is nothing but psychology projected to the outer world."[18] The human psyche, Freud seems to suggest, naturally creates (or "projects," in his term) the spiritual, regardless of religion and regardless of tradition. While in pretechnological times, an experience of the numinous may have arisen from a child's birth or a falling star or a volcanic explosion, today such experiences may be the awe and wonder of probing the machinery of the human mind or the workings of an atom or a black hole. Similarly, gods that were embodiments of light or darkness, lightning or thunder, may now be creatures of commerce, communications, or travel. While the ideas that were the seeds of the gods may have changed, the process of *anthropomorphization* of ideas into gods is built into the wiring of the human brain and continues to function even in an apparently godless world.

✤   ✤   ✤

Neil Gaiman was born in Portchester, Hampshire, England, in 1960, his family of Polish and other East European Jewish origins. Raised in East Grinstead, Sussex, he was educated in Church of England schools. Although Gaiman didn't attend college, he read voraciously, including fantasy and science fiction, and in his early twenties began to work as a journalist. He wrote and reviewed extensively for the British Fantasy Society, did many interviews, and had a few short stories published. His first book, in 1984, was a biography of the band Duran Duran, followed by a collaboration with Kim Newman on *Ghastly Be-*

---

17. New York: Ballantine Books (2003), p. 4.

18. Freud, Sigmund. *The Basic Writings of Sigmund Freud.* New York: Modern Library (1938), p. 164.

yond Belief, a collection of science-fiction quotations. The latter exhibited what would become his trademark British humor, very much in the style of Douglas Adams's *Hitchhiker's Guide to the Universe*, for which Gaiman wrote a companion in the 1980s, published in 1988. He contributed essays, interviews, and reviews to a wide variety of British magazines and began to write his first novel, *Good Omens*, on which he collaborated with Terry Pratchett, which was eventually published in 1990. *Good Omens* is, like almost all of Gaiman's writing, deeply spiritual and mythic, a darkly comic tale of angels and demons.

Gaiman first came to prominence as a comic-book writer. In January 1989, he began what would turn out to be a seven-year-long series of 78 comics under the collective title of *The Sandman*. The comics recorded a whole new mythology and a fresh look at a dozen other mythologies. Gaiman imagined a race of beings who were *above* the gods in the hierarchy of power and longevity, whom he called the Endless. The Endless—a family of seven beings—were, in their own words, anthropomorphizations of ideas: Dream, Death, Destiny, Desire, Despair, Delirium (originally known as Delight), and Destruction. They were thousands of years old, *predating* the gods, inherent in the wiring of mortal beings and so, endless. Dream, also known as Morpheus or the Sandman, is the titular hero of the saga, still grappling with the business of existence.

Although the story told in the comics is, in its roughest sense, a very, very long tragedy about the closing years of Dream's life and the travails of ruling the realm of dreams, the comics encompass dozens of other stories and hundreds of characters, including gods, fairies, demons, and mortals. Unquestionably, the story is about stories themselves, the process of story-telling, the shaping of myths, and the making of dreams. Into the tapestry of these new myths, Gaiman wove shards of the mythologies of the Norse, Greece, Rome, the Native Americans, the Japanese, and the Bible.

Gaiman's fascination with myth is also apparent in his post-*Sandman* novels. His first solo effort, *Neverwhere* (1996) is the novelization of a teleplay Gaiman wrote for the BBC, about a world apart from the world, peopled with angels and monsters. *Stardust* (1999) is based on Victorian fairy tales and adventure stories, exploring a world that is literally just beyond the mortal realm, featuring witches and pirates and magical beings. Such themes are not limited to his adult fiction: *Coraline* (2002) is a ten-year-old's perspective on another world, a shadow of her own, while such delights as *Wolves in the Walls* (2003) and *Fortunately, The Milk* (2013) show unimagined depths to ordinary lives.

American Gods was Gaiman's first major novel. Awarded the Hugo, Nebula, Locus, SFX Magazine, and Bram Stoker Awards, all for Best Novel, in 2002, it spent many weeks on various bestseller lists in 2001 and 2002, debuting at #10 on the *New York Times* bestseller list, only to return to those lists on reissue in 2011 and again when the Starz limited series began broadcasting in 2017. Yet despite its epic sweep—the War of the Gods!!!—the novel began as a personal odyssey, an attempt by Gaiman to find some perspective on his new home. In 1995, Gaiman emigrated not only to America but to its very heartland—Menomonie, a small town in northern Wisconsin an hour from Minneapolis—to be near his wife Mary's family and to bring up their youngest child, Madeline, who was born shortly after the Gaimans arrived in Wisconsin. In the introduction to the Tenth Anniversary Edition, Gaiman explains: "America was this strange, huge place where I now found myself living that I knew I didn't understand. But I wanted to understand it. More than that, I wanted to describe it. . . . I wanted to write a book that included all the parts of America that obsessed and delighted me . . ."

And so *American Gods* is in no small part a book about America, seen through fresh eyes. Many writers, such as Alexis de Tocqueville, whose *Democracy in America* revealed to his European readers a society markedly different from their own, had recorded American travels before. None, however, had previously seen *beneath* the landscape to the land itself. Gaiman took his discoveries of America and made them an *Odyssey*, near-Homeric in substance. Shadow's journey is a Hero's Journey, in the phrase of Joseph Campbell. It is also a reimagining of Odin's own path to knowledge. This, however, is a distinctly American trip, filled with roadside attractions and steeped in local histories—a trip so compelling that some of Gaiman's fans took to the road themselves, seeking to retrace Shadow's travels.

Not only fans and critics appreciated the book: Academics embraced it as a work of philosophy, exploring the role of gods in society, or new mythmaking, pushing the bounds of our understanding of mythology.[19] Folklorist Lynn Gelfand observes, "The popularity of Gaiman's stories demonstrates that people hunger for myths in the same way that they hunger to make sense of their universe; the two impulses, in fact, go hand in hand."[20] Compare the words

19. See, for example, *Neil Gaiman and Philosophy: Gods Gone Wild!*, edited by Tracy L. Bealer, Rachel Luria, and Wayne Yuen (Chicago and LaSalle, IL: Open Court Publishing Company, 2012), especially pp. 1–58; *The Mythological Dimensions of Neil Gaiman*, edited by Anthony S. Burdge, Jessica Burke, and Kristine Larsen (Crawfordville, FL: Kitsune Books, 2012), especially pp. 94–124; and *Neil Gaiman in the 21st Century*, edited by Tara Prescott (Jefferson, NC: McFarland & Company, Inc., Publishers, 2015), especially pp. 9–28 and 39–64.

20. "The End of the World as We Know It: Neil Gaiman and the Future of Mythology," in *The Mythological Dimensions of Neil Gaiman*, p. 237.

of American poet Muriel Rukeyser: "The Universe is made of stories, not of atoms."[21] And so, while *American Gods* is full of stories—the stories Americans tell each other about the land, the places, and the people—it is also *about* stories and their power to shape the world.

Fundamentally, *American Gods* is a mystery, or perhaps a series of mysteries: Why are there gods among us? Why are the gods preparing for war? What is Wednesday's game? And who is Shadow Moon? Although answers are to be found in the pages that follow, like all good mysteries, the answers breed more questions—about Shadow, about gods, and about ourselves. All books are journeys, and this one is filled with surprises, shocks, awe, inspiration, vulgarity, violence, love, power, beliefs, and truths.

Now journey on . . .

LESLIE S. KLINGER
Malibu, January 2019

21. *The Speed of Darkness: Poems* (New York: Random House, 1968).

A NOTE ON THE TEXT

THE FOLLOWING IS based on the Author's Preferred Text of *American Gods*, published as the Tenth Anniversary Edition, with a few corrections approved by Gaiman for the Folio Society edition in 2016. Significant changes from the first edition of *American Gods*, published in 2001, are noted.[22] These were derived largely from a computer comparison of the two texts. In addition, with the permission of Neil Gaiman, the editor was given the opportunity to examine the notes and handwritten manuscripts that were the original drafts of the book, as well as a typed "first draft" that had extensive handwritten changes by Gaiman. Significant changes—though far from all—are noted.

Please be warned that in order to provide meaningful comments, some of the notes necessarily contain "spoilers" regarding plot developments. As with many of my other annotated editions, new readers are encouraged to first enjoy this magnificent work of art *without* reading the notes. Hopefully, the notes will provide extra enjoyment to the reader who already appreciates the book.

LESLIE S. KLINGER

22. In a private conversation with this editor, Gaiman pointed out that virtually every word or sentence noted below as not appearing in the First Edition was material cut by the editor of the First Edition to shorten the book, not new material written by Gaiman after the First Edition was published.

THE TEXT OF
AMERICAN
GODS

For absent friends

KATHY ACKER[23]

AND

ROGER ZELAZNY[24]

and all points between

23. Kathy Acker (1947–1997) was an experimentalist who wrote fiction, essays, and plays. Winner of the Pushcart Prize in 1979, Acker's work was part of the "punk" aesthetic and drew influences from Jean Genet, Alain Robbe-Grillet, and Gertrude Stein, as well as pornography, mysticism, and philosophy. She was a friend of Alan Moore, one of Gaiman's mentors, and Gaiman.

24. Roger Zelazny (1937–1995) was a major writer of science fiction and fantasy, best remembered for his *Chronicles of Amber* (consisting of ten novels and numerous short stories) as well as two highly regarded novels, the serialized . . . *And Call Me Conrad* (1965, later published in 1966 as *This Immortal*) and *Lord of Light* (1967). Zelazny's work incorporated a pantheon of mythologies juxtaposed with contemporary dialogue and often contemporary settings. *Lord of Light*, for example, imagines a Hindu pantheon come to life on an alien planet. He was nominated for dozens of literary awards, winning six Hugos and three Nebulas in his career. Zelazny and Gaiman were friends as well.

AN INTRODUCTION
TO THE TENTH ANNIVERSARY EDITION

I DON'T KNOW WHAT it's like to read this book. I only know what it was like to live the writing of it.

I moved to America in 1992. Something started, in the back of my head. There were unrelated ideas that I knew were important and yet seemed unconnected: two men meeting on a plane; the car on the ice; the significance of coin tricks; and more than anything, America: this strange, huge place where I now found myself living that I knew I didn't understand. But I wanted to understand it. More than that, I wanted to describe it.

And then, during a stopover in Iceland I stared at a tourist diorama of the travels of Leif Erickson, and it all came together. I wrote a letter to my agent and my editor that explained what the book would be. I wrote "American Gods" at the top of the letter, certain I could come up with a better title.

A couple of weeks later, my editor sent me a mock-up of the book cover. It showed a road, and a lightning strike, and, at the top, it said, "American Gods." It seemed to be the cover of the book I had planned to write.

I found it both off-putting and exhilarating to have the cover before the book. I put it up on the wall and looked at it, intimidated, all thoughts of ever finding another title gone forever. This was the book cover. This was the book.

Now I just had to write it.

I wrote the first chapter on a train journey from Chicago to San Diego. And I kept traveling, and I kept writing. I drove from Minneapolis to Florida by back roads, following routes I thought Shadow would take in the book. I wrote, and sometimes, when I was stuck, I hit the road. I ate pasties in the Upper Peninsula and hush puppies in Cairo. I did my best not to write about any place I had not been.

I wrote my book in many places—houses in Florida, and in a cabin on a Wisconsin lake, and in a hotel room in Las Vegas.

I would follow Shadow on his journey, and when I did not know what happened to Shadow I would write a Coming to America story, and by the time I got to the end of that I would know what Shadow was doing, and so would return to him. I wanted to write two thousand words a day, and if I wrote a thousand words a day I was happy.

I remember when it was all done in first draft telling Gene Wolfe, who is the wisest writer I know and has written more excellent novels than any man I've met,[25] that I thought I had now learned how to write a novel. Gene looked at me, and smiled kindly. "You never learn how to write a novel," he told me. "You only learn to write the novel you're on."

He was right. I'd learned to write the novel I was writing, and nothing more. Still, it was a fine, strange novel to have learned how to write. I was always aware of how very far short it fell of the beautiful, golden, gleaming, perfect book I had in my head, but even so, it made me happy.

I grew a beard and I did not cut my hair while I was writing this book, and many people thought I was a trifle odd (although not the Swedes, who approved and told me that a king of theirs had done something very similar, only not with a novel). I shaved the beard off at the end of the first draft, and disposed of the unfeasibly long hair shortly after that.

The second draft was mostly a process of excavation and clarification. Moments that needed to grow grew and moments that needed to be shorter were trimmed.

I wanted it to be a number of things. I wanted to write a book that was big and odd and meandering, and I did and it was. I wanted to write a book that included all the parts of America that obsessed and delighted me, which tended to be the bits that never showed up in the films and television shows.

I finished it, eventually, and I handed it in, taking a certain amount of comfort in the old saying that a novel can best be defined as a long piece of prose with something wrong with it, and I was fairly sure that I'd written one of those.

My editor was concerned that the book I had given to her was slightly too big and too meandering (she didn't mind it being too odd), and she wanted me to trim it, and I did. I suspect her instincts may have been right, for the book

---

25. Sadly, Wolfe, born in 1931, named a Grand Master by the Science Fiction Writers of America and best known for his *Book of the New Sun* series of highly literate fantasy, died in April 2019.

was certainly successful—it sold many copies, and it was fortunate enough to receive a number of awards, including the Nebula and the Hugo (for, primarily, SF), the Bram Stoker (for horror), and the Locus (for fantasy), demonstrating that it may have been a fairly odd novel and that even if it was popular nobody was quite certain which box it belonged in.

But that would be in the future: first the book needed to be published. The publishing process fascinated me and I chronicled it on the web, on a blog I started for that reason (but which has continued to this day). When it was published I went on a book-signing tour, across the U.S., then to the U.K., then to Canada, and finally home. The first book signing I did was in June 2001, at the Borders Books in the World Trade Center. A couple of days after I returned home, on September 11, 2001, neither that bookstore nor the World Trade Center existed.

The reception the book was given surprised me.

I was used to telling stories that people liked, or that they didn't read. I'd never written anything divisive before. But with this book, people either loved it, or they hated it. The ones who hated it, even if they liked my other books, *really* hated it. Some people complained that the book was not American enough; others that it was too American; that Shadow was unsympathetic; that I had failed to understand that the true religion of America was sports; and so on. All, undoubtedly, valid criticisms. But in the end, mostly, it found its people. I think it's fair to say that more people loved it, and continue to love it.

One day, I hope, I will go back to that story. Shadow is ten years older now, after all. So is America. And the Gods are waiting.

NEIL GAIMAN
September 2010

CAVEAT, AND WARNING
FOR TRAVELERS

THIS IS A work of fiction, not a guidebook. While the geography of the United States of America in this tale is not entirely imaginary—many of the landmarks in this book can be visited, paths can be followed, ways can be mapped—I have taken liberties. Fewer liberties than you might imagine, but liberties nonetheless.

Permission has neither been asked nor given for the use of real places in this story when they appear. I expect that the owners of Rock City or the House on the Rock, and the hunters who own the motel in the center of America, are as perplexed as anyone would be to find their properties in here.

I have obscured the location of several of the places in this book: the town of Lakeside, for example, and the farm with the ash tree an hour south of Blacksburg. You may look for them if you wish. You might even find them.

Furthermore, it goes without saying that all of the people, living, dead, and otherwise, in this story are fictional or used in a fictional context. Only the gods are real.

*One question that has always intrigued me is what
happens to demonic beings when immigrants move
from their homelands. Irish-Americans remember
the fairies, Norwegian-Americans the nisser, Greek-
Americans the vrykólakas, but only in relation to
events remembered in the Old Country. When I once
asked why such demons are not seen in America,
my informants giggled confusedly and said "They're
scared to pass the ocean, it's too far," pointing out that
Christ and the apostles never came to America.*

—RICHARD DORSON,

"A Theory for American Folklore,"
American Folklore and the Historian

(University of Chicago Press, 1971)[26]

26. Richard Dorson (1916–1982) was the leading American folklorist of his day, as well as the author of 24 books on folklore. He served as director of the Folklore Institute at Indiana University at its founding in 1963, and in 1978 he became the first chair of the Folklore Department at IU. In a private conversation, Gaiman told this editor that Dorson's work—especially on "fake" folklore such as Paul Bunyan (see note 560, below)—was a major source for various aspects of *American Gods*.

PART ONE

SHADOWS

CHAPTER ONE

The boundaries of our country, sir? Why sir, onto the north we are bounded by the Aurora Borealis, on the east we are bounded by the rising sun, on the south we are bounded by the procession of the Equinoxes, and on the west by the Day of Judgement.

—THE AMERICAN, *Joe Miller's Jest Book*[27]

HADOW HAD DONE three years in prison. He was big enough, and looked don't-fuck-with-me enough that his biggest problem was killing time. So he kept himself in shape, and taught himself coin tricks, and thought a lot about how much he loved his wife.

The best thing—in Shadow's opinion, perhaps the only good thing—about being in prison was a feeling of relief.[28] The feeling that he'd plunged as low as he could plunge and he'd hit bottom. He didn't worry that the man was going to get him, because the man had got him. He did not awake in prison with a feeling of dread;[29] he was no longer scared of what tomorrow might bring, because yesterday had brought it.

It did not matter, Shadow decided, if you had done what you had been convicted of or not. In his experience everyone he met in prison was aggrieved about something: there was always something the authorities had got wrong,

27. "A Kentuckian was once asked what he considered the boundaries of the United States." Anecdote #394, *The American Joe Miller: A Collection of Yankee Wit and Humour.* Compiled by Robert Kempt (London: Adams and Francis, 1865).

28. *American Gods*, Notebook 1, is a first draft of the book (referred to here as the "Manuscript"). It begins: "The best thing, and I mean the *very* best thing, and it's pretty much the only good thing, about being in prison is the feeling of relief—that one has plunged as low as anyone can plunge, hit bottom, and that you're not worrying that the man is going to get you, because the man done got you, while all those feelings of nameless dread simply evaporate: you aren't scared of what tomorrow will bring, because it brought it." In the Manuscript, the entire first chapter is written in the first person; Gaiman abandoned this in later drafts for a third-person point of view.

29. The first half of this sentence does not appear in the First Edition.

30. Low Key's true identity does not occur to Shadow for some time. See text accompanying note 713, below.

31. The balance of this paragraph does not appear in the First Edition.

32. What state is this? Shadow is apparently in a state prison, rather than a federal penitentiary. The Starz version of *American Gods* clearly places Shadow in the Oklahoma State Penitentiary, probably the maximum security prison in McAlester, Oklahoma.

In 1972, the U.S. Supreme Court found the death penalty to be unconstitutional and suspended all executions. No hangings were conducted in any state until the death penalty was restored in 1976. Only three hangings have been conducted in any state since then, and none since 1996. At present, Washington and Delaware provide for the possibility of execution by hanging. The last *public* hanging was in 1936, in Kentucky; the execution of Rainey Bethea brought a crowd of over 20,000 people.

something they said you did when you didn't—or you didn't do quite like they said you did. What was important was that they had got you.

He had noticed it in the first few days, when everything, from the slang to the bad food, was new. Despite the misery and the utter skin-crawling horror of incarceration, he was breathing relief.

Shadow tried not to talk too much. Somewhere around the middle of year two he mentioned his theory to Low Key Lyesmith, his cellmate.[30]

Low Key, who was a grifter from Minnesota, smiled his scarred smile. "Yeah," he said. "That's true. It's even better when you've been sentenced to death. That's when you remember the jokes about the guys who kicked their boots off as the noose flipped around their necks, because their friends always told them they'd die with their boots on."

"Is that a joke?" asked Shadow.

"Damn right. Gallows humor. Best kind there is[31]—bang, the worst has happened. You get a few days for it to sink in, then you're riding the cart on your way to do the dance on nothing."

"When did they last hang a man in this state?" asked Shadow.[32]

The Oklahoma Department of Corrections
bus carrying Shadow away from prison
Photo copyright © 2018 Fremantle North America

The warden's office (note the Oklahoma-shaped
plaque on the wall)
Photo copyright © 2018 Fremantle North America

"How the hell should I know?" Lyesmith kept his orange-blond hair pretty much shaved. You could see the lines of his skull. "Tell you what, though. This country started going to hell when they stopped hanging folks. No gallows dirt. No gallows deals."[33]

Shadow shrugged. He could see nothing romantic in a death sentence.

If you didn't have a death sentence, he decided, then prison was, at best, only a temporary reprieve from life, for two reasons. First, life creeps back into prison. There are always places to go further down, even when you've been taken off the board; life goes on,[34] even if it's life under a microscope or life in a cage. And second, if you just hang in there, some day they're going to have to let you out.

In the beginning it was too far away for Shadow to focus on. Then it became a distant beam of hope, and he learned how to tell himself "this too shall pass" when the prison shit went down, as prison shit always did. One day the magic door would open and he'd walk through it. So he marked off the days on his *Songbirds of North America* calendar, which was the only calendar they sold in the prison commissary, and the sun went down and he didn't see it and the sun came up and he didn't see it. He practiced coin tricks from a book[35] he found in the wasteland of the prison library; and he worked out; and he made lists in his head of what he'd do when he got out of prison.

Shadow's lists got shorter and shorter. After two years he had it down to three things.

First, he was going to take a bath. A real, long, serious soak, in a tub with bubbles in it. Maybe read the paper, maybe not. Some days he thought one way, some days the other.

Second he was going to towel himself off, put on a robe. Maybe slippers. He liked the idea of slippers. If he smoked he would be smoking a pipe about now, but he didn't smoke. He would pick up his wife in his arms ("Puppy," she would squeal in mock horror and real delight, "what are you *doing*?"). He would carry her into the bedroom, and close the door. They'd call out for pizzas if they got hungry.

Third, after he and Laura had come out of the bedroom,

33. According to the *Poetic Edda*, a collection of Old Norse poems recorded in the *Codex Regius* in the 1270s C.E., Odin sacrificed himself by hanging on Yggdrasil, the "World-Tree," also known as "Odin's horse," and is known as the "gallows god." Gallows dirt or graveyard dirt was often an important ingredient in spells, for reasons unknown. While graveyard dirt was often consecrated soil, gallows dirt would be the soil associated with the unconsecrated, the criminal class. "Gallows deals" may refer to sacrifices such as Odin's.

34. In the First Edition, only the phrase "life goes on" appears; the rest of the sentence has been added.

35. Probably J. B. Bobo's classic *Modern Coin Magic* (Minneapolis: Carl W. Jones, 1952) or possibly the reissued "expanded and greatly enlarged" *New Modern Coin Magic* (Chicago: Magic, Inc., 1966).

36. Low Key does not appear in this scene in the Manuscript; rather, the entire conversation is with the Iceman, mentioned shortly.

37. Attributed to the Greek lawmaker Solon, in a conversation with Croesus, as recorded by Herodotus (1.32.12). Herodotus's *Histories*, recorded in 440 B.C.E., is regarded as the founding work of the history of Western civilizations. This statement is the judgment made by Solon when Croesus attempts to demonstrate to Solon that he is rich, powerful, and therefore the happiest of men. Solon's point is that chance or ill luck may strike a man at any time, and only at the end of his life can a summation be made. But, points out Elizabeth Swanstrom, in "Mr. Wednesday's Game of Chance," in *Neil Gaiman and Philosophy: Gods Gone Wild*, edited by Tracy L. Bealer, Rachel Luria, and Wayne Yuen (Chicago and LaSalle, Illinois: Open Court Publishing Co., 2012), p. 12, this is misdirection: In fact, Shadow is being manipulated.

38. Is the Iceman to be identified with the Norse god Ull, the god of winter, skiing, and archery? In the mythology of the *Poetic Edda* and the *Prose Edda*, also a thirteenth-century document, recorded by Snori Snurluson, Ull is one of the twelve major deities, which pantheon includes Odin and Thor.

39. The phrase "something meaningless" does not appear in the First Edition.

maybe a couple of days later, he was going to keep his head down and stay out of trouble for the rest of his life.

"And then you'll be happy?" asked Low Key Lyesmith.[36] That day they were working in the prison shop, assembling bird feeders, which was barely more interesting than stamping out license plates.

"Call no man happy," said Shadow, "until he is dead."[37]

"Herodotus," said Low Key. "Hey. You're learning."

"Who the fuck's Herodotus?" asked the Iceman, slotting together the sides of a bird feeder, and passing it to Shadow, who bolted and screwed it tight.

"Dead Greek," said Shadow.

"My last girlfriend was Greek," said the Iceman.[38] "The shit her family ate. You would not believe. Like rice wrapped in leaves. Shit like that."

The Iceman was the same size and shape as a Coke machine, with blue eyes and hair so blond it was almost white. He had beaten the crap out of some guy who had made the mistake of copping a feel off his girlfriend in the bar where she danced and the Iceman bounced. The guy's friends had called the police, who arrested the Iceman and ran a check on him, which revealed that the Iceman had walked from a work-release program eighteen months earlier.

"So what was I supposed to do?" asked the Iceman, aggrieved, when he had told Shadow the whole sad tale. "I'd told him she was my girlfriend. Was I supposed to let him disrespect me like that? Was I? I mean, he had his hands all over her."

Shadow had said something meaningless,[39] like "You tell 'em," and left it at that. One thing he had learned early, you do your own time in prison. You don't do anyone else's time for them.

Keep your head down. Do your own time.

Lyesmith had loaned Shadow a battered paperback copy of Herodotus's *Histories* several months earlier. "It's not boring. It's cool," he said, when Shadow protested that he didn't read books. "Read it first, then tell me it's cool."

Shadow had made a face, but he had started to read, and had found himself hooked against his will.

"Greeks," said the Iceman, with disgust. "And it ain't true what they say about them, neither. I tried giving it to my girlfriend in the ass, she almost clawed my eyes out."

Lyesmith was transferred one day, without warning. He left Shadow his copy of Herodotus with several actual coins hidden in the pages: two quarters, a penny, and a nickel.[40] Coins were contraband: you can sharpen the edges against a stone, slice open someone's face in a fight. Shadow didn't want a weapon; Shadow just wanted something to do with his hands.

Shadow was not superstitious. He did not believe in anything he could not see. Still, he could feel disaster hovering above the prison in those final weeks, just as he had felt it in the days before the robbery. There was a hollowness in the pit of his stomach, which he told himself was simply a fear of going back to the world on the outside. But he could not be sure. He was more paranoid than usual, and in prison usual is very, and is a survival skill. Shadow became more quiet, more shadowy, than ever. He found himself watching the body language of the guards, of the other inmates, searching for a clue to the bad thing that was going to happen, as he was certain that it would.

A month before he was due to be released. Shadow sat in a chilly office, facing a short man with a port-wine birthmark on his forehead.[41] They sat across a desk from each other; the man had Shadow's file open in front of him, and was holding a ballpoint pen. The end of the pen was badly chewed.

"You cold, Shadow?"

"Yes," said Shadow. "A little."

The man shrugged. "That's the system," he said. "Furnaces don't go on until December the first. Then they go off March the first. I don't make the rules." Social niceties done with,[42] he ran his forefinger down the sheet of paper stapled to the inside-left of the folder. "You're thirty-two years old?"[43]

"Yes, sir."

"You look younger."

"Clean living."

"Says here you've been a model inmate."

40. A nickel in the First Edition.

41. Ruddy birthmarks were usually taken as a sign of a werewolf.

42. The preceding phrase does not appear in the First Edition.

43. Shadow is 35 in the Manuscript.

44. This sentence does not appear in the First Edition.

45. So the prison is not in Indiana.

46. The Manuscript adds, "He's satisfied, as he should be, for I haven't had to lie to him yet, except for the thirty-five thing. And my name, of course."

47. In the Manuscript, included on the checklist is Shadow's address, which is 2209 Second Street, Haleyville. There is a Haleyville in Alabama, but there is no such address there.

"I learned my lesson, sir."

"Did you? Did you really?" He looked at Shadow intently, the birthmark on his forehead lowering. Shadow thought about telling the man some of his theories about prison, but he said nothing. He nodded, instead, and concentrated on appearing properly remorseful.

"Says here you've got a wife, Shadow."

"Her name's Laura."

"How's everything there?"

"Pretty good. She got kind of mad at me when I was arrested.[44] But she's come down to see me as much as she could—it's a long way to travel.[45] We write and I call her when I can."

"What does your wife do?"

"She's a travel agent. Sends people all over the world."

"How'd you meet her?"

Shadow could not decide why the man was asking. He considered telling him it was none of his business, then said, "She was my best buddy's wife's best friend. They set us up on a blind date. We hit it off."

"And you've got a job waiting for you?"

"Yessir. My buddy, Robbie, the one I just told you about, he owns the Muscle Farm, the place I used to train. He says my old job is waiting for me."

An eyebrow raised. "Really?"

"Says he figures I'll be a big draw. Bring back some old-timers, and pull in the tough crowd who want to be tougher."

The man seemed satisfied.[46] He chewed the end of his ballpoint pen, then turned over the sheet of paper.

"How do you feel about your offense?"

Shadow shrugged. "I was stupid," he said, and meant it.

The man with the birthmark sighed. He ticked off a number of items on a checklist.[47] Then he riffled through the papers in Shadow's file. "How're you getting home from here?" he asked. "Greyhound?"

"Flying home. It's good to have a wife who's a travel agent."

The man frowned, and the birthmark creased. "She sent you a ticket?"

"Didn't need to. Just sent me a confirmation number. Electronic ticket. All I have to do is turn up at the airport in a month and show 'em my ID, and I'm outta here."

The man nodded, scribbled one final note, then he closed the file and put down the ballpoint pen. Two pale hands rested on the gray desk like pink animals. He brought his hands close together, made a steeple of his forefingers, and stared at Shadow with watery hazel eyes.

"You're lucky," he said. "You have someone to go back to, you got a job waiting. You can put all this behind you. You got a second chance. Make the most of it."

The man did not offer to shake Shadow's hand as he rose to leave, nor did Shadow expect him to.

The last week was the worst. In some ways it was worse than the whole three years put together. Shadow wondered if it was the weather: oppressive, still and cold. It felt as if a storm was on the way, but the storm never came. He had the jitters and the heebie-jeebies, a feeling deep in his stomach that something was entirely wrong. In the exercise yard the wind gusted. Shadow imagined that he could smell snow on the air.

He called his wife collect. Shadow knew that the phone companies whacked a three-dollar surcharge on every call made from a prison phone. That's why operators are always real polite to people calling from prisons, Shadow had decided: they knew that he paid their wages.

"Something feels weird," he told Laura. That wasn't the first thing he said to her. The first thing was "I love you," because it's a good thing to say if you can mean it, and Shadow did.

"Hello," said Laura. "I love you too. What feels weird?"

"I don't know," he said. "Maybe the weather. It feels like if we could only get a storm, everything would be okay."

"It's nice here," she said. "The last of the leaves haven't quite fallen. If we don't get a storm, you'll be able to see them when you get home."

"Five days," said Shadow.

"A hundred and twenty hours, and then you come home," she said.

"Everything okay there? Nothing wrong?"

"Everything's fine. I'm seeing Robbie tonight. We're planning your surprise welcome-home party."

"Surprise party?"

"Of course. You don't know anything about it, do you?"

"Not a thing."

"That's my husband," she said. Shadow realized that he was smiling. He had been inside for three years, but she could still make him smile.

"Love you, babes," said Shadow.

"Love you, puppy," said Laura.

Shadow put down the phone.

When they got married Laura told Shadow that she wanted a puppy, but their landlord had pointed out they weren't allowed pets under the terms of their lease. "Hey," Shadow had said, "I'll be your puppy. What do you want me to do? Chew your slippers? Piss on the kitchen floor? Lick your nose? Sniff your crotch? I bet there's nothing a puppy can do I can't do!" And he picked her up as if she weighed nothing at all, and began to lick her nose while she giggled and shrieked, and then he carried her to the bed.

In the food hall Sam Fetisher sidled over to Shadow and smiled, showing his old teeth.[48] He sat down beside Shadow and began to eat his macaroni and cheese.

"We got to talk," said Sam Fetisher.

Sam Fetisher was one of the blackest men that Shadow had ever seen. He might have been sixty. He might have been eighty. Then again, Shadow had met thirty-year-old crack heads who looked older than Sam Fetisher.

"Mm?" said Shadow.

"Storm's on the way," said Sam.

"Feels like it," said Shadow. "Maybe it'll snow soon."

"Not that kind of storm. Bigger storms[49] than that coming. I tell you, boy, you're better off in here than out on the street when the big storm comes."

"Done my time," said Shadow. "Friday, I'm gone."

Sam Fetisher stared at Shadow. "Where you from?" he asked.

"Eagle Point. Indiana."[50]

---

48. "Fetishism" is the belief that objects have supernatural powers. As a religious system, Western historians relegated fetishism to an early stage of culture, said to be followed by polytheism and ultimately monotheism. Fetishism was observed in the eighteenth century in West African and later in Native American cultures and is an important part of voodoo, discussed later. In the Manuscript, the character's name was originally Boomer Sam, changed to Sam Fetisher.

49. The word is "storm" in the First Edition, and in fact several storms occur.

50. Eagle Point is a point of land on Webster Lake, in the northern part of Indiana, near Fort Wayne; it is about 130 miles from Chicago. It is an unincorporated community,

"You're a lying fuck," said Sam Fetisher. "I mean originally. Where are your folks from?"

"Chicago," said Shadow. His mother had lived in Chicago as a girl, and she had died there, half a lifetime ago.

"Like I said. Big storm coming. Keep your head down, Shadow-boy. It's like . . . what do they call those things continents ride around on? Some kind of plates?"

"Tectonic plates?"[51] Shadow hazarded.

"That's it. Tectonic plates. It's like when they go riding, when North America goes skidding into South America, you don't want to be in the middle. You dig me?"

"Not even a little."

One brown eye closed in a slow wink. "Hell, don't say I didn't warn you," said Sam Fetisher, and he spooned a trembling lump of orange Jell-O into his mouth.[52]

Shadow spent the night half-awake, drifting in and out of sleep, listening to his new cellmate grunt and snore in the bunk below him. Several cells away a man whined and howled and sobbed like an animal, and from time to time someone would scream at him to shut the fuck up. Shadow tried not to hear. He let the empty minutes wash over him, lonely and slow.

Two days to go. Forty-eight hours, starting with oatmeal and prison coffee and a guard named Wilson who tapped Shadow harder than he had to on the shoulder and said, "Shadow? This way."

Shadow checked his conscience. It was quiet, which did not, he had observed, in a prison, mean that he was not in deep shit. The two men walked more or less side by side, feet echoing on metal and concrete.

Shadow tasted fear in the back of his throat, bitter as old coffee. The bad thing was happening . . .

There was a voice in the back of his head whispering that they were going to slap another year onto his sentence, drop him into solitary, cut off his hands, cut off his head. He told himself he was being stupid, but his heart was pounding fit to burst out of his chest.

"I don't get you, Shadow," said Wilson, as they walked.

"What's not to get, sir?"

properly part of North Webster, Indiana. In the Manuscript, Shadow only says "Outside Chicago." Eagle Point is not identified until he is waiting to speak with the warden. In the typed first draft of the manuscript (the "First Draft"), the word "Indiana" does not appear. Instead, Shadow describes the town as located in "Northwest Illinois."

51. The lithosphere, the crust and upper mantle of a planet, is composed of "plates" of rock. Earth's lithosphere consists of seven or eight such plates, known as tectonic plates. The movement of these plates is caused by gravity, tidal forces, and mantle dynamics and results in earthquakes, tremors, and possibly even the shifting of continents and other landmasses.

52. In the First Edition, Shadow replies, "I won't."

"You. You're too fucking quiet. Too polite. You wait like the old guys, but you're what? Twenty-five? Twenty-eight?"

"Thirty-two, sir."

"And what are you? A spic? A gypsy?"

"Not that I know of, sir. Maybe."

"Maybe you got nigger blood in you. You got nigger blood in you, Shadow?"

"Could be, sir." Shadow stood tall and looked straight ahead, and concentrated on not allowing himself to be riled by this man.

"Yeah? Well, all I know is, you fucking spook me." Wilson had sandy blond hair and a sandy blond face and a sandy blond smile. "You leaving us soon?"

"Hope so, sir."

"You'll be back.[53] I can see it in your eyes. You're a fuckup, Shadow. Now, if I had my way, none of you assholes would ever get out. We'd drop you in the hole and forget you."

Oubliettes,[54] thought Shadow, and he said nothing. It was a survival thing: he didn't answer back, didn't say anything about job security for prison guards, debate the nature of repentance, rehabilitation, or rates of recidivism. He didn't say anything funny or clever, and, to be on the safe side, when he was talking to a prison official, whenever possible, he didn't say anything at all. Speak when you're spoken to. Do your own time. Get out. Get home. Have a long hot bath. Tell Laura you love her. Rebuild a life.

They walked through a couple of checkpoints. Wilson showed his ID each time. Up a set of stairs, and they were standing outside the prison warden's office. Shadow had never been there before, but he knew what it was.[55] It had the prison warden's name—G. Patterson—on the door in black letters, and beside the door, a miniature traffic light.

The top light burned red.

Wilson pressed a button below the traffic light.

They stood there in silence for a couple of minutes. Shadow tried to tell himself that everything was all right, that on Friday morning he'd be on the plane up to Eagle Point,[56] but he did not believe it himself.

53. This and the next paragraph do not appear in the First Edition.

54. A dungeon or cell accessible only through a hole in the ceiling. The first use of the term in English was in Sir Walter Scott's 1818 *Ivanhoe*. Of course, the guard is speaking figuratively: "The hole" was long in use as a term meaning solitary confinement (one source dates it to 1535), but by the late 1920s it meant simply "prison."

55. This sentence does not appear in the First Edition.

56. At this point in the Manuscript, "Haleyville" no longer is mentioned.

The red light went out and the green light went on, and Wilson opened the door. They went inside.

Shadow had seen the warden a handful of times in the last three years. Once he had been showing a politician around; Shadow had not recognized the man.[57] Once, during a lock-down, the warden had spoken to them in groups of a hundred, telling them that the prison was over-crowded, and that, since it would remain overcrowded, they had better get used to it. This was Shadow's first time up close to the man.

Up close, Patterson looked worse. His face was oblong, with gray hair cut into a military bristle cut. He smelled of Old Spice. Behind him was a shelf of books, each with the word *prison* in the title; his desk was perfectly clean, empty but for a telephone and a tear-off-the-pages *Far Side* calendar. He had a hearing aid in his right ear.

"Please, sit down."

Shadow sat down at the desk, noting the civility.[58]

Wilson stood behind him.

The warden opened a desk drawer and took out a file, placed it on his desk.

"Says here you were sentenced to six years for aggravated assault and battery. You've served three years. You were due to be released on Friday."

Were? Shadow felt his stomach lurch inside him. He wondered how much longer he was going to have to serve—another year? Two years? All three? All he said was "Yes, sir."

The warden licked his lips. "What did you say?"

"I said, 'Yes, sir.'"

"Shadow, we're going to be releasing you later this afternoon. You'll be getting out a couple of days early." The warden said this with no joy, as if he were intoning a death sentence.[59] Shadow nodded, and he waited for the other shoe to drop. The warden looked down at the paper on his desk. "This came from the Johnson Memorial Hospital[60] in Eagle Point . . . Your wife. She died in the early hours of this morning. It was an automobile accident. I'm sorry."

Shadow nodded once more.

Wilson walked him back to his cell, not saying anything.

57. The latter half of this sentence and the last sentence of this paragraph do not appear in the First Edition.

58. The phrase "noting the civility" does not appear in the First Edition.

59. This sentence does not appear in the First Edition.

60. This is a fictitious name; the real Johnson Memorial Hospital is south of Indianapolis.

He unlocked the cell door and let Shadow in. Then he said, "It's like one of them good-news, bad-news jokes, isn't it? Good news, we're letting you out early, bad news, your wife is dead." He laughed, as if it were genuinely funny.

Shadow said nothing at all.

✳ ✳ ✳

NUMBLY, HE PACKED up his possessions, gave several away. He left behind Low Key's Herodotus and the book of coin tricks, and, with a momentary pang, he abandoned the blank metal disks he had smuggled out of the workshop which had, until he had found Low Key's change in the book,[61] served him for coins. There would be coins, real coins, on the outside. He shaved. He dressed in civilian clothes. He walked through door after door, knowing that he would never walk back through them again, feeling empty inside.

The rain had started to gust from the gray sky, a freezing rain. Pellets of ice stung Shadow's face, while the rain soaked the thin overcoat as they walked away from the prison building, toward the yellow ex–school bus that would take them to the nearest city.[62]

By the time they got to the bus they were soaked. Eight of them were leaving, Shadow thought. Fifteen hundred still inside. He sat on the bus and shivered until the heaters started working, wondering what he was doing, where he was going now.

Ghost images filled his head, unbidden. In his imagination he was leaving another prison, long ago.

He had been imprisoned in a lightless garret room for far too long: his beard was wild and his hair was a tangle. The guards had walked him down a gray stone stairway and out into a plaza filled with brightly colored things, with people and with objects. It was a market day and he was dazzled by the noise and the color, squinting at the sunlight that filled the square, smelling the salt-wet air and all the good things of the market, and on his left the sun glittered from the water. . . .[63]

The bus shuddered to a halt at a red light.

The wind howled about the bus, and the wipers slooshed

61. The phrase "until he had found . . ." does not appear in the First Edition.

62. The nearest "city" to McAlester, Oklahoma, is Tulsa; Oklahoma City is only slightly farther away. Both would offer flights to Fort Wayne, Indiana, in most cases connecting through Chicago, and Shadow would then drive the approximately 40 miles to Eagle Point. A diversion of a Tulsa or Oklahoma City flight to St. Louis is quite possible.

63. In a private conversation with this editor, Gaiman described this as a deliberately ambiguous vision of Shadow's from a previous life. That he has had many past lives is evident from his dream of climbing the mountain of his own skulls—see note 491, below. Is he being led from a holding cell to the marketplace? Or to be punished? Or even executed? See "Coming to America 1778," below. A "garret" is an unlikely cell for a prisoner, but it may have been cheap temporary storage for a slaver's "goods." The word "garret" does not appear in the First Edition, though it appears in the Manuscript, and the vision begins "It was a big grey building . . ."

heavily back and forth across the windshield, smearing the city into a red and yellow neon wetness. It was early afternoon, but it looked like night through the glass.

"Shit," said the man in the seat behind Shadow, rubbing the condensation from the window with his hand, staring at a wet figure hurrying down the sidewalk. "There's pussy out there."

Shadow swallowed. It occurred to him that he had not cried yet—had in fact felt nothing at all. No tears. No sorrow. Nothing.

He found himself thinking about a guy named Johnnie Larch he'd shared a cell with when he'd first been put inside, who told Shadow how he'd once got out after five years behind bars, with $100 and a ticket to Seattle, where his sister lived.

Johnnie Larch had got to the airport, and he handed his ticket to the woman on the counter, and she asked to see his driver's license.

He showed it to her. It had expired a couple of years earlier. She told him it was not valid as ID. He told her it might not be valid as a driver's license, but it sure as hell was fine identification, and it had a photo of him on it, and his height and his weight,[64] and damn it, who else did she think he was, if he wasn't him?

She said she'd thank him to keep his voice down.

He told her to give him a fucking boarding pass, or she was going to regret it, and that he wasn't going to be disrespected. You don't let people disrespect you in prison.

Then she pressed a button, and a few moments later the airport security showed up, and they tried to persuade Johnnie Larch to leave the airport quietly, and he did not wish to leave, and there was something of an altercation.

The upshot of it all was that Johnnie Larch never actually made it to Seattle, and he spent the next couple of days in town in bars, and when his $100 was gone he held up a gas station with a toy gun for money to keep drinking, and the police finally picked him up for pissing in the street. Pretty soon he was back inside serving the rest of his sentence and a little extra for the gas station job.

64. The details of the ID card do not appear in the First Edition.

And the moral of this story, according to Johnnie Larch, was this: don't piss off people who work in airports.

"Are you sure it's not something like 'kinds of behavior that work in a specialized environment, such as a prison, can fail to work and in fact become harmful when used outside such an environment'?" said Shadow, when Johnnie Larch told him the story.

"No, listen to me, I'm *telling* you, man," said Johnnie Larch, "don't piss off those bitches in airports."

Shadow half-smiled at the memory. His own driver's license had several months still to go before it expired.

"Bus station! Everybody out!"

The building stank of piss and sour beer. Shadow climbed into a taxi and told the driver to take him to the airport. He told him that there was an extra five dollars if he could do it in silence. They made it in twenty minutes and the driver never said a word.

Then Shadow was stumbling through the brightly lit airport terminal. Shadow worried about the whole e-ticket business. He knew he had a ticket for a flight on Friday, but he didn't know if it would work today. Anything electronic seemed fundamentally magical to Shadow, and liable to evaporate at any moment. He liked things he could hold and touch.[65]

Still, he had his wallet, back in his possession for the first time in three years, containing several expired credit cards and one Visa card which, he was pleasantly surprised to discover, didn't expire until the end of January. He had a reservation number. And, he realized, he had the certainty that once he got home everything would, somehow, be right once more.[66] Laura would be fine again. Maybe it was some kind of scam to spring him a few days early. Or perhaps it was a simple mix-up: some other Laura Moon's body had been dragged from the highway wreckage.[67]

Lightning flickered outside the airport, through the windows-walls. Shadow realized he was holding his breath, waiting for something. A distant boom of thunder. He exhaled.

65. This sentence does not appear in the First Edition.

66. In the First Edition, the phrase "okay" appears instead of "right once more."

67. Laura's name in the Manuscript is "Laura Major."

A tired white woman stared at him from behind the counter.

"Hello," said Shadow. *You're the first strange woman I've spoken to, in the flesh, in three years.* "I've got an e-ticket number. I was supposed to be traveling on Friday but I have to go today. There was a death in my family."

"Mm. I'm sorry to hear that." She tapped at the keyboard, stared at the screen, tapped again. "No problem. I've put you on the three thirty. It may be delayed, because of the storm, so keep an eye on the screens. Checking any baggage?"

He held up a shoulder bag. "I don't need to check this, do I?"

"No," she said. "It's fine. Do you have any picture ID?"

Shadow showed her his driver's license.[68] Then he assured her that no one had given him a bomb to take onto the plane, and she, in return, gave him a printed boarding pass. Then he passed through the metal detector while his bag went through the X-ray machine.

It was not a big airport, but the number of people wandering, just wandering, amazed him. He watched people put down bags casually, observed wallets stuffed into back pockets, saw purses put down, unwatched, under chairs. That was when he realized he was no longer in prison.

Thirty minutes to wait until boarding. Shadow bought a slice of pizza and burned his lip on the hot cheese. He took his change and went to the phones. Called Robbie at the Muscle Farm, but the machine answered.

"Hey, Robbie," said Shadow. "They tell me that Laura's dead. They let me out early. I'm coming home."

Then, because people do make mistakes, he'd seen it happen, he called home, and listened to Laura's voice.

"Hi," she said. "I'm not here or I can't come to the phone. Leave a message and I'll get back to you. And have a *good* day."

Shadow couldn't bring himself to leave a message.

He sat in a plastic chair by the gate, and held his bag so tight he hurt his hand.

He was thinking about the first time he had ever seen

68. The balance of the paragraph does not appear in the First Edition.

69. The contents of what Shadow talked about does not appear in the First Edition.

Chi-Chi's was a real restaurant chain, with a Mexican theme. It was founded in 1975 in a suburb of Minneapolis, not far from Gaiman's residence, by Marno Mc-Dermott, who named it after his wife's nickname. The chain expanded throughout the world, with over 200 locations in 1995, but closed almost all of its North American operation in 2004; the last American store, in Utah, closed in 2011. It continues to operate in Belgium, Luxembourg, Austria, the United Arab Emirates, and Kuwait.

70. The two previous sentences and the paragraph before them do not appear in the First Draft.

71. The buffalo-man is not a specific figure of Native American mythology, though buffalos had great significance for the peoples of North America, who used the buffalo as food and its skin and bones for the manufacture of clothing, tools, and utensils. Some tribes venerated the buffalo as a spirit blessing the peoples with everything they needed to survive. In a private conversation with this editor, however, Gaiman indicated that the buffalo-man was *not* a god, but rather was intended to represent the spirit of the American land.

Laura. He hadn't even known her name then. She was Audrey Burton's friend. He had been sitting with Robbie in a booth at Chi-Chi's,[69] talking about something, probably how one of the other trainers had just announced she was opening her own dance studio, when Laura had walked in a pace or so behind Audrey, and Shadow had found himself staring. She had long, chestnut hair and eyes so blue Shadow mistakenly thought she was wearing tinted contact lenses. She had ordered a strawberry daiquiri, and insisted that Shadow taste it, and laughed delightedly when he did.

Laura loved people to taste what she tasted.

He had kissed her good night, that night, and she had tasted of strawberry daiquiris, and he had never wanted to kiss anyone else again.[70] A woman announced that his plane was boarding, and Shadow's row was the first to be called. He was in the very back, an empty seat beside him. The rain pattered continually against the side of the plane: he imagined small children tossing down dried peas by the handful from the skies.

As the plane took off he fell asleep.

Shadow was in a dark place, and the thing staring at him wore a buffalo's head, rank and furry with huge wet eyes. Its body was a man's body, oiled and slick.[71]

Arikaha medicine ceremony
Photograph by Edward Curtis, 1889

"Changes are coming," said the buffalo without moving its lips. "There are certain decisions that will have to be made."

Firelight flickered from wet cave walls.

"Where am I?" Shadow asked.

"In the earth and under the earth," said the buffalo man. "You are where the forgotten wait." His eyes were liquid black marbles, and his voice was a rumble from beneath the world. He smelled like wet cow. "Believe," said the rumbling voice. "If you are to survive, you must believe."

"Believe what?" asked Shadow. "What should I believe?"

He stared at Shadow, the buffalo man, and he drew himself up huge, and his eyes filled with fire. He opened his spit-flecked buffalo mouth and it was red inside with the flames that burned inside him, under the earth.

"*Everything*," roared the buffalo man.

The world tipped and spun, and Shadow was on the plane once more; but the tipping continued. In the front of the plane a woman screamed, half-heartedly.

Lightning burst in blinding flashes around the plane. The captain came on the intercom to tell them that he was going to try and gain some altitude, to get away from the storm.

The plane shook and shuddered, and Shadow wondered, coldly and idly, if he was going to die. It seemed possible, he decided, but unlikely. He stared out of the window and watched the lightning illuminate the horizon.

Then he dozed once more, and dreamed he was back in prison, and Low Key had whispered to him in the food line that someone had put out a contract on his life, but that Shadow could not find out who or why; and when he woke up they were coming in for a landing.

He stumbled off the plane, blinking and waking.

All airports, he had long ago decided, look very much the same. It doesn't actually matter where you are, you are in an airport: tiles and walkways and restrooms, gates and newsstands and fluorescent lights. This airport looked like an airport. The trouble is, this wasn't the airport he was going to. This was a big airport, with way too many people, and way too many gates.

72. This paragraph does not appear in the First Edition.

73. The balance of this paragraph does not appear in the First Edition.

The people had the glazed, beaten look you only see in airports and prisons. *If Hell is other people,* thought Shadow, *then Purgatory is airports.*[72]

"Excuse me, ma'am?"

The woman looked at him over the clipboard. "Yes?"

"What airport is this?"

She looked at him, puzzled, trying to decide whether or not he was joking, then she said, "St. Louis."

"I thought this was the plane to Eagle Point."

"It was. They redirected it here because of the storms. Didn't they make an announcement?"

"Probably. I fell asleep."

"You'll need to talk to that man over there, in the red coat."

The man was almost as tall as Shadow: he looked like the father from a seventies sitcom, and he tapped something into a computer and told Shadow to run—*run!*—to a gate on the far side of the terminal.

Shadow ran through the airport, but the doors were already closed when he got to the gate.[73] He watched the plane pull away from the gate, through the plate glass. Then he explained his problem to the gate attendant (calmly, quietly, politely) and she sent him to a passenger assistance desk, where Shadow explained that he was on his way home after a long absence and his wife had just been killed in a road accident, and that it was vitally important that he went home *now.* He said nothing about prison.

The woman at the passenger assistance desk (short and brown, with a mole on the side of her nose) consulted with another woman and made a phone call ("Nope, that one's out. They've just cancelled it") then she printed out another boarding card. "This will get you there," she told him. "We'll call ahead to the gate and tell them you're coming."

Shadow felt like a pea being flicked between three cups, or a card being shuffled through a deck. Again he ran through the airport, ending up near where he had gotten off in the first place.

A small man at the gate took his boarding pass. "We've been waiting for you," he confided, tearing off the stub of the boarding pass, with Shadow's seat assignment—17-D—on it. Shadow hurried onto the plane, and they closed the door behind him.

He walked through first class—there were only four first-class seats, three of which were occupied. The bearded man in a pale suit seated next to the unoccupied seat at the very front grinned at Shadow as he got onto the plane, then raised his wrist and tapped his watch as Shadow walked past.

Yeah, yeah, I'm making you late, thought Shadow. *Let that be the worst of your worries.*

The plane seemed pretty full, as he made his way down toward the back. Actually, Shadow quickly discovered, it was completely full, and there was a middle-aged woman sitting in seat 17-D. Shadow showed her his boarding card stub, and she showed him hers: they matched.

"Can you take your seat, please?" asked the flight attendant.

"No," he said, "I'm afraid I can't.[74] This lady is sitting in it."

She clicked her tongue and checked their boarding cards, then she led him back up to the front of the plane, and pointed him to the empty seat in first class. "Looks like it's your lucky day," she told him.

Shadow sat down. "Can I bring you something to drink?" she asked him. "We'll just have time before we take off. And I'm sure you need one after that."

"I'd like a beer, please," said Shadow. "Whatever you've got."

The flight attendant went away.

The man in the pale suit in the seat beside Shadow put out his arm and tapped his watch with his fingernail. It was a black Rolex. "You're late," said the man, and he grinned a huge grin with no warmth in it at all.

"Sorry?"

"I said, you're late."

The flight attendant handed Shadow a glass of beer. He

74. The next sentence does not appear in the First Edition.

31

Strangers on a plane (Mr. Wednesday, played by Ian McShane, and Shadow, played by
Ricky Whittle, from the Starz presentation of *American Gods*)
Photo copyright © 2018 Fremantle North America

sipped it. For one moment, he wondered if the man was crazy, and then he decided he must have been referring to the plane, waiting for one last passenger.

"Sorry if I held you up," he said, politely. "You in a hurry?"

The plane backed away from the gate. The flight attendant came back and took away Shadow's beer, half-finished. The man in the pale suit grinned at her and said, "Don't worry, I'll hold on to this tightly," and she let him keep his glass of Jack Daniel's, while protesting, weakly, that it violated airline regulations. ("Let me be the judge of that, m'dear.")

"Time is certainly of the essence," said the man. "But no, I am not in a hurry.[75] I was merely concerned that you would not make the plane."

75. In the First Edition, Wednesday does not say "I am not in a hurry."

"That was kind of you."

The plane sat restlessly on the ground, engines throbbing, aching to be off.

"Kind my ass," said the man in the pale suit. "I've got a job for you, Shadow."

A roar of engines. The little plane jerked forward into a take-off, pushing Shadow back into his seat. Then they were airborne, and the airport lights were falling away below them. Shadow looked at the man in the seat next to him.

His hair was a reddish-gray; his beard, little more than stubble, was grayish-red. He was smaller than Shadow, but he seemed to take up a hell of a lot of room.[76] A craggy, square face with pale gray eyes.[77] The suit looked expensive, and was the color of melted vanilla ice cream. His tie was dark gray silk, and the tiepin was a tree, worked in silver: trunk, branches, and deep roots.

He held his glass of Jack Daniel's as they took off, and did not spill a drop.

"Aren't you going to ask me what kind of job?"

"How do you know who I am?"

The man chuckled. "Oh, it's the easiest thing in the world to know what people call themselves. A little thought, a little luck, a little memory. Ask me what kind of job."

"No," said Shadow. The attendant brought him another glass of beer, and he sipped at it.

"Why not?"

"I'm going home. I've got a job waiting for me there. I don't want any other job."

The man's craggy smile did not change, outwardly, but now he seemed, actually, amused. "You don't have a job waiting for you at home," he said. "You have nothing waiting for you there. Meanwhile, I am offering you a perfectly legal job—good money, limited security, remarkable fringe benefits. Hell, if you live that long, I could throw in a pension plan. You think maybe you'd like one of them?"

Shadow said, "You could have seen my name on my boarding pass. Or on the side of my bag."[78]

The man said nothing.

"Whoever you are," said Shadow, "you couldn't have known

76. This sentence does not appear in the First Edition.

77. In one of Gaiman's journals, he notes that "Shadow has grey eyes." This trait is seen here in Wednesday, a suggestion of a blood relationship. In the Manuscript, Wednesday's eyes are blue.

78. In the First Edition, the sentence reads, "You must have seen my name on the side of my bag."

I was going to be on this plane. I didn't know I was going to be on this plane, and if my plane hadn't been diverted to St. Louis, I wouldn't have been. My guess is you're a practical joker. Maybe you're hustling something. But I think maybe we'll have a better time if we end this conversation here."

The man shrugged.

Shadow picked up the in-flight magazine. The little plane jerked and bumped through the sky, making it harder to concentrate. The words floated through his mind like soap bubbles, there as he read them, gone completely a moment later.

The man sat quietly in the seat beside him, sipping his Jack Daniel's. His eyes were closed.

Shadow read the list of in-flight music channels available on transatlantic flights, and then he was looking at the map of the world with red lines on it that showed where the airline flew. Then he had finished reading the magazine, and, reluctantly, he closed the cover, and slipped it into the pocket on the wall.

The man opened his eyes. There was something strange about his eyes, Shadow thought. One of them was a darker gray than the other.[79] He looked at Shadow. "By the way," he said, "I was sorry to hear about your wife, Shadow. A great loss."

Shadow nearly hit the man, then. Instead he took a deep breath. ("Like I said, don't piss off those bitches in airports," said Johnnie Larch, in the back of his mind, "or they'll haul your sorry ass back here before you can spit.") He counted to five.

"So was I," he said.

The man shook his head. "If it could but have been any other way," he said, and sighed.[80]

"She died in a car crash," said Shadow. "It's a fast way to go. Other ways could have been worse."[81]

The man shook his head, slowly. For a moment it seemed to Shadow as if the man was insubstantial; as if the plane had suddenly become more real, while his neighbor had become less so.

"Shadow," he said. "It's not a joke. It's not a trick. I can pay you better than any other job you'll find will pay you.

79. This is the first hint that Shadow is in the company of Odin, the All-Father, the chief of the Norse gods. According to legend, Odin "so thirsted after knowledge that he sacrificed an eye to his uncle, the giant Mimir, for a drink of the beverage of wisdom from Mimir's Well." *Dictionary of Ancient Deities*, p. 356. Odin appears several times in Gaiman's *Sandman*.

80. Wednesday implies that it was necessary that Laura die to bring Shadow to him.

81. In the First Edition, Shadow simply says, "There are worse ways to die."

You're an ex-con. There's not a long line of people elbowing each other out of the way to hire you."

"Mister whoever-the-fuck-you-are," said Shadow, just loud enough to be heard over the din of the engines, "there isn't enough money in the world."

The grin got bigger. Shadow found himself remembering a PBS show he had seen as a teenager,[82] about chimpanzees. The show claimed that when apes and chimps smile it's only to bare their teeth in a grimace of hate or aggression or terror. When a chimp grins, it's a threat. This grin was one of those.

"Sure there's money enough. And there are also bonuses. Work for me, and I'll tell you things.[83] There may be a little risk, of course, but if you survive you can have whatever your heart desires. You could be the next king of America. Now," said the man, "who else is going to pay you that well? Hmm?"

"Who are you?" asked Shadow.

"Ah, yes. The age of information—young lady, could you pour me another glass of Jack Daniel's? Easy on the ice—not, of course, that there has ever been any other kind of age. Information and knowledge: these are currencies that have never gone out of style."

"I said, who are you?"

"Let's see. Well, seeing that today certainly is my day—why don't you call me Wednesday?[84] Mister Wednesday. Although given the weather, it might as well be Thursday, eh?"

"What's your real name?"

"Work for me long enough and well enough," said the man in the pale suit, "and I may even tell you that. There. Job offer. Think about it. No one expects you to say yes immediately, not knowing whether you're leaping into a piranha tank or a pit of bears. Take your time." He closed his eyes and leaned back in his seat.

"I don't think so," said Shadow. "I don't like you. I don't want to work with you."

"Like I say," said the man, without opening his eyes, "don't rush into it. Take your time."

The plane landed with a bump, and a few passengers got off. Shadow looked out of the window: it was a little airport in the middle of nowhere, and there were still two little

82. The phrase "as a teenager" does not appear in the First Edition.

83. In the First Edition, in place of this and the preceding two sentences, Wednesday says, "Work for me." In the Manuscript, Wednesday says, "I'll tell you why you did that office robbery. I'll tell you why you don't remember anything before you were, what, twenty years old? Eighteen? Who else is going to pay you well? Huh? If you stick with me and show what you can do, you'll walk away knowing your real name, who you are, why Caleb Samuels tried to kill you."

84. "Woden's-day" (Wōdnesdæg in Old English) is the usual etymology of "Wednesday," just as "Thors-day" is given for Thursday. Woden is the Old English version of Odin. Thor is of course the god of thunder. The weekdays have other references to the Norse gods: Tuesday was named after Tiu, or Tiw, the Anglo-Saxon name for Tyr, the Norse god of war. Friday is explained at note 196, below. Saturday is the odd god out—it was named after Saturn, the Roman god of revelry (hence the word "saturnalia").

As will be seen, Wednesday is not the Norse god Odin—rather, he is the *American* version of Odin.

85. In the First Edition, the next two phrases do not appear.

86. The balance of this paragraph does not appear in the First Edition.

87. Eagle Point is about 375 miles from St. Louis. There are several possible destinations along the route that could be 250 miles away and feature airports: Terre Haute, Indiana; Springfield, Illinois; Decatur, Illinois; Champaign, Illinois. It is impossible to determine which of these was Shadow's initial destination.

88. There is no place in the U.S. named Nottamun. However, "Nottamun Town" is a traditional English folk ballad:

> In Nottamun Town, not a soul would
>   look up,
> Not a soul would look up, not a soul
>   would look down
> Not a soul would look up, not a soul
>   would look down
> To show me the way to fair Nottamun
>   Town
>
> I bought me a horse twas called a grey
>   mare
> Grey mane and grey tail and green
>   stripe on her back
> Grey mane and grey tail and green
>   stripe on her back
> Weren't a hair upon her that was not
>   coal black
>
> She stood so still threw me to the dirt
> She tore at my hide, she bruised my
>   shirt
> From saddle to stirrup I mounted again
> And on my ten toes I rode over the plain
>
> When I got there no one did I see
> They all stood around me just looking
>   at me

airports to go before Eagle Point. Shadow transferred his glance to the man in the pale suit—Mr. Wednesday? He seemed to be asleep.

Shadow stood up, grabbed his bag, and stepped off the plane, down the steps onto the slick wet tarmac, walking at an even pace toward the lights of the terminal. A light rain spattered his face.

Before he went inside the airport building, he stopped, and turned, and watched. No one else got off the plane. The ground crew rolled the steps away, the door was closed, and it taxied off down the runway. Shadow stared at it until it took off, then he walked inside,[85] to the Budget car rental desk, the only one open, and he rented what turned out, when he got to the parking lot, to be a small red Toyota.

Shadow unfolded the map they had given him. He spread it out on the passenger's seat. Eagle Point was about two hundred and fifty miles away,[86] most of the journey on the freeway.[87] He had not driven a car in three years.

The storms had passed, if they had come this far. It was cold and clear. Clouds scudded in front of the moon, and for a moment Shadow could not be certain whether it was the clouds or the moon that was moving.

He drove north for an hour and a half.

It was getting late. He was hungry, and when he realized how hungry he really was, he pulled off at the next exit, and drove into the town of Nottamun (pop. 1,301).[88] He filled the gas-tank at the Amoco, and asked the bored woman at the cash register[89] where the best bar in the area was—somewhere that he could get something to eat.

"Jack's Crocodile Bar," she told him. "It's west on County Road N."[90]

"Crocodile Bar?"

"Yeah. Jack says they add character." She drew him a map on the back of a mauve flyer, which advertised a chicken roast to raise money for a young girl who needed a new kidney. "He's got a couple of crocodiles, a snake, one a them big lizard things."

"An iguana?"

"That's him."

Through the town, over a bridge, on for a couple of miles, and he stopped at a low, rectangular building with an illuminated Pabst sign, and a Coca-Cola machine by the door.[91]

The parking lot was half-empty. Shadow parked the red Toyota and went inside.

The air was thick with smoke and "Walkin' after Midnight"[92] was playing on the jukebox. Shadow looked around for the crocodiles, but could not see them.

"Odin the Wanderer"
By Willy Pogany (1922)

Jack's Crocodile Bar
(from the Starz presentation of *American Gods*)
Photo copyright © 2018 Fremantle North America

I called for a cup to drive gladness away
And stifle the dust for it rained the whole day

And the King and the Queen and the company more
Came a riding behind and a walking before
Come a stark naked drummer beating a drum
With his hands in his bosom came marching along

Sat down on a hard hot cold frozen stone
Ten thousand stood round me but I was alone
Took my hat in my hand to keep my head warm
Ten thousand was drowned that never was born

In Nottamun Town, not a soul would look up,
Not a soul would look up, not a soul would look down
Not a soul would look up, not a soul would look down
To show me the way to fair Nottamun Town

The name "Nottamun" is probably a corruption of "Nottingham."

89. Shadow does not ask about a bar in the First Edition.

90. County Road N is a highway near Menomonie, Wisconsin, where Gaiman lived in 2000.

91. The Coca-Cola machine is absent from the First Edition.

92. "Walkin' After Midnight" by Alan Block and Donn Hecht was recorded in 1956 by Patsy Cline and became one of her biggest hits.

93. In the First Edition, Shadow does not ask the identity of the bartender, and he specifically asks for fries!

He wondered if the woman in the gas station had been pulling his leg.

"What'll it be?" asked the bartender.

"You Jack?" [93]

"It's Jack's night off. I'm Paul."

"Hi, Paul. House beer, and a hamburger with all the trimmings. No fries."

"Bowl of chili to start? Best chili in the state."

"Sounds good," said Shadow. "Where's the restroom?"

The man pointed to a door in the corner of the bar. There was a stuffed alligator head mounted on the door. Shadow went through the door.

It was a clean, well-lit restroom. Shadow looked around the room first; force of habit. ("Remember, Shadow, you can't fight back when you're pissing," Low Key said, low-key as always, in the back of his head.) He took the urinal stall on the left. Then he unzipped his fly and pissed for an age, relaxing, feeling relief. He read the yellowing press clipping framed at eye-level, with a photo of Jack and two alligators.

There was a polite grunt from the urinal immediately to his right, although he had heard nobody come in.

The man in the pale suit was bigger standing than he had seemed sitting on the plane beside Shadow. He was almost Shadow's height, and Shadow was a big man. He was staring ahead of him. He finished pissing, shook off the last few drops, and zipped himself up.

Then he grinned, like a fox eating shit from a barbed wire fence. "So," said Mr. Wednesday. "You've had time to think, Shadow. Do you want a job?"

Somewhere in America
LOS ANGELES, 11:26 P.M.

I n a dark red room—the color of the walls is close to that of raw liver—is a tall woman dressed cartoonishly in too-tight silk shorts, her breasts pulled up and pushed forward by the yellow blouse tied beneath them. Her black hair is piled high and knotted on top of her head. Standing beside her is a short man wearing an olive T-shirt and expensive blue jeans. He is holding, in his right hand, a wallet and a Nokia mobile phone with a red, white, and blue face-plate.

The red room contains a bed, upon which are white satin-style sheets and an ox-blood bedspread. At the foot of the bed is a small wooden table, upon which is a small stone statue of a woman with enormous hips, and a candle-holder.

The woman hands the man a small red candle. "Here," she says. "Light it."

"Me?"

"Yes," she says, "if you want to have me."

"I shoulda just got you to suck me off in the car."

"Perhaps," she says. "Don't you want me?" Her hand runs up her body from thigh to breast, a gesture of presentation, as if she were demonstrating a new product.

Red silk scarves over the lamp in the corner of the room make the light red.

The man looks at her hungrily, then he takes the candle

from her and pushes it into the candleholder. "You got a light?"

She passes him a book of matches. He tears off a match, lights the wick: it flickers and then burns with a steady flame, which gives the illusion of motion to the faceless statue beside it, all hips and breasts. "Put the money beneath the statue."

"Fifty bucks."

"Yes."

"When I saw you first, on Sunset, I almost thought you were a man." [94]

"But I have these," she says, unknotting the yellow blouse, freeing her breasts.

"So do a lot of guys, these days."

She stretches and smiles. "Yes," she says. "Now, come love me."

He unbuttons his blue jeans, and removes his olive T-shirt. She massages his white shoulders with her brown fingers; then she turns him over, and begins to make love to him with her hands, and her fingers, and her tongue.

It seems to him that the lights in the red room have been dimmed, and the sole illumination comes from the candle, which burns with a bright flame.

"What's your name?" he asks her.

"Bilquis," [95] she tells him, raising her head. "With a Q."

94. Neither this nor the next three sentences appear in the First Edition.

95. The historical facts regarding Bilquis (more properly, Bilqis, ملكة سبأ) are obscure. According to some historians, Bilqis, identified as the Queen of Sheba, was the daughter of Hudhad ben Sharahil, a descendant of Sam (Shem), the son of Nuh (Noah). She was a queen of the Himyarite tribe, ruling in Yemen for nine years. Some claim that one of her parents was a djinn; however, none have attributed any divinity to her. Bilqis was first a sun worshiper, but reportedly, after meeting Sulayman (Solomon, the Biblical king), she converted to monotheism. The Queen of Sheba is the only woman whose name appears in the Qur'an; she also appears in the Hebrew Bible.

Bilquis (played by Yetide Badaki,
from the Starz presentation of *American Gods*)
Photo copyright © 2018 Fremantle North America

"A what?"

"Never mind."

He is gasping now. "Let me fuck you," he says. "I have to fuck you."

"Okay, hon," she says. "We'll do it. But will you do something for me, while you're doing it?"

"Hey," he says, suddenly tetchy, "*I'm* paying *you,* you know."

She straddles him, in one smooth movement, whispering, "I know, honey, I know, you're paying me, and I mean, look at you, I should be paying you, I'm so lucky . . ."

He purses his lips, trying to show that her hooker talk is having no effect on him, he can't be taken; that she's a street whore for Chrissakes, while he's practically a *producer,* and he knows all about last-minute rip-offs, but she doesn't ask for money. Instead she says, "Honey, while you're giving it to me, while you're pushing that big hard thing inside of me, will you *worship* me?"

"Will I what?"

She is rocking back and forth on him: the engorged head of his penis is being rubbed against the wet lips of her vulva.

"Will you call me goddess? Will you pray to me? Will you worship me with your body?"

He smiles. Is that what[96] she wants? "Sure," he says. We've all got our kinks, at the end of the day. She reaches her hand between her legs and slips him inside her.

"Is that good, is it, goddess?" he asks, gasping.

"Worship me, honey," says Bilquis, the hooker.

"Yes," he says. "I worship your breasts and your eyes[97] and your cunt. I worship your thighs and your eyes and your cherry-red lips . . ."

"Yes . . . ," she croons,[98] riding him like a storm-tossed boat rides the waves.

"I worship your nipples, from which the milk of life flows. Your kiss is honey and your touch scorches like fire, and I worship it." His words are becoming more rhythmic now, keeping pace with the thrust and roll of their bodies. "Bring me your lust in the morning, and bring me relief and your blessing in the evening. Let me walk in dark places un-

The Queen of Sheba visits King Solomon
Julius Schnor von Carolsfeld, 19th century

96. "all" in the First Edition.

97. "hair" in the First Edition.

98. The balance of the sentence does not appear in the First Edition.

41

harmed and let me come to you once more and sleep beside you and make love with you again. I worship you with everything that is within me, and everything inside my mind, with everywhere I've been and my dreams and my . . ." He breaks off, panting for breath. ". . . What are you *doing*? That feels *amaz*ing. So *amaz*ing . . ." And he looks down at his hips, at the place where the two of them conjoin, but her forefinger touches his chin and pushes his head back, so he is looking only at her face and at the ceiling once again.

"Keep talking, honey," she says. "Don't stop. Doesn't it feel good?"

"It feels better than anything has ever felt," he tells her, meaning it as he says it. "Your eyes are stars, burning in the, shit, the firmament, and your lips are gentle waves that lick the sand, and I worship them," and now he's thrusting deeper and deeper inside her: he feels electric, as if his whole lower body has become sexually charged: priapic, engorged, blissful.

"Bring me your gift," he mutters, no longer knowing what he is saying, "your one true gift, and make me always this . . . always so . . . I pray . . . I . . ."

And then the pleasure crests into orgasm, blasting his mind into void, his head and self and entire beingness a perfect blank as he thrusts deeper into her and deeper still . . .

Eyes closed, spasming, he luxuriates in the moment; and then he feels a lurch, and it seems to him that he is hanging, head-down, although the pleasure continues.

He opens his eyes.

He thinks, grasping for thought and reason again, of birth, and wonders, without fear, in a moment of perfect postcoital clarity, whether what he sees is some kind of illusion.

This is what he sees:

He is inside her to the chest, and as he stares at this in disbelief and wonder she rests both hands upon his shoulders and puts gentle pressure on his body.

He slipslides further inside her.

"How are you doing this to me?" he asks, or he thinks he asks, but perhaps it is only in his head.

"You're doing it, honey," she whispers. He feels the lips of her vulva tight around his upper chest and back, constricting and enveloping him. He wonders what this would look like to somebody watching them. He wonders why he is not scared. And then he knows.

"I worship you with my body," he whispers, as she pushes him inside her. Her labia pull slickly across his face, and his eyes slip into darkness.

She stretches on the bed, like a huge cat, and then she yawns. "Yes," she says, "You do."

The Nokia phone plays a high, electrical transposition of the "Ode to Joy." She picks it up, and thumbs a key, and puts the telephone to her ear.

Her belly is flat, her labia small and closed. A sheen of sweat glistens on her forehead and on her upper lip.

"Yeah?" she says. And then she says, "No, honey, he's not here. He's gone away."

She turns the telephone off before she flops out on the bed in the dark red room, then she stretches once more, and she closes her eyes, and she sleeps.

CHAPTER TWO

99. While the exact source of the lyric is unknown, some suggest that it is a verse from the traditional "St. James Infirmary Blues," which mourns the death of the singer's girl. The first recorded version was in 1927, by Fess Williams and the Royal Flush Orchestra (as "Gambler's Blues"), around the time Cadillacs began to be used as hearses. However, that version specifically mentions a horse-drawn hearse. Here is a recording: https://www.youtube.com/watch?v=pnrT2U_pA0k

They took her to the cemet'ry
In a big ol' Cadillac
They took her to the cemet'ry
But they did not bring her back.
　　　　　—OLD SONG[99]

 HAVE TAKEN THE liberty," said Mr. Wednesday, washing his hands in the men's room of Jack's Crocodile Bar, "of ordering food for myself, to be delivered to your table. We have much to discuss, after all."

"I don't think so," said Shadow. He dried his own hands on a paper towel and crumpled it, and dropped it into the bin.

"You need a job," said Wednesday. "People don't hire ex-cons. You folk make them uncomfortable."

"I have a job waiting. A good job."

"Would that be the job at the Muscle Farm?"

"Maybe," said Shadow.

"Nope. You don't. Robbie Burton's dead. Without him the Muscle Farm's dead too."

"You're a liar."

"Of course. And a good one. The best you will ever meet. But, I'm afraid, I'm not lying to you about this." He reached into his pocket, produced a newspaper, much folded, and

Mr. Wednesday (played by Ian McShane, from the Starz presentation of *American Gods*)
Photo copyright © 2018 Fremantle North America

100. The song was a hit for the girl group in 1965. It is allegedly composed of several Mardi Gras traditional chants, used by Mardi Gras "Indians" to taunt each other. The authors—Sugar Boy Crawford and the members of the Dixie Cups—Barbara Ann Hawkins, Rosa Lee Hawkins, and Joan Marie Johnson—at various times all disavowed any knowledge of what the song's lyrics meant. In an interview, Barbara Ann Hawkins recalled that she had heard her grandmother sing the song. Dr. John (stage-name of Malcolm John Rebennack), who covered the song in 1972, explained in the liner notes to his recording, that the song had a good deal of Creole patois in it. "It is Mardi Gras music, and the Shaweez was one of many Mardi Gras groups who dressed up in far out Indian costumes and came on as Indian tribes. The tribes used to hang out on Claiborne Avenue and used to get juiced up there getting ready to perform and 'second line' in their own special style during Mardi Gras. That's dead and gone because there's a freeway where those grounds used to be. The tribes were like social clubs who lived all year for Mardi Gras, getting their costumes together. Many of them were musicians, gamblers, hustlers and pimps."

handed it to Shadow. "Page seven," he said. "Come on back to the bar. You can read it at the table." Shadow pushed open the door, back into the bar. The air was blue with smoke, and the Dixie Cups were on the jukebox singing "Iko Iko."[100] Shadow smiled, slightly, in recognition of the old children's song.

The barman pointed to a table in the corner. There was a bowl of chili and a burger at one side of the table, a rare steak and a bowl of fries laid in the place across from it.

Look at my King all dressed in Red,
Iko Iko all day,
I bet you five dollars he'll kill you dead,
Jockamo-feena-nay

Shadow took his seat at the table. He put the newspaper down. "I got out of prison this morning," he said.[101] "This is my first meal as a free man. You won't object if I wait until after I've eaten to read your page seven?"

"Not in the slightest bit."

Shadow ate his hamburger. It was better than prison hamburgers. The chili was good but, he decided, after a couple of mouthfuls, not the best in the state.

101. This sentence does not appear in the First Edition. In the First Edition, Shadow announces more forcefully that "I'll wait until . . ." and so Wednesday does not announce that he won't object.

Laura made a great chili. She used lean-cut meat, dark kidney beans, carrots cut small, a bottle or so of dark beer, and freshly sliced hot peppers. She would let the chili cook for a while, then add red wine, lemon juice, and a pinch of fresh dill, and, finally, measure out and add her chili powders. On more than one occasion Shadow had tried to get her to show him how she made it: he would watch everything she did, from slicing the onions and dropping them into the olive oil at the bottom of the pot. He had even written down the sequence of events,[102] ingredient by ingredient, and he had once made Laura's chili for himself on a weekend when she had been out of town. It had tasted okay—it was certainly edible, and he ate it, but it had not been Laura's chili.

The news item on page seven was the first account of his wife's death that Shadow had read. It felt strange, as if he were reading about someone in a story:[103] how Laura Moon, whose age was given in the article as twenty-seven, and Robbie Burton, thirty-nine, were in Robbie's car on the interstate, when they swerved into the path of a thirty-two wheeler, which sideswiped them as it tried to change lanes and avoid them. The truck brushed Robbie's car and sent it spinning off the side of the road, where the car had hit a road sign, hard, and stopped spinning.

Rescue crews were on the scene in minutes. They pulled Robbie and Laura from the wreckage. They were both dead by the time they arrived at the hospital.

Shadow folded the newspaper up once more, and slid it back across the table, toward Wednesday, who was gorging himself on a steak so bloody and so blue it might never have been introduced to a kitchen flame.

"Here. Take it back," said Shadow.

Robbie had been driving. He must have been drunk, although the newspaper account said nothing about this. Shadow found himself imagining Laura's face when she realized that Robbie was too drunk to drive. The scenario unfolded in Shadow's mind, and there was nothing he could do to stop it: Laura shouting at Robbie—shouting at him to

102. In the First Edition, Shadow merely writes down the "recipe." In one of the many examples of life imitating art that seem to surround Gaiman's work, there are numerous recipes online for "Laura's chili." See, e.g., http://www.innatthecrossroads.com/laura -moons-chili-american-gods-2-2/.

103. The preceding phrase does not appear in the First Edition, and the details of the accident are simplified.

pull off the road, then the thud of car against truck, and the steering wheel wrenching over . . .

. . . the car on the side of the road, broken glass glittering like ice and diamonds in the headlights, blood pooling in rubies on the road beside them. Two bodies, dead or soon-to-die,[104] being carried from the wreck, or laid neatly by the side of the road.

"Well?" asked Mr. Wednesday. He had finished his steak, sliced and devoured it like a starving man. Now he was munching the french fries, spearing them with his fork.

"You're right," said Shadow. "I don't have a job."

Shadow took a quarter from his pocket, tails up. He flicked it up in the air, knocking it against his finger as it left his hand to give it a wobble that made it look as if it were turning, caught it, slapped it down on the back of his hand.

"Call," he said.

"Why?" asked Wednesday.

"I don't want to work for anyone with worse luck than me. Call."

"Heads," said Mr. Wednesday.

"Sorry," said Shadow, revealing the coin without even bothering to glance at it. "It was tails. I rigged the toss."

"Rigged games are the easiest ones to beat," said Wednesday, wagging a square finger at Shadow. "Take another look at the quarter."

Shadow glanced down at it. The head was face-up.

"I must have fumbled the toss," he said, puzzled.

"You do yourself a disservice," said Wednesday, and he grinned. "I'm just a lucky, lucky guy." Then he looked up. "Well I never. Mad Sweeney.[105] Will you have a drink with us?"

"Southern Comfort and Coke, straight up," said a voice from behind Shadow.

"I'll go and talk to the barman," said Wednesday. He stood up, and began to make his way toward the bar.

"Aren't you going to ask what I'm drinking?" called Shadow.

"I already know what you're drinking," said Wednesday,

104. This phrase does not appear in the First Edition.

105. Mad Sweeney takes his name from the Suibhne mac Colmain, king of the Dál nAraidi, a character of medieval Irish literature. In the tale, the king interferes with the work of St. Ronan Finn, who is building a church. St. Ronan places a curse on him. Specifically, Suibhne is cursed to "fly through the air like the shaft of his spear and that he might die of a spear cast like the cleric whom he had slain." Suibhne abandons the Battle of Mag Rath and, changing to a bird, takes up a life of wandering. At the end of his travels, Suibhne arrives at County Carlow, where he stays with Moling, a priest. The priest directs his cook to provide the madman with a meal, which she does by pouring milk into a hole she made with her foot in a pile of cow dung. However, her husband (Moling's herder) believes that Suibhne and his wife are carrying on, and in a fit of jealousy, while Suibhne is drinking from the hole, the husband spears Suibhne. Thus Suibhne dies in the manner foretold by St. Ronan.

His story results in him being dubbed Suibhne Geilt or "Mad Sweeney." Note that there is nothing of leprechauns in this story; Mad Sweeney's deification occurs when he is transplanted to America.

Mad Sweeney
(played by Pablo Schreiber, from the Starz
presentation of *American Gods*)
*Photo copyright © 2018 Fremantle
North America*

106. This sentence does not appear in the First Edition.

107. In the First Edition, Shadow asks Sweeney, "What do you do?"

108. In the First Edition, Sweeney says this "with a grin."

and then he was standing by the bar. Patsy Cline started to sing "Walkin' after Midnight" on the jukebox again.

The man who had ordered Southern Comfort and Coke sat down beside Shadow. He had a short ginger-colored beard. He wore a denim jacket covered with bright sew-on patches, and under the jacket a stained white T-shirt. On the T-shirt was printed:

IF YOU CAN'T EAT IT, DRINK IT, SMOKE IT
OR SNORT IT . . . THEN F°CK IT!

He wore a baseball cap, on which was printed:

THE ONLY WOMAN I HAVE EVER LOVED
WAS ANOTHER MAN'S WIFE . . .
MY MOTHER!

He opened a soft pack of Lucky Strikes with a dirty thumbnail, took a cigarette, offered one to Shadow. Shadow was about to take one, automatically—he did not smoke, but a cigarette makes good barter material—when he realized that he was no longer inside. You could buy cigarettes here whenever you wanted.[106] He shook his head.

"You working for our man then?" asked the bearded man. He was not sober, although he was not yet drunk.

"It looks that way," said Shadow.[107]

The bearded man lit his cigarette. "I'm a leprechaun," he said.[108]

Shadow did not smile. "Really?" he said. "Shouldn't you be drinking Guinness?"

"Stereotypes. You have to learn to think outside the box," said the bearded man. "There's a lot more to Ireland than Guinness."

"You don't have an Irish accent."

"I've been over here too fucken long."

"So you *are* originally from Ireland?"

"I told you. I'm a leprechaun. We don't come from fucken Moscow."

"I guess not."

Wednesday returned to the table, three drinks held easily in his paw-like hands. "Southern Comfort and Coke for you, Mad Sweeney,[109] m'man, and a Jack Daniel's for me. And *this* is for you, Shadow."

"What is it?"

"Taste it."

The drink was a tawny golden color. Shadow took a sip, tasting an odd blend of sour and sweet on his tongue. He could taste the alcohol underneath, and a strange blend of flavors. It reminded him a little of prison hooch, brewed in a garbage bag from rotten fruit and bread and sugar and water, but it was smoother, sweeter, infinitely stranger.

"Okay," said Shadow. "I tasted it. What was it?"

"Mead,"[110] said Wednesday. "Honey wine. The drink of heroes. The drink of the gods."

Shadow took another tentative sip. Yes, he could taste the honey, he decided. That was one of the tastes. "Tastes kinda like pickle juice," he said. "Sweet pickle juice wine."

"Tastes like a drunken diabetic's piss," agreed Wednesday. "I hate the stuff."

"Then why did you bring it for me?" asked Shadow, reasonably.

Wednesday stared at Shadow with his mismatched eyes. One of them, Shadow decided, was a glass eye, but he could not decide which one. "I brought you mead to drink because it's traditional. And right now we need all the tradition we can get. It seals our bargain."

"We haven't made a bargain."

"Sure we have. You work for me. You protect me. You help me.[111] You transport me from place to place. You investigate, from time to time—go places and ask questions for me. You run errands. In an emergency, but only in an emergency, you hurt people who need to be hurt. In the unlikely event of my death, you will hold my vigil. And in return I shall make sure that your needs are adequately taken care of."

"He's hustling you," said Mad Sweeney, rubbing his bristly ginger beard. "He's a hustler."

109. His name is merely "Sweeney" in the Manuscript.

110. Mead, said to be the inspiration of poetry, was legendarily created by dwarves mixing honey with the blood of Kvasir, a well-known wise man. Odin stole mead from the dwarves. The tale is retold in Gaiman's *Norse Mythology* (New York: W. W. Norton, 2017).

111. This sentence and the sentence beginning "You investigate . . ." do not appear in the First Edition.

112. Wednesday never reveals what he knows, but the superstition prevails that "dead air"—sudden silence in a crowd—occurs at twenty minutes after the hour because Abraham Lincoln died at 7:20 a.m. on April 15, 1865. Another suggestion is that choruses of angels sing at exactly 20 minutes after the hour, and humans everywhere pause to listen. Dylan Thomas puts this superstition in the mouth of a character in *Portrait of the Artist as a Young Dog* (1940): "'A host of angels must be passing by! . . . What a silence there is!'"

Known also as the "20-minute-lull," some speculate that this is merely harmonic convergence, the natural result of ebbing and flowing noise; others suggest that the silence is a throwback to prehistoric man's need to pause to listen for predators. Neither of these scientific theories provide any support for the "20-minute" aspect of the phenomenon. Perhaps the simplest explanation is that while such silences occur around the clock, only those that fit the superstition are commented on!

The next three sentences do not appear in the First Edition.

113. It is unclear what kind of supernatural being Sweeney is, though he is definitely

A clurichaun
By Maclise and Green, 1888

"Damn straight I'm a hustler," said Wednesday. "That's why I need someone to look out for my best interests."

The song on the jukebox ended, and for a moment the bar fell quiet, every conversation at a lull.

"Someone once told me that you only get those everybody-shuts-up-at-once moments at twenty past or twenty to the hour," said Shadow.

Sweeney pointed to the clock above the bar, held in the massive and indifferent jaws of a stuffed alligator head. The time was 11:20.

"There," said Shadow. "Damned if I know why that happens."

"I know why," said Wednesday.[112]

"You going to share with the group?"

"I may tell you, one day, yes. Or I may not. Drink your mead."

Shadow knocked the rest of the mead back in one long gulp. "It might be better over ice," he said.

"Or it might not," said Wednesday. "It's terrible stuff."

"That it is," agreed Mad Sweeney. "You'll excuse me for a moment, gentlemen, but I find myself in deep and urgent need of a lengthy piss." He stood up and walked away, an impossibly tall man. He had to be almost seven feet tall, decided Shadow.[113]

A waitress wiped a cloth across the table and took their empty plates. She emptied Sweeney's ashtray, and asked if they would like to order any more drinks.[114] Wednesday told her to bring the same again for everyone, although this time Shadow's mead was to be on the rocks. "Anyway," said Wednesday, "that's what I need of you,[115] if you're working for me. Which, of course, you are."

"That's what you want," said Shadow. "Would you like to know what I want?"

"Nothing could make me happier."

The waitress brought the drink. Shadow sipped his mead on the rocks. The ice did not help—if anything it sharpened the sourness, and made the taste linger in the mouth after the mead was swallowed. However, Shadow consoled himself, it did not taste particularly alcoholic. He was not ready to be drunk. Not yet.

He took a deep breath.

"Okay," said Shadow. "My life, which for three years has been a long way from being the greatest life there has ever been, just took a distinct and sudden turn for the worse. Now there are a few things I need to do. I want to go to Laura's funeral. I want to say goodbye.[116] After that, if you still need me, I want to start at five hundred dollars a week." The figure was a stab in the dark, a made-up number. Wednesday's eyes revealed nothing. "If we're happy working together, in six months' time you raise it to a thousand a week."

He paused. It was the longest speech he'd made in years. "You say you may need people to be hurt. Well, I'll hurt people if they're trying to hurt you. But I don't hurt people for fun or for profit. I won't go back to prison. Once was enough."

"You won't have to," said Wednesday.

"No," said Shadow. "I won't." He finished the last of the mead. He wondered, suddenly, somewhere in the back of his head, whether the mead was responsible for loosening his tongue. But the words were coming out of him like the water spraying from a broken fire hydrant in summer, and he could not have stopped them if he had tried. "I don't like you, Mister Wednesday, or whatever your real name may be. We are not friends. I don't know how you got off that plane without me seeing you, or how you trailed me here. But I'm[117] impressed. You have class. And I'm at a loose end right now. You should know that when we're done, I'll be gone. And if you piss me off, I'll be gone too. Until then, I'll work for you."

Wednesday grinned. His smiles were strange things, Shadow decided. They contained no shred of humor, no happiness, no mirth. Wednesday looked like he had learned to smile from a manual.[118]

"Very good," he said. "Then we have a compact. And we are agreed."

"What the hell," said Shadow. Across the room, Mad

Irish, as will be confirmed later. Irish folklore speaks of leprechauns and clurichauns (the latter are especially associated with over-indulgence in alcoholic beverages, as is Sweeney), but William Butler Yeats thought these distinctions might be simply aspects of a single breed of Irish fairy. However, virtually all accounts ascribe smallness to the creatures—indeed, the word "leprechaun" is thought to be a corruption of Old Irish words meaning "small" and "body." Sweeney may have adapted in America to be quite different from one of the "little people."

114. This sentence does not appear in the First Edition.

115. The balance of this paragraph does not appear in the First Edition.

116. In the First Edition, the sentence "I should wind up her stuff." follows.

117. In the First Edition, Shadow says merely, "But I'm at a loose end right now."

118. This paragraph does not appear in the First Edition.

Sweeney was feeding quarters into the jukebox. Wednesday spat in his hand and extended it. Shadow shrugged. He spat in his own palm. They clasped hands. Wednesday began to squeeze. Shadow squeezed back. After a few seconds his hand began to hurt. Wednesday held the grip for another half-minute, and then he let go.

"Good," he said. "Good. Very good." He smiled, a brief flash, and Shadow wondered if there had been real humor in that smile, actual pleasure.[119] "So, one last glass of evil, vile fucking mead to seal our deal, and then we are done."

"It'll be a Southern Comfort and Coke for me," said Sweeney, lurching back from the jukebox.

The jukebox began to play the Velvet Underground's "Who Loves the Sun?"[120] Shadow thought it a strange song to find on a jukebox. It seemed very unlikely. But then, this whole evening had become increasingly unlikely.

Shadow took the quarter he had used for the coin-toss from the table, enjoying the sensation of a freshly milled coin against his fingers, producing it in his right hand between forefinger and thumb. He appeared to take it into his left hand in one smooth movement, while casually finger-palming it. He closed his left hand on the imaginary quarter. Then he took a second quarter in his right hand, between finger and thumb, and, as he pretended to drop that coin into the left hand, he let the palmed quarter fall into his right hand, striking the quarter he held there on the way. The chink confirmed the illusion that both coins were in his left hand, while they were now both held safely in his right.

"Coin tricks is it?" asked Sweeney, his chin raising, his scruffy beard bristling. "Why, if it's coin tricks we're doing, watch this."

He took a glass from the table, a glass that had once held mead,[121] and he tipped the ice-cubes into the ashtray. Then he reached out and took a large coin, golden and shining, from the air. He dropped it into the glass. He took another gold coin from the air and tossed it into the glass, where it clinked against the first. He took a coin from the candle flame of a candle on the wall, another from his beard, a third

119. This sentence does not appear in the First Edition.

120. Written by Lou Reed and recorded in 1970 by the Velvet Underground (making it unlikely to be found on a jukebox at this point in time), the song expresses a nihilistic point of view, denying the value of the sun or the wind after a broken heart.

121. In the First Edition, it is merely an empty glass.

from Shadow's empty left hand, and dropped them, one by one, into the glass. Then he curled his fingers over the glass, and blew hard, and several more golden coins dropped into the glass from his hand. He tipped the glass of sticky coins into his jacket pocket, and then tapped the pocket to show, unmistakably, that it was empty.

"There," he said. "*That's* a coin trick for you."

Shadow, who had been watching closely throughout the impromptu performance, put his head on one side. "We have to talk about that," he said.[122] "I need to know how you did it."

"I did it," said Sweeney, with the air of one confiding a huge secret, "with panache and style. That's how I did it."[123] He laughed, silently, rocking on his heels, his gappy teeth bared.

"Yes," said Shadow. "That is how you did it. You've got to teach me. All the ways of doing the Miser's Dream[124] that I've read about you'd be hiding the coins in the hand that holds the glass, and dropping them in while you produce and vanish the coin in your right hand."

"Sounds like a hell of a lot of work to me," said Mad Sweeney. "It's easier just to pick them out of the air." He picked up his half-finished Southern Comfort and Coke, looked at it, and put it down on the table.[125]

Wednesday stared at both of them as if he had just discovered new and previously unimagined life forms.[126] Then he said, "Mead for you, Shadow. I'll stick with Mister Jack Daniel's, and for the freeloading Irishman . . . ?"

"A bottled beer, something dark for preference," said Sweeney. "Freeloader, is it?" He picked up what was left of his drink, and raised it to Wednesday in a toast. "May the storm pass over us, and leave us hale and unharmed," he said, and knocked the drink back.

"A fine toast," said Wednesday. "But it won't."

Another mead was placed in front of Shadow.

"Do I have to drink this?"[127] he asked, without enthusiasm.

"Yes, I'm afraid you do. It seals our deal. Third time's the charm, eh?"

122. This sentence does not appear in the First Edition.

123. Said in true conjurer's fashion—the only response proper to a lay audience.

124. The classic production of dozens of coins apparently from thin air. It was first popularized by stage magician T. Nelson Downs in 1895.

125. This sentence does not appear in the First Edition.

126. This sentence does not appear in the First Edition, and the following reads, "Wednesday said, . . ."

127. The balance of this sentence does not appear in the First Edition.

"Shit," said Shadow. He swallowed the mead in two large gulps. The pickled honey taste filled his mouth.

"There," said Mr. Wednesday. "You're my man, now."

"So," said Sweeney, "you want to know the trick of how it's done?"

"Yes," said Shadow. "Were you loading them in your sleeve?"

"They were never in my sleeve," said Sweeney. He chortled to himself, rocking and bouncing as if he were a lanky, bearded, drunken volcano preparing to erupt with delight at his own brilliance. "It's the simplest trick in the world. I'll fight you for it."

Shadow shook his head. "I'll pass."

"Now *there's* a fine thing," said Sweeney to the room. "Old Wednesday gets himself a bodyguard, and the feller's too scared to put up his fists, even."

"I won't fight you," agreed Shadow.

Sweeney swayed and sweated. He fiddled with the peak of his baseball cap. Then he pulled one of his coins out of the air and placed it on the table. "Real gold, if you were wondering," said Sweeney. "Win or lose—and you'll lose—it's yours if you fight me. A big fellow like you— who'd'a thought you'd be a fucken coward?"

"He's already said he won't fight you," said Wednesday. "Go away, Mad Sweeney. Take your beer and leave us in peace."

Sweeney took a step closer to Wednesday. "Call me a freeloader, will you, you doomed old creature? You cold-blooded, heartless old tree-hanger." His face was turning a deep, angry red.

Wednesday put out his hands, palms up, pacific. "Foolishness, Sweeney. Watch where you put your words."

Sweeney glared at him. Then he said, with the gravity of the very drunk, "You've hired a coward. What would he do if I hurt you, do you think?"

Wednesday turned to Shadow. "I've had enough of this," he said. "Deal with it."

Shadow got to his feet and looked up into Mad Sweeney's face: how tall *was* the man? he wondered. "You're bothering us," he said. "You're drunk. I think you ought to leave now."

A slow smile spread over Sweeney's face. "There, now," he said.[128] "Like a little yapping dog, it's finally ready to fight. Hey, everybody," he called to the room, "there's going to be a lesson learned. Watch this!" He swung a huge fist at Shadow's face. Shadow jerked back: Sweeney's hand caught him beneath the right eye. He saw blotches of light, and felt pain.

And with that, the fight began.

Sweeney fought without style, without science, with nothing but enthusiasm for the fight itself: huge, barreling roundhouse blows that missed as often as they connected.

Shadow fought defensively, carefully, blocking Sweeney's blows or avoiding them. He became very aware of the audience around them. Tables were pulled out of the way with protesting groans, making a space for the men to spar. Shadow was aware at all times of Wednesday's eyes upon him, of Wednesday's humorless grin. It was a test, that was obvious, but what kind of a test? In prison Shadow had learned there were two kinds of fights: *don't fuck with me* fights, where you made it as showy and impressive as you could, and private fights, *real* fights which were fast and hard and nasty, and always over in seconds.

"Hey, Sweeney," said Shadow, breathless, "why are we fighting?"

"For the joy of it," said Sweeney, sober now, or at least, no longer visibly drunk. "For the sheer unholy fucken delight of it. Can't you feel the joy in your own veins, rising like the sap in the springtime?" His lip was bleeding. So was Shadow's knuckle.

"So how'd you do the coin production?" asked Shadow. He swayed back and twisted, took a blow on his shoulder intended for his face.

"To tell the truth," grunted Sweeney, "I told you how I did it when first we spoke. But there's none so blind—ow! Good one!—as those who will not listen."

Shadow jabbed at Sweeney, forcing him back into a table; empty glasses and ashtrays crashed to the floor. Shadow could have finished him off then.[129] The man was defenseless, in no position to be able to do anything, sprawled back as he was.[130]

128. The next two sentences do not appear in the First Edition.

129. This and the next four sentences were not in the First Draft.

130. This sentence does not appear in the First Edition.

Shadow glanced at Wednesday, who nodded. Shadow looked down at Mad Sweeney. "Are we done?" he asked. Mad Sweeney hesitated, then nodded. Shadow let go of him, and took several steps backward. Sweeney, panting, pushed himself back up to a standing position.

"Not on yer ass!" he shouted. "It ain't over till I say it is!" Then he grinned, and threw himself forward, swinging at Shadow. He stepped onto a fallen ice-cube, and his grin turned to open-mouthed dismay as his feet went out from under him, and he fell backward. The back of his head hit the barroom floor with a definite thud.

Shadow put his knee into Mad Sweeney's chest. "For the second time, are we done fighting?" he asked.

"We may as well be, at that," said Sweeney, raising his head from the floor, "for the joy's gone out of me now, like the pee from a small boy in a swimming pool on a hot day." And he spat the blood from his mouth and closed his eyes and began to snore, in deep and magnificent snores.

Somebody clapped Shadow on the back. Wednesday put a bottle of beer into his hand.

It tasted better than mead.

*　　*　　*

SHADOW WOKE UP stretched out in the back of a sedan car. The morning sun was dazzling, and his head hurt. He sat up awkwardly, rubbing his eyes.

Wednesday was driving. He was humming tunelessly as he drove. He had a paper cup of coffee in the cup holder. They were heading along what looked like an interstate highway, with the cruise control set to an even sixty-five.[131] The passenger seat was empty.

"How are you feeling, this fine morning?" asked Wednesday, without turning around.

"What happened to my car?" asked Shadow. "It was a rental."

"Mad Sweeney took it back for you. It was part of the deal the two of you cut last night."

"Deal?"

"After the fight."

131. The cruise control is not mentioned in the First Edition.

"Fight?" He put one hand up and rubbed his cheek, and then he winced. Yes, there had been a fight. He remembered a tall man with a ginger beard, and the cheering and whooping of an appreciative audience. "Who won?"

"You don't remember, eh?" Wednesday chuckled.

"Not so you'd notice," said Shadow.[132] Conversations from the night before began to jostle in his head uncomfortably. "You got any more of that coffee?"

The big man reached beneath the passenger seat and passed back an unopened bottle of water. "Here. You'll be dehydrated. This will help more than coffee, for the moment. We'll stop at the next gas station and get you some breakfast. You'll need to clean yourself up, too. You look like something the goat dragged in."

"Cat dragged in," said Shadow.

"Goat," said Wednesday. "Huge rank stinking goat with big teeth."[133]

Shadow unscrewed the top of the water and drank. Something clinked heavily in his jacket pocket. He put his hand into the pocket and pulled out a coin the size of a half-dollar. It was heavy, and a deep yellow in color.[134] It was also slightly sticky. Shadow palmed it in his right hand, classic palm, then produced it from between his third and fourth fingers. He front-palmed it, holding it between his first and his little finger, so it was invisible from behind, then slipped his two middle fingers under it, pivoting it smoothly into a back-palm. Finally he dropped the coin back into his left hand, and he placed it into his pocket.

"What the hell was I drinking last night?" asked Shadow. The events of the night were crowding around him now, without shape, without sense, but he knew they were there.

Mr. Wednesday spotted an exit sign promising a gas station, and he gunned the engine. "You don't remember?"

"No."

"You were drinking mead," said Wednesday. He grinned a huge grin.

Mead.

Yes.

Shadow leaned back in the seat, and sucked down water

132. This sentence and the two preceding paragraphs do not appear in the First Edition.

133. Goats were of course plentiful in Norway and thus in Norse myths. Probably the most useful was the goat Heidrun, mentioned in the *Poetic Edda,* who ate the leaves of the tree Læraðr and whose teats ran with mead.

134. The entire remainder of this section of the chapter does not appear in the First Edition.

from the bottle, and let the night before wash over him. Most of it, he remembered. Some of it, he didn't.

*   *   *

IN THE GAS station Shadow bought a Clean-U-Up Kit, which contained a razor, a packet of shaving cream, a comb, and a disposable toothbrush packed with a tiny tube of toothpaste. Then he walked into the men's restroom and looked at himself in the mirror.

He had a bruise under one eye—when he prodded it, experimentally, with one finger, he found it hurt deeply—and a swollen lower lip.[135] His hair was a tangle, and he looked as if he had spent the first half of last night fighting and then the rest of the night fast asleep, fully dressed, in the back seat of a car. Tinny music played in the background: it took him some moments to identify it as the Beatles' "Fool on the Hill."[136]

Shadow washed his face with the restroom's liquid soap, then he lathered his face and shaved. He wet his hair and combed it back.[137] He brushed his teeth. Then he washed the last traces of the soap and the toothpaste from his face with lukewarm water. Stared back at his reflection: clean-shaven, but his eyes were still red and puffy. He looked older than he remembered.

He wondered what Laura would say when she saw him, and then he remembered that Laura wouldn't say anything ever again and he saw his face, in the mirror, tremble, but only for a moment.

He went out.

"I look like shit," said Shadow.

"Of course you do," agreed Wednesday.

Wednesday took an assortment of snack-food up to the cash register, and paid for that and their gas, changing his mind twice about whether he was doing it with plastic or with cash, to the irritation of the gum-chewing young lady behind the till. Shadow watched as Wednesday became increasingly flustered and apologetic. He seemed very old, suddenly. The girl gave him his cash back, and put the purchase on the card, and then gave him the card receipt and

132. This sentence and the two preceding paragraphs do not appear in the First Edition.

135. The balance of this paragraph does not appear in the First Edition.

136. The song is credited to John Lennon and Paul McCartney, though McCartney apparently wrote it. The song was recorded, with McCartney as the lead, in 1967 and included on the *Magical Mystery Tour* album later that year. The lyrics of the song describe an outcast visionary like the Maharishi Mahesh Yogi, who influenced the Beatles.

137. The balance of this paragraph does not appear in the First Edition.

took his cash, then returned the cash and took a different card. Wednesday was obviously on the verge of tears, an old man made helpless by the implacable plastic march of the modern world.

Shadow checked out the payphone: an out-of-order sign hung on it.[138]

They walked out of the warm gas station, and their breath steamed in the air.

"You want me to drive?" asked Shadow.[139]

"Hell no," said Wednesday.

The freeway slipped past them: browning grass meadows on each side of them. The trees were leafless and dead. Two black birds stared at them from a telegraph wire.

"Hey, Wednesday."

"What?"

"The way I saw it in there, you never paid for the gas."

"Oh?"

"The way I saw it, she wound up paying you for the privilege of having you in her gas station. You think she's figured it out yet?"

"She never will."

"So what are you? A two-bit con artist?"

Wednesday nodded. "Yes," he said. "I suppose I am. Among other things."

He swung out into the left lane to pass a truck. The sky was a bleak and uniform gray.

"It's going to snow," said Shadow.

"Yes."

"Sweeney. Did he actually show me how he did that trick with the gold coins?"

"Oh yes."

"I can't remember."

"It'll come back. It was a long night."

Several small snowflakes brushed the windshield, melting in seconds.

"Your wife's body is on display at Wendell's Funeral Parlor at present," said Wednesday. "Then after lunch they will take her from there to the graveyard for the interment."

"How do you know?"

138. This sentence does not appear in the First Edition.

139. Shadow does not ask and Wednesday does not answer in the First Edition.

140. This sentence does not appear in the First Edition.

141. Concealment of a coin at the base of the first finger, held by the flesh of the thumb. The move is described carefully in Bobo's *Modern Coin Magic* and is generally attributed to T. Nelson Downs; it was first published in Camille Gaultier's *Magic Without Apparatus* in 1914.

"I called ahead while you were in the john. You know where Wendell's Funeral Parlor is?"

Shadow nodded. The snowflakes whirled and dizzied in front of them.

"This is our exit," said Shadow. The car stole off the interstate, and past the cluster of motels to the north of Eagle Point.

Three years had passed. Yes. The Super-8 motel had gone, torn down: in its place was a Wendy's.[140] There were more stoplights, unfamiliar storefronts. They drove downtown. Shadow asked Wednesday to slow as they drove past the Muscle Farm. CLOSED INDEFINITELY, said the hand-lettered sign on the door, DUE TO BEREAVEMENT.

Left on Main Street. Past a new tattoo parlor and the Armed Forces Recruitment Center, then the Burger King, and, familiar and unchanged, Olsen's Drug Store, and at last the yellow-brick facade of Wendell's Funeral Parlor. A neon sign in the front window said HOUSE OF REST. Blank tombstones stood unchristened and uncarved in the window beneath the sign.

Wednesday pulled up in the parking lot.

"Do you want me to come in?" he asked.

"Not particularly."

"Good." The grin flashed, without humor. "There's business I can be getting on with while you say your goodbyes. I'll get rooms for us at the Motel America. Meet me there when you're done."

Shadow got out of the car, and watched it pull away. Then he walked in. The dimly lit corridor smelled of flowers and of furniture polish, with just the slightest tang of formaldehyde and rot beneath the surface. At the far end was the Chapel of Rest.

Shadow realized that he was palming the gold coin, moving it compulsively from a back palm to a front palm to a Downs palm,[141] over and over. The weight was reassuring in his hand.

His wife's name was on a sheet of paper beside the door at the far end of the corridor. He walked into the Chapel of Rest. Shadow knew most of the people in the room: Laura's family, her workmates at the travel agency, several of her friends.

They all recognized him. He could see it in their faces. There were no smiles, though, no hellos.[142]

At the end of the room was a small dais, and, on it, a cream-colored casket with several displays of flowers arranged about it: scarlets and yellows and whites and deep, bloody purples. He took a step forward. He could see Laura's body from where he was standing. He did not want to walk forward; he did not dare to walk away.

A man in a dark suit—Shadow guessed he worked at the funeral home—said, "Sir? Would you like to sign the condolence and remembrance book?" and pointed him to a leather-bound book, open on a small lectern.

He wrote SHADOW[143] and the date in his precise handwriting, then, slowly, he wrote (PUPPY) beside it, putting off walking toward the end of the room, where the people were, and the casket, and the thing in the cream casket that was no longer Laura.

A small woman walked in from the corridor, and hesitated. Her hair was a coppery red, and her clothes were expensive and very black. *Widow's weeds,* thought Shadow, who knew her well: Audrey Burton, Robbie's wife.[144]

Audrey was holding a sprig of violets, wrapped at the base with silver foil. It was the kind of thing a child would make in June, thought Shadow. But violets were out of season.

Audrey looked directly at Shadow, and there was no recognition in her eyes.[145] Then she walked across the room, to Laura's casket. Shadow followed her.

Laura lay with her eyes closed, and her arms folded across her chest. She wore a conservative blue suit he did not recognize. Her long brown hair was out of her eyes. It was his Laura and it was not: her repose, he realized, was what was unnatural. Laura was always such a restless sleeper.

Audrey placed her sprig of summer violets on Laura's chest. Then she pursed her blackberry-colored lips, worked her mouth for a moment and spat, hard, onto Laura's dead face.

The spit caught Laura on the cheek, and began to drip down toward her ear.

142. This paragraph is not in the First Draft.

143. In the Manuscript, he writes "BURMA SHADOW."

144. In the Manuscript, her name is Anna-Louise. In the First Draft, it is Babette.

145. This sentence does not appear in the First Edition.

146. This sentence does not appear in the First Edition.

Audrey was already walking toward the door. Shadow hurried after her. "Audrey?" he said. This time she recognized him.[146] He wondered if she was taking tranquilizers. Her voice was distant and detached.

"Shadow? Did you escape? Or did they let you out?"

"Let me out yesterday. I'm a free man," said Shadow. "What the hell was that all about?"

She stopped in the dark corridor. "The violets? They were always her favorite flower. When we were girls we used to pick them together."

"Not the violets."

"Oh, *that*," she said. She wiped a speck of something invisible from the corner of her mouth. "Well, I would have thought that was obvious."

"Not to me, Audrey."

"They didn't tell you?" Her voice was calm, emotionless. "Your wife died with my husband's cock in her mouth, Shadow."

147. This sentence does not appear in the First Edition.

She turned away, walked out into the parking lot, and Shadow watched her leave.[147]

He went back into the funeral home. Someone had already wiped away the spit.

✦   ✦   ✦

148. This paragraph does not appear in the First Edition.

NONE OF THE people at the viewing were able to meet Shadow's eye. Those who came over and talked to him did so as little as they could, mumbled awkward commiserations and fled.[148]

After lunch—Shadow ate at the Burger King—was the burial. Laura's cream-colored coffin was interred in the small non-denominational cemetery on the edge of town: unfenced, a hilly woodland meadow filled with black granite and white marble headstones.

149. Mrs. Minos, in the First Draft.

He rode to the cemetery in the Wendell's hearse, with Laura's mother. Mrs. McCabe[149] seemed to feel that Laura's death was Shadow's fault. "If you'd been here," she said, "this would never have happened. I don't know why she married you. I told her. Time and again, I told her. But they don't listen to their mothers, do they?" She stopped, looked more closely at Shadow's face. "Have you been fighting?"

"Yes," he said.

"Barbarian," she said, then she set her mouth, raised her head so her chins quivered, and stared straight ahead of her.

To Shadow's surprise Audrey Burton was also at the funeral, standing toward the back. The short service ended, the casket was lowered into the cold ground. The people went away.

Shadow did not leave. He stood there with his hands in his pockets, shivering, staring at the hole in the ground.

Above him the sky was iron gray, featureless and flat as a mirror. It continued to snow, erratically, in ghost-like tumbling flakes.

There was something he wanted to say to Laura, and he was prepared to wait until he knew what it was. The world slowly began to lose light and color. Shadow's feet were going numb, while his hands and face hurt from the cold. He burrowed his hands into his pockets for warmth, and his fingers closed about the gold coin.

Shadow at Laura's funeral (played by Ricky Whittle, from the Starz presentation of *American Gods*)
Photo copyright © 2018 Fremantle North America

He walked over to the grave.

"This is for you," he said.

Several shovels of earth had been emptied onto the casket, but the hole was far from full. He threw the gold coin into the grave with Laura, then he pushed more earth into the hole, to hide the coin from acquisitive gravediggers. He brushed the earth from his hands, and said, "Good night, Laura." Then he said, "I'm sorry." He turned his face toward the lights of the town, and began to walk back into Eagle Point.

His motel was a good two miles away, but after spending three years in prison he was relishing the idea that he could simply walk and walk, forever if need be. He could keep walking north, and wind up in Alaska, or head south, to Mexico and beyond. He could walk to Patagonia, or to Tierra del Fuego.[150] The Land of Fire. He tried to remember how it had got its name: he remembered reading as a boy of naked men, crouched by fires to keep warm . . .

A car drew up beside him. The window hummed down.

"You want a lift, Shadow?" asked Audrey Burton.

"No," he said. "Not from you."

He continued to walk. Audrey drove beside him at three miles an hour. Snowflakes danced in the beams of her headlights.

"I thought she was my best friend," said Audrey. "We'd talk every day. When Robbie and I had a fight, she'd be the first one to know—we'd go down to Chi-Chi's for margaritas and to talk about what scumpots men can be. And all the time she was fucking him behind my back."

"Please go away, Audrey."

"I just want you to know I had good reason for what I did." He said nothing.

"Hey!" she shouted. "Hey! I'm talking to you!"

Shadow turned. "Do you want me to tell you that you were right when you spit in Laura's face? Do you want me to say it didn't hurt? Or that what you told me made me hate her more than I miss her? It's not going to happen, Audrey."

She drove beside him for another minute, not saying anything. Then she said, "So, how was prison, Shadow?"

---

150. The balance of this paragraph does not appear in the First Edition.

"It was fine," said Shadow. "You would have felt right at home."

She put her foot down on the gas then, making the engine roar, and drove on and away.

With the headlights gone, the world was dark. Twilight faded into night. Shadow kept expecting the act of walking to warm him, to spread warmth through his icy hands and feet. It didn't happen.

Back in prison, Low Key Lyesmith[151] had once referred to the little prison cemetery out behind the infirmary as the Bone Orchard, and the image had taken root in Shadow's mind. That night he had dreamed of an orchard under the moonlight, of skeletal white trees, their branches ending in bony hands, their roots going deep down into the graves. There was fruit that grew upon the trees in the bone orchard, in his dream, and there was something very disturbing about the fruit in the dream, but on waking he could no longer remember what strange fruit grew on the trees, or why he found it so repellent.

Cars passed him. Shadow wished that there was a sidewalk. He tripped on something that he could not see in the dark and sprawled into the ditch on the side of the road, his right hand sinking into several inches of cold mud. He climbed to his feet and wiped his hands on the leg of his pants. He stood there, awkwardly. He had only enough time to observe that there was someone beside him before something wet was forced over his nose and mouth, and he tasted harsh, chemical fumes.

This time the ditch seemed warm and comforting.

*   *   *

SHADOW'S TEMPLES FELT as if they had been reattached to the rest of his skull with roofing nails,[152] and his vision was blurred.

His hands were bound behind his back with what felt like some kind of straps. He was in a car, sitting on leather upholstery. For a moment he wondered if there was something wrong with his depth perception and then he understood that, no, the other seat really *was* that far away.

151. This is the first mention of Low-key in the Manuscript, and he is described here as a *"self-styled grifter extraordinaire."*

152. The sentence ends here in the First Edition.

There were people sitting beside him, but he could not turn to look at them.

The fat young man at the other end of the stretch limo took a can of Diet Coke from the cocktail bar and popped it open. He wore a long black coat, made of some silky material, and he appeared barely out of his teens: a spattering of acne glistened on one cheek. He smiled when he saw that Shadow was awake.

"Hello, Shadow," he said. "Don't fuck with me."

"Okay," said Shadow. "I won't. Can you drop me off at the Motel America, up by the interstate?"

"Hit him," said the young man to the person on Shadow's left. A punch was delivered to Shadow's solar plexus, knocking the breath from him, doubling him over. He straightened up, slowly.

"I said don't fuck with me. That was fucking with me. Keep your answers short and to the point or I'll fucking kill you. Or maybe I won't kill you. Maybe I'll have the children break every bone in your fucking body. There are two hundred and six of them. So don't fuck with me."

"Got it," said Shadow.

The ceiling lights in the limo changed color from violet to blue then to green and to yellow.

"You're working for Wednesday," said the young man.

"Yes," said Shadow.

"What the fuck is he after? I mean, what's he doing here? He must have a plan. What's the game plan?"

"I started working for Mister Wednesday this morning," said Shadow. "I'm an errand boy.[153] Maybe a driver, if he ever lets me drive. We've barely exchanged a dozen words."

"You're saying you don't know?"

"I'm saying I don't know."[154]

The boy stared at him. He swigged some Coke from the can, belched, stared some more. "Would you tell me if you did know?"

"Probably not," admitted Shadow. "As you say, I'm working for Mr. Wednesday."

The boy opened his jacket and took out a silver cigarette

153. The paragraph ends here in the First Edition.

154. The next two sentences do not appear in the First Edition.

The god of technology, who refers to himself later as "a technical boy"
(from the Starz presentation of *American Gods,* where he is played by Bruce Langley)
Photo copyright © 2018 Fremantle North America

case from an inside pocket. He opened it, and offered a cigarette to Shadow. "Smoke?"

Shadow thought about asking for his hands to be untied, but decided against it. "No thank you," he said.

The cigarette appeared to have been hand-rolled, and when the boy lit it, with a matte black Zippo lighter,[155] the odor that filled the limo was not tobacco. It was not pot either, decided Shadow. It smelled a little like burning electrical parts.

The boy inhaled deeply, then held his breath. He let the smoke trickle out from his mouth, pulled it back into his nostrils. Shadow suspected that he had practiced that in front of a mirror for a while before doing it in public.

"If you've lied to me," said the boy, as if from a long way away, "I'll fucking kill you. You know that."

"So you said."

155. The balance of this sentence and the next sentence do not appear in the First Edition.

The Zippo lighter has been described as "a legendary and distinct symbol of America." The company was founded in 1932, and when World War II broke out, the company devoted all of its resources to producing lighters for the military. The omnipresence of the lighter among the troops led to the legends of lives saved when bullets were deflected by the metal case or of long-lost lighters reappearing across continents. Because of its association with the military, the Zippo became a distinctly masculine symbol. It still sells widely today: In 2012, the company celebrated production of its 500,000,000th lighter. A museum called the "Zippo/Case Visitors Center" is at 1932 Zippo Drive in Bradford, Pennsylvania.

156. This sentence does not appear in the First Edition.

157. The sentences "And he better accept it." and "His time is over. Yes? You fucking tell him that, man." do not appear in the First Edition.

158. Bufotenin or bufotenine is an alkaloid found in the skin of some species of toads, and in mushrooms, higher plants, and mammals. Ingested or smoked by humans, it produces psychedelic reactions like LSD or mescalin. The alkaloid is used in snuff in Central American religions, the tree bark containing it is smoked by South American shamans, and the Church of the Toad of Light advocates extracting it from the toad skins and smoking it. It is illegal in the U.S. and other countries, and there is no known synthetic compound with the same chemical structure.

159. The balance of this paragraph does not appear in the First Edition.

The boy took another long drag on his cigarette. The lights inside the limo transmuted from orange, to red, and back to purple.[156] "You say you're staying at the Motel America?" He tapped on the driver's window, behind him. The glass window lowered. "Hey. Motel America, up by the interstate. We need to drop off our guest."

The driver nodded, and the glass rose up again.

The glinting fiber-optic lights inside the limo continued to change, cycling through their set of dim colors. It seemed to Shadow that the boy's eyes were glinting too, the green of an antique computer monitor.

"You tell Wednesday this, man. You tell him he's history. He's forgotten. He's old. And he better accept it.[157] Tell him that we are the future and we don't give a fuck about him or anyone like him. His time is over. Yes? You fucking tell him that, man. He has been consigned to the Dumpster of history while people like me ride our limos down the superhighway of tomorrow."

"I'll tell him," said Shadow. He was beginning to feel light-headed. He hoped that he was not going to be sick.

"Tell him that we have fucking reprogrammed reality. Tell him that language is a virus and that religion is an operating system and that prayers are just so much fucking spam. Tell him that or I'll fucking kill you," said the young man mildly, from the smoke.

"Got it," said Shadow. "You can let me out here. I can walk the rest of the way."

The young man nodded. "Good talking to you," he said. The smoke had mellowed him. "You should know that if we do fucking kill you then we'll just delete you. You got that? One click and you're overwritten with random ones and zeros. Undelete is not an option." He tapped on the window behind him. "He's getting off here," he said. Then he turned back to Shadow, pointed to his cigarette. "Synthetic toad-skins," he said. "You know they can synthesize bufotenin[158] now?"

The car stopped. The person to Shadow's right got out and held the door open for Shadow. Shadow climbed out awkwardly,[159] his hands tied behind his back. He realized that he had not yet got a clear look at either of the people who had been in the back seat with him. He did not know if they were men or women, old or young.

Shadow's bonds were cut. The nylon strips fell to the tarmac. Shadow turned around. The inside of the car was now one writhing cloud of smoke in which two lights glinted, copper-colored, like the beautiful eyes of a toad. "It's all about the dominant fucking paradigm, Shadow. Nothing else is important. And hey, sorry to hear about your old lady."

The door closed, and the stretch limo drove off, quietly. Shadow was a couple of hundred yards away from his motel, and he walked there, breathing the cold air, past red and yellow and blue lights advertising every kind of fast food a man could imagine, as long as it was a hamburger; and he reached the Motel America without incident.

CHAPTER THREE

160. This is usually rendered as a Latin proverb: *Vulnerant omnia, ultima necat.* (All the hours wound you, the last one kills.)

Every hour wounds. The last one kills.
—OLD SAYING[160]

 HERE WAS A thin young woman behind the counter at the Motel America. She told Shadow he had already been checked in by his friend, and gave him his rectangular plastic room key. She had pale blonde hair and a rodent-like quality to her face that was most apparent when she looked suspicious, and eased when she smiled. Most of the time she looked at Shadow, she looked suspicious.[161] She refused to tell him Wednesday's room number, and insisted on telephoning Wednesday on the house phone to let him know his guest was here.

161. This sentence does not appear in the First Edition.

Wednesday came out of a room down the hall, and beckoned to Shadow.

"How was the funeral?" he asked.

"It's over," said Shadow.

162. This sentence does not appear in the First Edition.

"That shitty, huh?[162] You want to talk about it?"

"No," said Shadow.

"Good." Wednesday grinned. "Too much talking these days. Talk talk talk. This country would get along much better if people learned how to suffer in silence.[163] You hungry?"

163. The following four sentences do not appear in the First Edition.

"A little."

70

"There's no food here. But you can order a pizza and they'll put it on the room."

Wednesday led the way back to his room, which was across the hall from Shadow's. There were maps all over the room, unfolded, spread out on the bed, taped to the walls. Wednesday had drawn all over the maps in bright marking pens, fluorescent greens and painful pinks and vivid oranges.

"I got hijacked by a fat kid in a limo," said Shadow. "He says to tell you that you have been consigned to the dung heap of history while people like him ride in their limos down the superhighways of life. Something like that."

"Little snot," said Wednesday.

"You know him?"

Wednesday shrugged. "I know who he is." He sat down, heavily, on the room's only chair. "They don't have a clue," he said. "They don't have a fucking clue. How much longer do you need to stay in town?"

"I don't know. Maybe another week. I guess I need to wrap up Laura's affairs. Take care of the apartment, get rid of her clothes, all that. It'll drive her mother nuts, but the woman deserves it."

Wednesday nodded his huge head. "Well, the sooner you're done, the sooner we can move out of Eagle Point. Good night."

Shadow walked across the hall. His room was a duplicate of Wednesday's room, down to the print of a bloody sunset on the wall above the bed. He ordered a cheese and meatball pizza, then he ran a bath, pouring all the motel's little plastic bottles of shampoo into the water, making it foam.

He was too big to lie down in the bathtub, but he sat in it and luxuriated as best he could. Shadow had promised himself a bath when he got out of prison, and Shadow kept his promises.

The pizza arrived shortly after he got out of the bath, and Shadow ate it, washing it down with a can of root beer.[164]

He turned on the television, and watched an episode of Jerry Springer he remembered from before he went to prison. The theme of the show was "I want to be a prosti-

164. The following paragraph does not appear in the First Edition.

165. Jerry Springer was born in the U.K. but raised in the United States. He practiced law in Cincinnati, Ohio, for more than a decade, while he also pursued a career in journalism. He became a local newscaster and eventually the political reporter and commentator for NBC's Cincinnati television station WLWT. This platform launched Springer into politics, including public service as a member of the City Council and as the mayor of Cincinnati. He ran unsuccessfully for governor of Ohio in 1982.

In 1991, the television station developed a talk show, *The Jerry Springer Show*, featuring extended versions of Springer's political commentaries, and cast him as a local version of the popular television host Phil Donahue. In 1994, however, the show changed course radically, shifting focus to sex and relationships. Unlike many other talk shows, it featured non-celebrity guests, usually persons who were in relationships or families or had similar lifestyles. For example, "My boyfriend turned out to be a girl" was a popular episode, as was "I want my man to stop watching porn." Embracing its branding as "tabloid" and "sensational," the show also seemed to celebrate deviant behavior on- and off-stage. In its new incarnation, *The Jerry Springer Show* was wildly successful, running in many markets throughout the U.S. daily until 2018. It was copied extensively outside the U.S., and reruns aired widely.

Springer thrived on confrontations between the guests, and there was often scripted brawling on stage or in the audience. In 2002, Nancy Campbell-Panitz, who appeared on the show with her former husband Ralf Panitz and his new girlfriend, was murdered by her ex-husband within hours of the appearance, and Campbell-Panitz's sons sued the show, claiming that it fostered such violence. The incident did nothing to diminish the show's audience, however, although one critic called the show "the worst in the history of television."

The programs invariably concluded with tute" and several would-be whores, most of them female, were brought out, shouted at and hectored by the audience; then a gold-draped pimp came out and offered them employment in his stable, and an ex-hooker ran out and pleaded with them all to get real jobs. Shadow turned it off before Jerry got to his thought for the day.[165]

Shadow lay in bed, thinking, *This is my first bed as a free man,* and the thought gave him less pleasure than he had imagined that it would. He left the drapes open, watched the lights of the cars and of the fast food joints through the window glass, comforted to know there was another world out there, one he could walk to any time he wanted.

Shadow could have been in his bed at home, he thought, in the apartment that he had shared with Laura—in the bed that he had shared with Laura. But the thought of being there without her, surrounded by her things, her scent, her life, was simply too painful . . .

Don't go there, thought Shadow. He decided to think about something else. He thought about coin tricks. Shadow knew that he did not have the personality to be a magician: he could not weave the stories that were so necessary for belief, nor did he wish to do card tricks, or produce paper flowers. But he liked to manipulate coins; he enjoyed the craft of it. He started to list the coin vanishes he had mastered, which reminded him of the coin he had tossed into Laura's grave, and then, in his head, Audrey was telling him that Laura had died with Robbie's cock in her mouth, and once again he felt a small hurt in his chest. In his heart.

Every hour wounds. The last one kills. Where had he heard that?[166] He could no longer remember. He could feel, somewhere deep inside him, anger and pain building, a knot of tension at the base of his skull, a tightness at the temples. He breathed in through his nose, out through his mouth, forcing himself to let the tension go.

He thought of Wednesday's comment and smiled, despite himself: Shadow had heard too many people telling each other not to repress their feelings, to let their emotions out, let the pain go. Shadow thought there was a lot to be said for bottling up emotions. If you did it long enough and deep enough, he suspected, pretty soon you wouldn't feel anything at all.

Sleep took him then, without Shadow noticing.

He was walking . . .

He was walking through a room bigger than a city, and everywhere he looked there were statues and carvings and rough-hewn images. He was standing beside a statue of a woman-like thing: her naked breasts hung, flat and pendulous on her chest, around her waist was a chain of severed hands, both of her own hands held sharp knives, and, instead of a head, rising from her neck there were twin serpents, their bodies arched, facing each other, ready to attack.[167] There was something profoundly disturbing about the statue, a deep and violent wrongness. Shadow backed away from it.

He began to walk through the hall. The carved eyes of those statues that had eyes seemed to follow his every step.

In his dream, he realized that each statue had a name burning on the floor in front of it. The man with the white hair, with a necklace of teeth about his neck, holding a drum, was *Leucotios;*[168] the broad-hipped woman, with monsters dropping from the vast gash between her legs, was *Hubur;*[169] the ram-headed man holding the golden ball was *Hershef.*[170]

A precise voice, fussy and exact, was speaking to him, in his dream, but he could see no one.[171]

"These are gods who have been forgotten, and now might as well be dead. They can be found only in dry histories. They are gone, all gone, but their names and their images remain with us."

Shadow turned a corner, and knew himself to be in another room, even vaster than the first. It went on further than the eye could see. Close to him was the skull of a mammoth, polished and brown, and a hairy ocher cloak, being worn by a small woman with a deformed left hand.[172] Next to that were three women, each carved from the same granite boulder, joined at the waist: their faces had an unfinished, hasty look to them, although their breasts and genitalia had been carved with elaborate care;[173] and there

Springer's "Final Thought," a personal lecture to the guests on the moral values that Springer thought they should espouse, and Springer's trademark sign-off: "Till next time, take care of yourselves and each other."

166. The balance of this paragraph does not appear in the First Edition.

167. Coatlicue, in Aztec mythology, is described as having a skirt of snakes, a necklace of hearts and hands supporting a skull pendant, clawed hands and feet, with flabby breasts. She was the magically impregnated mother of Huitzilopochtli, the earth serpent deity, and one of the wives of Mixcoatl, the Cloud Serpent of the Milky Way.

168. A god with many variant names, including Cocidius (British), Alator (Celtic), Loucetius (Celtic), Totates or Teutates (Celtic), but in each case a war god, identified with Mars.

Aztec statue of Coatlicue
Museo Nacional de Antropología e Historia de la Ciudad de México

Drawing of plaque dedication to Cocidius,
ca. 43–410 C.E., at Bewcastle, England

169. Hubur or Hubar, which means "river" in ancient Sumerian, was identified as the river of the underworld and is also identified with Tiamat, the goddess of the primeval sea, a mother-goddess, credited with populating the world with monsters and creatures such as scorpions, spiders, and other pests.

170. The god appears as Arsaphes among the Greeks and Harsaphes in Egypt. He was a god of fertility and water and was principally worshipped at Heracleopolis Magna; the god was also known as "Terrible Face."

171. In light of Shadow's complicated relationship with time, this is likely Mr. Ibis, whom Shadow has not yet met.

172. See text accompanying note 664, below.

173. Triple female deities, sometimes conjoined, sometimes morphing into other shapes, are common in the pantheon of ancient deities. The Morrigan and the Norn, both discussed below, are, respectively, Irish and Norse; the

was a flightless bird which Shadow did not recognize, twice his height, with a beak made for rending, like a vulture's, but with human arms:[174] and on, and on.

The voice spoke once more, as if it were addressing a class, saying, "These are the gods who have passed out of memory. Even their names are lost. The people who worshiped them are as forgotten as their gods. Their totems are long since broken and cast down. Their last priests died without passing on their secrets.

"Gods die. And when they truly die they are unmourned and unremembered. Ideas are more difficult to kill than people, but they can be killed, in the end."

There was a whispering noise that began then to run through the hall, a low susurrus that caused Shadow, in his dream, to experience a chilling and inexplicable fear. An all-engulfing panic took him, there in the halls of the Gods whose very existence had been forgotten—octopus-faced gods and gods who were only mummified hands or falling rocks or forest fires . . .

Shadow woke with his heart jackhammering in his chest, his forehead clammy, entirely awake. The red numerals on the bedside clock told him the time was 1:03 A.M. The light of the Motel America sign outside shone through his bedroom window. Disoriented, Shadow got up and walked into the tiny motel bathroom. He pissed without turning on the lights, and returned to the bedroom. The dream was still fresh and vivid in his mind's eye, but he could not explain to himself why it had scared him so.

The light that came into the room from outside was not bright, but Shadow's eyes had become used to the dark. There was a woman sitting on the side of his bed.

He knew her. He would have known her in a crowd of a thousand, or of a hundred thousand. She sat straight on the side of his bed.[175] She was still wearing the navy-blue suit they had buried her in.

Her voice was a whisper, but a familiar one. "I guess," said Laura, "you're going to ask what I'm doing here."

Shadow said nothing.

He sat down on the room's only chair, and, finally, asked, "Babe? Is that you?"

"Yes," she said. "I'm cold, puppy."

"You're dead, babe."

"Yes," she said. "Yes. I am." She patted the bed next to her. "Come and sit by me," she said.

"No," said Shadow. "I think I'll stay right here for now. We have some unresolved issues to address."

"Like me being dead?"

"Possibly, but I was thinking more of how you died. You and Robbie."

"Oh," she said. "That."

Shadow could smell—or perhaps, he thought, he simply imagined that he smelled—an odor of rot, of flowers and preservatives. His wife—his ex-wife . . . no, he corrected himself, his *late* wife . . . sat on the bed and stared at him, unblinking.

"Puppy," she said. "Could you—do you think you could possibly get me—a cigarette?"

Hershef or Harsaphes, from E. A. Wallis Budge's *The Gods of the Egyptians* (1904)

Shadow meets the walking dead (Shadow, played by Ricky Whittle, and Laura Moon, played by Emily Browning, from the Starz presentation of *American Gods*)
Photo copyright © 2018 Fremantle North America

75

Triple goddesses—here, the Graiae
Perseus and the Graiae by
Edward Burne-Jones, 1892

Greeks included the Erinyes (the Fates) as well as Hecate, a single deity with three aspects, and the Egyptians worshipped the triple-goddess Qudshu-Astarte-Anat (Qetesh, also known as Athirat and Asherah, Astoreth, and Anath). Triple-goddesses feature prominently in Gaiman's *Sandman* chronicles.

174. Again, there are numerous bird-headed gods in various cultures, including the Egyptians Horus and Thoth, both discussed below, and in India, the Garuda, often depicted with partially human features including hands.

175. This sentence does not appear in the First Edition.

176. This and the preceding two sentences do not appear in the First Edition.

177. The following two sentences do not appear in the First Edition.

178. The next three sentences do not appear in the First Edition.

179. In the Manuscript, the conversation is accusatory: "You went to prison," says Laura. "You know what you did was wrong."

"I thought you gave them up."

"I did," she said. "But I'm no longer concerned about the health risks. And I think it would calm my nerves. There's a machine in the lobby."

Shadow pulled on his jeans and a T-shirt and went, barefoot, into the lobby. The night clerk was a middle-aged man, reading a book by John Grisham. Shadow bought a pack of Virginia Slims from the machine. He asked the night clerk for a book of matches.

The man stared at him, asked for his room number. Shadow told him. The man nodded.[176] "You're in a non-smoking room," he said. "You make sure you open the window, now." He passed Shadow a book of matches and a plastic ashtray with the Motel America logo on it.

"Got it," said Shadow.

He went back into his bedroom.[177] He did not turn the light on. His wife was still on the bed. She had stretched out now, on top of his rumpled covers. Shadow opened the window and then passed her the cigarettes and the matches. Her fingers were cold. She lit a match and he saw that her nails, usually pristine, were battered and chewed, and there was mud under them.

Laura lit the cigarette, inhaled, blew out the match. She took another puff. "I can't taste it," she said. "I don't think this is doing anything."

"I'm sorry," he said.

"Me too," said Laura.

When she inhaled the cigarette tip glowed, and he was able to see her face.

"So," she said. "They let you out." [178]

"Yes."

"How was prison?"

"Could have been worse."

"Yes." The tip of the cigarette glowed orange. "I'm still grateful. I should never have got you mixed up in it."[179]

"Well," he said, "I agreed to do it. I could have said no." He wondered why he wasn't scared of her: why a dream of a museum could leave him terrified, while he seemed to be coping with a walking corpse without fear.

"Yes," she said. "You could have. You big galoot." Smoke wreathed her face. She was very beautiful in the dim light. "You want to know about me and Robbie?"

"Yes." It was Laura, he realized. Living or dead, he couldn't fear her.[180]

She stubbed out the cigarette in the ashtray. "You were in prison," she said. "And I needed someone to talk to. I needed a shoulder to cry on. You weren't there. I was upset."

"I'm sorry." Shadow realized something was different about her voice, and he tried to figure out what it was.

"I know. So we'd meet for coffee. Talk about what we'd do when you got out of prison. How good it would be to see you again. He really liked you, you know. He was looking forward to giving you back your old job."

"Yes."

"And then Audrey went to visit her sister for a week. This was, oh, a year, thirteen months after you'd gone away." Her voice lacked expression; each word was flat and dull, like pebbles dropped, one by one, into a deep well. "Robbie came over. We got drunk together. We did it on the floor of the bedroom. It was good. It was really good."

"I didn't need to hear that."

"No? I'm sorry. It's harder to pick and choose when you're dead. It's like a photograph, you know. It doesn't matter as much."

"It matters to me."

Laura lit a second cigarette. Her movements were fluid and competent, not stiff. Shadow wondered, for a moment, if she was dead at all. Perhaps this was some kind of elaborate trick. "Yes," she said. "I see that. Well, we carried on our affair—although we didn't call it that, we did not call it anything—for most of the last two years."

"Were you going to leave me for him?"

"Why would I do that? You're my big bear. You're my puppy. You did what you did for me. I waited three years for you to come back to me. I love you."

He stopped himself from saying *I love you, too.* He wasn't going to say that. Not any more. "So what happened the other night?"

A garuda, by Louis Le Breton (1863)

180. In the First Edition, the sentence "I guess" appears in place of the entire paragraph.

"The night I was killed?"

"Yes."

"Well, Robbie and I went out to talk about your welcome-back surprise party. It would have been so good. And I told him that we were done. Finished. That now that you were back that was the way it had to be."

"Mm. Thank you, babe."

"You're welcome, darling." The ghost of a smile crossed her face. "We got maudlin. It was sweet. We got stupid. I got very drunk. He didn't. He had to drive. We were driving home and I announced that I was going to give him a good-bye blowjob, one last time with feeling, and I unzipped his pants, and I did."

"Big mistake."

"Tell me about it. I knocked the gearshift with my shoulder, and then Robbie was trying to push me out of the way to put the car back in gear, and we were swerving, and there was a loud crunch and I remember the world started to roll and to spin, and I thought, *I'm going to die.* It was very dispassionate. I remember that. I wasn't scared. And then I don't remember anything more."

There was a smell like burning plastic. It was the cigarette, Shadow realized: it had burned down to the filter. Laura did not seem to have noticed.

"What are you doing here, Laura?"

"Can't a wife come and see her husband?"

"You're dead. I went to your funeral this afternoon."

"Yes." She stopped talking, stared into nothing. Shadow stood up and walked over to her. He took the smoldering cigarette butt from her fingers and threw it out of the window.

"Well?"

Her eyes sought his. "I don't know much more than I did when I was alive. Most of the stuff I know now that I didn't know then I can't put into words."

"Normally people who die stay in their graves," said Shadow.

"Do they? Do they really, puppy? I used to think they did too. Now I'm not so sure. Perhaps." She climbed off the bed and walked over to the window. Her face, in the light of the motel sign, was as beautiful as it had ever been. The face of the woman he had gone to prison for.

His heart hurt in his chest as if someone had taken it in a fist and squeezed. "Laura . . . ?"

She did not look at him. "You've gotten yourself mixed up in some bad things, Shadow. You're going to screw it up, if someone isn't there to watch out for you. I'm watching out for you. And thank you for my present."

"What present?"

She reached into the pocket of her blouse, and pulled out the gold coin he had thrown into the grave earlier that day. There was still black dirt on it. "I may have it put on a chain. It was very sweet of you."

"You're welcome."

She turned then and looked at him with eyes that seemed both to see and not to see him. "I think there are several aspects of our marriage we're going to have to work on."

"Babes," he told her. "You're dead."

"That's one of those aspects, obviously." She paused. "Okay," she said. "I'm going now. It will be better if I go." And, naturally and easily, she turned and put her hands on Shadow's shoulders, and went up on tiptoes to kiss him goodbye, as she had always kissed him goodbye.

Awkwardly he bent to kiss her on the cheek, but she moved her mouth as he did so and pushed her lips against his. Her breath smelled, faintly, of mothballs.

Laura's tongue flickered into Shadow's mouth. It was cold, and dry, and it tasted of cigarettes and of bile. If Shadow had had any doubts as to whether his wife was dead or not, they ended then.

He pulled back.

"I love you," she said, simply. "I'll be looking out for you." She walked over to the motel room door. There was a strange taste in his mouth. "Get some sleep, puppy," she told him. "And stay out of trouble."

She opened the door to the hall. The fluorescent light in the hallway was not kind: beneath it, Laura looked dead, but then, it did that to every one.

"You could have asked me to stay the night," she said, in her cold-stone voice.

"I don't think I could," said Shadow.

"You will, hon," she said. "Before all this is over. You will." She turned away from him, and walked down the corridor.

Shadow looked out of the doorway. The night clerk kept on reading his John Grisham novel, and barely looked up as she walked past him. There was thick graveyard mud clinging to her shoes. And then she was gone.

Shadow breathed out, a slow sigh. His heart was pounding arrhythmically in his chest. He walked across the hall, and knocked on Wednesday's door. As he knocked he got the weirdest notion: that he was being buffeted by black wings, as if an enormous crow was flying through him, out into the hall and the world beyond.

Wednesday opened the door. He had a white motel towel wrapped around his waist, but was otherwise naked. "What the hell do you want?" he asked.

"Something you should know," said Shadow. "Maybe it was a dream—but it wasn't—or maybe I inhaled some of the fat kid's synthetic toad-skin smoke, or probably I'm just going mad . . ."

"Yeah, yeah. Spit it out," said Wednesday. "I'm kind of in the middle of something here."

Shadow glanced into the room. He could see someone in the bed, watching him. A sheet pulled up over small breasts. Pale blonde hair, something rattish about the face. The girl from the motel desk.[181] He lowered his voice. "I just saw my wife," he said. "She was in my room."

"A ghost, you mean? You saw a ghost?"

"No. Not a ghost. She was solid. It was her. She's dead all right, but it wasn't any kind of a ghost. I touched her. She kissed me."

"I see." Wednesday darted a look at the woman in the bed. "Be right back, m'dear," he said.

They crossed the hall to Shadow's room. Wednesday turned on the lamps. He looked at the cigarette butt in the ashtray. He scratched his chest. His nipples were dark, old-

181. This sentence does not appear in the First Edition.

man nipples, and his chest hair was grizzled. There was a white scar down one side of his torso.[182] He sniffed the air. Then he shrugged.

"Okay," he said. "So your dead wife showed up. You scared?"

"A little."

"Very wise. The dead always give me the screaming mimis. Anything else?"

"I'm ready to leave Eagle Point. Laura's mother can sort out the apartment, all that. She hates me anyway. I'm ready to go when you are."

Wednesday smiled. "Good news, my boy. We'll leave in the morning.[183] Now, you should get some sleep. I have some scotch in my room, if you need help sleeping. Yes?"

"No. I'll be fine."

"Then do not disturb me further. I have a long night ahead of me."

"No sleep?" asked Shadow, smiling.[184]

182. Another clue to the identity of Wednesday: In the Old Norse poem Hávamál ("Sayings of the Wise One"), Odin recounts his self-sacrifice: "I know that I hung on a wind-rocked tree, nine whole nights, with a spear wounded and to Odin offered, myself to myself." (Benjamin Thorpe 1866 translation) The wound was self-inflicted, by Odin's spear Gungnir.

183. The Manuscript reads, "An eyeball sat in a glass of water beside the bed. Shadow winked at it, but it could not wink back."

184. This sentence and the next paragraph do not appear in the First Edition.

Shadow contemplating his future (played by Ricky Whittle, from the Starz presentation of *American Gods*)
Photo copyright © 2018 Fremantle North America

"I don't sleep. It's overrated. A bad habit I do my best to avoid—in company, wherever possible, and the young lady may go off the boil if I don't get back to her."

"Good night," said Shadow.

"Exactly," said Wednesday, and he closed the door as he went out.

Shadow sat down on the bed. The smell of cigarettes and preservatives lingered in the air. He wished that he were mourning Laura: it seemed more appropriate than being troubled by her or, he admitted it to himself now that she had gone, just a little scared by her. It was time to mourn. He turned the lights out, and lay on the bed, and thought of Laura as she was before he went to prison. He remembered their marriage when they were young and happy and stupid and unable to keep their hands off each other.

It had been a very long time since Shadow had cried, so long he thought he had forgotten how. He had not even cried when his mother died.[185] But he began to cry then, in painful, lurching sobs. He missed Laura and the days that were forever gone.[186]

For the first time since he was a small boy, Shadow cried himself to sleep.

185. The Manuscript refers to Shadow's grandparents dying, not his mother. Also, the Manuscript has a deleted passage regarding a boy named Jack Robinson, who bullied Shadow from the age of 11 on.

186. This sentence does not appear in the First Edition.

Coming to America

813 A.D.

They navigated the green sea by the stars and by the shore, and when the shore was only a memory and the night sky was overcast and dark they navigated by faith, and they called on the all-father[187] to bring them safely to land once more.

A bad journey they had of it, their fingers numb and with a shiver in their bones that not even wine could burn off. They would wake in the morning to see that the rime had frosted their beards, and, until the sun warmed them, they looked like old men, white-bearded before their time.

Teeth were loosening and eyes were deep-sunken in their sockets when they made landfall on the green land to the West. The men said, "We are far, far from our homes and our hearths, far from the seas we know and the lands we love. Here on the edge of the world we will be forgotten by our gods."

Their leader clambered to the top of a great rock, and he mocked them for their lack of faith. "The all-father made the world," he shouted. "He built it with his hands from the shattered bones and the flesh of Ymir, his grandfather.[188] He placed Ymir's brains in the sky as clouds, and his salt blood became the seas we crossed. If he made the world, do you not realize that he created this land as well? And if we die here as men, shall we not be received into his hall?"

And the men cheered and laughed. They set to, with a

187. Another name for Odin, as chief of the Norse gods.

188. Ymir was a frost giant, grandfather to Odin—see note 438, below.

will, to build a hall out of split trees and mud, inside a small stockade of sharpened logs, although as far as they knew they were the only men in the new land.

On the day that the hall was finished there was a storm: the sky at midday became as dark as night, and the sky was rent with forks of white flame, and the thunder-crashes were so loud that the men were almost deafened by them, and the ship's cat they had brought with them for good fortune hid beneath their beached longboat. The storm was hard enough and vicious enough that the men laughed and clapped each other on the back, and they said, "The thunderer is here with us, in this distant land," and they gave thanks, and rejoiced, and they drank until they were reeling.

In the smoky darkness of their hall, that night, the bard sang them the old songs. He sang of Odin, the all-father, who was sacrificed to himself as bravely and as nobly as others were sacrificed to him. He sang of the nine days that the all-father hung from the world-tree, his side pierced and dripping from the spear-point (at this point his song became, for a moment, a scream),[189] and he sang them all the things the all-father had learned in his agony: nine names, and nine runes, and twice-nine charms. When he told them of the spear piercing Odin's side, the bard shrieked in pain, as the all-father himself had called out in his agony, and all the men shivered, imagining his pain.

They found the scraeling[190] the following day, which was the all-father's own day. He was a small man, his long hair black as a crow's wing, his skin the color of rich red clay. He spoke in words none of them could understand, not even their bard, who had been on a ship that had sailed through the pillars of Hercules,[191] and who could speak the trader's pidgin men spoke all across the Mediterranean. The stranger was dressed in feathers and in furs, and there were small bones braided into his long hair.

They led him into their encampment, and they gave him roasted meat to eat, and strong drink to quench his thirst. They laughed riotously at the man as he stumbled and sang, at the way his head rolled and lolled, and this on less than

189. The parenthetical explanation does not appear in the First Edition.

190. Usually spelled "skraeling," this is the name that the Norse applied to the inhabitants of Greenland and North America, from the Old Norse *Skrælingja*, meaning "little men."

191. The Pillars of Hercules or Heracles are mentioned by Plato and Aristotle as the boundaries of the Greek world, and the location of the "pillars" referred to by them (which may have been figurative) is widely disputed. However, by the time of the Norsemen travelling to North America, the "Pillars of Hercules" most likely referred to twin promontories at the end of the Strait of Gibraltar: One is the Rock of Gibraltar, the other either Jebel Moussa (Musa, Musain) in Morocco or Mount Acha or Hacho (near the Spanish-controlled city of Ceuta, on the Moroccan coast).

a drinking-horn of mead. They gave him more drink, and soon enough he lay beneath the table with his head curled under his arm.

Then they picked him up, a man at each shoulder, a man at each leg, carried him at shoulder height, the four men making him an eight-legged horse, and they carried him at the head of a procession to an ash tree on the hill over-looking the bay, where they put a rope around his neck and hung him high in the wind, their tribute to the all-father, the gallows lord. The scraeling's body swung in the wind, his face blackening, his tongue protruding, his eyes pop-ping, his penis hard enough to hang a leather helmet on, while the men cheered and shouted and laughed, proud to be sending their sacrifice to the Heavens.

And, the next day, when two huge ravens[192] landed upon the scraeling's corpse, one on each shoulder, and com-menced to peck at its cheeks and eyes, the men knew their sacrifice had been accepted.

It was a long winter, and they were hungry, but they were cheered by the thought that, when spring came, they would send the boat back to the northlands, and it would bring settlers, and bring women. As the weather became colder, and the days became shorter, some of the men took to searching for the scraeling village, hoping to find food, and women. They found nothing, save for the places where fires had been, where small encampments had been abandoned.

One midwinter's day, when the sun was as distant and cold as a dull silver coin, they saw that the remains of the scraeling's body had been removed from the ash tree. That afternoon it began to snow, in huge, slow flakes.

The men from the northlands closed the gates of their encampment, retreated behind their wooden wall.

The scraeling war party fell upon them that night: five hundred men to thirty. They climbed the wall, and, over the following seven days, they killed each of the thirty men, in thirty different ways. And the sailors were forgotten, by history and their people.

The wall they tore down, and the village they burned. The longboat, upside-down and pulled high on the shingle,

192. The ravens Huginn, the personification of thought, and Muninn, the personification of memory, accompany Odin and were said to be sent out by him daily to scout the world and bring him news.

they also burned, hoping that the pale strangers had but one boat, and that by burning it they were ensuring that no other Northmen would come to their shores.

It was more than a hundred years before Leif the Fortunate, son of Erik the Red, rediscovered that land, which he would call Vineland.[193] His gods were already waiting for him when he arrived: Tyr, one-handed,[194] and gray Odin gallows-god, and Thor of the thunders.

They were there.

They were waiting.

193. Ca. 1000 C.E., long before John Cabot and Christopher Columbus, the Viking Leif Erikson led an expedition to North America—probably Newfoundland and the Gulf of St. Lawrence—and named the land discovered there "Vinland" or "Vineland." Although Old Norse literature wrote of the voyage, confirming archaeological evidence was not found until 1960. Thomas Pynchon's 1990 novel, *Vineland*, explores a dark America in the 1980s, a "scabland garrison state," where dissent is sought out and destroyed and the counterculture is suppressed.

194. Tyr, generally said to be a son of Odin, lost his hand to the wolf Fenrir in the act of binding him. Occasionally identified with Mars, Tyr may have been a god *senior* to Odin in early Germanic myths, but in Norse mythology he was relegated to a minor role.

CHAPTER FOUR

Let the Midnight Special
Shine its light on me
Let the Midnight Special
Shine its ever-lovin' light on me
— "THE MIDNIGHT SPECIAL,"
traditional song [195]

HADOW AND WEDNESDAY ate breakfast at a Country Kitchen across the street from their motel. It was eight in the morning, and the world was misty and chill.

"You still ready to leave Eagle Point?" asked Wednesday, at the breakfast bar. "I have some calls to make, if you are. Friday today. Friday's a free day. A woman's day.[196] Saturday tomorrow. Much to do on Saturday."

"I'm ready," said Shadow. "Nothing keeping me here."

Wednesday heaped his plate high with several kinds of breakfast meats. Shadow took some melon, a bagel, and a packet of cream cheese. They went and sat down in a booth.

"That was some dream you had last night," said Wednesday.

"Yes," said Shadow. "It was." Laura's muddy footprints had been visible on the motel carpet when he got up that morning, leading from his bedroom to the lobby and out the door.

195. Portions of the lyrics of the song were first published in 1905; the song itself was first published by Carl Sandburg in *The American Songbag* in 1927. The train that is the subject of the song was probably an invention of Southern prisoners rather than a real train, though several actual passenger trains were dubbed "the Midnight Special." John and Alan Lomax, in their book, *Best Loved American Folk Songs*, identify the Midnight Special as a particular train from Houston that shone its light into a cell in the Sugar Land Prison. The light, they suggest, signified freedom, as do beams of light in other songs. Sandburg, on the other hand, saw the song as a testimony that the prisoner singing would rather be run over by the train than remain in jail.

196. Wednesday refers to "Freya's-day," Freya or Frigga being his wife (or one of them, depending on the source). See note 84, above, for the other days of the week.

Freya
By Johannes Gehrts, 1901

197. See note 79, above, for the location!

198. This sentence does not appear in the First Edition.

199. This and the next sentence do not appear in the First Edition.

200. This sentence does not appear in the First Edition.

"So," said Wednesday. "Why'd they call you Shadow?"

Shadow shrugged. "It's a name," he said. Outside the plate glass the world in the mist had become a pencil drawing executed in a dozen different grays with, here and there, a smudge of electric red or pure white. "How'd you lose your eye?"

Wednesday shoveled half a dozen pieces of bacon into his mouth, chewed, wiped the fat from his lips with the back of his hand. "Didn't lose it," he said. "I still know exactly where it is."[197]

"So what's the plan?"

Wednesday looked thoughtful. He ate several vivid pink slices of ham, picked a fragment of meat from his beard, dropped it onto his plate. "Plan is as follows. On Saturday night, which, as I have already remarked, is tomorrow, we shall be meeting with a number of persons preeminent in their respective fields—do not let their demeanor intimidate you. We shall meet at one of the most important places in the entire country. Afterward we shall wine and dine them. There will be, at a guess, thirty or forty of them.[198] Perhaps more. I need to enlist them in my current enterprise."

"And where is the most important place in the country?"

"One of them, m'boy. I said one of them. Opinions are justifiably divided. I have sent word to my colleagues. We'll stop off in Chicago on the way, as I need to pick up some money. Entertaining, in the manner we shall need to entertain, will take more ready cash than I happen to have available. Then on to Madison."

"I see."[199]

"No, you don't. But all will become clear in time."

Wednesday paid and they left, walked back across the road to the motel parking lot. Wednesday tossed Shadow the car keys. He drove down to the freeway and out of town.

"You going to miss it?" asked Wednesday. He was sorting through a folder filled with maps.

"The town? No. Too many Laura memories.[200] I didn't really ever have a life here. I was never in one place too long as a kid, and I didn't get here until I was in my twenties. So this town is Laura's."

"Let's hope she stays here," said Wednesday.

"It was a dream," said Shadow. "Remember."

"That's good," said Wednesday. "Healthy attitude to have. Did you fuck her last night?"

Shadow took a breath. Then, "That is none of your damn business. And no."

"Did you want to?"

Shadow said nothing at all. He drove north, toward Chicago.[201] Wednesday chuckled, and began to pore over his maps, unfolding and refolding them, making occasional notes on a yellow legal pad with a large silver ballpoint pen.

Eventually he was finished. He put his pen away, put the folder on the back seat. "The best thing about the states we're heading for," said Wednesday, "Minnesota, Wisconsin, all around there, is it has the kind of women I liked when I was younger. Pale-skinned and blue-eyed, hair so fair it's almost white, wine-colored lips, and round, full breasts with the veins running through them like a good cheese."

"Only when you were younger?" asked Shadow. "Looked like you were doing pretty good last night."

"Yes." Wednesday smiled. "Would you like to know the secret of my success?"

"You pay them?"

"Nothing so crude. No, the secret is charm. Pure and simple."

"Charm, huh? Well, like they say, you either got it or you ain't."

"Charms can be learnt," said Wednesday.

"So where are we going?" asked Shadow.[202]

"There's an old friend of mine we need to talk to. He's one of the people who'll be coming to the get-together. Old man, now. He's expecting us for dinner."

They drove north and west, toward Chicago.

"Whatever's happening with Laura," said Shadow, breaking the silence. "Is it your fault? Did you make it happen?"

"No," said Wednesday.

"Like the kid in the car asked me: would you tell me if it was?"

201. In the First Draft, Shadow drove "east."

202. This sentence and the next six paragraphs do not appear in the First Edition.

203. Bob Dylan wrote the classic protest song "A Hard Rain's a-Gonna Fall" in 1962, and the song refers to "a highway of diamonds with nobody on it."

204. As will be seen, Wednesday and Shadow visit Slavic gods. It is likely that they have settled in the Ukrainian Village, a Chicago neighborhood located on the near west side of Chicago, bounded by Division Street to the north, Chicago Avenue to the south, Western Avenue to the west, and Damen Avenue to the east.

205. The balance of this sentence does not appear in the First Edition.

"I'm as puzzled as you are."

Shadow tuned the radio to an oldies station, and listened to songs that were current before he was born. Bob Dylan sang about a hard rain that was going to fall,[203] and Shadow wondered if that rain had fallen yet, or if it was something that was still going to happen. The road ahead of them was empty and the ice crystals on the asphalt glittered like diamonds in the morning sun.

✤ ✤ ✤

CHICAGO HAPPENED SLOWLY, like a migraine. First they were driving through countryside, then, imperceptibly, the occasional town became a low suburban sprawl, and the sprawl became the city.

They parked outside a squat black brownstone.[204] The sidewalk was clear of snow. They walked to the lobby. Wednesday pressed the top button on the gouged metal intercom box. Nothing happened. He pressed it again. Then, experimentally, he began to press the other buttons, for other tenants, with no response.

"It's dead," said a gaunt old woman, coming down the steps. "Doesn't work. We call the super, ask him when he going to fix, when he going to mend the heating, he does not care, goes to Arizona for the winter for his chest." Her accent was thick, Eastern European, Shadow guessed.

Wednesday bowed low. "Zorya, my dear, may I say how unutterably beautiful you look? A radiant creature. You have not aged."

The old woman glared at him. "He don't want to see you. I don't want to see you neither. You bad news."

"That's because I don't come if it isn't important."

The woman sniffed. She carried an empty string shopping bag, and wore an old red coat, buttoned up to her chin,[205] and, perched on her gray hair, a green velvet hat that was, in appearance, a little bit flowerpot, a little bit bread-loaf. She looked at Shadow suspiciously.

"Who is the big man?" she asked Wednesday. "Another one of your murderers?"

"You do me a deep disservice, good lady. This gentleman

is called Shadow. He is working for me, yes, but on your behalf. Shadow, may I introduce you to the lovely Miss Zorya Vechernyaya."[206]

"Good to meet you," said Shadow.

Bird-like, the old woman peered up at him. "Shadow," she said. "A good name. When the shadows are long, that is my time. And you are the long shadow." She looked him up and down, then she smiled. "You may kiss my hand," she said, and extended a cold hand to him.

Shadow bent down and kissed her thin hand. She had a large amber ring on her middle finger.

"Good boy," she said. "I am going to buy groceries. You see, I am the only one of us who brings in any money. The other two cannot make money fortune-telling. This is because they only tell the truth, and the truth is not what people want to hear. It is a bad thing, and it troubles people, so they do not come back. But I can lie to them, tell them what they want to hear. I tell the pretty fortunes.[207] So I bring home the bread. Do you think you will be here for supper?"

"I would hope so," said Wednesday.

"Then you had better give me some money to buy more food," she said. "I am proud, but I am not stupid. The others are prouder than I am, and he is the proudest of all. So give me money and do not tell them that you give me money."

Wednesday opened his wallet, and reached in. He took out a twenty. Zorya Vechernyaya plucked it from his fingers, and waited. He took out another twenty and gave it to her.

"Is good," she said. "We will feed you like princes. Like we would feed our own father.[208] Now, go up the stairs to the top. Zorya Utrennyaya[209] is awake, but our other sister is still asleep, so do not be making too much noise, when you get to the top."

Shadow and Wednesday climbed the dark stairs. The landing two stories up was half-filled with black plastic garbage bags and it smelled of rotting vegetables.

"Are they gypsies?" asked Shadow.

"Zorya and her family? Not at all. They're not *Rom*. They're Russian. Slavs, I believe."[210]

"But she does fortune-telling."

206. The Zorya, also known as the Aurora in Greek mythology, were goddesses charged with guarding the universe. Their task was to keep watch over the hound Simargl, chained to Polaris in the constellation of Ursa Minor, the Little Bear. If the hound escaped, he would devour the constellation and bring about the end of the world. This is the Evening Star. Gaiman spoke of his research into the Zorya: "The most frustrating of my research was Czernobog and the Zorya, the Slavic Gods, because there's so little about them actually known. I ran across them while I was beginning the book, and I loved the idea of Czernobog the black god and his brother Bielobog the white god, and the Zorya, these sisters of the dawn—the morning star, the evening star, and the mysterious midnight sister. And then I spent weeks trying to research them more. At the end of three weeks of solid research I had nothing I hadn't had in some little Peterson's book of gods at the start. There's so little known about the Russian Gods. The Catholic church and the Russian Orthodox church stamped out most of it, and then Napoleon burned the rest of it on his way to and from Moscow." ("Dreaming *American Gods*: An Interview with Neil Gaiman" (2001), in *Conversations with Neil Gaiman*. Edited by Joseph Michael Sommers (Jackson, MS: University Press of Mississippi, 2018), p. 94.)

207. This sentence does not appear in the First Edition.

208. This sentence does not appear in the First Edition.

209. The Morning Star.

210. The Zoryas serve the sun god Dažbog, who in some myths is described as their father. Zorya Utrennyaya opens the gates to the god's palace every morning for the sun-chariot's departure. At dusk, Zorya Vechernyaya closes the palace gates once more after its return.

211. Czernobog (from Proto-Slavic °čĭrnŭ "black" and °bogŭ "god")—also spelled as Chernabog, Chernobog, Chornoboh, Czorneboh, Čiernoboh, Crnobog, Tchernobog and Zcerneboch among other variants—is a Slavic deity, the "black god." Christian historical sources interpret him as a dark, accursed god, but this may be a modern aspect. He is likely the counterpart of Byelobog or Bielobog, the "white god," a benevolent deity. Chernabog is also the malevolent demon that rules Bald Mountain, in the "Night on Bald Mountain" segment of Disney's animated 1940 film *Fantasia*. The segment features the Russian composer Modest Moussorgsky's 1867 series of compositions known as *St. John's Eve on Bald Mountain*, sadly never performed during his lifetime, as well as Franz Schubert's 1825 *Ave Maria*. There is no specific connection in Slavic mythology between the Zoryas and these other gods.

212. Grimnir or Grimmir ("the hooded") is the name Odin assumed when he visited the hall of Geirod. In the First Edition, the name is Votan (the Slavic pronunciation of Wotan or Woden).

Chernabog, from *Fantasia*
Walt Disney Productions, 1940

"Lots of people do fortune-telling. I dabble in it myself." Wednesday was panting as they went up the final flight of stairs. "I'm out of condition."

The landing at the top of the stairs ended in a single door painted red, with a peephole in it.

Wednesday knocked at the door. There was no response. He knocked again, louder this time.

"Okay! Okay! I heard you! I heard you!" The sound of locks being undone, of bolts being pulled, the rattle of a chain. The red door opened a crack.

"Who is it?" A man's voice, old and cigarette-roughened.

"An old friend, Czernobog.[211] With an associate."

The door opened as far as the security chain would allow. Shadow could see a gray face, in the shadows, peering out at them. "What do you want, Grimnir?"[212]

"Initially, simply the pleasure of your company. And I have information to share. What's that phrase . . . oh yes. You may learn something to your advantage."

The door opened all the way. The man in the dusty bathrobe was short, with iron-gray hair and craggy features. He wore gray pinstripe pants, shiny from age, and slippers. He held an unfiltered cigarette with square-tipped fingers, sucking the tip while keeping it cupped in his fist—like a convict, thought Shadow, or a soldier. He extended his left hand to Wednesday.

"Welcome then, Grimnir."

"They call me Wednesday these days," he said, shaking the old man's hand.

A narrow smile; a flash of yellow teeth. "Yes," he said. "Very funny. And this is?"

"This is my associate. Shadow, meet Mister Czernobog."

"Well met," said Czernobog. He shook Shadow's left hand with his own. His hands were rough and callused, and the tips of his fingers were as yellow as if they had been dipped in iodine.

"How do you do, Mister Czernobog."

"I do old. My guts ache, and my back hurts, and I cough my chest apart every morning."

"Why you are standing at the door?" asked a woman's

voice. Shadow looked over Czernobog's shoulder, at the old woman standing behind him. She was smaller and frailer than her sister, but her hair was long and still golden. "I am Zorya Utrennyaya," she said. "You must not stand there in the hall. You must come in, go through to the sitting room, through there, I will bring you coffee, go, go in, through there."

Through the doorway into an apartment that smelled like over-boiled cabbage and cat-box and unfiltered foreign cigarettes, and they were ushered through a tiny hallway past several closed doors to the sitting room at the far end of the corridor, and were seated on a huge old horsehair sofa, disturbing an elderly gray cat in the process, who stretched, stood up, and walked, stiffly, to a distant part of the sofa, where he lay down, warily stared at each of them in turn, then closed one eye and went back to sleep. Czernobog sat in an armchair across from them.

Zorya Utrennyaya found an empty ashtray and placed it beside Czernobog. "How you want your coffee?" she asked her guests. "Here we take it black as night, sweet as sin."

"That'll be fine, ma'am," said Shadow. He looked out of the window, at the buildings across the street.

Zorya Utrennyaya went out. Czernobog stared at her as she left. "That's a good woman," he said. "Not like her sisters. One of them is a harpy, the other, all she does is sleep." He put his slippered feet up on a long, low coffee table, a chess board inset in the middle, cigarette burns and mug rings on its surface.

"Is she your wife?" asked Shadow.

"She's nobody's wife." The old man sat in silence for a moment, looking down at his rough hands. "No. We are all relatives. We come over here together, long time ago."

From the pocket of his bathrobe, Czernobog produced a pack of unfiltered cigarettes. Shadow did not recognize the brand.[213] Wednesday pulled out a narrow gold lighter from the pocket of his pale suit, and lit the old man's cigarette. "First we come to New York," said Czernobog. "All our countrymen go to New York. Then, we come out here, to Chicago. Everything got very bad. In the old country,

213. This sentence does not appear in the First Edition.

Czernobog (played by Peter Stormare, from the Starz presentation of *American Gods*)
Photo copyright © 2018 Fremantle North America

214. In the First Edition, the sentence ends with "bad memory."

they had nearly forgotten me. Here, I am a bad memory no one wants to remember.[214] You know what I did when I got to Chicago?"

"No," said Shadow.

"I get a job in the meat business. On the kill floor. When the steer comes up the ramp, I was a knocker. You know why we are called knockers? Is because we take the sledge-hammer and we knock the cow down with it. *Bam!* It takes strength in the arms. Yes? Then the shackler chains the beef up, hauls it up, then they cut the throat. They drain the blood first before they cut the head off. We were the strongest, the knockers." He pushed up the sleeve of his bath-robe, flexed his upper arm to display the muscles still visible under the old skin. "Is not just strong though. There was an art to it. To the blow. Otherwise the cow is just stunned, or angry. Then, in the fifties, they give us the bolt gun. You put it to the forehead, *bam! Bam!* Now you think, anybody can kill. Not so." He mimed putting a metal bolt through a cow's head. "It still takes skill." He smiled at the memory, displaying an iron-colored tooth.[215]

"Don't tell them cow-killing stories." Zorya Utrennyaya carried in their coffee on a red wooden tray. Small brightly enameled cups[216] filled with a brown liquid so dark it was almost black. She gave them each a cup, then sat beside Czernobog.

"Zorya Vechernyaya is doing shopping," she said. "She will be soon back."

"We met her downstairs," said Shadow. "She says she tells fortunes."

"Yes," said her sister. "In the twilight, that is the time for lies. I do not tell good lies, so I am a poor fortune-teller. And our sister, Zorya Polunochnaya,[217] she can tell no lies at all."

The coffee was even sweeter and stronger than Shadow had expected.

Shadow excused himself to use the bathroom—a cramped, closet-like room near the front door, hung with several brown-spotted framed photographs.[218] It was early afternoon, but already the daylight was beginning to fade. He heard voices raised from down the hall. He washed his hands in icy-cold water with a sickly-smelling sliver of pink soap.

Czernobog was standing in the hall as Shadow came out.

"You bring trouble!" he was shouting. "Nothing but trouble! I will not listen! You will get out of my house!"

Wednesday was still sitting on the sofa, sipping his coffee, stroking the gray cat. Zorya Utrennyaya stood on the thin carpet, one hand nervously twining in and out of her long yellow hair.

"Is there a problem?" asked Shadow.

"*He* is the problem!" shouted Czernobog. "*He* is! You tell him that there is nothing will make me help him! I want him to go! I want him out of here! Both of you go!"

"Please," said Zorya Utrennyaya, "please be quiet, you wake up Zorya Polunochnaya."

215. Many countries now require humane slaughter of cattle, so that the animal is minimally excited en route to the slaughterhouse and is quickly anesthetized by either mechanical or electrical means. Czernobog's recital of the replacement of hammers with so-called captive bolt stunners is an accurate history of meat-packing industry practices.

Chicago was for many years the largest center of meat-packing in the United States. Philip Armour and others organized the construction of the Union Stockyards in 1865, and Gustavus Swift followed suit with stockyards in 1875. The public was stunned, however, by the publication of Sinclair Lewis's muck-raking novel *The Jungle* in 1906, which revealed the shocking sanitary and working conditions prevalent in the stockyards. The result was passage by Congress that year of the Meat Inspection Act and the Pure Food and Drug Act. However, even today, working conditions remain dangerous, with higher rates of injuries than many other industries, and the industry employs many undocumented workers and recent immigrants.

216. The contents of the cups is not described in the First Edition.

217. There is of course no celestial body known as the Midnight Star (the word "polunochnaya" means midnight). Slavic myths do not mention a third sister, but as noted above, triple-deities are common throughout mythology. Subsequent to publication of *American Gods*, despite Gaiman's admitted pure invention of the figure, Zorya Polunochnaya seems to have entered mythology. See, e.g., https://www.bustle.com/p/what-god-is-zorya-polunochnaya-based-on-this-american-gods-stargazer-is-celestial-herself-57462 and https://www.crystalinks.com/zorya.html. Some sources fail to even mention her first appearance in the novel.

218. In the First Edition, the photos are described as pictures "of men and women in stiff Victorian poses."

"You are like him, you want me to join his madness!" shouted Czernobog. He looked as if he was on the verge of tears. A pillar of ash tumbled from his cigarette onto the threadbare hall carpet.

Wednesday stood up, walked over to Czernobog. He rested his hand on Czernobog's shoulder. "Listen," he said, peaceably. "Firstly, it's not madness. It's the only way. Secondly, everyone will be there. You would not want to be left out, would you?"

"You know who I am," said Czernobog. "You know what these hands have done. You want my brother, not me. And he's gone."

A door in the hallway opened, and a sleepy female voice said, "Is something wrong?"

"Nothing is wrong, my sister," said Zorya Utrennyaya. "Go back to sleep." Then she turned to Czernobog. "See? See what you do with all your shouting? You go back in there and sit down. Sit!" Czernobog looked as if he were about to protest; and then the fight went out of him. He looked frail, suddenly: frail, and lonely.

The three men went back into the shabby sitting room. There was a brown nicotine ring around that room that ended about a foot from the ceiling, like the tide-line in an old bathtub.

"It doesn't have to be for you," said Wednesday to Czernobog, unfazed. "If it is for your brother, it's for you as well. That's one place you dualistic types have it over the rest of us, eh?"

Czernobog said nothing.

"Talking of Bielebog, have you heard anything from him?"

Czernobog shook his head. Then he spoke, staring down at the threadbare carpet. "None of us have heard of him.[219] I am almost forgotten, but still, they remember me a little, here and in the old country." He looked up at Shadow. "Do you have a brother?"

"No," said Shadow. "Not that I know of."

"I have a brother. They say, you put us together, we are like one person, you know? When we are young, his hair, it is very blond, very light,[220] and people say, he is the good

---

219. Czernobog means that they have lost touch with one another. Of course, if Bielobog is merely an aspect of Czernobog, no one would see them together. This and the following sentence do not appear in the First Edition.

220. In the First Edition, Bielobog has blue eyes. Czernobog's eyes are gray.

one. And my hair it is very dark, darker than yours even, and people say I am the rogue, you know? I am the bad one. And now time passes, and my hair is gray. His hair, too, I think, is gray. And you look at us, you would not know who was light, who was dark."

"Were you close?" asked Shadow.

"Close?" asked Czernobog. "No. We were not close.[221] How could we be? We cared about such different things."

There was a clatter from the end of the hall, and Zorya Vechernyaya came in. "Supper in one hour," she said. Then she went out.

Czernobog sighed. "She thinks she is a good cook," he said. "She was brought up, there were servants to cook. Now, there are no servants. There is nothing."

"Not nothing," said Wednesday. "Never nothing."

"You," said Czernobog. "I shall not listen to you." He turned to Shadow. "Do you play checkers?" he asked.

"Yes," said Shadow.

"Good. You shall play checkers with me," he said, taking a wooden box of pieces from the mantelpiece, and shaking them out onto the table. "I shall play black."

Wednesday touched Shadow's arm. "You don't have to do this, you know," he said.

"Not a problem. I want to," said Shadow. Wednesday shrugged, and picked up an old copy of the *Reader's Digest* from a small pile of yellowing magazines on the windowsill. Czernobog's brown fingers finished arranging the pieces on the squares, and the game began.

✢   ✢   ✢

IN THE DAYS that were to come, Shadow often found himself remembering that game. Some nights he dreamed of it. His flat, round pieces were the color of old, dirty wood, nominally white. Czernobog's were a dull, faded black. Shadow was the first to move. In his dreams, there was no conversation as they played, just the loud click as the pieces were put down, or the hiss of wood against wood as they were slid from square to adjoining square.

For the first half-dozen moves each of the men slipped

221. This sentence does not appear in the First Edition.

222. In the First Edition, the sentence reads, "he was not temperamentally suited to planning ahead."

223. The rules of checkers (draughts in England) are simple: Each player has twelve pieces, arranged on the colored or black squares of a checker/chessboard in rows of four on the side closest to the player. Pieces may be moved only away from the player's side along the diagonal lines of the colored squares. When one player moves his or her piece to abut a piece of the other's, and there is an empty square on the other side of the other's piece, the moving player must move his or her piece to the other side ("jump" the piece). The jumped piece is removed from the board. When a player moves his or her piece to the last row on the opposite side of the board, the piece is "kinged" (a second piece is placed on top to denote a "king"), and that "king" is thereafter permitted to move in either direction along the diagonals. The game ends when one player has "jumped" all of the other player's pieces.

224. A long-running feature of *Reader's Digest* (now retitled "Offbase"), it consisted of humorous stories about life in military service contributed by readers. For example, David Denbek sent in this anecdote: "*From an Army Soldier*: Our Army Unit was overseas conducting maneuvers with the Marines. On shift one night, a Marine asked my sergeant where he was from. 'I'm originally from Central America,' said the sergeant. 'Oh, yeah?' asked the Marine. 'Kansas?'"

pieces out onto the board, into the center, leaving the back rows untouched. There were pauses between the moves, long, chess-like pauses, while each man watched, and thought.

Shadow had played checkers in prison: it passed the time. He had played chess, too, but he was not temperamentally suited to chess. He did not like planning ahead.[222] He preferred picking the perfect move for the moment. You could win in checkers like that, sometimes.

There was a click, as Czernobog picked up a black piece and jumped it over one of Shadow's white pieces, placing it on the square on the other side.[223] The old man picked up Shadow's white piece and put it on the table at the side of the board.

"First blood. You have lost," said Czernobog. "The game is done."

"No," said Shadow. "Game's got a long way to go yet."

"Then would you care for a wager? A little side bet, to make it more interesting?"

"No," said Wednesday, without looking up from a "Humor in Uniform" column.[224] "He wouldn't."

"I am not playing with you, old man. I play with him. So, you want to bet on the game, Mister Shadow?"

"What were you two arguing about, before?" asked Shadow.

Czernobog raised a craggy eyebrow. "Your master wants me to come with him. To help him with his nonsense. I would rather die."

"You want to make a bet. Okay. If I win, you come with us."

The old man pursed his lips. "Perhaps," he said. "But only if you take my forfeit, when you lose."

"And that is?"

There was no change in Czernobog's expression. "If I win, I get to knock your brains out. With the sledgehammer. First you go down on your knees. Then I hit you a blow with it, so you don't get up again." Shadow looked at the man's old face, trying to read him. He was not joking, Shadow was certain of that: there was a hunger there for something, for pain, or death or retribution.

Wednesday closed the *Reader's Digest*. "This is getting ridiculous," he said. "I was wrong to come here. Shadow, we're leaving." The gray cat, disturbed, got to its feet and leapt onto the table beside the checkers game. It stared at the pieces, then leapt down onto the floor and, tail held high, it stalked from the room.

"No," said Shadow. He was not scared of dying. After all, it was not as if he had anything left to live for. "It's fine. I accept. If you win the game, you get the chance to knock my brains out with one blow of your sledgehammer." And he moved his next white piece to the adjoining square on the edge of the board.

Nothing more was said, but Wednesday did not pick up his *Reader's Digest* again. He watched the game with his glass eye and his true eye, with an expression that betrayed nothing.

Czernobog took another of Shadow's pieces. Shadow took two of Czernobog's. From the corridor came the smell of unfamiliar foods cooking. While not all of the smells were appetizing, Shadow realized suddenly how hungry he was.

The two men moved their pieces, black and white, turn and turn-about. A flurry of pieces taken, a blossoming of two-piece-high kings: no longer forced to move only forward on the board, a sideways slip at a time, the kings could move forward or back, which made them doubly dangerous. They had reached the furthest row, and could go where they wanted. Czernobog had three kings, Shadow had two.

Czernobog moved one of his kings around the board, eliminating Shadow's remaining pieces, while using the other two kings to keep Shadow's pieces pinned down.

And then Czernobog made a fourth king, and returned down the board to Shadow's two kings, and, unsmiling, took them both. And that was that.

"So," said Czernobog. "I get to knock out your brains. And you will go on your knees willingly. Is good." He reached out an old hand, and patted Shadow's arm with it.

"We've still got time before dinner's ready," said Shadow. "You want another game? Same terms?"

Czernobog lit another cigarette, from a kitchen box of

matches. "How can it be same terms? You want I should kill you twice?"

"Right now, you have one blow, that's all. You told me yourself that it's not just strength, it's skill too. This way, if you win this game, you get two blows to my head."

Czernobog glowered. "One blow, is all it takes, one blow. That is the art." He patted his upper right arm, where the muscles were, with his left, scattering gray ash from the cigarette in his left hand.

"It's been a long time. If you've lost your skill you might simply bruise me. How long has it been since you swung a killing hammer in the stock-yards? Thirty years? Forty?"

Czernobog said nothing. His closed mouth was a gray slash across his face. He tapped his fingers on the wooden table, drumming out a rhythm with them. Then he pushed the twenty-four checkers pieces back to their home squares on the board.

"Play," he said. "Again, you are light. I am dark."

Shadow pushed his first piece out. Czernobog pushed one of his own pieces forward. And it occurred to Shadow that Czernobog was going to try to play the same game again, the one that he had just won, that this would be his limitation.

This time Shadow played recklessly. He snatched tiny opportunities, moved without thinking, without a pause to consider. And this time, as he played, Shadow smiled; and whenever Czernobog moved a piece, Shadow smiled wider.

Soon, Czernobog was slamming his pieces down as he moved them, banging them down on the wooden table so hard that the remaining pieces shivered on their black squares.

"There," said Czernobog, taking one of Shadow's men with a crash, slamming the black piece down. "There. What do you say to that?"

Shadow said nothing: he simply smiled, and jumped the piece that Czernobog had put down, and another, and another, and a fourth, clearing the center of the board of black pieces. He took a white piece from the pile beside the board and kinged his man.

After that, it was just a mopping-up exercise: another handful of moves, and the game was done.

Shadow said, "Best of three?"

Czernobog simply stared at him, his gray eyes like points of steel. And then he laughed, clapped his hands on Shadow's shoulders. "I like you!" he exclaimed. "You have balls."

Then Zorya Utrennyaya put her head around the door to tell them that dinner was ready, and they should clear their game away, and put the tablecloth down on the table.

"We have no dining room," she said. "I am sorry. We eat in here."

Serving dishes were placed on the table. Each of the diners was given a small painted tray on which was some tarnished cutlery, to place on his or her lap.

Zorya Vechernyaya took five wooden bowls and placed an unpeeled boiled potato in each, then ladled in a healthy serving of a ferociously crimson borscht. She plopped a spoonful of white sour cream in, and handed the bowls to each of them.

"I thought there were six of us," said Shadow.

"Zorya Polunochnaya is still asleep," said Zorya Vechernyaya. "We keep her food in the refrigerator. When she wakes, she will eat."

The borscht was vinegary, and tasted like pickled beets. The boiled potato was mealy.

The next course was a leathery pot roast, accompanied by greens of some description—although they had been boiled so long and so thoroughly that they were no longer, by any stretch of the imagination, greens, and were in fact well on their way to becoming browns.

Then there were cabbage leaves stuffed with ground meat and rice, cabbage leaves of such a toughness that they were almost impossible to cut without spattering ground meat and rice all over the carpet. Shadow pushed his around his plate.

"We played checkers," said Czernobog, hacking himself another lump of pot roast. "The young man and me. He won a game, I won a game. Because he won a game, I have agreed to go with him and Wednesday, and help them in their madness. And because I won a game, when this is all done, I get to kill the young man, with a blow of a hammer."

The two Zoryas nodded gravely. "Such a pity," said Zorya Vechernyaya. "In my fortune for you, I should have said you would have a long life and a happy one, with many children."

"That is why you are a good fortune-teller," said Zorya Utrennyaya. She looked sleepy, as if it were an effort for her to be up so late. "You tell the best lies."

It was a long meal,[225] and at the end of it, Shadow was still hungry. Prison food had been pretty bad, and prison food was better than this.

"Good food," said Wednesday, who had cleaned his plate with every evidence of enjoyment. "I thank you, ladies. And now, I am afraid that it is incumbent upon us to ask you to recommend to us a fine hotel in the neighborhood."

Zorya Vechernyaya looked offended at this. "Why should you go to a hotel?" she said. "We are not your friends?"

"I couldn't put you to any trouble . . ." said Wednesday.

"Is no trouble," said Zorya Utrennyaya, one hand playing with her incongruously golden hair, and she yawned.

"You can sleep in Bielebog's room," said Zorya Vechernyaya, pointing to Wednesday. "Is empty. And for you, young man, I make up a bed on sofa. You will be more comfortable than in feather bed. I swear."

"That would be really kind of you," said Wednesday. "We accept."

"And you pay me only no more than what you pay for hotel," said Zorya Vechernyaya, with a triumphant toss of her head. "A hundred dollars."

"Thirty," said Wednesday.

"Fifty."

"Thirty-five."

"Forty-five."

"Forty."

"Is good. Forty-five dollar." Zorya Vechernyaya reached across the table and shook Wednesday's hand. Then she began to clean the pots off the table. Zorya Utrennyaya

225. The phrase "It was a long meal" does not appear in the First Edition.

yawned so hugely Shadow worried that she might dislocate her jaw, and announced that she was going to bed before she fell asleep with her head in the pie, and she said good night to them all.

Shadow helped Zorya Vechernyaya to take the plates and dishes into the little kitchen. To his surprise there was an elderly dishwashing machine beneath the sink, and he filled it. Zorya Vechernyaya looked over his shoulder, tutted, and removed the wooden borscht bowls.

"Those, in the sink," she told him.

"Sorry."

"Is not to worry. Now, back in there, we have pie," she said,[226] and she took the pie from the oven.

The pie—it was an apple pie—had been bought in a store and oven-warmed, and was very, very good indeed. The four of them ate it with ice cream, and then Zorya Vechernyaya made everyone go out of the sitting room, and made up a very fine-looking bed on the sofa for Shadow.

Wednesday spoke to Shadow as they stood in the corridor.

"What you did in there, with the checkers game," he said. "Yes?"

"That was good. Very, very stupid of you. But good. Sleep safe."

Shadow brushed his teeth and washed his face in the cold water of the little bathroom, and then walked back down the hall to the sitting room, turned out the light, and was asleep before his head touched the pillow.

❊   ❊   ❊

THERE WERE EXPLOSIONS in Shadow's dream: he was driving a truck through a minefield, and bombs were going off on each side of him. The windshield shattered and he felt warm blood running down his face.

Someone was shooting at him.

A bullet punctured his lung, a bullet shattered his spine, another hit his shoulder. He felt each bullet strike. He collapsed across the steering wheel.

The last explosion ended in darkness.

226. The balance of this sentence does not appear in the First Edition.

I must be dreaming, thought Shadow, alone in the darkness. *I think I just died.* He remembered hearing and believing, as a child, that if you died in your dreams, you would die in real life. He did not feel dead. He opened his eyes, experimentally.

There was a woman in the little sitting room, standing against the window, with her back to him. His heart missed a half-beat, and he said, "Laura?"

She turned, framed by the moonlight. "I'm sorry," she said. "I did not mean to wake you." She had a soft, Eastern European accent. "I will go."

"No, it's okay," said Shadow. "You didn't wake me. I had a dream."

"Yes," she said. "You were crying out, and moaning. Part of me wanted to wake you, but I thought, no, I should leave him."

Her hair was pale and colorless in the moon's thin light. She wore a thin white cotton nightgown, with a high, lace neck, and a hem that swept the ground. Shadow sat up, entirely awake. "You are Zorya Polu . . ." He hesitated. "The sister who was asleep."

"I am Zorya Polunochnaya, yes. And you are called Shadow, yes? That was what Zorya Vechernyaya told me, when I woke."

"Yes. What were you looking at, out there?"

She looked at him, then she beckoned him to join her by the window. She turned her back while he pulled on his jeans. He walked over to her. It seemed a long walk, for such a small room.

He could not tell her age. Her skin was unlined, her eyes were dark, her lashes were long, her hair was to her waist, and white. The moonlight drained colors into ghosts of themselves. She was taller than either of her sisters.

She pointed up into the night sky. "I was looking at that," she said, pointing to the Big Dipper. "See?"

"Ursa Major," he said. "The Great Bear."

"That is one way of looking at it," she said. "But it is not the way from where I come from. I am going to sit on the roof. Would you like to come with me?"

"I guess," said Shadow.[227]

"Is good," she said.

She lifted the window and clambered, barefoot, out onto the fire escape. A freezing wind blew through the window. Something was bothering Shadow, but he did not know what it was; he hesitated, then pulled on his sweater, socks, and shoes and followed her out onto the rusting fire escape. She was waiting for him. His breath steamed in the chilly air. He watched her bare feet pad up the icy metal steps, and followed her up to the roof.

The wind gusted cold, flattening her nightgown against her body, and Shadow became uncomfortably aware that Zorya Polunochnaya was wearing nothing at all underneath.

"You don't mind the cold?" he said, as they reached the top of the fire escape, and the wind whipped his words away.

"Sorry?"

She bent her face close to his. Her breath was sweet.

"I said, doesn't the cold bother you?"

In reply, she held up a finger: *Wait*. She stepped, lightly, over the side of the building and onto the flat roof. Shadow stepped over a little more clumsily, and followed her across the roof, to the shadow of the water-tower. There was a wooden bench waiting for them there, and she sat down on it, and he sat down beside her.

The water-tower acted as a windbreak, for which Shadow was grateful.[228] The lights of the city smudged the sky with yellow, swallowing half the stars he had been able to see from the open country. Still, he could see the Big Dipper and the North Star, and he found the three stars of Orion's belt, which allowed him to see Orion, which he always saw as a man running to kick a football—

"No," she said. "The cold does not bother me. This time is my time: I could no more feel uncomfortable in the night than a fish could feel uncomfortable in the deep water."

"You must like the night," said Shadow, wishing that he had said something wiser, more profound.

"My sisters are of their times. Zorya Utrennyaya is of the dawn. In the old country she would wake to open the gates,

227. This and the next sentence do not appear in the First Edition.

228. The balance of this paragraph does not appear in the First Edition.

and let our father drive his—um, I forget the word, like a car but with horses?"

"Chariot?"

"His chariot. Our father would ride it out. And Zorya Vechernyaya, she would open the gates for him at dusk, when he returned to us."

"And you?"

She paused. Her lips were full, but very pale. "I never saw our father. I was asleep."

"Is it a medical condition?"

She did not answer. The shrug, if she shrugged, was imperceptible. "So. You wanted to know what I was looking at."

"The Big Dipper."

She raised an arm to point to it, and the wind flattened her nightgown against her body. Her nipples, every goosebump on the areolae, were visible momentarily, dark against the white cotton. Shadow shivered.

"Odin's Wain, they call it.[229] And the Great Bear. Where we come from, we believe that is a, a thing, a, not a god, but like a god, a bad thing, chained up in those stars. If it escapes, it will eat the whole of everything. And there are three sisters who must watch the sky, all the day, all the night. If he escapes, the thing in the stars, the world is over. *Pf!*, like that."

"And people believe that?"

"They did. A long time ago."

"And you were looking to see if you could see the monster in the stars?"

"Something like that. Yes."

He smiled. If it were not for the cold, he decided, he would have thought he was dreaming. Everything felt so much like a dream.

"Can I ask how old you are? Your sisters seem so much older."

She nodded her head. "I am the youngest. Zorya Utrennyaya was born in the morning, and Zorya Vechernyaya was born in the evening, and I was born at midnight. I am the midnight sister: Zorya Polunochnaya. Are you married?"

229. This is the name given to the "Big Dipper" in Scandinavian myth, based on the shape of the constellation as a wagon or wheelbarrow. Its Old English name was Charles's Wain—reportedly from "churl's waggen," meaning the farmer's wagon. However, Richard Hinckley Allen, in his comprehensive *Star Names and Their Meanings* (New York and London: G. E. Stechert, 1899), concludes instead that the name Charles (Charlemagne, Charles the Great) arose "out of the verbal association of the star-name *Arcturus* with *Arturus* or Arthur, and the legendary association of Arthur and Charlemagne; so that what was originally the wain of Arcturus . . . became at length the wain of Carl or Charlemagne" (p. 428). The constellation's Latin name is of course *Ursa major*, the "great bear," and while the "Big Dipper" and "Ursa major" are often used synonymously, the constellation actually consists of many more stars than form the Dipper.

"My wife is dead. She died last week in a car accident. It was her funeral yesterday."

"I'm so sorry."

"She came to see me last night." It was not hard to say, in the darkness and the moonlight; it was not as unthinkable as it was by daylight.

"Did you ask her what she wanted?"

"No. Not really."

"Perhaps you should. It is the wisest thing to ask the dead. Sometimes they will tell you. Zorya Vechernyaya tells me that you played checkers with Czernobog."

"Yes. He won the right to knock in my skull with a sledge."

"In the old days, they would take people up to the top of the mountains. To the high places. They would smash the back of their skulls with a rock. For Czernobog."

Shadow glanced about. No, they were alone on the roof.

Zorya Polunochnaya laughed. "Silly, he is not here. And you won a game also. He may not strike his blow until this is all over. He said he would not. And you will know. Like the cows he killed. They always know, first. Otherwise, what is the point?"

"I feel," Shadow told her, "like I'm in a world with its own sense of logic. Its own rules. Like when you're in a dream, and you know there are rules you mustn't break, but you don't know what they are[230] or what they mean. I have no idea what we're talking about, or what happened today, or pretty much anything since I got out of jail. I'm just going along with it, you know?"

"I know," she said. She held his hand, with a hand that was icy cold. "You were given protection once, but you lost it already. You gave it away. You had the sun in your hand. And that is life itself.[231] All I can give you is much weaker protection. The daughter, not the father. But all helps. Yes?" Her white hair blew about her face in the chilly wind,[232] and Shadow knew that it was time to go back inside.

"Do I have to fight you? Or play checkers?" he asked.

"You do not even have to kiss me," she told him. "Just take the moon."[233]

"How?"

230. The phrase "what they are" does not appear in the First Edition, nor does the next sentence.

231. Zorya Polunochnaya refers to the gold coin that Shadow received from Mad Sweeney. In the First Edition, she says, "You were given the sun itself" and says nothing about life.

232. The balance of this sentence does not appear in the First Edition.

233. In the First Edition, Zorya says, "Just take the moon from me."

Peace dollar

*With permission of
National Numismatic Collection,
National Museum of American History.*

234. Properly known as the Peace Dollar, the coin was minted from 1921–1928 and then again from 1934–1935. The obverse bears the head of Libertas, the Roman goddess of liberty (the same represented by the Statue of Liberty); the reverse bears an image of an American bald eagle. The coin was designed by the Italian immigrant Antonio de Francisci. The 1921 version was high-relief, expensive to make, and in 1922, it was recast as a low-relief coin.

The 1922 version especially seems to feature a halo-like crown around the head of Libertas.

1922 silver dollar

"Take the moon."

"I don't understand."

"Watch," said Zorya Polunochnaya. She raised her left hand and held it in front of the moon, so that her forefinger and thumb seemed to be grasping it. Then, in one smooth movement, she plucked at it. For a moment, it looked like she had taken the moon from the sky, but then Shadow saw that the moon shone still, and Zorya Polunochnaya opened her hand to display a silver Liberty-head dollar[234] resting between finger and thumb.

"That was beautifully done," said Shadow. "I didn't see you palm it. And I don't know how you did that last bit."

"I did not palm it," she said. "I took it. And now I give it to you, to keep safe. Here. Don't give this one away."

She placed it in his right hand and closed his fingers around it. The coin was cold in his hand. Zorya Polunochnaya leaned forward, and closed his eyes with her fingers, and kissed him, lightly, once upon each eyelid.

✴   ✴   ✴

SHADOW AWOKE ON the sofa, fully dressed. A narrow shaft of sunlight streamed in through the window, making the dust motes dance.

He got out of bed, and walked over to the window. The room seemed much smaller in the daylight.

The thing that had been troubling him since last night came into focus as he looked out and down and across the street. There was no fire escape outside this window: no balcony, no rusting metal steps.

Still, held tight in the palm of his hand, bright and shiny as the day it had been minted, was a 1922 Liberty-head silver dollar.

"Oh. You're up," said Wednesday, putting his head around the door. "That's good. You want coffee? We're going to rob a bank."

Coming to America[235]
1721

The important thing to understand about American history, *wrote Mr. Ibis, in his leather-bound journal*, is that it is fictional, a charcoal-sketched simplicity for the children, or the easily bored. For the most part it is uninspected, unimagined, unthought, a representation of the thing, and not the thing itself. It is a fine fiction, *he continued, pausing for a moment to dip his pen in the inkwell, and to collect his thoughts*, that America was founded by pilgrims, seeking the freedom to believe as they wished, that they came to the Americas, spread and bred and filled the empty land.

In truth, the American colonies were as much a dumping ground as an escape, a forgetting place. In the days where you could be hanged in London from Tyburn's triple-crowned tree for the theft of twelve pennies, the Americas became a symbol of clemency, of a second chance. But the conditions of transportation were such that, for some, it was easier to take the leap from the leafless and dance on nothing until the dancing was done. Transportation it was called: for five years, for ten years, for life. That was the sentence.[236]

You were sold to a captain, and would ride in his ship, crowded tight as a slaver's, to the colonies or to the West Indies; off the boat the captain would sell you on as an indentured servant to one who would take the cost of your

235. In a private conversation with this editor, Gaiman expressed that as a youth, his favorite reading was the *Newgate Calendar*, subtitled *The Malefactors' Bloody Register*, a chapbook of crime and criminals that was as popular as the Bible in eighteenth-century and early nineteenth-century England. He intended the "Coming to America" interludes as homages to the moralistic, editorializing tales recounted in the *Calendar*.

236. "Transportation" as a means of punishing criminals and political dissidents was effectively invented by England, which began transporting persons to its colonies in North America in 1610. The American Revolution ended the practice as to the United States, but Australia and Tasmania became popular "dumping-grounds" after 1786, and England transported criminals from India to the Andaman Islands (see Conan Doyle's *The Sign of the Four* for a tale of an escapee from the Andamans). France instituted the practice later, using its colonies New Caledonia and Guiana (in particular Devil's Island, the resting place of the celebrated political prisoner Alfred Dreyfus in 1894). Penal transportation did not cease everywhere until 1897.

237. We may estimate that Essie was born around 1660 and lived to around age 61, an average life expectancy for the era.

238. Pixies, pisgies, or piskies may simply be a West Country name for fairies. The most abundant stories of pixies are found in the west counties of Devon, Somerset, and Cornwall, and one account tells of a war between the pixies and the fairies, resulting in a geographical division. Pixies are best known for causing people to lose their way, although single pixies have been said to be helpful.

239. Spriggans are ugly, malicious fairies said to be the ghosts of giants and, though naturally small, able to transform into gigantic shapes. Legend assigns them the role of bodyguard to other fairies.

240. For a detailed discussion of this legend, this editor suggests his *New Annotated Sherlock Holmes: The Novels* (New York: W. W. Norton, 2005), for Conan Doyle's *Hound of the Baskervilles*, included in the volume, is drawn from legends of black dogs upon the moors.

241. Selkies—"seal-women"—are creatures, male and female, who can change from seals in the sea to humans on the land. The principal legends of the selkies are found in Scotland and the Shetland and Orkney Islands, not the English Channel; however, myths of seal-men and seal-women are found in

skin out in your labor until the years of your indenture were done. But at least you were not waiting to hang in an English prison (for in those days prisons were places where you stayed until you were freed, transported, or hanged: you were not sentenced there for a term), and you were free to make the best of your new world. You were also free to bribe a sea captain to return you to England before the terms of your transportation were over and done. People did. And if the authorities caught you returning from transportation—if an old enemy, or an old friend with a score to settle, saw you and peached on you—then you were hanged without a blink.

I am reminded, *he continued, after a short pause, during which he refilled the inkwell on his desk from the bottle of umber ink from the closet, and dipped his pen once more,* of the life of Essie Tregowan, who came from a chilly little cliff-top village in Cornwall, in the Southwest of England, where her family had lived from time out of mind.[237] Her father was a fisherman, and it was rumored that he was one of the wreckers—those who would hang their lamps high on the dangerous coast when the storm winds raged, luring ships onto the rocks, for the goods on shipboard. Essie's mother was in service as a cook at the squire's house, and, at the age of twelve, Essie began to work there, in the scullery. She was a thin little thing, with wide brown eyes and dark brown hair; and she was not a hard worker but was forever slipping off and away to listen to stories and tales, if there was anyone who would tell them: tales of the piskies[238] and the spriggans,[239] of the black dogs of the moors[240] and the seal-women of the Channel.[241] And, though the squire laughed at such things, the kitchen-folk always put out a china saucer of the creamiest milk at night, put it outside the kitchen door, for the piskies.

Several years passed, and Essie was no longer a thin little thing: now she curved and billowed like the swell of the green sea, and her brown eyes laughed, and her chestnut hair tossed and curled. Essie's eyes lighted on Bartholomew, the squire's eighteen-year-old son, home from Rugby,[242] and she went at night to the standing stone on the edge of the woodland, and she put some bread that Bartholomew had been eating but had left unfinished on the stone, wrapped in a cut strand of her own hair. And on the very next day Bartholomew came and talked to her, and looked on her approvingly with his own eyes, the dangerous blue of a sky when a storm is coming, while she was cleaning out the grate in his bedroom.

He had such dangerous eyes, said Essie Tregowan.

Soon enough Bartholomew went up to Oxford, and, when Essie's condition became apparent, she was dismissed. But the babe was stillborn, and, as a favor to Essie's mother, who was a very fine cook, the squire's wife prevailed upon her husband to return the former maiden to her former position in the scullery.

Even so, Essie's love for Bartholomew had turned to hatred for his family, and within the year she took for her new beau a man from a neighboring village, with a bad reputation, who went by the name of Josiah Horner. And one night, when the family slept, Essie arose in the night and unbolted the side door, to let her lover in. He rifled the house while the family slept on.

Suspicion immediately fell upon someone in the house, for it was apparent that someone must have opened the door (which the squire's wife distinctly remembered having bolted herself) and someone must have known where the squire kept his silver plate, and the drawer in which he kept his coins and his promissory notes. Still, Essie, by resolutely denying everything, was convicted of nothing until Master Josiah Horner was caught, in a chandler's in Exeter, passing one of the squire's notes. The squire identified it as his, and Horner and Essie went to trial.

Horner was convicted at the local assizes, and was, as the slang of the time so cruelly and so casually had it, turned off,[243] but the judge took pity on Essie, because of her age or her chestnut hair, and he sentenced her to seven years' transportation. She was to be transported on a ship called the *Neptune*, under the command of one Captain Clarke. So Essie went to the Carolinas[244]; and on the way she conceived an alliance with the selfsame captain, and prevailed

Fairies
Maclise and Green, 1888

Scandinavian cultures as well. Male selkies were said to be amorous, stealing ashore to court mortal women, with their offspring often displaying webbed hands or feet. The typical tale of the "seal-maiden" is that of a young selkie found by a fisherman, deprived of her seal-skin, and brought (usually forcibly) to the fisherman's home. Though the seal-maiden might marry the fisherman and even have children, her longing for the sea was always evident and occasionally overwhelming, resulting in the wife's unexplained disappearance. See Katharine Briggs's *An Encyclopedia of Fairies* (New York: Pantheon Books, 1976), pp. 353–55.

242. A famous independent school in the south of England, Rugby was founded in 1567 as a free grammar school for local boys. In 1667, after extensive litigation between the founder's family and the trust he had created, the courts ruled in favor of the trust, and the school began to grow. When Matthew Arnold took on the role of Headmaster in 1828, he expanded the curriculum and established strict standards, leading to the school becoming a forerunner of the Victorian "public school" system. The sport of rugby was invented there, and the 1857 novel by Thomas Hughes, *Tom Brown's School Days*, captures life at the school in 1830.

243. The word "turn" in connection with executions has been traced back to 1542, in Hall's *Henry VIII* (which refers to the "turning-tree" as the fate of criminals) and Shakespeare's *Measure for Measure* (1603), in which the phrase "good turn" is used in its punning form as meaning both "a favor" and "a hanging." See J. S. Farmer and W. E. Henley's *Historical Dictionary of Slang* (originally published as *Slang and Its Analogues*, 1890).

244. The Carolinas were the colony split in 1729 into the colonies of North and South Carolina.

upon him to return her to England with him, as his wife, and to take her to his mother's house in London, where no man knew her. The journey back, when the human cargo had been exchanged for cotton and tobacco, was a peaceful time, and a happy one, for the captain and his new bride, who were as two lovebirds or courting butterflies, unable to cease from touching each other or giving each other little gifts and endearments.

When they reached London, Captain Clarke lodged Essie with his mother, who treated her in all ways as her son's new wife. Eight weeks later, the *Neptune* set sail again, and the pretty young bride with the chestnut hair waved her husband goodbye from dockside. Then she returned to her mother-in-law's house, where, the old woman being absent, Essie helped herself to a length of silk, several gold coins, and a silver pot in which the old woman kept her buttons, and pocketing these things Essie vanished into the stews of London.

Over the following two years Essie became an accomplished shop-lifter, her wide skirts capable of concealing a multitude of sins, consisting chiefly of stolen bolts of silk and lace, and she lived life to the full. Essie gave thanks for her escapes from her vicissitudes to all the creatures that she had been told of as a child, to the piskies (whose influence, she was certain, extended as far as London), and she would put a wooden bowl of milk on a window-ledge each night, although her friends laughed at her; but she had the last laugh, as her friends got the pox or the clap and Essie remained in the peak of health.

She was a year shy of her twentieth birthday when fate dealt her an ill-blow: she sat in the Crossed Forks Inn off Fleet Street, in Bell Yard, when she saw a young man enter and seat himself near the fireplace, fresh down from the University. "Oho! A pigeon ripe for the plucking," thinks Essie to herself, and she sits next to him, and tells him what a fine young man he is, and with one hand she begins to stroke his knee, while her other hand, more carefully, goes in search of his pocket-watch. And then he looked her full in the face, and her heart leapt and sank as eyes the dangerous blue of the summer sky before a storm gazed back into hers, and Master Bartholomew said her name.

She was taken to Newgate and charged with returning from transportation. Found guilty, Essie shocked no one by pleading her belly, although the town matrons, who assessed such claims (which were usually spurious), were surprised when they were forced to agree that Essie was indeed with child; although who the father was, Essie declined to say.

Her sentence of death was once more commuted to transportation, this time for life.

She rode out this time on the *Sea-Maiden*. There were two hundred transportees on that ship, packed into the hold like so many fat hogs on their way to market. Fluxes and fevers ran rampant; there was scarcely room to sit, let alone to lie down; a woman died in childbirth in the back of the hold, and, the people being pushed in too tightly to pass her body forward, she and the infant were forced out of a small porthole in the back, directly into the choppy gray sea. Essie was eight months gone, and it was a wonder she kept the baby, but keep it she did.

In her life ever after she would have nightmares of her time in that hold, and she would wake up screaming with the taste and stench of the place in her throat.

The *Sea-Maiden* landed at Norfolk in Virginia, and Essie's indenture was bought by a "small planter," a tobacco farmer named John Richardson, for his wife had died of the childbirth fever a week after giving birth to his daughter, and he had need of a wet-nurse and a maid of all work upon his smallholding.

So Essie's baby boy, whom she called Anthony, after, she said, her late husband his father (knowing there was none there to contradict her, and perhaps she had known an Anthony once), sucked at Essie's breast alongside of Phyllida Richardson, and her employer's child always got first suck, so she grew into a healthy child, tall and strong, while Essie's son grew weak and rickety on what was left.

And along with the milk, the children as they grew drank Essie's tales: of the knockers and the blue-caps who live down the mines;[245] of the Bucca,[246] the tricksiest spirit of

245. The knockers were helpful mine-based spirits who would hammer if a good lode was found or knock out a warning of danger. "Blue-caps" were also said to be mine-spirits who would work the mines, but blue-caps expected to be paid! See *Encyclopedia of Fairies*, pp. 27–28.

246. A hobgoblin or storm spirit that required propitiation. The name "Bucca-boo" seems to have degraded into the common word "bugaboo," an object of fear or alarm.

247. The stories of "apple-tree men," usually the oldest tree in the orchard, are traced to Somerset and reported in *Folktales of England* by Katharine Briggs and Ruth Tongue.

248. *Cf.* the malicious trees in the Old Forest and elsewhere, described by J. R. R. Tolkien in *Lord of the Rings* (1954–55).

the land, much more dangerous than the red-headed, snub-nosed piskies, for whom the first fish of the catch was always left upon the shingle, and for whom a fresh-baked loaf of bread was left in the field, at reaping time, to ensure a fine harvest; she told them of the apple-tree men[247]—old apple trees who talked when they had a mind, and who needed to be placated with the first cider of the crop, which was poured onto their roots as the year turned, if they were to give you a fine crop for the next year. She told them, in her mellifluous Cornish drawl, which trees they should be wary of, in the old rhyme:

Elm, he do brood
And Oak, he do hate,
But the willow-man goes walking,
If you stays out late.[248]

She told them all these things, and they believed, because she believed.

The farm prospered, and Essie Tregowan placed a china saucer of milk outside the back door, each night, for the piskies. And after eight months John Richardson came a-knocking quietly on Essie's bedroom door, and asked her for favors of the kind a woman shows a man, and Essie told him how shocked and hurt she was, a poor widow-woman, and an indentured servant no better than a slave, to be asked to prostitute herself for a man whom she had had so much respect for—and an indentured servant could not marry, so how he could even think to torment an indentured transportee girl so she could not bring herself to think—and her nut-brown eyes filled with tears, such that Richardson found himself apologizing to her, and the upshot of it was that John Richardson wound up, in that corridor, of that hot summer's night, going down on one knee to Essie Tregowan and proposing an end to her indenture and offering his hand in marriage. Now, although she accepted him, she would not sleep a night with him until it was legal, whereupon she moved from the little room in the attic to the master bedroom in the front of the house; and if some of Farmer Richardson's friends and their wives cut him when next they saw him in town, many more of them were of the opinion that the new Mistress Richardson was a damn fine-looking woman, and that Johnnie Richardson had done quite well for himself.

Within a year, she was delivered of another child, another boy, but as blond as his father and his half-sister, and they named him John, after his father.

The three children went to the local church to hear the traveling preacher on Sundays, and they went to the little school to learn their letters and their numbers with the children of the other small farmers; while Essie also made sure they knew the mysteries of the piskies, which were the most important mysteries there were: red-headed men, with eyes and clothes as green as a river, with turned-up noses, funny, squinting men who would, if they got a mind to, turn you and twist you and lead you out of your way, unless you had salt in your pocket, or a little bread. When the children went off to school, they each of them carried a little salt in one pocket, a little bread in the other, the old symbols of life and the earth, to make sure they came safely home once more, and they always did.

The children grew in the lush Virginia hills, grew tall and strong (although Anthony, her first son, was always weaker, paler, more prone to disease and bad airs) and the Richardsons were happy; and Essie loved her husband as best she could. They had been married a decade when John Richardson developed a toothache so bad it made him fall from his horse. They took him to the nearest town, where his tooth was pulled; but it was too late, and the blood-poisoning carried him off, black-faced and groaning, and they buried him beneath his favorite willow tree.

The widow Richardson was left the farm to manage until Richardson's two children were of age: she managed the indentured servants and the slaves, and brought in the tobacco crop, year in, year out; she poured cider on the roots of the apple trees on New Year's Eve, and placed a loaf of new-baked bread in the fields at harvest-time, and she always left a saucer of milk at the back door. The farm flourished, and the widow Richardson gained a reputation as a hard bargainer, but one whose crop was always good, and who never sold shoddy for better merchandise.

So all went well for another ten years; but after that was a bad year, for Anthony, her son, slew Johnnie, his half-brother, in a furious quarrel over the future of the farm and the disposition of Phyllida's hand; and some said he had not meant to kill his brother, and that it was a foolish blow that struck too deep, and some said otherwise. Anthony fled, leaving Essie to bury her youngest son beside his father. Now, some said Anthony fled to Boston, and some said he went south, to Florida,[249] and his mother was of the opinion that he had taken ship to England, to enlist in George's army and fight the rebel Scots.[250] But with both sons gone the farm was an empty place, and a sad one, and Phyllida pined and plained as if her heart had been broken, while nothing that her stepmother could say or do would put a smile back on her lips again.

But heartbroken or not, they needed a man about the farm, and so Phyllida married Harry Soames, a ship's carpenter by profession, who had tired of the sea and who dreamed of a life on land on a farm like the Lincolnshire farm upon which he had grown up. And although the Richardsons' farm was little enough like that, Harry Soames found correspondences enough to make him happy. Five children were born to Phyllida and Harry, three of whom lived.

The widow Richardson missed her sons, and she missed her husband, although he was now little more than a memory of a fair man who treated her kindly. Phyllida's children would come to Essie for tales, and she would tell them of the Black Dog of the Moors, and of Raw-Head and Bloody-Bones,[251] or the Apple Tree Man, but they were not interested; they only wanted tales of Jack—Jack up the Beanstalk,[252] or Jack Giant-killer, or Jack and his Cat and the King. She loved those children as if they were her own flesh and blood, although sometimes she would call them by the names of those long dead.

It was May, and she took her chair out into the kitchen

249. "to Florida" does not appear in the First Edition.

250. This is presumably in 1715, when a Jacobite rebellion, seeking to put Queen Anne's Catholic half-brother James Stuart (known as James III and VIII) on the throne in place of George I, broke out in Scotland. By the end of the year the rebellion was all but over.

251. Despite the compound name, this is a single figure: John Locke's 1693 *Some Thought Concerning Education* mentions that "Raw-Head and Bloody-Bones, and such other Names" were used by servants "to awe children, and keep them in subjection." Samuel Johnson's *Dictionary of the English Language* (first published in 1755) identified this as "the name of a spectre, mentioned to fright children," and E. Cobham Brewer's *Dictionary of Phrase and Fable* (1894) names it as "a bogie at one time the terror of children." "Bloodybone" appears in print as early as 1548, but the details of the creature are lost.

252. The first published version did not appear until 1734, but the tale is said to be thousands of years old. See http://www.bbc.com/news/uk-35358487, in which one folklorist claims that the story is a version of the "Boy Who Stole Ogre's Treasure" group of tales.

garden, to pick peas and to shuck them in the sunlight, for even in the lush heat of Virginia the cold had entered her bones as the frost had entered her hair, and a little warmth was a fine thing.

As the widow Richardson shucked the peas with her old hands, she got to thinking about how fine it would be to walk once more on the moors and the salty cliffs of her native Cornwall, and she thought of sitting on the shingle as a little girl, waiting for her father's boat to return from the gray seas. Her hands, blue-knuckled and clumsy, opened the pea-pods, forced the full peas into an earthenware bowl, and dropped the empty pea-pods onto her aproned lap. And then she found herself remembering, as she had not remembered for a long time, a life well lost: how she had twitched purses and filched silks with her clever fingers; and now she remembers the warden of Newgate telling her that it would be a good twelve weeks before her case would be heard, and that she could escape the gallows if she could plead her belly, and what a pretty thing she was—and how she had turned to the wall and bravely lifted her skirts, hating herself and hating him, but knowing he was right; and the feel of the life, quickening inside her, that meant that she could cheat death for a little longer . . .

"Essie Tregowan?" said the stranger.

The widow Richardson looked up, shading her eyes in the May sunshine. "Do I know you?" she asked. She had not heard him approach.

The man was dressed all in green: dusty green trews, green jacket, and a dark green coat. His hair was a carroty red, and he grinned at her all lopsided. There was something about the man that made her happy to look at him, and something else that whispered of danger. "You might say that you know me," he said.[253]

He squinted down at her, and she squinted right back up at him, searching his moon-face for a clue to his identity. He looked as young as one of her own grandchildren, yet he had called her by her old name, and there was a burr in his voice she knew from her childhood, from the rocks and the moors of her home.

253. In the Starz version of *American Gods*, Essie has become a "MacGowan," a fine Irish name, and relocated to Ireland. At the end of her life she meets Mad Sweeney. Tellingly, Essie is played by Emily Browning, the same actress who plays Laura Moon, and in the teleplay, Laura develops a relationship with Mad Sweeney.

254. A nickname for the Cornish, its origin is obscure. "Jack" is a common name, and some attribute the nickname to the habit of addressing fellow miners as "Cousin"; others suggest that Cornish immigrants were continually asking about jobs "for Cousin Jack back home." Brewer's *Dictionary of Phrase and Fable* (1894) merely states that in the western provinces (of England), Cornishmen are so-called.

"You're a Cornishman?" she asked.

"That I am, a Cousin Jack,"[254] said the red-haired man. "Or rather, that I was, but now I'm here in this new world, where nobody puts out ale or milk for an honest fellow, or a loaf of bread come harvest time."

The old woman steadied the bowl of peas upon her lap. "If you're who I think you are," she said, "then I've no quarrel with you." In the house, she could hear Phyllida grumbling to the housekeeper.

"Nor I with you," said the red-haired fellow, a little sadly, "although it was you that brought me here, you and a few like you, into this land with no time for magic and no place for piskies and such folk."

"You've done me many a good turn," she said.

"Good and ill," said the squinting stranger. "We're like the wind. We blows both ways."

Essie nodded.

"Will you take my hand, Essie Tregowan?" And he reached out a hand to her. Freckled it was, and although Essie's eyesight was going she could see each orange hair on the back of his hand, glowing golden in the afternoon sunlight. She bit her lip. Then, hesitantly, she placed her blue-knotted hand in his.

She was still warm when they found her, although the life had fled her body and only half the peas were shelled.

CHAPTER FIVE

Madam Life's a piece in bloom
Death goes dogging everywhere:
She's the tenant of the room,
He's the ruffian on the stair.
        —W. E. HENLEY,
          "Madam Life's a piece in bloom"[255]

NLY ZORYA UTRENNYAYA was awake to say goodbye to them, that Saturday morning. She took Wednesday's forty-five dollars and insisted on writing him out a receipt for it in wide, looping handwriting, on the back of an expired soft-drink coupon. She looked quite doll-like in the morning light, with her old face carefully made-up and her golden hair piled high upon her head.

Wednesday kissed her hand. "Thank you for your hospitality, dear lady," he said. "You and your lovely sisters remain as radiant as the sky itself."

"You are a bad old man," she told him, and shook a finger at him. Then she hugged him. "Keep safe," she instructed him. "I would not like to hear that you were gone for good."

"It would distress me equally, my dear."

She shook hands with Shadow. "Zorya Polunochnaya thinks very highly of you," she said. "I also."

"Thank you," said Shadow. "Thanks for the dinner."

255. The full untitled poem by William E. Henley (1849–1903) reads:

> *Madam Liziece in bloom*
> *Death goes dogging everywhere:*
> *She's the tenant of the room,*
> *He's the ruffian on the stair.*
>
> *You shall see her as a friend,*
> *You shall bilk him once or twice;*
> *But he'll trap you in the end,*
> *And he'll stick you for her price.*
>
> *With his kneebones at your chest,*
> *And his knuckles in your throat,*
> *You would reason—plead—protest!*
> *Clutching at her petticoat;*
>
> *But she's heard it all before,*
> *Well she knows you've had your fun,*
> *Gingerly she gains the door,*
> *And your little job is done.*

The poem was reportedly written in 1877 and may have appeared in the magazine *The London*, of which Henley was the editor at the time. It is not collected in his *A Book of Verses* (1888) but does appear in the larger collection of his poetry, titled *Poems* (1898), and is inserted into the section titled "Life and Death (Echoes)" as poem IX.

Henley is best remembered for his 1875 poem "Invictus," but he was also the co-editor (with John Stephen Farmer) of the influential seven-volume *Slang and Its Analogues* (1890–1904). Though his role in the compilation of the slang dictionary is not well understood, Henley clearly made corrections and additions to the volumes. In the course of a lawsuit brought by Farmer against the publisher (who had refused to print what he deemed to be "indecent" terms in the second volume), Farmer argued that Henley was the "evil genius" behind the volume in question. He pointed out that the first volume, in which Henley had been less involved, was less "obscene." Farmer lost the case and was ordered to pay the defendant's costs, but publication went forward with a different publisher. After Henley's death, revisions continued, but critics have noted that the dictionary became less polished. Nonetheless, their overall critical judgment is that Henley's and Farmer's work has yet to be surpassed for its detail and scope.

Henley was also close friends for a time with Robert Louis Stevenson, who partially modeled the pirate Long John Silver (*Treasure Island*) on the one-legged Henley.

256. The "slide vanish" is described by Bobo in *Modern Coin Magic* and first attributed to John Mulholland (1898–1970). Bobo calls it a "retention of vision vanish."

257. It is not often remembered that the "Statue of Liberty," as it is commonly known, that well-known symbol of America, was a gift from the people of France to the people of the United States. The gift was inspired by Édouard René de Laboulaye, who in 1865 suggested that any monument raised

She raised an eyebrow at him. "You liked? You must come again."

Wednesday and Shadow walked down the stairs. Shadow put his hands in his jacket pockets. The silver dollar was cold in his hand. It was bigger and heavier than any coins he'd used so far. He classic-palmed it, let his hand hang by his side naturally, then straightened his hand as the coin slipped down to a front-palm position. It felt natural there, held between his forefinger and his little finger by the slightest of pressure.

"Smoothly done," said Wednesday.

"I'm just learning," said Shadow. "I can do a lot of the technical stuff. The hardest part is making people look at the wrong hand."

"Is that so?"

"Yes," said Shadow. "It's called misdirection." He slipped his middle fingers under the coin, pushing it into a back palm, and fumbled his grip on it, ever-so-slightly. The coin dropped from his hand to the stairwell with a clatter and bounced down half a flight of stairs. Wednesday reached down and picked it up.

"You cannot afford to be careless with people's gifts," said Wednesday. "Something like this, you need to hang on to it. Don't go throwing it about." He examined the coin, looking first at the eagle side, then at the face of Liberty on the obverse. "Ah, Lady Liberty. Beautiful, is she not?" He tossed the coin to Shadow, who picked it from the air, did a slide vanish—seeming to drop it into his left hand while actually keeping it in his right—and then appeared to pocket it with his left hand.[256] The coin sat in the palm of his right hand, in plain view. It felt comforting there.

"Lady Liberty," said Wednesday. "Like so many of the gods that Americans hold dear, a foreigner. In this case, a Frenchwoman, although, in deference to American sensibilities, the French covered up her magnificent bosom on that statue they presented to New York.[257] Liberty," he continued, wrinkling his nose at the used condom that lay on the bottom flight of steps, toeing it to the side of the stairs with distaste. "Someone could slip on that. Break their necks," he muttered, interrupting himself. "Like a banana peel, only with bad taste and irony thrown in." He pushed open the door, and the sunlight hit them. The world outside was colder than it had looked from indoors: Shadow wondered if there was more snow to come.[258] "Liberty," boomed Wednesday, as they walked to his car, "is a bitch who must be bedded on a mattress of corpses."

"Yeah?" said Shadow.

"Quoting," said Wednesday. "Quoting someone French.[259] That's who they have a statue to, in their New York harbor: a bitch, who liked to be fucked on the refuse from the tumbril. Hold your torch as high as you want to, m'dear, there's still rats in your dress and cold jism dripping down your leg." He unlocked the car, and pointed Shadow to the passenger seat.

"I think she's beautiful," said Shadow, holding the coin up close. Liberty's silver face reminded him a little of Zorya Polunochnaya.

"That," said Wednesday, driving off, "is the eternal folly of man. To be chasing after the sweet flesh, without realizing that it is simply a pretty cover for the bones. Worm food. At night, you're rubbing yourself against worm food. No offense meant."

Shadow had never seen Wednesday quite so expansive. His new boss, he decided, went through phases of extroversion followed by periods of intense quiet. "So you aren't American?" asked Shadow.

"Nobody's American," said Wednesday. "Not originally. That's my point." He checked his watch. "We still have several hours to kill before the banks close. Good job last night with Czernobog, by the way. I would have closed him on coming eventually, but you enlisted him more wholeheartedly than ever I could have."

"Only because he gets to kill me afterward."

"Not necessarily. As you yourself so wisely pointed out, he's old, and the killing stroke might merely leave you, well, paralyzed for life, say. A hopeless invalid. So you have much to look forward to, should Mister Czernobog survive the coming difficulties."

to U.S. independence would properly be a joint project of the French and Americans. In 1875, Laboulaye further proposed that the French finance the gift. The Americans were charged with raising the funds for the pedestal, but donations proved difficult to attract. American publisher Joseph Pulitzer mounted a drive that brought the pedestal to completion.

The statue was designed by French sculptor Frédéric Auguste Bartholdi and its metal framework was built by Gustave Eiffel, the maker of the "Eiffel Tower" in Paris. A dedication ceremony on October 28, 1886, under the aegis of President Grover Cleveland, was the occasion of New York's first "ticker-tape" parade.

Wednesday is correct that other versions of "Lady Liberty" (Marianne in France) are depicted with bare or semi-naked breasts. However, there is no evidence that Bartholdi ever considered a version of "Liberty Enlightening the World," as the statue is properly known, with bare breasts.

258. This sentence does not appear in the First Edition.

259. Attributed to Louis-Antoine Saint-Just (in 1793, year two of the French Republican calendar). Saint-Just (1767–1794) was an outspoken ideologue and principal architect of the so-called Reign of Terror. His rise to power in revolutionary France was very swift. In 1791, he published *Esprit de la révolution et de la constitution de France* (*The Spirit of the Revolution and the Constitution of France*), an idealistic volume that won him national attention. He was elected to the National Convention shortly after his 25th birthday (the minimum age for such office), and in 1793, he was elected president of the National Convention. As president, he urged ruthless steps, including execution of the king without a trial. St. Just said to the Convention, "We must not only punish traitors, but all people who are not enthusiastic. There are only two kinds of citizens: the good and the bad. The Republic owes to the good its protection. To the bad it owes only death." Dreaded and detested, when the Montagnards lost office and the Convention turned to more moderate views, he was arrested in July 1794 and soon put to death. The story of St. Just is part of the *Sandman* tales told by Gaiman.

"And there is some question about this?" said Shadow, echoing Wednesday's manner, then hating himself for it.

"Fuck yes," said Wednesday. He pulled up in the parking lot of a bank. "This," he said, "is the bank I shall be robbing. They don't close for another few hours. Let's go in and say hello."

He gestured to Shadow. Reluctantly, Shadow got out of the car and followed Wednesday in. If the old man was going to do something stupid, Shadow could see no reason why his face should be on the camera; but curiosity pulled him in and he walked into the bank. He looked down at the floor, rubbed his nose with his hand, doing his best to keep his face hidden.

"Deposit forms, ma'am?" said Wednesday to the lone teller.

"Over there."

"Very good. And if I were to need to make a night deposit . . . ?"

"Same forms." She smiled at him. "You know where the night deposit slot is, hon? Left out the main door, it's on the wall."

"My thanks."

Wednesday picked up several deposit forms. He grinned a goodbye at the teller, and he and Shadow walked out.

Wednesday stood there on the sidewalk for a moment, scratching his beard meditatively. Then he walked over to the ATM machine, and to the night safe, set in the side of the wall, and inspected them. He led Shadow across the road to the supermarket, where he bought a chocolate fudge Popsicle for himself, and a cup of hot chocolate for Shadow. There was a payphone set in the wall of the entryway, as you went in, below a notice board with rooms to rent, and puppies and kittens in need of good homes. Wednesday wrote down the telephone number of the payphone. They crossed the road once more. "What we need," said Wednesday, suddenly, "is snow. A good, driving, irritating snow. Think 'snow' for me, will you?"

"Huh?"

"Concentrate on making those clouds—the ones over

there, in the west—making them bigger and darker. Think gray skies and driving winds coming down from the arctic. Think snow."

"I don't think it will do any good."

"Nonsense. If nothing else, it will keep your mind occupied," said Wednesday, unlocking the car. "Kinko's next.**260** Hurry up."

Snow, thought Shadow, in the passenger seat, sipping his hot chocolate. *Huge, dizzying, clumps and clusters of snow falling through the air, patches of white against an iron-gray sky, snow that touches your tongue with cold and winter, that kisses your face with its hesitant touch before freezing you to death. Twelve cotton-candy inches of snow, creating a fairy-tale world, making everything unrecognizably beautiful . . .*

Wednesday was talking to him.

"I'm sorry?" said Shadow.

"I said we're here," said Wednesday. "You were somewhere else."

"I was thinking about snow," said Shadow.

In Kinko's, Wednesday set about photocopying the deposit slips from the bank. He had the clerk instant-print him two sets of ten business cards. Shadow's head had begun to ache, and there was an uncomfortable feeling between his shoulder blades; he wondered if he had slept on it wrong, if it was an awkward legacy of the night before's sofa.

Wednesday sat at the computer terminal, composing a letter, and, with the clerk's help, making several large-sized signs.

Snow, thought Shadow. *High in the atmosphere, perfect, tiny crystals that form about a minute piece of dust, each a lace-like work of unique, six-sided fractal art. And the snow crystals clump together into flakes as they fall, covering Chicago in their white plenty, inch upon inch . . .*

"Here," said Wednesday. He handed Shadow a cup of Kinko's coffee, a half-dissolved lump of non-dairy creamer powder floating on the top. "I think that's enough, don't you?"

"Enough what?"

260. Kinko's, now known as FedEx Office, is a chain of stores providing photocopying, printing, binding, and other office services. It was founded in 1970 by Paul Orfalea, whose nickname was "Kinko" because of his curly hair. The first shop had a sidewalk copy machine and was located in Isla Vista, next to the campus of the University of California, Santa Barbara. Orfalea left the company in 2000, and in 2004, it was purchased by FedEx, the world's largest freight airline.

"Enough snow. Don't want to immobilize the city, do we?"

The sky was a uniform battleship gray. Snow was coming. Yes.

"I didn't really do that?" said Shadow. "I mean, I didn't. Did I?"

"Drink the coffee," said Wednesday. "It's foul stuff, but it will ease the headache." Then he said, "Good work."

Wednesday paid the Kinko's clerk, and he carried his signs and letters and cards outside to the car. He opened the trunk of his car, put the papers in a large black metal case of the kind carried by payroll guards, and closed the trunk. He passed Shadow a business card.

"Who," said Shadow, "is A. Haddock, Director of Security, A1 Security Services?"

"You are."

"A. Haddock?"[261]

"Yes."

"What does the A stand for?"

"Alfredo? Alphonse? Augustine? Ambrose? Your call entirely."

"Oh. I see."

"I'm James O'Gorman," said Wednesday. "Jimmy to my friends. See? I've got a card too."

They got back in the car. Wednesday said, "If you can think 'A. Haddock' as well as you thought 'snow,' we should have plenty of lovely money with which to wine and dine my friends of tonight."

"And if we're in jail by this evening?"[262]

"Then my friends will just have to make do without us."

"I'm not going back to prison."

"You won't be."

"I thought we had agreed that I wouldn't be doing anything illegal."

"You aren't. Possibly aiding and abetting, a little conspiracy to commit, followed of course by receiving stolen money, but trust me, you'll come out of this smelling like a rose."

"Is that before or after your elderly Slavic Charles Atlas[263] crushes my skull with one blow?"

"His eyesight's going," said Wednesday reassuringly.

---

261. Albert Haddock is the protagonist of *Uncommon Law*, a book by A. P. Herbert first published in 1935 (the title is a play on the concept of the "common law," the non-statutory law of England). The book is a collection of humorous reports of absurd and comical aspects of the law, first published in *Punch* as *Misleading Cases*. Of course, "A. Haddock" is also a fish!

262. This sentence and the next do not appear in the First Edition.

263. Charles Atlas, formerly Angelo Siciliano (1892–1972), who plainly named himself after the Titan Atlas, was a popular bodybuilder. His widely advertised mail-order exercise program—ads appeared commonly on the back of comic books—focused on convincing "97-pound weaklings" to take steps to gain musculature that would allow them to repel thugs and win popularity.

"He'll probably miss you entirely. Now, we still have a little time to kill—the bank closes at midday on Saturdays, after all. Would you like lunch?"

"Yes," said Shadow. "I'm starving."

"I know just the place," said Wednesday. He hummed as he drove, some cheerful song that Shadow could not identify. Snowflakes began to fall, just as Shadow had imagined them, and he felt strangely proud. He knew, rationally, that he had nothing to do with the snow, just as he knew the silver dollar he carried in his pocket was not, and never had been, the moon. But still . . .

They stopped outside a large shed-like building. A sign said that the All-U-Can-Eat lunch buffet was $4.99. "I love this place," said Wednesday.

"Good food?" asked Shadow.

"Not particularly," said Wednesday. "But the ambience is unmissable."

The ambience that Wednesday loved, it turned out, once lunch had been eaten—Shadow had the fried chicken, and enjoyed it—was the business that took up the rear of the shed: it was, the hanging flag across the center of the room announced, a Bankrupt and Liquidated Stock Clearance Depot.

Wednesday went out to the car, and reappeared with a small suitcase, which he took into the men's room. Shadow figured he'd learn soon enough what Wednesday was up to, whether he wanted to or not, and so he prowled the liquidation aisles, staring at the things for sale: boxes of coffee "for use in airline filters only," Teenage Mutant Ninja Turtle toys and Xena: Warrior Princess harem dolls, teddy bears that played patriotic tunes on the xylophone when plugged in, and other teddy bears that played seasonal songs on the xylophone when plugged in,[264] cans of processed meat, galoshes and sundry overshoes, marshmallows, Bill Clinton presidential wristwatches,[265] artificial miniature Christmas trees, salt and pepper shakers in the shapes of animals, body parts, fruit and nuts, and, Shadow's favorite, a "just add real carrot" snowman kit, with plastic coal eyes, a corn-cob pipe, and a plastic hat.

Charles Atlas advertisement, ca. 1950

264. The "other" teddy bears are not mentioned in the First Edition.

265. William Jefferson Clinton was president of the United States from 1993 to 2001, his last few months of office being just after publication of *American Gods*. How quickly history "liquidates" its actors! Interestingly, in the Manuscript, the watches were "George W. Bush" models. In a private conversation with this editor, Gaiman expressed that he changed the reference to Clinton because he thought that by 2000, when *American Gods* was published, Bush would have passed from the reader's memory!

Shadow thought about how you made the moon seem to come out of the sky and become a silver dollar, and what made a woman get out of her grave and walk across town to talk to you.

"Isn't it a wonderful place?" asked Wednesday when he came out of the men's room. His hands were still wet, and he was drying them off on a handkerchief. "They're out of paper towels in there," he said. He had changed his clothes. He was now wearing a dark blue jacket, with matching trousers, a blue knit tie, a thick blue sweater, a white shirt, and black shoes. He looked like a security guard, and Shadow said so.

"What can I possibly say to that, young man," said Wednesday, picking up a box of floating plastic aquarium fish (*They'll never fade—and you'll never have to feed them!!*"), "other than to congratulate you on your perspicacity. How about Arthur Haddock? Arthur's a good name."

"Too mundane."

"Well, you'll think of something. There. Let us return to town. We should be in perfect time for our bank robbery, and then I shall have a little spending money."

"Most people," said Shadow, "would simply take it from the ATM."

"Which is, oddly enough, more or less exactly what I was planning to do."

Wednesday parked the car in the supermarket lot across the street from the bank. From the trunk of the car Wednesday brought out the metal case and a clipboard, and a pair of handcuffs. He handcuffed the case to his left wrist. He attached the other end of the cuff to the metal case's handle. The snow continued to fall. Then he put a peaked blue cap on, and Velcroed a patch to the breast pocket of his jacket. A1 SECURITY was written on the cap and the patch. He put the deposit slips on his clipboard. Then he slouched. He looked like a retired beat cop, and appeared somehow to have gained himself a paunch.

"Now," he said, "you do a little shopping in the food store, then hang out by the phone. If anyone asks, you're waiting for a call from your girlfriend, whose car has broken down."

"So why's she calling me there?"

"How the hell should you know?"

Wednesday put on a pair of faded pink earmuffs. He closed the trunk. Snowflakes settled on his dark blue cap, and on his earmuffs.

"How do I look?" he asked.

"Ludicrous," said Shadow.

"Ludicrous?"

"Or goofy, maybe," said Shadow.

"Mm. Goofy and ludicrous. That's good." Wednesday smiled. The earmuffs made him appear, at the same time, reassuring, amusing, and, ultimately, loveable. He strode across the street and walked along the block to the bank building, while Shadow walked into the supermarket hall and watched.

Wednesday taped a large red OUT OF ORDER notice to the ATM. He put a red ribbon across the night deposit slot, and he taped a photocopied sign up above it. Shadow read it with amusement.

FOR YOUR CONVENIENCE, it said, WE ARE WORKING TO MAKE ONGOING IMPROVEMENT'S.[266] WE APOLOGIZE FOR THE TEMPORARY INCONVENIENCE.

Then Wednesday turned around and faced the street. He looked cold and put-upon.

A young woman came over to use the ATM. Wednesday shook his head, explained that it was out of order. She cursed, apologized for cursing, and ran off.

A car drew up, and a man got out holding a small gray sack and a key. Shadow watched as Wednesday apologized to the man, then made him sign the clipboard, checked his deposit slip, painstakingly wrote him out a receipt and puzzled over which copy to keep, and, finally, opened his big black metal case and put the man's sack inside.

The man shivered in the snow, stamping his feet, waiting for the old security guard to be done with this administrative nonsense, so he could leave his takings and get out of the cold and be on his way, then he took his receipt and got back into his warm car and drove off.

Wednesday walked across the street carrying the metal case, and bought himself a coffee at the supermarket.

266. Gaiman reported to this editor, in private conversation, that he fought hard to retain the incorrect apostrophe in various editions. For other examples, see the chapter on apostrophes in Lynn Truss's *Eats, Shoots & Leaves: The Zero Tolerance Approach to Punctuation* (2003).

"Afternoon, young man," he said, with an avuncular chuckle, as he passed Shadow. "Cold enough for you?"

He walked back across the street, and took gray sacks and envelopes from people coming to deposit their earnings or their takings on this Saturday afternoon, a fine old security man in his funny pink earmuffs.

Shadow bought some things to read—*Turkey Hunting,*[267] *People,* and because the cover picture of Bigfoot was so endearing, the *Weekly World News*[268]—and stared out of the window.

"Anything I can do to help?" asked a middle-aged black man with a white mustache. He seemed to be the manager.

"Thanks, man, but no. I'm waiting for a phone call. My girlfriend's car broke down."

"Probably the battery," said the man. "People forget those things only last three, maybe four years. It's not like they cost a fortune."

"Tell me about it," said Shadow.

"Hang in there, big guy," said the manager, and he went back into the supermarket.

The snow had turned the street scene into the interior of a snowglobe, perfect in all its details.

Shadow watched, impressed. Unable to hear the conversations across the street, he felt it was like watching a fine silent movie performance, all pantomime and expression: the old security guard was gruff, earnest—a little bumbling perhaps, but enormously well-meaning. Everyone who gave him their money walked away a little happier from having met him.

And then the cops drew up outside the bank, and Shadow's heart sank. Wednesday tipped his cap to them and ambled over to the police car. He said his hellos and shook hands through the open window, and nodded, then hunted through his pockets until he found a business card and a letter, and passed them through the window of the car. Then he sipped his coffee.

The telephone rang. Shadow picked up the hand piece and did his best to sound bored. "A1 Security Services," he said.

267. Actually, it was *Turkey & Turkey Hunting*, now out of print but continuing online. The magazine billed itself as the #1 source of "practical & comprehensive information for wild turkey hunters," including discussions of weapons, decoys, camouflage, hunting grounds, and recipes.

268. The *Weekly World News* was a tabloid-style newspaper with outlandish covers that featured stories of extraterrestrials, mythical creatures, urban legends, and other fiction. Its sister publication, the *National Enquirer*, took a similar approach to celebrity news. Branded as "The World's Only Reliable Newspaper," it appeared from 1979 to 2007; in 2009, it reappeared as an online journal. The mythical "Bigfoot" and other cryptids such as the popular "Bat Boy" were featured on the cover of *WWN* many times.

"Can I speak to A. Haddock?" asked the cop across the street.

"This is Andy Haddock speaking," said Shadow.

"Yeah, Mister Haddock, this is the police," said the cop in the car across the street. "You've got a man at the First Illinois Bank on the corner of Market and Second."

"Uh, yeah. That's right. Jimmy O'Gorman. And what seems to be the problem, officer? Jim behaving himself? He's not been drinking?" "No problem, sir. Your man is just fine, sir. Just wanted to make certain everything was in order."

"You tell Jim that if he's caught drinking again, officer, he's fired. You got that? Out of a job. Out on his ass. We have zero tolerance at A1 Security."

"I really don't think it's really my place to tell him that, sir. He's doing a fine job. We're just concerned because something like this really ought to be done by two personnel. It's risky, having one unarmed guard dealing with such large amounts of money."

"Tell me about it. Or more to the point, you tell those cheapskates down at the First Illinois about it. These are my men I'm putting on the line, officer. Good men. Men like you." Shadow found himself warming to this identity. He could feel himself becoming Andy Haddock, chewed cheap cigar in his ashtray, a stack of paperwork to get to this Saturday afternoon, a home in Schaumburg and a mistress in a little apartment on Lake Shore Drive. "Y'know, you sound like a bright young man, officer, uh . . ."

"Myerson."

"Officer Myerson. You need a little weekend work, or you wind up leaving the force, any reason, you give us a call. We always need good men. You got my card?"

"Yes, sir."

"You hang on to it," said Andy Haddock. "You call me."

The police car drove off, and Wednesday shuffled back through the snow to deal with the small line of people who were waiting to give him their money.

"She okay?" asked the manager, putting his head around the door. "Your girlfriend?"

Bat Boy

"It was the battery," said Shadow. "Now I just got to wait."

"Women," said the manager. "I hope yours is worth waiting for."

Winter darkness descended, the afternoon slowly graying into night. Lights went on. More people gave Wednesday their money. Suddenly, as if at some signal Shadow could not see, Wednesday walked over to the wall, removed the OUT OF ORDER signs, and trudged across the slushy road, heading for the car park. Shadow waited a minute, then followed him.

Wednesday was sitting in the back of the car. He had opened the metal case and was methodically laying everything he had been given out on the back seat in neat piles.

"Drive," he said. "We're heading for the First Illinois Bank over on State Street."[269]

"Repeat performance?" asked Shadow. "Isn't that kind of pushing your luck?"

"Not at all," said Wednesday. "We're going to do a little banking."

While Shadow drove, Wednesday sat in the back seat and removed the bills from the deposit bags in handfuls, leaving the checks and the credit card slips, and taking the cash from some, although not all, of the envelopes. He dropped the cash back into the metal case. Shadow pulled up outside the bank, stopping the car about fifty yards down the road, well out of camera range. Wednesday got out of the car, and pushed the envelopes through the night deposit slot. Then he opened the night safe, and dropped in the gray bags. He closed it again.

He climbed into the passenger seat. "You're heading for I-90," said Wednesday. "Follow the signs west for Madison."

Shadow began to drive.

Wednesday looked back at the bank they were leaving. "There, my boy," he said, cheerfully, "that will confuse everything. Now, to get the really big money, you need to do that at about 4:30 on a Sunday morning, when the clubs and the bars drop off their Saturday night's takings. Hit the right bank, the right guy making the drop off—they tend to pick them big and honest, and sometimes have a couple

269. There was a real First Illinois Bank, in East St. Louis, Illinois, but it had no Chicago branches. It was acquired in 2017, and its name was retired.

of bouncers accompany them, but they aren't necessarily smart—and you can walk away with a quarter of a million dollars for an evening's work."

"If it's that easy," said Shadow, "how come everybody doesn't do it?"

"It's not an entirely risk-free occupation," said Wednesday, "especially not at 4:30 in the morning."

"You mean the cops are more suspicious at 4:30 in the morning?"

"Not at all. But the bouncers are. And things can get awkward."

He flicked through a sheaf of fifties, added a smaller stack of twenties, weighed them in his hand, then passed them over to Shadow. "Here," he said. "Your first week's wages."

Shadow pocketed the money without counting it. "So, that's what you do?" he asked. "To make money?"

"Rarely. Only when a great deal of cash is needed fast. On the whole, I make my money from people who never know they've been taken, and who never complain, and who will frequently line up to be taken when I come back that way again."

"That Sweeney guy said you were a hustler."

"He was right. But that is the least of what I am. And the least of what I need you for, Shadow."

✦   ✦   ✦

SNOW SPUN THROUGH their headlights and into the windshield as they drove through the darkness. The effect was almost hypnotic.

"This is the only country in the world," said Wednesday, into the stillness, "that worries about what it is."

"What?"

"The rest of them know what they are. No one ever needs to go searching for the heart of Norway. Or looks for the soul of Mozambique. They know what they are."[270]

"And . . . ?"

"Just thinking out loud."

"So you've been to lots of other countries, then?"

270. This speech occurs earlier in the Manuscript, and is followed by these remarks: "This place, they don't know what they are. So they need relevance." "You're not American?" asked Shadow. "Nobody's American," said Wednesday. "That's my point. This country's like the bottom of a well. Once you're here you never leave."

271. The House on the Rock is located near Spring Green, Wisconsin. It first opened in 1959 but has grown considerably by accretion. Supposedly built single-handedly by Alex Johnson, Jr. (1914–1989), who owned it until 1988, it is at best an eccentric tourist attraction. American novelist Jane Smiley wrote about it for *The New Yorker* in 1993: "Though most people outside of the Midwest have never heard of it, the House on the Rock is said to draw more visitors every year than any other spot in Wisconsin. Also in the Wyoming Valley, but on top of a huge monolith, the House on the Rock reveals the spirit of its builder, Alex Jordan Jr., to be as single-minded and eccentric as Frank Lloyd Wright's, but in substance almost absurdly opposed.

". . . And it is hard not to be overwhelmed by the House on the Rock. The sheer abundance of objects is impressive, and the warmth most of the objects exude, the way that the toys ask to be played with, for example, makes the displays inherently inviting. But almost from the beginning, it is too much. The house itself is dusty. Windowpanes are cracked. Books are water damaged. The collections seem disordered, not curated. In fact, there is no effort to explore the objects as cultural artifacts, or to use them to educate the passing hordes. If there were informative cards, it would be impossible to read them in the dark. Everything is simply massed together, and Alex Jordan comes to seem like the manifestation of pure American acquisitiveness, and acquisitiveness of a strangely boyish kind, as if he had finalized all his desires in childhood and never grown into any others."

For an extensive photo record of a visit to the House (with references to *American Gods*), see https://www.fangirlquest.com /travel/house-on-the-rock-wisconsin/.

Wednesday said nothing. Shadow glanced at him. "No," said Wednesday, with a sigh. "No. I never have."

They stopped for gas, and Wednesday went into the restroom in his security guard jacket with his suitcase, and came out in a crisp, pale suit, brown shoes, and a knee-length brown coat that looked like it might be Italian.

"So when we get to Madison, what then?"

"Take Highway 14 west to Spring Green. We'll be meeting everyone at a place called the House on the Rock.[271] You been there?"

"No," said Shadow. "But I've seen the signs."

The signs for the House on the Rock were all around that part of the world: oblique, ambiguous signs all across Illinois and Minnesota and Wisconsin, probably as far away as Iowa, Shadow suspected, signs alerting you to the existence of the House on the Rock. Shadow had seen the signs, and wondered about them. Did the House balance perilously upon the Rock? What was so interesting about the Rock? About the House? He had given it a passing thought, but then forgotten it. Shadow was not in the habit of visiting roadside attractions.

They drove past the capitol dome of Madison, another perfect snowglobe scene in the falling snow, and then they were off the interstate, and driving down country roads. After almost an hour of driving through towns with names like Black Earth, they turned down a narrow driveway, past several enormous, snow-dusted flowerpots entwined with lizard-like dragons. The tree-lined parking lot was almost empty.

"They'll be closing soon," said Wednesday.

"So what is this place?" asked Shadow, as they walked through the parking lot toward a low, unimpressive wooden building.

"This is a roadside attraction," said Wednesday. "One of the finest. Which means it is a place of power."

"Come again?"

"It's perfectly simple," said Wednesday. "In other countries, over the years, people recognized the places of power. Sometimes it would be a natural formation, sometimes it

Exterior of House on the Rock
Courtesy, HOTR, 2018

would just be a place that was, somehow, special. They knew that something important was happening there, that there was some focusing point, some channel, some window to the Immanent. And so they would build temples, or cathedrals, or erect stone circles, or . . . well, you get the idea."

"There are churches all across the States, though," said Shadow.

"In every town. Sometimes on every block. And about as significant, in this context, as dentists' offices. No, in the USA, people still get the call, or some of them, and they feel themselves being called to from the transcendent void, and they respond to it by building a model out of beer bottles of somewhere they've never visited, or by erecting a gigantic bat-house in some part of the country that bats have traditionally declined to visit. Roadside attractions: people feel themselves being pulled to places where, in other parts of the world, they would recognize that part of themselves that is truly transcendent, and buy a hot dog and walk around, feeling satisfied on a level they cannot truly describe, and profoundly dissatisfied on a level beneath that."

"You have some pretty whacked-out theories," said Shadow.

"Nothing theoretical about it, young man," said Wednesday. "You should have figured that out by now."

There was only one ticket window open. "We stop selling tickets in half an hour," said the girl. "It takes at least two hours to walk around, you see."

Wednesday paid for their tickets in cash.

"Where's the rock?" asked Shadow.

"Under the house," said Wednesday.

"Where's the house?"

Wednesday put his finger to his lips, and they walked forward. Farther in, a player piano was playing something that was intended to have been Ravel's "Bolero."[272] The place seemed to be a geometrically reconfigured 1960s bachelor pad, with open stonework, pile carpeting, and magnificently ugly mushroom-shaped stained glass lampshades. Up a winding staircase was another room, filled with knickknacks.

"They say this was built by Frank Lloyd Wright's evil twin," said Wednesday. "Frank Lloyd Wrong." He chuckled at his joke.

"I saw that on a T-shirt," said Shadow.

Up and down more stairs, and now they were in a long, long room, made of glass, that protruded, needlelike, out over the leafless black-and-white countryside hundreds of feet below them. Shadow stood and watched the snow tumble and spin.

"This is the House on the Rock?" he asked, puzzled.

"More or less. This is the Infinity Room, part of the actual house, although a late addition.[273] But no, my young friend, we have not scratched the tiniest surface of what the house has to offer."

"So according to your theory," said Shadow, "Walt Disney World would be the holiest place in America."

272. A classical piece composed by French composer Maurice Ravel (1875–1937) and first performed in 1928, it was originally intended as a ballet.

273. It was built in 1985.

Infinity Room
Courtesy, HOTR, 2018

Wednesday frowned, and stroked his beard. "Walt Disney bought some orange groves in the middle of Florida and built a tourist town on them. No magic there of any kind, although I think there might be something real in the original Disneyland. There may be some power there, although twisted, and hard to access. There's definitely nothing out of the ordinary about Disney World.[274] But some parts of Florida are filled with real magic. You just have to keep your eyes open. Ah, for the mermaids of Weeki Wachee . . .[275] Follow me, this way."

Everywhere was the sound of music: jangling, awkward music, ever-so-slightly off the beat and out of time. Wednesday took a five-dollar bill and put it into a change machine, receiving a handful of brass-colored metal coins in return. He tossed one to Shadow, who caught it, and, realizing that a small boy was watching him, held it up between forefinger and thumb and vanished it. The small boy ran over to his mother, who was inspecting one of the ubiquitous Santa

274. This sentence does not appear in the First Edition.

275. Wednesday undoubtedly means Weeki Wachee Springs State Park, an attraction in Hernando County, Florida, that features underwater shows performed by women in mermaid costumes.

A vintage picture advertising Weeki Wachee Springs State Park, ca. 1947

*Artistic concepts reflect the many forms that Alex's
dream took on the way to a final reality.*

Design of the Infinity Room
Courtesy, HOTR, 2018

Clauses—OVER 6000 ON DISPLAY! the signs said—and he tugged urgently at the hem of her coat.

Shadow followed Wednesday outside briefly, and then followed the signs to the Streets of Yesterday.

"Forty years ago Alex Jordan—his face is on the token you have palmed in your right hand, Shadow—began to build a house on a high jut of rock in a field he did not own, and even he could not have told you why. And people came to see him build it—the curious, and the puzzled, and those who were neither and who could not honestly have told you why they came. So he did what any sensible American male of his generation would do: he began to charge them money—nothing much. A nickel each, perhaps. Or

Streets of Yesterday
Courtesy, HOTR, 2018

a quarter. And he continued building, and the people kept coming.

"So he took those quarters and nickels and made something even bigger and stranger. He built these warehouses on the land beneath the house, and filled them with things for people to see, and then the people came to see them. Millions of people come here every year."

"Why?"

But Wednesday simply smiled, and they walked into the dimly lit, tree-lined Streets of Yesterday.

Prim-lipped Victorian china dolls stared in profusion through dusty store windows, like so many props from respectable horror films. Cobblestones under their feet, the darkness of a roof above their heads, jangling mechanical music in the background. They passed a glass box of broken puppets, and an overgrown golden music box in a glass case. They passed the dentist's and the drugstore (RESTORE POTENCY! USE O'LEARY'S MAGNETICAL BELT!).[276]

At the end of the street was a large glass box with a female mannequin inside it, dressed as a gypsy fortune-teller.

"Now," boomed Wednesday, over the mechanical music, "at the start of any quest or enterprise it behooves us to consult the Norns.[277] So let us designate this Sybil our *Urd,* eh?" He dropped a brass-colored House on the Rock coin

276. While "O'Leary's Magnetical Belt" may be lumped in with other quack nostrums of the nineteenth and early twentieth century, "magnetic belts" are still widely sold today to relieve pain in affected body parts. See, e.g., https://bit.ly/2J4IutQ.

277. The goddesses of destiny. Though there were many Norns, the three most prominent are Urd ("fate," the past), Verdandi ("becoming," the present), and Skuld ("that which is intended," the future). They are said to reside under Yggdrasil, the World Tree, near Urd's well, where they water the roots of the Tree from the well. According to the *Dictionary of Ancient Deities*, they "control the unchanging universal laws and the fate of mortals and the Aesirs, the race of gods of which Odin was the chief. Urd and Verdandi were beneficial, but Skuld was said to undo the good work of the other two" (p. 351). We will meet the Norns later.

The Norns
Johannes Gehrts, 1889

Dolls
Courtesy, HOTR, 2018

278. The fortune clearly speaks truly. In the Manuscript, however, it reads: "EVERY DEATH IS A NEW BEGINNING. Lucky number 1. Lucky colour BLACK. A STORM IS COMING. KEEP YOUR OWN COUNSEL." In the First Draft, it reads: "EVERY DEATH IS A NEW BEGINNING. YOUR LUCKY NUMBER IS ONE. YOUR LUCKY COLOUR IS BLACK. IT'S A WISE CHILD KNOWS ITS OWN FATHER. THE APPLE DOES NOT FALL FAR FROM THE TREE." Gaiman wrote in by hand another version of the final message: "YOU WILL DIE THREE TIMES."

into the slot. With jagged, mechanical motions, the gypsy lifted her arm and lowered it once more. A slip of paper chunked out of the slot.

Wednesday took it, read it, grunted, folded it up, and put it in his pocket.

"Aren't you going to show it to me? I'll show you mine," said Shadow.

"A man's fortune is his own affair," said Wednesday, stiffly. "I would not ask to see yours."

Shadow put his own coin in the slot. He took his slip of paper. He read it.

EVERY ENDING IS A NEW BEGINNING.

YOUR LUCKY NUMBER IS NONE.

YOUR LUCKY COLOR IS DEAD.

MOTTO: LIKE FATHER, LIKE SON.[278]

Shadow made a face. He folded the fortune up and put it in his inside pocket.

They went further in, down a red corridor, past rooms filled with empty chairs upon which rested violins and violas and cellos which played themselves, or seemed to, when fed a coin. Keys depressed, cymbals crashed, pipes blew compressed air into clarinets and oboes. Shadow observed, with a wry amusement, that the bows of the stringed instruments, played by mechanical arms, never actually touched the strings, which were often loose or missing. He wondered whether all the sounds he heard were made by wind and percussion, or whether there were tapes as well.

They had walked for what felt like several miles when they came to a room called the Mikado,[279] one wall of which was a nineteenth-century pseudo-Oriental nightmare, in which beetle-browed mechanical drummers banged cymbals and drums while staring out from their dragon-encrusted lair. Currently, they were majestically torturing Saint-Saëns's "Danse Macabre."[280]

Czernobog sat on a bench in the wall facing the Mikado machine, tapping out the time with his fingers. Pipes fluted, bells jangled.[281]

Wednesday sat next to him. Shadow decided to remain standing. Czernobog extended his left hand, shook Wednesday's, shook Shadow's. "Well met," he said. Then he sat back, apparently enjoying the music.

The "Danse Macabre" came to a tempestuous and discordant end. That all the artificial instruments were ever-so-slightly out of tune added to the otherworldliness of the place. A new piece began.

"How was your bank robbery?" asked Czernobog. "It went well?" He stood, reluctant to leave the Mikado and its thundering, jangling music.

"Slick as a snake in a barrel of butter," said Wednesday.

"I get a pension from the slaughterhouse," said Czernobog. "I do not ask for more."

"It won't last forever," said Wednesday. "Nothing does."

More corridors, more musical machines. Shadow be-

279. A famous comic opera by Arthur Sullivan and W. S. Gilbert, first performed in 1875. It is set in Japan and rode the wave of fascination with all things Japanese that swept England. The titular Mikado is the Emperor of Japan; the setting is the fictional town of Titipu.

280. Written in 1874 by the French composer Emile Saint-Saëns (1835–1921), this tone poem for orchestra is based on the legend that Death appears at midnight on Halloween Eve and causes the dead to rise from their graves and dance while Death fiddles.

281. In the Manuscript, this is the first time Shadow meets Czernobog.

came aware that they were not following the path through the rooms intended for tourists, but seemed to be following a different route of Wednesday's own devising. They were going down a slope, and Shadow, confused, wondered if they had already been that way.

Czernobog grasped Shadow's arm. "Quickly, come here," he said, pulling him over to a large glass box by a wall. It contained a diorama of a tramp asleep in a churchyard in front of a church door. THE DRUNKARD'S DREAM said the label, which explained that it was a nineteenth-century penny-in-the-slot machine,[282] originally from an English railway station. The coin slot had been modified to take the brass House on the Rock coins.

"Put in the money," said Czernobog.

"Why?" asked Shadow.

"You must see. I show you."

Shadow inserted his coin. The drunk in the graveyard raised his bottle to his lips. One of the gravestones flipped over, revealing a grasping corpse; a headstone turned around, flowers replaced by a grinning skull. A wraith appeared on the right of the church, while on the left of the church *something* with a half-glimpsed pointed, unsettlingly bird-like face, a pale, Boschian nightmare, glided smoothly from a headstone into the shadows and was gone. Then the church door opened, a priest came out, and the ghosts, haunts, and corpses vanished, and only the priest and the drunk were left alone in the graveyard. The priest looked down at the drunk disdainfully, and backed through the open door, which closed behind him, leaving the drunk on his own.

The clockwork story was deeply unsettling. Much more unsettling, thought Shadow, than clockwork has any right to be.

"You know why I show that to you?" asked Czernobog.

"No."

"That is the world as it is. That is the real world. It is there, in that box."

They wandered through a blood-colored room filled with old theatrical organs, huge organ pipes, and what ap-

282. Known as an automaton, such coin-operated machines often showed elaborate scenes (for example, here is a set of figures in action at the St. Dennistoun Mortuary: https://www.youtube.com/watch?v=nsqFuU2OFNQ).

The organ room
Courtesy, HOTR, 2018

peared to be enormous copper brewing vats, liberated from a brewery.

"Where are we going?" asked Shadow.

"The carousel," said Czernobog.

"But we've passed signs to the carousel a dozen times already."

"He goes his way. We travel a spiral. The quickest way is sometimes the longest."

Shadow's feet were beginning to hurt, and he found this sentiment to be extremely unlikely.

A mechanical machine played "Octopus's Garden"[283] in a room that went up for many stories, the center of which was filled entirely with a replica of a great black whale-like beast, with a life-sized replica of a boat in its vast fiberglass mouth. They passed on from there to a Travel Hall, where

283. Written and sung by Ringo Starr, the Beatles recorded this popular, upbeat song about visiting an underwater garden in 1969, and it was included in the *Abbey Road* album later that year. Starr indicated later that the refrain, "I'd like to be / under the sea," reflected his desire to avoid the growing disharmony among the group.

284. Reuben "Rube" Goldberg (1883–1970) was an American cartoonist who "invented" complicated machines, usually involving many moving parts, to accomplish simple tasks. Many of these appeared in his popular strip *The Inventions of Professor Lucifer Gorgonzola Butts*, drawn from 1914 to 1964. Goldberg won many awards for his work, including the Pulitzer Prize for his political cartoons, and the phrase "Rube Goldberg machine" passed into the vernacular in the 1920s. Interestingly, there is a corresponding expression common in England during World War I, a "Heath Robinson machine," named after an English cartoonist (1872–1944) with a similar penchant for odd inventions.

285. Between 1925 and 1963, the Burma-Vita company advertised its brushless shaving cream via slogans or rhymes on sequential highway signs. About 600 of the slogans are reproduced in Frank Rowsome, and Carl Rose's *The Verse by the Side of the Road: The Story of the Burma-Shave Signs and Jingles*. (Brattleboro, Vermont: Stephen Greene Press, 1965). Possibly the best of the signs read: "If you / Don't know / Whose signs / These are / You can't have / Driven very far"

The two slogans here, however, were invented by Gaiman (according to a private conversation with this editor).

they saw the car covered with tiles, and the functioning Rube Goldberg[284] chicken device and the rusting Burma Shave ads on the wall.

LIFE IS HARD

IT'S TOIL AND TROUBLE

KEEP YOUR JAWLINE

FREE FROM STUBBLE

BURMA SHAVE[285]

read one, and

HE UNDERTOOK TO OVERTAKE

THE ROAD WAS ON A BEND

FROM NOW ON THE UNDERTAKER

IS HIS ONLY FRIEND

BURMA SHAVE

and they were at the bottom of a ramp now, with an ice-cream shop in front of them. It was nominally open, but the girl washing down the surfaces had a closed look on her face, so they walked past it into the pizzeria-cafeteria, empty but for an elderly black man wearing a bright check suit and canary-yellow gloves. He was a small man, the kind of little old man who looked as if the passing of the years had shrunk him, eating an enormous, many-scooped ice-cream sundae, drinking a supersized mug of coffee. A black cigarillo was burning in the ashtray in front of him.

"Three coffees," said Wednesday to Shadow. He went to the restroom.

Shadow bought the coffees and took them over to Czernobog, who was sitting with the old black man, and was smoking a cigarette surreptitiously, as if he were scared of being caught. The other man, happily toying with his sundae, mostly ignored his cigarillo, but as Shadow approached he picked it up, inhaled deeply, and blew two smoke rings—first one large one, then another, smaller one, which passed neatly through the first—and he grinned, as if he were astonishingly pleased with himself.

Mr. Nancy (played by Orlando Jones, from the Starz presentation of *American Gods*)
Photo copyright © 2018 Fremantle North America

"Shadow, this is Mister Nancy," said Czernobog.**286**

The old man got to his feet, and thrust out his yellow-gloved right hand. "Good to meet you," he said with a dazzling smile. "I know who you must be. You're working for the old one-eye bastard, aren't you?" There was a faint twang in his voice, a hint of a patois that might have been West Indian.

"I work for Mister Wednesday," said Shadow. "Yes. Please, sit down."

Czernobog inhaled on his cigarette.

"I think," he pronounced, gloomily, "that our kind, we like the cigarettes so much because they remind us of the offerings that once they burned for us, the smoke rising up as they sought our approval or our favor."

"They never gave me nothin' like that," said Nancy. "Best I could hope for was a pile of fruit to eat, maybe curry goat, something slow and cold and tall to drink, and a big old high-titty woman to keep me company." He grinned white teeth, and winked at Shadow.

"These days," said Czernobog, his expression unchanged, "we have nothing."

"Well, I don't get anywhere near as much fruit as I used to," said Mr. Nancy, his eyes shining. "But there still ain't

286. Mister Nancy, we will learn, is Anansi (Ananse or Annancy), the creator and trickster spider-god who is the spirit of storytelling. Anansi, like Br'er Rabbit, weak and vulnerable, survives by his wit and wisdom and is the subject of many tales in folklore. Anansi tales originated in West Africa and crossed to the New World with the slave trade.

HER CHARIOT	A MAN A MISS
RACED 80 PER	A CAR - A CURVE
THEY HAULED AWAY	HE KISSED THE MISS
WHAT HAD	AND MISSED
BEN HUR	THE CURVE
Burma Shave	*Burma Shave*

Burma-Shave signs, probably ca. 1960s

Scepter with Anansi
(from the Gold Coast, now Ghana)

287. Gaiman's fine 2005 novel, *Anansi Boys* (New York: Morrow), a sort of sequel to *American Gods*, addresses the issue of exactly how many sons Anansi has.

nothing out there in the world for my money that can beat a big old high-titty woman. Some folk you talk to, they say it's the booty you got to inspect at first, but I'm here to tell you that it's the titties that still crank my engine on a cold morning." Nancy began to laugh, a wheezing, rattling, good-natured laugh, and Shadow found himself liking the old man despite himself.

Wednesday returned from the restroom, and shook hands with Nancy. "Shadow, you want something to eat? A slice of pizza? Or a sandwich?"

"I'm not hungry," said Shadow.

"Let me tell you somethin'," said Mr. Nancy. "It can be a long time between meals. Someone offers you food, you say yes. I'm no longer young as I was, but I can tell you this, you never say no to the opportunity to piss, to eat, or to get half an hour's shut-eye. You follow me?"

"Yes. But I'm really not hungry."

"You're a big one," said Nancy, staring into Shadow's light-gray eyes with old eyes the color of mahogany, "a tall drink of water, but I got to tell you, you don't look too bright. I got a son, stupid as a man who bought his stupid at a two-for-one sale, and you remind me of him."[287]

"If you don't mind, I'll take that as a compliment," said Shadow.

"Being called dumb as a man who slept late the mornin' they handed out brains?"

"Being compared to a member of your family."

Mr. Nancy stubbed out his cigarillo, then he flicked an imaginary speck of ash off his yellow gloves. "You may not be the worst choice old one-eye could have made, come to that." He looked up at Wednesday. "You got any idea how many of us there's goin' to be here tonight?"

"I sent the message out to everyone I could find," said Wednesday. "Obviously not everyone is going to be able to come. And some of them," he said with a pointed look at Czernobog, "might not want to. But I think we can confidently expect several dozen of us. And the word will travel."

They made their way past a display of suits of armor ("Victorian fake," pronounced Wednesday as they passed

Wooden horses
Courtesy, HOTR, 2018

the glassed-in display, "modern fake, twelfth-century helm
on a seventeenth-century reproduction, fifteenth-century
left gauntlet . . .") and then Wednesday pushed through an
exit door, circled them around the outside of the building
("I can't be doin' with all these ins and outs," said Nancy,
"I'm not as young as I used to be, and I come from warmer
climes,") along a covered walk-way, in through another exit
door, and they were in the Carousel room.

Calliope music played: a Strauss waltz, stirring and occasionally discordant. The wall as they entered was hung with
antique carousel horses, hundreds of them, some in need
of a lick of paint, others in need of a good dusting; above
them hung dozens of winged angels constructed rather
obviously from female store window mannequins; some of

The Carousel
Courtesy, HOTR, 2018

them bared their sexless breasts; some had lost their wigs and stared baldly and blindly down from the darkness.

And then there was the Carousel.

A sign proclaimed it was the largest in the world, said how much it weighed, how many thousand light bulbs were to be found in the chandeliers that hung from it in gothic profusion, and forbade anyone from climbing on it or from riding on the animals.

And such animals! Shadow stared, impressed in spite of himself, at the hundreds of full-sized creatures who circled on the platform of the carousel. Real creatures, imaginary creatures, and transformations of the two: each creature was different—he saw mermaid and merman, centaur and unicorn, elephants (one huge, one tiny), bulldog, frog and phoenix, zebra, tiger, manticore and basilisk, swans pulling a carriage, a white ox, a fox, twin walruses, even a sea serpent,[288] all of them brightly colored and more than real: each rode the platform as the waltz came to an end and a new waltz began. The carousel did not even slow down.

288. Other animals of note: A dragon, pigs with fangs, a two-headed mer-unicorn, a lynx, twin armored unicorns, twin rabbits, and a gryphon.

Carousel animals
Courtesy, HOTR, 2018

More Carousel animals
Courtesy, HOTR, 2018

"What's it for?" asked Shadow. "I mean, okay, world's biggest, hundreds of animals, thousands of light bulbs, and it goes around all the time, and no one ever rides it."

"It's not there to be ridden, not by people," said Wednesday. "It's there to be admired. It's there to *be*."

"Like a prayer wheel goin' round and round," said Mr. Nancy. "Accumulating power."

"So where are we meeting everyone?" asked Shadow. "I

289. In the First Edition, Shadow was "amused, and a little puzzled."

290. In Norse mythology, Odin was frequently accompanied by Geri and Freki, two wolves. References to the wolves may be found in the *Poetic Edda* and the *Prose Edda* as well as later poetry. In the Manuscript, Wednesday mounts a dragon, Czernobog a two-headed bull.

Note that the actual carousel had no wolf figure at the time of these events. However, in furtherance of the observation that life imitates art imitating life, a wolf was added to the carousel by the House on the Rock management as part of an event in 2010 celebrating the tenth anniversary of *American Gods*.

291. Nancy, originating in West Africa, would of course like the idea of riding on lion's-back.

The Griffin at Temple Bar
C. B. Birch (ca. 1890)

thought you said that we were meeting them here. But the place is empty."

Wednesday grinned his scary grin. "Shadow," he said. "You're asking too many questions. You're paid not to ask questions."

"Sorry."

"Now, stand over here and help us up," said Wednesday, and he walked over to the platform on one side, with a description of the Carousel on it, and a warning that the Carousel was not to be ridden.

Shadow thought of saying something, but instead he helped them, one by one, up onto the ledge. Wednesday seemed profoundly heavy, Czernobog climbed up himself, only using Shadow's shoulder to steady himself, Nancy seemed to weigh nothing at all. Each of the old men climbed out onto the ledge, and then, with a step and a hop, they walked out onto the circling Carousel platform.

"Well?" barked Wednesday. "Aren't you coming?"

Shadow, not without a certain amount of hesitation, and a hasty look around for any House on the Rock personnel who might be watching, swung himself up onto the ledge beside the World's Largest Carousel. Shadow was puzzled[289] to realize that he was far more concerned with breaking the rules by climbing onto the Carousel than he had been aiding and abetting this afternoon's bank robbery.

Each of the old men selected a mount. Wednesday climbed onto a golden wolf.[290] Czernobog climbed onto an armored centaur, its face hidden by a metal helmet. Nancy, chuckling, slithered up onto the back of an enormous, leaping lion, captured by the sculptor mid-roar.[291] He patted the side of the lion. The Strauss waltz carried them around, majestically.

Wednesday was smiling, and Nancy was laughing delightedly, an old man's cackle, and even the dour Czernobog seemed to be enjoying himself. Shadow felt as if a weight were suddenly lifted from his back: three old men were enjoying themselves, riding the world's biggest carousel. So what if they did all get thrown out of the place? Wasn't it worth it, worth anything, to say that you had ridden on the

World's Largest Carousel? Wasn't it worth it to have traveled on one of those glorious monsters?

Shadow inspected a bulldog, and a mer-creature, and an elephant with a golden howdah, and then he climbed on the back of a creature with an eagle's head and the body of a tiger,[292] and held on tight.

The rhythm of the "Blue Danube" waltz rippled and rang and sang in his head, the lights of a thousand chandeliers glinted and prismed, and for a heartbeat Shadow was a child again, and all it took to make him happy was to ride the Carousel: he stayed perfectly still, riding his eagle-tiger at the center of everything, and the world revolved around him.

Shadow heard himself laugh, over the sound of the music. He was happy. It was as if the last thirty-six hours had never happened, as if the last three years had not happened, as if his life had evaporated into the daydream of a small child, riding the carousel in Golden Gate Park in San Francisco,[293] on his first trip back to the States, a marathon journey by ship and by car, his mother standing there, watching him proudly, and himself sucking his melting Popsicle, holding on tightly, hoping that the music would never stop, the carousel would never slow, the ride would never end. He was going around and around and around again . . .

Then the lights went out, and Shadow saw the gods.

292. This is a kind of *griffin*, usually depicted as having an eagle's head and lion's body.

In the Manuscript, Shadow chooses the elephant. His mother is not mentioned in the Manuscript.

293. According to the website for Golden Gate Park, "Since the playground opened in 1888, there have been three carousels at Golden Gate Park. The current jewel that literally glistens in the park is a 1914 beauty built by the Herschell-Spillman Company . . .

"The illustrious, original carousel showcased 62 animal figures, decorative benches, alluring picture panels, and even an organ. The Herschell-Spillman creation enjoyed a long, continuous run until 1977 when a mechanism failed to work. Dubbed mechanically deficient, as well as lacking its initial visual appeal, the original carousel was sent to a restoration team for repair." https://goldengatepark.com/golden-gate-park-carousel.html

Shadow, who was born around 1968, would have ridden on the unrestored version.

Golden Gate Park carousel, 2009
(Photo by Joe Mabel, GFDL, CC-BY-SA-3.0)
https://commons.wikimedia.org/wiki
/File:Golden_Gate_Park_carousel_01.jpg

CHAPTER SIX

294. The poem was first published in the *Atlantic Monthly* for July 1892 (p. 57) and is dated April 1892. Aldrich made minor edits (for example, changing the phrase "strange tongues are these" to "strange tongues are loud" and adding the phrase "alien to" in place of "in" in the following line) in the 1895 collected version of his poem, and the Folio Society edition of *American Gods* uses this later version. The poem is often read as an anti-immigration polemic, consistent with the new "nativism" that was sweeping the United States at the end of the nineteenth century. A more careful reading, however, suggests that Aldrich was concerned only with dissident voices, those who publicly espoused anti-American ideals. Bailey was a prolific writer, poet, and critic and edited the *Atlantic Monthly* from 1881 to 1890. He refused to publish works by the publisher's friends and set a high bar for the magazine. His 1862 novel, *Out of His Head*, contains one of the earliest examples of American detective fiction.

Wide open and unguarded stand our gates,
And through them passes a wild motley throng.
Men from the Volga and the Tartar steppes.
Featureless figures of the Hoang-ho,
Malayan, Scythian, Teuton, Kelt and Slav,
Flying the Old World's poverty and scorn;
These bringing with them unknown gods and rites,
Those, tiger passions, here to stretch their claws,
In street and alley what strange tongues are loud,[294]
Accents of menace alien to our ear,
Voices that once the Tower of Babel knew.

—THOMAS BAILEY ALDRICH,
"Unguarded Gates," 1895

 NE MOMENT SHADOW was riding the World's Largest Carousel, holding on to his eagle-headed tiger, and then the red and white lights of the Carousel stretched and shivered and went out, and he was falling through an ocean of stars, while the mechanical waltz was replaced by a pounding rhythmic roll and crash, as of cymbals or the breakers on the shores of a far ocean.

The only light was starlight, but it illuminated everything with a cold clarity. Beneath him his mount stretched, and padded, its warm fur under his left hand, its feathers beneath his right.

"It's a good ride, isn't it?" The voice came from behind him, in its ears and in his mind.

Shadow turned, slowly, streaming images of himself as he moved, frozen moments, each him captured in a fraction of a second, every tiny movement lasting for an infinite period. The images that reached his mind made no sense: it was like seeing the world through the multifaceted jeweled eyes of a dragonfly, but each facet saw something completely different, and he was unable to combine the things he was seeing, or thought he was seeing, into a whole that made any sense.

He was looking at Mr. Nancy, an old black man with a pencil mustache, in his check sports jacket and his lemon-yellow gloves, riding a carousel lion as it rose and lowered, high in the air; and, at the same time, in the same place, he saw a jeweled spider as high as a horse, its eyes an emerald nebula, strutting, staring down at him; and simultaneously he was looking at an extraordinarily tall man with teak-colored skin and three sets of arms, wearing a flowing ostrich-feather headdress, his face painted with red stripes, riding an irritated golden lion, two of his six hands holding on tightly to the beast's mane; and he was also seeing a young black boy, dressed in rags, his left foot all swollen and crawling with black flies; and last of all, and behind all these things, Shadow was looking at a tiny brown spider, hiding under a withered ocher leaf.

Shadow saw all these things, and he knew they were the same thing.

"If you don't close your mouth," said the many things that were Mr. Nancy, "somethin's goin' to fly in there."

Shadow closed his mouth and swallowed, hard.

There was a wooden hall on a hill, a mile or so from them. They were trotting toward the hall, their mounts' hooves and feet padding noiselessly on the dry sand at the sea's edge.

Czernobog trotted up on his centaur. He tapped the human arm of his mount. "None of this is truly happening," he said to Shadow. He sounded miserable. "Is all in your head. Best not to think of it."

Shadow saw a gray-haired old east-European immigrant, with a shabby raincoat and one iron-colored tooth, true. But he also saw a squat black thing, darker than the darkness that surrounded them, its eyes two burning coals; and he saw a prince, with long flowing black hair, and long black mustaches, blood on his hands and his face, riding, naked but for a bearskin over his shoulder, on a creature half-man, half-beast, its face and torso blue-tattooed with swirls and spirals.

"Who are you?" asked Shadow. "What are you?"

Their mounts padded along the shore. Waves broke and crashed implacably on the night beach.

Wednesday guided his wolf—now a huge and charcoal-gray beast with green eyes—over to Shadow. Shadow's mount caracoled[295] away from it, and Shadow stroked its neck and told it not to be afraid. Its tiger tail swished, aggressively. It occurred to Shadow that there was another wolf, a twin to the one that Wednesday was riding, keeping pace with them in the sand dunes, just a moment out of sight.

"Do you know me, Shadow?" said Wednesday. He rode his wolf with his head high. His right eye glittered and flashed, his left eye was dull. He wore a cloak, with a deep, monk-like cowl, and his face stared out at them from the shadows. "I told you I would tell you my names. This is what they call me. I am called Glad-of-War, Grim, Raider, and Third. I am One-eyed. I am called Highest, and True-Guesser. I am Grimnir, and I am the Hooded One. I am All-Father, and I am Gondlir Wand-bearer.[296] I have as many names as there are winds, as many titles as there are ways to die. My ravens are Huginn and Muninn: Thought and Memory; my wolves are Freki and Geri; my horse is the gallows." Two ghostly-gray ravens, like transparent skins of birds, landed on Wednesday's shoulders, pushed their beaks *into* the side of Wednesday's head as if tasting his mind, and flapped out into the world once more.

What should I believe? thought Shadow, and the voice came back to him from somewhere deep beneath the world, in a bass rumble: *Believe everything.*

295. A half-turn to the right or left—the term applies only to mounted horses.

296. Gondlir (Göndlir in Old Norse) means "wand-bearer" and refers to Odin's magic staff. According to Old Norse poetry, the name was applied to him "midst gods."

"Odin?" said Shadow, and the wind whipped the word from his lips.

"Odin," whispered Wednesday, and the crash of the breakers on the beach of skulls was not loud enough to drown that whisper. "Odin," said Wednesday, tasting the sound of the words in his mouth.[297] "Odin," said Wednesday, his voice a triumphant shout that echoed from horizon to horizon. His name swelled and grew and filled the world like the pounding of blood in Shadow's ears.[298]

And then, as in a dream, they were no longer riding toward a distant hall. They were already there, and their mounts were tied in the shelter beside the hall.

The hall was huge but primitive. The roof was thatched, the walls were wooden. There was a fire burning in the center of the hall, and the smoke stung Shadow's eyes.

"We should have done this in my mind, not in his," muttered Mr. Nancy to Shadow. "It would have been warmer there."

"We're in his mind?"

"More or less. This is Valaskjalf.[299] It's his old hall."

Shadow was relieved to see that Nancy was now once more an old man wearing yellow gloves, although his shadow shook and shivered and changed in the flames of the fire, and what it changed into was not always entirely human.

There were wooden benches against the walls, and, sitting on them or standing beside them, perhaps ten people. They kept their distance from each other: a mixed lot, who included a dark-skinned, matronly woman in a red sari, several shabby-looking businessmen, and others, too close to the fire for Shadow to be able to make them out.

"Where are they?" whispered Wednesday fiercely, to Nancy. "Well? Where are they? There should be scores of us here. Dozens!"

"You did all the inviting," said Nancy. "I think it's a wonder you got as many here as you did. You think I should tell a story, to start things off?"

Wednesday shook his head. "Out of the question."

"They don't look very friendly," said Nancy. "A story's a

297. According to Old Norse/Icelandic scholars, the correct spelling is Oⅾinn and pronounced "Othinn," though it has become conventionalized as "Oh-din."

298. The First Draft continues with the following paragraph: "'If you got so many bloody names, then why are you shoutin' about one of them?' called Nancy. 'Settle down. We'll leave the beasts out here, and go see your guests. They're waitin' for us.'"

299. "The Shelf of the Slain," Valaskjalf was one of Odin's halls of legend, supposed to be roofed with silver.

good way of gettin' someone on your side. And you don't have a bard to sing to them."

"No stories," said Wednesday. "Not now. Later, there will be time for stories. Not now."

"No stories. Right. I'll just be the warm-up man." And Mr. Nancy strode out into the firelight with an easy smile.

"I know what you are all thinking," he said. "You are thinking, what is Compé Anansi doing, coming out to talk to you all, when the All-Father called you all here, just like he called me here? Well, you know, sometimes people need reminding of things. I look around when I come in, and I thought, *Where's the rest of us?* But then I thought, just because we are few and they are many, we are weak, and they are powerful, it does not mean that we are lost.

"You know, one time I saw Tiger down at the waterhole: he had the biggest testicles of any animal, and the sharpest claws, and two front teeth as long as knives and as sharp as blades. And I said to him, 'Brother Tiger, you go for a swim, I'll look after your balls for you.' He was so proud of his balls. So he got into the waterhole for a swim, and I put his balls on, and left him my own little spider-balls. And then, you know what I did? I ran away, fast as my legs would take me.

"I didn't stop till I got to the next town. And I saw Old Monkey there. 'You lookin' mighty fine, Anansi,' said Old Monkey. I said to him, 'You know what they all singin' in the town over there?' 'What are they singin'?' he asks me. 'They singin' the funniest song,' I told him. Then I did a dance, and I sings,

> *Tiger's balls, yeah,*
> *I ate Tiger's balls*
> *Now ain't nobody gonna stop me ever at all*
> *Nobody put me up against the big black wall*
> *Cos I ate that Tiger's testimonials*
> *I ate Tiger's balls.*

"Old Monkey he laughs fit to bust, holding his side and shakin', and stampin', then he starts singin', *'Tiger's Balls, I ate tiger's balls,'* snappin' his fingers, spinnin' around on his two feet. 'That's a fine song,' he says, 'I'm going to sing it to all my friends.' 'You do that,' I tell him, and I head back to the waterhole.

"There's Tiger, down by the waterhole, walking up and down, with his tail switchin' and swishin' and his ears and the fur on his neck up as far as they can go, and he's snappin' at every insect comes by with his huge old saber-teeth, and his eyes flashin' orange fire. He looks mean and scary and big, but danglin' between his legs, there's the littlest balls in the littlest blackest most wrinkledy ball-sack you ever did see.

"'Hey, Anansi,' he says, when he sees me. 'You were supposed to be guarding my balls while I went swimming. But when I got out of the swimming hole, there was nothing on the side of the bank but these little black shriveled-up good-for-nothing spider balls I'm wearing.'

"'I done my best,' I tells him, 'but it was those monkeys, they come by and eat your balls all up, and when I tell them off, then they pulled off my own little balls. And I was so ashamed I ran away.'

"'You a liar, Anansi,' says Tiger. 'I'm going to eat your liver.' But then he hears the monkeys coming from their town to the waterhole. A dozen happy monkeys, boppin' down the path, clickin' their fingers and singin' as loud as they could sing,

Tiger's balls, yeah,
I ate Tiger's balls
Now ain't nobody gonna stop me ever at all
Nobody put me up against the big black wall
Cos I ate that Tiger's testimonials
I ate Tiger's balls.

"And Tiger, he growls, and he roars and he's off into the forest after them, and the monkeys screech and head for the highest trees. And I scratch my nice new big balls, and damn they felt good hangin' between my skinny legs, and I walk on home. And even today, Tiger keeps chasin' monkeys. So you all remember: just because you're small, doesn't mean you got no power."

Thor and Loki confront the giant Skyrmir
Elmer Boyd Smith, 1902

300. The phrase "and I'm not sure . . ." does not appear in the First Edition.

301. Loki is one of the more prominent gods in Norse mythology, of uncertain lineage (though most sources say he is the child of a giant); he is a trickster god, sometimes working with the other gods, sometimes opposing them. Known also as the "Prince of Lies," a title sometimes ascribed to Satan, he is said to have given birth to the monsters Fenrir, a wolf, Nithog, a giant serpent, and Hel, the mistress of the underworld. Loki is slated to lead the forces of Midgard, the world of man, at Ragnarok, the battle that will take place at the end of the world. For more on the Norse gods, see *Norse Mythology*. Loki is a significant player in Gaiman's *Sandman*.

Mr. Nancy smiled, and bowed his head, and spread his hands, accepting the applause and laughter like a pro, and then he turned and walked back to where Shadow and Czernobog were standing.

"I thought I said no stories," said Wednesday.

"You call that a story?" said Nancy. "I barely cleared my throat. Just warmed them up for you. Go knock them dead."

Wednesday walked out into the firelight, a big old man with a glass eye in a brown suit and an old Armani coat. He stood there, looking at the people on the wooden benches, saying nothing for longer than Shadow could believe someone could comfortably say nothing. And, finally, he spoke.

"You know me," he said. "You all know me. Some of you have no cause to love me, and I'm not sure I can blame you for that,[300] but love me or not, you know me."

There was a rustling, a stir among the people on the benches.

"I've been here longer than most of you. Like the rest of you, I figured we could get by on what we got. Not enough to make us happy, but enough to keep going.

"That may not be the case any more. There's a storm coming, and it's not a storm of our making."

He paused. Now he stepped forward, and folded his arms across his chest.

"When the people came to America they brought us with them. They brought me, and Loki[301] and Thor,[302] Anansi and the Lion-God,[303] Leprechauns and Cluracans[304] and Banshees,[305] Kubera[306] and Frau Holle[307] and Ashtaroth,[308] and they brought you. We rode here in their minds, and we took root. We traveled with the settlers to the new lands across the ocean.

"The land is vast. Soon enough, our people abandoned us, remembered us only as creatures of the old land, as things that had not come with them to the new. Our true believers passed on, or stopped believing, and we were left, lost and scared and dispossessed, to get by on what little smidgens of worship or belief we could find. And to get by as best we could.

"So that's what we've done, gotten by, out on the edges of things, where no one was watching us too closely.

"We have, let us face it and admit it, little influence. We prey on them, and we take from them, and we get by; we strip and we whore and we drink too much; we pump gas and we steal and we cheat and we exist in the cracks at the edges of society. Old gods, here in this new land without gods."

Wednesday paused. He looked from one to another of his listeners, grave and statesmanlike. They stared back at him impassively, their faces masklike and unreadable. Wednesday cleared his throat, and he spat, hard, into the fire. It flared and flamed, illuminating the inside of the hall.

"Now, as all of you will have had reason aplenty to discover for yourselves, there are new gods growing in America, clinging to growing knots of belief: gods of credit-card and freeway, of internet and telephone, of radio and hospital and television, gods of plastic and of beeper and of neon. Proud gods, fat and foolish creatures, puffed up with their own newness and importance.

"They are aware of us, and they fear us, and they hate us," said Odin. "You are fooling yourselves if you believe otherwise. They will destroy us, if they can. It is time for us to band together. It is time for us to act."

The old woman in the red sari stepped into the fire-light.[309] On her forehead was a small dark blue jewel. She said, "You called us here for this nonsense?" And then she snorted, a snort of mingled amusement and irritation.

Wednesday's brows lowered. "I called you here, yes. But this is sense, Mama-ji,[310] not nonsense. Even a child could see that."

"So I am a child, am I?" She wagged a finger at him. "I was old in Kalighat[311] before you were dreamed of, you foolish man. I am a child? Then I *am* a child, for there is nothing in your foolish talk to see."

Again, a moment of double-vision: Shadow saw the old woman, her dark face pinched with age and disapproval, but behind her he saw something huge, a naked woman with skin as black as a new leather jacket, and lips and

Thor, the Thunder-God
Johannes Gehrts, 1884

302. The Norse god of thunder and lightning, he is said to be one of Odin's sons and frequently accompanies him on adventures.

303. Probably the ancient Egyptian son of Ra and Bast, known as Maahes, he was viewed as a deity of war, protection, and the weather.

304. In the First Edition, Kobolds are mentioned in place of Cluracans. See note 866, below.

305. The Banshee is an Irish death spirit; the word literally means "fairy woman" ("Bean Sidhe"). For more on leprechauns and cluracans, see note 113, above.

306. The hideous dwarf son of Visravas and Idavida and perhaps an aspect of Shiva, Kubera or Kuvera is the Hindu god of wealth and treasures.

A banshee (artist unknown)

Kubera, in 10th-century sandstone
from northern India
San Antonio Museum of Art

307. Also known as Holda, she is a Teutonic god of weather and the dispenser of gifts.

308. Also known as Ishtar or Astarte, she is the Near Eastern goddess of love, battle, war, fertility, sex, and maternity. See also note 173, above. She appears in *Sandman* as Ishtar.

tongue the bright red of arterial blood. Around her neck were skulls, and her many hands held knives, and swords, and severed heads.

"I did not call you a child, Mama-ji," said Wednesday, peaceably. "But it seems self-evident—"

"The only thing that seems self-evident," said the old woman, pointing (as behind her, through her, above her, a black finger, sharp-taloned, pointed in echo), "is your own desire for glory. We've lived in peace in this country for a long time. Some of us do better than others, I agree. I do well. Back in India, there is an incarnation of me who does much better, but so be it. I am not envious. I've watched the new ones rise, and I've watched them fall again." Her hand fell to her side. Shadow saw that the others were looking at her, a mixture of expressions—respect, amusement, embarrassment—in their eyes. "They worshiped the railroads here, only a blink of an eye ago. And now the iron gods are as forgotten as the emerald hunters . . ."

"Make your point, Mama-ji," said Wednesday.

"My point?" Her nostrils flared. The corners of her mouth turned down. "I—and I am *obviously* only a child— say that we wait. We do nothing. We don't know that they mean us harm."

"And will you still counsel waiting when they come in the night and they kill you, or they take you away?"

Her expression was disdainful and amused: it was all in the lips and the eyebrows and the set of the nose. "If they try such a thing," she said, "they will find me hard to catch, and harder still to kill."

A squat young man sitting on the bench behind her harrumphed for attention, then said, with a booming voice, "All-Father, my people are comfortable. We make the best of what we have. If this war of yours goes against us, we could lose everything."

Wednesday said, "You have already lost everything. I am offering you the chance to take something back."

The fire blazed high as he spoke, illuminating the faces of the audience.

I don't really believe, Shadow thought. *I don't believe*

any of this. Maybe I'm still fifteen. Mom's still alive and I haven't even met Laura yet. Everything that's happened so far has been some kind of especially vivid dream. And yet he could not believe that either. All we have to believe with is our senses: the tools we use to perceive the world, our sight, our touch, our memory. If they lie to us, then nothing can be trusted. And even if we do not believe, then still we cannot travel in any other way than the road our senses show us; and we must walk that road to the end.

Then the fire burned out, and there was darkness in Valaskjalf, Odin's Hall.

"Now what?" whispered Shadow.

"Now we go back to the Carousel room," muttered Mr. Nancy, "and old One-Eye buys us all dinner, greases some palms, kisses some babies, and no one says the G-word any more."

"G-word?"

"*Gods.* What *were* you doin' the day they handed out brains, boy, anyway?"

"Someone was telling a story about stealing a tiger's balls, and I had to stop and find out how it ended."

Mr. Nancy chuckled.

"But nothing was resolved. Nobody agreed to anything."

"He's working them slowly. He'll land 'em one at a time. You'll see. They'll come around in the end."

Shadow could feel that a wind was coming up from somewhere, stirring his hair, touching his face, pulling at him.

They were standing in the room of the biggest Carousel in the world, listening to "The Emperor Waltz."

There was a group of people, tourists by the look of them, talking with Wednesday over at the other side of the room, by the wall covered with all the wooden carousel horses: as many people as there had been shadowy figures in Wednesday's Hall. "Through here," boomed Wednesday, and he led them through the only exit, formed to look like the gaping mouth of a huge monster, its sharp teeth ready to rend them all to slivers. He moved among them like a politician, cajoling, encouraging, smiling, gently disagreeing, pacifying.

"Did that happen?" asked Shadow.

Ishtar, on the back of a lion
(6th century B.C.E.)

309. This argument with Mama-ji does not appear in the First Draft.

310. "Mama-ji" is a masculine title, meaning mother's brother, not a name. In a private conversation with this editor, Gaiman explained that various texts use this misnomer, and that in the Hindi equivalent of "franglais," the word has taken on the feminine gender.

311. Kalighat is in the Kolkata region of West Bengal, India, and is the home of an ancient temple of Kali. Kali is an Indian goddess, the destroyer of evil forces.

159

"Did what happen, shit-for-brains?" asked Mr. Nancy.

"The hall. The fire. Tiger balls. Riding the Carousel."

"Heck, nobody's allowed to ride the Carousel. Didn't you see the signs? Now hush."

The monster's mouth led to the Organ Room, which puzzled Shadow—hadn't they already come through that way? It was no less strange the second time. Wednesday led them all up some stairs, past life-sized models of the four horsemen of the apocalypse hanging from the ceiling, and they followed the signs to an early exit.

Shadow and Nancy brought up the rear. And then they were out of the House on the Rock, walking past the gift store and heading back into the parking lot.

"Pity we had to leave before the end," said Mr. Nancy. "I was kind of hoping to see the biggest artificial orchestra in the whole world."

"I've seen it," said Czernobog. "It's not so much."[312]

✦   ✦   ✦

THE RESTAURANT WAS a big and barn-like structure, ten minutes up the road. Wednesday had told each of his guests that tonight's dinner was on him, and had organized rides to the restaurant for any of them that didn't have their own transportation.

Shadow wondered how they had gotten to the House on the Rock without their own transportation, and how they were going to get away again, but he said nothing. It seemed the smartest thing to say.

Shadow had a carful of Wednesday's guests to ferry to the restaurant: the woman in the red sari sat in the front seat beside him. There were two men in the back seat: a peculiar-looking young man[313] whose name Shadow had not properly caught, but thought might be Elvis, and another man, in a dark suit, who Shadow could not remember.[314]

He had stood beside the man as he got into the car, had opened and closed the door for him, and was unable to remember anything about him. He turned around in the driver's seat and looked at him, carefully noting his face, his hair, his clothes, making certain he would know him if

312. The version of the conference that appears in the Manuscript is considerably different, with only four people attending besides Wednesday, Nancy, and Czernobog: Mama-ji, the king of the dwarves, the nameless god, and a young woman who is described as like a niece of Czernobog, with dark hair and a crimson slash of a mouth.

313. He is described as "squat" in the First Edition.

314. This is the first appearance of the "nameless god." For more on his identity, see note 482, below.

he met him again, and turned back to start the car, to find that the man had slipped from his mind. An impression of wealth was left behind, but nothing more.

I'm tired, thought Shadow. He glanced to his right and snuck a glance at the Indian woman. He noted the tiny silver necklace of skulls that circled her neck, her charm bracelet of heads and hands that jangled, like tiny bells, when she moved. There was a dark blue jewel on her forehead. She smelled of spices, of cardamom and nutmeg and flowers. Her hair was pepper-and-salt, and she smiled when she saw him look at her.

"You call me Mama-ji," she said.

"I am Shadow, Mama-ji," said Shadow.

"And what do you think of your employer's plans, Mister Shadow?"

He slowed, as a large black truck sped past, overtaking them with a spray of slush. "I don't ask, he don't tell," he said.

"If you ask me, he wants a last stand. He wants us to go out in a blaze of glory. That's what he wants. And we are old enough, or stupid enough, that maybe some of us will say yes."

"It's not my job to ask questions, Mama-ji," said Shadow. The inside of the car filled with her tinkling laughter.

The man in the back seat—not the peculiar-looking young man, the other one—said something, and Shadow replied to him, but a moment later he was damned if he could remember what had been said.

The peculiar-looking young man had said nothing, but now he started to hum to himself, a deep, melodic, bass humming that made the interior of the car vibrate and rattle and buzz.

The peculiar-looking man was of average height, but of an odd shape: Shadow had heard of men who were barrel-chested before, but had no image to accompany the metaphor. This man was barrel-chested, and he had legs like, yes, like tree-trunks, and hands like, exactly, ham-hocks. He wore a black parka with a hood, several sweaters, thick dungarees, and, incongruously, in the winter and with those

315. The "peculiar-looking" man is later revealed to be Alviss, the dwarf-king. See note 673, below.

316. The Manuscript refers to nine at the restaurant, but the four who met them plus Wednesday, Shadow, Czernobog, and Nancy makes only eight . . .

clothes, a pair of white tennis shoes, which were the same size and shape as shoe boxes. His fingers resembled sausages, with flat, squared-off fingertips.[315]

"That's some hum you got," said Shadow from the driver's seat.

"Sorry," said the peculiar young man, in a deep, deep voice, embarrassed. He stopped humming.

"No, I enjoyed it," said Shadow. "Don't stop."

The peculiar young man hesitated, then commenced to hum once more, his voice as deep and reverberant as before. This time there were words interspersed in the humming. "Down down down," he sang, so deeply that the windows rattled. "Down down down, down down, down down."

Christmas lights were draped across the eaves of every house and building that they drove past. They ranged from discreet golden lights that dripped twinkles to giant displays of snowmen and teddy bears and multicolored stars.

Shadow pulled up at the restaurant and he let his passengers off by the front door, then he got back into the car.[316] He would park it at the back of the parking lot. He wanted to make the short walk back to the restaurant on his own, in the cold, to clear his head.

He parked the car beside a black truck. He wondered if it was the same one that had sped past him earlier.

He closed the car door, and stood there in the parking lot, his breath steaming.

Inside the restaurant, Shadow could imagine Wednesday already sitting all his guests down around a big table, working the room. Shadow wondered whether he had really had Kali in the front of his car, wondered what he had been driving in the back . . .

"Hey, bud, you got a match?" said a voice that was half-familiar, and Shadow turned to apologize and say no, he didn't have a match, but the gun barrel hit him over the left eye, and he started to fall. He put out an arm to steady himself as he went down. Someone pushed something soft into his mouth, to stop him crying out, and taped it into position: easy, practiced moves, like a butcher gutting a chicken.

Shadow tried to shout, to warn Wednesday, to warn them all, but nothing came out of his mouth but a muffled noise.

"The quarry are all inside," said the half-familiar voice. "Everyone in position?" A crackle of a voice, half-audible through a radio. "Let's move in and round them all up."

"What about the big guy?" said another voice.

"Package him up, take him out," said the first voice.

They put a bag-like hood over Shadow's head, and bound his wrists and ankles with tape, and put him in the back of a truck, and drove him away.

*   *   *

THERE WERE NO windows in the tiny room in which they had locked Shadow. There was a plastic chair, a lightweight folding table, and a bucket with a cover on it, which served Shadow as a makeshift toilet. There was also a six-foot-long strip of yellow foam on the floor, and a thin blanket with a long-since-crusted brown stain in the center: blood or shit or food, Shadow didn't know and didn't care to investigate. There was a naked bulb behind a metal grille high in the room, but no light switch that Shadow had been able to find. The light was always on. There was no door handle on his side of the door.

He was hungry.

The first thing he had done, when the spooks had pushed him into the room, after they'd ripped off the tape from his ankles and wrists and mouth and left him alone, was to walk around the room and inspect it, carefully. He tapped the walls. They sounded dully metallic. There was a small ventilation grid at the top of the room. The door was soundly locked.

He was bleeding above the left eyebrow in a slow ooze. His head ached.

The floor was uncarpeted. He tapped it. It was made of the same metal as the walls.

He took the top off the bucket, pissed in it, and covered it once more. According to his watch only four hours had passed since the raid on the restaurant.

His wallet was gone, but they had left him his coins.

He sat on the chair, at the card-table. The table was covered with a cigarette-burned green baize. Shadow practiced appearing to push coins through the table. Then he took two quarters and made up a Pointless Coin Trick.

He concealed a quarter in his right palm, and openly displayed the other quarter in his left hand, between finger and thumb. Then he appeared to take the quarter from his left hand, while actually letting it drop back into his left hand. He opened his right hand to display the quarter that had been there all along.

The thing about coin manipulation was that it took all Shadow's head to do it; or rather, he could not do it if he was angry or upset, so the action of practicing an illusion, even one with no possible use on its own—consider, he had expended an enormous amount of effort and skill to make it appear that he had moved a quarter from one hand to the other, something that it takes no skill whatever to do for real—calmed him, cleared his mind of turmoil and fear.

He began a trick even more pointless: a one-handed half-dollar-to-penny transformation, but with his two quarters. Each of the coins was alternately concealed and revealed as the trick progressed: he began with one quarter visible, held between the tips of his forefingers, the other hidden horizontally in the fork of his thumb, a Downs palm. He raised his hand to his mouth and blew on the coin, while slipping the visible quarter onto the tip of his third finger and pushing it into a classic palm, as the first two fingers took the hidden quarter out of the Downs palm and presented it.[317] The effect was that he displayed a quarter in his hand, raised it to his mouth, blew on it, and lowered it again, displaying the same quarter all the while.

He did it over and over and over again.

He wondered if they were going to kill him, and his hand trembled, just a little, and one of the quarters dropped from his fingertip onto the stained green baize of the card table.

And then, because he just couldn't do it any more, he put the coins away, and took out the Liberty-head dollar that Zorya Polunochnaya had given him, and held on to it tightly, and waited.

317. The manipulation is much less detailed in the First Edition.

✦ ✦ ✦

AT THREE IN the morning, by his watch, the spooks returned to interrogate him. Two men in dark suits, with dark hair and shiny black shoes. Spooks. One was square-jawed, wide-shouldered, great hair, looked like he had played football in high school, badly bitten fingernails, the other had a receding hairline, silver-rimmed round glasses, manicured nails. While they looked nothing alike, Shadow found himself suspecting that, on some level, possibly cellular, the two men were identical. They stood on each side of the card table, looking down at him.

"How long have you been working for Cargo, sir?" asked one.

"I don't know what that is," said Shadow.

"He calls himself Wednesday. Grimm. Olfather. Old guy. You've been seen with him, sir."

"I've been working for him for three days."[318]

"Don't lie to us, sir," said the spook with the glasses.

"Okay," said Shadow. "I won't. But it's still three days."

The clean-jawed spook reached down and twisted Shadow's ear between finger and thumb. He squeezed as he twisted. The pain was intense. "We told you not to lie to us, sir," he said, mildly. Then he let go.

Each of the spooks had a gun-bulge under his jacket. Shadow did not try to retaliate. He pretended he was back in prison. *Do your own time,* thought Shadow. *Don't tell them anything they don't know already. Don't ask questions.*

"These are dangerous people you're palling around with, sir," said the spook with glasses. "You will be doing your country a service by turning state's evidence." He smiled, sympathetically: *I'm the good cop,* said the smile.

"I see," said Shadow.

"And if you don't want to help us, sir," said the clean-jawed spook, "you can see what we're like when we're not happy." He hit Shadow with an open-handed blow across the stomach, knocking the breath from him. It wasn't torture, Shadow thought, just punctuation: *I'm the bad cop.* He retched.

318. Shadow describes his employment less accurately as "a couple of days" in the First Edition.

"I would like to make you happy," said Shadow, as soon as he could speak.

"All we ask is your cooperation, sir."

"Can I ask . . ." gasped Shadow (*don't ask questions*, he thought, but it was too late, the words were already spoken), "can I ask who I'll be cooperating with?"

"You want us to tell you our names?" asked the clean-jawed spook. "You have to be out of your mind."

"No, he's got a point," said the spook with glasses. "It may make it easier for him to relate to us." He looked at Shadow and smiled like a man advertising toothpaste. "Hi. I'm Mister Stone, sir. My colleague is Mister Wood."

"Actually," said Shadow, "I meant, what agency are you with? CIA? FBI?"

Stone shook his head. "Chee. It's not as easy as that, any more, sir. Things just aren't that simple."

"The private sector," said Wood, "the public sector. You know. There's a lot of interplay these days."

"But I can assure you," said Stone, with another smiley smile, "we *are* the good guys. Are you hungry, sir?" He reached into a pocket of his jacket, pulled out a Snickers bar. "Here. A gift."

"Thanks," said Shadow. He unwrapped the Snickers bar and ate it.

"I guess you'd like something to drink with that. Coffee? Beer?"

"Water, please," said Shadow.

Stone walked to the door, knocked on it. He said something to the guard on the other side of the door, who nodded and returned a minute later with a polystyrene cup filled with cold water.

"CIA," said Wood. He shook his head, ruefully. "Those bozos. Hey, Stone. I heard a new CIA joke. Okay: how can we be sure the CIA wasn't involved in the Kennedy assassination?"

"I don't know," said Stone. "How *can* we be sure?"

"He's dead, isn't he?" said Wood.

They both laughed.

"Feeling better now, sir?" asked Stone.

"I guess."

"So why don't you tell us what happened this evening, sir?"

"We did some tourist stuff. Went to the House on the Rock. Went out for some food. You know the rest."

Stone sighed, heavily. Wood shook his head, as if disappointed, and kicked Shadow in the kneecap. The pain was excruciating. Then Wood pushed a fist slowly into Shadow's back, just above the right kidney, and he twisted his fist, and the pain was worse for Shadow than the pain in his knee.

I'm bigger than either of them, he thought. *I can take them.* But they were armed; and even if he—somehow—killed or subdued them both, he'd still be locked in the cell with them. (But he'd have a gun. He'd have two guns.) (*No.*)

Wood was keeping his hands away from Shadow's face. No marks. Nothing permanent: just fists and feet on his torso and knees. It hurt, and Shadow clutched the Liberty dollar tight in the palm of his hand, and waited for it to be over.

And after far too long a time the beating ended.

"We'll see you in a couple of hours, sir," said Stone. "You know, Woody really hated to have to do that. We're reasonable men. Like I said, we are the good guys. You're on the wrong side. Meantime, why don't you try to get a little sleep?"

"You better start taking us seriously," said Wood.

"Woody's got a point there, sir," said Stone. "Think about it."

The door slammed closed behind them. Shadow wondered if they would turn out the light, but they didn't, and it blazed into the room like a cold eye. Shadow crawled across the floor to the yellow foam-rubber pad and climbed onto it, pulling the thin blanket over himself, and he closed his eyes, and he held on to nothing, and he held on to dreams.

Time passed.

He was fifteen again, and his mother was dying, and she was trying to tell him something very important, and he couldn't understand her. He moved in his sleep and a shaft of pain moved him from half-sleep to half-waking, and he winced.

Shadow shivered under the thin blanket. His right arm covered his eyes, blocking out the light of the bulb. He wondered whether Wednesday and the others were still at liberty, if they were even still alive. He hoped that they were.

The silver dollar remained cold in his left hand. He could feel it there, as it had been during the beating. He wondered idly why it did not warm to his body temperature. Half-asleep, now, and half-delirious, the coin, and the idea of Liberty, and the moon, and Zorya Polunochnaya somehow became intertwined in one woven beam of silver light that shone from the depths to the heavens, and he rode the silver beam up and away from the heartache and the fear, away from the pain and, blessedly, back into dreams . . .

From far away he could hear some kind of noise, but it was too late to think about it: he belonged to sleep now.

A half-thought: he hoped it was not people coming to wake him up, to hit him or to shout at him. And then, he noticed with pleasure, he was really asleep, and no longer cold.

✦ ✦ ✦

SOMEBODY SOMEWHERE WAS shouting for help, in his dream or out of it.

Shadow rolled over on the foam rubber, finding new places that hurt as he rolled,[319] hoping that he had not woken fully and relieved to find sleep was enfolding him once more.

Someone was shaking his shoulder.

He wanted to ask them not to wake him, to let him sleep and leave him be, but it came out as a grunt.

"Puppy?" said Laura. "You have to wake up. Please wake up, hon."

And there was a moment's gentle relief. He had had such a strange dream, of prisons and con-men and down-at-heel gods, and now Laura was waking him to tell him it was time for work, and perhaps there would be time enough before

319. The balance of the sentence does not appear in the First Edition.

work to steal some coffee and a kiss, or more than a kiss; and he put out his hand to touch her.

Her flesh was cold as ice, and sticky.

Shadow opened his eyes.

"Where did all the blood come from?" he asked.

"Other people," she said. "It's not mine. I'm filled with formaldehyde, mixed with glycerin and lanolin."[320]

"Which other people?" he asked.

"The guards," she said. "It's okay. I killed them. You better move. I don't think I gave anyone a chance to raise the alarm. Take a coat from out there, or you'll freeze your butt off."

"You killed them?"

She shrugged, and half-smiled, awkwardly. Her hands looked as if she had been finger-painting, composing a picture that had been executed solely in crimsons, and there were splashes and spatters on her face and clothes (the same blue suit in which she had been buried) that made Shadow think of Jackson Pollock,[321] because it was less problematic to think of Jackson Pollock than to accept the alternative.

"It's easier to kill people, when you're dead yourself," she told him. "I mean, it's not such a big deal. You're not so prejudiced any more."

"It's still a big deal to me," said Shadow.

"You want to stay here until the morning crew comes?" she said. "You can if you like. I thought you'd like to get out of here."

"They'll think I did it," he said, stupidly.

"Maybe," she said. "Put on a coat, hon. You'll freeze."

He walked out into the corridor. At the end of the corridor was a guardroom. In the guardroom were four dead men: three guards, and the man who had called himself Stone. His friend was nowhere to be seen. From the blood-colored skid-marks on the floor, two of them had been dragged into the guardroom, and dropped onto the floor.

Shadow's coat was hanging from the coat rack. His wallet was still in the inside pocket, apparently untouched. Laura pulled open a couple of cardboard boxes, filled with candy bars.

320. Many embalming fluids are mixtures of formaldehyde and modifying agents, designed to prevent the drying out of the skin. A standard formula for medical corpse donations (modified for funerals) is an arterial injection of a water-based solution of formaldehyde 5% (mixed with methanol 5%, glycerine 10%, lanolin 1%, potassium nitrate and dyes).

321. Pollock (1912–1956) was a major force in the abstract expressionist movement. His most famous paintings are seemingly random, tangled drippings of multi-colored paint. Pollock himself described his art as "motion made visible memories, arrested in space."

Lavender Mist by Jackson Pollock (1950)

The guards, now he could see them properly, were wearing dark camouflage uniforms, but there were no official tags on them, nothing to say for whom they were working. They might have been weekend duck hunters, dressed for the shoot.

Laura reached out her cold hand, and squeezed Shadow's hand in hers. She had the gold coin he had given her around her neck, on a golden chain.

"That looks nice," he said.

"Thanks." She smiled, prettily.

"What about the others?" he asked. "Wednesday, and the rest of them? Where are they?" Laura passed him a handful of candy bars, and he filled his pockets with them.

"There wasn't anybody else here. A lot of empty cells, and one with you in it. Oh, and one of the men had gone into the cell down there to jack off with a magazine. He got such a shock."

"You killed him while he was jerking himself off?"

She shrugged. "I guess," she said, uncomfortably. "I was worried they were hurting you. Someone has to watch out for you, and I told you I would, didn't I? Here, take these." They were chemical hand- and footwarmers: thin pads— you broke the seal and they heated up to a little above body temperature and stayed that way for hours. Shadow pocketed them.

"Look out for me. Yes," he said, "you did."

She reached out a finger, stroked him above his left eyebrow. "You're hurt," she said.

"I'm okay," he said.

He opened a metal door in the wall. It swung open slowly. There was a four-foot drop to the ground, and he swung himself down to what felt like gravel. He picked up Laura by the waist, swung her down, as he used to swing her, easily, without a second thought . . .

The moon came out from behind a thick cloud. It was low on the horizon, ready to set, but the light it cast onto the snow was enough to see by.

They had emerged from what turned out to be the black-painted metal car of a long freight train, parked or abandoned in a woodland siding. The series of cars went on as far as he could see, into the trees and away. Of course he had been on a train. He should have known.

"How the hell did you find me here?" he asked his dead wife.

She shook her head slowly, amused. "You shine like a beacon in a dark world," she told him. "It wasn't that hard. Now," she told him, "you need to go. Just go. Go as far and as fast as you can. Don't use your credit cards and you should be fine."

"Where should I go?"

She pushed a hand through her matted hair, flicking it back out of her eyes. "The road's that way," she told him. "Do whatever you can. Steal a car if you have to. Go south."

"Laura," he said, and hesitated. "Do you know what's going on? Do you know who these people are? Who did you kill?"

"Yeah," she said. "I think I know."

"I owe you," said Shadow. "I'd still be in there if it wasn't for you. I don't think they had anything good planned for me."

"No," she said. "I don't think they did."

They walked away from the empty train cars. Shadow wondered about the other trains he'd seen, blank windowless metal cars which went on for mile after mile hooting their lonely way through the night. His fingers closed around the Liberty dollar in his pocket, and he remembered Zorya Polunochnaya, and the way she had looked at him in the moonlight. *Did you ask her what she wanted? . . . It is the wisest thing to ask the dead. Sometimes they will tell you.*

"Laura . . . What do you want?" he asked.

"You really want to know?"

"Yes. Please."

Laura looked up at him with dead blue eyes. "I want to be alive again," she said. "Not in this half-life. I want to be *really* alive. I want to feel my heart pumping in my chest again. I want to feel blood moving through me—hot, and salty, and real. It's weird, you don't think you can feel it, the blood, but believe me, when it stops flowing, you'll know."

322. This sentence does not appear in the First Edition.

She rubbed her eyes, smudging her face with red from the mess on her hands. "Look, I don't know why this happened to me.[322] But it's hard. You know why dead people only go out at night, puppy? Because it's easier to pass for real, in the dark. And I don't want to have to pass. I want to be alive."

"I don't understand what you want me to do."

"Make it happen, hon. You'll figure it out. I know you will."

"Okay," he said. "I'll try. And if I do figure it out, how do I find you?"

But she was gone, and there was nothing left in the woodland but a gentle gray in the sky to show him where east was, and on the bitter December wind a lonely wail that might have been the cry of the last night bird or the call of the first bird of dawn.

Shadow set his face to the south, and he began to walk.

CHAPTER SEVEN

As the Hindu gods are "immortal" only in a very particular sense—for they are born and they die—they experience most of the great human dilemmas and often seem to differ from mortals in a few trivial details . . . and from demons even less. Yet they are regarded by the Hindus as a class of beings by definition totally different from any other; they are symbols in a way that no human being, however "archetypal" his life story, can ever be. They are actors playing parts that are real only for us; they are the masks behind which we see our own faces.

—WENDY DONIGER O'FLAHERTY,
Introduction, *Hindu Myths* (Penguin Books, 1975)[323]

323. Wendy Doniger is a leading Indologist, who teaches at the University of Chicago. Since the early 2000s her work has been criticized by some in the Hindu community, who disparage her application of Western psychology to Hindu myths. She has also been accused of misquoting traditional sources and has been the center of controversies over whether Westerners can and should write about topics central to Indian self-identity.

HADOW HAD BEEN walking south, or what he hoped was more or less south, for several hours, heading along a narrow and unmarked road through the woods somewhere in, he imagined, southern Wisconsin. Several jeeps came down the road toward him at one point, headlights blazing, and he ducked well back into the trees until they had passed. The early morning mist hung at waist level. The cars were black.

When, thirty minutes later, he heard the noise of distant helicopters coming from the west, he struck out away from the timber trail and into the woods. There were two helicopters, and he lay, crouched in a hollow beneath a fallen tree, and listened to them pass over. As they moved away, he looked out and looked up, for one hasty glance at the gray winter sky. He was satisfied to observe that the helicopters were painted a matte black. He waited beneath the tree until the noise of the helicopters was completely gone.

Under the trees the snow was little more than a dusting, which crunched underfoot. He was deeply grateful for the chemical hand- and feetwarmers, which kept his extremities from freezing. Beyond that, he was numb: heart-numb, mind-numb, soul-numb. And the numbness, he realized, went a long way down, and a long way back.

So what do I want? he asked himself. He couldn't answer, so he just kept on walking, a step at a time, on and on through the woods. Trees looked familiar, moments of landscape were perfectly déjà-vued. Could he be walking in circles? Maybe he would just walk and walk and walk until the warmers and the candy bars ran out and then sit down and never get up again.

He reached a large stream, of the kind the locals called a creek and pronounced *crick*, and decided to follow it. Streams led to rivers, rivers all led to the Mississippi, and if he kept walking, or stole a boat or built a raft, eventually he'd get to New Orleans, where it was warm, an idea which seemed both comforting and unlikely.

There were no more helicopters. He had the feeling that the ones that had passed overhead had been cleaning up the mess at the freight train siding, not hunting for him, otherwise they would have returned; there would have been tracker dogs and sirens and the whole paraphernalia of pursuit. Instead, there was nothing.

What did *he* want? Not to get caught. Not to get blamed for the deaths of the men on the train. "It wasn't me," he heard himself saying, "it was my dead wife." He could imagine the expressions on the faces of the law officers. Then people could argue about whether he was crazy or not while he went to the chair . . .

He wondered whether Wisconsin had the death penalty.[324] He wondered whether that would matter. He wanted to understand what was going on—and to find out how it

324. The death penalty was abolished in Wisconsin in 1853, five years after its admission to the Union, and only one execution ever took place in the state, in 1851.

was all going to end. And finally, producing a half-rueful grin, he realized that most of all he wanted everything to be normal. He wanted never to have gone to prison, for Laura to still be alive, for none of this ever to have happened.

"I'm afraid that's not exactly an option, m'boy," he thought to himself, in Wednesday's gruff voice, and he nodded agreement. *Not an option. You burned your bridges. So keep walking. Do your own time . . .*

A distant woodpecker drummed against a rotten log.

Shadow became aware of eyes on him: a handful of red cardinals stared at him from a skeletal elder bush, then returned to pecking at the clusters of black elderberries. They looked like the illustrations in the *Songbirds of North America* calendar. He heard the birds' video-arcade trills and zaps and whoops follow him along the side of the creek. Eventually, they faded away.

The dead fawn lay in a glade in the shadow of a hill, and a black bird the size of a small dog was picking at its side with a large, wicked beak, rending and tearing gobbets of red meat from the corpse. Its eyes were gone, but its head was untouched, and white fawn-spots were visible on its rump. Shadow wondered how it had died.

The black bird cocked its head onto one side, and then said, in a voice like stones being struck, "You shadow man."

"I'm Shadow," said Shadow. The bird hopped up onto the fawn's rump, raised its head, ruffled its crown and neck feathers. It was enormous and its eyes were black beads. There was something intimidating about a bird that size, this close.

"Says he will see you in Kay-ro," tokked the raven. Shadow wondered which of Odin's ravens this was: Huginn or Muninn: Memory or Thought.

"Kay-ro?" he asked.

"In Egypt."

"How am I going to go to Egypt?"

"Follow Mississippi. Go south. Find Jackal."

"Look," said Shadow, "I don't want to seem like I'm . . . Jesus, look . . ." He paused. Regrouped. He was cold, stand-

325. Frederick Forsyth wrote a global best-seller called *Day of the Jackal* in 1971, based on an actual attempt to assassinate Charles de Gaulle by a real organization known as the OAS and an actual assassin named Jean-Marie Bastien-Thiry. In Forsyth's book, the attack was carried out by a fictional assassin nicknamed "the Jackal." The book inspired several copycats: Would-be assassin Vladimir Arutinian, who attempted to kill U.S. President George W. Bush during his 2005 visit to the Republic of Georgia, read the novel obsessively, annotating it heavily during his planning for the attmpt. A copy of the Hebrew translation of the book was owned by Yigal Amir, who assassinated Yitzhak Rabin, prime minister of Israel, in 1995. Ilich Ramirez Sanchez, the international terrorist dubbed "Carlos" by one of his employers, was given the name "the Jackal" by *The Guardian* at the time of his arrest when a correspondent reported that he owned a copy of Forsyth's novel.

326. An apocryphal line from the television show *Lassie*, in which the dog's barking always seemed to be a message to an adult about someone in need of rescue. "Timmy" was of course Lassie's youthful owner. The phrase has become the anchor of many jokes, and when Jon Provost, who played Timmy on the original show, wrote his memoirs in 2007 (with Laurie Jacobson), he titled the book *Timmy's in the Well: The Jon Provost Story.*

327. The balance of this paragraph and the next do not appear in the First Edition.

328. This is a real chain of fast-food restaurants, with almost 700 stores throughout the Midwest. The chain was founded in 1984 in Sauk City, Wisconsin. In addition to the ButterBurgers and frozen custard, the menu features cheese curds, a distinctly Wisconsin dish.

ing in a wood, talking to a big black bird who was currently brunching on Bambi. "Okay. What I'm trying to say is, I don't want mysteries."

"Mysteries," agreed the bird, helpfully.

"What I want is explanations. Jackal in Kay-ro. This does not help me. It's a line from a bad spy thriller."[325]

"Jackal. Friend. *Tok*. Kay-ro."

"So you said. I'd like a little more information than that."

The bird half-turned, and pulled another bloody strip of raw venison from the fawn's ribs. Then it flew off into the trees, the red strip dangling from its beak like a long, bloody worm.

"Hey! Can you at least get me back to a real road?" called Shadow.

The raven flew up and away. Shadow looked at the corpse of the baby deer. He decided that if he were a real woodsman, he would slice off a steak and grill it over a wood fire. Instead, he sat on a fallen tree and ate a Snickers bar and knew that he really wasn't a real woodsman.

The raven cawed from the edge of the clearing.

"You want me to follow you?" asked Shadow. "Or has Timmy fallen down another well?"[326] The bird cawed again, impatiently. Shadow started walking toward it. It waited until he was close, then flapped heavily into another tree, heading somewhat to the left of the way Shadow had originally been going.

"Hey," said Shadow. "Huginn or Muninn, or whoever you are."

The bird turned, head tipped, suspiciously, on one side, and it stared at him with bright eyes.

"Say 'Nevermore,'" said Shadow.

"Fuck you," said the raven. It said nothing else as they went through the woodland together,[327] the raven in the lead and flying from tree to tree, the man stomping heavily through the undergrowth trying to catch up.

The sky was a uniform gray. It was almost midday.

In half an hour they reached a blacktop road on the edge of a town, and the raven flew back into the wood. Shadow observed a Culver's Frozen Custard ButterBurgers sign,[328] and, next to it, a gas station. He went into the Culver's, which was empty of customers. There was a keen young man with a shaven head behind the cash register. Shadow ordered two ButterBurgers and french fries. Then he went into the restroom to clean up. He looked a real mess. He did an inventory of the contents of his pockets: he had a few coins, including the silver Liberty dollar, a disposable toothbrush and toothpaste, three Snickers bars, five chemical heater pads, a wallet (with nothing more in it than his driver's license and a credit card—he wondered how much longer the credit card had to live), and in the coat's inside pocket, a thousand dollars in fifties and twenties, his take from yesterday's bank job. He washed his face and hands in hot water, slicked down his dark hair, then went back into the restaurant and ate his burgers and fries, and drank his coffee.

He went back to the counter. "You want frozen custard?" asked the keen young man.

"No. No thanks. Is there anywhere around here I could rent a car? My car died, back down the road a way."

The young man scratched his head-stubble. "Not around here, mister. If your car died you could call Triple-A. Or talk to the gas station next door about a tow."

"A fine idea," said Shadow. "Thanks."

He walked across the melting snow, from the Culver's parking lot to the gas station. He bought candy bars and beef jerky sticks and more chemical hand- and feetwarmers.

"Anywhere hereabouts I could rent a car?" he asked the woman behind the cash register. She was immensely plump, and bespectacled, and was delighted to have someone to talk to.

"Let me think," she said. "We're kind of out of the way here. They do that kind of thing over in Madison. Where you going?"

"Kay-ro," he said. "Wherever that is."

"I know where that is," she said. "Hand me that map from that rack over there." Shadow passed her a plastic-coated map of Illinois. She unfolded it, then pointed in triumph to the bottommost corner of the state. "There it is."

Historic downtown Cairo, Illinois
(*Wikimedia Commons*)

"Cairo?"

"That's how they pronounce the one in Egypt. The one in Little Egypt, they call that one Kayro. They got a Thebes down there, all sorts. My sister-in-law comes from Thebes. I asked her about the one in Egypt, she looked at me as if I had a screw loose." The woman chuckled like a drain.

"Any pyramids?" The city was five hundred miles away, almost directly south.

"Not that they ever told me. They call it Little Egypt because back, oh, mebbe a hundred, hundred and fifty years back, there was a famine all over. Crops failed. But they didn't fail down there. So everyone went there to buy food. Like in the Bible. Joseph and the Technicolor Dreamcoat. Off we go to Egypt, bad-a-boom."[329]

"So if you were me, and you needed to get there, how would you go?" asked Shadow.

"Drive."

329. This is one version of the origin of the name. See note 335, below, for another. In the Douglas-Lincoln debates in 1858, Douglas referred to southern Illinois as "Egypt" at least in part because of the strong pro-slavery sentiments common there, though it seems likely that Douglas was merely playing on an already current nickname.

Map of Cairo, Illinois (1885)

"Car died a few miles down the road. It was a pieceashit if you'll pardon my language," said Shadow.

"Pee-Oh-Esses," she said. "Yup. That's what my brother-in-law calls 'em. He buys and sells cars in a small way. He'll call me up, say, 'Mattie, I just sold another Pee-Oh-Ess.' Say, maybe he'd be interested in your old car. For scrap or something."

"It belongs to my boss," said Shadow, surprising himself with the fluency and ease of his lies. "I need to call him, so he can come pick it up." A thought struck him. "Your brother-in-law, is he around here?"

"He's in Muscoda.[330] Ten minutes south of here. Just over the river. Why?"

"Well, does he have a Pee-Oh-Ess he'd like to sell me for, mm, five, six hundred bucks?"

She smiled sweetly. "Mister, he doesn't have a car on that back lot you couldn't buy with a full tank of gas for five hundred dollars. But don't you tell him I said so."

"Would you call him?" asked Shadow.

"I'm way ahead of you," she told him, and she picked up the phone. "Hon? It's Mattie. You get over here this minute. I got a man here wants to buy a car."

✻   ✻   ✻

THE PIECE OF shit he chose was a 1983 Chevy Nova, which he bought, with a full tank of gas, for four hundred

330. A town in the southwestern corner of Wisconsin, it is about 23 miles from Spring Green, and the gas station couldn't be much farther. Although Shadow may have been on a train, he was evidently not held captive far from the restaurant near the House on the Rock.

and fifty dollars. It had almost a quarter of a million miles on the clock, and smelled faintly of bourbon, tobacco, and more strongly of something that reminded Shadow of bananas. He couldn't tell what color it was, under the dirt and the snow. Still, of all the vehicles in Mattie's brother-in-law's back lot, it was the only one that looked like it might take him five hundred miles.

The deal was done in cash, and Mattie's brother-in-law never asked for Shadow's name or social security number or for anything except the money.

Shadow drove west, then south, with five hundred and fifty dollars in his pocket, keeping off the interstate. The piece of shit had a radio, but nothing happened when he turned it on. A sign said he'd left Wisconsin and was now in Illinois. He passed a strip-mining works, huge blue arc lights burning in the dim midwinter daylight.

He stopped and ate lunch at a place called Mom's, catching them just before they closed for the afternoon. The food was okay.[331]

Each town he passed through had an extra sign up beside the sign telling him that he was now entering Our Town (pop. 720). The extra sign announced that the town's Under-14s team was the third runner-up in the interstate Hundred-Yard Sprint, or that the town was the home of the Illinois Girls' Under-16s Wrestling semifinalist.

He drove on, head nodding, feeling more drained and exhausted with every minute that passed. He ran a stoplight, and was nearly sideswiped by a woman in a Dodge. As soon as he got out into open country he pulled off onto an empty tractor path on the side of the road, and he parked by a snow-spotted stubbly field in which a slow procession of fat black wild turkeys walked like a line of mourners; he turned off the engine, stretched out in the back seat, and fell asleep.

Darkness; a sensation of falling—as if he were tumbling down a great hole, like Alice. He fell for a hundred years into darkness. Faces passed him, swimming out of the black, then each face was ripped up and away before he could touch it . . .

331. This sentence does not appear in the First Edition.

Abruptly, and without transition, he was not falling. Now he was in a cave, and he was no longer alone. Shadow stared into familiar eyes: huge, liquid black eyes. They blinked.

Under the earth: yes. He remembered this place. The stink of wet cow. Firelight flickered on the wet cave walls, illuminating the buffalo head, the man's body, skin the color of brick clay.

"Can't you people leave me be?" asked Shadow. "I just want to sleep."

The buffalo man nodded, slowly. His lips did not move, but a voice in Shadow's head said, "Where are you going, Shadow?"

"Cairo."

"Why?"

"Where else have I got to go? It's where Wednesday wants me to go. I drank his mead." In Shadow's dream, with the power of dream-logic behind it, the obligation seemed unarguable: he drank Wednesday's mead three times, and sealed the pact—what other choice of action did he have?

The buffalo-headed man reached a hand into the fire, stirring the embers and the broken branches into a blaze. "The storm is coming," he said. Now there was ash on his hands, and he wiped it onto his hairless chest, leaving soot-black streaks.

"So you people keep telling me. Can I ask you a question?"

There was a pause. A fly settled on the furry forehead. The buffalo man flicked it away. "Ask."

"Is this true? Are these people really gods? It's all so . . ." He paused. Then he said, "Unlikely,"[332] which was not exactly the word he had been going for but seemed to be the best he could do.

"What are gods?" asked the buffalo man.

"I don't know," said Shadow.

There was a tapping, relentless and dull. Shadow waited for the buffalo man to say something more, to explain what gods were, to explain the whole tangled nightmare that his life seemed to have become. He was cold. The fire no longer burned.[333]

332. In the First Edition, Shadow says, "Impossible," not "Unlikely."

333. This sentence does not appear in the First Edition.

Tap. Tap. Tap.

Shadow opened his eyes, and, groggily, sat up. He was freezing, and the sky outside the car was the deep luminescent purple that divides the dusk from the night.

Tap. Tap. Someone said, "Hey, mister," and Shadow turned his head. The someone was standing beside the car, no more than a darker shape against the darkling sky. Shadow reached out a hand and cranked down the window a few inches. He made several waking-up noises, and then he said, "Hi."

"You all right? You sick? You been drinking?" The voice was high—a woman's or a boy's.

"I'm fine," said Shadow. "Hold on." He opened the door, and got out, stretching his aching limbs and neck as he did so. Then he rubbed his hands together, to get the blood circulating and to warm them up.

"Whoa. You're pretty big."

"That's what they tell me," said Shadow. "Who are you?"

"I'm Sam," said the voice.

"Boy Sam or girl Sam?"

"Girl-Sam. I used to be Sammi with an i, and I'd do a smiley face over the i, but then I got completely sick of it because like absolutely everybody was doing it, so I stopped."

"Okay, girl-Sam. You go over there, and look out at the road."

"Why? Are you a crazed killer or something?"

"No," said Shadow, "I need to take a leak and I'd like just the smallest amount of privacy."

"Oh. Right. Okay. Got it. No problem. I am so with you. I can't even pee if there's someone in the next stall. Major shy bladder syndrome."

"Now, please."

She walked to the far side of the car, and Shadow took a few steps closer to the field, unzipped his jeans, and pissed against a fencepost for a very long time. He walked back to the car. The last of the gloaming had become night.

"You still there?" he asked.

"Yes," she said. "You must have a bladder like Lake Erie. I think empires rose and fell in the time it took you to pee. I could hear it the whole time."

"Thank you. Do you want something?"

"Well, I wanted to see if you were okay. I mean, if you were dead or something I would have called the cops. But the windows were kind of fogged up so I thought, well, he's probably still alive."

"You live around here?"

"Nope. Hitchhiking down from Madison."

"That's not safe."

"I've done it five times a year for three years now. I'm still alive. Where are you headed?"

"I'm going as far as Cairo."

"Thank you," she said. "I'm going to El Paso. Staying with my aunt for the holidays."

"I can't take you all the way," said Shadow.

"Not El Paso, Texas. The other one, in Illinois. It's a few hours south. You know where you are now?"

"No," said Shadow. "I have no idea. Somewhere on Highway Fifty-two?"

"The next town's Peru," said Sam. "Not the one in Peru. The one in Illinois. Let me smell you. Bend down." Shadow bent down, and the girl sniffed his face. "Okay. I don't smell booze. You can drive. Let's go."

"What makes you think I'm giving you a ride?"

"Because I'm a damsel in distress," she said, "and you are a knight in whatever. A really dirty car. You know someone wrote *Wash Me!* on your rear windshield?" Shadow got into the car and opened the passenger door. The light that goes on in cars when the front door is opened did not go on in this car.

"No," he said, "I didn't."

She climbed in. "It was me," she said. "I wrote it. While there was still enough light to see."

Shadow started the car, turned on the headlights, and headed back onto the road. "Left," said Sam helpfully. Shadow turned left, and he drove. After several minutes the heater started to work, and blessed warmth filled the car.

"You haven't said anything yet," said Sam. "Say something."

"Are you human?" asked Shadow. "An honest-to-

334. At this point, Shadow thinks he is asking whether Sam is like him. There has been much debate among fans whether Sam's answer is true. Like Shadow, she was raised by a single mother, and some speculate that her father may have been a Native American god. The context of her sudden appearance at the car window appears to them to be an answer to the Buffalo Man's question "What are gods?"

goodness, born-of-man-and-woman, living breathing human being?"[334]

"Sure," she said.

"Okay. Just checking. So what would you like me to say?"

"Something to reassure me, at this point. I suddenly have that *oh shit I'm in the wrong car with a crazy man* feeling."

"Yeah," he said. "I've had that one. What would you find reassuring?"

"Just tell me you're not an escaped convict or a mass murderer or something."

He thought for a moment. "You know, I'm really not."

"You had to think about it though, didn't you?"

"Done my time. Never killed anybody."

"Oh."

They entered a small town, lit up by streetlights and blinking Christmas decorations, and Shadow glanced to his right. The girl had a tangle of short dark hair and a face that was both attractive and, he decided, faintly mannish: her features might have been chiseled out of rock. She was looking at him.

"What were you in prison for?"

"I hurt a couple of people real bad. I got angry."

"Did they deserve it?"

Shadow thought for a moment. "I thought so at the time."

"Would you do it again?"

"Hell, no. I lost three years of my life in there."

"Mm. You got Indian blood in you?"

"Not that I know of."

"You looked like it, was all."

"Sorry to disappoint you."

"S'okay. You hungry?"

Shadow nodded. "I could eat," he said.

"There's a good place just past the next set of lights. Good food. Cheap, too."

Shadow pulled up in the parking lot. They got out of the car. He didn't bother to lock it, although he pocketed the keys. He pulled out some coins to buy a newspaper. "Can you afford to eat here?" he asked.

"Yeah," she said, raising her chin. "I can pay for myself."

Shadow nodded. "Tell you what. I'll toss you for it," he said. "Heads you pay for my dinner, tails, I pay for yours."

"Let me see the coin first," she said, suspiciously. "I had an uncle had a double-headed quarter."

She inspected it, satisfied herself there was nothing strange about the quarter. Shadow placed the coin head-up on his thumb and cheated the toss, so it wobbled and looked like it was spinning, then he caught it and flipped it over onto the back of his left hand, and uncovered it with his right, in front of her.

"Tails," she said, happily. "Dinner's on you."

"Yup," he said. "You can't win them all."

Shadow ordered the meatloaf, Sam ordered lasagna. Shadow flipped through the newspaper to see if there was anything in it about dead men in a freight train. There wasn't. The only story of interest was on the cover: crows in record numbers were infesting the town. Local farmers wanted to hang dead crows around the town on public buildings to frighten the others away; ornithologists said that it wouldn't work, that the living crows would simply eat the dead ones. The locals were implacable. "When they see the corpses of their friends," said a spokesman, "they'll know that we don't want them here."

The food was good, and it came mounded on steaming plates, more than any one person could eat.

"So what's in Cairo?" asked Sam, with her mouth full.

"No idea. I got a message from my boss saying he needs me down there."

"What do you do?"

"I'm an errand boy."

She smiled. "Well," she said, "you aren't Mafia, not looking like that and driving that piece of shit. Why does your car smell like bananas, anyway?"

He shrugged, carried on eating.

Sam narrowed her eyes. "Maybe you're a banana smuggler," she said. "You haven't asked me what I do yet."

"I figure you're at school."

"UW Madison."

"Where you are undoubtedly studying art history,

185

women's studies, and probably casting your own bronzes. And you probably work in a coffee house to help cover the rent."

She put down her fork, nostrils flaring, eyes wide. "How the fuck did you do that?"

"What? Now you say, no, actually I'm studying Romance languages and ornithology."

"So you're saying that was a lucky guess or something?"

"What was?"

She stared at him with dark eyes. "You are one peculiar guy, Mister . . . I don't know your name."

"They call me Shadow," he said.

She twisted her mouth wryly, as if she were tasting something she disliked. She stopped talking, put her head down, finished her lasagna.

"Do you know why it's called Egypt?" asked Shadow, when Sam finished eating.

"Down Cairo way? Yeah. It's in the delta of the Ohio and the Mississippi. Like Cairo in Egypt, in the Nile delta."[335]

"That makes sense."

She sat back in her chair, ordered coffee and chocolate cream pie, ran a hand through her black hair. "You married, Mister Shadow?" And then, as he hesitated, "Gee. I just asked another tricky question, didn't I?"

"They buried her on Thursday," he said, picking his words with care. "She was killed in a car crash."

"Oh. God. Jesus. I'm sorry."

"Me too."

An awkward pause. "My half-sister lost her kid, my nephew, end of last year. It's rough."

"Yeah. It is. What did he die of?"

She sipped her coffee. "We don't know. We don't even really know that he's dead. He just vanished. But he was only thirteen. It was the middle of last winter. My sister was pretty broken up about it."

"Were there any, any clues?" He sounded like a TV cop. He tried again. "Did they suspect foul play?" That sounded worse.

"They suspected my non-custodial asshole brother-in-

335. Sam expresses another common theory: that the nickname arose from the nature of the terrain, which resembled the Nile delta. The name "Cairo" was given to the town in 1818 by its developers, perhaps because of the terrain.

law, his father. Who was asshole enough to have stolen him away. Probably did. But this is in a little town in the North-woods. Lovely, sweet, pretty little town where no one ever locks their doors."[336] She sighed, shook her head. She held her coffee cup in both hands. Then she looked up at him, changing the subject. "How did you know I cast bronzes?"

"Lucky guess. It was just something to say."

"Are you sure you aren't part Indian?"

"Not that I know. It's possible. I never met my father.[337] I guess my ma would have told me if he was Native American, though. Maybe."

Again the mouth-twist. Sam gave up halfway through her chocolate cream pie: the slice was half the size of her head. She pushed the plate across the table to Shadow. "You want?" He smiled, said, "Sure," and finished it off.

The waitress handed them the check, and Shadow paid.

"Thanks," said Sam.

It was getting colder now. The car coughed a couple of times before it started. Shadow drove back onto the road, and kept going south. "You ever read a guy named Herodotus?" he asked.

"Jesus. What?"

"Herodotus. You ever read his *Histories*?"

"You know," she said, dreamily, "I don't get it. I don't get how you talk, or the words you use or anything. One moment you're a big dumb guy, the next you're reading my friggin' mind, and the next we're talking about Herodotus. So no. I have not read Herodotus. I've heard about him. Maybe on NPR. Isn't he the one they call the father of lies?"[338]

"I thought that was the Devil."

"Yeah, him too. But they were talking about Herodotus saying there were giant ants and gryphons guarding gold mines, and how he made this stuff up."

"I don't think so. He wrote what he'd been told. It's like, he's writing these histories. And they're mostly pretty good histories. Loads of weird little details—like, did you know, in Egypt, if a particularly beautiful girl, or the wife of a lord or whatever, died, they wouldn't send her to the embalmer for three days? They'd let her body spoil in the heat first."

336. The balance of this paragraph and the next do not appear in the First Edition.

337. In the First Edition, Shadow responds, "I don't know much about my father." This sentence and the next do not appear in the First Draft.

338. Herodotus was called the "Father of History" by Cicero. For almost as long, detractors have referred to him as "Father of Lies." One of the earliest of Herodotus's critics was Lucian of Samosata, who, in *Verae Historiae*, denied him a place among the famous on the Island of the Blessed. While some of the criticism was aimed at perceived bias against or in favor of specific nationalities, much of the criticism was directed against what many believe to be the "tall tales" repeated by Herodotus as factual, such as his report of fox-sized ants in Persia.

339. Herodotus, *Histories*, II, chapter 89: "Wives of notable men, and women of great beauty and reputation, are not at once given to the embalmers, but only after they have been dead for three or four days; this is done to deter the embalmers from having intercourse with the women. For it is said that one was caught having intercourse with the fresh corpse of a woman, and was denounced by his fellow-workman." (Translation by A. D. Godley, Cambridge: Harvard University Press, 1920)

340. The theory is called "bicameralism" and the book is *The Origin of Consciousness in the Breakdown of the Bicameral Mind* by Julian Jaynes (New York: Houghton Mifflin Harcourt Publishing Company, 1976), revised in 1990. Bicameralism remains highly controversial.

"Why? Oh, hold on. Okay, I think I know why.[339] Oh, that's disgusting."

"And there're battles in there, all sorts of normal things. And then there are the gods. Some guy is running back to report on the outcome of a battle and he's running and running, and he sees Pan in a glade. And Pan says, 'Tell them to build me a temple here.' So he says okay, and runs the rest of the way back. And he reports the battle news, and then says, 'Oh, and by the way, Pan wants you to build him a temple.' It's really matter-of-fact, you know?"

"So there are stories with gods in them. What are you trying to say? That these guys had hallucinations?"

"No," said Shadow. "That's not it."

She chewed a hangnail. "I read some book about brains," she said. "My roommate had it and she kept waving it around. It was like, how five thousand years ago the lobes of the brain fused and before that people thought when the right lobe of the brain said anything it was the voice of some god telling them what to do. It's just brains."[340]

"I like my theory better," said Shadow.

"What's your theory?"

"That back then people used to run into the gods from time to time."

"Oh." Silence: only the rattling of the car, the roar of the engine, the growling of the muffler—which did not sound healthy. Then, "Do you think they're still there?"

"Where?"

"Greece. Egypt. The islands. Those places. Do you think if you walked where those people walked you'd see the gods?"

"Maybe. But I don't think people'd know that was what they'd seen."

"I bet it's like space aliens," she said. "These days, people see space aliens. Back then they saw gods. Maybe the space aliens come from the right side of the brain."

"I don't think the gods ever gave rectal probes," said Shadow. "And they didn't mutilate cattle themselves. They got people to do it for them."

She chuckled. They drove in silence for a few minutes,

and then she said, "Hey, that reminds me of my favorite god story, from Comparative Religion 101. You want to hear it?"

"Sure," said Shadow.

"Okay. This is one about Odin. The Norse god. You know? There was some Viking king on a Viking ship—this was back in the Viking times, obviously—and they were becalmed, so he says he'll sacrifice one of his men to Odin if Odin will send them a wind, and get them to land. Okay. The wind comes up, and they get to land. So, on land, they draw lots to figure out who gets sacrificed—and it's the king himself. Well, he's not happy about this, but they figure out that they can hang him in effigy and not hurt him. They take a calf's intestines and loop them loosely around the guy's neck, and they tie the other end to a thin branch, and they take a reed instead of a spear and poke him with it and go, 'Okay, you've been hung'—hanged?—whatever—'you've been sacrificed to Odin.'"[341]

The road curved: Another Town, pop. 300, home of the runner-up to the State Under-12s speed-skating championship, two huge giant economy-sized funeral parlors on each side of the road, and how many funeral parlors do you need, Shadow wondered, when you only have three hundred people . . . ?

"Okay. As soon as they say Odin's name, the reed transforms into a spear and stabs the guy in the side, the calf intestines become a thick rope, the branch becomes a bough of a tree, and the tree pulls up, and the ground drops away, and the king is left hanging there to die with a wound in his side and his face going black. End of story. White people have some fucked-up gods, Mister Shadow."

"Yes," said Shadow. "You're not white?"

"I'm a Cherokee," she said.

"Full-blooded?"

"Nope. Only four pints.[342] My mom was white. My dad was a real reservation Indian. He came out this way, eventually married my mom, had me, then when they split he went back to Oklahoma."[343]

"He went back to the reservation?"

"No. He borrowed money and opened a Taco Bell knock-

341. Sam is referring to the tale of Víkar, a Norse king who, according to the late-thirteenth century Scandinavian poem known as *Gautreks saga*, suffered a terrible fate on an ill-starred voyage when his ships were becalmed. She has the details correct but omits mentioning the human co-conspirator. King Víkar knew that to raise a wind, a human sacrifice would be required, and as fate would have it, Víkar himself was chosen by lot. The king's counselor Starkad proposed a mock hanging from a tree in place of an actual sacrifice, but according to legend, the real author of the suggestion was Odin, who desired Víkar's death (as perhaps did Starkad as well). According to the account in *Gautreks saga*, when Starkad let loose a branch of the tree, invoking Odin, the reed-stalk he held was transformed into a real spear, the stump under Víkar's feet fell away, and the calf intestines by which he had been hanged turned into a stout gallows rope.

342. Yes, the human body contains 10 to 12 pints of blood, but who cares if Sam's math is slightly off?

343. By 1907, when Oklahoma became a state, almost all of the former Indian reservations that dominated the territory were dissolved, with the exception of the Osage Nation, the so-called Underground Reservation (the Osage retained extensive mineral rights). However, in 2017, the 10th Circuit Court of Appeals ruled that the Muscogee (Creek) Nation reservation had never been legally dissolved. Sam probably did not mean that her father had been raised on an *Oklahoma* reservation, only that he had lived there after leaving another reservation and returned to his former home. Not all Cherokees are from Oklahoma—for example, many of the Eastern Band of Cherokee Indians reside on a reservation in northwestern North Carolina.

off called Taco Bill's. He does okay. He doesn't like me. Says I'm half-breed."

"I'm sorry."

"He's a jerk. I'm proud of my Indian blood. It helps pay my college tuition. Hell, one day it'll probably help get me a job, if I can't sell my bronzes."

"There's always that," said Shadow.

He stopped in El Paso, IL (pop. 2,500),[344] to let Sam out at a down-at-heel house on the edge of the town. A large wire-framed model of a reindeer covered in twinkling lights stood in the front yard. "You want to come in?" she asked. "My aunt would give you a coffee."

"No," he said. "I've got to keep moving."

She smiled at him, looking suddenly, and for the first time, vulnerable. She patted him on the arm. "You're fucked up, mister. But you're cool."

"I believe that's what they call the human condition," said Shadow. "Thanks for the company."

"No problem," she said. "If you see any gods on the road to Cairo, you make sure and say hi to them from me." She got out of the car, and went to the door of the house. She pressed a doorbell and stood there at the door, without looking back. Shadow waited until the door was opened and she was safely inside before he put his foot down and headed back for the highway. He passed through Normal, and Bloomington, and Lawndale.[345]

At eleven that night Shadow started shaking. He was just entering Middletown. He decided he needed sleep, or just not to drive any longer, and he pulled up in front of a Night's Inn, paid thirty-five dollars, cash in advance, for his ground-floor room, and went into the bathroom. A sad cockroach lay on its back in the middle of the tiled floor. Shadow took a towel and cleaned off the inside of the tub with it, then ran a bath. In the main room he took off his clothes and put them on the bed. The bruises on his torso were dark and vivid. He sat in the bath, watching the color of the bathwater change. Then, naked, he washed his socks and briefs and T-shirt in the basin, wrung them out and hung them on the clothesline that pulled out from the wall

344. A town just north of Bloomington and east of Peoria. El Paso is about 240 miles from Muscoda, where Shadow bought his car.

345. These are all northeast of Springfield, Illinois—Normal and Bloomington are towns in McLean County, and Lawndale is an unincorporated township in Logan County just to the southwest of McLean County. Middletown, mentioned next, is also in Logan County.

above the bathtub. He left the cockroach where it was, out of respect for the dead.

Shadow climbed into the bed. He wondered about watching an adult movie, but the pay-per-view device by the phone needed a credit card.[346] Then again, he was not convinced that it would make him feel any better to watch other people have sex that he wasn't having. He turned on the TV for company, pressed the Sleep button on the remote three times, which would make the TV set turn itself off automatically in forty-five minutes, by which time he figured he'd be fast asleep. It was a quarter to midnight.

The picture was motel-fuzzy, and the colors swam across the screen. He flipped from late show to late show in the televisual wasteland, unable to focus. Someone was demonstrating something that did something in the kitchen, and replaced a dozen other kitchen utensils, none of which Shadow possessed. Flip. A man in a suit explained that these were the end times and that Jesus—a four-or five-syllable word the way the man pronounced it—would make Shadow's business prosper and thrive if Shadow sent him money. Flip: an episode of *M*A*S*H*[347] ended and a *Dick Van Dyke* episode began.

Shadow hadn't seen an episode of *The Dick Van Dyke Show* for years, but there was something comforting about the 1965 black-and-white world it painted, and he put the channel changer down beside the bed, and turned off the bedside light. He watched the show, eyes slowly closing, aware that something was odd. He had not seen many episodes of *The Dick Van Dyke Show*, so he was not surprised that it was an episode he could not remember seeing before. What he found strange was the tone.

All the regulars were concerned about Rob's drinking: he was missing days at work. They went to his home: he had locked himself in the bedroom, and had to be persuaded to come out: he was staggering drunk, but still pretty funny. His friends, played by Morey Amsterdam and Rose Marie, left after getting some good gags in. Then, when Rob's wife went to remonstrate with him, he hit her, hard, in the face. She sat down on the floor and began to cry, not in that fa-

346. In the First Edition, Shadow adds the thought "and it was too risky." Laura previously warned him not to use a credit card.

347. Based on the 1970 feature film *M*A*S*H* (which, in turn, was based on Richard Hooker's 1968 novel *MASH: A Novel About Three Army Doctors*), the irreverent show, about a mobile army surgical hospital in Korea, was one of the highest-rated television series in history, airing from 1972 to 1983.

348. New episodes of the shows did not air simultaneously: *I Love Lucy* ran from 1951 to 1957, while *The Dick Van Dyke* show was first aired from 1961 to 1966. However, both shows were so popular that reruns air virtually continuously, on some channel somewhere.

349. This does not occur in any of the 180 episodes. Gaiman, in a private conversation with this editor, expressed that while he invented the plot, he liked to imagine that it could have been used for an early 1950s comedy series; while refrigerators replaced iceboxes in many homes long before the 1950s, mass production of consumer refrigerators did not truly begin until after World War II, and for many households, the refrigerator was still an innovation.

350. That is, it's the fictional character talking, not the actress. On the television show, Lucy Ricardo was a regular American housewife married to a Cuban bandleader, Ricky Ricardo (played by Desi Arnaz, Lucille Ball's husband).

mous Mary Tyler Moore wail, but in small, helpless sobs, hugging herself and whispering, "Don't hit me, please, I'll do anything, just don't hit me any more."

"What the fuck is this?" said Shadow, aloud.

The picture dissolved into phosphor-dot fuzz. When it came back, *The Dick Van Dyke Show* had, inexplicably, become *I Love Lucy*.[348] Lucy was trying to persuade Ricky to let her replace their old icebox with a new refrigerator.[349] When he left, however, she walked over to the couch and sat down, crossing her ankles, resting her hands in her lap, and staring out patiently in black and white across the years.

"Shadow?" she said. "We need to talk."

Shadow said nothing. She opened her purse and took out a cigarette, lit it with an expensive silver lighter, put the lighter away. "I'm talking to you," she said. "Well?"

"This is crazy," said Shadow.

"Like the rest of your life is sane? Give me a fucking break."

"Whatever. Lucille Ball talking to me from the TV is weirder by several orders of magnitude than anything that's happened to me so far," said Shadow.

"It's not Lucille Ball. It's Lucy Ricardo.[350] And you know something—I'm not even her. It's just an easy way to look, given the context. That's all." She shifted uncomfortably on the sofa.

"Who are you?" asked Shadow.

"Okay," she said. "Good question. I'm the idiot box. I'm the TV. I'm the all-seeing eye and the world of the cathode ray. I'm the boob tube. I'm the little shrine the family gathers to adore."

"You're the television? Or someone in the television?"

"The TV's the altar. I'm what people are sacrificing to."

"What do they sacrifice?" asked Shadow.

"Their time, mostly," said Lucy. "Sometimes each other." She raised two fingers, blew imaginary gun smoke from the tips. Then she winked, a big old *I Love Lucy* wink.

"You're a god?" said Shadow.

Lucy smirked, and took a lady-like puff of her cigarette. "You could say that," she said.

"Sam says hi," said Shadow.

"What? Who's Sam? What are you talking about?"

Shadow looked at his watch. It was twenty-five past twelve. "Doesn't matter," he said. "So, Lucy-on-the-TV. What do we need to talk about? Too many people have needed to talk recently. Normally it ends with someone hitting me."

The camera moved in for a close-up: Lucy looked concerned, her lips pursed. "I hate that. I hate that people were hurting you, Shadow. I'd never do that, honey. No, I want to offer you a job."

"Doing what?"

"Working for me. I'm really sorry.[351] I heard about the trouble you had with the Spookshow, and I was impressed with how you dealt with it. Efficient, no-nonsense, effective. Who'd've thought you had it in you? They are really pissed."

"Really?"

"They underestimated you, sweetheart. Not a mistake I'm going to make. I want you in my camp." She stood up, walked toward the camera. "Look at it like this, Shadow: we are the coming thing. We're shopping malls—your friends are crappy roadside attractions. Hell, we're online malls, while your friends are sitting by the side of the highway selling homegrown produce from a garden cart. No—they aren't even fruit sellers. Buggy-whip vendors. Whalebone-corset repairers. We are now and tomorrow. Your friends aren't even yesterday any more."

It was a strangely familiar speech. Shadow asked, "Did you ever meet a fat kid in a limo?"

She spread her hands and rolled her eyes comically, funny Lucy Ricardo washing her hands of a disaster. "The technical boy? You met the technical boy? Look, he's a good kid.[352] He's one of us. He's just not good with people he doesn't know. When you're working for us, you'll see how amazing he is."

"And if I don't want to work for you, I-Love-Lucy?"

There was a knock on the door of Lucy's apartment, and Ricky's voice could be heard off-stage, asking Loo-cy what

351. This apology does not appear in the First Edition.

352. In the Manuscript, in the scene at the motel, the boy's name is revealed to be Gen Eric.

was *keepin'* her so long, they was due down at the club in the next scene; a flash of irritation touched Lucy's cartoonish face. "Hell," she said. "Look, whatever the old guys are paying you, I can pay you double. Treble. A hundred times. Whatever they're giving you, I can give you so much more." She smiled, a perfect, roguish, Lucy Ricardo smile. "You name it, honey. What do you need?" She began to undo the buttons of her blouse. "Hey," she said. "You ever wanted to see Lucy's tits?"

The screen went black. The sleep function had kicked in and the set turned itself off. Shadow looked at his watch: it was half past midnight. "Not really," said Shadow.

He rolled over in bed and closed his eyes. It occurred to him that the reason he liked Wednesday and Mr. Nancy and the rest of them better than their opposition was pretty straightforward: they might be dirty, and cheap, and their food might taste like shit, but at least they didn't speak in clichés.

And he would take a roadside attraction, no matter how cheap, how crooked, or how sad, over a shopping mall, any day.

✢   ✢   ✢

MORNING FOUND SHADOW back on the road, driving through a gently undulating brown landscape of winter grass and leafless trees. The last of the snow had vanished. He filled up the tank of the piece of shit in a town which was home to the runner-up of the State Women's Under-16s three-hundred-meter dash, and, hoping that the dirt wasn't all that was holding it together, he ran the car through the gas station car wash, and was surprised to discover that the car was, when clean, against all reason, white, and pretty much free of rust. He drove on.

The sky was impossibly blue, and white industrial smoke rising from factory chimneys was frozen in the sky, like a photograph. A hawk launched itself from a dead tree and flew toward him, wings strobing in the sunlight like a series of stop-motion photographs.[353]

At some point he found himself heading into East

353. This is possibly Horus. See note 380, below.

St. Louis. He attempted to avoid it and instead found himself driving through what appeared to be a red-light district in an industrial park. Eighteen-wheelers and huge rigs were parked outside buildings that looked like temporary warehouses, that claimed to be 24 HOUR NITE CLUBs and, in one case, THE BEST PEAP SHOW IN TOWN. Shadow shook his head, and drove on. Laura had loved to dance, clothed or naked (and, on several memorable evenings, moving from one state to the other), and he had loved to watch her.

Lunch was a sandwich and a can of Coke in a town called Red Bud.

He passed a valley filled with the wreckage of thousands of yellow bulldozers, tractors and Caterpillars. He wondered if this was the bulldozers' graveyard, where the bulldozers went to die.

He drove past the Pop-a-Top Lounge. He drove through Chester ("Home of Popeye").[354] He noticed that the houses had started to gain pillars out front, that even the shabbiest, thinnest house now had its white pillars, proclaiming it, in someone's eyes, a mansion. He drove over a big, muddy river, and laughed out loud when he saw that the name of it, according to the sign, was the Big Muddy River.[355] He saw a covering of brown kudzu over three winter-dead trees, twisting them into strange, almost human shapes: they could have been witches, three bent old crones ready to reveal his fortune.

He drove alongside the Mississippi. Shadow had never seen the Nile, but there was a blinding afternoon sun burning on the wide brown river which made him think of the muddy expanse of the Nile: not the Nile as it is now, but as it was long ago, flowing like an artery through the papyrus marshes, home to cobra and jackal and wild cow . . .

A road sign pointed to Thebes.

The road was built up about twelve feet, so he was driving above the marshes. Clumps and clusters of birds in flight were questing back and forth, black dots against the blue sky, moving in some kind of desperate Brownian motion.

In the late afternoon the sun began to lower, gilding the

354. Chester, Illinois, was the birthplace of Elzie Crisler Segar (1894–1938), who created the cartoon character "Popeye" for his strip *Thimble Theatre* in 1929. Segar is memorialized by a statue of Popeye in Elzie Segar Memorial Park, erected in the late 1970s. In 2006, townspeople began the construction of statues of all of the other characters that appeared in the cartoon strip, one new statue appearing each year.

355. This is an actual river in southern Illinois, with a length of 156 miles. It does indeed feature a mud bottom.

world in elf-light, a thick warm custardy light that made the world feel unearthly and more than real, and it was in this light that Shadow passed the sign telling him he was Now Entering Historical Cairo. He drove under a bridge and found himself in a small port town. The imposing structure of the Cairo courthouse and the even more imposing customs house looked like enormous freshly baked cookies in the syrupy gold of the light at the end of the day.

He parked his car in a side street and walked to the embankment at the edge of a river, unsure whether he was gazing at the Ohio or the Mississippi. A small brown cat nosed and sprang among the trashcans at the back of a building, and the light made even the garbage magical.

A lone seagull was gliding along the river's edge, flipping a wing to correct itself as it went.

Shadow realized that he was not alone. A small girl, wearing old tennis shoes on her feet and a man's gray woolen sweater as a dress, was standing on the sidewalk, ten feet away from him, staring at him with the somber gravity of a six-year-old. Her hair was black, and straight, and long; her skin was as brown as the river.

He grinned at her. She stared back at him, defiantly.

There was a squeal and a yowl from the waterfront, and the little brown cat shot away from a spilled garbage can, pursued by a long-muzzled black dog. The cat scurried under a car.

"Hey," said Shadow to the girl. "You ever seen invisible powder before?"

She hesitated. Then she shook her head.

"Okay," said Shadow. "Well, watch this." Shadow pulled out a quarter with his left hand, held it up, tilting it from one side to another, then appeared to toss it into his right hand, closing his hand hard on nothing, and putting the hand forward. "Now," he said, "I just take some invisible powder from my pocket"—and he reached his left hand into his breast pocket, dropping the quarter into the pocket as he did so—"and I sprinkle it on the hand with the coin"—and he mimed sprinkling, —"and look—now the quarter's invisible too." He opened his empty right hand, and, in astonishment, his empty left hand as well.

The little girl just stared.

Shadow shrugged and put his hands back in his pockets, loading a quarter in one hand, a folded-up five-dollar bill in the other. He was going to produce them from the air, and then give the girl the five bucks: she looked like she needed it. "Hey," he said, "we've got an audience."

The black dog and the little brown cat were watching him as well, flanking the girl, looking up at him intently. The dog's huge ears were pricked up, giving it a comically alert expression. A crane-like man with gold-rimmed spectacles was coming up the sidewalk toward them, peering from side to side as if he were looking for something. Shadow wondered if he was the dog's owner.

"What did you think?" Shadow asked the dog, trying to put the little girl at her ease. "Was that cool?"

The black dog licked its long snout. Then it said, in a deep, dry voice, "I saw Harry Houdini once, and believe me, man, you are no Harry Houdini."[356]

The little girl looked at the animals, she looked up at Shadow, and then she ran off, her feet pounding the sidewalk as if all the powers of hell were after her. The two animals watched her go. The crane-like man had reached the dog. He leaned down and scratched its high, pointed ears.

"Come on," said the man in the gold-rimmed spectacles to the dog. "It was only a coin trick. It's not like he was doing an underwater escape."

"Not yet," said the dog. "But he will." The golden light was done, and the gray of twilight had begun.

Shadow dropped the coin and the folded bill back into his pocket. "Okay," he said. "Which one of you is Jackal?"

"Use your eyes," said the black dog with the long snout. "This way." It began to amble along the sidewalk, beside the man in the gold-rimmed glasses, and, after a moment's hesitation, Shadow followed them. The cat was nowhere to be seen. They reached a large old building on a row of boarded-up houses.

Anubis and Thoth participating in the weighing of souls ceremony (Book of the Dead of Hunefer, 19th dynasty). This depiction shows the scribe Hunefer's heart being weighed on the scale of Maat against the feather of truth, by the jackal-headed Anubis. The ibis-headed Thoth, scribe of the gods, records the result. If his heart equals exactly the weight of the feather, Hunefer is allowed to pass into the afterlife. If not, he is eaten by the waiting Ammet. This scene is mirrored in the text at note 778, below.

356. This, it will be seen, is Jacquel, or Anubis. Anubis is the Egyptian god of funerals and mummification, who led the soul through the land of shades, to the place of judgment by Osiris. Anubis is usually depicted as a bushy-tailed black jackal or a black man with the head of a dog or jackal.

Jacquel's remark is a paraphrase of the famous comment by Senator Lloyd Bentsen about Senator Dan Quayle, in their vice presidential debate in 1988. Quayle remarked, "I have as much experience in the Congress as Jack Kennedy did when he sought the presidency." Bentsen replied: "Senator, I served with Jack Kennedy, I knew Jack Kennedy, Jack Kennedy was a friend of mine. Senator, you are no Jack Kennedy." The exchange has been endlessly repeated, modified, repurposed, and parodied since.

Harry Houdini (1874–1926) was clearly the most famous magician and escape artist of the twentieth century.

357. The ibis is a long-billed water fowl, venerated in ancient Egypt as the symbol of Thoth, a god of unknown parentage and a protector of Horus. Thoth is associated with the moon and the sciences, including writing, mathematics, measurement, and timekeeping. In late Egyptian art, Thoth is usually shown as an ibis-headed man in the act of writing.

358. In the Manuscript, different versions of Chapters 7 and 8 are written out. Four people live in the house in Cairo: Isis (in the form of a little girl), Jacquel (Anubis), Ibis (Thoth), and the little brown cat (Bast). The events that occur are approximately the same.

The sign beside the door said IBIS AND JACQUEL. A FAMILY FIRM. FUNERAL PARLOR. SINCE 1863.

"I'm Mister Ibis," said the man in the gold-rimmed glasses.[357] "I think I should buy you a spot of supper. I'm afraid my friend here has some work that needs doing."[358]

Somewhere in America

N ew York scares Salim, and so he clutches his
sample case protectively with both hands, holding it to his chest. He is scared of black people,
the way they stare at him, and he is scared of the Jews,
the ones dressed all in black with hats and beards and side
curls he can identify and how many others that he cannot;
he is scared of the sheer quantity of the people, all shapes
and sizes of people, as they spill from their high, high, filthy
buildings onto the sidewalks; he is scared of the honking
hullabaloo of the traffic, and he is even scared of the air,
which smells both dirty and sweet, and nothing at all like
the air of Oman.

Salim has been in New York, in America, for a week. Each
day he visits two, perhaps three different offices, opens his
sample case, shows them the copper trinkets, the rings and
bottles and tiny flashlights, the models of the Empire State
Building, the Statue of Liberty, the Eiffel Tower, gleaming
in copper inside; each night he writes a fax to his brother-
in-law, Fuad, at home in Muscat,[359] telling him that he has
taken no orders, or, on one happy day, that he had taken
several orders (but, as Salim is painfully aware, not yet
enough even to cover his airfare and hotel bill).

For reasons Salim does not understand, his brother-in-
law's business partners have booked him into the Para-

359. The capital city of Oman and also its
largest. The Sultanate of Oman is situated
on the southeastern coast of the Arabian
Peninsula.

360. The balance of the sentence does not appear in the First Edition.

mount Hotel on Forty-sixth Street. He finds it confusing, claustrophobic, expensive, alien.

Fuad is Salim's sister's husband. He is not a rich man, but he is the co-owner of a small trinket factory,[360] making knickknacks from copper, brooches and rings and bracelets and statues. Everything is made for export, to other Arab countries, to Europe, to America.

Salim has been working for Fuad for six months. Fuad scares him a little. The tone of Fuad's faxes is becoming harsher. In the evening, Salim sits in his hotel room, reading his Qur'an, telling himself that this will pass, that his stay in this strange world is limited and finite.

His brother-in-law gave him a thousand dollars for miscellaneous traveling expenses and the money, which seemed so huge a sum when first he saw it, is evaporating faster than Salim can believe. When he first arrived, scared of being seen as a cheap Arab, he tipped everyone, handing extra dollar bills to everyone he encountered; and then he decided that he was being taken advantage of, that perhaps they were even laughing at him, and he stopped tipping entirely.

On his first and only journey by subway he got lost and confused, and missed his appointment; now he takes taxis only when he has to, and the rest of the time he walks. He stumbles into overheated offices, his cheeks numb from the cold outside, sweating beneath his coat, shoes soaked by slush; and when the winds blow down the avenues (which run from north to south, as the streets run west to east, all so simple, and Salim always knows where to face Mecca) he feels a cold on his exposed skin that is so intense it is like being struck.

He never eats at the hotel (for while the hotel bill is being covered by Fuad's business partners, he must pay for his own food); instead he buys food at falafel houses and at little food stores, smuggles it up to the room beneath his coat for days before he realizes that no one cares. And even then he feels strange about carrying the bags of food into the dimly lit elevators (Salim always has to bend and squint to find the button to press to take him to his floor) and up to the tiny white room in which he stays.

Salim is upset. The fax that was waiting for him when he woke this morning was curt, and alternately chiding, stern, and disappointed: Salim was letting them down—his sister, Fuad, Fuad's business partners, the Sultanate of Oman, the whole Arab world. Unless he was able to get the orders, Fuad would no longer consider it his obligation to employ Salim. They depended upon him. His hotel was too expensive. What was Salim doing with their money, living like a sultan in America? Salim read the fax in his room (which has always been too hot and stifling, so last night he opened a window, and was now too cold) and sat there for a time, his face frozen into an expression of complete misery.

Then Salim walked downtown, holding his sample case as if it contained diamonds and rubies, trudging through the cold for block after block until, on Broadway and Nineteenth Street, he finds a squat building over a Laundromat and walks up the stairs to the fourth floor, to the office of Panglobal Imports.[361]

The office is dingy, but he knows that Panglobal handles almost half of the ornamental souvenirs that enter the U.S. from the Far East. A real order, a significant order, from Panglobal could redeem Salim's journey, could make the difference between failure and success, so Salim sits on an uncomfortable wooden chair in an outer office, his sample case balanced on his lap, staring at the middle-aged woman with her hair dyed too bright a red who sits behind the desk, blowing her nose on Kleenex after Kleenex. After she blows her nose she wipes it, and drops the Kleenex into the trash.

Salim got there at 10:30 A.M., half an hour before his appointment. Now he sits there, flushed and shivering, wondering if he is running a fever. The time ticks by so slowly.

Salim looks at his watch. Then he clears his throat.

The woman behind the desk glares at him. "Yes?" she says. It sounds like *Yed*.

"It is eleven thirty-five," says Salim.

The woman glances at the clock on the wall, and says, "Yed," again. "Id id."

"My appointment was for eleven," says Salim with a placating smile.

361. In the First Edition, the Laundromat is a deli, but in fact, this is a relatively upscale corner, two blocks from Union Square Park.

"Mister Blanding knows you're here," she tells him, re-provingly. *Bidter Bladdig dode you're here.*

Salim picks up an old copy of the *New York Post* from the table. He speaks English better than he reads it, and he puzzles his way through the stories like a man doing a cross-word puzzle. He waits, a plump young man with the eyes of a hurt puppy, glancing from his watch to his newspaper to the clock on the wall.

At twelve thirty several men come out from the inner office. They talk loudly, jabbering away to each other in American. One of them, a big, paunchy man, has a cigar, unlit, in his mouth. He glances at Salim as he comes out. He tells the woman behind the desk to try the juice of a lemon, and zinc, as his sister swears by zinc, and vitamin C. She promises him that she will, and gives him several en-velopes. He pockets them and then he, and the other men, go out into the hall. The sound of their laughter disappears down the stairwell.

It is one o'clock. The woman behind the desk opens a drawer and takes out a brown paper bag, from which she removes several sandwiches, an apple, and a Milky Way. She also takes out a small plastic bottle of freshly squeezed orange juice.

"Excuse me," says Salim, "but can you perhaps call Mis-ter Blanding and tell him that I am still waiting?"

She looks up at him as if surprised to see that he is still there, as if they have not been sitting five feet apart for two and a half hours. "He's at lunch," she says. *He'd ad dudge.*

Salim knows, knows deep down in his gut, that Blanding was the man with the unlit cigar. "When will he be back?"

She shrugs, takes a bite of her sandwich. "He's busy with appointments for the rest of the day," she says. *He'd biddy wid abboidmeds for the red ob the day.*

"Will he see me, then, when he comes back?" asks Salim.

She shrugs, and blows her nose.

Salim is hungry, increasingly so, and frustrated, and pow-erless.

At three o'clock the woman looks at him and says, "He wode be gubbig bag."

"Excuse?"

"Bidder Bladdig. He wode be gubbig bag today."

"Can I make an appointment for tomorrow?"

She wipes her nose. "You hab to teddephode. Appoid-beds odly by teddephode."

"I see," says Salim. And then he smiles: a salesman, Fuad had told him many times before he left Muscat, is naked in America without his smile. "Tomorrow I will telephone," he says. He takes his sample case, and he walks down the many stairs to the street, where the freezing rain is turning to sleet. Salim contemplates the long, cold walk back to the Forty-sixth Street hotel, and the weight of the sample case, then he steps to the edge of the sidewalk and waves at every yellow cab that approaches, whether the light on top is on or off, and every cab drives past him.

One of them accelerates as it passes; a wheel dives into a water-filled pothole, spraying freezing muddy water over Salim's pants and coat. For a moment, he contemplates throwing himself in front of one of the lumbering cars, and then he realizes that his brother-in-law would be more concerned with the fate of the sample case than that of Salim himself, and that he would bring grief to no one but his beloved sister, Fuad's wife (for Salim had always been a slight embarrassment to his father and mother, and his romantic encounters had always, of necessity, been both brief and relatively anonymous): also, he doubts that any of the cars is going fast enough actually to end his life.

A battered yellow taxi draws up beside him and, grateful to be able to abandon his train of thought, Salim gets in.

The back seat is patched with gray duct tape; the half-open Plexiglas barrier is covered with notices warning him not to smoke, telling him how much to pay to the various airports. The recorded voice of somebody famous he has never heard of tells him to remember to wear his seatbelt.

"The Paramount Hotel, please," says Salim.

The cab driver grunts, and pulls away from the curb, into the traffic. He is unshaven, and he wears a thick, dust-colored sweater, and black plastic sunglasses. The weather is gray, and night is falling: Salim wonders if the man has a

362. In the First Edition, it is unclear whether the driver swears in English or in Arabic, but Salim speaks to him "in his own language," presumably moved to do so by the nature of the driver's oath.

363. "Ubar" was discovered in the 1990s by an expedition including Dr. Juris Zarins. In a September 1996 interview, Dr. Zarins answered the question of whether they had found Ubar: "There's a lot of confusion about that word. If you look at the classical texts and the Arab historical sources, Ubar refers to a region and a group of people, not to a specific town. People always overlook that. It's very clear on Ptolemy's second century map of the area. It says in big letters 'Iobaritae.' And in his text that accompanied the maps, he's very clear about that. It was only the late Medieval version of *The One Thousand and One Nights*, in the fourteenth or fifteenth century, that romanticized Ubar and turned it into a city, rather than a region or a people." However, the expedition did find a city, possibly the lost city of Irem or Iram, the "City of a Thousand Pillars." Irem is mentioned in the Q'uran: "Have you not considered how your Lord dealt with Aad / With Irem of lofty pillars / the like of which has never been seen in the Land?" (Q'uran, chapter 89, 6–14). There is some suggestion that Irem may be "The Nameless City" of which H. P. Lovecraft wrote in 1921. See this editor's *New Annotated H. P. Lovecraft* (New York: Liveright Publishing Co., 2014), pp. 80–93.

problem with his eyes. The wipers smear the street scene into grays and smudged lights.

From nowhere, a truck pulls out in front of them, and the cab driver swears in Arabic,[362] by the beard of the Prophet.

Salim stares at the name on the dashboard, but he cannot make it out from here. "How long have you been driving a cab, my friend?" he asks the man, in Arabic.

"Ten years," says the driver, in the same language. "Where are you from?"

"Muscat," says Salim. "In Oman."

"From Oman. I have been in Oman. It was a long time ago. Have you heard of the city of Ubar?" asks the taxi driver.

"Indeed I have," says Salim. "The Lost City of Towers. They found it in the desert five, ten years ago, I do not remember exactly. Were you with the expedition that excavated it?"

"Something like that. It was a good city," says the taxi driver. "On most nights there would be three, maybe four thousand people camped there: every traveler would rest at Ubar, and the music would play, and the wine would flow like water and the water would flow as well, which was why the city existed."

"That is what I have heard," says Salim. "And it perished, what, a thousand years ago? Two thousand?"[363]

The taxi driver says nothing. They are stopped at a red traffic light. The light turns green, but the taxi driver does not move, despite the immediate discordant blare of horns behind them. Hesitantly, Salim reaches through the hole in the Plexiglas and he touches the driver on the shoulder. The man's head jerks up, with a start, and he puts his foot down on the gas, lurching them across the intersection.

"Fuckshitfuckfuck," he says, in English.

"You must be very tired, my friend," says Salim.

"I have been driving this Allah-forgotten taxi for thirty hours," says the driver. "It is too much. Before that, I sleep for five hours, and I drove fourteen hours before that. We are shorthanded, before Christmas."

"I hope you have made a lot of money," says Salim.

The driver sighs. "Not much. This morning I drove a man from Fifty-first Street to Newark airport. When we got there, he ran off into the airport, and I could not find him again. A fifty-dollar fare gone, and I had to pay the tolls on the way back myself."

Salim nods. "I had to spend today waiting to see a man who will not see me. My brother-in-law hates me. I have been in America for a week, and it has done nothing but eat my money. I sell nothing."

"What do you sell?"

"Shit," says Salim. "Worthless gewgaws and baubles and tourist trinkets. Horrible, cheap, foolish, ugly shit."

The taxi driver wrenches the wheel to the right, swings around something, drives on. Salim wonders how he can see to drive, between the rain, the night, and the thick sunglasses.

"You try to sell shit?"

"Yes," says Salim, thrilled and horrified that he has spoken the truth about his brother-in-law's samples.

"And they will not buy it?"

"No."

"Strange. You look at the stores here, that is all they sell."

Salim smiles nervously.

A truck is blocking the street in front of them: a red-faced cop standing in front of it waves and shouts and points them down the nearest street.

"We will go over to Eighth Avenue, come uptown that way," says the taxi driver. They turn onto the street, where the traffic has stopped completely. There is a cacophony of horns, but the cars do not move.

The driver sways in his seat. His chin begins to descend to his chest, one, two, three times. Then he begins, gently, to snore. Salim reaches out to wake the man, hoping that he is doing the right thing. As he shakes his shoulder the driver moves, and Salim's hand brushes the man's face, knocking the man's sunglasses from his face onto his lap.

The taxi driver opens his eyes and reaches for, and replaces, the black plastic sunglasses, but it is too late. Salim has seen his eyes.

364. In the First Edition, the driver says this "very quietly."

365. A spirit from Arabian mythology, also spelled *afrit*, *afreet*, or *afrite*, *efreet*, or *ifreet*. According to the *Encyclopedia Britannica*, "As with the jinn, an ifrit may be either a believer or an unbeliever, good or evil, but is most often depicted as a wicked and ruthless being." An ifrit is mentioned in the Qur'an. *The Encyclopedia of the Occult*, by Lewis Spence (London: Bracken Books, 1994) states, "They assume diverse forms, and frequent ruins, woods, and wild desolate places, for the purpose of preying on men and other living things." (p. 223) The *Dictionary of Ancient Deities* adds the assertion that they are made of fire but live lives much as humans do. (p. 251) Yet the *Encyclopedia of Spirits and Ghosts in World Mythology*, by Theresa Bane (Jefferson, NC: McFarland Books, 2016) claims that the ifrit appears as a large winged demon made of smoke, lives underground, and is immortal. (p. 75) Clearly there is no consensus.

366. The word "marid" means rebellious, and it is a common Arabic adjective for all classes of demons; the word has taken on a secondary meaning of a specific class of demon or spirit, usually evil, and according to most sources, is the most powerful class of djinn. The marid are said to be the shock troops of Iblis (Eblis), the chief djinn and ruler of the lower world; Iblis is a fallen angel formerly known as Azazel.

The car crawls forward in the rain. The numbers on the meter increase.

"Are you going to kill me?" asks Salim.

The taxi driver's lips are pressed together. Salim watches his face in the driver's mirror.

"No," says the driver.[364]

The car stops again. The rain patters on the roof.

Salim begins to speak. "My grandmother swore that she had seen an ifrit,[365] or perhaps a marid,[366] late one evening, on the edge of the desert. We told her that it was just a sandstorm, a little wind, but she said no, she saw its face, and its eyes, like yours, were burning flames."

The driver smiles, but his eyes are hidden behind the black plastic glasses, and Salim cannot tell whether there is any humor in that smile or not. "The grandmothers came here too," he says.

"Are there many jinn in New York?" asks Salim.

"No. Not many of us."

"There are the angels, and there are men, who Allah made from mud, and then there are the people of the fire, the jinn," says Salim.

"People know nothing about my people here," says the driver. "They think we grant wishes. If I could grant wishes do you think I would be driving a cab?"

"I do not understand."

The taxi driver seems gloomy. Salim watches his face in the mirror as he speaks, staring at the ifrit's dark lips.

"They believe that we grant wishes. Why do they believe that? I sleep in one stinking room in Brooklyn. I drive this taxi for any stinking freak who has the money to ride in it, and for some who don't. I drive them where they need to go, and sometimes they tip me. Sometimes they pay me." His lower lip began to tremble. The ifrit seemed on edge. "One of them shat on the back seat once. I had to clean it before I could take the cab back. How could he do that? I had to clean the wet shit from the seat. Is that right?"

Salim puts out a hand, pats the ifrit's shoulder. He can feel solid flesh through the wool of the sweater. The ifrit raises his hand from the wheel, rests it on Salim's hand for a moment.

Salim thinks of the desert then: red sands blow a dust-storm through his thoughts, and the scarlet silks of the tents that surrounded the lost city of Ubar flap and billow through his mind.

They drive up Eighth Avenue.

"The old believe. They do not piss into holes, because the Prophet told them that jinn live in holes. They know that the angels throw flaming stars at us when we try to listen to their conversations. But even for the old, when they come to this country we are very, very far away. Back there, I did not have to drive a cab."

"I am sorry," says Salim.

"It is a bad time," says the driver. "A storm is coming. It scares me. I would do anything to get away."

The two of them say nothing more on their way back to the hotel.

When Salim gets out of the cab he gives the ifrit a twenty-dollar bill, tells him to keep the change. Then, with a sudden burst of courage, he tells him his room number. The taxi driver says nothing in reply. A young woman clambers into the back of the cab, and it pulls out into the cold and the rain.

Six o'clock in the evening. Salim has not yet written the fax to his brother-in-law. He goes out into the rain, buys himself this night's kebab and french fries. It has only been a week, but he feels that he is becoming heavier, rounder, softening in this country of New York.

When he comes back to the hotel he is surprised to see the taxi driver standing in the lobby, hands deep into his pockets. He is staring at a display of black-and-white post-cards. When he sees Salim he smiles, self-consciously. "I called your room," he says, "but there was no answer. So I thought I would wait."

Salim smiles also, and touches the man's arm. "I am here," he says.

Together they enter the dim, green-lit elevator, ascend

The black king of the djinns, Al-Malik al-Aswad, an ifrit, depicted in *Kitab al-Bulhan*, a late-14th-century Arabic manuscript

207

to the fifth floor holding hands. The ifrit asks if he may use Salim's bathroom. "I feel very dirty," he says. Salim nods. He sits on the bed, which fills most of the small white room, and listens to the sound of the shower running. Salim takes off his shoes, his socks, and then the rest of his clothes.

The taxi driver comes out of the shower, wet, with a towel wrapped about his mid-section. He is not wearing his sunglasses, and in the dim room his eyes burn with scarlet flames.

Salim blinks back tears. "I wish you could see what I see," he says.

"I do not grant wishes," whispers the ifrit, dropping his towel and pushing Salim gently, but irresistibly, down onto the bed.

It is an hour or more before the ifrit comes, thrusting and grinding into Salim's mouth. Salim has already come twice in this time. The jinn's semen tastes strange, fiery, and it burns Salim's throat.

Salim goes to the bathroom, washes out his mouth. When he returns to the bedroom the taxi driver is already asleep in the white bed, snoring peacefully. Salim climbs into the bed beside him, cuddles close to the ifrit, imagining the desert on his skin.

As he starts to fall asleep he realizes that he still has not written his fax to Fuad, and he feels guilty. Deep inside he feels empty and alone: he reaches out, rests his hand on the ifrit's tumescent cock and, comforted, he sleeps.

They wake in the small hours, moving against each other, and they make love again. At one point Salim realizes that he is crying, and the ifrit is kissing away his tears with burning lips. "What is your name?" Salim asks the taxi driver.

"There is a name on my driving permit, but it is not mine," the ifrit says.

Afterward, Salim could not remember where the sex had stopped and the dreams began.

When Salim wakes, the cold sun creeping into the white room, he is alone.

Also, he discovers, his sample case is gone, all the bottles and rings and souvenir copper flashlights, all gone, along with his suitcase, his wallet, his passport, and his air tickets back to Oman.

He finds a pair of jeans, the T-shirt, and the dust-colored woolen sweater discarded on the floor. Beneath them he finds a driver's license in the name of Ibrahim bin Irem, a taxi permit in the same name, and a ring of keys with an address written on a piece of paper attached to them in English. The photographs on the license and the permit ID do not look much like Salim, but then, they did not look much like the ifrit.

The telephone rings: it is the front desk calling to point out that Salim has already checked out, and his guest needs to leave soon so that they can service the room, to get it ready for another occupant.

"I do not grant wishes," says Salim, tasting the way the words shape themselves in his mouth.

He feels strangely light-headed as he dresses.

New York is very simple: the avenues run north to south, the streets run west to east. How hard can it be? he asks himself.

He tosses the car keys into the air and catches them. Then he puts on the black plastic sunglasses he found in the pockets, and leaves the hotel room to go and look for his cab.

CHAPTER EIGHT

367. The poem consists of two cantos, "The Witch of Coös" and "The Pauper Witch of Grafton," and it first appeared in *Poetry: A Magazine of Verse* in 1922. The quoted lines appear in the first canto.

He said the dead had souls, but when I asked him
How that could be—I thought the dead were souls,
He broke my trance. Don't that make you suspicious
That there's something the dead are keeping back?
Yes, there's something the dead are keeping back.

—ROBERT FROST,
"*Two Witches*"[367]

HE WEEK BEFORE Christmas is often a quiet one in a funeral parlor, Shadow learned, over supper. Mr. Ibis explained it to him. "The lingering ones are holding on for one final Christmas," said Mr. Ibis, "or even for New Year's, while the others, the ones for whom other people's jollity and celebration will prove too painful, have not yet been tipped over the edge by that last showing of *It's a Wonderful Life,* have not quite encountered the final straw, or should I say, the final *sprig of holly* that breaks not the camel's but the *reindeer's* back." And he made a little noise as he said it, half smirk, half snort, which suggested that he had just uttered a well-honed phrase of which he was particularly fond.

Ibis and Jacquel was a small, family-owned funeral home: one of the last truly independent funeral homes in the area, or so Mr. Ibis maintained. "Most fields of human merchandising value nationwide brand identities," he said. Mr. Ibis spoke in explanations: a gentle, earnest lecturing that put Shadow in mind of a college professor who used to work out at the Muscle Farm and who could not talk, could only discourse, expound, explain. Shadow had figured out within the first few minutes of meeting Mr. Ibis that his expected part in any conversation with the funeral director was to say as little as possible. They were sitting in a small restaurant, two blocks from Ibis and Jacquel's funeral home. Shadow's supper consisted of an all-day full breakfast—it came with hush puppies—while Mr. Ibis picked and pecked at a slice of coffeecake. "This, I believe, is because people like to know what they are getting ahead of time. Thus McDonald's, Wal-Mart, F. W. Woolworth (of blessed memory): store-brands maintained and visible across the entire country. Wherever you go, you will get something that is, with small regional variations, the same.

"In the field of funeral homes, however, things are, perforce, different. You need to feel that you are getting small-town personal service from someone who has a calling to the profession. You want personal attention to you and your loved one in a time of great loss. You wish to know that your grief is happening on a local level, not on a national one. But in all branches of industry—and death is an industry, my young friend, make no mistake about that—one makes one's money from operating in bulk, from buying in quantity, from centralizing one's operations. It's not pretty, but it's true. Trouble is, no one wants to know that their loved ones are traveling in a cooler-van to some big old converted warehouse where they may have twenty, fifty, a hundred cadavers on the go. No, sir. Folks want to think they're going to a family concern, somewhere they'll be treated with respect by someone who'll tip his hat to them if he sees them in the street."

Mr. Ibis wore a hat. It was a sober brown hat that matched his sober brown blazer and his sober brown face. Small gold-rimmed glasses perched on his nose. In Shadow's memory Mr. Ibis was a short man; whenever he would stand beside him, Shadow would rediscover that Mr. Ibis was well over six feet in height, with a crane-like stoop.[368]

368. In the First Edition, the following sentence follows: "Sitting opposite him now, across the shiny red table, Shadow found himself staring into the man's face."

"So when the big companies come in they buy the name of the company, they pay the funeral directors to stay on, they create the apparency of diversity. But that is merely the tip of the gravestone. In reality, they are as local as Burger King. Now, for our own reasons, we *are* truly an independent. We do all our own embalming, and it's the finest embalming in the country, although nobody knows it but us. We don't do cremations, though. We could make more money if we had our own crematorium, but it goes against what we're good at. What my business partner says is, if the Lord gives you a talent or a skill, you have an obligation to use it as best you can. Don't you agree?"

"Sounds good to me," said Shadow.

"The Lord gave my business partner dominion over the dead, just as he gave me skill with words. Fine things, words. I write books of tales, you know. Nothing literary. Just for my own amusement. Accounts of lives." He paused. By the time Shadow realized that he should have asked if he might be allowed to read one, the moment had passed. "Anyway, what we give them here is continuity: there's been an Ibis and Jacquel in business here for almost two hundred years. We weren't always funeral directors, though. We used to be morticians, and before that, undertakers."

"And before that?"

"Well," said Mr. Ibis, smiling just a little smugly, "we go back a very long way. Of course, it wasn't until after the War Between the States that we found our niche here. That was when we became the funeral parlor for the colored folks hereabouts. Before that no one thought of us as colored—foreign maybe, exotic and dark, but not colored. Once the war was done, pretty soon, no one could remember a time when we weren't perceived as black. My business partner, he's always had darker skin than mine. It was an easy transition. Mostly you are what they think you are. It's just strange when they talk about African-Americans. Makes me think of the people from Punt, Ophir, Nubia. We never thought of ourselves as Africans—we were the people of the Nile."

"So you were Egyptians," said Shadow.

Mr. Ibis pushed his lower lip upward, then let his head bob from side to side, as if it were on a spring, weighing the pluses and minuses, seeing things from both points of view. "Well, yes and no. 'Egyptians' makes me think of the folk who live there now. The ones who built their cities over our graveyards and palaces. Do they look like me?"

Shadow shrugged. He'd seen black guys who looked like Mr. Ibis. He'd seen white guys with tans who looked like Mr. Ibis.

"How was your coffee-cake?" asked the waitress, refilling their coffees.

"Best I ever had," said Mr. Ibis. "You give my best to your ma."

"I'll do that," she said, and bustled away.

"You don't want to ask after the health of anyone, if you're a funeral director. They think maybe you're scouting for business," said Mr. Ibis, in an undertone. "Shall we see if your room is ready?"

Their breath steamed in the night air. Christmas lights twinkled in the windows of the stores they passed. "It's good of you, putting me up," said Shadow. "I appreciate it."

"We owe your employer a number of favors. And Lord knows, we have the room. It's a big old house. There used to be more of us, you know. Now it's just the three of us. You won't be in the way."

"Any idea how long I'm meant to stay with you?"

Mr. Ibis shook his head. "He didn't say. But we are happy to have you here, and we can find you work. If you are not squeamish. If you treat the dead with respect."

"So," asked Shadow, "what are you people doing here in Cairo? Was it just the name or something?"

"No. Not at all. Actually this region takes its names from us, although people barely know it. It was a trading post back in the old days."

"Frontier times?"

"You might call it that," said Mr. Ibis. "*Evening, Mizz*

369. There is strong evidence that Upper Michigan was mined extensively for copper by Native Americans from 2500 B.C.E. onwards, for more than a thousand years, and new evidence suggests that as long as 6,000 years ago, the mining around the Great Lakes was so extensive as to leave a pollution trail. See https://eos.org/articles/miners-left-pollution-trail-great-lakes-6000-years-ago.
Fringe scientists have argued that some of the deposits extracted made their way to the Mediterranean, via "fair-haired marine men" reported in the region. See https://grahamhancock.com/wakefieldjs1/ for an extended discussion of the theory. In addition to the www.grahamhancock.com website generally, see also www.atlantisrising magazine.com for numerous discussions of ancient American mysteries.

370. In 1996, a skeleton was found at the Lake Wallula section of the Columbia River in Kennewick, Washington. Known as the Kennewick Man, the skeleton was reasonably intact, missing the sternum and some hand and foot bones. When studied, anthropologists noted that the skeleton lacked many distinctive Native American features but exhibited some Caucasian features. The teeth were thought to evidence a diet different from the typical Native American regime. Preliminary radio carbon dating suggested that the remains were around 9,000 years old. Also, a projectile tip of a type used from around 8,500 B.C.E. to 4,500 B.C.E. was found lodged in the hip. All of this evidence led to the theory that this was the skeleton of a Stone Age man with physical characteristics different from later Native Americans. Among all modern populations, the remains most closely resembled that of the Ainu, indigenous to the northern island of Hokkaido as well as the Kuril Islands and Sakhalin. Of course, many scientists argue that the sample is too small to jump to the conclusion that the Ainu were in America.

Simmons! And a merry Christmas to you too! The folk who brought me here came up the Mississippi a long time back."

Shadow stopped in the street, and stared. "Are you trying to tell me that ancient Egyptians came here to trade five thousand years ago?"

Mr. Ibis said nothing, but he smirked loudly. Then he said, "Three thousand five hundred and thirty years ago. Give or take."

"Okay," said Shadow. "I'll buy it, I guess. What were they trading?"

"Not much," said Mr. Ibis. "Animal skins. Some food. Copper from the mines in the upper peninsula.[369] The whole thing was rather a disappointment. Not worth the effort. They stayed here long enough to believe in us, to sacrifice to us, and for a handful of the traders to die of fever and be buried here, leaving us behind them." He stopped dead in the middle of the sidewalk, turned around slowly, arms extended. "This country has been Grand Central Station for ten thousand years or more. You say to me, what about Columbus?"

"Sure," said Shadow, obligingly. "What about him?"

"Columbus did what people had been doing for thousands of years. There's nothing special about coming to America. I've been writing stories about it, from time to time." They began to walk again.

"True stories?"

"Up to a point, yes. I'll let you read one or two, if you like. It's all there for anyone who has eyes to see it. Personally— and this is speaking as a subscriber to *Scientific American,* here—I feel very sorry for the professionals whenever they find another confusing skull, something that belonged to the wrong sort of people, or whenever they find statues or artifacts that confuse them—for they'll talk about the odd, but they won't talk about the impossible, which is where I feel sorry for them, for as soon as something becomes impossible it slipslides out of belief entirely, whether it's true or not. I mean, here's a skull that shows the Ainu, the Japanese aboriginal race, were in America nine thousand years ago.[370] Here's another that shows there were Polynesians in California nearly two thousand years later.[371] And all the scientists mutter and puzzle over who's descended from whom, missing the point entirely. Heaven knows what'll happen if they ever actually find the Hopi emergence tunnels.[372] That'll shake a few things up, you just wait.

"Did the Irish come to America in the dark ages, you ask me? Of course they did, and the Welsh, and the Vikings, while the Africans from the west coast—what in later days they called the slave coast or the ivory coast—they were trading with South America, and the Chinese visited Oregon a couple of times: they called it Fu Sang.[373] The Basque established their secret sacred fishing grounds off the coast of Newfoundland twelve hundred years back.[374] Now, I suppose you're going to say, but, Mister Ibis, these people were primitives, they didn't have radio controls and vitamin pills and jet airplanes."

Shadow hadn't said anything, and hadn't planned to say anything, but he felt it was required of him, so he said, "Well, weren't they?" The last dead leaves of the autumn crackled underfoot, winter-crisp.

"The misconception is that men didn't travel long distances in boats before the days of Columbus. Yet New Zealand and Tahiti and countless Pacific islands were settled by people in boats whose navigation skills would have put Columbus to shame; and the wealth of Africa was from trading, although that was mostly to the East, to India and China. My people, the Nile folk, we discovered early on that a reed boat will take you around the world, if you have the patience and enough jars of sweet water. You see, the biggest problem with coming to America in the old days was that there wasn't a lot here that anyone wanted to trade, and it was much too far away."[375]

They had reached a large house, built in the style people called Queen Anne. Shadow wondered who Queen Anne was, and why she had been so fond of Addams Family–style houses.[376] It was the only building on the block that wasn't locked up with boarded-over windows. They went through the gate and walked around the back of the building.

Through large double doors, which Mr. Ibis unlocked

371. The evidence for Polynesians in California is thin and controversial: Linguist Kathryn A. Klar and archaeologist Terry L. Jones argue that there is a linguistic link between the Polynesian and Chumash words for long-boats. This link is supported, they argue, by carbon-dating shells and bones forming part of a Chumash headdress that must have been exchanged when Polynesians visited California between 500 and 700 C.E. See *Polynesians in America: Pre-Columbian Contacts with the New World.* Edited by Terry L. Jones, Alice A. Storey, Elizabeth A. Matisoo-Smith, and José Miguel Ramírez-Aliaga (Lanham, PA: Alta-Mira Press, 2011).

372. Hopi mythology expresses that Spider Woman, an intermediary between the deity and the people, caused a hollow reed (tunnel) to grow into the sky of a prior, subterranean world. The tunnel emerged in the present world at the *sipapu.* The worthy occupants of the prior world, the Hopi people, emerged into this world through the tunnel, leaving the old world to flood and the destruction of its wicked inhabitants. The location of the *sipapu* is usually said to be the Grand Canyon.

373. A country named Fusang was described by the native Buddhist missionary Hui Shen in 499 C.E. as a place 20,000 Chinese *li* east of Da-han, and also east of China. This would place it either on the west coast of America or British Columbia (or perhaps the Sakhalin Islands). The theory of a Chinese presence in America was not taken seriously after the beginning of the twentieth century, and there is no physical evidence of such presence.

374. In his *History of Brittany* (1582), the French jurist and historian Bertrand d'Argentré (1519–1590) claimed that the Basques, Bretons, and Normans reached Newfoundland and were whaling there "before any other people." Bordeaux jurist

Etienne de Cleirac (1647) similarly claimed that in pursuing whales in the North Atlantic, French Basques discovered North America a century before Columbus. The evidence is weighed in Jean-Pierre Proulx's *Basque Whaling in Labrador in the 16th Century* (Accents Publications Service, 1993). This sentence does not appear in the First Draft.

375. Discovery of traces of tobacco and coca in ancient Egyptian mummies has also led to speculation that Egyptian traders visited the Americas thousands of years ago.

376. Anne was the queen of England from 1702 to 1714. Despite her short reign, it was stable and prosperous, and her monarchy fostered artistic, literary, scientific, economic, and political advancement. Blenheim Palace and Castle Howard were built, and Queen Anne–style architecture and Queen Anne–style furniture flourished and found favor long after her death.

The so-called Queen Anne–style home, asymmetric, half-timbered, cross-gabled, was popular in America from 1876 to 1915. However, Charles Addams's cartoons did not appear until 1938 and ran until his death in 1988; the family, unnamed until the eponymous television show in the 1960s, lived in a large *Gothic*-appearing home. The cartoons depicted an inversion of a typical American family and therefore the house Addams chose for the family was of the style long *discarded* by "modern" Americans. Shadow is undoubtedly aware of the historical order (Anne preceded the Addams family by almost 250 years) and is making a joke here.

with a key from his keychain, and they were in a large, unheated room, occupied by two people: a very tall, dark-skinned man, holding a large metal scalpel, and a dead girl in her late teens, lying on a long, porcelain object that resembled both a table and a sink.

There were several photographs of the dead girl pinned up on a cork-board on the wall above the body. She was smiling in one, a high school head shot. In another she was standing in a line with three other girls; they were wearing what might have been prom dresses, and her black hair was tied above her head in an intricate knot-work.

Cold on the porcelain, her hair was down, loose around her shoulders, and matted with dried blood.

"This is my partner, Mister Jacquel," said Ibis.

"We met already," said Jacquel. "Forgive me if I don't shake hands."

Shadow looked down at the girl on the table. "What happened to her?" he asked.

"Poor taste in boyfriends," said Jacquel.

"It's not always fatal," said Mr. Ibis, with a sigh. "This time it was. He was drunk, and he had a knife, and she told him that she thought she was pregnant. He didn't believe it was his."

"She was stabbed . . . ," said Mr. Jacquel, and he counted. There was a click as he stepped on a footswitch, turning on a small Dictaphone on a nearby table. "Five times. There are three knife wounds in the left anterior chest wall. The first is between the fourth and fifth intercostal spaces at the medial border of the left breast, two point two centimeters in length; the second and third are through the inferior portion of the left mid-breast penetrating at the sixth interspace, overlapping, and measuring three centimeters. There is one wound two centimeters long in the upper anterior left chest in the second interspace, and one wound five centimeters long and a maximum of one point six centimeters deep in the anteromedial left deltoid, a slashing injury. All the chest wounds are deep penetrating injuries. There are no other visible wounds externally." He released pressure from the foot switch. Shadow noticed a small microphone dangling above the embalming table by its cord.

"So you're the coroner as well?" asked Shadow.

"Coroner's a political appointment around here," said Ibis. "His job is to kick the corpse. If it doesn't kick him back, he signs the death certificate. Jacquel's what they call a prosector.[377] He works for the county medical examiner. He does autopsies, and saves tissue samples for analysis. He's already photographed her wounds."

Jacquel ignored them. He took a big scalpel and made a deep incision in a large V which began at both collarbones and met at the bottom of her breastbone, and then he turned the V into a Y, another deep incision that continued from her breastbone to her pubis. He picked up what looked like a small, heavy chrome drill with a medallion-sized round saw blade at the business end. He turned it on, and cut through the ribs at both sides of her breastbone.

The girl opened like a purse.

Shadow suddenly was aware of a mild but unpleasantly penetrating, pungent, meaty smell.

"I thought it would smell worse," said Shadow.

"She's pretty fresh," said Jacquel. "And the intestines weren't pierced, so it doesn't smell of shit."

Shadow found himself looking away, not from revulsion, as he would have expected, but from a strange desire to give the girl some privacy. It would be hard to be nakeder than this open thing.

Jacquel tied off the intestines, glistening and snakelike in her belly, below the stomach and deep in the pelvis. He ran them through his fingers, foot after foot of them, described them as "normal" to the microphone, put them in a bucket on the floor. He sucked all the blood out of her chest with a vacuum pump, and measured the volume. Then he inspected the inside of her chest. He said to the microphone, "There are three lacerations in the pericardium, which is filled with clotted and liquefied blood."

Jacquel grasped her heart, cut it at its top, turned it about in his hand, examining it. He stepped on his switch and

377. A person who dissects corpses for examination or demonstration.

said, "There are two lacerations of the myocardium; a one-point-five-centimeter laceration in the right ventricle and a one-point-eight-centimeter laceration penetrating the left ventricle."

Jacquel removed each lung. The left lung had been stabbed and was half collapsed. He weighed them, and the heart, and he photographed the wounds. From each lung he sliced a small piece of tissue, which he placed into a jar.

"Formaldehyde," whispered Mr. Ibis, helpfully.

Jacquel continued to talk to the microphone, describing what he was doing, what he saw, as he removed the girl's liver, the stomach, spleen, pancreas, both kidneys, the uterus and the ovaries.

He weighed each organ, reported them as normal and uninjured. From each organ he took a small slice and put it into a jar of formaldehyde.

From the heart, the liver, and from one of the kidneys, he cut an additional slice. These pieces he chewed, slowly, making them last, and ate while he worked.

Somehow it seemed to Shadow a good thing for him to do: respectful, not obscene.

"So you want to stay here with us for a spell?" said Jacquel, masticating the slice of the girl's heart.

"If you'll have me," said Shadow.

"Certainly we'll have you," said Mr. Ibis. "No reasons why not and plenty of reasons why. You'll be under our protection as long as you're here."

"I hope you don't mind sleeping under the same roof as the dead," said Jacquel.

Shadow thought of the touch of Laura's lips, bitter and cold. "No," he said. "Not as long as they stay dead, anyhow."

Jacquel turned and looked at him with dark brown eyes as quizzical and cold as a desert dog's. "They stay dead here," was all he said.

"Seems to me," said Shadow. "Seems to me that the dead come back pretty easy."

"Not at all," said Ibis. "Even zombies, they make them out of the living, you know. A little powder, a little chanting, a little push, and you have a zombie. They live, but they believe they are dead. But to truly bring the dead back to life, in their bodies. That takes power." He hesitates, then, "In the old land, in the old days, it was easier then."

"You could bind the *ka* of a man to his body for five thousand years," said Jacquel. "Binding or loosing. But that was a long time ago." He took all the organs that he had removed and replaced them, respectfully, in the body cavity. He replaced the intestines and the breastbone and pulled the skin edges near each other. Then he took a thick needle and thread and, with deft, quick strokes, he sewed it up, like a man stitching a baseball: the cadaver transformed from meat into girl once again.

"I need a beer," said Jacquel. He pulled off his rubber gloves and dropped them into the bin. He dropped his dark brown overalls into a hamper. Then he took the cardboard tray of jars filled with little red and brown and purple slices of the organs. "Coming?"

They walked up the back stairs to the kitchen. It was brown and white, a sober and respectable room that looked to Shadow as if it had last been decorated in 1920. There was a huge Kelvinator[378] rattling to itself by one wall. Jacquel opened the Kelvinator's door, put the plastic jars with their slivers of spleen, of kidney, of liver, of heart, inside. He took out three brown bottles. Ibis opened a glass-fronted cupboard, removed three tall glasses. Then he gestured for Shadow to sit down at the kitchen table.

Ibis poured the beer and passed a glass to Shadow, a glass to Jacquel. It was a fine beer, bitter and dark.

"Good beer," said Shadow.

"We brew it ourselves," said Ibis. "In the old days the women did the brewing. They were better brewers than we are. But now it is only the three of us here. Me, him, and her." He gestured toward the small brown cat, fast asleep in a cat-basket in the corner of the room. "There were more of us, in the beginning. But Set[379] left us to explore, what, two hundred years ago? Must be, by now. We got a postcard from him from San Francisco in 1905, 1906. Then nothing. While poor Horus . . ."[380] He trailed off, in a sigh, and shook his head.

378. Kelvinator began manufacturing iceboxes and refrigerators in 1914 and continues in some markets to this day.

379. Set or Seth was the Egyptian god of darkness and evil. Originally the patron of Lower Egypt, when Upper Egypt conquered Lower Egypt, he became the enemy of his nephew Horus. Set's brother is Osiris and his son is Anubis. As Set represented darkness, so Osiris personified light and goodness. According to *Britannica.com*, "Seth's appearance poses a problem for Egyptologists. He is often depicted as an animal or as a human with the head of an animal. But they can't figure out what animal he's supposed to be. He usually has a long snout and long ears that are squared at the tips. In his fully animal form, he has a thin doglike body and a straight tail with a tuft on the end. Many scholars now believe that no such animal ever existed and that the Seth animal is some sort of mythical composite."

380. In most versions, Horus is the son of Osiris and Isis and is one of the principal Egyptian deities. Horus is always represented as a falcon or falcon-headed.

Set and Horus adoring Ramses II (from the small temple at Abu Simbel)

"I still see him, on occasion," said Jacquel. "On my way to a pickup." He sipped his beer.

"I'll work for my keep," said Shadow. "While I'm here. You tell me what you need doing, and I'll do it."

"We'll find work for you," agreed Jacquel.

The small brown cat opened her eyes and stretched to her feet. She padded across the kitchen floor and pushed at Shadow's boot with her head. He put down his left hand and scratched her forehead and the back of her ears and the scruff of her neck. She arched ecstatically, then sprang into his lap, pushed herself up against his chest, and touched her cold nose to his. Then she curled up in his lap and went back to sleep. He put his hand down to stroke her: her fur was soft, and she was warm and pleasant in his lap: she acted like she was in the safest place in the world, and Shadow felt comforted.

The beer left a pleasant buzz in Shadow's head.

"Your room is at the top of the stairs, by the bathroom," said Jacquel. "Your work clothes will be hanging in the closet—you'll see. You'll want to wash up and shave first, I guess."

Shadow did. He showered standing in the cast-iron tub and he shaved, very nervously, with a straight razor that Jacquel loaned him. It was obscenely sharp, and had a mother-of-pearl handle, and Shadow suspected it was usually used to give dead men their final shave. He had never used a straight razor before, but he did not cut himself. He washed off the shaving cream, looked at himself naked in the fly-specked bathroom mirror. He was bruised: fresh bruises on his chest and arms overlaying the fading bruises that Mad Sweeney had left him. He looked at his wet, black hair and the dark gray eyes which looked back mistrustfully from the mirror at him, looked at the marks on his coffee-colored skin.[381]

And then, as if someone else were holding his hand, he raised the straight razor, placed it, blade open, against his throat.

It would be a way out, he thought. *An easy way out. And if there's anyone who'd simply take it in their stride, who'd*

---

381. This sentence does not appear in the First Edition. This is the first explicit description of Shadow's appearance; *cf.* the prison guard suggesting to Shadow after visiting the warden that Shadow might have "nigger blood," and Shadow's response "could be." We will learn later that Shadow's mother contracted sickle-cell anemia, a disease that commonly afflicts black people, and her skin turned a "yellowish gray" on her sickbed.

just clean up the mess and get on with things, it's the two guys sitting downstairs at the kitchen table drinking their beer. No more worries. No more Laura. No more mysteries and conspiracies. No more bad dreams. Just peace and quiet and rest forever. One clean slash, ear to ear. That's all it'll take.

He stood there with the razor against his throat. A tiny smudge of blood came from the place where the blade touched the skin. He had not even noticed a cut. *See,* he told himself, and he could almost hear the words being whispered in his ear. *It's painless. Too sharp to hurt. I'll be gone before I know it.*

Then the door to the bathroom swung open, just a few inches, enough for the little brown cat to put her head around the doorframe and "Mrr?" up at him, curiously.

"Hey," he said to the cat. "I thought I locked that door."

He closed the cut-throat razor, put it down on the side of the sink, dabbed at his tiny cut with a toilet paper swab. Then he wrapped a towel around his waist and went into the bedroom next door.

His bedroom, like the kitchen, seemed to have been decorated some time in the 1920s: there was a washstand and a pitcher beside the chest of drawers and mirror. The room itself smelled faintly musty, as if it was too infrequently aired, and the sheets of the bed seemed faintly damp when he touched them.[382]

Someone had already laid out clothes for him on the bed: a black suit, white shirt, black tie, white undershirt and underpants, black socks. Black shoes sat on the worn Persian carpet beside the bed.

He dressed himself. The clothes were of good quality, although none of them were new. He wondered who they had belonged to. Was he wearing a dead man's socks? Would he be stepping into a dead man's shoes?[383] Then he put the clothes on and looked at himself in the mirror. The clothes fit perfectly: there was not even the stretching around the chest or the shortness in the arms he had expected. He adjusted the tie in the mirror and now it seemed to him that his reflection was smiling at him, sardonically. He scratched

382. This sentence does not appear in the First Edition.

383. The balance of the paragraph is substantially absent from the First Edition. Only the sentence beginning "He adjusted . . ." appears.

the side of his nose, was actually relieved when his reflection did the same.

Now it seemed inconceivable to him that he had ever thought of cutting his throat. His reflection continued to smile as he adjusted his tie.

"Hey," he said to it, "you know something that I don't?" and immediately felt foolish.

The door creaked open and the cat slipped between the doorpost and the door and padded across the room, then up on the windowsill. "Hey," he said to the cat. "I did shut that door. I know I shut that door." She looked at him, interested. Her eyes were dark yellow, the color of amber. Then she jumped down from the sill, onto the bed, where she wrapped herself into a curl of fur and went back to sleep, a circle of cat upon the old counterpane.

Shadow left the bedroom door open, so the cat could leave and the room air a little, and he walked downstairs. The stairs creaked and grumbled as he walked down them, protesting his weight, as if they just wanted to be left in peace.

"*Damn* you look good," said Jacquel. He was waiting at the bottom of the stairs, and was now himself dressed in a black suit, similar to Shadow's. "You ever driven a hearse?"

"No."

"First time for everything, then," said Jacquel. "It's parked out front."

✦   ✦   ✦

AN OLD WOMAN had died. Her name had been Lila Goodchild. At Mr. Jacquel's direction, Shadow carried the folded aluminum gurney up the narrow stairs to her bedroom and unfolded it next to her bed. He took out a translucent blue plastic body bag, laid it next to the dead woman on the bed, and unzipped it open. She wore a pink nightgown and a quilted robe. Shadow lifted her and wrapped her, fragile and almost weightless, in a blanket, and placed it onto the bag. He zipped the bag shut and put it on the gurney. While Shadow did this, Jacquel talked to a very old man who had, when she was alive, been married to Lila

Goodchild. Or rather, Jacquel listened while the old man talked. As Shadow had zipped Mrs. Goodchild away the old man had been explaining how ungrateful his children had been, and grandchildren too, though that wasn't their fault, that was their parents', the apple didn't fall far from the tree, and he thought he'd raised them better than that.

Shadow and Jacquel wheeled the loaded gurney to the narrow flight of stairs. The old man followed them, still talking, mostly about money, and greed, and ingratitude. He wore bedroom slippers. Shadow carried the heavier bottom end of the gurney down the stairs and out onto the street, then he wheeled it along the icy sidewalk to the hearse. Jacquel opened the hearse's rear door. Shadow hesitated, and Jacquel said, "Just push it on in there. The supports'll fold up out of the way." Shadow pushed the gurney, and the supports snapped up, the wheels rotated, and the gurney rolled right on to the floor of the hearse. Jacquel showed him how to strap it in securely, and Shadow closed up the hearse while Jacquel listened to the old man who had been married to Lila Goodchild, unmindful of the cold, an old man in his slippers and his bathrobe out on the wintry sidewalk telling Jacquel how his children were vultures, no better than hovering vultures, waiting to take what little he and Lila had scraped together, and how the two of them had fled to St. Louis, to Memphis, to Miami, and how they wound up in Cairo, and how relieved he was that Lila had not died in a nursing home, how scared he was that he would.

They walked the old man back into the house, up the stairs to his room. A small TV set droned from one corner of the couple's bedroom. As Shadow passed it he noticed that the newsreader was grinning and winking at him. When he was sure that no one was looking in his direction he gave the set the finger.

"They've got no money," said Jacquel when they were back in the hearse. "He'll come in to see Ibis tomorrow. He'll choose the cheapest funeral. Her friends will persuade him to do her right, give her a proper sendoff in the front room, I expect. But he'll grumble. Got no money. No-

384. Or Ammit or Ammut, part crocodile, part hippopotamus, part lion, usually characterized as a demoness or goddess. Thus Shadow's "he must have eaten a lot of people" is an incorrect gender reference, but Jacquel is too polite to correct him.

385. Mithras was a Babylonian sun god, the god of light and fertility and, in Indian mythology, the ruler of the day. His birthday is said to be December 25, and his birth was witnessed by magi and shepherds. Mithraism was widespread five hundred years before Jesus's birth and was the principal active religion competing with the spread of Christianity. See Appendix for a tale of the meeting of Shadow and Jesus.

A depiction of Mithras killing a bull, from the Mithraeum near Heidelberg

body around here's got money these days. Anyway, he'll be dead in six months. A year at the outside."

Snowflakes tumbled and drifted in front of the headlights. The snow was coming south. Shadow said, "Is he sick?"

"It ain't that. Women survive their men. Men—men like him—don't live long when their women are gone. You'll see—he'll just start wandering, all the familiar things are going to be gone with her. He gets tired and he fades and then he gives up and then he's gone. Maybe pneumonia will take him or maybe it'll be cancer, or maybe his heart will stop. Old age, and all the fight gone out of you. Then you die."

Shadow thought. "Hey, Jacquel?"

"Yeah."

"Do you believe in the soul?" It wasn't quite the question he had been going to ask, and it took him by surprise to hear it coming from his mouth. He had intended to say something less direct, but there was nothing less direct that he could say.

"Depends. Back in my day, we had it all set up. You line up when you die, and you answer for your evil deeds and for your good deeds, and if your evil deeds outweighed a feather, we'd feed your soul and your heart to Ammet, the Eater of Souls."[384]

"He must have eaten a lot of people."

"Not as many as you'd think. It was a really heavy feather. We had it made special. You had to be pretty damn evil to tip the scales on that baby. Stop here, that gas station. We'll put in a few gallons."

The streets were quiet, in the way that streets only are when the first snow falls. "It's going to be a white Christmas," said Shadow as he pumped the gas.

"Yup. Shit. That boy was one lucky son of a virgin."

"Jesus?"

"Lucky, lucky guy. He could fall in a cesspit and come up smelling like roses. Hell, it's not even his birthday, you know that? He took it from Mithras.[385] You run into Mithras yet? Red cap. Nice kid."

"No, I don't think so."

"Well . . . I've never seen Mithras around here. He was an army brat. Maybe he's back in the Middle East, taking it easy, but I expect he's probably gone by now. It happens. One day every soldier in the empire has to shower in the blood of your sacrificial bull. The next they don't even re-member your birthday."

Swish went the windshield wipers, pushing the snow to the side, bunching the flakes up into knots and swirls of clear ice.

A traffic light turned momentarily yellow and then red, and Shadow put his foot on the brake. The hearse fishtailed and swung around on the empty road before it stopped.

The light turned green. Shadow took the hearse up to ten miles per hour, which seemed enough on the slippery roads. It was perfectly happy cruising in second gear: he guessed it must have spent a lot of its time at that speed, holding up traffic.

"That's good," said Jacquel. "So, yeah, Jesus does pretty good over here. But I met a guy who said he saw him hitch-hiking by the side of the road in Afghanistan and nobody was stopping to give him a ride. You know? It all depends on where you are."

"I think a real storm's coming," said Shadow. He was talking about the weather.

Jacquel, when, eventually, he began to answer, wasn't talking about the weather at all. "You look at me and Ibis," he said. "We'll be out of business in a few years. We got savings put aside for the lean years, but the lean years have been here for a long while, and every year they just get leaner. Horus is crazy, really bugfuck crazy, spends all his time as a hawk, eats roadkill, what kind of a life is that? You've seen Bast.[386] And *we're* in better shape than most of them. At least we've got a little belief to be going along with. Most of the suckers out there have barely got that. It's like the funeral business—the big guys are going to buy you up one day, like it or not, because they're bigger and more efficient and because they *work*. Fighting's not going to change a damned thing, because we lost this particular

Statue of Bastet, ca. 500 B.C.E.
Photo by Einsamer Schütze,
C.C.A.-Share Alike 3.0
https://en.wikipedia.org/wiki/Gayer
-Anderson_cat#/media/File:British
_Museum_Egypt_101-black.jpg

386. Another Egyptian deity, the goddess of fruitfulness, pleasure, dance, music, and cats. Bast is said to have been Set's wife and is usually depicted either as a cat or as a cat-headed woman. She appears several times in *Sandman*.

battle when we came to this green land a hundred years ago or a thousand or ten thousand. We arrived and America just didn't care that we'd arrived. So we get bought out, or we press on, or we hit the road. So, yes. You're right. The storm's coming."

Shadow turned onto the street where the houses were, all but one of them, dead, their windows blind and boarded. "Take the back alley," said Jacquel.

He backed the hearse up until it was almost touching the double doors at the rear of the house. Ibis opened the hearse, and the mortuary doors, and Shadow unbuckled the gurney and pulled it out. The wheeled supports rotated and dropped as they cleared the bumper. He wheeled the gurney to the embalming table. He picked up Lila Goodchild, cradling her in her opaque bag like a sleeping child, and placed her carefully on the table in the chilly mortuary, as if he were afraid to wake her.

"You know, I have a transfer board," said Jacquel. "You don't have to carry her."

"Ain't nothing," said Shadow. He was starting to sound more like Jacquel. "I'm a big guy. It doesn't bother me."

As a kid Shadow had been small for his age, all elbows and knees. The only photograph of Shadow as a kid that Laura had liked enough to frame showed a serious child with unruly hair and dark eyes standing beside a table, laden high with cakes and cookies. Shadow thought the picture might have been taken at an embassy Christmas party, as he had been dressed in a bowtie and his best clothes,[387] as one might dress a doll. He was looking solemnly out at the adult world that surrounded him.

They had moved too much, his mother and Shadow, first around Europe, from embassy to embassy, where his mother had worked as a communicator in the Foreign Service, transcribing and sending classified telegrams across the world, and then, when he was eight years old, back to the U.S., where his mother, now too sporadically sick to hold down a steady job, had moved from city to city restlessly spending a year here or a year there, temping when

387. The balance of this paragraph does not appear in the First Edition.

she was well enough. They never spent long enough in any place for Shadow to make friends, to feel at home, to relax. And Shadow had been a small child . . .

He had grown so fast. In the spring of his thirteenth year the local kids had been picking on him, goading him into fights they knew they could not fail to win and after which Shadow would run, angry and often weeping, to the boys' room to wash the mud or the blood from his face before anyone could see it. Then came summer, a long, magical, thirteenth summer, which he spent keeping out of the way of the bigger kids, swimming in the local pool, reading library books at poolside. At the start of the summer he could barely swim. By the end of August he was swimming length after length in an easy crawl, diving from the high board, ripening to a deep brown from the sun and the water.[388] In September, he had returned to school to discover that the boys who had made him miserable were small, soft things no longer capable of upsetting him. The two who tried it were taught better manners, hard and fast and painfully, and Shadow found that he had redefined himself: he could no longer be a quiet kid, doing his best to remain unobtrusively at the back of things. He was too big for that, too obvious. By the end of the year he was on the swimming team and on the weight-lifting team, and the coach was courting him for the triathlon team. He liked being big and strong. It gave him an identity. He'd been a shy, quiet, bookish kid, and that had been painful; now he was a big dumb guy, and nobody expected him to be able to do anything more than move a sofa into the next room on his own.

Nobody until Laura, anyway.

*   *   *

MR. IBIS HAD prepared dinner: rice and boiled greens for himself and Mr. Jacquel. "I am not a meat eater," he explained, "while Jacquel gets all the meat he needs in the course of his work." Beside Shadow's place was a carton of chicken pieces from KFC, and a bottle of beer.

There was more chicken than Shadow could eat, and he

388. There is a myth that people with dark skin do not tan from the sun. This is simply not true. The sun increases the amount of melanin in everyone's skin, making people with "coffee-colored" skin like Shadow darker.

shared the leftovers with the cat, removing the skin and crusty coating then shredding the meat for her with his fingers.

"There was a guy in prison named Jackson," said Shadow, as he ate, "worked in the prison library. He told me that they changed the name from Kentucky Fried Chicken to KFC because they don't serve real chicken any more. It's become this genetically modified mutant thing, like a giant centipede with no head, just segment after segment of legs and breasts and wings. It's fed through nutrient tubes. This guy said the government wouldn't let them use the word *chicken*."[389]

Mr. Ibis raised his eyebrows. "You think that's true?"

"Nope. Now, my old cellmate, Low Key, he said they changed the name because the word *fried* had become a bad word. Maybe they wanted people to think that the chicken cooked itself."

After dinner Jacquel excused himself and went down to the mortuary. Ibis went to his study to write. Shadow sat in the kitchen for a little longer, feeding fragments of chicken breast to the little brown cat, sipping his beer. When the beer and the chicken were gone, he washed up the plates and cutlery, put them on the rack to dry, and went upstairs.

He took a bath in the claw-footed bathtub, brushed his teeth with his disposable toothbrush and toothpaste. Tomorrow, he decided, he would buy a new toothbrush.[390]

When he returned to the bedroom the little brown cat was once more asleep at the bottom of the bed, curled into a fur crescent. In the middle drawer of the vanity he found several pairs of striped cotton pajamas. They looked seventy years old, but smelled fresh, and he pulled on a pair which, like the black suit, fitted him as if they had been tailored for him.

There was a small stack of *Reader's Digest*s on the little table beside the bed, none of them dated later than March 1960. Jackson, the library guy—the same one who had sworn to the truth of the Kentucky Fried Mutant Chicken Creature story, who had told him the story of the black freight trains that the government uses to haul political

389. In 1991, the fast-food chain known as "Kentucky Fried Chicken" changed its name to "KFC." In fact, this decision was likely made partly to remove the stigma of the word "fried" in an age of diet-conscious customers and partly to allow the company to offer a broader menu. However, urban legends immediately sprang up that the company was forced by the government to remove the word "chicken" because the company had been serving "mutant" chickens— genetically engineered six-legged fowls or birds with gigantic plumped breasts. The myth became so widespread that the company posted a detailed denial: http://chick enchattin.kfc.com/where-does-kfc-chicken -come-from/

390. This paragraph does not appear in the First Edition.

prisoners off to Secret Northern Californian Concentration Camps, moving across the country in the dead of the night—Jackson had also told him that the CIA used the *Reader's Digest* as a front for their branch offices around the world. He said that every *Reader's Digest* office in every country was really CIA.

"A joke," said the late Mr. Wood, in Shadow's memory. "How can we be sure the CIA wasn't involved in the Kennedy assassination?" Shadow cracked the window open a few inches—enough for fresh air to get in, enough for the cat to be able to get out onto the balcony outside.

He turned on the bedside lamp, climbed into bed and read for a little, trying to turn off his mind, to get the last few days out of his head, picking the dullest-looking articles in the dullest-looking *Digests*. He noticed he was falling asleep halfway through "I Am John's Pancreas."[391] He barely had time enough to turn out the bedside light and put his head down on the pillow before his eyes closed for the night.

* * *

LATER HE WAS never able to recollect the sequences and details of that dream: attempts to remember it produced nothing more than a tangle of dark images, underexposed in the darkroom of his mind. There was a girl. He had met her somewhere, and now they were walking across a bridge. It spanned a small lake, in the middle of a town. The wind was ruffling the surface of the lake, making waves tipped with whitecaps, which seemed to Shadow to be tiny hands reaching for him.[392]

—*Down there,* said the woman. She was wearing a leopard-print skirt which flapped and tossed in the wind, and the flesh between the top of her stockings and her skirt was creamy and soft and in his dream, on the bridge, before God and the world, Shadow went down to his knees in front of her, burying his head in her crotch, drinking in the intoxicating jungle female scent of her. He became aware, in his dream, of his erection in real life, a rigid, pounding, monstrous thing as painful in its hardness as the erections

391. *Reader's Digest* famously included numerous health articles, including "I am Joe's Pancreas." The reference to *John's* pancreas, according to Gaiman in a private conversation with this editor, may have been a misrecollection on his part, inspired by the 1986 alternative rock album *I Am John's Pancreas* by A Witness.

392. Later Shadow will take this very walk in Lakeside with Sam Black Crow.

393. The balance of the sentence does not appear in the First Edition.

he'd had as a boy, when he was crashing into puberty[393] with no idea of what the unprompted rigidities were, knowing only that they scared him.

He pulled away and looked upward, and still he could not see her face. But his mouth was seeking hers and her lips were soft against his, and his hands were cupping her breasts, and then they were running across the satin smoothness of her skin, pushing into and parting the furs that hid her waist, sliding into the wonderful cleft of her which warmed and wetted and parted for him, opening to his hand like a flower.

The woman purred against him ecstatically, her hand moving down to the hardness of him and squeezing it. He pushed the bed sheets away and rolled on top of her, his hand parting her thighs, her hand guiding him between her legs, where one thrust, one magical push . . .

Now he was back in his old prison cell with her, and he was kissing her deeply. She wrapped her arms tightly around him, clamped her legs about his legs to hold him tight, so he could not pull out, not even if he wanted to.

Never had he kissed lips so soft. He had not known that there were lips so soft in the whole world. Her tongue, though, was sandpaper-rough as it slipped against his.

—*Who are you?* he asked.

She made no answer, just pushed him onto his back and, in one lithe movement, straddled him and began to ride him. No, not to ride him: to insinuate herself against him in series of silken-smooth waves, each more powerful than the one before, strokes and beats and rhythms which crashed against his mind and his body just as the wind-waves on the lake splashed against the shore. Her nails were needle-sharp and they pierced his sides, raking them, but he felt no pain, only pleasure, everything was transmuted by some alchemy into moments of utter pleasure.

He struggled to find himself, struggled to talk, his head now filled with sand dunes and desert winds.

—*Who are you?* he asked again, gasping for the words.

She stared at him with eyes the color of dark amber, then lowered her mouth to his and kissed him with a passion, kissed him so completely and so deeply that there, on the bridge over the lake, in his prison cell, in the bed in the Cairo funeral home, he almost came. He rode the sensation like a kite riding a hurricane, willing it not to crest, not to explode, wanting it never to end. He pulled it under control. He had to warn her.

—*My wife, Laura. She will kill you.*

—*Not me,* she said.

A fragment of nonsense bubbled up from somewhere in his mind: in medieval days it was said that a woman on top during coitus would conceive a bishop. That was what they called it: trying for a bishop . . .[394]

He wanted to know her name, but he dared not ask her a third time, and she pushed her chest against his, and he could feel the hard nubs of her nipples against his chest, and she was squeezing him, somehow squeezing him *down there* deep inside her and this time he could not ride it or surf it, this time it picked him up and spun and tumbled him away, and he was arching up, pushing into her as deeply as he could imagine, as if they were, in some way, part of the same creature, tasting, drinking, holding, *wanting . . .*

—*Let it happen,* she said, her voice a throaty feline growl. *Give it to me. Let it happen.* And he came, spasming and dissolving, the back of his mind itself liquefying then sublimating slowly from one state to the next.

Somewhere in there, at the end of it, he took a breath, a clear draught of air he felt all the way down to the depths of his lungs, and he knew that he had been holding his breath for a long time now. Three years, at least. Perhaps even longer.

—*Now rest,* she said, and she kissed his eyelids with her soft lips. *Let it go. Let it all go.*

The sleep he slept after that was deep and dreamless and comforting, and Shadow dived deep and embraced it.

✤ ✤ ✤

THE LIGHT WAS strange. It was—he checked his watch—six forty-five A.M., and still dark outside, but the room was filled with a pale blue dimness. He climbed out of bed. He

394. Religious and secular literature emphasized the male superior as the normative position. For example, the *Alphabet of Ben Sira* (9th or 10th century C.E.) tells of Lilith, Adam's first wife, fleeing Eden and becoming a demon because Adam refused to have intercourse with her in a female-superior position. Because the female superior was supposed to reduce the risk of pregnancy, the position was viewed as improper, the approved purpose of intercourse between married persons being solely procreative. Indeed Gulielmus Peraldus's influential treatise on sin made a distinction between sexual sins against nature "according to the substance," meaning non-vaginal intercourse, and those "according to the manner, as when a woman mounts." Gulielmus Peraldus (William Perault), *Summa de vitiis* (probably first published 1255–65, republished Venice 1492), 3:2:2, quoted in Ruth Mazo Karras's *Sexuality in Medieval Europe: Doing Unto Others* (London and New York: Routledge, 2017), p. 111.

Shadow did not make up this phrase, however. In the 1796 edition of Captain Francis Groses's renowned *A Classical Dictionary of the Vulgar Tongue*, the earliest dictionary of English slang and cant (first published in 1785), an entry may be found for "Riding St. George": "The woman uppermost in the amorous congress; that is, the dragon upon St. George. *This is said to be the way to get a bishop.*" (Emphasis added.) However, it is still difficult to understand how a position that was regarded as sinful became known as the means of giving birth to a clergyman.

Interestingly, early sex manuals refer to the female-superior position as "equestrian" (the modern slang terminology is "cowgirl").

was certain that he had been wearing pajamas when he went to bed, but now he was naked, and the air was cold on his skin. He walked to the window and closed it.

There had been a snowstorm in the night: six inches had fallen, perhaps more. The corner of the town that Shadow could see from his window, dirty and run-down, had been transformed into somewhere clean and different: these houses were not abandoned and forgotten, they were frosted into elegance. The streets had vanished completely, lost beneath a white field of snow.

There was an idea that hovered at the edge of his perception. Something about *transience*. It flickered and was gone.

He could see as well as if it were full daylight.

In the mirror, Shadow noticed something strange. He stepped closer, and stared, puzzled. All his bruises had vanished. He touched his side, pressing firmly with his fingertips, feeling for one of the deep pains that told him he had encountered Mr. Stone and Mr. Wood, hunting for the greening blossoms of bruise that Mad Sweeney had gifted him with, and finding nothing. His face was clear and unmarked. His sides, however, and his back (he twisted to examine it) were scratched with what looked like claw marks.

He hadn't dreamed it, then. Not entirely.

Shadow opened the drawers, and put on what he found: an ancient pair of blue-denim Levis, a shirt, a thick blue sweater, and a black undertaker's coat he found hanging in the wardrobe at the back of the room. He wondered again who the clothes had belonged to.[395]

He wore his own old shoes.

The house was still asleep. He crept through it, willing the floorboards not to creak, and then he was outside (out through the front door, not the mortuary, not this morning, not when he didn't have to),[396] and he walked through the snow, his feet leaving deep prints in the virgin snow, his steps crunching as they pushed the soft snow deep onto the sidewalk. It was lighter out than it had seemed from inside the house, and the snow reflected the light from the sky.

After fifteen minutes walking, Shadow came to a bridge, with a big sign on the side of it warning him he was now

395. This sentence does not appear in the First Edition.

396. The parenthetical phrase does not appear in the First Edition.

leaving historical Cairo. A man stood under the bridge, tall and gangling, sucking on a cigarette and shivering continually. Shadow thought he recognized the man,[397] but the light on the snow was playing tricks on his eyes, and he walked closer and closer in order to be sure. The man wore a patched denim jacket and a baseball cap.

And then, under the bridge in the winter darkness he was close enough to see the purple smudge of bruise around the man's eye, and he said, "Good morning, Mad Sweeney."

The world was so quiet. Not even cars disturbed the snowbound silence.

"Hey, man," said Mad Sweeney. He did not look up. The cigarette had been rolled by hand. Shadow wondered if the man was smoking a joint.[398] No, the smell was tobacco.

"You keep hanging out under bridges, Mad Sweeney," said Shadow, "people gonna think you're a troll."

This time Mad Sweeney looked up. Shadow could see the whites of his eyes all around his irises. The man looked scared. "I was lookin' for you," he said. "You gotta help me, man. I fucked up big-time." He sucked on his hand-rolled cigarette, pulled it away from his mouth. The cigarette paper stuck to his lower lip, and the cigarette fell apart, spilling its contents onto his ginger beard and down the front of his filthy T-shirt. Mad Sweeney brushed it off, convulsively, with blackened hands, as if it were a dangerous insect.

"My resources are pretty much tapped out, Mad Sweeney," said Shadow. "But why don't you tell me what it is you need. You want me to get you a coffee?"

Mad Sweeney shook his head. He took out a tobacco pouch and papers from the pocket of his denim jacket and began to roll himself another cigarette. His beard bristled and his mouth moved as he did this, although no words were said aloud. He licked the adhesive side of the cigarette paper and rolled it between his fingers. The result looked only distantly like a cigarette. Then he said, "'M not a troll. Shit. Those bastards're fucken *mean*."

"I know you're not a troll, Sweeney," said Shadow, gently,[399] hoping that he did not sound as if he were patronizing the man. "How can I help you?"

397. The balance of the paragraph does not appear in the First Edition.

398. This sentence and the next do not appear in the First Edition.

399. The balance of the sentence does not appear in the First Edition.

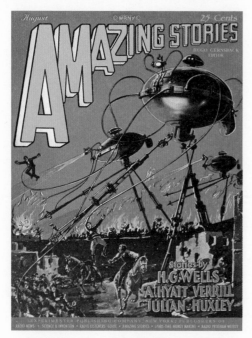

Frank Paul's cover for the Aug. 1927
Amazing Stories, illustrating H. G. Wells's
War of the Worlds

400. The balance of the paragraph does not appear in the First Edition.

401. Frank Rudolph Paul (1884–1963) was an influential illustrator of pulp magazines, especially *Amazing Stories,* and a protégé of its groundbreaking editor Hugo Gernsback. His covers often depicted futuristic buildings, robots, spaceships, and aliens and made use of his architectural training.

402. Who exactly is Mad Sweeney in trouble with? The laws of the universe? As we will see, Mad Sweeney *did* give the coin to the "King of America," in some sense.

403. Brân is a gigantic Celtic deity, the "crowned king over this island of Britain," according to the medieval *Mabinogion* (a collection of Welsh tales).

Mad Sweeney flicked his Zippo, and the first inch of his cigarette flamed and then subsided to ash. "You remember I showed you how to get a coin? You remember?"

"Yes," said Shadow. He saw the gold coin in his mind's eye, watched it tumble into Laura's casket, saw it glitter around her neck. "I remember."

"You took the wrong coin, man."

A car approached the gloom beneath the bridge, blinding them with its lights. It slowed as it passed them, then stopped, and a window slid down. "Everything okay here, gentlemen?"

"Everything's just peachy thank you, officer," said Shadow. "Just out for a morning walk."

"Okay now," said the cop. He did not look as if he believed that everything was okay. He waited. Shadow put a hand on Mad Sweeney's shoulder, and walked him forward, out of town, away from the police car. He heard the window hum closed, but the car remained where it was.

Shadow walked. Mad Sweeney walked, and sometimes he staggered.[400] They passed a sign saying FUTURE CITY. Shadow imagined a city of spires and Frank R. Paul towers,[401] all gleaming in gentle primary colors, bubble-domed air-cars flitting from tower to tower like glittering hover-flies. That was Future City and somehow Shadow didn't think it was ever going to be built in Cairo.

The police car cruised past them slowly, then turned, and went back into the city, accelerating down the snowy road.

"Now, why don't you tell me what's troubling you," said Shadow.

"I did it like he said. I did it all like he said, but I gave you the wrong coin. It wasn't meant to be that coin. That's for royalty. You see? I shouldn't even have been able to take it. That's the coin you'd give to the King of America himself. Not some pissant bastard like you or me. And now I'm in big trouble.[402] Just give me the coin back, man. You'll never see me again, if you do, I sweartofuckenBran,[403] okay? I swear by the years I spent in the fucken trees."

"You did it like who said, Sweeney?"

"Grimnir. The dude you call Wednesday. You know who he is? Who he really is?"

"Yeah. I guess."

There was a panicked look in the Irishman's crazy blue eyes. "It was nothing bad. Nothing you can—nothing bad. He just told me to be there at that bar and to pick a fight with you. He said he wanted to see what you were made of."

"He tell you to do anything else?"

Sweeney shivered and twitched; Shadow thought it was the cold for a moment, then knew where he'd seen that shuddering shiver before. In prison: it was a junkie shiver. Sweeney was in withdrawal from something, and Shadow would have been willing to bet it was heroin. A junkie leprechaun? Mad Sweeney pinched off the burning head of his cigarette, dropped it on the ground, put the unfinished yellowing rest of it into his pocket. He rubbed his filthy fingers together, breathed on them to try and rub warmth into them. His voice was a whine now. "Listen, just give me the fucken coin, man.[404] What do you want it for? Huh? Hey, you know there's more where that came from. I'll give you another, just as good. Hell, I'll give you a shitload, man."

He took off his filthy baseball cap—then, with his right hand, he stroked the air, producing a large golden coin. He dropped it into his cap. And then he took another from a wisp of breath steam, and another, catching and grabbing them from the still morning air until the baseball cap was brimming with them and Sweeney was forced to hold it with both hands.

He extended the baseball cap filled with gold to Shadow. "Here," he said. "Take them, man. Just give me back the coin I gave to you." Shadow looked down at the cap, wondered how much its contents would be worth.

"Where am I going to spend those coins, Mad Sweeney?" Shadow asked. "Are there a lot of places you can turn your gold into cash?"

He thought the Irishman was going to hit him for a moment, but the moment passed and Mad Sweeney just stood there, holding out his gold-filled cap with both hands like

404. The next three sentences do not appear in the First Edition.

Oliver Twist. And then tears swelled in his blue eyes and began to spill down his cheeks. He took the cap and put it—now empty of everything except a greasy sweatband—back over his thinning scalp. "You gotta, man," he was saying. "Didn't I show you how to do it? I showed you how to take coins from the hoard. I showed you where the hoard was. The treasure of the sun.[405] Just give me that first coin back. It didn't belong to me."

"I don't have it any more."

Mad Sweeney's tears stopped, and spots of color appeared in his cheeks. "You, you fucken—" he said, and then the words failed him and his mouth opened and closed, soundlessly.

"I'm telling you the truth," said Shadow. "I'm sorry. If I had it, I'd give it back to you. But I gave it away."

Sweeney's filthy hands clamped on Shadow's shoulders, and the pale blue eyes stared into his. The tears had made streaks in the dirt on Mad Sweeney's face. "Shit," he said. Shadow could smell tobacco and stale beer and whiskey-sweat. "You're telling the truth, you fucker. Gave it away and freely and of your own will. Damn your dark eyes, you gave it a-fucken-way."

"I'm sorry." Shadow remembered the whispering thump the coin had made as it landed in Laura's casket.

"Sorry or not, I'm damned and I'm doomed."[406] The tears were flowing once more, and clear snot began to run from the man's nose. His words dissolved, then, into syllables which never quite congealed together into words. "Bah-bah-bah-bah-bah," he said. "Muh-muh-muh-muh-muh." He wiped his nose and his eyes on his sleeves, muddying his face into strange patterns, wiping the snot all over his beard and mustache.

Shadow squeezed Mad Sweeney's upper arm in an awkward male gesture. *I'm here*, it said.[407]

"'Twere better I had never been conceived," said Mad Sweeney, at length. Then he looked up. "The fellow you gave it to. Would he give it back?"

"It's a woman. And I don't know where she is. But no, I don't believe she would."

405. This sentence does not appear in the First Edition.

406. Most of the balance of the paragraph does not appear in the First Edition.

407. This sentence does not appear in the First Edition.

Sweeney sighed, mournfully. "When I was but a young pup," he said, "there was a woman I met, under the stars, who let me play with her bubbies, and she told me my fortune. She told me that I would be undone and abandoned west of the sunrise, and that a dead woman's bauble would seal my fate. And I laughed and poured more barley wine and played with her bubbies some more, and I kissed her full on her pretty lips. Those were the good days—the first of the gray monks had not yet come to our land,[408] nor had they ridden the green sea to westward. And now." He stopped, mid-sentence. His head turned and he focused on Shadow. "You shouldn't trust him," he said, reproachfully.

"Who?"

"Wednesday. You mustn't trust him."

"I don't have to trust him. I work for him."

"Do you remember how to do it?"

"What?" Shadow felt he was having a conversation with half a dozen different people. The self-styled leprechaun sputtered and jumped from persona to persona, from theme to theme, as if the remaining clusters of brain cells were igniting, flaming, and then going out for good.

"The coins, man. The coins. I showed you, remember?" He raised two fingers to his face, stared at them, then pulled a gold coin from his mouth. He tossed the coin to Shadow, who stretched out a hand to catch it, but no coin reached him.

"I was drunk," said Shadow. "I don't remember."

Sweeney stumbled across the road. It was light now and the world was white and gray. Shadow followed him. Sweeney walked in a long, loping stride, as if he were always falling, but his legs were there to stop him, to propel him into another stumble. When they reached the bridge, he held on to the bricks with one hand, and turned and said, "You got a few bucks? I don't need much. Just enough for a ticket out of this place. Twenty bucks will do me fine. You got a twenty? Just a lousy twenty?"

"Where can you go on a twenty-dollar bus-ticket?" asked Shadow.

"I can get out of here," said Sweeney. "I can get away

408. Mad Sweeney refers to the introduction of Christianity to Ireland by monks before the fifth century C.E. Contrary to popular belief, St. Patrick did not introduce Christianity to Ireland; monasteries were already present when he arrived sometime in the fifth century.

409. Mad Sweeney makes a play on the famous aphorism attributed to Karl Marx, "Religion is the opiate of the masses." Marx's true expression may be translated: "Religion is the sigh of the oppressed creature, the heart of a heartless world, and the soul of soulless conditions. It is the opiate of the masses." From Marx's introduction to his work *A Contribution to the Critique of Hegel's Philosophy of Right*, separately published in 1844.

410. The image first appeared on a poster by Art Bevacqua in 1970 and was widely copied on teeshirts.

before the storm hits. Away from a world in which opiates have become the religion of the masses.[409] Away from." He stopped, wiped his nose on the side of his hand, then wiped his hand on his sleeve.

Shadow reached into his jeans, pulled out a twenty and passed it to Sweeney. "Here."

Sweeney crumpled it up and pushed it deep into the breast pocket of his oil-stained denim jacket, under the sew-on patch showing two vultures on a dead branch and, barely legible beneath them, the words PATIENCE MY ASS! I'M GOING TO KILL SOMETHING![410] He nodded. "That'll get me where I need to go," he said.

He leaned against the brick, fumbled in his pockets until he found the unfinished stub of cigarette he had abandoned earlier. He lit it carefully, trying not to burn his fingers or his beard. "I'll tell you something," he said, as if he had said nothing that day. "You're walking on gallows ground, and there's a hempen rope around your neck and a raven-bird on each shoulder, waiting for your eyes, and the gallows tree has deep roots, for it stretches from heaven to hell, and our world is only the branch from which the rope is swinging." He stopped. "I'll rest here a spell," he said, crouching down, his back resting against the black brickwork.

"Good luck," said Shadow.

"Hell, I'm fucked," said Mad Sweeney. "Whatever. Thanks."

Shadow walked back toward the town. It was 8:00 A.M. and Cairo was waking like a tired beast. He glanced back to the bridge, and saw Sweeney's pale face, striped with tears and dirt, watching him go.

It was the last time Shadow saw Mad Sweeney alive.

✢   ✢   ✢

THE BRIEF WINTER days leading up to Christmas were like moments of light between the winter darknesses, and they fled fast in the house of the dead.

It was the twenty-third of December, and Jacquel and Ibis's played host to a wake for Lila Goodchild. Bustling women filled the kitchen with tubs and with saucepans and with skillets and with Tupperware, and the deceased was laid out in her casket in the funeral home's front room with hothouse flowers around her. There was a table on the other side of the room laden high with coleslaw and beans and cornmeal hush puppies and chicken and ribs and black-eyed peas, and by mid-afternoon the house was filled with people weeping and laughing and shaking hands with the minister, everything being quietly organized and overseen by the sober-suited Messrs. Jacquel and Ibis. The burial would be on the following morning.

When the telephone in the hall rang (it was Bakelite and black and had an honest-to-goodness rotary dial on the front) Mr. Ibis answered. Then he took Shadow aside. "That was the police," he said. "Can you make a pickup?"

"Sure."

"Be discreet. Here." He wrote down an address on a slip of paper, then passed it to Shadow, who read the address, written in perfect copperplate handwriting, and then folded it up and put it in his pocket. "There'll be a police car," Ibis added.

Shadow went out back and got the hearse. Mr. Jacquel and Mr. Ibis had each made a point, individually, of explaining that, really, the hearse should only be used for funerals, and they had a van that they used to collect bodies, but the van was being repaired, had been for three weeks now, and could he be very careful with the hearse? Shadow drove carefully down the street. The snowplows had cleaned the roads by now, but he was comfortable driving slowly. It seemed right to go slow in a hearse, although he could barely remember the last time he had seen a hearse on the streets. Death had vanished from the streets of America, thought Shadow; now it happened in hospital rooms and in ambulances. *We must not startle the living,* thought Shadow. Mr. Ibis had told him that they move the dead about in some hospitals on the lower level of apparently empty covered gurneys, the deceased traveling their own paths in their own covered ways.

A dark blue police cruiser was parked on a side street, and Shadow pulled up the hearse behind it. There were two cops inside the cruiser, drinking their coffee from thermos tops. They had the engine running to keep warm. Shadow tapped on the side window.

"Yeah?"

"I'm from the funeral home," said Shadow.

"We're waiting for the medical examiner," said the cop. Shadow wondered if it was the same man who had spoken to him under the bridge. The cop, who was black, got out of the car, leaving his colleague in the driver's seat, and walked Shadow back to a Dumpster. Mad Sweeney was sitting in the snow beside the Dumpster. There was an empty green bottle in his lap,[411] a dusting of snow and ice on his face and baseball cap and shoulders. He didn't blink.

"Dead wino," said the cop.

"Looks like it," said Shadow.

"Don't touch anything yet," said the cop. "Medical examiner should be here any time now. You ask me, the guy drank himself into a stupor and froze his ass."

"Yes," agreed Shadow. "That's certainly what it looks like."

He squatted down and looked at the bottle in Mad Sweeney's lap. Jameson Irish whiskey: a twenty-dollar ticket out of this place. A small green Nissan pulled up, and a harassed middle-aged man with sandy hair and a sandy mustache got out, walked over. He touched the corpse's neck. *He kicks the corpse,* thought Shadow, *and if it doesn't kick him back . . .*

"He's dead," said the medical examiner. "Any ID?"

"He's a John Doe," said the cop.

The medical examiner looked at Shadow. "You working for Jacquel and Ibis?" he asked.

"Yes," said Shadow.

"Tell Jacquel to get dentals and prints for ID and identity photos. We don't need a post. He should just draw blood for toxicology. Got that? Do you want me to write it down for you?"

"No," said Shadow. "It's fine. I can remember."

The man scowled fleetingly, then pulled a business card from his wallet, scribbled on it, and gave it to Shadow, say-

411. This is the empty Jameson Irish whiskey bottle that Shadow kindly replaces when Mad Sweeney is reanimated at the mortuary, below.

ing, "Give this to Jacquel." Then the medical examiner said "Merry Christmas" to everyone, and was on his way. The cops kept the empty bottle.

Shadow signed for the John Doe and put it on the gurney. The body was pretty stiff, and Shadow couldn't get it out of a sitting position. He fiddled with the gurney, and found out that he could prop up one end. He strapped John Doe, sitting, to the gurney and put him in the back of the hearse, facing forward. Might as well give him a good ride. He closed the rear curtains. Then he drove back to the funeral home.

The hearse was stopped at a traffic light—the same lights he'd fishtailed at, several nights earlier—when Shadow heard a voice croak, "And it's a fine wake I'll be wanting, with the best of everything, and beautiful women shedding tears and their clothes in their distress, and brave men lamenting and telling fine tales of me in my great days."

"You're dead, Mad Sweeney," said Shadow. "You take what you're given when you're dead."

"Aye, that I shall," sighed the dead man sitting in the back of the hearse. The junkie whine had vanished from his voice now, replaced with a resigned flatness, as if the words were being broadcast from a long, long way away, dead words being sent out on a dead frequency.

The light turned green and Shadow put his foot gently down on the gas.

"But give me a wake tonight, nonetheless," said Mad Sweeney. "Set me a place at table, and give me a stinking drunk wake tonight. You killed me, Shadow, you owe me that much."

"I never killed you, Mad Sweeney," said Shadow. *It's twenty dollars,* he thought, *for a ticket out of here.* "It was the drink and the cold killed you, not me."

There was no reply, and there was silence in the car for the rest of the journey. After he parked at the back, Shadow wheeled the gurney out of the hearse and into the mortuary. He manhandled Mad Sweeney onto the embalming table as if he were hauling a side of beef.

He covered the John Doe with a sheet and left him there,

with the paperwork beside him. As he went up the back stairs he thought he heard a voice, quiet and muted, like a radio playing in a distant room, which said, "And what would drink or cold be doing killing me, a leprechaun of the blood? No, it was you losing the little golden sun killed me, Shadow, killed me dead as sure as water's wet and days are long and a friend will always disappoint you in the end."

Shadow wanted to point out to Mad Sweeney that that was a kind of bitter philosophy, but he suspected it was the being dead that made you bitter.

He went upstairs to the main house, where a number of middle-aged women were putting Saran wrap on casserole dishes, popping the Tupperware tops onto plastic pots of cooling fried potatoes and macaroni and cheese.

Mr. Goodchild, the husband of the deceased, had Mr. Ibis against a wall, and was telling him how he knew none of his children would come out to pay their respects to their mother. The apple don't fall far from the tree, he told anyone who would listen to him. The apple don't fall far from the tree.

✴ ✴ ✴

THAT EVENING SHADOW laid an extra place at the table. He put a glass at each place, and a new bottle of Jameson Gold in the middle of the table. It was the most expensive Irish whiskey they sold at the liquor store. After they ate (a large platter of leftovers left for them by the middle-aged women) Shadow poured a generous tot into each glass—his, Ibis's, Jacquel's and Mad Sweeney's.

"So what if he's sitting on a gurney in the cellar," said Shadow, as he poured, "on his way to a pauper's grave? To-night we'll toast him, and give him the wake he wanted."

Shadow raised his glass to the empty place at the table. "I only met Mad Sweeney twice, alive," he said. "The first time I thought he was a world-class jerk with the devil in him. The second time I thought he was a major fuckup and I gave him the money to kill himself. He showed me a coin trick I don't remember how to do, gave me some bruises, and claimed he was a leprechaun. Rest in peace,

Mad Sweeney." He sipped the whiskey, letting the smoky taste evaporate in his mouth. The other two drank, toasting the empty chair along with him.

Mr. Ibis reached into an inside pocket and pulled out a notebook, which he flipped through until he found the appropriate page, and he read out a summarized version of Mad Sweeney's life.

According to Mr. Ibis, Mad Sweeney had started his life as the guardian of a sacred rock in a small Irish glade, over three thousand years ago. Mr. Ibis told them of Mad Sweeney's love affairs, his enmities, the madness that gave him his power ("a later version of the tale is still told, although the sacred nature, and the antiquity, of much of the verse has long been forgotten"), the worship and adoration in his own land that slowly transmuted into a guarded respect and then, finally, into amusement; he told them the story of the girl from Bantry who came to the New World, and who brought her belief in Mad Sweeney the leprechaun with her, for hadn't she seen him of a night, down by the pool, and hadn't he smiled at her and called her by her own true name? She had become a refugee, in the hold of a ship of people who had watched their potatoes turn to black sludge in the ground, who had watched friends and lovers die of hunger, who dreamed of a land of full stomachs. The girl from Bantry Bay dreamed, specifically, of a city where a girl would be able to earn enough to bring her family over to the New World. Many of the Irish coming in to America thought of themselves as Catholics, even if they knew nothing of the catechism, even if all they knew of religion was the Bean Sidhe,[412] the banshee, who came to wail at the walls of a house where death soon would be, and Saint Bride,[413] who was once Bridget of the two sisters (each of the three was a Brigid, each was the same woman), and tales of Finn,[414] of Oisín,[415] of Conan the Bald[416]—even of the leprechauns, the little people (and was that not the biggest joke of the Irish, for the leprechauns in their day were the tallest of the mound folk) . . .[417]

All this and more Mr. Ibis told them in the kitchen that night. His shadow on the wall was stretched and bird-like,

412. See note 305, above.

413. Brigid was an early Irish goddess, whose demesnes included poetry, smithing, medicine, arts and crafts, livestock, and sacred wells. She was said to have two sisters named Brigid, one a goddess of healing and another a goddess of smithing, and so she may have truly been a triple goddess, embodying all of these attributes. (See note 173, above.) Saint Bride, whose pre-canonization name was Bridget, was an Irish abbess in the Middle Ages who became a patron saint of Ireland.

414. Finn or Fionn, also called Finn Mc-Cool (the Anglicized version of Fionn mac Cumhaill), was a popular giant, rogue, lover, poet, and hero, leader of the Fenians, and the subject of many tales. He shares some traits with King Arthur and is said to have lived for over 200 years.

A probable statue of Brigid,
2nd century C.E., in Rennes, Brittany

Fionn
Beatrice Elvery, in Heroes of the Dawn, *1914*

415. Also known as Ossian or Osheen or Usheen, he is remembered as Ireland's greatest poet and the principal recorder of the Fenian cycle. In the 1760s, James MacPherson published a series of highly influential poems that he claimed were translations of Ossian's work, though it seems clear that MacPherson freely adapted many Gallic ballads.

416. Conán mac Morna, also known as Conan Maol (the "bald"), is another member of the Fenian circle. No relation to Conan the Barbarian or Conan the Doyle, he is usually depicted as a fat, greedy troublemaker, unafraid of a fight, Falstaffian in nature or akin to Friar Tuck of the Robin Hood legends.

417. See note 113, above, regarding the size of leprechauns.

and as the whiskey flowed Shadow imagined it the head of a huge waterfowl, beak long and curved, and it was somewhere in the middle of the second glass that Mad Sweeney himself began to throw both details and irrelevancies into Ibis's narrative (". . . such a girl she was, with breasts cream-colored and spackled with freckles, with the tips of them the rich reddish pink of the sunrise on a day when it'll be bucketing down before noon but glorious again by supper . . .") and then Sweeney was trying, with both hands, to explain the history of the gods in Ireland, wave after wave of them as they came in from Gaul and from Spain and from every damn place, each wave of them transforming the last gods into trolls and fairies and every damn creature until Holy Mother Church herself arrived and every god in Ireland was transformed into a fairy or a saint or a dead king without so much as a by-your-leave . . .**418**

Mr. Ibis polished his gold-rimmed spectacles and explained—enunciating even more clearly and precisely than usual, so Shadow knew he was drunk (his words and the sweat that beaded on his forehead in that chilly house were the only indications of this)—with forefinger wagging, explained that he was an artist and that his tales should not be seen as literal constructs but as imaginative re-creations, truer than the truth, and Mad Sweeney said, "I'll show you an imaginative re-creation, my fist imaginatively re-creating your fucken face for starters," and Mr. Jacquel bared his teeth and growled at Sweeney, the growl of a huge dog who's not looking for a fight but can always finish one by ripping out your throat, and Sweeney took the message and sat down and poured himself another glass of whiskey.

"Have you remembered how I do my little coin trick?" he asked Shadow with a grin.

"I have not."

"If you can guess how I did it," said Mad Sweeney, his lips purple, his blue eyes beclouded, "I'll tell you if you get warm."

"It's not a palm is it?" asked Shadow.

"It is not."

"Is it a gadget of some kind? Something up your sleeve

or elsewhere that shoots the coins up for you to catch? Or a coin on a wire that swings in front of and behind your hand?"[419]

"It is not that neither. More whiskey, anybody?"

"I read in a book about a way of doing the Miser's Dream with latex covering the palm of your hand, making a skin-colored pouch for the coins to hide behind."

"This is a sad wake for Great Sweeney who flew like a bird across all of Ireland and ate watercress in his madness:[420] to be dead and unmourned save for a bird, a dog, and an idiot. No, it is not a pouch."

"Well, that's pretty much it for ideas," said Shadow. "I expect you just take them out of nowhere." It was meant to be sarcasm, but then he saw the expression on Sweeney's face. "You *do*," he said. "You do take them from nowhere."

"Well, not exactly nowhere," said Mad Sweeney. "But now you're getting the idea. You take them from the hoard."

"The hoard," said Shadow, starting to remember. "Yes."

"You just have to hold it in your mind, and it's yours to take from. The sun's treasure. It's there in those moments when the world makes a rainbow. It's there in the moment of eclipse and the moment of the storm."

And he showed Shadow how to do the thing.

This time Shadow got it.

✦   ✦   ✦

SHADOW'S HEAD ACHED and pounded, and his tongue tasted and felt like flypaper. He squinted at the glare of the daylight. He had fallen asleep with his head on the kitchen table. He was fully dressed, although he had at some point taken off his black tie.

He walked downstairs, to the mortuary, and was relieved but unsurprised to see that John Doe was still on the embalming table. Shadow pried the empty bottle of Jameson Gold from the corpse's rigor-mortised fingers, and threw it away. He could hear someone moving about in the house above.

Mr. Wednesday was sitting at the kitchen table when Shadow went upstairs. He was eating leftover potato salad

Finn McCool Comes to Aid the Fianna
Stephen Reid (1932)

418. Ireland had a long history of invasion (in both military and cultural senses) from its beginnings. The earliest occupants have been traced to around 7,900 B.C.E., when Mesolithic hunter-gatherers moved onto the island. These established communities, but after 600 B.C.E. groups of Celtic-speaking people began to arrive. Kingdoms emerged, many including Druidic upper classes, and the influence of the Roman empire on Ireland spread. By medieval times, there were myths of ancient Spanish migrations to Ireland, but modern historians give them little credence.

These cultures brought their gods with them. The primitive gods of Ireland became overlaid with Celtic gods, and Roman gods appeared as well. By the early fifth century, Christianity was making much headway in Ireland, and the early Church began to conflict with these older religions.

419. This sentence does not appear in the First Edition.

420. See Mad Sweeney's true history at note 105, above.

"Sometimes a maiden held up an apple of gold to Niam and Usheen, as their slender white horse dashed across the waves of the ocean."
Albert Herter, Tales of the Enchanted Islands of the Atlantic, *1899*

from a Tupperware container with a plastic spoon. He wore a dark gray suit, a white shirt and a deep gray tie: the morning sun glittered on the silver tiepin in the shape of a tree. He smiled at Shadow when he saw him.

"Ah, Shadow m'boy, good to see you're up. I thought you were going to sleep forever."

"Mad Sweeney's dead," said Shadow.

"So I heard," said Wednesday. "A great pity. Of course it will come to all of us, in the end." He tugged on an imaginary rope, somewhere on the level of his ear, and then jerked his neck to one side, tongue protruding, eyes bulging. As quick pantomimes went, it was disturbing. And then he let go of the rope and smiled his familiar grin. "Would you like some potato salad?"

"I would not." Shadow darted a look around the kitchen and out into the hall. "Do you know where Ibis and Jacquel are?"

"Indeed I do. They are burying Mrs. Lila Goodchild—something that they would probably have liked your help in doing, but I asked them not to wake you. You have a long drive ahead of you."

"We're leaving?"

"Within the hour."

"I should say goodbye."

"Goodbyes are overrated. You'll see them again, I have no doubt, before this affair is done with."

For the first time since that first night, Shadow observed, the small brown cat was curled up in her basket. She opened her incurious amber eyes and watched him go.

So Shadow left the house of the dead. Ice sheathed the winter-black bushes and trees as if they'd been insulated, made into dreams. The path was slippery.

Wednesday led the way to Shadow's white Chevy Nova, parked out on the road. It had been recently cleaned, and the Wisconsin plates had been removed, replaced with Minnesota plates. Wednesday's luggage was already stacked in the back seat. Wednesday unlocked the car with keys that were duplicates of the ones Shadow had in his own pocket.

"I'll drive," said Wednesday. "It'll be at least an hour before you're good for anything."

They drove north, the Mississippi on their left, a wide silver stream beneath a gray sky. Shadow saw, perched on a leafless gray tree beside the road, a huge brown and white hawk, which stared down at them with mad eyes as they drove toward it, then took to the wing and rose in slow and powerful circles[421] and, in moments, was out of sight.

Shadow realized it had only been a temporary reprieve, his time in the house of the dead; and already it was beginning to feel like something that happened to somebody else, a long time ago.

421. In the First Edition, this sentence ends here.

PART TWO

MY AINSEL [422]

CHAPTER NINE

Not to mention mythic creatures in the rubble. . . .
—WENDY COPE,
"A Policeman's Lot"[423]

 S THEY DROVE out of Illinois late that evening, Shadow asked Wednesday his first question. He saw the WELCOME TO WISCONSIN sign, and said, "So who were the bunch that grabbed me in the parking lot? Mister Wood and Mister Stone? Who were they?"

The lights of the car illuminated the winter landscape. Wednesday had announced that they were not to take freeways because he didn't know whose side the freeways were on, so Shadow was sticking to back roads. He didn't mind. He wasn't even sure that Wednesday was crazy.

Wednesday grunted. "Just spooks. Members of the opposition. Black hats."

"I think," said Shadow, "that they think they're the white hats."

"Of course they do. There's never been a true war that wasn't fought between two sets of people who were certain they were in the right. The really dangerous people believe that they are doing whatever they are doing solely and only because it is without question the right thing to do. And that is what makes them dangerous."

422. "My Own Self," "Me A'an Sel'," or "My Ainsel" is a Northumbrian fairy tale about a child who outwits a fairy with word-play, and giving him the name "Mike Ainsel" is Wednesday naming Shadow as his duplicate or stand-in—a role that is evident later in the story.

423. From Cope's collection *Making Cocoa for Kingsley Amis* (London: Faber & Faber, 1985). The poem, a parody of Gilbert and Sullivan's "Policeman's Song" from the 1879 operetta *The Pirates of Penzance*, expresses her views about the poet Ted Hughes (also published by Faber & Faber) and art in general.

"And you?" asked Shadow. "Why are you doing what you're doing?"

"Because I want to," said Wednesday. And then he grinned. "So that's all right."

Shadow said, "How did you all get away? Or did you all get away?"

"We did," said Wednesday. "Although it was a close thing. If they'd not stopped to grab you, they might have taken the lot of us. It convinced several of the people who had been sitting on the fence that I might not be completely crazy."

"So how did you get out?"

Wednesday shook his head. "I don't pay you to ask questions," he said. "I've told you before."

Shadow shrugged.

They spent the night in a Super 8 motel, south of La Crosse.

Christmas Day was spent on the road, driving north and east. The farmland became pine forest. The towns seemed to come farther and farther apart.

They ate their Christmas lunch late in the afternoon in a hall-like family restaurant in northern central Wisconsin. Shadow picked cheerlessly at the dry turkey, jam-sweet red lumps of cranberry sauce, tough-as-wood roasted potatoes and the violently green canned peas. From the way he attacked it, and the way he smacked his lips, Wednesday seemed to be enjoying the food. As the meal progressed he became positively expansive—talking, joking, and, whenever she came close enough, flirting with the waitress, a thin blonde girl who looked scarcely old enough to have dropped out of high school.

"Excuse me, m'dear, but might I trouble you for another cup of your delightful hot chocolate? And I trust you won't think me too forward if I say what a mightily fetching and becoming dress that is. Festive, yet classy."

The waitress, who wore a bright red and green skirt edged with glittering silver tinsel, giggled and colored and smiled happily, and went off to get Wednesday another mug of hot chocolate.

"Fetching," said Wednesday, thoughtfully, watching her

go. "Becoming," he said. Shadow did not think he was talking about the dress. Wednesday shoveled the final slice of turkey into his mouth, flicked at his beard with his napkin, and pushed his plate forward. "Aaah. Good." He looked around him, at the family restaurant. In the background a tape of Christmas songs was playing: the little drummer boy had no gifts to bring, *parupapom-pom, rapappom pom, rapappom pom.*[424]

"Some things may change," said Wednesday, abruptly. "People, however . . . people stay the same. Some grifts last forever, others are swallowed soon enough by time and by the world. My favorite grift of all is no longer practical. Still, a surprising number of grifts are timeless—the Spanish Prisoner,[425] the Pigeon Drop,[426] the Fawney Rig (that's the Pigeon Drop but with a gold ring instead of a wallet),[427] the Fiddle Game . . ."

"I've never heard of the Fiddle Game," said Shadow. "I think I've heard of the others. My old cellmate said he'd actually done the Spanish Prisoner. He was a grifter."

"Ah," said Wednesday, and his left eye sparkled. "The Fiddle Game was a fine and wonderful con. In its purest form it is a two-man grift. It trades on cupidity and greed, as all great grifts do. You can always cheat an honest man, but it takes more work. So. We are in a hotel, or an inn, or a fine restaurant, and, dining there, we find a man—shabby, but shabby genteel, not down-at-heel but certainly down on his luck. We shall call him Abraham. And when the time comes to settle his bill—not a huge bill, you understand, fifty, seventy-five dollars—an embarrassment! Where is his wallet? Good Lord, he must have left it at a friend's, not far away. He shall go and obtain his wallet forthwith! But here, mine host, says Abraham, take this old fiddle of mine for security. It's old, as you can see, but it's how I make my living."

Wednesday's smile when he saw the waitress approaching was huge and predatory. "Ah, the hot chocolate! Brought to me by my Christmas Angel! Tell me, my dear, could I have some more of your delicious bread when you get a moment?"

The waitress—what was she, Shadow wondered: sixteen,

424. "The Little Drummer Boy," originally known as "Carol of the Drum," was written by Katherine Kennicott Davis in 1941, based on a traditional Czech tune. It was first popularized in the 1950s by the Trapp Family Singers (of *Sound of Music* fame) and today seems to be inescapable during the holiday season—over 220 cover versions of the song have been noted.

425. A fine version of the scam is told by Arthur Train, in "The Spanish Prisoner," first published in *The Cosmopolitan Magazine* (Mar. 1910) and reproduced in full here: http://www.hidden-knowledge.com/fun stuff/spanishprisoner/spanishprisoner1.html. The con lives on in the form of e-mails from *faux*-Nigerian officials desiring a "processing fee" to obtain an allegedly stolen fortune.

426. The con artist offers the victim a large sum of money that the grifter has "found" in some fashion. Unlike the "processing fee" scam, both the grifter and the victim must put up some money to get the fortune. Invariably, the con takes place when the supposed fortune is finally delivered to the victim by a so-called expert or neutral person (such as a "lawyer" with whom they have deposited their funds), only to prove worthless, while the grifter and the "expert" (acting in concert) depart with the victim's share of the deposited funds as well as recovering their own. See mystery-thriller writer Duane Swierczynski's *The Complete Idiot's Guide to Frauds, Scams, and Cons* (Indianapolis: Alpha Books, 2002).

427. Fawney Rig is also the joking name of the home of the head of the Order of Ancient Mysteries, Roderick Burgess, who captures Morpheus in Gaiman's *Sandman*. A "fawney rig" is thieves' cant for "a common fraud, thus practised: A fellow drops a brass ring, double gilt, which he picks up before the party meant to be cheated, and to whom he disposes of it for less than its supposed, and ten times more than its real, value." (Francis Grose's *1811 Dictionary of the Vulgar Tongue*.)

seventeen?—looked at the floor and her cheeks flushed crimson. She put down the chocolate with shaking hands and retreated to the edge of the room, by the slowly rotating display of pies, where she stopped and stared at Wednesday. Then she slipped into the kitchen, to fetch Wednesday his bread.

"So. The violin—old, unquestionably, perhaps even a little battered—is placed away in its case, and our temporarily impecunious Abraham sets off in search of his wallet. But a well-dressed gentleman, only just done with his own dinner, has been observing this exchange, and now he approaches our host: could he, perchance, inspect the violin that honest Abraham left behind?

"Certainly he can. Our host hands it over, and the well-dressed man—let us call him Barrington—opens his mouth wide, then remembers himself and closes it, examines the violin reverentially, like a man who has been permitted into a holy sanctum to examine the bones of a prophet. 'Why,' he says, 'this is—it must be—no, it cannot be—but yes, there it is—my lord! But this is unbelievable!" and he points to the maker's mark, on a strip of browning paper inside the violin—but still, he says, even without it he would have known it by the color of the varnish, by the scroll, by the shape.

"Now Barrington reaches inside his pocket and produces an engraved business card, proclaiming him to be a preeminent dealer in rare and antique musical instruments. 'So this violin is rare?' asks mine host. 'Indeed it is,' says Barrington, still admiring it with awe, 'and worth in excess of a hundred thousand dollars, unless I miss my guess. Even as a dealer in such things I would pay fifty—no, seventy-five thousand dollars, good cash money for such an exquisite piece. I have a man on the West Coast who would buy it tomorrow, sight unseen, with one telegram, and pay whatever I asked for it.' And then he consults his watch, and his face falls. 'My train—' he says. 'I have scarcely enough time to catch my train! Good sir, when the owner of this inestimable instrument should return, please give him my card, for, alas, I must be away.' And with that, Barrington leaves, a man who knows that time and the train wait for no man.

"Mine host examines the violin, curiosity mingling with cupidity in his veins, and a plan begins to bubble up through his mind. But the minutes go by, and Abraham does not return. And now it is late, and through the door, shabby but proud, comes our Abraham, our fiddle-player, and he holds in his hands a wallet, a wallet that has seen better days, a wallet that has never contained more than a hundred dollars on its best day, and from it he takes the money to pay for his meal or his stay, and he asks for the return of his violin.

"Mine host puts the fiddle in its case on the counter, and Abraham takes it like a mother cradling her child. 'Tell me,' says the host (with the engraved card of a man who'll pay fifty thousand dollars, good cash money, burning in his inside breast pocket), 'how much is a violin like this worth? For my niece has a yearning on her to play the fiddle, and it's her birthday coming up in a week or so.'

"'Sell this fiddle?' says Abraham. 'I could never sell her. I've had her for twenty years I have, fiddled all over the country with her. And to tell the truth, she cost me all of five hundred dollars back when I bought her.'

"Mine host keeps the smile from his face. 'Five hundred dollars? What if I were to offer you a thousand dollars for it, here and now?'

"The fiddle player looks delighted, then crestfallen, and he says, 'But lordy, I'm a fiddle player, sir, it's all I know how to do. This fiddle knows me and she loves me, and my fingers know her so well I could play an air upon her in the dark. Where will I find another that sounds so fine? A thousand dollars is good money, but this is my livelihood. Not a thousand dollars, not for five thousand.'"

"Mine host sees his profits shrinking, but this is business, and you must spend money to make money. 'Eight thousand dollars,' he says. 'It's not worth that, but I've taken a fancy to it, and I do love and indulge my niece.'

"Abraham is almost in tears at the thought of losing his beloved fiddle, but how can he say no to eight thousand dollars?—especially when mine host goes to the wall safe, and removes not eight but nine thousand dollars, all neatly banded and ready to be slipped into the fiddle player's threadbare pocket. 'You're a good man,' he tells his host. 'You're a saint! But you must swear to take care of my girl!' and, reluctantly, he hands over his violin."

"But what if mine host simply hands over Barrington's card and tells Abraham that he's come into some good fortune?" asked Shadow.

"Then we're out the cost of two dinners," said Wednesday. He wiped the remaining gravy and leftovers from his plate with a slice of bread, which he ate with lip-smacking relish.

"Let me see if I've got it straight," said Shadow. "So Abraham leaves, nine thousand dollars the richer, and in the parking lot by the train station he and Barrington meet up. They split the money, get into Barrington's Model A Ford and head for the next town. I guess in the trunk of that car they must have a box filled with hundred-dollar violins."

"I personally made it a point of honor never to pay more than five dollars for any of them," said Wednesday. Then he turned to the hovering waitress. "Now, my dear, regale us with your description of the sumptuous desserts available to us on this, our Lord's natal day." He stared at her—it was almost a leer—as if nothing that she could offer him would be as toothsome a morsel as herself. Shadow felt deeply uncomfortable: it was like watching an old wolf stalking a fawn too young to know that if it did not run, and run now, it would wind up in a distant glade with its bones picked clean by the ravens.

The girl blushed once more and told them that dessert was apple pie, apple pie à la mode—"That's with a scoop of vanilla ice cream"—Christmas Cake, Christmas Cake à la mode, or a red and green whipped pudding. Wednesday stared into her eyes and told her that he would try the Christmas Cake à la mode. Shadow passed.

"Now, as grifts go," said Wednesday, "the Fiddle Game goes back three hundred years or more. And if you pick your chicken correctly you could still play it tomorrow anywhere in America."

"I thought you said that your favorite grift was no longer practical," said Shadow.

"I did indeed. However, that is not my favorite. It was fine and enjoyable, but not my favorite.[428] No, my favorite was one they called the Bishop Game. It had everything: excitement, subterfuge, portability, surprise. Perhaps, I think from time to time, perhaps with a little modification, it might . . ." He thought for a moment, then shook his head. "No. Its time has passed. It is, let us say, 1920, in a city of medium to large size—Chicago, perhaps, or New York, or Philadelphia. We are in a jeweler's emporium. A man dressed as a clergyman—and not just any clergyman, but a bishop, in his purple—enters and picks out a necklace, a gorgeous and glorious confection of diamonds and pearls, and pays for it with a dozen of the crispest hundred-dollar bills.

"There's a smudge of green ink on the topmost bill and the store owner, apologetically but firmly, sends the stack of bills to the bank on the corner to be checked. Soon enough, the store clerk returns with the bills. The bank says they are none of them counterfeit. The owner apologizes again, and the bishop is most gracious, he well understands the problem, there are such lawless and ungodly types in the world today, such immorality and lewdness abroad in the world—and shameless women, and now that the underworld has crawled out of the gutter and come to live on the screens of the picture palaces what more could anyone expect? And the necklace is placed in its case, and the store owner does his best not to ponder why a bishop of the church would be purchasing a twelve-hundred-dollar diamond necklace, nor why he would be paying good cash money for it.

"The bishop bids him a hearty farewell, and walks out on the street, only for a heavy hand to descend on his shoulder. 'Why, Soapy, yez spalpeen, up to your old tricks are you?' and a broad beat cop with an honest Irish face walks the bishop back into the jewelry store.

"'Beggin' your pardon, but has this man just bought anything from you?' asks the cop. 'Certainly not,' says the bishop. 'Tell him I have not.' 'Indeed he has,' says the

428. This sentence does not appear in the First Edition.

257

jeweler. 'He bought a pearl and diamond necklace from me—paid for it in cash as well.' 'Would you have the bills available, sir?' asks the cop.

"So the jeweler takes the twelve hundred-dollar bills from the cash register and hands them to the cop, who holds them up to the light and shakes his head in wonder. 'Oh, Soapy, Soapy,' he says, 'these are the finest that you've made yet! You're a craftsman, that you are!'

"A self-satisfied smile spreads across the bishop's face. 'You can't prove nothing,' says the bishop. 'And the bank said that they were on the level. It's the real green stuff.' 'I'm sure they did,' agrees the cop on the beat, 'but I doubt that the bank had been warned that Soapy Sylvester was in town, nor of the quality of the hundred-dollar bills he'd been passing in Denver and in St. Louis.' And with that he reaches into the bishop's pocket and pulls out the necklace. 'Twelve hundred dollars' worth of diamonds and pearls in exchange for fifty cents' worth of paper and ink,' says the policeman, who is obviously a philosopher at heart. 'And passing yourself off as a man of the church. You should be ashamed,' he says, as he claps the handcuffs on the bishop, who is obviously no bishop, and he marches him away, but not before he gives the jeweler a receipt for both the necklace and the twelve hundred counterfeit dollars. It's evidence, after all."

"Was it really counterfeit?" asked Shadow.

"Of course not! Fresh banknotes, straight from the bank, only with a thumbprint and a smudge of green ink on a couple of them to make them a little more interesting."

Shadow sipped his coffee. It was worse than prison coffee. "So the cop was obviously no cop. And the necklace?"

"Evidence," said Wednesday. He unscrewed the top from the salt-shaker, poured a little heap of salt on the table. "But the jeweler gets a receipt, and assurance that he'll get the necklace straight back as soon as Soapy comes to trial. He is congratulated on being a good citizen, and he watches, proudly, already thinking of the tale he'll have to tell at the next meeting of the Oddfellows[429] tomorrow night, as the policeman marches the man pretending to be a bishop out

429. Odd Fellows, or Oddfellows, also Odd Fellowship or Oddfellowship, is an international social/benevolent fraternity with local lodges (like the Masons or the Optimists). The American-based organization has about 600,000 members internationally; other Oddfellows organizations bring the international total to millions of members. It was first documented in 1730 in London.

of the store, twelve hundred dollars in one pocket, a twelve-hundred-dollar diamond necklace in the other, on their way to a police station that'll never see hide nor hair of either of them."

The waitress had returned to clear the table. "Tell me, my dear," said Wednesday. "Are you married?"

She shook her head.

"Astonishing that a young lady of such loveliness has not yet been snapped up." He was doodling with his fingernail in the spilled salt, making squat, blocky rune-like shapes. The waitress stood passively beside him, reminding Shadow less of a fawn and more of a young rabbit caught in an eighteen-wheeler's headlights, frozen in fear and indecision.

Wednesday lowered his voice, so much so that Shadow, only across the table, could barely hear him. "What time do you get off work?"

"Nine," she said, and swallowed. "Nine thirty latest."

"And what is the finest motel in this area?"

"There's a Motel 6,"[430] she said. "It's not much."

Wednesday touched the back of her hand, fleetingly, with the tips of his fingers, leaving crumbs of salt on her skin. She made no attempt to wipe them off. "To us," he said, his voice an almost inaudible rumble, "it shall be a pleasure-palace."

The waitress looked at him. She bit her thin lips, hesitated, then nodded and fled for the kitchen.

"C'mon," said Shadow. "She looks barely legal."

"I've never been overly concerned about legality," Wednesday told him. "Not as long as I get what I want.[431] Sometimes the nights are long and cold. And I need her, not as an end in herself, but to wake me up a little. Even King David knew that there is one easy prescription to get warm blood flowing through an old frame: take one virgin, call me in the morning."

Shadow caught himself wondering if the girl on night duty in the hotel back in Eagle Point had been a virgin. "Don't you ever worry about disease?" he asked. "What if you knock her up? What if she's got a brother?"

430. The Motel 6 chain of budget hospitality was founded in Santa Barbara in 1972, and the "6" originally reflected the rate of a base room. By 1980, the chain had expanded to 300 locations, and it now has facilities around the world. In 2018, Motel 6 ranked last in one prominent customer satisfaction survey, and, among other complaints, was allegedly aiding the U.S. government in tracking down illegal immigrants by reporting its guests to the Immigration and Customs Enforcement agency.

431. This and the next sentence do not appear in the First Edition.

432. This sentence does not appear in the First Edition.

433. As we will later see, Wednesday is lying about this.

434. This sentence does not appear in the First Edition.

435. In the Manuscript, the name is Jack Emerson, changed to Ainsell, with two *L*'s.

436. Where indeed? Although Gaiman warns in "Caveat, and Warning for Travelers," at p. 7, above, that he has "obscured" the location of Lakeside, readers have hunted inexhaustibly for the town. Gaiman has obscured it by providing contradictory locational clues: (1) Hinzelmann describes Lakeside as south of Rhinelander, a town about 40 miles south of the northern edge of Wisconsin, the Michigan border. Similarly, Mabel describes the Upper Peninsula of Michigan as being "to the northeast." (2) Chad Mulligan describes Stevens Point as south of Lakeside; Stevens Point is roughly in the center of Wisconsin. This is confirmed by his comment that Marguerite's ex-husband drove "up to Ironwood" or "down to Green Bay." Based on (1) and (2), then, Lakeside must be in the northeastern part of Wisconsin. (3) Earlier, the drive to Lakeside is described as follows: From a motel south of La Crosse, Wisconsin, Wednesday and Shadow drive "north and east." This is followed by Wednesday describing Shadow's upcoming bus trip as "north." This confirms Lakeside as being in the northeast corner of Wisconsin. Yet these clues are contradicted by a number of other points: (a) There is a real Lakeside, in Douglas County in northwest Wisconsin. However, that Lakeside is on the shores of Lake Superior, a complete misfit for the lake described as being "at the center of everything" in Lakeside. (b) References to County W and County Q place Lakeside near the town of Wisconsin Rapids, in Wood County (see note 520, below);

"No," said Wednesday. "I don't worry about diseases. I don't catch them. People like me avoid them.[432] Unfortunately, for the most part people like me fire blanks, so there's not a great deal of interbreeding. It used to happen in the old days. Nowadays, it's possible, but so unlikely as to be almost unimaginable. So no worries there.[433] And many girls have brothers, and fathers. Some even have husbands.[434] It's not my problem. Ninety-nine times out of a hundred, I've left town already."

"So we're staying here for the night?"

Wednesday rubbed his chin. "I shall stay in the Motel 6," he said. Then he put his hand into his coat pocket. He pulled out a front-door key, bronze-colored, with a card tag attached on which was typed an address: 502 NORTHRIDGE RD, APT #3. "You, on the other hand, have an apartment waiting for you, in a city far from here." Wednesday closed his eyes for a moment. Then he opened them, gray and gleaming and fractionally mismatched, and he said, "The Greyhound bus will be coming through town in twenty minutes. It stops at the gas station. Here's your ticket." He pulled out a folded bus ticket, passed it across the table. Shadow picked it up and looked at it.

"Who's Mike Ainsel?" he asked. That was the name on the ticket.[435]

"You are. Happy Christmas."

"And where's Lakeside?"[436]

"Your happy home in the months to come. And now, because good things come in threes . . ." He took a small, gift-wrapped package from his pocket, pushed it across the table. It sat beside the ketchup bottle with the black smears of dried ketchup on the top. Shadow made no move to take it.

"Well?"

Reluctantly, Shadow tore open the red wrapping paper, to reveal a fawn-colored calfskin wallet, shiny from use. It was obviously somebody's wallet. Inside the wallet was a driver's license with Shadow's photograph on it, in the name of Michael Ainsel, with a Milwaukee address, a MasterCard for M. Ainsel, and twenty crisp fifty-dollar bills. Shadow closed the wallet, put it into an inside pocket.

"Thanks," he said.

"Think of it as a Christmas bonus. Now, let me walk you down to the Greyhound. I shall wave to you as you ride the gray dog north."

They walked outside the restaurant. Shadow found it hard to believe how much colder it had gotten in the last few hours. It felt too cold to snow, now. Aggressively cold. This was a bad winter.

"Hey. Wednesday. Both of the scams you were telling me about—the violin scam and the bishop one, the bishop and the cop—" He hesitated, trying to form his thought, to bring it into focus.

"What of them?"

Then he had it. "They're both two-man scams. One guy on each side. Did you used to have a partner?" Shadow's breath came in clouds. He promised himself that when he got to Lakeside he would spend some of his Christmas bonus on the warmest, thickest winter coat that money could buy.

"Yes," said Wednesday. "Yes. I had a partner. A junior partner.[437] But, alas, those days are gone. *There's* the gas station, and *there*, unless my eye deceives me, is the bus." It was already signaling its turn into the parking lot. "Your address is on the key," said Wednesday. "If anyone asks, I am your uncle, and I shall be rejoicing in the unlikely name of Emerson Borson.[438] Settle in, in Lakeside, nephew Ainsel. I'll come for you within the week. We shall be traveling together. Visiting the people I have to visit. In the meantime, keep your head down and stay out of trouble."

"My car—?" said Shadow.

"I'll take good care of it. Have a good time in Lakeside," said Wednesday. He thrust out his hand, and Shadow shook it. Wednesday's hand was colder than a corpse's.

"Jesus," said Shadow. "You're cold."

"Then the sooner I am making the two-backed beast with the little hotsy-totsy lass from the restaurant in a back room of the Motel 6, the better." And he reached out his other hand and squeezed Shadow's shoulder.

Shadow experienced a dizzying moment of double vision:

however, this is in the center of the state. (c) Mulligan comments that runaways might go to the Twin Cities (rather than suggesting Milwaukee or Madison), suggesting a proximity to the northwestern part of Wisconsin rather than the northeastern. Jake La Jeunesse argues that these contradictions are deliberate. "*All* of these details describe Lakeside. If any single location cannot fit all the characteristics, then in order to reconcile all the discrepancies, Lakeside must exist nowhere because nowhere can fit the characteristics. Since the Greek term utopia translates to 'no place,' the town can be associated with the concept of utopia." "Locating Lakeside, Wisconsin: Neil Gaiman's *American Gods* and the American Small-town Utopia," pp. 54–55.

437. Odin had two frequent partners in his tales, Loki and Thor. Loki was known as the trickster, whose cleverness often landed him and his companions in trouble. Wednesday's use of the past tense suggests that he may be speaking of Thor, whom we know killed himself more than 80 years previously. Loki, as we know, has been in prison.

438. The human Bor was indeed said to be Odin's father; Bor was the offspring of the frost giant Ymir, the first of the supreme Norse gods. Gaiman's *Norse Mythology* calls him "the first being, a giant bigger than worlds, the ancestor of all giants." (p. 293) So: "Ymir's-son Bor's-son" . . . is not an unlikely name for Odin.

he saw the grizzled man facing him, squeezing his shoulder, but he saw something else: so many winters, hundreds and hundreds of winters, and a gray man in a broad-brimmed hat walking from settlement to settlement, leaning on his staff, staring in through windows at the firelight, at a joy and a burning life he would never be able to touch, never even be able to feel . . .

"Go," said Wednesday, his voice a reassuring growl. "All is well, and all is well, and all shall be well."

Shadow showed his ticket to the driver. "Hell of a day to be traveling," she said. And then she added, with a certain grim satisfaction, "Merry Christmas."

The bus was almost empty. "When will we get in to Lakeside?" asked Shadow.

"Two hours. Maybe a bit more," said the driver. "They say there's a cold snap coming." She thumbed a switch and the doors closed with a hiss and a thump.

Shadow walked halfway down the bus, put the seat back as far as it would go, and he started to think. The motion of the bus and the warmth combined to lull him, and before he was aware that he was becoming sleepy, he was asleep.

✢   ✢   ✢

IN THE EARTH, and under the earth. The marks on the wall were the red of wet clay: hand prints, finger-marks and, here and there, crude representations of animals and people and birds.

The fire still burned and the buffalo man still sat on the other side of the fire, staring at Shadow with huge eyes, eyes like pools of dark mud. The buffalo lips, fringed with matted brown hair, did not move as the buffalo voice said, "Well, Shadow? Do you believe yet?"

"I don't know," said Shadow. His mouth had not moved either, he observed. Whatever words were passing between the two of them were not being spoken, not in any way that Shadow understood speech. "Are you real?"

"Believe," said the buffalo man.

"Are you . . ." Shadow hesitated, and then he asked, "Are you a god too?"

The buffalo man reached one hand into the flames of the fire and he pulled out a burning brand. He held the brand in the middle. Blue and yellow flames licked his red hand, but they did not burn.

"This is not a land for gods," said the buffalo man. But it was not the buffalo man talking any more, Shadow knew, in his dream: it was the fire speaking, the crackling and the burning of the flame itself that spoke to Shadow in the dark place under the earth.

"This land was brought up from the depths of the ocean by a diver," said the fire. "It was spun from its own substance by a spider. It was shat by a raven. It is the body of a fallen father, whose bones are mountains, whose eyes are lakes.

"This is a land of dreams and fire," said the flame.

The buffalo man put the brand back on the fire.

"Why are you telling me this stuff?" said Shadow. "I'm not important. I'm not anything. I was an okay physical trainer, a really lousy smalltime crook and maybe not so good a husband as I thought I was . . ." He trailed off.

"How do I help Laura?" Shadow asked the buffalo man. "She wants to be alive again. I said I'd help her. I owe her that."

The buffalo man said nothing. He pointed up[439] with his soot-blackened palm facing Shadow, his index finger pointing toward the roof of the cave. Shadow's eyes followed. There was a thin, wintry light, coming from a tiny opening far above.

"Up there?" asked Shadow, wishing that one of his questions would be answered. "I'm supposed to go up there?"

The dream took him then, the idea becoming the thing itself, and Shadow was crushed into the rock and earth. He was like a mole, trying to push through the earth, like a badger, climbing through the earth, like a groundhog, pushing the earth out of his way, like a bear, but the earth was too hard, too dense, and his breath was coming in gasps, and soon he could go no further, dig and climb no more, and he knew then that he would die, somewhere in the deep place beneath the world.

439. In the First Edition, the sentence reads simply, "He pointed up toward the roof of the cave."

His own strength was not enough. His efforts became weaker. He knew that though his body was riding in a hot bus through cold woods if he stopped breathing here, beneath the world, he would stop breathing there as well, that even now his breath was coming in shallow panting gasps.

He struggled and he pushed, ever more weakly, each movement using precious air. He was trapped: could go no further, and could not return the way that he had come.

"Now bargain," said a voice in his mind.[440] It might have been his own voice. He could not tell.

"What do I have to bargain with?" Shadow asked. "I have nothing."

He could taste the clay now, thick and mud-gritty in his mouth[441]; he could taste the sharp mineral tang of the rocks that surrounded him.

And then Shadow said, "Except myself. I have myself, don't I?"

It seemed as if everything was holding its breath[442]—not just Shadow, but the whole world under the earth, every worm, every crevice, every cavern, holding its breath.

"I offer myself," he said.

The response was immediate. The rocks and the earth that had surrounded him began to push down on Shadow, squeezed him so hard that the last ounce of air in his lungs was crushed out of him. The pressure became pain, pushing him on every side[443], and he felt he was being mashed, a fern becoming coal. He reached the zenith of pain and hung there, cresting, knowing that he could take no more, that no one could take more than this,[444] and at that moment the spasm eased and Shadow could breathe again. The light above him had grown larger.

He was being pushed toward the surface.

As the next earth-spasm hit, Shadow tried to ride with it. This time he felt himself being pushed upward,[445] the pressure of the earth pushing him out, expelling him, pushing him closer to the light. And then a moment for a breath.

The spasms took him and rocked him, each harder, each more painful than the one before it.

He rolled and writhed through the earth, and now his

440. The balance of the paragraph does not appear in the First Edition.

441. The balance of the sentence does not appear in the First Edition.

442. The balance of the sentence does not appear in the First Edition.

443. The balance of the sentence does not appear in the First Edition.

444. This phrase about "no one" does not appear in the First Edition.

445. The balance of this paragraph and the next two paragraphs do not appear in the First Edition.

face was pushed against the opening, a gap in the rock scarcely larger than the span of his hand, through which a muted gray light came, and air, blessed air.

The pain, on that last awful contraction, was impossible to believe as he felt himself being squeezed, crushed and pushed through that unyielding rock gap, his bones shattering, his flesh becoming something shapeless and snakelike,[446] and as his mouth and ruined head cleared the hole he began to scream, in fear and pain.

He wondered, as he screamed, whether, back in the waking world, he was also screaming—if he were screaming in his sleep back on the darkened bus.

And as that final spasm ended Shadow was on the ground, his fingers clutching the red earth,[447] grateful only that the pain was over and he could breathe once more, deep lungfuls of warm, evening air.

He pulled himself into a sitting position, wiped the earth from his face with his hand and looked up at the sky. It was twilight, a long, purple twilight, and the stars were coming out, one by one, stars so much brighter and more vivid than any stars he had ever seen or imagined.

"Soon," said the crackling voice of the flame, coming from behind him, "they will fall. Soon they will fall and the star people will meet the earth people. There will be heroes among them, and men who will slay monsters and bring knowledge, but none of them will be gods. This is a poor place for gods."[448]

A blast of air, shocking in its coldness, touched his face. It was like being doused in ice water. He could hear the driver's voice saying that they were in Pinewood, anyone who needs a cigarette or wants to stretch their legs, we'll be stopping here for ten minutes then we'll be back on the road.

Shadow stumbled off the bus. They were parked outside another rural gas station, almost identical to the one they had left. The driver was helping a couple of teenage girls onto the bus, putting their suitcases away in the luggage compartment.

"Hey," the driver said, when she saw Shadow. "You're getting off at Lakeside, right?"

446. The word "snakelike" does not appear in the First Edition.

447. The balance of the sentence does not appear in the First Edition.

448. In the First Draft, this sentence does not appear, though Gaiman wrote in "We have no time for gods, here."

Shadow agreed, sleepily, that he was.

"Heck, that's a good town," said the bus-driver. "I think sometimes that if I were just going to pack it all in, I'd move to Lakeside. Prettiest town I've ever seen. You've lived there long?"

"My first visit."

"You have a pasty at Mabel's for me, you hear?"

Shadow decided not to ask for clarification. "Tell me," said Shadow, "was I talking in my sleep?"

"If you were, I didn't hear you." She looked at her watch. "Back on the bus. I'll call you when we get to Lakeside."

The two girls—he doubted that either of them was much more than fourteen years old—who had got on in Pinewood were now in the seat in front of him. They were friends, Shadow decided, eavesdropping without meaning to, not sisters. One of them knew almost nothing about sex, but knew a lot about animals, helped out or spent a lot of time at some kind of animal shelter, while the other was not interested in animals, but, armed with a hundred tidbits gleaned from the Internet and from daytime television, thought she knew a great deal about human sexuality. Shadow listened with a horrified and amused fascination to the one who thought she was wise in the ways of the world detail the precise mechanics of using Alka-Seltzer tablets to enhance oral sex.

He listened to both of them—the girl who liked animals, and the one who knew why Alka-Seltzer gave you more oral bang for your buck than, like, even Altoids—dishing the dirt on the current Miss Lakeside, who had, like, everybody knew, only gotten her greasy hands on the coronet and sash by flirtin' up to the judges.[449]

Shadow started to tune them out, blanked everything except the noise of the road, and now only fragments of conversation would come back every now and again.

Goldie is, like, such a good dog, and he was a purebred retriever, if only my dad would say okay, he wags his tail whenever he sees me.

It's Christmas, he has to let me use the snowmobile.

449. This paragraph does not appear in the First Edition.

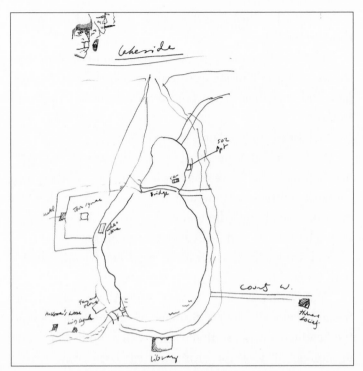

Lakeside (map by Neil Gaiman)

You can write your name with your tongue on the side of his thing.

I miss Sandy.

Yeah, I miss Sandy too.

Six inches tonight they said, but they just make it up, they make up the weather and nobody ever calls them on it . . .

And then the brakes of the bus were hissing and the driver was shouting "Lakeside!" and the doors clunked open. Shadow followed the girls out into the floodlit parking lot of a video store and tanning salon that functioned, Shadow guessed, as Lakeside's Greyhound station. The air was dreadfully cold, but it was a fresh cold. It woke him up. He stared at the lights of the town to the south and the west, and the pale expanse of a frozen lake to the east.

The girls were standing in the lot, stamping and blowing on their hands dramatically. One of them, the younger one, snuck a look at Shadow, smiled awkwardly when she realized that he had seen her do so.

450. This sentence does not appear in the First Edition.

"Merry Christmas," said Shadow. It seemed like a safe thing to say.[450]

"Yeah," said the other girl, perhaps a year or so older than the first, "merry Christmas to you too." She had carroty red hair and a snub nose covered with a hundred thousand freckles.

"Nice town you got here," said Shadow.

"We like it," said the younger one. She was the one who liked animals. She gave Shadow a shy grin, revealing blue rubber-band braces stretching across her front teeth. "You look like somebody," she told him, gravely. "Are you somebody's brother or somebody's son or something?"

"You are such a spaz, Alison," said her friend. "Everybody's somebody's son or brother or something."

"That wasn't what I meant," said Alison. Headlights framed them all for one brilliant white moment. Behind the headlights was a station wagon with a mother in it, and in moments it took the girls and their bags away, leaving Shadow standing alone in the parking lot.

"Young man? Anything I can do for you?" The old man was locking up the video store. He pocketed his keys. "Store ain't open Christmas," he told Shadow cheerfully. "But I come down to meet the bus. Make sure everything was okay. Couldn't live with myself if some poor soul'd found 'emselves stranded on Christmas Day." He was close enough that Shadow could see his face: old but contented, the face of a man who had sipped life's vinegar and found it, by and large, to be mostly whiskey, and good whiskey at that.

"Well, you could give me the number of the local taxi company," said Shadow.

"I could," said the old man, doubtfully, "but Tom'll be in his bed this time of night, and even if you could rouse him you'll get no satisfaction—I saw him down at the Buck Stops Here earlier this evening, and he was very merry. Very merry indeed. Where is it you're aiming to go?"

Shadow showed him the address tag on the door key.

"Well," he said, "that's a ten-, mebbe a twenty-minute walk over the bridge and around. But it's no fun when it's this cold, and when you don't know where you're going it always seems longer—you ever notice that? First time takes forever, and then ever after it's over in a flash?"

"Yes," said Shadow. "I've never thought of it like that. But I guess it's true."

The old man nodded. His face cracked into a grin. "What the heck, it's Christmas. I'll run you over there in Tessie."

"Tessie?" said Shadow, and then he said, "I mean, thank you."[451]

"You're welcome."

Shadow followed the old man to the road, where a huge old roadster was parked. It looked like something that gangsters might have been proud to drive in the Roaring Twenties, running boards and all. It was a deep dark color under the sodium lights[452] that might have been red and might have been green. "This is Tessie," the old man said. "Ain't she a beaut?" He patted her proprietarily, where the hood curved up and arched over the front nearside wheel.

"What make is she?" asked Shadow.

"She's a Wendt Phoenix.[453] Wendt went under in '31, name was bought by Chrysler, but they never made any more Wendts. Harvey Wendt, who founded the company, was a local boy. Went out to California, killed himself in, oh, 1941, '42. Great tragedy."

The car smelled of leather and old cigarette smoke—not a fresh smell, but as if enough people had smoked enough cigarettes and cigars in the car over the years that the smell of burning tobacco had become part of the fabric of the car. The old man turned the key in the ignition and Tessie started first time.

"Tomorrow," he told Shadow, "she goes into the garage. I'll cover her with a dust sheet, and that's where she'll stay until spring. Truth of the matter is, I shouldn't be driving her right now, with the snow on the ground."

"Doesn't she ride well in snow?"

"Rides just fine. It's the salt they put on the roads to melt the snow. Rusts these old beauties faster than you could believe. You want to go door to door, or would you like the moonlight grand tour of the town?"

"I don't want to trouble you—"

451. This sentence and the next do not appear in the First Edition.

452. Sodium lamps were first produced commercially by Philips in Holland in 1932. The lamp works by creating an electric arc through vaporized sodium metal. While the lamps are cost-efficient and can be readily seen at a distance, sodium lamps—especially low-pressure sodium lamps, the most common type—produce a limited spectrum of light and so inhibit color vision at night.

453. A fictional car, made by a fictional person. The car is a Packard in the Manuscript. Gaiman expressed to this editor in a private conversation that he delighted in the pun of a car called a "Wendt."

454. As we will learn later, Hinzelmann is a hinzelmann. The *heinselmännchen* are the legendary sprites/house gnomes of the town of Cologne, Germany. It is told that during the night, the *heinselmännchen* would do all of the work of the townspeople, allowing them to be lazy. One day, the tailor's wife set a trap for them, spreading peas on the floor. When the trap was discovered, the *heinselmännchen* were so angry that they refused to do any more work for the townspeople. This editor was taught by his father, who was born near Cologne, that whenever anything was found to be out of place or lost in the morning, it was clearly a prank played by the *heinselmännchen*.

For more on the *heinselmännchen*, see note 866, below.

455. His name is Harry in the Manuscript.

456. Hinzelmann's saying has "gone viral," as is said, since *American Gods* was first published, and bookstores across America—especially those in financial difficulties—have adopted the motto.

"It's no trouble. You get to be my age, you're grateful for the least wink of sleep. I'm lucky if I get five hours a night nowadays—wake up and my mind is just turning and turning. Where are my manners? My name's Hinzelmann.[454] I'd say, call me Richie,[455] but round here folks who know me just call me plain Hinzelmann. I'd shake your hand, but I need two hands to drive Tessie. She knows when I'm not paying attention."

"Mike Ainsel," said Shadow. "Pleased to meet you, Hinzelmann."

"So we'll go round the lake. Grand tour," said Hinzelmann.

Main Street, which they were on, was a pretty street, even at night, and it looked old-fashioned in the best sense of the word—as if, for a hundred years, people had been caring for that street and they had not been in a hurry to lose anything they liked.

Hinzelmann pointed out the town's two restaurants as they passed them (a German restaurant and what he described as "Greek, Norwegian, bit of everything, and a popover at every plate"); he pointed out the bakery and the bookstore ("What I say is, a town isn't a town without a bookstore. It may call itself a town, but unless it's got a bookstore, it knows it's not foolin' a soul").[456] He slowed Tessie as they passed the library so Shadow could get a good look at it. Antique gaslights flickered over the doorway—Hinzelmann proudly called Shadow's attention to them. "Built in the 1870s by John Henning, local lumber baron. He wanted it called the Henning Memorial Library, but when he died they started calling it the Lakeside Library, and I guess it'll be the Lakeside Library now until the end of time. Isn't it a dream?" He couldn't have been prouder of it if he had built it himself. The building reminded Shadow of a castle, and he said so. "That's right," agreed Hinzelmann. "Turrets and all. Henning wanted it to look like that on the outside. Inside they still have all the original pine shelving. Miriam Shultz wants to tear the insides out and modernize, but it's on the register of historic places, and there's not a damn thing she can do."

They drove around the south side of the lake. The town

circled the lake, which was a thirty-foot drop below the level of the road. Shadow could see the patches of white ice dulling the surface of the lake with, here and there, a shiny patch of water reflecting the lights of the town.

"Looks like it's freezing over," he said.

"It's been frozen over for a month now," said Hinzelmann. "The dull spots are snowdrifts and the shiny spots are ice. It froze just after Thanksgiving in one cold night, froze smooth as glass. You do much ice-fishing, Mister Ainsel?"

"Never."

"Best thing a man can do. It's not the fish you catch, it's the peace of mind that you take home at the end of the day."

"I'll remember that." Shadow peered down at the lake through Tessie's window. "Can you actually walk on it already?"

"You can walk on it. Drive on it too, but I wouldn't want to risk it yet. It's been cold up here for six weeks," said Hinzelmann. "But you also got to allow that things freeze harder and faster up here in northern Wisconsin than they do most anyplace else there is. I was out hunting once—hunting for deer, and this was oh, thirty, forty years back, and I shot at a buck, missed him and sent him running off through the woods—this was over acrost the north end of the lake, up near where you'll be living, Mike. Now he was the finest buck I ever did see, twenty point, big as a small horse, no lie. Now, I'm younger and feistier back then than I am now, and though it had started snowing before Halloween that year, now it was Thanksgiving and there was clean snow on the ground, fresh as anything, and I could see the buck's footprints. It looked to me like the big fellow was heading for the lake in a panic.

"Well, only a damn fool tries to run down a buck, but there am I, a damn fool, running after him, and there he is, standing in the lake, in oh, eight, nine inches of water, and he's just looking at me. That very moment, the sun goes behind a cloud, and the freeze comes—temperature must have fallen thirty degrees in ten minutes, not a word of a lie. And that old stag, he gets ready to run, and he can't move. He's frozen into the ice.

"Die heinzelmännchen"
Theodor Hosemann, Deutsche Gedichte mit Illustrationen, *ca. 1870*

"Me, I just walk over to him slowly. You can see he wants to run, but he's iced in and it just isn't going to happen. But there's no way I can bring myself to shoot a defenseless critter when he can't get away—what kind of man would I be if I done that, heh? So I takes my shotgun and I fires off one shell, straight up into the air.

"Well the noise and the shock is enough to make that buck just about jump out of his skin, and seein' that his legs are iced in, that's just what he proceeds to do. He leaves his hide and his antlers stuck to the ice, while he charges back into the woods, pink as a newborn mouse and shivering fit to bust.

"I felt bad enough for that old buck that I talked the Lakeside Ladies Knitting Circle into making him something warm to wear all the winter, and they knitted him an all-over one-piece woolen suit, so he wouldn't freeze to death. Course the joke was on us, because they knitted him a suit of bright orange wool so no hunter ever shot at it. Hunters in these parts wear orange at hunting season," he added, helpfully. "And if you think there's a word of a lie in that, I can prove it to you. I've got the antlers up on my rec room wall to this day."

Shadow laughed, and the old man smiled the satisfied smile of a master craftsman. They pulled up outside a brick building with a large wooden deck, from which golden holiday lights hung and twinkled invitingly.

"That's Five-oh-two," said Hinzelmann. "Apartment three would be on the top floor, round the other side, overlooking the lake. There you go, Mike."

"Thank you, Mister Hinzelmann. Can I give you anything toward gas?"

"Just Hinzelmann. And you don't owe me a penny. Merry Christmas from me and from Tessie."

"Are you sure you won't accept anything?"

The old man scratched his chin. "Tell you what," he said. "Sometime in the next week or so I'll come by and sell you some tickets. For our raffle. Charity. For now, young man, you can be getting on to bed."

Shadow smiled. "Merry Christmas, Hinzelmann," he said.

The old man shook Shadow's hand with one red-knuckled hand. It felt as hard and as callused as an oak branch. "Now, you watch the path as you go up there, it's going to be slippery. I can see your door from here, at the side there, see it? I'll just wait in the car down here until you're safely inside. You just give me the thumbs-up when you're in okay, and I'll drive off."

He kept the Wendt idling until Shadow was safely up the wooden steps on the side of the house, and had opened the apartment door with his key. The door to the apartment swung open. Shadow made a thumbs-up sign and the old man in the Wendt—*Tessie*, thought Shadow, and the thought of a car with a name made him smile one more time— Hinzelmann and Tessie swung around and made their way back across the bridge.

Shadow shut the front door. The room was freezing. It smelled of people who had gone away to live other lives, and of all they had eaten and dreamed. He found the thermostat and cranked it up to 70 degrees. He went into the tiny kitchen, checked the drawers, opened the avocado-colored refrigerator, but it was empty. No surprise there. At least the fridge smelled clean inside, not musty.

There was a small bedroom with a bare mattress in it, beside the kitchen, next to an even tinier bathroom that was mostly shower stall. An aged cigarette butt floated in the toilet bowl, staining the water brown. Shadow flushed it away.

He found sheets and blankets in a closet, and made the bed. Then he took off his shoes, his jacket and his watch, and he climbed into the bed fully dressed, wondering how long it would take him to get warm.

The lights were off, and there was silence, mostly, nothing but the hum of the refrigerator, and somewhere in the building, a radio playing. He lay there in the darkness, wondering if he had slept himself out on the Greyhound, if the hunger and the cold and the new bed and the craziness of the last few weeks would combine to keep him awake that night.

In the stillness he heard something snap like a shot. A branch, he thought, or the ice. It was freezing out there.

He wondered how long he would have to wait until Wednesday came for him. A day? A week? However long he had, he knew he had to focus on something in the meantime. He would start to work out again, he decided, and practice his coin sleights and palms until he was smooth as anything (*Practice all your tricks*, somebody whispered inside his head, in a voice that was not his own, *all of them but one, not the trick that poor dead Mad Sweeney showed you, dead of exposure and the cold and of being forgotten and surplus to requirements, not that trick. Oh not that one*).

But this *was* a good town. He could feel it.

He thought of his dream, if it had been a dream, that first night in Cairo. He thought of Zorya . . . what the hell was her name? The midnight sister. And then he thought of Laura . . .

It was as if thinking of her opened a window in his mind. He could see her. He could, somehow, see her.

She was in Eagle Point, in the backyard outside her mother's big house.

She stood in the cold, which she did not feel any more, or which she felt all the time, she stood outside the house that her mother had bought in 1989 with the insurance money after Laura's father, Harvey McCabe, had passed on, a heart attack while straining on the can, and she was staring in, her cold hands pressed against the glass, her breath not fogging it, not at all, watching her mother, and her sister and her sister's children and husband in from Texas, home for Christmas. Out in the darkness, that was where Laura was, unable not to look.

Tears prickled in Shadow's eyes, and he rolled over in his bed.

Wednesday, he thought, and with just a thought a window opened and he was watching from a corner of the room in the Motel 6, watching two figures thrusting and rolling in the semi-darkness.[457]

He felt like a Peeping Tom, turned his thoughts away, willed them to come back to him. He could imagine huge black wings pounding through the night toward him,[458] he could see the lake spread out below him as the wind blew down from the Arctic, breathed its cold on the land, forcing any remaining liquids to become solid,[459] prying jack-frost fingers a hundred times colder than the fingers of any corpse.

Shadow's breath came shallowly now,[460] and he was no longer cold. He could hear a wind rising, a bitter screaming around the house, and for a moment he thought he could hear words on the wind.

If he was going to be anywhere, he might as well be here, he thought, and then he slept.

457. This paragraph does not appear in the First Edition.

458. The preceding phrase does not appear in the First Edition.

459. This and the preceding phrase do not appear in the First Edition.

460. The balance of this sentence does not appear in the First Edition.

Meanwhile. A Conversation.

D*ingdong.*
"Miz Crow?"
"Yes."
"You are Samantha Black Crow?"
"Yes."
"Do you mind if we ask you a few questions, ma'am?"[461]
"Yeah. I do, actually."
"There's no need to take that attitude, ma'am."
"Are you cops? What are you?"
"My name is Town. My colleague here is Mister Road. We're investigating the disappearance of two of our associates."
"What were their names?"
"I'm sorry?"
"Tell me their names. I want to know what they were called. Your associates. Tell me their names and maybe I'll help you."
". . . Okay. Their names were Mister Stone, and Mister Wood. Now, can we ask you some questions?"
"Do you guys just see things and pick names? 'Oh, you be Mister Sidewalk, he's Mister Carpet, say hello to Mister Airplane'?"
"Very funny, young lady. First question: we need to know if you've seen this man. Here. You can hold the photograph."

461. This sentence and the next do not appear in the First Edition.

"Whoa. Straight on and profile, with numbers on the bottom . . . and big. He's cute, though. What did he do?"[462]

"He was mixed up in a small-town bank robbery, as a driver, some years ago. His two colleagues decided to keep all the loot for themselves and ran out on him. He got angry. Found them. Came close to killing them with his hands. The state cut a deal with the men he hurt: they testified and got a suspended sentence, Shadow here got six years. He served three. You ask me, guys like that, they should just lock them up and throw away the key."

"I've never heard anyone say that in real life, you know. Not out loud."

"Say what, Miz Crow?"

"Loot. It's not a word you ever hear people say. Maybe in movies people say it. Not for real."

"This isn't a movie, Miz Crow."

"Black Crow. It's Miz Black Crow. My friends call me Sam."

"Got it, Sam. Now about this man—"

"But you aren't my friends. You can call me Miz Black Crow."

"Listen, you snot-nosed little—"

"It's okay, Mister Road. Sam here—pardon, ma'am,—I mean, Miz Black Crow wants to help us. She's a law-abiding citizen."

"Ma'am, we know you helped Shadow. You were seen with him, in a white Chevy Nova. He gave you a ride. He bought you dinner. Did he say anything that could help us in our investigation? Two of our best men have vanished."

"I never met him."

"You met him. Please don't make the mistake of thinking we're stupid. We aren't stupid."

"Mm. I meet a lot of people. Maybe I met him and forgot already."

"Ma'am, it really is to your advantage to cooperate with us."

"Otherwise, you'll have to introduce me to your friends Mister Thumbscrews and Mister Pentothal?"

"Ma'am, you aren't making this any easier on yourself."

462. The following is the only place in the text in which we learn the official details of Shadow's crime.

"Gee. I'm sorry. Now, is there anything else? Cos I'm going to say 'buh-bye now' and close the door and I figure you two are going to go and get into Mister Car and drive away."

"Your lack of cooperation has been noted, ma'am."

"Buh-bye now."

Click.

CHAPTER TEN

I'll tell you all my secrets
But I lie about my past
So send me off to bed for evermore
　　　—TOM WAITS,
　　　　"Tango Till They're Sore"[463]

whole life in darkness, surrounded by filth,
that was what Shadow dreamed, his first night
in Lakeside.[464] *A child's life, long ago and far*
away, in a land across the ocean, in the lands where the
sun rose. But this life contained no sunrises, only dimness
by day and blindness by night.

Nobody spoke to him. He heard human voices, from out-
side, but he could understand human speech no better than
he understood the howling of the owls or the yelps of dogs.
He remembered, or thought he remembered, one night,
half a lifetime ago, when one of the big people had entered,
quietly, and had not cuffed him or fed him, but had picked
him up to her breast and embraced him. She smelled good.
She had made crooning noises.[465] *Hot drops of water had*
fallen from her face to his. He had been scared, and had
wailed loudly in his fear.

She put him down on the straw, hurriedly, and left the
hut, fastening the door behind her.

He remembered that moment, and he treasured it, just

463. This is the chorus of Waits's 1985 song, from the album *Rain Dogs.*

464. The dream does not appear in the First Draft, only a note in Gaiman's hand to insert a dream—"something of the kobold—a dream of childhood and knives perhaps."

465. This sentence does not appear in the First Edition.

279

as he remembered the sweetness of a cabbage-heart, the tart taste of plums, the crunch of apples, the greasy delight of roasted fish.

And now he saw the faces in the firelight, all of them looking at him as he was led out from the hut for the first time, which was the only time. So that was what people looked like. Raised in darkness, he had never seen faces. Everything was so new. So strange. The bonfire light hurt his eyes. They pulled on the rope around his neck, to lead him to the space between the two bonfires, where the man waited for him.

And when the first blade was raised in the firelight, what a cheer went up from the crowd and the child from the darkness began to laugh and laugh with them, in delight and in freedom.

And then the blade came down.

Shadow opened his eyes and realized that he was hungry and cold, in an apartment with a layer of ice clouding the inside of the window glass. His frozen breath, he thought. He got out of bed, pleased he did not have to get dressed. He scraped at a window with a fingernail as he passed, felt the ice collect under the nail, then melt to water.

He tried to remember his dream, but remembered nothing but misery and darkness.

He put on his shoes. He figured he would walk into the town center, walk over the bridge across the northern end of the lake, if he had the geography of the town right. He put on his thin jacket, remembering his promise to himself that he would buy a warm winter coat, opened the apartment door and stepped out onto the wooden deck. The cold took his breath away: he breathed in, and felt every hair in his nostrils freeze into rigidity. The deck gave him a fine view of the lake, irregular patches of gray surrounded by an expanse of white.

466. This sentence does not appear in the First Edition.

He wondered how cold it was.[466] The cold snap had come, that was for sure. It could not be much above zero, and it would not be a pleasant walk, but he was certain he could make it into town without too much trouble. What did Hinzelmann say last night—a ten-minute walk? And

Shadow was a big man. He would walk briskly and keep himself warm.

He set off south, heading for the bridge.

Soon he began to cough, a dry, thin cough, as the bitterly cold air touched his lungs. Soon his ears and face and lips hurt, and then his feet hurt. He thrust his ungloved hands deep into his coat pockets, clenched his fingers together trying to find some warmth. He found himself remembering Low Key Lyesmith's tall tales of the Minnesota winters—particularly the one about a hunter treed by a bear during a hard freeze who took out his dick and pissed an arching yellow stream of steaming urine that was already frozen hard before it hit the ground, then slid down the rock-hard frozen-piss-pole to freedom. A wry smile at the memory and another dry, painful cough.

Step after step after step. He glanced back. The apartment building was not as far away as he had expected.

This walk, he decided, was a mistake. But he was already three or four minutes from the apartment, and the bridge over the lake was in sight. It made as much sense to press on as to go home (and then what? Call a taxi on the dead phone? Wait for spring? He had no food in the apartment, he reminded himself).

He kept walking, revising his estimates of the temperature downward as he walked. Minus 10? Minus 20? Minus 40, maybe, that strange point on the thermometer when Celsius and Fahrenheit say the same thing. Probably not that cold. But then there was wind chill, and the wind was now hard and steady and continuous, blowing over the lake, coming down from the Arctic across Canada.

He remembered, enviously, the chemical hand- and foot-warmers he had taken from the men in the black train. He wished he had them now.

Ten more minutes of walking, he guessed, and the bridge seemed to be no nearer. He was too cold to shiver. His eyes hurt. This was not simply cold: this was science fiction. This was a story set on the dark side of Mercury, back when they thought Mercury had a dark side.[467] This was somewhere out on rocky Pluto, where the sun is just another star, shin-

467. Mercury *does* have a dark side, inasmuch as it rotates around its axis only every 59 Earth days. Temperatures on the side away from the Sun drop to almost 300 degrees Fahrenheit below zero (about −184 degrees Celsius).

468. Written in 1934 by Felix Bernard and Richard B. Smith, the song begins, "Sleigh bells ring, are you listening? / In the lane, snow is glistening . . ." It has been covered by more than 200 artists and, despite no mention of the holiday, is a popular tune during the Christmas season.

469. The title song from the eponymous film, first released in 1965. The chorus ends, "Won't you please, please help me!"

ing only a little more brightly in the darkness. This, thought Shadow, is just a hair away from the places where air comes in buckets and pours just like beer.

The occasional cars that roared past him seemed unreal: spaceships, little freeze-dried packages of metal and glass, inhabited by people dressed more warmly than he was. An old song his mother had loved, "Winter Wonderland,"[468] began to run through his head, and he hummed it through closed lips, kept pace to it as he walked.

He had lost all sensation in his feet. He looked down at his black leather shoes, at the thin cotton socks, and began, seriously, to worry about frostbite.

This was beyond a joke. This had moved beyond foolishness, slipped over the line into genuine twenty-four-karat Jesus-Christ-I-fucked-up-big-time territory. His clothes might as well have been netting or lace: the wind blew through him, froze his bones and the marrow in his bones, froze the lashes of his eyes, froze the warm place under his balls, which were retreating into his pelvic cavity.

Keep walking, he told himself. *Keep walking. I can stop and drink a pail of air when I get home.* A Beatles song started in his head, and he adjusted his pace to match it. It was only when he got to the chorus that he realized that he was humming "Help!"[469]

He was almost at the bridge now. Then he had to walk across it, and he would still be another ten minutes from the stores on the west of the lake—maybe a little more . . .

A dark car passed him, stopped, then reversed in a foggy cloud of exhaust smoke and came to a halt beside him. A window slid down, and the haze and steam from the window mixed with the exhaust to form a dragon's breath that surrounded the car. "Everything okay here?" said a cop inside.

Shadow's first, automatic instinct was to say *Yup, everything's just fine and jim-dandy thank you, officer, nothing's happening here. Move on. Nothing to see.* But it was too late for that, and he started to say, "I think I'm freezing. I was walking into Lakeside to buy food and clothes, but I underestimated the length of the walk"—he was that far through the sentence in his head, when he realized that all that had come out was "F-f-freezing," and a chattering noise, and he said, "So s-sorry. Cold. Sorry."

The cop pulled open the back door of the car, and said, "You get in there this moment and warm yourself up, okay?" Shadow climbed in gratefully, and he sat in the back and rubbed his hands together, trying not to worry about frost-bitten toes. The cop got back in the driver's seat. Shadow stared at him through the metal grille. Shadow tried not to think about the last time he'd been in the back of a police car, or to notice that there were no door handles in the back, and to concentrate instead on rubbing life back into his hands. His face hurt and his red fingers hurt, and now, in the warmth, his toes were starting to hurt once more. That was, Shadow figured, a good sign.

The cop put the car in drive and moved off. "You know, that was," he said, not turning to look at Shadow, just talking a little louder, "if you'll pardon me saying so, a real stupid thing to do. You didn't hear any of the weather advisories? It's minus thirty out there. God alone knows what the wind chill is, minus sixty, minus seventy, although I figure when you're down at minus thirty, wind chill's the least of your worries."

"Thanks," said Shadow. "Thanks for stopping. Very, very grateful."

"Woman in Rhinelander went out this morning to fill her bird feeder in her robe and carpet slippers and she froze, literally froze, to the sidewalk. She's in intensive care now. It was on the radio this morning. You're new in town." It was almost a question, but the man knew the answer already.

"I came in on the Greyhound last night. Figured today I'd buy myself some warm clothes, food, and a car. Wasn't expecting this cold."

"Yeah," said the cop. "It took me by surprise as well. I was too busy worrying about global warming. I'm Chad Mulligan. I'm the chief of police here in Lakeside."

"Mike Ainsel."

"Hi, Mike. Feeling any better?"

"A little, yes."

"So where would you like me to take you first?"

Shadow put his hands down to the hot air stream, painful on his fingers, then he pulled them away. Let it happen in its own time. "Can you just drop me off in the town center?"

"Wouldn't hear of it. Long as you don't need me to drive a getaway car for your bank robbery I'll happily take you wherever you need to go. Think of it as the town welcome wagon."

"Where would you suggest we start?"

"You only moved in last night."

"That's right."

"You eaten breakfast yet?"

"Not yet."

"Well, that seems like a heck of a good starting place to me," said Mulligan.

They were over the bridge now, and entering the northwest side of the town. "This is Main Street," said Mulligan, "and this," he said, crossing Main Street and turning right, "is the town square."

Even in the winter the town square was impressive, but Shadow knew that this place was meant to be seen in summer: it would be a riot of color, of poppies and irises and flowers of every kind, and the clump of birch trees in one corner would be a green and silver bower. Now it was a colorless place, beautiful in a skeletal way, the band shell empty, the fountain turned off for the winter, the brownstone city hall capped by white snow.

". . . and this," concluded Chad Mulligan, bringing the car to a stop outside a high glass-fronted old building on the west of the square, "is Mabel's."

He got out of the car, opened the rear door for Shadow. The two men put their heads down against the cold and the wind, and hurried across the sidewalk and into a warm room, fragrant with the smells of new-baked bread, of pastry and soup and bacon.

The place was almost empty. Mulligan sat down at a table and Shadow sat opposite him. He suspected that Mulligan was doing this to get a feel for the stranger in town. Then again, the police chief might simply be what he appeared: friendly, helpful, good.

A woman bustled over to their table, not fat but *big,* a big woman in her sixties, her hair bottle-bronze.

"Hello, Chad," she said. "You'll want a hot chocolate while you're thinking." She handed them two laminated menus.

"No cream on the top, though," he agreed. "Mabel knows me too well," he said to Shadow. "What'll it be, pal?"

"Hot chocolate sounds great," said Shadow. "And I'm happy to have the whipped cream on the top."

"That's good," said Mabel. "Live dangerously, hon. Are you going to introduce me, Chad? Is this young man a new officer?"

"Not yet," said Chad Mulligan, with a flash of white teeth. "This is Mike Ainsel. He moved to Lakeside last night. Now, if you'll excuse me." He got up, walked to the back of the room, through the door marked POINTERS. It was next to a door marked SETTERS.[470]

"You're the new man in the apartment up on Northridge Road. The old Pilsen place. Oh yes," she said, happily, "I know *just* who you are. Hinzelmann was by this morning for his morning pasty, he told me all about you. You boys only having hot chocolate or you want to look at the breakfast menu?"

"Breakfast for me," said Shadow. "What's good?"

"Everything's good," said Mabel. "I make it. But this is the furthest south and east of the yoopie you can get pasties, and they are particularly good. Warming and filling too. My specialty."

Shadow had no idea what a pasty was, but he said that would be fine, and in a few moments Mabel returned with a plate with what looked like a folded-over pie on it. The lower half was wrapped in a paper napkin. Shadow picked it up with the napkin and bit into it: it was warm and filled with meat, potatoes, carrots, onions. "First pasty I've ever had," he said. "It's real good."

"They're a yoopie thing," she told him. "Mostly you need to be at least up Ironwood way to get one. The Cornish

470. "Pointers" and "setters" restrooms first appear in print in Donald E. Westlake's fourth comic-crime novel featuring the thief John Dortmunder, *Nobody's Perfect,* first published in 1977.

471. Little can be definitely said about the history of the pasty, other than its origins in Cornwall, though there are traces of pasties in accounts, chronicles, and cookbooks from England and France as early as the thirteenth century. The traditional recipe is a circle of dough with a filling of meat, onions, "Swede" (rootabaga), and potatoes, cooked in the dough, though nineteenth-century recipes have been found for "full meal" or "two-course" pasties that are half meat-and-potatoes and half jam or fruit. The pasty was probably originally made as lunch ("croust" or "crib" in the Cornish language) for Cornish tin miners, whose jobs kept them down in the mines during the midday break. One explanation for the shape of the pasty is this: Though the men were filthy with dirt and tin leavings (including arsenic), the folded crust of the pasty permitted them to eat the food without touching it and, when finished, discard the dirty pastry covering. The knockers (see note 245, above) were appeased, it was said, by these offerings. Other cultural historians point out that the pasty's dense, folded pastry could stay warm for 8 to 10 hours and, if carried next to the body, could help warm the miners.

As tin mining in Cornwall waned in the early nineteenth century, Cornish miners (Cousin Jacks) migrated to various regions around the world where their mining expertise was appreciated. The pasty followed. In the Upper Peninsula, pasties are a significant tourist attraction, including an annual Pasty Fest in Calumet, Michigan, in early July. Curiously, when Finnish immigrants followed the Cornish miners in 1864 and began to work the Copper Country mines of the Peninsula, the Finns (and other ethnic groups) adopted the pasty. When Finnish immigration into the Peninsula peaked at the end of the nineteenth century, the newly arrived settlers found their countrymen baking pasties and assumed that it was a Finnish invention. Today, the pasty is strongly associated with Finnish culture in upper Michigan.

men who came over to work the iron mines brought them over." 471

"Yoopie?"

"Upper Peninsula. UP. Yoopie. Where the Yoopers come from. 472 It's the little chunk of Michigan to the northeast."

The chief of police came back. He picked up the hot chocolate and slurped it. "Mabel," he said, "are you forcing this nice young man to eat one of your pasties?"

"It's good," said Shadow. It was, too—a savory delight wrapped in hot pastry.

"They go straight to the belly," said Chad Mulligan, patting his own stomach. "I warn you. Okay. So, you need a car?" With his parka off, he was revealed as a lanky man with a round, apple-belly gut on him. He looked harassed and competent, more like an engineer than a cop.

Shadow nodded, mouth full.

"Right. I made some calls. Justin Liebowitz's selling his jeep, wants four thousand dollars for it, will settle for three. The Gunthers have had their Toyota 4Runner for sale for eight months, ugly sonofabitch, but at this point they'd probably pay you to take it out of their driveway. And if you don't care about ugly, it's got to be a great deal. I used the phone in the men's room, left a message for Missy Gunther down at Lakeside Realty, but she wasn't in yet, probably getting her hair done down at Sheila's."

The pasty remained good as Shadow chewed his way through it. It was astonishingly filling. "Stick-to-your-ribs food," as his mother would have said. "Sticks to your sides."

"So," said Chief of Police Chad Mulligan, wiping the hot chocolate foam from around his lips. "I figure we stop off next at Henning's Farm and Home Supplies, get you a real winter wardrobe, swing by Dave's Finest Food, so you can fill your larder, then I'll drop you up by Lakeside Realty. If you can put down a thousand up front for the car they'll be happy, otherwise five hundred a month for four months should see them okay. It's an ugly car, like I said, but if the kid hadn't painted it purple it'd be a ten-thousand-dollar car, and reliable, and you'll need something like that to get around this winter, you ask me."

"This is very good of you," said Shadow. "But shouldn't you be out catching criminals, not helping newcomers? Not that I'm complaining, you understand."

Mabel chuckled. "We all tell him that," she said.

Mulligan shrugged. "It's a good town," he said, simply. "Not much trouble. You'll always get someone speeding within city limits—which is a good thing, as traffic tickets pay my wages. Friday, Saturday nights you get some jerk who gets drunk and beats on a spouse—and that one can go both ways, believe me. Men and women. And I learned when I was on the force in Green Bay, I'd rather attend a bank robbery than a domestic in a big city.[473] But out here things are quiet. They call me out when someone's locked their keys in their vehicle. Barking dogs. Every year there's a couple of high school kids caught with weed behind the bleachers. Biggest police case we've had here in five years was when Dan Schwartz got drunk and shot up his own trailer, then he went on the run, down Main Street, in his wheelchair, waving this darn shotgun, shouting that he would shoot anyone who got in his way, that no one would stop him from getting to the interstate. I think he was on his way to Washington to shoot the president. I still laugh whenever I think of Dan heading down the interstate in that wheelchair of his with the bumper sticker on the back. MY JUVENILE DELINQUENT IS SCREWING YOUR HONOR STUDENT. You remember, Mabel?"

She nodded, lips pursed. She did not seem to find it as funny as Mulligan did.

"What did you do?" asked Shadow.

"I talked to him. He gave me the shotgun. Slept it off down at the jail. Dan's not a bad guy, he was just drunk and upset."

Shadow paid for his own breakfast and, over Chad Mulligan's halfhearted protests, both hot chocolates.

Henning's Farm and Home was a warehouse-sized building on the south of the town that sold everything from tractors to toys (the toys, along with the Christmas ornaments, were already on sale). The store was bustling with post-Christmas shoppers. Shadow recognized the younger of the

The depth of international devotion to the pasty may be seen on websites such as www .cornishpasties.org.uk and www.pasty.com.

472. This sentence does not appear in the First Edition.

473. This sentence does not appear in the First Edition.

girls who had sat in front of him on the bus. She was trailing after her parents. He waved at her and she gave him a hesitant, blue-rubber-banded smile. Shadow wondered idly what she'd look like in ten years' time.

Probably as beautiful as the girl at the Henning's Farm and Home checkout counter, who scanned in his purchases with a chattering hand-held gun, capable, Shadow had no doubt, of ringing up a tractor if someone drove it through.

"Ten pairs of long underwear?" said the girl. "Stocking up, huh?" She looked like a movie starlet.

Shadow felt fourteen again, and tongue-tied and foolish. He said nothing while she rang up the thermal boots, the gloves, the sweaters, and the goose-down-filled coat.

He had no wish to put the credit card that Wednesday had given him to the test, not with Chief of Police Mulligan standing helpfully beside him, so he paid for everything in cash. Then he took his bags into the men's restroom, and came out wearing many of his purchases.

"Looking good, big fella," said Mulligan.

"At least I'm warm," said Shadow, and outside, in the parking lot, although the wind burned cold on the skin of his face, the rest of him was warm enough. At Mulligan's invitation, he put his shopping bags in the back of the police car, and rode in the passenger seat, in the front.

"So, what do you do, Mister Ainsel?" asked the chief of police. "Big guy like you. What's your profession, and will you be practicing it in Lakeside?"

Shadow's heart began to pound, but his voice was steady. "I work for my uncle. He buys and sells stuff all over the country. I just do the heavy lifting."

"Does he pay well?"

"I'm family. He knows I'm not going to rip him off, and I'm learning a little about the trade on the way. Until I figure out what it is I really want to do." It was coming out of him with conviction, smooth as a snake. He knew everything about big Mike Ainsel in that moment, and he liked Mike Ainsel. Mike Ainsel had none of the problems that Shadow had. Ainsel had never been married. Mike Ainsel had never been interrogated on a freight train by Mr. Wood and Mr. Stone. Televisions did not speak to Mike Ainsel. (*You want to see Lucy's tits?* asked a voice in his head.) Mike Ainsel didn't have bad dreams, or believe that there was a storm coming.

He filled his shopping basket at Dave's Finest Foods, doing what he thought of as a gas-station stop—milk, eggs, bread, apples, cheese, cookies. Just some food. He'd do a real one later. As Shadow moved around, Chad Mulligan said hello to people and introduced Shadow to them. "This is Mike Ainsel, he's taken the empty apartment at the old Pilsen place. Up around the back," he'd say. Shadow gave up trying to remember names. He just shook hands with people and smiled, sweating a little, uncomfortable in his insulated layers in the hot store.

Chad Mulligan drove Shadow across the street to Lakeside Realty. Missy Gunther, her hair freshly set and lacquered, did not need an introduction—she knew exactly who Mike Ainsel was. Why that nice Mr. Borson, his uncle Emerson, such a nice man, he'd been by, what, about six, eight weeks ago now, and rented the apartment up at the old Pilsen place, and wasn't the view just to die for up there? Well, honey, just wait until the spring, and we're so lucky, so many of the lakes in this part of the world go bright green from the algae in the summer, it would turn your stomach, but our lake, well, come fourth of July you could still practically *drink* it, and Mr. Borson had paid for a whole year's lease in advance, and as for the Toyota 4Runner, she couldn't believe that Chad Mulligan still remembered it, and yes, she'd be delighted to get rid of it. Tell the truth, she'd pretty much resigned herself to giving it to Hinzelmann as this year's klunker and just taking the tax write-off, not that the car was a *klunker*, far from it, no, it was her son's car before he went to school in Green Bay, and, well, he'd painted it purple one day and, ha-ha, she certainly hoped that Mike Ainsel liked purple, that was all she had to say, and if he didn't she wouldn't blame him . . .

Chief of Police Mulligan excused himself near the middle of this litany. "Looks like they need me back at the office, good meeting you, Mike," he said, and he moved

Shadow's shopping bags into the back of Missy Gunther's station wagon.

Missy drove Shadow back to her place, where, in the drive, he saw an elderly SUV. The blown snow had bleached half of it to a blinding white, while the rest of it was painted the kind of drippy purple that someone would need to be very stoned, very often, to even begin to be able to find attractive.

Still, the car started up on the first try, and the heater worked, although it took almost ten minutes of running the engine with the heater on full before it even started to change the interior of the car from unbearably cold to merely chilly. While this was happening, Missy Gunther took Shadow into her kitchen—excuse the mess, but the little ones just leave their toys all over after Christmas and she just doesn't have the heart, would he care for some leftover turkey dinner? Last year they did goose but this year it was a big old turkey,[474] well, coffee then, won't take a moment to brew a fresh pot—and Shadow took a large red toy car off a window seat and sat down, while Missy Gunther asked if he had met his neighbors yet, and Shadow confessed that he hadn't.

There were, he was informed, while the coffee dripped and brewed, four other inhabitants of his apartment building—back when it was the Pilsen place the Pilsens lived in the downstairs flat and rented out the upper two flats, now their apartment, that was the downstairs one[475] and that was taken by a couple of young men, Mr. Holz and Mr. Neiman, they actually are a couple and when she said *couple,* Mr. Ainsel, heavens, we have all kinds here, more than one kind of tree in the forest, although mostly those kind of people wind up in Madison or the Twin Cities, but truth to tell, nobody here gives it a second thought. They're in Key West for the winter, they'll be back in April, he'll meet them then. The thing about Lakeside is that it's a good town. Now next door to Mr. Ainsel, that's Marguerite Olsen and her little boy, a sweet lady, sweet, sweet lady, but she's had a hard life, still sweet as pie, and she works for the *Lakeside News.* Not the most exciting newspaper in

474. The beginning of this sentence does not appear in the First Edition.

475. This clarification does not appear in the First Edition.

the world, but truth to tell Missy Gunther thought that was probably the way most folk around here liked it.

Oh, she said, and poured him coffee, she just wished that Mr. Ainsel could see the town in the summer or late in the spring, when the lilacs and the apple and the cherry blossoms were out, she thought there was nothing like it for beauty, nothing like it anywhere in the world.

Shadow gave her a five-hundred-dollar deposit, and he climbed up into the car and started to back it up, out of her front yard and onto the driveway proper. Missy Gunther tapped on his front window. "This is for you," she said. "I nearly forgot." She handed him a buff envelope. "It's kind of a gag. We had them printed up a few years back. You don't have to look at it now."

He thanked her, and drove, cautiously, back into the town. He took the road that ran around the lake. He wished he could see it in the spring, or the summer, or the fall: it would be very beautiful, he had no doubt of that.

In ten minutes he was home.

He parked the car out on the street and walked up the outside steps to his cold apartment. He unpacked his shopping, put the food into the cupboards and the fridge, and then he opened the envelope Missy Gunther had given him.

It contained a passport. Blue, laminated cover and, inside, a proclamation that *Michael Ainsel* (his name handwritten in Missy Gunther's precise handwriting) was a citizen of Lakeside. There was a map of the town on the next page. The rest of it was filled with discount coupons for various local stores.

"I think I may like it here," said Shadow, aloud. He looked out of the icy window at the frozen lake. "If it ever warms up."

There was a bang at the front door at around 2:00 P.M. Shadow had been practicing the Sucker Vanish with a quarter, tossing it from one hand to the other undetectably. His hands were cold enough and clumsy enough that he kept dropping the coin onto the table, and the knock at the door made him drop it again.

He went to the door and opened it.

A moment of pure fear: the man at the door wore a black mask which covered the lower half of his face. It was the kind of mask that a bank robber might wear on TV, or a serial killer from a cheap movie might wear to scare his victims. The top of the man's head was covered by a black knit cap.

Still, the man was smaller and slighter than Shadow, and he did not appear to be armed. And he wore a bright plaid coat, of the kind that serial killers normally avoid.

"Ih hihelhan," said the visitor.

"Huh?"

The man pulled the mask downward, revealing Hinzelmann's cheerful face. "I said, it's Hinzelmann. You know, I don't know what we did before they came up with these masks. Well, I do remember what we did. Thick knitted caps that went all around your face, and scarves and you don't want to know what else. I think it's a miracle what they come up with these days. I may be an old man, but I'm not going to grumble about progress, not me."

He finished this speech by thrusting a basket at Shadow, filled high with local cheeses, bottles, jars, and several small salamis that proclaimed themselves to be venison summer sausage, and by coming inside. "Merry Day after Christmas," he said. His nose and ears and cheeks were red as raspberries, mask or no mask. "I hear you already ate a whole one of Mabel's pasties. Brought you a few things."

"That's very kind of you," said Shadow.

"Kind, nothing. I'm going to stick it to you next week for the raffle. The chamber of commerce runs it, and I run the chamber of commerce. Last year we raised almost seventeen thousand dollars for the children's ward of Lakeside Hospital."

"Well, why don't you put me down for a ticket now?"

"It don't start until the day the klunker hits the ice," said Hinzelmann. He looked out of Shadow's window toward the lake. "Cold out there. Must have dropped fifty degrees last night."

"It happened really fast," agreed Shadow.

"We used to pray for freezes like this back in the old

days," said Hinzelmann. "My daddy told me.[476] When the settlers were first coming into these parts, farming people and lumber people, long before ever the mining people came out, although the mines never really happened in this county, which they could have done, for there's iron enough under there . . ."

"You'd pray for days like this?" interrupted Shadow.

"Well, yah, it was the only way the settlers survived back then. Weren't enough food for everyone, and you couldn't just go down to Dave's and fill up your shopping trolley in the old days, no, sir. So my grampaw, he got to thinking, and when a really cold day like this come along he'd take my grammaw, and the kids, my uncle and my aunt and my daddy—he was the youngest—and the serving girl and the hired man, and he'd go down with them to the creek, give 'em a little rum-and-herbs drink, it was a recipe he'd got from the old country, then he'd pour creek water over them. Course they'd freeze in seconds, stiff and blue as so many popsicles. He'd haul them to a trench they'd already dug and filled with straw, and he'd stack 'em down there, one by one, like so much cordwood in the trench, and he'd pack straw around them, then he'd cover the top of the trench with two-b'-fours to keep the critters out—in those days there were wolves and bears and all sorts you never see any more around here, no hodags though, that's just a story about the hodags[477] and I wouldn't ever stretch your credulity by telling you no stories, no, sir,—he'd cover the trench with two-b'-fours and the next snowfall would cover it up completely, save for the flag he'd planted to show him where the trench was.

"Then my grampaw would ride through the winter in comfort and never have to worry about running out of food or out of fuel. And when he saw that the true spring was coming he'd go to the flag, and he'd dig his way down through the snow, and he'd move the two-b'-fours, and he'd carry them in one by one and set the family in front of the fire to thaw. Nobody ever minded except one of the hired men who lost half an ear to a family of mice who nibbled it off one time my grampaw didn't push those two-b'-fours all

476. The balance of this paragraph does not appear in the First Edition.

477. In 1893, Eugene Shephard, a well-known Wisconsin surveyor, announced the discovery of a beast near Rhinelander, Wisconsin, with "the head of a frog, the grinning face of a giant elephant, thick short legs set off by huge claws, the back of a dinosaur, and a long tail with spears at the end." Shephard, who termed it a "hodag," and a group of his friends reported that, with the use of dynamite, they had killed the beast. The newspaper ran a photo of the kill.

When the Smithsonian Institute announced that it would send a team of scientists to examine the unlikely creature, Shephard admitted the hoax, but the hodag lives on as the official mascot of the local high school.

A hodag, in front of the Rhinelander chamber of commerce
Wisconsin Chamber of Commerce (Photo by Gourami Watcher, 2013, CCA-3.0 Share-Alike license, https://commons .wikimedia.org/wiki/File:Hodag_002.jpg)

the way closed. Of course, in those days we had *real* winters. You could do that back then. These pussy winters we get nowadays it don't hardly get cold enough."

"No?" asked Shadow. He was playing straight-man, and enjoying it enormously.

"Not since the winter of '49 and you'd be too young to remember that one. *That* was a winter. I see you bought yourself a vee-hicle."

"Yup. What do you think?"

"Truth to tell, I never liked that Gunther boy. I had a trout stream down in the woods a way, on back of my property, way back, well it's town land but I'd put down stones in the river, made little pools and places where the trout liked to live. Caught me some beauties too—one fellow must have been pretty much thirty inches long, and that little Gunther so-an'-so he kicked down each of the pools and threatened to report me to the DNR.[478] Now he's in Green Bay, and soon enough he'll be back here. If there were any justice in the world he'd've gone off into the world as a winter runaway, but nope, sticks like a cockleburr to a woolen vest." He began to arrange the contents of Shadow's welcome basket on the counter. "This is Katherine Powdermaker's crab apple jelly. She's been giving me a pot for Christmas for longer than you've been alive, and the sad truth is I've never opened a one. They're down in my basement, forty, fifty pots. Maybe I'll open one and discover that I like the stuff. Meantime, here's a pot for you. Maybe you'll like it."

Shadow put the jar away in the fridge, along with the other presents that Hinzelmann had brought him. "What's this?" he asked, holding up a tall, unlabeled bottle filled with a greenish buttery substance.[479]

"Olive oil. That's how it looks when it gets this cold. Don't worry, it'll cook up fine."

"Okay. What are winter runaways?"

"Mm." The old man pushed his woolen cap above his ears, rubbed his temple with a pink forefinger. "Well, it ain't unique to Lakeside—we're a good town, better than most,

---

478. The "Department of Natural Resources."

479. This and the next two paragraphs do not appear in the First Edition.

but we're not perfect. Some winters, well, maybe a kid gets a bit stir-crazy, when it gets so cold that you can't go out, and the snow's so dry that you can't make so much as a snowball without it crumbling away . . ."

"They run off?"

The old man nodded, gravely. "I blame the television, showing all the kids things they'll never have—*Dallas* and *Dynasty* and *Beverly Hills* and *Hawaii Five-O,* all of that nonsense.[480] I've not had a television since the fall of '83, except for a black-and-white set I keep in the closet for if folk come in from out of town and there's a big game on."

"Can I get you anything, Hinzelmann?"

"Not coffee. Gives me heartburn. Just water." Hinzelmann shook his head. "Biggest problem in this part of the world is poverty. Not the poverty we had in the Depression but something more in . . . what's the word, means it creeps in at the edges, like cock-a-roaches?"

"*Insidious*?"

"Yeah. Insidious. Logging's dead. Mining's dead. Tourists don't drive further north than the Dells, 'cept for a handful of hunters and some kids going to camp on the lakes—and they aren't spending their money in the towns."

"Lakeside seems kind of prosperous, though."

The old man's blue eyes blinked. "And believe me, it takes a lot of work," he said. "Hard work. But this is a good town, and all the work all the people here put into it is worthwhile. Not that my family weren't poor as kids. Ask me how poor we was as kids."

Shadow put on his straight-man face and said, "How poor were you as kids, Mister Hinzelmann?"

"Just Hinzelmann, Mike. We were so poor that we couldn't afford a fire. Come New Year's Eve my father would suck on a peppermint, and us kids, we'd stand around with our hands outstretched, basking in the glow."

Shadow made a rim-shot noise. Hinzelmann put on his ski-mask and did up his huge plaid coat, pulled out his car keys from his pocket and then, last of all, pulled on his great gloves. "You get too bored up here, you just come down

480. Hinzelmann means *Beverly Hills 90210.* The other shows all had ended by 1991; *90210* aired until 2000 and was not on the air in 1983, when Hinzelmann last owned a television. In the First Edition, only the first two shows are mentioned, while the Manuscript lists the first three.

to the store and ask for me. I'll show you my collection of hand-tied fishing flies. Bore you so much that getting back here will be a relief." His voice was muffled, but audible.

"I'll do that," said Shadow with a smile. "How's Tessie?"

"Hibernating. She'll be out in the spring. You take care now, Mister Ainsel." And he closed the door behind him as he left.

The apartment grew ever colder.

Shadow put on his coat and his gloves. Then he put on his boots. He could hardly see through the windows now for the ice on the inside of the panes which turned the view of the lake into an abstract image.

His breath was clouding in the air.

He went out of his apartment onto the wooden deck and knocked on the door next door. He heard a woman's voice shouting at someone *to for heaven's sake shut up and turn that television down*—a kid he thought, adults don't shout like that at other adults, not with that tone in their voice.[481] The door opened and a tired woman with very long, very black hair was staring at him warily.

"Yes?"

"How do you do, ma'am. I'm Mike Ainsel. I'm your next-door neighbor."

Her expression did not change, not by a hair. "Yes?"

"Ma'am. It's freezing in my apartment. There's a little heat coming out of the grate, but it's not warming the place up, not at all."

She looked him up and down, then a ghost of a smile touched the edges of her lips and she said, "Come in, then. If you don't there'll be no heat in here, either."

He stepped inside her apartment. Plastic, multicolored toys were strewn all over the floor. There were small heaps of torn Christmas wrapping paper by the wall. A small boy sat inches away from the television set, a video of the Disney *Hercules* playing, an animated satyr stomping and shouting his way across the screen. Shadow kept his back to the TV set.

"Okay," she said. "This is what you do. First you seal the windows, you can buy the stuff down at Henning's, it's just

481. The last phrase does not appear in the First Edition.

like Saran wrap but for windows. Tape it to the windows, then if you want to get fancy you run a blow-dryer on it, it stays there the whole winter. That stops the heat leaving through the windows. Then you buy a space heater or two. The building's furnace is old, and it can't cope with the real cold. We've had some easy winters recently, I suppose we should be grateful." Then she put out her hand. "Marguerite Olsen."

"Good to meet you," said Shadow. He pulled off a glove and they shook hands. "You know, ma'am, I'd always thought of Olsens as being blonder than you."

"My ex-husband was as blond as they came. Pink and blond. Couldn't tan at gunpoint."

"Missy Gunther told me you write for the local paper."

"Missy Gunther tells everybody everything. I don't see why we need a local paper with Missy Gunther around." She nodded. "Yes. Some news reporting here and there, but my editor writes most of the news. I write the nature column, the gardening column, an opinion column every Sunday and the 'News From the Community' column which tells, in mind-numbing detail, who went to dinner with who for fifteen miles around. Or is that *whom*?"

"*Whom*," said Shadow, before he could stop himself. "It's the objective case."

She looked at him with her black eyes, and Shadow experienced a moment of pure déjà vu. *I've been here before,* he thought.

No, she reminds me of someone.

"Anyway, that's how you heat up your apartment," she said.

"Thank you," said Shadow. "When it's warm you and your little one must come over."

"His name's Leon," she said. "Good meeting you, Mister . . . I'm sorry . . ."

"Ainsel," said Shadow. "Mike Ainsel."

"And what sort of a name is Ainsel?" she asked.

Shadow had no idea. "My name," he said. "I'm afraid I was never very interested in family history."

"Norwegian, maybe?" she said.

"We were never close," he said. Then he remembered Uncle Emerson Borson, and added, "On that side, anyway."

✦ ✦ ✦

BY THE TIME that Mr. Wednesday arrived, Shadow had put clear plastic sheeting across all the windows and had one space heater running in the main room and one in the bedroom at the back. It was practically cozy.

"What the hell is that purple piece of shit you're driving?" asked Wednesday, by way of greeting.

"Well," said Shadow, "you drove off with my white piece of shit. Where is it, by the way?"

"I traded it in in Duluth," said Wednesday. "You can't be too careful. Don't worry—you'll get your share when all this is done."

"What am I doing here?" asked Shadow. "In Lakeside, I mean. Not in the world."

Wednesday smiled his smile, the one that made Shadow want to hit him. "You're living here because it's the last place they'll look for you. I can keep you out of sight here."

"By *they* you mean the black hats?"

"Exactly. I'm afraid the House on the Rock is now out of bounds. It's a little difficult, but we'll cope. Now it's just stamping our feet and flag-waving, caracole and saunter until the action starts—a little later than any of us expected. I think they'll hold off until spring. Nothing big can happen until then."

"How come?"

"Because they may babble on about micro-milliseconds and virtual worlds and paradigm shifts and what-have-you, but they still inhabit this planet and are still bound by the cycle of the year. These are the dead months. A victory in these months is a dead victory."

"I have no idea what you're talking about," said Shadow. That was not entirely true. He had a vague idea, and he hoped it was wrong.

"It's going to be a bad winter, and you and I are going to use our time as wisely as we can. We shall rally our troops and pick our battleground."

"Okay," said Shadow. He knew that Wednesday was telling him the truth, or a part of a truth. War was coming. No, that was not it: the war had already begun. The battle was coming. "Mad Sweeney said that he was working for you when we met him that first night. He said that before he died."

"And would I have wanted to employ someone who could not even best a sad case like that in a bar fight? But never fear, you've repaid my faith in you a dozen times over. Have you ever been to Las Vegas?"

"Las Vegas, Nevada?"

"That's the one."

"No."

"We're flying in there from Madison later tonight, on a gentleman's red-eye, a charter plane for High Rollers. I've convinced them that we should be on it."

"Don't you ever get tired of lying?" asked Shadow. He said it gently, curiously.

"Not in the slightest. Anyway, it's true. We are playing for the highest stakes of all. It shouldn't take us more than a couple of hours to get to Madison, the roads are clear. So lock your door and turn off the heaters. It would be a terrible thing if you burned down the house in your absence."

"Who are we going to see in Las Vegas?"

Wednesday told him.

Shadow turned off the heaters, packed some clothes into an overnight bag, then turned back to Wednesday and said, "Look, I feel kind of stupid. I know you just told me who we're going to see, but I dunno. I just had a brain-fart or something. It's gone. Who is it again?"

Wednesday told him once more.

This time Shadow almost had it. The name was there on the tip of his mind. He wished he'd been paying closer attention when Wednesday told him. He let it go.[482]

"Who's driving?" he asked Wednesday.

"You are," said Wednesday. They walked out of the house, down the wooden stairs and the icy path to where a black Lincoln town car was parked.

Shadow drove.

482. The following is the second appearance in the text of the "nameless god," first seen in the back seat of the car at the House on the Rock (see note 314, above). For the details of his identity, see note 814, below.

299

✢   ✢   ✢

Entering the casino one is beset at every side by invitation— invitations such that it would take a man of stone, heartless, mindless, and curiously devoid of avarice, to decline them. Listen: a machine gun rattle of silver coins as they tumble and spurt down into a slot machine tray and overflow onto monogrammed carpets is replaced by the siren clangor of the slots, the jangling, blippeting chorus swallowed by the huge room, muted to a comforting background chatter by the time one reaches the card tables, the distant sounds only loud enough to keep the adrenaline flowing through the gamblers' veins.

There is a secret that the casinos possess, a secret they hold and guard and prize, the holiest of their mysteries. For most people do not gamble to win money, after all, although that is what is advertised, sold, claimed and dreamed. But that is merely the easy lie that allows the gamblers to lie to themselves, the big lie that gets them through the enormous, ever-open, welcoming doors.

The secret is this: people gamble to lose money. They come to the casinos for the moment in which they feel alive, to ride the spinning wheel and turn with the cards and lose themselves, with the coins, in the slots. They want to know they matter. They may brag about the nights they won, the money they took from the casino, but they treasure, secretly treasure, the times they lost. It's a sacrifice, of sorts.

The money flows through the casino in an uninterrupted stream of green and silver, streaming from hand to hand, from gambler to croupier, to cashier, to the management, to security, finally ending up in the Holy of Holies, the innermost sanctum, the Counting Room. And it is here, in the counting room of this casino, that you come to rest, here, where the greenbacks are sorted, stacked, indexed, here in a space that is slowly becoming redundant as more and more of the money that flows through the casino is imaginary: an electrical sequence of ons and offs, sequences that flow down telephone lines.

In the Counting Room you see three men, counting money under the glassy stare of the cameras they can see, the insectile gazes of the tiny cameras they cannot see. During the course of one shift each of the men counts more money than he will see in all the pay packets of his life. Each man, when he sleeps, dreams of counting money, of stacks and paper bands and numbers which climb inevitably, which are sorted and lost. Each of the three men has idly wondered, not less than once a week, how to evade the casino's security systems and run off with as much money as he could haul; and, reluctantly, each man has inspected the dream and found it impractical, has settled for a steady paycheck, avoided the twin specters of prison and an unmarked grave.

And here, in the sanctum sanctorum, there are the three men who count the money, and there are the guards who watch and who bring money and take it away; and then there is another person. His charcoal-gray suit is immaculate, his hair is dark, he is clean-shaven, and his face, and his demeanor, are, in every sense, forgettable. None of the other men has even observed that he is there, or if they have noticed him, they have forgotten him on the instant.

As the shift ends the doors are opened, and the man in the charcoal suit leaves the room and walks, with the guards, through the corridors, their feet shushing along the monogrammed carpets. The money, in strongboxes, is wheeled to an interior loading bay, where it is loaded into armored cars. As the ramp door swings open, to allow the armored car out onto the early streets of Las Vegas, the man in the charcoal suit walks, unnoticed, through the doorway, and saunters up the ramp, out onto the sidewalk. He does not even glance up to see the imitation of New York on his left.

Las Vegas has become a child's picture book dream of a city—here a storybook castle, there a sphinx-flanked black pyramid beaming white light into the darkness as a landing beam for UFOs, and everywhere neon oracles and twisting screens predict happiness and good fortune, announce singers and comedians and magicians in residence or on their way, and the lights always flash and beckon and call. Once every hour a volcano erupts in light and flame. Once every hour a pirate ship sinks a man o' war.

The man in the charcoal suit ambles comfortably along the sidewalk, feeling the flow of the money through the town. In the summer the streets are baking, and each store doorway he passes breathes wintry A/C out into the sweaty warmth and chills the sweat on his face. Now, in the desert winter, there's a dry cold, which he appreciates. In his mind the movement of money forms a fine lattice-work, a three-dimensional cat's-cradle of light and motion. What he finds attractive about this desert city is the speed of movement, the way the money moves from place to place and hand to hand: it's a rush for him, a high, and it pulls him like an addict to the street.

A taxi follows him slowly down the street, keeping its distance. He does not notice it; it does not occur to him to notice it: he is so rarely noticed himself that he finds the concept that he could be being followed almost inconceivable.

It's four in the morning, and he finds himself drawn to a hotel and casino that has been out of style for thirty years, still running until tomorrow or six months from now when they'll implode it and knock it down and build a pleasure palace where it was, and forget it forever. Nobody knows him, nobody remembers him, but the lobby bar is tacky and quiet, and the air is blue with old cigarette smoke and someone's about to drop several million dollars on a poker game in a private room upstairs. The man in the charcoal suit settles himself in the bar several floors below the game, and is ignored by a waitress. A Muzak version of "Why Can't He Be You"[483] *is playing, almost subliminally. Five Elvis Presley impersonators, each man wearing a different colored jumpsuit, watch a late-night rerun of a football game on the bar TV.*[484]

A big man in a light gray suit sits at the man in the charcoal suit's table, and, noticing him even if she does not notice the man in the charcoal suit, the waitress, who is too thin to be pretty, too obviously anorectic to work

483. A song recorded by Patsy Cline in 1962, written by Hank Cochran. Among its verses is the following, a fitting tribute to the "nameless god":

> *He's not the one who dominates my*
> > *mind and soul*
> *And I should love him so, 'cause he loves*
> > *me, I know*
> *But his kisses leave me cold*
> *He sends me flowers, calls on the hour,*
> > *just to prove his love*
> *And my friends say when he's around,*
> > *I'm all he speaks of*
> *And he does all the things that you*
> > *would never do*
> *He loves me too, his love is true*
> *Why can't he be you*

484. There are numerous academic and literary studies of the phenomenon of "Elvis impersonators," tribute artists who ape the look and performances of recording star Elvis Presley. The most comprehensive is probably Gilbert B. Rodman's *Elvis After Elvis: The Posthumous Career of a Living Legend* (New York: Routledge, 1996). According to *The Guinness Book of Records*, the largest gathering of Elvis impersonators took place in 2014 when 895 impersonators assembled at a casino in Cherokee, North Carolina.

Luxor or the Tropicana, and who is counting the minutes until she gets off work, comes straight over and smiles. He grins widely at her. "You're looking a treat tonight, m'dear, a fine sight for these poor old eyes," he says, and, scenting a large tip, she smiles broadly at him. The man in the light gray suit orders a Jack Daniel's for himself and a Laphroaig and water for the man in the charcoal suit sitting beside him.

"You know," says the man in the light gray suit, when his drink arrives, "the finest line of poetry ever uttered in the history of this whole damn country was said by Canada Bill Jones in 1853, in Baton Rouge, while he was being robbed blind in a crooked game of faro. George Devol, who was, like Canada Bill, not a man who was averse to fleecing the odd sucker, drew Bill aside and asked him if he couldn't see that the game was crooked. And Canada Bill sighed, and shrugged his shoulders, and said, 'I know. But it's the only game in town.' And he went back to the game."[485]

Dark eyes stare at the man in the light gray suit distrustfully. The man in the charcoal suit says something in reply. The man in the light suit, who has a graying reddish beard, shakes his head.

"Look," he says, "I'm sorry about what went down in Wisconsin. But I got you all out safely, didn't I? No one was hurt."

The man in the dark suit sips his Laphroaig and water, savoring the marshy taste, the body-in-the-bog quality of the whisky. He asks a question.

"I don't know. Everything's moving faster than I expected. Everyone's got a hard-on for the kid I hired to run errands—I've got him outside, waiting in the taxi. Are you still in?"

The man in the dark suit replies.

The bearded man shakes his head. "She's not been seen for two hundred years. If she isn't dead she's taken herself out of the picture."

Something else is said.

"Look," says the bearded man, knocking back his Jack Daniel's. "You come in, be there when we need you, and I'll

485. The story is from George Devol's *Forty Years a Gambler on the Mississippi* (Cincinnati: Devol & Haynes, 1887). William "Canada Bill Jones" (1837–1877) was reputed to be the best three-card monte dealer on the river. Born in Yorkshire, England, he migrated to Canada at the age of 20 and made his reputation. Canada Bill died of consumption in Reading, Pennsylvania, a pauper—his funeral expenses were allegedly covered by the gamblers of Chicago.

486. Soma (named from the Sanskrit word meaning to distill or extract) is, in ancient Vedic tradition, a ritualistic drink associated with immortality and light. While it was clearly drunk by humans, it was also imbibed by gods and may be said to be the "drink of the gods." Soma was extracted from a plant which scholars have failed to definitely identify, but which might be cannabis or psychoactive mushrooms. Aldous Huxley, in his 1932 novel, *Brave New World*, gave the name "soma" to the drug used by the government to control the masses.

take care of you. Whaddayou want? Soma? I can get you a bottle of Soma.[486] *The real stuff."*

The man in the dark suit stares. Then he nods his head, reluctantly, and makes a comment.

"Of course I am," says the bearded man, smiling like a knife. "What do you expect? But look at it this way: it's the only game in town." He reaches out a paw-like hand and shakes the other man's well-manicured hand. Then he walks away.

The thin waitress comes over, puzzled: there's now only one man at the corner table, a sharply dressed man with dark hair in a charcoal-gray suit. "You doing okay?" she asks. "Is your friend coming back?"

The man with the dark hair sighs, and explains that his friend won't be coming back, and thus she won't be paid for her time, or for her trouble. And then, seeing the hurt in her eyes, and taking pity on her, he examines the golden threads in his mind, watches the matrix, follows the money until he spots a node, and tells her that if she's outside Treasure Island at 6:00 A.M., thirty minutes after she gets off work, she'll meet an oncologist from Denver who will just have won $40,000 at a craps table, and will need a mentor, a partner, someone to help him dispose of it all in the forty-eight hours before he gets on the plane home.

The words evaporate in the waitress's mind, but they leave her happy. She sighs and notes that the guys in the corner have done a runner, and have not even tipped her; and it occurs to her that, instead of driving straight home when she gets off shift, she's going to drive over to Treasure Island; but she would never, if you asked her, be able to tell you why.

✳   ✳   ✳

"SO WHO WAS that guy you were seeing?" asked Shadow as they walked back down the Las Vegas concourse. There were slot machines in the airport. Even at this time of the morning people stood in front of them, feeding them coins. Shadow wondered if there were those who never left the airport, who got off their planes, walked along the Jetway into the airport building and stopped there, trapped by the spinning images and the flashing lights; people who would stay in the airport until they had fed their last quarter to the machines, and then would turn around and get onto the plane back home.

He guessed it must have happened. He suspected that there wasn't much that hadn't happened in Las Vegas at some point or other. And America was so damn big that with so many people there was always bound to be *somebody*.[487]

And then he realized that he had zoned out just as Wednesday had been telling him who the man in the dark suit they had followed in the taxi had been, and he had missed it.

"So he's in," said Wednesday. "It'll cost me a bottle of Soma, though."

"What's Soma?"

"It's a drink." They walked onto the charter plane, empty but for them and a trio of corporate big spenders who needed to be back in Chicago by the start of the next business day.

Wednesday got comfortable, ordered himself a Jack Daniel's. "My kind of people see your kind of people . . ." He hesitated. "It's like bees and honey. Each bee makes only a tiny, tiny drop of honey. It takes thousands of them, millions perhaps, all working together to make the pot of honey you have on your breakfast table. Now imagine that you could eat nothing but honey. That's what it's like for my kind of people . . . we feed on belief, on prayers, on love.[488] It takes a lot of people believing just the tiniest bit to sustain us. That's what we need, instead of food. Belief."

"And Soma is . . ."

"To take the analogy further, it's honey wine. Mead." He chuckled. "It's a drink. Concentrated prayer and belief, distilled into a potent liqueur."

They were somewhere over Nebraska eating an unimpressive in-flight breakfast when Shadow said, "My wife."

"The dead one."

"Laura. She doesn't want to be dead. She told me. After she got me away from the guys on the train."

487. This paragraph does not appear in the First Edition.

488. The balance of this paragraph does not appear in the First Edition.

489. An indefinitely long prison sentence. *The Oxford English Dictionary* traces the earliest usage in print to 1791.

490. The next two sentences do not appear in the First Edition.

491. The recital of the "charms" that Odin learned is drawn from the Hávamál, the "Sayings of the High One." The oldest text version is part of the *Codex Regius*. The following is the translation of verses 148 through 165 by the English scholar Benjamin Thorpe in 1866:

148. Those songs I know
which the king's wife knows not
nor son of man.
Help the first is called,
for that will help thee
against strifes and cares.

149. For the second I know,
what the sons of men require,
who will as leeches live.

150. For the third I know,
if I have great need
to restrain my foes,
the weapons' edge I deaden:
of my adversaries
nor arms nor wiles harm aught.

151. For the fourth I know,
if men place
bonds on my limbs,
I so sing
that I can walk;
the fetter starts from my feet,
and the manacle from my hands.

152. For the fifth I know,
I see a shot from a hostile hand,
a shaft flying amid the host,
so swift it cannot fly
that I cannot arrest it,
if only I get sight of it.

"The action of a fine wife. Freeing you from durance vile[489] and murdering those who would have harmed you. You should treasure her, Nephew Ainsel."

"She wants to be really alive.[490] Not one of the walking dead, or whatever she is. She wants to live again. Can we do that? Is that possible?"

Wednesday said nothing for long enough that Shadow started to wonder if he had heard the question, or if he had, possibly, fallen asleep with his eyes open. Then he said, staring ahead of him as he talked,[491] "I know a charm that can cure pain and sickness, and lift the grief from the heart of the grieving.

"I know a charm that will heal with a touch.

"I know a charm that will turn aside the weapons of an enemy.

"I know another charm to free myself from all bonds and locks.

"A fifth charm: I can catch a bullet in flight and take no harm from it."

His words were quiet, urgent. Gone was the hectoring tone, gone was the grin. Wednesday spoke as if he were reciting the words of a religious ritual, as if he were speaking something dark and painful.

"A sixth: spells sent to hurt me will hurt only the sender.

"A seventh charm I know: I can quench a fire simply by looking at it.

"An eighth: if any man hates me, I can win his friendship.

"A ninth: I can sing the wind to sleep and calm a storm for long enough to bring a ship to shore.

"Those were the first nine charms I learned. Nine nights I hung on the bare tree, my side pierced with a spear's point. I swayed and blew in the cold winds and the hot winds, without food, without water, a sacrifice of myself to myself, and the worlds opened to me.[492]

"For a tenth charm, I learned to dispel witches, to spin them around in the skies so that they will never find their way back to their own doors again.

"An eleventh: if I sing it when a battle rages it can take

153. For the sixth I know,
if one wounds me
with a green tree's roots;
also if a man
declares hatred to me,
harm shall consume them sooner
    than me.

154. For the seventh I know,
if a lofty house I see
blaze o'er its inmates,
so furiously it shall not burn
that I cannot save it.
That song I can sing.

155. For the eighth I know,
what to all is
useful to learn:
where hatred grows
among the sons of men –
that I can quickly assuage.

156. For the ninth I know,
if I stand in need
my bark on the water to save,
I can the wind
on the waves allay,
and the sea lull.

157. For the tenth I know,
if I see troll-wives
sporting in air,
I can so operate
that they will forsake
their own forms,
and their own minds.

158. For the eleventh I know,
if I have to lead
my ancient friends to battle,
under their shields I sing,
and with power they go
safe to the fight,
safe from the fight;
safe on every side they go.

159. For the twelfth I know,
if on a tree I see

a corpse swinging from a halter,
I can so grave
and in runes depict,
that the man shall walk,
and with me converse.

160. For the thirteenth I know,
if on a young man
I sprinkle water,
he shall not fall,
though he into battle come:
that man shall not sink before swords.

161. For the fourteenth I know,
if in the society of men
I have to enumerate the gods,
Æsir and Alfar,
I know the distinctions of all.
This few unskilled can do.

162. For the fifteenth I know
what the dwarf Thiodreyrir sang
before Delling's doors.
Strength he sang to the Æsir,
and to the Alfar prosperity,
wisdom to Hroptatýr.

163. For the sixteenth I know,
if a modest maiden's favour and
    affection
I desire to possess,
the soul I change
of the white-armed damsel,
and wholly turn her mind.

164. For the seventeenth I know,
that that young maiden will
reluctantly avoid me.
These songs, Loddfafnir!
thou wilt long have lacked;
yet it may be good if thou understandest
    them,
profitable if thou learnest them.

165. For the eighteenth I know
that which I never teach
to maid or wife of man,
(all is better

what one only knows.
This is the closing of the songs)
save her alone
who clasps me in her arms,
or is my sister.

492. See note 182, above, where we first glimpse this wound.

warriors through the tumult unscathed and unhurt, and bring them safely back to their hearth and their home.

"A twelfth charm I know: if I see a hanged man I can bring him down from the gallows to whisper to us all he remembers.

"A thirteenth: if I sprinkle water on a child's head, that child will not fall in battle.

"A fourteenth: I know the names of all the gods. Every damned one of them.

"A fifteenth: I have a dream of power, of glory, and of wisdom, and I can make people believe my dreams."

His voice was so low now that Shadow had to strain to hear it over the plane's engine noise.

"A sixteenth charm I know: if I need love I can turn the mind and heart of any woman.

"A seventeenth, that no woman I want will ever want another.

"And I know an eighteenth charm, and that charm is the greatest of all, and that charm I can tell to no man, for a secret that no one knows but you is the most powerful secret there can ever be."

He sighed, and then stopped talking.

Shadow could feel his skin crawl. It was as if he had just seen a door open to another place, somewhere worlds away where hanged men blew in the wind at every crossroads, where witches shrieked overhead in the night.

"Laura," was all he said.

Wednesday turned his head, stared into Shadow's pale gray eyes with his own. "I can't make her live again," he said. "I don't even know why she isn't as dead as she ought to be."

"I think I did it," said Shadow. "It was my fault."

Wednesday raised a bushy eyebrow.

"Mad Sweeney gave me a golden coin, back when he showed me how to do that trick. From what he said, he gave me the wrong coin. What he gave me was something more powerful than what he thought he was giving me. I passed it on to Laura."

Wednesday grunted, lowered his chin to his chest, frowned. Then he sat back. "That could do it," he said. "And no, I can't help you. What you do in your own time is your own affair, of course."

"What," asked Shadow, "is that supposed to mean?"

"It means that I can't stop you from hunting eagle stones or thunderbirds. But I would infinitely prefer that you spend your days quietly sequestered in Lakeside, out of sight, and, I hope, out of mind. When things get hairy we'll need all hands to the wheel."

He looked very old as he said this, and fragile, and his skin seemed almost transparent, and the flesh beneath was gray.

Shadow wanted, wanted very much, to reach out and put his hand over Wednesday's gray hand. He wanted to tell him that everything would be okay—something that Shadow did not feel, but that he knew had to be said. There were men in black trains out there. There was a fat kid in a stretch limo and there were people in the television who did not mean them well.

He did not touch Wednesday. He did not say anything.

Later, he wondered if he could have changed things, if that gesture would have done any good, if it could have averted any of the harm that was to come. He told himself it wouldn't. He knew it wouldn't. But still, afterward, he wished that, just for a moment on that slow flight home, he had touched Wednesday's hand.

✢   ✢   ✢

THE BRIEF WINTER daylight was already fading when Wednesday dropped Shadow outside his apartment. The freezing temperature when Shadow opened the car door felt even more science fictional when compared to Las Vegas.

"Don't get into any trouble," said Wednesday. "Keep your head below the parapet. Make no waves."

"All at the same time?"

"Don't get smart with me, m'boy. You can keep out of

sight in Lakeside. I pulled in a big favor to keep you here, safe and sound. If you were in a city they'd get your scent in minutes."

"I'll stay put and keep out of trouble." Shadow meant it as he said it. He'd had a lifetime of trouble and he was ready to let it go forever. "When are you coming back?" he asked.

"Soon," said Wednesday, and he gunned the Lincoln's engine, slid up the window and drove off into the frigid night.

CHAPTER ELEVEN

Three may keep a secret, if two of them are dead.
—BEN FRANKLIN,
Poor Richard's Almanack **493**

HREE COLD DAYS passed. The thermometer never made it up to the zero mark, not even at midday. Shadow wondered how people had survived this weather in the days before electricity, before thermal face masks and lightweight thermal underwear, before easy travel.

He was down at the Video, Tanning, Bait, and Tackle store, being shown Hinzelmann's hand-tied trout flies. They were more interesting than he had expected: colorful fakes of life, made of feather and thread, each with a hook hidden inside it.

He asked Hinzelmann.

"For real?" asked Hinzelmann.

"For real," said Shadow.

"Well," said the older man. "Sometimes they didn't survive it, and they died. Leaky chimneys and badly ventilated stoves and ranges killed as many people as the cold. But those days were hard—they'd spend the summer and the fall laying up the food and the firewood for the winter. The worst thing of all was the madness. I heard on the radio, they were saying how it was to do with the sunlight, how

493. First published in 1732, the 1733 edition featured the pseudonymous Richard Saunders as the editor. The last edition was published in 1758. The quoted aphorism is one of the more popular from the *Almanack*, and its first appearance is not noted.

there isn't enough of it in the winter. My daddy, he said folk just went stir-crazy—winter madness they called it. Lakeside always had it easy, but some of the other towns around here, they had it hard. There was a saying still had currency when I was a kid, that if the serving girl hadn't tried to kill you by February she hadn't any backbone.

"Storybooks were like gold-dust—anything you could read was treasured, back before the town had a lending library. When my grampaw got sent a storybook from his brother in Bavaria, all the Germans in town met up in the town hall to hear him read it, and the Finns and the Irish and the rest of them, they'd make the Germans tell them the stories.

"Twenty miles south of here, in Jibway, they found a woman walking mother-naked in the winter with a dead babe at her breast, and she'd not suffer them to take it from her." He shook his head meditatively, closed the fly cabinet with a click. "Bad business. You want a video rental card? Eventually they'll open a Blockbuster here,[494] and then we'll soon be out of business. But for now we got a pretty fair selection."

Shadow reminded Hinzelmann that he had no television and no VCR. He enjoyed Hinzelmann's company—the reminiscences, the tall tales, the goblin grin of the old man. It could make things awkward between them were Shadow to admit that television had made him uncomfortable ever since it had started to talk to him.

Hinzelmann fished in a drawer, and took out a tin box—by the look of it, it had once been a Christmas Box, of the kind that contained chocolates or cookies: a mottled Santa Claus, holding a tray of Coca-Cola bottles, beamed up from its lid. Hinzelmann eased off the metal top of the box, revealing a notebook and books of blank tickets, and said, "How many you want me to put you down for?"

"How many of what?"

"Klunker tickets. She'll go out onto the ice today, so we've started selling tickets. Each ticket is ten dollars, five for forty, ten for seventy-five. One ticket buys you five minutes. Of course we can't promise it'll go down in your five min-

494. Blockbuster was a big-box store renting videos and games. Blockbuster expanded internationally throughout the 1990s, and by 2004, Blockbuster employed 84,300 people worldwide and had 9,094 stores in total. Ironically, today, only one remains, in Bend, Oregon.

utes, but the person who's closest stands to win five hundred bucks, and if it goes down in your five minutes, you win a thousand dollars. The earlier you buy your tickets, the more times aren't spoken for. You want to see the info sheet?"

"Sure."

Hinzelmann handed Shadow a photocopied sheet. The klunker was an old car with its engine and fuel tank removed, which would be parked out on the ice for the winter. Sometime in the spring the lake ice would melt, and when it was too thin to bear the car's weight the car would fall into the lake. The earliest the klunker had ever tumbled into the lake was February the twenty-seventh ("That was the winter of 1998. I don't think you could rightly call that a winter at all"), the latest was May the first ("That was 1950. Seemed that year that the only way that winter would end was if somebody hammered a stake through its heart"). The beginning of April appeared to be the most common time for the car to sink—normally in mid-afternoon.

All of the mid-afternoons in April had already gone, marked off in Hinzelmann's lined notebook. Shadow bought a twenty-five-minute period on the morning of March the twenty-third, from 9:00 A.M. to 9:25 A.M. He handed Hinzelmann forty dollars.

"I just wish everybody in town was as easy a sell as you are," said Hinzelmann.

"It's a thank-you for that ride you gave me that first night I was in town."

"No, Mike," said Hinzelmann. "It's for the children." For a moment he looked serious, with no trace of impishness on his creased old face. "Come down this afternoon, you can lend a hand pushing the klunker out onto the lake."

He passed Shadow five blue cards, each with a date and time written on it in Hinzelmann's old-fashioned handwriting, then entered the details of each in his notebook.

"Hinzelmann," asked Shadow. "Have you ever heard of eagle stones?"

"Up north of Rhinelander? Nope, that's Eagle River. Can't say I have."

"How about thunderbirds?"

"Well, there was the Thunderbird Framing Gallery up on Fifth Street, but that closed down. I'm not helping, am I?"

"Nope."

"Tell you what, why don't you go look at the library. Good people, although they may be kind of distracted by the library sale on this week. I showed you where the library was, didn't I?"

Shadow nodded, and said so long. He wished he'd thought of the library himself. He got into the purple 4Runner and drove south on Main Street, following the lake around to the southernmost point, until he reached the castle-like building which housed the city library. He walked inside. A sign pointed to the basement: LIBRARY SALE, it said. The library proper was on the ground floor, and he stamped the snow off his boots and went in.

A forbidding woman with pursed, crimson-colored lips asked him pointedly if she could help him.

"I suppose I need a library card," he said. "And I want to know all about thunderbirds."

The woman had him fill out a form, then she told him it would take a week until he could be issued with his card.[495] Shadow wondered if they spent the week sending out inquiries to ensure that he was not wanted in any other libraries across America for failure to return library books.

He had known a man in prison who had been imprisoned for stealing library books.

"Sounds kind of rough," said Shadow, when the man told him why he was inside.

"Half a million dollars' worth of books," said the man, proudly. His name was Gary McGuire. "Mostly rare and antique books from libraries and universities. They found a whole storage locker filled with books from floor to ceiling. Open and shut case."

"Why did you take them?" asked Shadow.

"I wanted them," said Gary.

"Jesus. Half a million dollars' worth of books."

Gary flashed him a grin, lowered his voice and said, "That was just in the storage locker they *found*. They never found the garage in San Clemente with the *really* good stuff in it."

495. This and the succeeding paragraphs—the entire story about the book thief—do not appear in the First Edition.

Gary had died in prison, when what the infirmary had told him was just a malingering, feeling-lousy kind of day turned out to be a ruptured appendix. Now, here in the Lakeside library, Shadow found himself thinking about a garage in San Clemente with box after box of rare, strange and beautiful books in it rotting away, all of them browning and wilting and being eaten by mold and insects in the darkness, waiting for someone who would never come to set them free.

Native American Beliefs and Traditions was on a single shelf in one castle-like turret. Shadow pulled down some books and sat in the window seat. In several minutes he had learned that thunderbirds were mythical gigantic birds who lived on mountaintops, who brought the lightning and who flapped their wings to make the thunder. There were some tribes, he read, who believed that the thunderbirds had made the world. Another half-hour's reading did not turn up anything more, and he could find no mention of eagle stones anywhere in the books' indexes.[496]

Shadow was putting the last of the books back on the shelf when he became aware of somebody staring at him. Someone small and grave was peeking at him from around the heavy shelves. As he turned to look, the face vanished. He turned his back on the boy, then glanced around to see that he was being watched once more.

In his pocket was the Liberty dollar. He took it out of his pocket, held it up in his right hand, making sure the boy could see it. He finger-palmed it into his left hand, displayed both hands empty, raised his left hand to his mouth and coughed once, letting the coin tumble from his left hand into his right.

The boy looked at him wide-eyed and scampered away, returning a few moments later, dragging an unsmiling Marguerite Olsen, who looked at Shadow suspiciously and said, "Hello, Mister Ainsel. Leon says you were doing magic for him."

"Just a little prestidigitation, ma'am."[497]

"Please don't," she said.

"I'm sorry. I was just trying to entertain him."

496. In European tradition, eagle stones—aetites, hollow geodes—were said to promote childbirth and relieve pain. There is no traceable connection to Native American mythology.

497. The succeeding five sentences do not appear in the First Edition.

498. The balance of this paragraph does not appear in the First Edition.

499. Jenny Kerton is a character in Gaiman's short story "Wall: A Prologue," first published as a chapbook in Charles Vess's portfolio *A Fall of Stardust* (1999). *What My Heart Meant* is fictional, with a title in the form of a "romance" novel.

She shook her head, tautly. *Drop it.* Shadow dropped it. He said, "I never did say thank you for your advice about heating the apartment. It's warm as toast in there right now."

"That's good." Her icy expression had not begun to thaw.

"It's a lovely library," said Shadow.

"It's a beautiful building. But the city needs something more efficient and less beautiful. You going to the library sale downstairs?"

"I wasn't planning on it."

"Well, you should. It's for a good cause.[498] Makes money for new books, cleans out shelf space, and it's raising money to put in computers for the children's section. But the sooner we get a whole new library built, the better."

"I'll make a point of getting down there."

"Head out into the hall and then go downstairs. Good seeing you, Mister Ainsel."

"Call me Mike," he said.

She said nothing, just took Leon's hand and walked the boy over to the children's section.

"But, Mom," Shadow heard Leon say, "it wasn't *pressed igitation.* It wasn't. I saw it vanish and then it fell out of his *nose.* I *saw* it."

An oil portrait of Abraham Lincoln gazed down from the wall at him. Shadow walked down the marble and oak steps to the library basement, through a door into a large room filled with tables, each table covered with books of all kinds, indiscriminately assorted and promiscuously arranged: paperbacks and hardcovers, fiction and non-fiction, periodicals and encyclopedias all side by side upon the tables, spines up or spines out.

Shadow wandered to the back of the room where there was a table covered with old-looking leather-bound books, each with a library catalog number painted in white on the spine. "You're the first person over in that corner all day," said the man sitting by the stack of empty boxes and bags and the small, open, metal cashbox. "Mostly folk just take the thrillers and the children's books and the Harlequin Romances. Jenny Kerton,[499] Danielle Steel, all that." The man was reading Agatha Christie's *The Murder of Roger*

Ackroyd.[500] "Everything on the tables is fifty cents a book, or you can take three for a dollar."

Shadow thanked him and continued to browse. He found a copy of Herodotus's *Histories* bound in peeling brown leather. It made him think of the paperback copy he had left behind in prison. There was a book called *Perplexing Parlour Illusions,*[501] which looked like it might have some coin effects. He carried both the books over to the man with the cashbox.

"Buy one more, it's still a dollar," said the man. "And if you take another book away, you'll be doing us a favor. We need the shelf-space."

Shadow walked back to the old leather-bound books. He decided to liberate the book that was least likely to be bought by anyone else, and found himself unable to decide between *Common Diseases of the Urinary Tract with Illustrations by a Medical Doctor* and *Minutes of the Lakeside City Council 1872–1884.* He looked at the illustrations in the medical book and decided that somewhere in the town there was a teenage boy who could use the book to gross out his friends. He took the *Minutes* to the man on the door, who took his dollar and put all the books into a Dave's Finest Food brown paper sack.

Shadow left the library. He had a clear view of the lake, all the way to the northeastern corner. He could even see his apartment building, a small brown box[503] on the bank up past the bridge. And there were men on the ice near the bridge, four or five of them, pushing a dark green car into the center of the white lake.

"March the twenty-third," Shadow said to the lake, under his breath. "Nine A.M. to nine twenty-five A.M." He wondered if the lake or the klunker could hear him—and if they would pay any attention to him, even if they could. He doubted it. In Shadow's world, luck, the good kind, was something that other people had, not him.[504]

The wind blew bitter against his face.

Officer Chad Mulligan was waiting outside Shadow's apartment when he got back. Shadow's heart began to pound when he saw the police car, to relax a little when he

500. One of Agatha Christie's most famous novels, first published in 1926, only the third to feature the Belgian detective Hercule Poirot. Its unreliable narrator was an important innovation in the genre, and in a 2013 survey, members of the British Crime Writers Association named it the best crime novel of all time (and Christie the greatest crime writer—the Sherlock Holmes canon was named the best series).

501. This appears to be a fictional book.

502. Another pair of fictional books.

503. The building is described as "like a doll's house" in the First Edition.

504. This sentence does not appear in the First Edition.

observed that the policeman was doing paperwork in the front seat.

He walked over to the car, carrying his paper sack of books.

Mulligan lowered his window. "Library sale?" he said.

"Yes."

"I bought a box of Robert Ludlum books there two, three years back. Keep meaning to read them. My cousin swears by the guy. These days I figure if I ever get marooned on a desert island and I got my box of Robert Ludlum books with me, I can catch up on my reading."

"Something particular I can do for you, Chief?"

"Not a damn thing, pal. Thought I'd stop by and see how you were settling in. You remember that Chinese saying, 'You save a man's life, you're responsible for him'? Well, I'm not saying I saved your life last week. But I still thought I should check in. How's the Gunther Purple-mobile doing?"

"Good," said Shadow. "It's good. Running fine."

"Pleased to hear it."

"I saw my next-door neighbor in the library," said Shadow. "Miz Olsen. I was wondering . . ."

"What crawled up her butt and died?"

"If you want to put it like that."

"Long story. You want to ride along for a spell, and I'll tell you all about it."

Shadow thought about it for a moment. "Okay," he said. He got into the car, sat in the front passenger seat. Mulligan drove north of town. Then he turned off his lights and parked beside the road.

"Darren Olsen met Marge at UW Stevens Point and he brought her back north to Lakeside. She was a journalism major. He was studying, shit, hotel management, something like that. When they got here, jaws dropped. This was, what, thirteen, fourteen years ago. She was so beautiful . . . that black hair . . ." He paused. "Darren managed the Motel America over in Camden, twenty miles west of here. Except nobody ever seemed to want to stop in Camden and eventually the motel closed. They had two boys. At that time Sandy was eleven. The little one—Leon is it?—was just a babe in arms.

"Darren Olsen wasn't a brave man. He'd been a good high school football player, but that was the last time he was flying high. Whatever. He couldn't find the courage to tell Margie that he'd lost his job. So for a month, maybe for two months, he'd drive off early in the morning, come home late in the evening complaining about the hard day he'd had at the motel."

"What was he doing?" asked Shadow.

"Mm. Couldn't say for certain. I reckon he was driving up to Ironwood, maybe down to Green Bay. Guess he started out as a job hunter. Pretty soon he was drinking the time away, getting stoned, more than probably meeting the occasional working girl for a little instant gratification. He could have been gambling. What I do know for certain is that he emptied out their joint account in about ten weeks. It was only a matter of time before Margie figured out—there we go!"

He swung the car out, flicked on the siren and the lights, and scared the daylights out of a small man with Iowa plates who had just come down the hill at seventy.

The rogue Iowan ticketed, Mulligan returned to his story.

"Where was I? Okay. So Margie kicks him out, sues for divorce. It turned into a vicious custody battle. That's what they call 'em when they get into *People* magazine. Vicious Custody Battle. Always makes me think of lawyers with knives and assault weapons and brass knuckles.[505] She got the kids. Darren got visitation rights and precious little else. Now, back then Leon was pretty small. Sandy was older, a good kid, the kind of boy who worships his daddy. Wouldn't let Margie say nothing bad about him. They lost the house—had a nice place down on Daniels Road. She moved into the apartments. He left town. Came back every few months to make everybody miserable.

"This went on for a few years. He'd come back, spend money on the kids, leave Margie in tears. Most of us just started wishing he'd never come back at all. His mom and pop had moved to Florida when they retired, said they

505. This sentence does not appear in the First Edition.

couldn't take another Wisconsin winter. So last year he came out, said he wanted to take the boys to Florida for Christmas. Margie said not a hope, told him to get lost. It got pretty unpleasant—at one point I had to go over there. Domestic dispute. By the time I got there Darren was standing in the front yard shouting stuff, the boys were barely holding it together, Margie was crying.

"I told Darren he was shaping up for a night in the cells. I thought for a moment he was going to hit me, but he was sober enough not to do that. I gave him a ride down to the trailer park south of town, told him to shape up. That he'd hurt her enough . . . Next day he left town."

"Two weeks later, Sandy vanished. Didn't get onto the school bus. Told his best friend that he'd be seeing his dad soon, that Darren was bringing him a specially cool present to make up for having missed Christmas in Florida. Nobody's seen him since. Non-custodial kidnappings are the hardest. It's tough to find a kid who doesn't want to be found, y'see?"

Shadow said that he did. He saw something else as well. Chad Mulligan was in love with Marguerite Olsen himself. He wondered if the man knew how obvious it was.

Mulligan pulled out once more, lights flashing, and pulled over some teenagers doing sixty. He didn't ticket them, "just put the fear of God in them."

*   *   *

THAT EVENING SHADOW sat at the kitchen table trying to figure out how to transform a silver dollar into a penny. It was a trick he had found in *Perplexing Parlour Illusions* but the instructions were infuriating, unhelpful, and vague. Phrases like "then vanish the penny in the usual way" occurred every sentence or so. In this context, Shadow wondered, what was "the usual way"? A French drop? Sleeving it? Shouting "Oh my god, look out—a mountain lion!" and dropping the coin into his side pocket while the audience's attention was diverted?

He tossed his silver dollar into the air, caught it, remembering the moon and the woman who gave it to him, then he attempted the illusion. It didn't seem to work. He walked into the bathroom and tried it in front of the mirror, and confirmed that he was right. The trick as written simply didn't work. He sighed, dropped the coins in his pocket and sat down on the couch. He spread the cheap throw rug over his legs and flipped open the *Minutes of the Lakeside Council 1872–1884*. The type, in two columns, was so small as to be almost unreadable. He flipped through the book, looking at the reproductions of the photographs of the period, at the several incarnations of the Lakeside city council therein: long side-whiskers and clay pipes and battered hats and shiny hats, worn with faces which were, many of them, peculiarly familiar. He was unsurprised to see that the portly secretary of the 1882 city council was a Patrick Mulligan: shave him, make him lose twenty pounds and he'd be a dead ringer for Chad Mulligan, his—what, great-great-grandson? He wondered if Hinzelmann's pioneer grandfather was in the photographs, but it did not appear that he had been city council material. Shadow thought he had seen a reference to a Hinzelmann in the text, while flipping from photograph to photograph, but it eluded him when he leafed back for it, and the tiny type made Shadow's eyes ache.

He put the book down on his chest and realized his head was nodding. It would be foolish to fall asleep on the couch, he decided, soberly. The bedroom was only a few feet away. On the other hand, the bedroom and the bed would still be there in five minutes, and anyway, he was not going to go to sleep, only to close his eyes for a moment . . .

Darkness roared.

He stood on an open plain. Beside him was the place from which he had once emerged, from which the earth had squeezed him. Stars were still falling from the sky and each star that touched the red earth became a man or a woman. The men had long black hair and high cheekbones. The women all looked like Marguerite Olsen. These were the star people.

They looked at him with dark, proud eyes.

"Tell me about the thunderbirds," said Shadow. "Please. It's not for me. It's for my wife."

One by one they turned their backs on him, and as he lost their faces they were gone, one with the landscape. But the last of them, her hair streaked white on dark gray, pointed before she turned away, pointed into the wine-colored sky.

"Ask them yourself," she said. Summer lightning flickered, momentarily illuminating the landscape from horizon to horizon.

There were high rocks near him, peaks and spires of sandstone, and Shadow began to climb the nearest. The spire was the color of old ivory. He grabbed at a handhold, and felt it slice into his hand. It's bone, thought Shadow. Not stone. It's old dry bone.

But it was a dream, and in dreams, sometimes, you have no choices: either there are no decisions to be made, or they were made for you long before ever the dream began. Shadow continued to climb, pulling himself up. His hands hurt. Bone popped and crushed and fragmented under his bare feet, cutting them painfully. The wind tugged at him, and he pressed himself to the spire, and he continued to climb the tower.

It was made of only one kind of bone, he realized, repeated over and over. Each of the bones was dry and ball-like. For a moment he had imagined they might be old yellow shells or the eggs of some dreadful bird. But another flare of lightning told him differently: they had holes for eyes, and they had teeth, which grinned without humor.

Somewhere birds were calling. Rain spattered his face.

He was hundreds of feet above the ground, clinging to the side of the tower of skulls, while flashes of lightning burned in the wings of the shadowy birds who circled the spire—enormous black, condor-like birds, each with a ruff of white at its neck. They were huge, graceful, awful birds, and the beats of their wings crashed like thunder on the night air.

They were circling the spire.

They must be fifteen, twenty feet from wingtip to wingtip, *thought Shadow.*

Then the first bird swung out of its glide toward him, blue lightning crackling in its wings. He pushed himself into a crevice of skulls, hollow eye-holes stared at him, a clutter of ivory teeth smiled at him, but he kept climbing, pulling himself up the mountain of skulls, every sharp edge cutting into his skin, feeling revulsion and terror and awe.

Another bird came at him, and one hand-sized talon sank into his arm.

He reached out and tried to grasp a feather from its wing. If he returned to his tribe without a thunderbird's feather he would be disgraced, he would never be a man, but the bird pulled up, so that he could not grasp even one feather. The thunderbird loosened its grip and swung back onto the wind. Shadow continued to climb.

There must be a thousand skulls, *thought Shadow.* A thousand thousand. And not all of them are human. *He stood at last on the top of the spire, the great birds, the thunderbirds, circling him slowly, navigating the gusts of the storm with tiny flicks of their wings.*

He heard a voice, the voice of the buffalo man, calling to him on the wind, telling him who the skulls belonged to . . .[506]

The tower began to tumble, and the biggest bird, its eyes the blinding blue-white of forked lightning, plummeted down toward him in a rush of thunder, and Shadow was falling, tumbling down the tower of skulls . . .

The telephone shrilled. Shadow had not even known that it was connected. Groggy, shaken, he picked it up.

"What the fuck," shouted Wednesday, angrier than Shadow had ever heard him. "What the almighty flying fuck do you think you are playing at?"

"I was asleep," said Shadow into the receiver, stupidly.

"What do you think is the fucking point of stashing you in a hiding place like Lakeside, if you're going to raise such a ruckus that not even a dead man could miss it?"

"I dreamed of thunderbirds . . . ," said Shadow. "And a

506. Shadow later tells Easter that the voice confirmed that the skulls belonged to Shadow himself. The skulls suggest that he has been reincarnated many, many times.

Thunderbird
Artistic rendering by Carnby, licensed under CCA-Share Alike 4.0
https://commons.wikimedia.org/wiki/File:Thunderbird
_(artistic_rendition).jpg

tower. Skulls . . ." It seemed to him very important to re-count his dream.

"I know what you were dreaming. Everybody damn well knows what you were dreaming. Christ almighty. What's the point in hiding you, if you're going to start to fucking advertise?"

Shadow said nothing.

There was a pause at the other end of the telephone. "I'll be there in the morning," said Wednesday. It sounded like the anger had died down. "We're going to San Francisco. The flowers in your hair are optional."[507] And the line went dead.

Shadow put the telephone down on the carpet, and sat up, stiffly. It was six A.M. and still night-dark outside. He got up from the sofa, shivering. He could hear the wind as it screamed across the frozen lake. And he could hear some-body nearby, crying, only the thickness of a wall away. He

507. "San Francisco (Be Sure to Wear Flow-ers in Your Hair)" is a 1967 American pop song recorded by Scott McKenzie, written by John Phillips of The Mamas & the Papas. It advised: "If you're going to San Francisco, be sure to wear some flowers in your hair." The song celebrated San Francisco as the center of the late 1960s counterculture.

324

was certain it was Marguerite Olsen, and her sobbing was insistent and low and heartbreaking.

Shadow walked into the bathroom and pissed, then went into his bedroom and closed the door, blocking off the sound of the crying woman. Outside the wind howled and wailed as if it, too, was seeking for a lost child,[508] and he slept no more that night.

✢   ✢   ✢

SAN FRANCISCO IN January was unseasonably warm, warm enough that the sweat prickled on the back of Shadow's neck. Wednesday was wearing a deep blue suit, and a pair of gold-rimmed spectacles that made him look like an entertainment lawyer.[509]

They were walking along Haight Street. The street people and the hustlers and the moochers watched them go by, and no one shook a paper cup of change at them, no one asked them for anything at all.

Wednesday's jaw was set. Shadow had seen immediately that the man was still angry, and had asked no questions when the black Lincoln town car had pulled up outside the apartment that morning. They had not talked on the way to the airport. He had been relieved that Wednesday was in first class and he was back in coach.

Now it was late in the afternoon. Shadow, who had not been in San Francisco since he was a boy, who had only seen it since then as a background to movies, was astonished at how familiar it was, how colorful and unique the wooden houses, how steep the hills, how very much it didn't feel like anywhere else.

"It's almost hard to believe that this is in the same country as Lakeside," he said.

Wednesday glared at him. Then he said, "It's not. San Francisco isn't in the same country as Lakeside any more than New Orleans is in the same country as New York or Miami is in the same country as Minneapolis."

"Is that so?" said Shadow, mildly.

"Indeed it is. They may share certain cultural signifiers—money, a federal government, entertainment; it's the same

508. The balance of this sentence does not appear in the First Edition.

509. In the Manuscript, the meeting with Easter takes place in New Orleans. The array of food in which she is indulging is much more likely to be found in a courtyard restaurant in the French Quarter, such as the Court of Two Sisters, an historic venue on Royal Street. Gaiman made a note to himself in the Manuscript to consider moving the scene to San Francisco or Seattle.

land, obviously—but the only things that give it the illusion of being one country are the green-back, *The Tonight Show*, and McDonald's." They were approaching a park at the end of the road. "Be nice to the lady we are visiting. But not too nice."

"I'll be cool," said Shadow.

They stepped onto the grass.

A young girl, no older than fourteen, her hair dyed green and orange and pink, stared at them as they went by. She sat beside a dog, a mongrel, with a piece of string for a collar and a leash. She looked hungrier than the dog did. The dog yapped at them, then wagged its tail.[510]

Shadow gave the girl a dollar bill. She stared at it as if she was not sure what it was. "Buy dog food with it," Shadow suggested. She nodded, and smiled.

"Let me put it bluntly," said Wednesday. "You must be very cautious around the lady we are visiting. She might take a fancy to you, and that would be bad."

"Is she your girlfriend or something?"

"Not for all the little plastic toys in China," said Wednesday, agreeably. His anger seemed to have dissipated, or perhaps to have been invested for the future. Shadow suspected that anger was the engine that made Wednesday run.

There was a woman sitting on the grass, under a tree, with a paper tablecloth spread in front of her, and a variety of Tupperware dishes on the cloth.

She was—not fat, no, far from fat: what she was, a word that Shadow had never had cause to use until now, was curvaceous. Her hair was so fair that it was white, the kind of platinum-blonde tresses that should have belonged to a long-dead movie starlet, her lips were painted crimson, and she looked to be somewhere between twenty-five and fifty.

As they reached her she was selecting from a plate of deviled eggs. She looked up as Wednesday approached her, and put down the egg she had chosen, and wiped her hand. "Hello, you old fraud," she said, but she smiled as she said it, and Wednesday bowed low, took her hand and raised it to his lips.

510. The description is startlingly like Delirium, one of the Endless—see Gaiman's *Sandman*.

He said, "You look divine."

"How the hell else should I look?" she demanded, sweetly. "Anyway, you're a liar. New Orleans was *such* a mistake—I put on, what, thirty pounds there? I swear. I knew I had to leave when I started to waddle. The tops of my thighs rub together when I walk now, can you believe that?" This last was addressed to Shadow. He had no idea what to say in reply, and felt a hot flush suffuse his face. The woman laughed delightedly. "He's *blushing*! Wednesday my sweet, you brought me a *blusher*. How perfectly wonderful of you. What's he called?"

"This is Shadow," said Wednesday. He seemed to be enjoying Shadow's discomfort. "Shadow, say hello to Easter."[511]

Shadow said something that might have been Hello, and the woman smiled at him again. He felt like he was caught in headlights—the blinding kind that poachers use to freeze deer before they shoot them. He could smell her perfume from where he was standing, an intoxicating mixture of jasmine and honeysuckle, of sweet milk and female skin.

"So, how's tricks?" asked Wednesday.

The woman—Easter—laughed a deep and throaty laugh, full-bodied and joyous. How could you not like someone who laughed like that? "Everything's fine," she said. "How about you, you old wolf?"

"I was hoping to enlist your assistance."

"Wasting your time."

"At least hear me out before dismissing me."

"No point. Don't even bother."

She looked at Shadow. "Please, sit down here and help yourself to some of this food. Here, take a plate and pile it high. It's all good. Eggs, roast chicken, chicken curry, chicken salad, and over here is lapin—rabbit, actually, but cold rabbit is a delight, and in that bowl over there is the jugged hare,[512] well, why don't I just fill a plate for you?" And she did, taking a plastic plate and piling it high with foods and passing it to him. Then she looked at Wednesday. "Are you eating?" she asked.

"I am at your disposal, my dear," said Wednesday.

511. Eastre, Eostre, or Ostara was a Norse/Germanic goddess of spring, rebirth, and fertility and friend to all children. Saint Bede's *The Reckoning of Time* (eighth century C.E.) reports that during Ēosturmōnaþ (modern April), early Anglo-Saxons had held feasts in Ēostre's honor. These feasts, he claimed, had faded away with the spread of celebrations of the Christian Paschal month and the resurrection of Jesus. However, the evidence of worship of Eostre or Ostara is thin and controversial.

512. Stewed rabbit, cooked with red wine and juniper berries, and traditionally served with the rabbit's blood added at the end. "Jugged" dishes are cooked in a tall jug that is placed in heated water.

The goddess Ostara
Johannes Gehrts, 1884

"You," she told him, "are so full of shit it's a wonder your eyes don't turn brown." She passed him an empty plate. "Help yourself," she said.

The afternoon sun at her back burned her hair into a platinum aura. "Shadow," she said, chewing a chicken leg with gusto. "That's a sweet name. Why do they call you Shadow?"

Shadow licked his lips to moisten them. "When I was a kid," he said. "We lived, my mother and I, we were, I mean, she was, well, like a secretary, at a bunch of U.S. embassies, we went from city to city all over Northern Europe. Then she got sick and had to take early retirement and we came back to the States. I never knew what to say to the other kids, so I'd just find adults and follow them around, not saying anything. I just needed the company, I guess. I don't know. I was a small kid."

"You grew," she said.

"Yes," said Shadow. "I grew."

She turned back to Wednesday, who was spooning down a bowl of what looked like cold gumbo. "Is this the boy who's got everybody so upset?"

"You heard?"

"I keep my ears pricked up," she said. Then to Shadow, "You keep out of their way. There are too many secret societies out there, and they have no loyalties and no love. Commercial, independent, government, they're all in the same boat. They range from the barely competent to the deeply dangerous. Hey, old wolf, I heard a joke you'd like the other day. How do you know the CIA wasn't involved in the Kennedy assassination?"

"I've heard it," said Wednesday.

"Pity." She turned her attention back to Shadow. "But the spookshow, the ones you met, they're something else. They exist because everyone knows they must exist." She drained a paper cup of something that looked like white wine, and then she got to her feet. "Shadow's a good name," she said. "I want a mochaccino. Come on."

She began to walk away. "What about the food?" asked Wednesday. "You can't just leave it here."

She smiled at him, and pointed to the girl sitting by the dog, and then extended her arms to take in the Haight and the world. "Let it feed them," she said, and she walked, with Wednesday and Shadow trailing behind her.

"Remember," she said to Wednesday, as they walked, "*I'm* rich. I'm doing just peachy. Why should I help you?"

"You're one of us," he said. "You're as forgotten and as unloved and unremembered as any of us. It's pretty clear whose side you should be on."

They reached a sidewalk coffeehouse, went inside. There was only one waitress, who wore her eyebrow ring as a mark of caste, and a woman making coffee behind the counter. The waitress advanced upon them, smiling automatically, sat them down, took their orders.

Easter put her slim hand on the back of Wednesday's square gray hand. "I'm telling you," she said, "I'm doing *fine*. On my festival days they still feast on eggs and rabbits, on candy and on flesh, to represent rebirth and copulation. They wear flowers in their bonnets and they give each other flowers. They do it in my name. More and more of them every year. In my name, old wolf."

"And you wax fat and affluent on their worship and their love?" he said, dryly.

"Don't be an asshole." Suddenly she sounded very tired. She sipped her mochaccino.

"Serious question, m'dear. Certainly I would agree that millions upon millions of them give each other tokens in your name, and that they still practice all the rites of your festival, even down to hunting for hidden eggs. But how many of them know who you are? Eh? Excuse me, miss?" This to their waitress.

She said, "You need another espresso?"

"No, my dear. I was just wondering if you could solve a little argument we were having over here. My friend and I were disagreeing over what the word 'Easter' means. Would you happen to know?"

The girl stared at him as if green toads had begun to push their way between his lips. Then she said, "I don't know about any of that Christian stuff. I'm a pagan."

The woman behind the counter said, "I think it's like Latin or something for 'Christ has risen' maybe."

"Really?" said Wednesday.

"Yeah, sure," said the woman. "Easter. Just like the sun rises in the east, you know."

"The risen son. Of course—a most logical supposition." The woman smiled and returned to her coffee grinder. Wednesday looked up at their waitress. "I think I *shall* have another espresso, if you do not mind. And tell me, as a pagan, who do you worship?"

"Worship?"

"That's right. I imagine you must have a pretty wide-open field. So to whom do you set up your household altar? To whom do you bow down? To whom do you pray at dawn and at dusk?"

Her lips described several shapes without saying anything before she said, "The female principle. It's an empowerment thing. You know."

"Indeed. And this female principle of yours. Does she have a name?"

"She's the goddess within us all," said the girl with the eyebrow ring, color rising to her cheek. "She doesn't need a name."

"Ah," said Wednesday, with a wide monkey grin, "so do you have mighty bacchanals in her honor? Do you drink blood wine under the full moon, while scarlet candles burn in silver candleholders? Do you step naked into the seafoam, chanting ecstatically to your nameless goddess while the waves lick at your legs, lapping your thighs like the tongues of a thousand leopards?"

"You're making fun of me," she said. "We don't do any of that stuff you were saying." She took a deep breath. Shadow suspected she was counting to ten. "Any more coffees here? Another mochaccino for you, ma'am?" Her smile was a lot like the one she had greeted them with when they had entered.

They shook their heads, and the waitress turned to greet another customer.

"There," said Wednesday, "is one who 'does not have the faith and will not have the fun.' Chesterton.[513] Pagan indeed. So. Shall we go out onto the street, Easter my dear, and repeat the exercise? Find out how many passers-by know that their Easter festival takes its name from Eostre of the Dawn? Let's see—I have it. We shall ask a hundred people. For every one that knows the truth, you may cut off one of my fingers, and when I run out of them, toes; for every twenty who don't know you spend a night making love to me. And the odds are certainly in your favor here—this is San Francisco, after all.[514] There are heathens and pagans and Wiccans aplenty on these precipitous streets."

Her green eyes looked at Wednesday. They were, Shadow decided, the exact same color as a leaf in spring with the sun shining through it. She said nothing.

"We *could* try it," continued Wednesday. "But I would end up with ten fingers, ten toes, and five nights in your bed. So don't tell me they worship you and keep your festival day. They mouth your name, but it has no meaning to them. Nothing at all."

Tears stood out in her eyes. "I know that," she said, quietly. "I'm not a fool."

"No," said Wednesday. "You're not."

He's pushed her too far, thought Shadow.[515]

Wednesday looked down, ashamed. "I'm sorry," he said. Shadow could hear the real sincerity in his voice. "We *need* you. We need your energy. We need your power. Will you fight beside us when the storm comes?"

She hesitated. She had a chain of blue forget-me-nots tattooed around her left wrist.

"Yes," she said, after a while. "I guess I will."[516]

Wednesday kissed his finger, touched it to her cheek. Then he called their waitress over and paid for their coffees, counting out the money carefully, folding it over with the check and presenting it to her.

As she walked away, Shadow said, "Ma'am? Excuse me? I think you dropped this." He picked up a ten-dollar bill from the floor.

513. From "The Song of the Strange Ascetic," first published in 1913:

If I had been a Heathen,
I'd have praised the purple vine,
My slaves should dig the vineyards,
And I would drink the wine.
But Higgins is a Heathen,
And his slaves grow lean and grey,
That he may drink some tepid milk
Exactly twice a day.

If I had been a Heathen,
I'd have crowned Neaera's curls,
And filled my life with love affairs,
My house with dancing girls;
But Higgins is a Heathen,
And to lecture rooms is forced,
Where his aunts, who are not married,
Demand to be divorced.

If I had been a Heathen,
I'd have sent my armies forth,
And dragged behind my chariots
The Chieftains of the North.
But Higgins is a Heathen,
And he drives the dreary quill,
To lend the poor that funny cash
That makes them poorer still.

If I had been a Heathen,
I'd have piled my pyre on high,
And in a great red whirlwind
Gone roaring to the sky;
But Higgins is a Heathen,
And a richer man than I:
And they put him in an oven,
Just as if he were a pie.

Now who that runs can read it,
The riddle that I write,
Of why this poor old sinner,
Should sin without delight—
But I, I cannot read it
(Although I run and run),
Of them that do not have the faith,
And will not have the fun.

514. The Manuscript shifts at this point to San Francisco.

515. In the Manuscript, Shadow tries to break the moment, saying, "'Easter. Eostre. I suppose that would be where we get words like oestrogen and oestus from.' It was a safe bet. Wednesday said, 'Not at all. They come from *oestrus*, gadfly, and from *oistrus*, a frenzy. That last one: Greek. Don't they teach you anything in school these days?' 'I have little Latin,' said Shadow, remembering something he had heard, 'and less Greek.' 'Touché,' said Wednesday." Shadow's recollected quotation is from Thomas Hood's 1832 comic essay "The Schoolmaster Abroad," from his *Comic Annual*.

516. In the First Edition, this is followed by the paragraph: "*It's true what they say*, thought Shadow. *If you can fake sincerity, you've got it made.* Then he felt guilty for thinking it." This paragraph has been moved to text accompanying note 518, below, without the final sentence.

"No," she said, looking at the wrapped bills in her hand.

"I saw it fall, ma'am," said Shadow, politely. "You should count them."

She counted the money in her hand, looked puzzled and said, "Jesus. You're right. I'm sorry." She took the ten-dollar bill from Shadow, and walked away.

Easter walked out onto the sidewalk with them. The light was just starting to fade. She nodded to Wednesday, then she touched Shadow's hand and said, "What did you dream about, last night?"

"Thunderbirds," he said. "A mountain of skulls."

She nodded. "And do you know whose skulls they were?"

"There was a voice," he said. "In my dream. It told me."

She nodded and waited.

He said, "It said they were mine. Old skulls of mine. Thousands and thousands of them."

She looked at Wednesday, and said, "I think this one's a keeper." She smiled her bright smile. Then she patted Shadow's arm and walked away down the sidewalk. He watched her go, trying—and failing—not to think of her thighs rubbing together as she walked.

In the taxi on the way to the airport, Wednesday turned to Shadow. "What the hell was that business with the ten dollars about?"

"You shortchanged her. It comes out of her wages if she's short."

"What the hell do you care?" Wednesday seemed genuinely irate.

Shadow thought for a moment. Then he said, "Well, I wouldn't want anyone to do it to me. She hadn't done anything wrong."

"No?" Wednesday stared off into the middle-distance, and said, "When she was seven years old she shut a kitten in a closet. She listened to it mew for several days. When it ceased to mew, she took it out of the closet, put it into a shoebox, and buried it in the back yard. She wanted to bury something. She consistently steals from everywhere she works. Small amounts, usually. Last year she visited her grandmother in the nursing home to which the old woman is confined. She took an antique gold watch from her grand-mother's bedside table, and then went prowling through several of the other rooms, stealing small quantities of money and personal effects from the twilight folk in their golden years. When she got home she did not know what to do with her spoils, scared someone would come after her, so she threw everything away except the cash."

"I get the idea," said Shadow.

"She also has asymptomatic gonorrhea," said Wednesday. "She suspects she might be infected but does nothing about it. When her last boyfriend accused her of having given him a disease she was hurt, offended, and refused to see him again."

"This isn't necessary," said Shadow. "I said I get the idea. You could do this to anyone, couldn't you? Tell me bad things about them."

"Of course," agreed Wednesday. "They all do the same things. They may think their sins are original, but for the most part they are petty and repetitive."

"And that makes it okay for you to steal ten bucks from her?"

Wednesday paid the taxi and the two men walked into the airport, wandered up to their gate. Boarding had not yet begun. Wednesday said, "What the hell else can I do? They don't sacrifice rams or bulls to me. They don't send me the souls of killers and slaves, gallows-hung and raven-picked. *They* made me. *They* forgot me. Now I take a little back from them. Isn't that fair?"

"My mom used to say, 'Life isn't fair,'" said Shadow.

"Of course she did," said Wednesday. "It's one of those things that moms say, right up there with 'If all your friends jumped off a cliff would you do it too?'"

"You stiffed that girl for ten bucks, I slipped her ten bucks," said Shadow, doggedly. "It was the right thing to do, and I did it."

Someone announced that their plane was boarding. Wednesday stood up. "May your choices always be so clear," he said,[517] and once again, he sounded totally sincere.

It's true what they say, thought Shadow. *If you can fake sincerity, you've got it made.*[518]

517. The balance of this sentence does not appear in the First Edition.

518. This comment has been moved from earlier in the novel. See note 516, above.

✤   ✤   ✤

THE COLD SNAP was easing when Wednesday dropped Shadow off, in the small hours of the morning. It was still obscenely cold in Lakeside, but it was no longer impossibly cold. The lighted sign on the side of the M&I Bank flashed alternately 3:30 A.M. and −5° F as they drove through the town.

It was 9:30 A.M. when Chief of Police Chad Mulligan knocked on the apartment door and asked Shadow if he knew a girl named Alison McGovern.

"I don't think so," said Shadow, sleepily.

"This is her picture," said Mulligan. It was a high school photograph. Shadow recognized the person in the picture immediately: the girl with the blue rubber-band braces on her teeth, the one who had been learning all about the oral uses of Alka-Seltzer from her friend.

"Oh yeah. Okay. She was on the bus when I came into town."

"Where were you yesterday, Mister Ainsel?"

Shadow felt his world begin to spin away from him. He knew he had nothing to feel guilty about (*You're a parole-violating felon living under an assumed name*, whispered a calm voice in his mind. *Isn't that enough?*).

"San Francisco," he said. "California.[519] Helping my uncle transport a four-poster bed."

"You got any way of proving it? Ticket stubs? Anything like that?"

"Sure." He had both his boarding pass stubs in his back pocket, pulled them out. "What's going on?"

Chad Mulligan examined the boarding passes. "Alison McGovern's vanished. She helped out up at the Lakeside Humane Society. Feed animals, walk dogs. She'd come out for a few hours after school. One of those animal kids. So. Dolly Knopf, who runs the Humane Society, she'd always run her home when they closed up for the night. Yesterday Alison never got there."

"She's vanished."

"Yup. Her parents called us last night. Silly kid used to

519. Inexplicably, the Manuscript reads, "Portland, Oregon."

hitchhike up to the Humane Society. It's out on County W, pretty isolated. Her parents told her not to, but this isn't the kind of place where things happen . . . people here don't lock their doors, you know? And you can't tell kids. So, look at the photo again."

Alison McGovern was smiling. The rubber bands on her teeth in the photograph were red, not blue.

"You can honestly say you didn't kidnap her, rape her, murder her, anything like that?"

"I was in San Francisco. And I wouldn't do that shit."

"That was what I figured, pal. So you want to come help us look for her?"

"Me?"

"You. We've had the K-9 guys out this morning—nothing so far." He sighed. "Heck, Mike. I just hope she turns up in the Twin Cities with some dopey boyfriend."

"You think it's likely?"

"I think it's possible. You want to join the hunting party?"

Shadow remembered seeing the girl in Henning's Farm and Home Supplies, the flash of a shy blue-braced smile, how beautiful he had known she was going to be one day. "I'll come," he said.

There were two dozen men and women waiting in the lobby of the fire station. Shadow recognized Hinzelmann, and several other faces looked familiar. There were several police officers, dressed in blue, and some men and women from the Lumber County[520] sheriff's department, dressed in brown.

Chad Mulligan told them what Alison was wearing when she vanished (a scarlet snowsuit, green gloves, blue woolen hat under the hood of her snowsuit) and divided the volunteers into groups of three. Shadow, Hinzelmann, and a man named Brogan comprised one of the groups. They were reminded how short the daylight period was, told that if, god forbid, they found Alison's body they were not repeat not to disturb anything, just to radio back for help, but that if she was alive they were to keep her warm until help came.

They were dropped off out on County W.

Hinzelmann, Brogan and Shadow walked along the edge

520. There is no "Lumber County" in Wisconsin, but there is a "Wood County" in the middle of the state.

of a frozen creek. Each group of three had been issued a small hand-held walkie-talkie before they left.

The cloud cover was low, and the world was gray. No snow had fallen in the last thirty-six hours. Footprints stood out in the glittering crust of the crisp snow.

Brogan looked like a retired army colonel, with his slim mustache and white temples. He drove them, told Shadow he was a retired high school principal. "I took early retirement when I saw I wasn't getting any younger. These days I still teach a little, do the school play—that was always the high point of the year anyhow—and now I hunt a little and have a cabin down on Pike Lake, spend too much time there." As they set out Brogan said, "On the one hand, I hope we find her. On the other, if she's going to be found, I'd be very grateful if it was someone else who got to find her, and not us. You know what I mean?"

Shadow knew exactly what he meant.

The three men did not talk much. They walked, looking for a red snowsuit, or green gloves, or a blue hat, or a white body. Now and again Brogan, who had the walkie-talkie, would check in with Chad Mulligan.

At lunchtime they sat with the rest of the search party on a commandeered school bus and ate hot dogs and drank hot soup. Someone pointed out a red-tailed hawk in a bare tree, and someone else said that it looked more like a falcon, but it flew away and the argument was abandoned.

Hinzelmann told them a story about his grandfather's trumpet, and how he tried playing it during a cold snap, and the weather was so cold outside by the barn, where his grandfather had gone to practice, that no music came out.

"Then after he came inside he put the trumpet down by the wood-stove to thaw. Well, the family're all in bed that night and suddenly the unfrozen tunes start coming out of that trumpet. Scared my grandmother so much she nearly had kittens." [521]

The afternoon was endless, unfruitful, and depressing. The daylight faded slowly: distances collapsed and the world turned indigo and the wind blew cold enough to burn the

521. This is a variation of the story told by Baron Munchausen regarding his servant's French horn on a trip to Russia (*The Surprising Adventures of Baron Munchausen* by Ruldoph Erich Raspe (1895), Chapter VI).

skin on your face. When it was too dark to continue, Mulligan radioed to them to call it off for the evening, and they were picked up and driven back to the fire station.

In the block next to the fire station was the Buck Stops Here Tavern, and that was where most of the searchers wound up. They were exhausted and dispirited, talking to each other of the bald eagle that had circled them,[522] how cold it had become, how more than likely Alison would show up in a day or so, no idea of how much trouble she'd caused everyone.

"You shouldn't think badly of the town because of this," said Brogan. "It is a good town."

"Lakeside," said a trim woman whose name Shadow had forgotten, if ever they'd been introduced, "is the best town in the Northwoods. You know how many people are unemployed in Lakeside?"

"No," said Shadow.

"Less than twenty," she said. "There's over five thousand people live in and around this town. We may not be rich, but everyone's working. It's not like the mining towns up in the northeast—most of them are ghost towns now. There were farming towns that were killed by the falling cost of milk, or the low price of hogs. You know what the biggest cause of unnatural death is among farmers in the Midwest?"

"Suicide?" Shadow hazarded.

She looked almost disappointed. "Yeah. That's it. They kill themselves." She shook her head. Then she continued, "There are too many towns hereabouts that only exist for the hunters and the vacationers, towns that just take their money and send them home with their trophies and their bug bites. Then there are the company towns, where everything's just hunky-dory until Wal-Mart relocates their distribution center or 3M stops manufacturing CD cases there or whatever and suddenly there's a boatload of folks who can't pay their mortgages. I'm sorry, I didn't catch your name."

"Ainsel," said Shadow. "Mike Ainsel." The beer he was drinking was a local brew, made with spring water. It was good.

522. This phrase does not appear in the First Edition.

"I'm Callie Knopf," she said. "Dolly's sister." Her face was still ruddy from the cold. "So what I'm saying is that Lakeside's lucky. We've got a little of everything here—farm, light industry, tourism, crafts. Good schools."

Shadow looked at her in puzzlement. There was something empty at the bottom of all her words. It was as if he were listening to a salesman, a good salesman, who believed in his product, but still wanted to make sure you went home with all the brushes or the full set of encyclopedias. Perhaps she could see it in his face. She said, "I'm sorry. When you love something you just don't want to stop talking about it. What do you do, Mister Ainsel?"

"Heavy lifting," said Shadow.[523] "My uncle buys and sells antiques all over the country. He uses me to move big, heavy things. Without breaking them too badly. It's a good job, but not steady work." A black cat, the bar mascot, wound between Shadow's legs, rubbing its forehead on his boot. It leapt up beside him onto the bench and went to sleep.

"At least you get to travel," said Brogan. "You do anything else?"

"You got eight quarters on you?" asked Shadow. Brogan fumbled for his change. He found five quarters, pushed them across the table to Shadow. Callie Knopf produced another three quarters.

He laid out the coins, four in each row. Then, with scarcely a fumble, he did the Coins Through the Table, appearing to drop half the coins through the wood of the table, from his left hand into his right.

After that, he took all eight coins in his right hand, an empty water glass in his left, covered the glass with a napkin and appeared to make the coins vanish one by one from his right hand and land in the glass beneath the napkin with an audible clink. Finally, he opened his right hand to show it was empty, then swept the napkin away to show the coins in the glass.

He returned their coins—three to Callie, five to Brogan—then took a quarter back from Brogan's hand, leaving four

523. This sentence does not appear in the First Edition, nor does the sentence "Without breaking them too badly."

coins. He blew on it, and it was a penny, which he gave to Brogan, who counted his quarters and was dumbfounded to find that he still had all five in his hand.

"You're a Houdini," cackled Hinzelmann in delight. "That's what you are!"

"Just an amateur," said Shadow. "I've got a long way to go." Still, he felt a smidgen of pride. It had, he realized, been his first adult audience.

He stopped at the food store on the way home to buy a carton of milk. The ginger-haired girl on the checkout counter looked familiar, and her eyes were red-rimmed from crying. Her face was one big freckle.

"I know you," said Shadow. "You're—" And he was about to say the Alka-Seltzer girl, but bit it back and finished, "You're Alison's friend. From the bus. I hope she's going to be okay."

She sniffed and nodded. "Me too." She blew her nose on a tissue, hard, and pushed it back into her sleeve.

Her badge said HI! I'M SOPHIE! ASK ME HOW YOU CAN LOSE 20 LBS. IN 30 DAYS!

"I spent today looking for her. No luck yet."

Sophie nodded, blinked back tears. She waved the milk carton in front of a scanner and it chirped its price at them. Shadow passed her two dollars.

"I'm leaving this fucking town," said the girl in a sudden, choked voice. "I'm going to live with my mom in Ashland. Alison's gone. Sandy Olsen went last year. Jo Ming the year before that. What if it's me next year?"

"I thought Sandy Olsen was taken by his father."

"Yes," said the girl, bitterly. "I'm sure he was. And Jo Ming went out to California, and Sarah Lindquist got lost on a trail hike and they never found her. Whatever. I want to go to Ashland."

She took a deep breath and held it for a moment. Then she smiled at him. There was nothing insincere about that smile. It was just the smile of someone who knew that it was her job to smile when she gave someone their change, and as she put Shadow's change and receipt into his hand she told him to have a nice day. Then she turned to the woman with the full shopping cart behind him and began to unload-and-scan. A boy no older than Sophie sauntered over to bag the groceries.[524]

Shadow took his milk and drove away, past the gas station and the klunker on the ice, and over the bridge and home.

524. This sentence does not appear in the First Edition.

Coming to America
1778

There was a girl, and her uncle sold her, *wrote Mr. Ibis in his perfect copperplate handwriting.*

That is the tale; the rest is detail.[525]

There are stories that are true, in which each individual's tale is unique and tragic, and the worst of the tragedy is that we have heard it before, and we cannot allow ourselves to feel it too deeply. We build a shell around it like an oyster dealing with a painful particle of grit, coating it with smooth pearl layers in order to cope. This is how we walk and talk and function, day in, day out, immune to others' pain and loss. If it were to touch us it would cripple us or make saints of us; but, for the most part, it does not touch us. We cannot allow it to.

Tonight, as you eat, reflect if you can: there are children starving in the world, starving in numbers larger than the mind can easily hold, up in the big numbers where an error of a million here, a million there, can be forgiven. It may be uncomfortable for you to reflect upon this or it may not, but still, you will eat.

There are accounts which, if we open our hearts to them, will cut us too deeply. Look—here is a good man, good by his own lights and the lights of his friends: he is faithful and true to his wife, he adores and lavishes attention on his little children, he cares about his country, he does his job punctiliously, as best he can. So, efficiently and good-naturedly,

525. The next two paragraphs do not appear in the First Edition.

341

526. This sentence does not appear in the First Edition.

527. This sentence does not appear in the First Edition.

528. The English poet John Donne wrote, in 1624, as part of his *Devotions Upon Emergent Occasions*, Meditation 17:

> *No man is an Iland, intire of itselfe;*
>   *every man*
> *is a peece of the Continent, a part of the*
>   *maine;*
> *if a Clod bee washed away by the Sea,*
>   *Europe*
> *is the lesse, as well as if a Promontorie*
>   *were, as*
> *well as if a Manor of thy friends or of*
>   *thine*
> *owne were; any mans death*
>   *diminishes me,*
> *because I am involved in Mankinde;*
> *And therefore never send to know for*
>   *whom*
> *the bell tolls; It tolls for thee.*

he exterminates Jews: he appreciates the music that plays in the background to pacify them; he advises the Jews not to forget their identification numbers as they go into the showers—many people, he tells them, forget their numbers, and take the wrong clothes, when they come out of the showers. This calms the Jews: there will be life, they assure themselves, after the showers. And they are wrong.[526] Our man supervises the detail taking the bodies to the ovens; and if there is anything he feels bad about, it is that he still allows the gassing of vermin to affect him. Were he a truly good man, he knows, he would feel nothing but joy, as the earth is cleansed of its pests.

Leave him; he cuts too deep. He is too close to us and it hurts.[527]

There was a girl, and her uncle sold her. Put like that it seems so simple.

No man, proclaimed Donne, *is an Island*,[528] and he was wrong. If we were not islands, we would be lost, drowned in each other's tragedies. We are insulated (a word that means, literally, remember, *made into an island*) from the tragedy of others, by our island nature, and by the repetitive shape and form of the stories. We know the shape, and the shape does not change. There was a human being who was born, lived, and then, by some means or other, died. There. You may fill in the details from your own experience. As unoriginal as any other tale, as unique as any other life. Lives are snowflakes—unique in detail, forming patterns we have seen before, but as like one another as peas in a pod (and have you ever looked at peas in a pod? I mean, really *looked* at them? There's not a chance you'd mistake one for another, after a minute's close inspection.)

We need individual stories. Without individuals we see only numbers: a thousand dead, a hundred thousand dead, "casualties may rise to a million." With individual stories, the statistics become people—but even that is a lie, for the people continue to suffer in numbers that themselves are numbing and meaningless. *Look*, see the child's swollen, swollen belly, and the flies that crawl at the corners of his eyes, his skeletal limbs: will it make it easier for you to know his name, his age, his dreams, his fears? To see him from the inside? And if it does, are we not doing a disservice to his sister, who lies in the searing dust beside him, a distorted, distended caricature of a human child? And there, if we feel for them, are they now more important to us than a thousand other children touched by the same famine, a thousand other young lives who will soon be food for the flies' own myriad squirming children?

We draw our lines around these moments of pain, and remain upon our islands, and they cannot hurt us. They are covered with a smooth, safe, nacreous layer to let them slip, pearl-like, from our souls without real pain.

Fiction allows us to slide into these other heads, these other places, and look out through other eyes. And then in the tale we stop before we die, or we die vicariously and unharmed, and in the world beyond the tale we turn the page or close the book, and we resume our lives.

A life, which is, like any other, unlike any other.

And the simple truth is this: *there was a girl and her uncle sold her.*

This is what they used to say, where the girl came from: no man may be certain who fathered a child, but the mother, ah, that you could be certain of. Lineage and property was something that moved in the matrilineal line, but power remained in the hands of the men: a man had complete ownership of his sister's children.

There was a war in that place, and it was a small war, no more than a skirmish between the men of two rival villages. It was almost an argument. One village won the argument, one village lost it.

Life as a commodity, people as possessions. Enslavement had been part of the culture of those parts for thousands of years. The Arab slavers had destroyed the last of the great kingdoms of East Africa, while the West African nations had destroyed each other.

There was nothing untoward or unusual about their uncle selling the twins, although twins were considered magical beings, and their uncle was scared of them, scared enough that he did not tell them that they were to be sold in case they harmed his shadow and killed him. They were twelve years old. She was called Wututu, the messenger bird; he was called Agasu, the name of a dead king. They were healthy children, and, because they were twins, male and female, they were told many things about the gods, and because they were twins they listened to the things that they were told, and they remembered.

Their uncle was a fat and lazy man. If he had owned more cattle, perhaps he would have given up one of his cattle instead of the children, but he did not. He sold the twins. Enough of him: he shall not enter further into this narrative. We follow the twins.

They were marched, with several other slaves taken or sold in the war, for a dozen miles to a small outpost. Here they were traded, and the twins, along with thirteen others, were bought by six men with spears and knives who marched them to the west, toward the sea, and then for many miles along the coast. There were fifteen slaves now altogether, their hands loosely bound, tied neck to neck.

Wututu asked her brother Agasu what would happen to them.[529]

"I do not know," he said. Agasu was a boy who smiled often: his teeth were white and perfect, and he showed them as he grinned, his happy smiles making Wututu happy in her turn. He was not smiling now. Instead he tried to show bravery for his sister, his head back and shoulders spread, as proud, as menacing, as comical as a puppy with its hackles raised.

The man in the line behind Wututu, his cheeks scarred, said, "They will sell us to the white devils, who will take us to their home across the water."

"And what will they do to us there?" demanded Wututu.

The man said nothing.

"Well?" asked Wututu. Agasu tried to dart a glance over his shoulder. They were not allowed to talk or sing as they walked.

"It is possible they will eat us," said the man. "That is what I have been told. That is why they need so many slaves. It is because they are always hungry."

529. In the Manuscript, their names are Redflower and Leaf.

Wututu began to cry as she walked. Agasu said, "Do not cry, my sister. They will not eat you. I shall protect you. Our gods will protect you."

But Wututu continued to cry, walking with a heavy heart, feeling pain and anger and fear as only a child can feel it: raw and overwhelming. She was unable to tell Agasu that she was not worried about the white devils eating her. She would survive, she was certain of it. She cried because she was scared that they would eat her brother, and she was not certain that she could protect him.

They reached a trading post, and they were kept there for ten days. In the morning of the tenth day they were taken from the hut in which they had been imprisoned (it had become very crowded in the final days, as men arrived from far away, some of them from hundreds of miles, bringing their own strings and skeins of slaves). They were marched to the harbor, and Wututu saw the ship that was to take them away.

Her first thought was how big a ship it was, her second that it was too small for all of them to fit inside. It sat lightly on the water. The ship's boat came back and forth, ferrying the captives to the ship where they were manacled and arranged in low decks by sailors, some of whom were brick-red or tan skinned, with strange pointy noses and beards that made them look like beasts. Several of the sailors looked like her own people, like the men who had marched her to the coast. The men and the women and the children were separated, forced into different areas on the slave deck. There were too many slaves for the ship to hold easily, so another dozen men were chained up on the deck in the open, beneath the places where the crew would sling their hammocks.

Wututu was put in with the children, not with the women; and she was not chained, merely locked in. Agasu, her brother, was forced in with the men, in chains, packed like herrings. It stank under that deck, although the crew had scrubbed it down since their last cargo. It was a stink that had entered the wood: the smell of fear and bile and diarrhea and death, of fever and madness and hate. Wututu sat in the hot hold with the other children. She could feel the children on each side of her sweating. A wave tumbled a small boy into her, hard, and he apologized in a tongue that Wututu did not recognize. She tried to smile at him in the semi-darkness.

The ship set sail. Now it rode heavy in the water.

Wututu wondered about the place the white men came from (although none of them were truly white: sea-burned and sunburned they were, and their skins were dark). Were they so short of food that they had to send all the way to her land for people to eat? Or was it that she was to be a delicacy, a rare treat for a people who had eaten so many things that only black-skinned flesh in their cook pots made their mouths water?

On the second day out of port the ship hit a squall, not a bad one, but the ship's decks lurched and tumbled, and the smell of vomit joined the mixed smells of urine and liquid feces and fear-sweat. Rain poured down on them in bucketloads from the air gratings set in the ceiling of the slave deck.

A week into the voyage, and well out of sight of land, the slaves were allowed out of irons. They were warned that any disobedience, any trouble, and they would be punished more than they had ever imagined.

In the morning the captives were fed beans and ship's biscuits, and a mouthful each of vinegared lime juice, harsh enough that their faces would twist, and they would cough and splutter, and some of them would moan and wail as the lime juice was spooned out. They could not spit it out, though: if they were caught spitting or dribbling it out they were lashed or beaten.

The night brought them salted beef. It tasted unpleasant, and there was a rainbow sheen to the gray surface of the meat. That was at the start of the voyage. As the voyage continued, the meat grew worse.

When they could, Wututu and Agasu would huddle together, talking of their mother and their home and their playfellows. Sometimes Wututu would tell Agasu the stories their mother had told them, like those of Elegba, the trickiest of the gods, who was Great Mawu's eyes and ears in the world, who took messages to Mawu and brought back Mawu's replies.[530]

In the evenings, to while away the monotony of the voyage, the sailors would make the slaves sing for them and dance the dances of their native lands.

Wututu was lucky that she had been put in with the children. The children were packed in tightly and ignored; the women were not always so fortunate. On some slave ships the female slaves were raped repeatedly and continually by the crew, simply as an unspoken perquisite of the voyage. This was not one of those ships, which is not to say that there were no rapes.

A hundred men, women and children died on that voyage and were dropped over the side; and some of the captives who were dropped over the side had not yet died, but the green chill of the ocean cooled their final fever and they went down flailing, choking, lost.

Wututu and Agasu were traveling on a Dutch ship, but they did not know this, and it might as easily have been British, or Portuguese, or Spanish, or French.

The black crewmen on the ship, their skins even darker than Wututu's, told the captives where to go, what to do, when to dance. One morning Wututu caught one of the black guards staring at her. When she was eating, the man came over to her and stared down at her, without saying anything.

"Why do you do this?" she asked the man. "Why do you serve the white devils?"

He grinned at her as if her question was the funniest thing he ever had heard. Then he leaned over, so his lips were almost brushing her ears, so his hot breath on her ear made her suddenly feel sick. "If you were older," he told her, "I would make you scream with happiness from my penis. Perhaps I will do it tonight. I have seen how well you dance."

She looked at him with her nut-brown eyes and she said, unflinching, smiling even, "If you put it in me down there I will bite it off with my teeth down there. I am a witch girl,

530. Mawu is an orisha, a deity of the West African tribes, generally described as the twin sister of the male African deity Lisa (or androgynous and known as Mawu-Lisa) or the mate of Lisa. She created the earth and is associated with the sun and the moon. Elegba, more commonly called Eshu-Elegba, is a messenger of Mawu and often tempts humans to test them.

Temple of Shango, at Ibadan, Nigeria
African Mythology, p. 82

347

and I have very sharp teeth down there." She took pleasure in watching his expression change. He said nothing and walked away.

The words had come out of her mouth, but they had not been her words: she had not thought them or made them. No, she realized, those were the words of Elegba the trickster. Mawu had made the world and then, thanks to Elegba's trickery, had lost interest in it. It was Elegba of the clever ways and the iron-hard erection who had spoken through her, who had ridden her for a moment, and that night before she slept she gave thanks to Elegba.

Several of the captives refused to eat. They were whipped until they put food into their mouths and swallowed, although the whipping was severe enough that two men died of it. Still, no one else on the ship tried to starve themselves to freedom. A man and a woman tried to kill themselves by leaping over the side. The woman succeeded. The man was rescued and he was tied to the mast and lashed for the better part of a day, until his back ran with blood, and he was left there as the day became night. He was given no food to eat, and nothing to drink but his own piss. By the third day he was raving, and his head had swollen and grown soft, like an old melon. When he stopped raving they threw him over the side. Also, for five days following the escape attempt the captives were returned to their manacles and chains.

It was a long journey and a bad one for the captives, and it was not pleasant for the crew, although they had learned to harden their hearts to the business, and pretended to themselves that they were no more than farmers, taking their livestock to the market.

They made harbor on a pleasant, balmy day in Bridgetown, Barbados, and the captives were carried from the ship to the shore in low boats sent out from the dock, and taken to the market square, where they were, by dint of a certain amount of shouting, and blows from cudgels, arranged into lines. A whistle blew, and the market square filled with men, poking, prodding, red-faced men, shouting, inspecting, calling, appraising, grumbling.

Wututu and Agasu were separated then. It happened so fast—a big man forced open Agasu's mouth, looked at his teeth, felt his arm muscles, nodded, and two other men hauled Agasu away. He did not fight them. He looked at Wututu and called "Be brave," to her. She nodded, and then her vision smeared and blurred with tears, and she wailed. Together they were twins, magical, powerful. Apart they were two children in pain.

She never saw him again but once, and never in life.

This is what happened to Agasu. First they took him to a seasoning farm, where they whipped him daily for the things he did and didn't do, they taught him a smattering of English and they gave him the name of Inky Jack, for the darkness of his skin. When he ran away they hunted him down with dogs and brought him back, and cut off a toe with a chisel, to teach him a lesson he would not forget. He would have starved himself to death, but when he refused to eat his front teeth were broken and thin gruel was forced into his mouth, until he had no choice but to swallow or to choke.

Even in those times they preferred slaves born into captivity to those brought over from Africa. The free-born slaves tried to run, or they tried to die, and either way, there went the profits.

When Inky Jack was sixteen he was sold, with several other slaves, to a sugar plantation on St. Domingue.[531] They called him Hyacinth, the big, broken-toothed slave. He met an old woman from his own village on that plantation—she had been a house slave before her fingers became too gnarled and arthritic—who told him that the whites intentionally split up captives from the same towns and villages and regions, to avoid insurrection and revolts. They did not like it when slaves spoke to each other in their own languages.

Hyacinth learned some French, and was taught a few of the teachings of the Catholic Church. Each day he cut sugar cane from well before the sun rose until after the sun had set.

He fathered several children. He went with the other

531. Saint-Domingue has a history of violence. Originally claimed by the Spanish (after the "discovery" of the island of Hispaniola by Columbus), it was ceded to France as a colony in 1659, and French control was recognized by Spain in the Treaty of Ryswick of 1697. In 1791, slaves and free people of color began a rebellion against French authority. In response, France abolished slavery in the colony in 1793, though this alienated the dominant class of slaveholders. In 1802, rebellion began again, ousting the last French troops in late 1803. The following year, the colony later declared its independence and retook the indigenous name of Haiti. As Mama Zouzou points out later, U.S. president Thomas Jefferson and other European nations refused to recognize the Haitian republic, out of fear of the influence of a slave revolution. Recognition of the Haitian government was delayed until after the start of the American Civil War.

532. The "dance" was originally the martial art of stick-fighting, originating in the Kongo kingdom of West Africa, that evolved into a ritualized dance among the African slaves.

533. A patron of rains, streams, and rivers, Damballah is a Haitian god, though probably brought from the Yoruba tribes of Africa.

534. Also known as Ogue, Ogun, Oggun, Ogoun, or Gu, a god of warriors, smithing, and iron. He is said to have been born from a volcano.

535. Another god of the Yoruba people brought to Haiti, the god of thunder and lightning, war, and justice, said to be the brother of Ogun.

536. Also known as Azaka or Azacca, a god of the harvest and agriculture.

Vèvè for Damballah-wèdo,
drawn by the houngan Abraham

slaves, in the small hours of the night, to the woods, although it was forbidden, to dance the Calinda,[532] to sing to Damballa-Wedo,[533] the serpent god, in the form of a black snake. He sang to Elegba, to Ogu,[534] Shango,[535] Zaka,[536] and to many others, all the gods the captives had brought with them to the island, brought in their minds and their secret hearts.

The slaves on the sugar plantations of St. Domingue rarely lived more than a decade. The free time they were given—two hours in the heat of noon, and five hours in the dark of the night (from eleven until four)—was also the only time they had to grow and tend the food they would eat (for they were not fed by their masters, merely given small plots of land to cultivate, with which to feed themselves), and it was also the time they had to sleep and to dream. Even so, they would take that time and they would gather and dance, and sing and worship. The soil of St. Domingue was a fertile soil and the gods of Dahomey and the Congo and the Niger put down thick roots there and grew lush and huge and deep, and they promised freedom to those who worshiped them at night in the groves.

Hyacinth was twenty-five years of age when a spider bit the back of his right hand. The bite became infected and the flesh on the back of his hand was necrotic: soon enough his whole arm was swollen and purple, and the hand stank. It throbbed and it burned.

They gave him crude rum to drink, and they heated the blade of a machete in the fire until it glowed red and white. They cut his arm off at the shoulder with a saw, and they cauterized it with the burning blade. He lay in a fever for a week. Then he returned to work.

The one-armed slave called Hyacinth took part in the slave revolt of 1791.

Elegba himself took possession of Hyacinth in the grove, riding him as a white man rode a horse, and spoke through him. He remembered little of what was said, but the others who were with him told him that he had promised them freedom from their captivity. He remembered only his erection, rod-like and painful; and raising both hands—

the one he had, and the one he no longer possessed—to the moon.

A pig was killed, and the men and the women of that plantation drank the hot blood of the pig, pledging themselves and binding themselves into a brotherhood. They swore that they were an army of freedom, pledged themselves once more to the gods of all the lands from which they had been dragged as plunder.

"If we die in battle with the whites," they told each other, "we will be reborn in Africa, in our homes, in our own tribes."

There was another Hyacinth in the uprising, so they now called Agasu by the name of Big One-Arm. He fought, he worshiped, he sacrificed, he planned. He saw his friends and his lovers killed, and he kept fighting.

They fought for twelve years, a maddening, bloody struggle with the plantation owners, with the troops brought over from France. They fought, and they kept fighting, and, impossibly, they won.

On January the first, 1804, the independence of St. Domingue, soon to be known to the world as the Republic of Haiti, was declared. Big One-Arm did not live to see it. He had died in August 1802, bayoneted by a French soldier.

At the precise moment of the death of Big One-Arm (who had once been called Hyacinth, and before that, Inky Jack, and who was forever in his heart Agasu), his sister, whom he had known as Wututu, who had been called Mary on her first plantation in the Carolinas, and Daisy when she had become a house slave, and Sukey when she was sold to the Lavere family down the river in New Orleans, felt the cold bayonet slide between her ribs and started to scream and weep uncontrollably. Her twin daughters woke and began to howl. They were cream-and-coffee colored, her new babies, not like the black children she had borne when she was on the plantation and little more than a girl herself—children she had not seen since they were fifteen and ten years old. The middle girl had been dead for a year, when she was sold away from them.

Sukey had been whipped many times since she had come ashore—once, salt had been rubbed into the wounds, on another occasion she had been whipped so hard and for so long that she could not sit, or allow anything to touch her back, for several days. She had been raped several times when younger: by black men who had been ordered to share her wooden palette, and by white men. She had been chained. She had not wept then, though. Since her brother had been taken from her she had only wept once. It was in North Carolina, when she had seen the food for the slave children and the dogs poured into the same trough, and she had seen her little children scrabbling with the dogs for the scraps. She saw that happen one day—and she had seen it before, every day on that plantation, and she would see it again many times before she left—she saw it that one day and it broke her heart.

She had been beautiful for a while. Then the years of pain had taken their toll, and she was no longer beautiful. Her face was lined, and there was too much pain in those brown eyes.

Eleven years earlier, when she was twenty-five, her right arm had withered. None of the white folk had known what to make of it. The flesh seemed to melt from the bones, and now her right arm hung by her side, little more than a skeletal arm covered in skin, and almost immobile. After this she had become a house-slave.

The Casterton family, who had owned the plantation, were impressed by her cooking and house skills, but Mrs. Casterton found the withered arm unsettling, and so she was sold to the Lavere family, who were out for a year from Louisiana: M. Lavere was a fat, cheerful man, who was in need of a cook and a maid of all work, and who was not in the slightest repulsed by the slave Daisy's withered arm. When, a year later, they returned to Louisiana, slave Sukey went with them.

In New Orleans the women came to her, and the men also, to buy cures and love charms and little fetishes, black folks, yes, of course, but white folks too. The Lavere family turned a blind eye to it. Perhaps they enjoyed the prestige of having a slave who was feared and respected. They would not, however, sell her her freedom.

Sukey went into the bayou late at night, and she danced the Calinda and the Bamboula.[537] Like the dancers of St. Domingue and the dancers of her native land, the dancers in the bayou had a black snake as their *voudon*;[538] even so, the gods of her homeland and of the other African nations did not possess her people as they had possessed her brother and the folk of St. Domingue. She would still invoke them and call their names, to beg them for favors.

She listened when the white folk spoke of the revolt in St. Domingo (as they called it), and how it was doomed to fail—"Think of it! A cannibal land!"—and then she observed that they no longer spoke of it.

Soon, it seemed to her that they pretended that there never had been a place called St. Domingo, and as for Haiti, the word was never mentioned. It was as if the whole American nation had decided that they could, by an effort of belief, command a good-sized Caribbean island to no longer exist merely by willing it so.

A generation of Lavere children grew up under Sukey's watchful eye. The youngest, unable to say "Sukey" as a child, had called her Mama Zouzou, and the name had stuck. Now the year was 1821, and Sukey was in her mid-fifties. She looked much older.

She knew more of the secrets than old Sanité Dédé, who sold candies in front of the Cabildo, more than Marie Saloppé, who called herself the voodoo queen: both were free women of color, while Mama Zouzou was a slave, and would die a slave, or so her master had said.

The young woman who came to her to find what had happened to her husband styled herself the Widow Paris.[539] She was high-breasted and young and proud. She had African blood in her, and European blood, and Indian blood. Her skin was reddish, her hair was a gleaming black. Her eyes were black and haughty. Her husband, Jacques Paris, was, perhaps, dead. He was three-quarters white as these

537. The latter is a dance accompanied by drums, originating in Africa.

538. *Voudon* in this sense means the divine spirits and elements that formed the core of the belief system, here fetishized in the snake.

539. The Widow Paris, as the story styles her, was born Marie Catherine Laveau in 1801, according to official records, of African, Native American, and French descent. She was a renowned practitioner of what became known as New Orleans Voodoo. In 1819, she married Jacques (or Santiago) Paris; he died around 1820, having fathered two children with Marie, of whom nothing is known except their names. Marie then took a lover, Christophe Dominick Duminy de Glapion, a white nobleman. They reportedly had fifteen children, though that number may include grandchildren. One of their children was a daughter, born in 1827, also named Marie Laveau. This daughter, who occasionally used the surname of Paris, was also a renowned practitioner of Voodoo. While the mother Marie lived to the ripe old age of 79, her daughter Marie died ca. 1861. It is impossible at this remove to separate legend and lore from historical fact regarding the magical careers of either Marie.

Marie Laveau, from a 1920 painting
by Frank Schneider, based on a
reportedly lost 19th-century (1835)
painting by George Catlin

things were calculated, and the bastard of a once-proud family, one of the many immigrants who had fled from St. Domingo, and as freeborn as his striking young wife.

"My Jacques. Is he dead?" asked the Widow Paris. She was a hair-dresser who went from home to home, arranging the coiffures of the elegant ladies of New Orleans before their demanding social engagements.

Mama Zouzou consulted the bones, then shook her head. "He is with a white woman, somewhere north of here," she said. "A white woman with golden hair. He is alive." This was not magic. It was common knowledge in New Orleans just with whom Jacques Paris had run off, and the color of her hair.

Mama Zouzou was surprised to realize that the Widow Paris did not already know that Jacques was sticking his quadroon little pipi into a pink-skinned girl up in Colfax every night. Well, on the nights that he was not so drunk he could use it for nothing better than pissing. Perhaps she did know. Perhaps she had another reason for coming.

The Widow Paris came to see the old slave woman one or two times a week. After a month she brought gifts for the old woman: hair ribbons, and a seed-cake, and a black rooster.

"Mama Zouzou," said the girl, "it is time for you to teach me what you know."

"Yes," said Mama Zouzou, who knew which way the wind blew. And besides, the Widow Paris had confessed that she had been born with webbed toes, which meant that she was a twin and she had killed her twin in the womb. What choice did Mama Zouzou have?

She taught the girl that two nutmegs hung upon a string around the neck until the string breaks will cure heart murmurs, while a pigeon that has never flown, cut open and laid on the patient's head, will draw a fever. She showed her how to make a wishing bag, a small leather bag containing thirteen pennies, nine cotton seeds and the bristles of a black hog, and how to rub the bag to make wishes come true.

The Widow Paris learned everything that Mama Zouzou told her. She had no real interest in the gods, though. Not really. Her interests were in the practicalities. She was delighted to learn that if you dip a live frog in honey and place it in an ants' nest, then, when the bones are cleaned and white, a close examination will reveal a flat, heart-shaped bone, and another with a hook on it: the bone with the hook on it must be hooked onto the garment of the one you wish to love you, while the heart-shaped bone must be kept safely (for if it is lost, your loved one will turn on you like an angry dog). Infallibly, if you do this, the one you love will be yours.

She learned that dried snake powder, placed in the face powder of an enemy, will produce blindness, and that an enemy can be made to drown herself by taking a piece of her underwear, turning it inside out, and burying it at midnight under a brick.

Mama Zouzou showed the Widow Paris the World Wonder Root, the great and the little roots of John the Conqueror, she showed her dragon's blood, and valerian and five-finger grass. She showed her how to brew waste-away tea, and follow-me water and faire-Shingo water.

All these things and more Mama Zouzou showed the Widow Paris. Still, it was disappointing for the old woman. She did her best to teach her the hidden truths, the deep knowledge, to tell her of Elegba, of Mawu, of Aido-Hwedo the *voudon* serpent, and the rest, but the Widow Paris (I shall now tell you the name she was born with, and the name she later made famous: it was Marie Laveau. But this was not the great Marie Laveau, the one you have heard of, this was her mother, who eventually became the Widow Glapion), she had no interest in the gods of the distant land. If St. Domingo had been a lush black earth for the African gods to grow in, this land, with its corn and its melons, its crawfish and its cotton, was barren and infertile.

"She does not want to know," complains Mama Zouzou to Clémentine, her confidant, who took in the washing for many of the houses in that district, washing their curtains and coverlets. Clémentine had a blossom of burns on her cheek, and one of her children had been scalded to death when a copper overturned.

"Then do not teach her," says Clémentine.

"I teach her, but she does not see what is valuable—all she sees is what she can do with it. I give her diamonds, but she cares only for pretty glass. I give her a demi-*bouteille* of the best claret and she drinks river water. I give her quail and she wishes to eat only rat."

"Then why do you persist?" asks Clémentine.

Mama Zouzou shrugs her thin shoulders, causing her withered arm to shake.

She cannot answer. She could say that she teaches because she is grateful to be alive, and she is: she has seen too many die. She could say that she dreams that one day the slaves will rise, as they rose (and were defeated) in LaPlace, but that she knows in her heart that without the gods of Africa they will never overcome their white captors, will never return to their homelands.

When she woke that terrible night almost twenty years earlier, and felt the cold steel between her ribs, that was when Mama Zouzou's life had ended. Now she was someone who did not live, who simply hated. If you asked her about the hate she would have been unable to tell you about a twelve-year-old girl on a stinking ship: that had scabbed over in her mind—there had been too many whippings and beatings, too many nights in manacles, too many partings, too much pain. She could have told you about her son, though, and how his thumb had been cut off when their master discovered the boy was able to read and to write. She could have told you of her daughter, twelve years old and already eight months pregnant by an overseer, and how they dug a hole in the red earth to take her daughter's pregnant belly, and then they whipped her until her back had bled. Despite the carefully dug hole, her daughter had lost her baby and her life on a Sunday morning, when all the white folks were in church . . .

Too much pain.

"Worship them," Mama Zouzou told the young Widow Paris in the bayou, one hour after midnight. They were both naked to the waist, sweating in the humid night, their skins given accents by the white moonlight.

The Widow Paris's husband Jacques (whose own death,

three years later, would have several remarkable features)[540] had told Marie a little about the gods of St. Domingo, but she did not care. Power came from the rituals, not from the gods.

Together Mama Zouzou and the Widow Paris crooned and stamped and keened in the swamp. They were singing in the blacksnakes, the free woman of color and the slave woman with the withered arm.

"There is more to it than just, you prosper, your enemies fail," said Mama Zouzou.

Many of the words of the ceremonies, words she knew once, words her brother had also known, these words had fled from her memory. She told pretty Marie Laveau that the words did not matter, only the tunes and the beats, and there, singing and tapping in the blacksnakes, in the swamp, she has an odd vision. She sees the beats of the songs, the Calinda beat, the Bamboula beat, all the rhythms of equatorial Africa spreading slowly across this midnight land until the whole country shivers and swings to the beats of the old gods whose realms she had left. And even that, she understands somehow, in the swamp, even that will not be enough.

She turns to pretty Marie and sees herself through Marie's eyes, a black-skinned old woman, her face lined, her bony arm hanging limply by her side, her eyes the eyes of one who has seen her children fight in the trough for food from the dogs. She saw herself, and she knew then for the first time the revulsion and the fear the younger woman had for her.

Then she laughed, and crouched, and picked up in her good hand a blacksnake as tall as a sapling and as thick as a ship's rope.

"Here," she said. "Here will be our *voudon*."

She dropped the unresisting snake into a basket that yellow Marie was carrying.

And then, in the moonlight, the second sight possessed her for a final time, and she saw her brother Agasu, not the twelve-year-old boy she had last seen in the Bridgetown market so long ago, but a huge man, bald and grinning with

540. Jacques and Marie were only married for about a year; their relationship was more than three years, however, for they had a daughter in 1817. The "remarkable features" to which Mama Zouzou alludes are unremembered.

broken teeth, his back lined with deep scars. In one hand he held a machete-knife. His right arm was barely a stump.

She reached out her own good left hand.

"Stay, stay a while," she whispered. "I will be there. I will be with you soon."

And Marie Paris thought the old woman was speaking to her.

CHAPTER TWELVE

America has invested her religion as well as her morality in sound income-paying securities. She has adopted the unassailable position of a nation blessed because it deserves to be blessed; and her sons, whatever other theologies they may affect or disregard, subscribe unreservedly to this national creed.

—AGNES REPPLIER,
Times and Tendencies[541]

HADOW DROVE WEST, across Wisconsin and Minnesota and into North Dakota, where the snow-covered hills looked like huge sleeping buffalo, and he and Wednesday saw nothing but nothing and plenty of it for mile after mile. They went south, then, into South Dakota, heading for reservation country.

Wednesday had traded in the Lincoln town car, which Shadow had liked driving, for a lumbering and ancient Winnebago,[542] which smelled non-specifically but pervasively and unmistakably of male cat, and which he didn't enjoy driving at all.

As they passed their first signpost for Mount Rushmore, still several hundred miles away, Wednesday grunted. "Now that," he said, "is a holy place."

Shadow had thought Wednesday was asleep. He said, "I know it used to be sacred to the Indians."[543]

"It's a holy place," said Wednesday. "That's the American

541. The American essayist Agnes Repplier (1855–1950) was, in the words of historian John Lukacs, a *"moraliste* in the French tradition," commenting on a wide variety of subjects, in the judgment of critic Michael Dirda, "with discrimination and understated wit." This oft-quoted phrase is from her essay "On a Certain Condescension in Americans," which first appeared in the *Atlantic Monthly* for May 1926 and is collected in her 1931 volume *Times and Tendencies*.

542. A brand of recreational vehicle, generically now referring to a midsized RV.

543. The Black Hills were sacred to the Lakota Sioux, and the building of Mount Rushmore thus memorialized for them the white men's usurpation of the lands of the Native Americans.

544. John Gutzon de la Mothe Borglum (1867–1941), descended from Danish immigrants, was the designer and sculptor of the Mount Rushmore National Memorial. The project was conceived by local historian Doane Robinson, who wanted to promote the economy of the South Dakota region. Robinson originally proposed that the sculpture depict Lewis and Clark, the Native American leader Red Cloud, and "Buffalo" Bill Cody, but Borglum concluded that a more national focus would be needed to raise the funds required. He achieved federal funding, and the project began in 1927. Borglum died in March 1941 before completion. The original plan was to show the presidents from head to waist, but when funding ran out after Borglum's death, his son Lincoln Borglum reduced the scope of the project and concluded it in October 1941.

Way—they need to give people an excuse to come and worship. These days, people can't just go and see a mountain. Thus, Mister Gutzon Borglum's tremendous presidential faces.[544] Once they were carved, permission was granted, and now the people drive out in their multitudes to see something in the flesh that they've already seen on a thousand postcards."

"I knew a guy once. He did weight training at the Muscle Farm, years back. He said that the Dakota Indians, the young men climb up the mountain, then form death-defying human chains off the heads, just so that the guy at the end of the chain can piss on the president's nose."

Wednesday guffawed. "Oh, fine! Very fine! Is any specific president the particular butt of their ire?"

Shadow shrugged. "He never said."

Miles vanished beneath the wheels of the Winnebago. Shadow began to imagine that he was staying still while the American landscape moved past them at a steady sixty-seven miles per hour. A wintry mist fogged the edges of things.

It was midday on the second day of the drive, and they were almost there. Shadow, who had been thinking, said, "A girl vanished from Lakeside last week. When we were in San Francisco."

"Mm?" Wednesday sounded barely interested.

"Kid named Alison McGovern. She's not the first kid to vanish there. There have been others. They go in the wintertime."

Wednesday furrowed his brow. "It is a tragedy, is it not? The little faces on the milk-cartons—although I can't remember the last time I saw a kid on a milk-carton—and on the walls of freeway rest areas. *Have you seen me?* they ask. A deeply existential question at the best of times. *Have you seen me?* Pull off at the next exit."

Shadow thought he heard a helicopter pass overhead, but the clouds were too low to see anything.

"Why did you pick Lakeside?" asked Shadow.

"I told you. It's a nice quiet place to hide you away. You're off the board there, under the radar."

"Why?"

"Because that's the way it is. Now hang a left," said Wednesday.

Shadow turned left.

"There's something wrong," said Wednesday. "Fuck. Jesus fucking Christ on a bicycle. Slow down, but don't stop."

"Care to elaborate?"

"Trouble. Do you know any alternative routes?"

"Not really. This is my first time in South Dakota," said Shadow. "Also I don't know where we're going."

On the other side of the hill something flashed redly, smudged by the mist.

"Roadblock," said Wednesday. He pushed his hand deeply into first one pocket of his suit then another, searching for something.

"I can stop and turn around.[545] If we had a jeep I'd go off-road, but the Winnebago's just going to tip if I try and drive her across that ditch."

"We can't turn. They're behind us as well," said Wednesday. "Take your speed down to ten, fifteen miles per hour."

Shadow glanced into the mirror. There were headlights behind them, under a mile back. "Are you sure about this?" he asked.

Wednesday snorted. "Sure as eggs is eggs," he said. "As the turkey-farmer said when he hatched his first turtle. Ah, success!" and from the bottom of a pocket he produced a small piece of white chalk.

He started to scratch with the chalk on the dashboard of the camper, making marks as if he were solving an algebraic puzzle—or perhaps, Shadow thought, as if he were a hobo, scratching long messages to the other hobos in hobo code—*bad dog here, dangerous town, nice woman, soft jail in which to overnight* . . .[546]

"Okay," said Wednesday. "Now increase your speed to thirty. And don't slow down from that."

One of the cars behind them turned on its lights and siren and accelerated toward them. "Do not slow down," repeated Wednesday. "They just want us to slow before we get to the roadblock." *Scratch. Scratch. Scratch.*

545. The balance of this paragraph does not appear in the First Edition.

546. "Hobos" were not homeless persons, in the modern sense; rather, they were migrant workers who traveled America throughout the Depression era—often by rail—seeking temporary employment. To help each other out, hobos developed a secret language providing information to other hobos about the availability of food, water, or work or warning of dangerous situations. The code was pictographic, and messages left for others were often designed to appear to be random markings.

They crested the hill. The roadblock was less than a quarter of a mile away. Twelve cars arranged across the road, and on the side of the road, police cars, and several big black SUVs.

"There," said Wednesday, and he put his chalk away. The dashboard of the Winnebago was now covered with rune-like scratchings.

The car with the siren was just behind them. It had slowed to their speed, and an amplified voice was shouting, "Pull over!" Shadow looked at Wednesday.

"Turn right," said Wednesday. "Just pull off the road."

"I can't take this thing off-road. We'll tip."

"It'll be fine. Take a right. Now!"

Shadow pulled the wheel down with his right hand, and the Winnebago lurched and jolted. For a moment he thought he had been correct, that the camper was going to tip, and then the world through the windshield dissolved and shimmered, like the reflection in a clear pool when the wind brushes the surface,[547] and the Dakotas stretched and shifted.

The clouds and the mist and the snow and the day were gone.

Now there were stars overhead, hanging like frozen spears of light, stabbing the night sky.

"Park here," said Wednesday. "We can walk the rest of the way."

Shadow turned off the engine. He went into the back of the Winnebago, pulled on his coat, his Sorel winter boots, and his gloves. Then he climbed out of the vehicle and waited. "Okay," he said. "Let's go."

Wednesday looked at him with amusement and something else—irritation perhaps. Or pride. "Why don't you argue?" asked Wednesday. "Why don't you exclaim that it's all impossible? Why the hell do you just do what I say and take it all so fucking calmly?"

"Because you're not paying me to ask questions," said Shadow. And then he said, realizing the truth as the words came out of his mouth, "Anyway, nothing's really surprised me since Laura."

547. The balance of this sentence does not appear in the First Edition.

"Since she came back from the dead?"

"Since I learned she was screwing Robbie. That one hurt. Everything else just sits on the surface. Where are we going now?"

Wednesday pointed, and they began to walk. The ground beneath their feet was rock of some kind, slick and volcanic, occasionally glassy. The air was chilly, but not winter-cold. They sidestepped their way awkwardly down a hill. There was a rough path, and they followed it. Shadow looked down to the bottom of the hill,[548] and realized that what he was looking at was impossible.

"What the hell is that?" asked Shadow, but Wednesday touched his finger to his lips, shook his head sharply. Silence.

It looked like a mechanical spider, blue metal, glittering LED lights, and it was the size of a tractor. It squatted at the bottom of the hill. Beyond it were an assortment of bones, each with a flame beside it little bigger than a candle-flame, flickering.

Wednesday gestured for Shadow to keep his distance from these objects. Shadow took an extra step to the side, which was a mistake on that glassy path, as his ankle twisted and he tumbled down the slope as if he had been dropped, rolling and slipping and bouncing. He grabbed at a rock as he went past, and the obsidian snag ripped his leather glove as if it were paper.

He came to rest at the bottom of the hill, between the mechanical spider and the bones.

He put a hand down to push himself to his feet, and found himself touching what appeared to be a thighbone with the palm of his hand, and he was . . .

. . . standing in the daylight, smoking a cigarette, and looking at his watch. There were cars all around him, some empty, some not. He was wishing he had not had that last cup of coffee, for he dearly needed a piss, and it was starting to become uncomfortable.

One of the local law enforcement people came over to him, a big man with frost in his walrus mustache. He had already forgotten the man's name.

548. The balance of this sentence does not appear in the First Edition.

363

549. This paragraph and the next do not appear in the First Edition.

550. A spy-themed television series that ran from 1964 to 1968, featuring Napoleon Solo (Robert Vaughn) and Ilya Kuryakin (David McCallum) as agents of the U.N.C.L.E. agency run by Mr. Waverly (Leo G. Carroll). One secret entrance to U.N.C.L.E. headquarters was through Del Floria's Tailor Shop.

551. *Get Smart*, a parody of spy shows, ran from 1965 through 1970 and featured Don Adams as agent Maxwell Smart and Barbara Feldon as Agent 99, with Edward Platt playing the Chief. The show was created by Mel Brooks and Buck Henry and was broadly satirical. Smart always entered through a series of unmarked doors (no laundry), stepped into a phone booth, dialed a special number, and dropped from sight.

552. Agent Smart's "shoephone" was a running gag on *Get Smart*, but phones were secreted in many other places, including Agent 99's compact and her fingernail; Smart's tie, belt, wallet, garter, handkerchief, and eyeglasses; and even inside a regular telephone!

"I don't know how we could have lost them," says Local Law Enforcement, apologetic and puzzled.

"It was an optical illusion," he replies. "You get them in freak weather conditions. The mist. It was a mirage. They were driving down some other road. We thought they were on this one."

Local Law Enforcement looks disappointed. "Oh. I thought it was maybe like an *X-Files* kinda thing," he says.

"Nothing so exciting, I'm afraid." He suffers from occasional hemorrhoids and his ass has just started itching in the way that signals that a flare-up is coming. He wants to be back inside the Beltway. He wishes there was a tree to go and stand behind: the urge to piss is getting worse. He drops the cigarette and steps on it.

Local Law Enforcement walks over to one of the police cars and says something to the driver. They both shake their heads.

He wonders if he should simply grit his teeth, try to imagine that he is in Maui with no one else around, and piss against the rear wheel of the car.[549] He wishes he weren't so utterly pee-shy, and he thinks maybe he can hold it in for longer but he finds himself remembering a newspaper clipping that someone had tacked up in the lounge in his frat house, thirty years before: the cautionary tale of an old man who had been on a long bus ride with a busted rest-room, who had held it in, and, at the end of his journey, needed to be catheterized in order ever to piss again . . .

That was ridiculous. He isn't that old. He is going to celebrate his fiftieth birthday in April, and his waterworks work just fine. Everything works just fine.

He pulls out his telephone, touches the menu, pages down, and finds the address entry marked "Laundry" which had amused him so much when he typed it in—a reference to *The Man from U.N.C.L.E.*,[550] and as he looks at it he realizes that it's not from that at all, that was a *tailor's*, he's thinking of *Get Smart*,[551] and he still feels weird and slightly embarrassed after all these years about not realizing it was a comedy when he was a kid, and just wanting a shoephone . . .[552]

Mr. World (played by Crispin Glover, from the Starz presentation of *American Gods*)
Photo copyright © 2018 Fremantle North America

A woman's voice on the phone. "Yes?"

"This is Mister Town, for Mister World."

"Hold please. I'll see if he's available."

There is silence. Town crosses his legs, tugs his belt higher on his belly—got to lose these last ten pounds—and away from his bladder. Then an urbane voice says, "Hello, Mister Town."

"We lost them," says Town. He feels a knot of frustration in his gut: these were the bastards, the lousy dirty sons of bitches who killed Woody and Stone, for Chrissakes. Good men. Good men. He badly wants to fuck Mrs. Wood, but knows it's still too soon after Woody's death to make a move, so he is taking her out for dinner every couple of weeks, an investment in the future, she's just grateful for the attention . . .

"How?"

"I don't know. We set up a roadblock, there was nowhere they could have gone and they went there anyway."

"Just another one of life's little mysteries. Not to worry. Have you calmed the locals?"

"Told 'em it was an optical illusion."

"They buy it?"

"Probably."

There was something very familiar about Mr. World's voice—which was a strange thing to think, he'd been working for him directly for two years now, spoken to him every day, of *course* there was something familiar about his voice.

"They'll be far away by now."

"Should we send people down to the rez to intercept them?"

"Not worth the aggravation. Too many jurisdictional issues, and there are only so many strings we can pull in a morning. We have plenty of time. Just get back here. I've got my hands full at this end trying to organize the policy meeting."

"Trouble?"

"It's a pissing contest. I've proposed that we have it out here. The techies want it in Austin, or maybe San Jose, the players want it in Hollywood, the intangibles want it on Wall Street. Everybody wants it in their own back yard. Nobody's going to give."

"You need me to do anything?"

"Not yet. I'll growl at some of them, stroke others. You know the routine."

"Yes, sir."

"Carry on, Town."

The connection is broken.

Town thinks he should have had a SWAT team to pick off that fucking Winnebago, or land-mines on the road, or a tactical friggin' nukuler device, that would have showed those bastards they meant business. It was like Mr. World had once said to him, *We are writing the future in Letters of Fire*, and Mr. Town thinks that Jesus Christ if he doesn't piss now he'll lose a kidney, it'll just burst, and it was like his pop had said when they were on long journeys, when Town was a kid, out on the interstate, his pop would always say, "My back teeth are afloat," and Mr. Town could hear that voice even now, that sharp Yankee accent saying, "I got to take a leak soon. My back teeth are afloat" . . .

. . . and it was then that Shadow felt a hand opening his own hand, prising it open one finger at a time, off the thigh-bone it was clutching. He no longer needed to urinate; that was someone else. He was standing under the stars on a glassy rock plain,[553] and the bone was down on the ground beside the other bones.

Wednesday made the signal for silence again. Then he began to walk, and Shadow followed.

There was a creak from the mechanical spider, and Wednesday froze. Shadow stopped and waited with him. Green lights flickered and ran up and along its side in clusters. Shadow tried not to breathe too loudly.

He thought about what had just happened. It had been like looking through a window into someone else's mind. And then he thought, *Mr. World. It was me who thought his voice sounded familiar. That was my thought, not Town's. That was why that seemed so strange.* He tried to identify the voice in his mind, to put it into the category in which it belonged, but it eluded him.

It'll come to me, thought Shadow. Sooner or later, it'll come to me.

The green lights went blue, then red, then faded to a dull red, and the spider settled down on its metallic haunches. Wednesday began to walk forward, a lonely figure beneath the stars, in a broad-brimmed hat, his frayed dark cloak gusting randomly in the nowhere wind, his staff tapping on the glassy rock floor.

When the metallic spider was only a distant glint in the starlight, far back on the plain, Wednesday said, "It should be safe to speak, now."

"Where are we?"

"Behind the scenes," said Wednesday.

"Sorry?"

"Think of it as being behind the scenes. Like in a theatre

553. The balance of this sentence does not appear in the First Edition.

or something. I just pulled us out of the audience and now we're walking about backstage. It's a shortcut."

"When I touched that bone. I was in the mind of a guy named Town. He's with that spookshow. He hates us."

"Yes."

"He's got a boss named Mister World. He reminds me of someone, but I don't know who. I was looking into Town's head—or maybe I was in his head. I'm not certain."

"Do they know where we're headed?"

"I think they're calling off the hunt right now. They didn't want to follow us to the reservation. Are we going to a reservation?"

"Maybe." Wednesday leaned on his staff for a moment, then continued to walk.

"What was that spider thing?"

"A pattern manifestation. A search engine."

"Are they dangerous?"

"You only get to be my age by assuming the worst."

Shadow smiled. "And how old would that be?"

"Old as my tongue," said Wednesday. "And a few months older than my teeth."

"You play your cards so close to your chest," said Shadow, "that I'm not even sure that they're really cards at all."

Wednesday only grunted.

Each hill they came to was harder to climb.

Shadow began to feel headachy. There was a pounding quality to the starlight, something that resonated with the pulse in his temples and his chest. At the bottom of the next hill he stumbled, opened his mouth to say something and, without warning, he vomited.

Wednesday reached into an inside pocket, and produced a small hip flask. "Take a sip of this," he said. "Only a sip."

The liquid was pungent, and it evaporated in his mouth like a good brandy, although it did not taste like alcohol.[554] Wednesday took the flask away, and pocketed it. "It's not good for the audience to find themselves walking about backstage. That's why you're feeling sick. We need to hurry to get you out of here."

They walked faster—Wednesday at a solid trudge,

554. Is this soma? See note 486, above.

Shadow stumbling from time to time, but feeling better for the drink, which left his mouth tasting of orange peel, of rosemary oil and peppermint and cloves.

Wednesday took his arm. "There," he said, pointing to two identical hillocks of frozen rock-glass to their left. "Walk between those two mounds. Walk beside me."

They walked, and the cold air and bright daylight smashed into Shadow's face at the same time. He stopped, closed his eyes, dazzled and light-blinded, then, shading his eyes with his hand, he opened them once more.[555]

They were standing halfway up a gentle hill. The mist had gone, the day was sunny and chill, the sky was a perfect blue. At the bottom of the hill was a gravel road, and a red station wagon bounced along it like a child's toy car. A gust of wood smoke stung Shadow's face, making his eyes tear. The smoke came from a building nearby, which looked as if someone had picked up a mobile home and dropped it on the side of the hill thirty years ago. It was much repaired, patched, and, in places, added onto: Shadow was certain that the galvanized tin chimney, from which the wood smoke was coming, was not part of the original structure.[556]

As they reached the door it opened, and a middle-aged man with dark skin, sharp eyes and a mouth like a knife-slash looked down at them and said, "Eyah, I heard that there were two white men on their way to see me. Two whites in a Winnebago. And I heard that they got lost, like white men always get lost if they don't put up their signs everywhere. And now look at these two sorry beasts at the door. You know you're on Lakota land?" His hair was gray, and long.

"Since when were you Lakota, you old fraud?" said Wednesday. He was wearing a coat and a flap-eared cap, and already it seemed to Shadow unlikely that only a few moments ago under the stars he had been wearing a broad-brimmed hat and a tattered cloak. "So, Whiskey Jack.[557] You sad bastard. I'm starving, and my friend here just threw up his breakfast. Are you going to invite us in?"

Whiskey Jack scratched an armpit. He was wearing blue

555. This sentence does not appear in the First Edition.

556. This sentence does not appear in the First Edition.

557. The creator-god of the Cree People. *Encyclopedia of Ancient Deities* recounts this tale: "When Wisagatcak also known as Wisakedjak attempted to catch one of the beavers who lived at the beginning of the world, he failed. The beavers used magic against him and caused water to cover the land. Wisagatcak made a raft. Many varieties of animals climbed aboard. After a time, a muskrat dove into the water looking for land. He drowned. A raven flew about in search of land, without luck. Wisagatcak with the help of a wolf magically made a ball of moss which turned into earth. It spread across the whole world and rested on water." (p. 506) According to the *Dictionary of Native American Mythology*, he is also known as Wesucechak and usually appears in the guise of a wolf or moose but occasionally takes human form. He is known for his disguises, storytelling ability, and hunger, and therefore shares many characteristics with his fellow trickster-god Anansi. (p. 334)

558. John Chapman (1774–1845) was an American pioneer who introduced apple trees to Pennsylvania, Ohio, Indiana, Illinois, and parts of West Virginia as well as the Canadian province of Ontario. He became an American legend during his lifetime, known as "Johnny Appleseed." Chapman did not indiscriminately sow apple seeds; rather, he founded numerous nurseries across the territory. He was also a Swedenborgian missionary, spreading the Christian gospel as he sowed apples.

In 1948, Walt Disney Studios produced an animated segment (of its film *Melody Time*) featuring Dennis Day in "The Legend of Johnny Appleseed." The Disney version has a farmer inspired by an angel to go west and sow apple seeds across the country. He befriends a skunk and becomes a favorite of animals everywhere. No mention is made of his apostolic zeal. Thus, "Johnny Appleseed" has become fake folklore in the same manner as Paul Bunyan, notwithstanding his historical roots.

jeans and an undershirt the gray of his hair. He wore moccasins, and he seemed not to notice the cold. Then he said, "I like it here. Come in, white men who lost their Winnebago."

There was more wood smoke in the air inside the trailer, and there was another man in there, sitting at a table. The man wore stained buckskins, and was barefoot. His skin was the color of bark.

Wednesday seemed delighted. "Well," he said, "it seems our delay was fortuitous. Whiskey Jack and Apple Johnny. Two birds with one stone."

The man at the table, Apple Johnny, stared at Wednesday, then he reached down a hand to his crotch, cupped it and said, "Wrong again. I jes' checked and I got both of my stones, jes' where they oughta be." He looked up at Shadow, raised his hand, palm out. "I'm John Chapman.[558] You don't mind anything your boss says about me. He's an asshole. Always was an asshole. Always goin' to be an asshole. Some people is jes' assholes, and that's an end of it."

"Mike Ainsel," said Shadow.

Chapman rubbed his stubbly chin. "Ainsel," he said. "That's not a name. But it'll do at a pinch. What do they call you?"

"Shadow."

"I'll call you Shadow, then. Hey, Whiskey Jack"—but it wasn't really *Whiskey Jack* he was saying, Shadow realized; too many syllables—"how's the food looking?"

Whiskey Jack took a wooden spoon and lifted the lid off a black iron pot, bubbling away on the range of the wood-burning stove. "It's ready for eating," he said.

He took four plastic bowls and spooned the contents of the pot into the bowls, put them down on the table. Then he opened the door, stepped out into the snow, and pulled a plastic gallon jug from the snow bank. He brought it inside, and poured four large glasses of a cloudy yellow-brown liquid, which he put beside each bowl. Last of all, he found four spoons. He sat down at the table with the other men.

Wednesday raised his glass suspiciously. "Looks like piss," he said.

"You still drinking that stuff?" asked Whiskey Jack. "You white men are crazy. This is better." Then, to Shadow, "The stew is mostly wild turkey. John here brought the applejack."

"It's a soft apple cider," said John Chapman. "I never believed in hard liquor. Makes men mad."

The stew was delicious, and it was very good apple cider. Shadow forced himself to slow down, to chew his food, not to gulp it, but he was more hungry than he would have believed. He helped himself to a second bowl of the stew and a second glass of the cider.

"Dame Rumor says that you've been out talking to all manner of folk, offering them all manner of things. Says you're takin' the old folks on the war path," said John Chapman. Shadow and Whiskey Jack were washing up, putting the leftover stew into Tupperware bowls. Whiskey Jack put the bowls into the snowdrifts outside his front door, and put a milk crate on top of the place he'd pushed them, so he could find them again.

"I think that's a fair and judicious summary of events," said Wednesday.

"They will win," said Whiskey Jack flatly. "They won already. You lost already. Like the white man and my people. They won. And when they lost, they made treaties. Then they broke the treaties. And they won again. I'm not fighting for another lost cause."

"And it's no use you lookin' at me," said John Chapman, "for even if I fought for you—which'n I won't—I'm no use to you. Mangy rat-tailed bastards jes' picked me off and clean forgot me." He stopped. Then he said, "Paul Bunyan." He shook his head slowly and he said it again. "Paul Bunyan." Shadow had never heard two such innocuous words made to sound so damning.

"Paul Bunyan?" Shadow said. "What did he ever do?"

"He took up head space," said Whiskey Jack. He bummed a cigarette from Wednesday and the two men sat and smoked.

"It's like the idiots who figure that hummingbirds worry about their weight or tooth decay or some such nonsense, maybe they just want to spare hummingbirds the evils of

Johnny Appleseed
H. S. Knapp's A History of the Pioneer and Modern Times of Ashland County *(1862)*

559. This is not fiction: The internet is filled with warnings about the dangers of using artificial sweeteners, organic sugar, brown sugar, and honey in hummingbird feeders—they contain substances harmful to hummingbirds. See, e.g., https://www.humming birdsociety.org/feeding-hummingbirds/

560. Paul Bunyan was a creature of "tall tales," a legendary woodsman who worked in the lumbering trade, though there is scant evidence of an oral tradition of Bunyan tales predating 1910. The first Bunyan stories were published by James MacGillivray in "The Round River Drive" (*Detroit News-Tribune*, July 24, 1910). W. B. Laughead, a Minnesota advertising man, wrote a series of pamphlets between 1914 and 1944 using Bunyan as a figurehead to publicize the products of the Red River Lumber Company. His mythology has since spread in poetry, prose, and animated films.

561. This phrase does not appear in the First Edition.

A statue of Paul Bunyan, in Bangor, Maine
(Photo by Owlsmcgee, CCA-SA 4.0) https:// commons.wikimedia.org/wiki/File:Paul _Bunyan_statue_in_Bangor,_Maine.JPG

sugar," explained Wednesday. "So they fill the hummingbird feeders with fucking NutraSweet.[559] The birds come to the feeders and they drink it. Then they die, because their food contains no calories even though their little tummies are full. That's Paul Bunyan for you. Nobody ever told Paul Bunyan stories. Nobody ever believed in Paul Bunyan. He came staggering out of a New York ad agency in 1910 and filled the nation's myth stomach with empty calories."[560]

"I like Paul Bunyan," said Whiskey Jack. "I went on his ride at the Mall of America, few years back. You see big old Paul Bunyan at the top then you come crashing down. Splash. He's okay by me. I don't mind that he never existed, means he never cut down any trees. Not as good as planting trees though. That's better."

"You said a mouthful," said Johnny Chapman.

Wednesday blew a smoke ring. It hung in the air like something from a Warner Bros. cartoon,[561] dissipating slowly in wisps and curls. "Damn it, Whiskey Jack, that's not the point and you know it."

"I'm not going to help you," said Whiskey Jack. "When you get your ass kicked, you can come back here and if I'm still here I'll feed you again. You get the best food in the fall."

Wednesday said, "All the alternatives are worse."

"You have no idea what the alternatives are," said Whiskey Jack. Then he looked at Shadow. "You are hunting," he said. His voice was cigarette-roughened, and it resonated in that space, smoky with leaking wood smoke and cigarettes.

"I'm working," said Shadow.

Whiskey Jack shook his head. "You are also hunting something," he said. "There is a debt that you wish to pay."

Shadow thought of Laura's blue lips and the blood on her hands, and he nodded.

"Listen. Fox was here first, and his brother was the wolf. Fox said, people will live forever. If they die they will not die for long. Wolf said, no, people will die, people must die, all things that live must die, or they will spread and cover the world, and eat all the salmon and the caribou and the buffalo, eat all the squash and all the corn. Now one day Wolf died, and he said to the fox, quick, bring me back to life. And Fox said, No, the dead must stay dead. You convinced me. And he wept as he said this. But he said it, and it was final. Now Wolf rules the world of the dead and Fox lives always under the sun and the moon, and he still mourns his brother."

Wednesday said, "If you won't play, you won't play. We'll be moving on."

Whiskey Jack's face was impassive. "I'm talking to this young man," he said. "You are beyond help. He is not." He turned back to Shadow. "You know, you cannot come to me here unless I wish it."[562]

Shadow realized that he did know this. "Yes."

"Tell me your dream," said Whiskey Jack.

Shadow said, "I was climbing a tower of skulls. There were huge birds flying around it. They had lightning in their wings. They were attacking me. The tower fell."

"Everybody dreams," said Wednesday. "Can we hit the road?"

"Not everybody dreams of the Wakinyau,[563] the thunderbirds," said Whiskey Jack. "We felt the echoes of it here."

"I told you," said Wednesday. "Jesus."

"There's a clutch of thunderbirds in West Virginia," said Chapman, idly. "A couple of hens and an old cock-bird at least. There's also a breeding pair in the land, they used to call it the State of Franklin, but old Ben never got his state, up between Kentucky and Tennessee.[564] Course, there was never a great number of them, even at the best of times."

Whiskey Jack reached out a hand the color of the red clay, and he touched Shadow's face, gently. His irises were light brown banded with dark brown, and in that face those eyes seemed luminous.[565] "Eyah," he said. "It's true. If you hunt the thunderbird you could bring your woman back. But she belongs to the wolf, in the dead places, not walking the land."

"How do you know?" asked Shadow.

Whiskey Jack's lips did not move. "What did the Buffalo tell you?"

"To believe."

562. This sentence and the next do not appear in the First Edition.

563. Also called Wakinyan, Waukkeon, or Waukheon, these were thunder spirits or thunder birds, part of the Native American Lakota mythology.

564. The state of Frankland, later renamed Franklin, consisted of four western counties of North Carolina. Between 1784 and 1788, the territory, with its own governor, petitioned to join the fledgling colonies but could not get the requisite two-thirds approval. After its economy struggled and Indian raids pressed the territory, it rejoined North Carolina. Soon after its acquisition, North Carolina ceded the land to the United States to become part of the Southwest Territory, later the State of Tennessee. The area is now the northeastern part of Tennessee.

565. This sentence does not appear in the First Edition.

"Good advice. Are you going to follow it?"

"Kind of. I guess." They were talking without words, without mouths, without sound. Shadow wondered if, for the other two men in the room, they were standing, unmoving, for a heartbeat or for a fraction of a heartbeat.

"When you find your tribe, come back and see me," said Whiskey Jack. "I can help."

"I shall."

Whiskey Jack lowered his hand. Then he turned to Wednesday. "Are you going to fetch your Ho Chunk?"

"My what?"

"*Ho Chunk*.[566] It's what the Winnebago call themselves."

Wednesday shook his head. "It's too risky. Retrieving it could be problematic. They'll be looking for it."

"Is it stolen?"

Wednesday looked affronted. "Not a bit of it. The papers are in the glove compartment."

"And the keys?"

"I've got them," said Shadow.

"My nephew, Harry Bluejay, has an '81 Buick. Why don't you give me the keys to your camper? You can take his car."

Wednesday bristled. "What kind of trade is that?"

Whiskey Jack shrugged. "You know how hard it will be to bring back your camper from where you abandoned it? I'm doing you a favor. Take it or leave it. I don't care." He closed his knife-wound mouth.

Wednesday looked angry, and then the anger became rue, and he said, "Shadow, give the man the keys to the Winnebago." Shadow passed the car keys to Whiskey Jack.

"Johnny," said Whiskey Jack, "will you take these men down to find Harry Bluejay? Tell him I said for him to give them his car."

"Be my pleasure," said John Chapman.

He got up and walked to the door, picked up a small burlap sack sitting next to it, opened the door and walked outside. Shadow and Wednesday followed him. Whiskey Jack waited in the doorway. "Hey," he said to Wednesday. "Don't come back here, you. You are not welcome."

566. Whiskey Jack is making a joke here. The Ho-Chunk, also known as Hoocąągra or Winnebago, are Native Americans from the Midwest, part of the Sioux-speaking peoples.

Wednesday extended his middle finger heavenward. "Rotate on this," he said affably.

They walked downhill through the snow, pushing their way through the drifts. Chapman walked in front, his bare feet red against the crust-topped snow. "Aren't you cold?" asked Shadow.

"My wife was Choctaw," said Chapman.

"And she taught you mystical ways to keep out the cold?"

"Nope. She thought I was crazy," said Chapman. "She used t'say, 'Johnny, why don't you jes' put on boots?'" The slope of the hill became steeper, and they were forced to stop talking. The three men stumbled and slipped on the snow, using the trunks of birch trees on the hillside to steady themselves, and to stop themselves from falling. When the ground became slightly more level, Chapman said, "She's dead now, a'course. When she died I guess maybe I went a mite crazy. It could happen to anyone. It could happen to you." He clapped Shadow on the arm. "By Jesus and Jehosophat, you're a big man."

"So they tell me," said Shadow.[567]

They trudged down that hill for another half an hour, until they reached the gravel road that wound around the base of it, and the three men began to walk along it, toward the cluster of buildings they had seen from high on the hill.

A car slowed and stopped. The woman driving it reached over, wound down the passenger window, and said, "You bozos need a ride?"

"You are very gracious, madam," said Wednesday. "We're looking for a Mister Harry Bluejay."

"He'll be down at the rec hall," said the woman. She was in her forties, Shadow guessed. "Get in."

They got in. Wednesday took the passenger seat, John Chapman and Shadow climbed into the back. Shadow's legs were too long to sit in the back comfortably, but he did the best he could. The car jolted forward, down the gravel road.

"So where did you three come from?" asked the driver.

"Just visiting with a friend," said Wednesday.

"Lives on the hill back there," said Shadow.

567. The following nineteen paragraphs do not appear in the First Draft.

"What hill?" she asked.

Shadow looked back through the dusty rear window, looking back at the hill. But there was no high hill back there; nothing but clouds on the plains.

"Whiskey Jack," he said.

"Ah," she said. "We call him Inktomi here. I think it's the same guy. My grandfather used to tell some pretty good stories about him. Of course, all the best of them were kind of dirty." They hit a bump in the road, and the woman swore. "You okay back there?"

"Yes, ma'am," said Johnny Chapman. He was holding on to the back seat with both hands.

"Rez roads," she said. "You get used to them."

"Are they all like this?" asked Shadow.

"Pretty much," said the woman. "All the ones round here. And don't you go asking about all the money from casinos, because who in their right mind wants to come all the way out here to go to a casino? We don't see none of that money out here."

"I'm sorry."

"Don't be." She changed gears with a crash and a groan. "You know the white population all round here is falling? You go out there, you find ghost towns. How you going to keep them down on the farm, after they seen the world on their television screens? And it's not worth anyone's while to farm the Badlands anyhow. They took our lands, they settled here, now they're leaving. They go south. They go west. Maybe if we wait for enough of them to move to New York and Miami and L.A. we can take the whole of the middle back without a fight."

"Good luck," said Shadow.

They found Harry Bluejay in the rec hall, at the pool table, doing trick shots to impress a group of several girls. He had a blue jay tattooed on the back of his right hand, and multiple piercings in his right ear.

"*Ho hoka*, Harry Bluejay," said John Chapman.

"Fuck off, you crazy barefoot white ghost," said Harry Bluejay, conversationally. "You give me the creeps."

There were older men at the far end of the room, some of

them playing cards, some of them talking. There were other men, younger men of about Harry Bluejay's age, waiting for their turn at the pool table. It was a full-sized pool table, and a rip in the green baize on one side had been repaired with silver-gray duct tape.

"I got a message from your uncle," said Chapman, unfazed. "He says you're to give these two your car."

There must have been thirty, maybe even forty people in that hall, and now they were every one of them looking intently at their playing cards, or their feet, or their fingernails, and pretending as hard as they could not to be listening.

"He's not my uncle."

A cigarette-smoke fug hung over the hall like a cirrus cloud. Chapman smiled widely, displaying the worst set of teeth that Shadow had seen in a human mouth. "You want to tell your uncle that? He says you're the only reason he stays among the Lakota."

"Whiskey Jack says a lot of things," said Harry Bluejay, petulantly. But he did not say Whiskey Jack either. It sounded almost the same, to Shadow's ear, but not quite: *Wisakedjak*, he thought. That's what they're saying. Not Whiskey Jack at all.

Shadow said, "Yeah. And one of the things he said was that we're trading our Winnebago for your Buick."

"I don't see a Winnebago."

"He'll bring you the Winnebago," said John Chapman. "You know he will."

Harry Bluejay attempted a trick shot and missed. His hand was not steady enough. "I'm not the old fox's nephew," said Harry Bluejay. "I wish he wouldn't say that to people."

"Better a live fox than a dead wolf," said Wednesday, in a voice so deep it was almost a growl. "Now, will you sell us your car?"

Harry Bluejay shivered, visibly and violently. "Sure," he said. "Sure. I was only kidding. I kid a lot, me." He put down the pool cue on the pool table, and took a thick jacket, pulling it out from a cluster of similar jackets hanging from pegs by the door. "Let me get my shit out of the car first," he said.

He kept darting glances at Wednesday, as if he were concerned that the older man was about to explode.

Harry Bluejay's car was parked a hundred yards away. As they walked toward it, they passed a small whitewashed Catholic church, and a fair-haired man in a priest's collar who stared at them from the doorway as they went past. He was sucking on a cigarette as if he did not enjoy smoking it.

"Good day to you, father!" called Johnny Chapman, but the man in the dog-collar made no reply; he crushed his cigarette under his heel, picked up the butt, and dropped it into the bin beside the door, and went inside.

"I told you not to give him those pamphlets last time you were here," said Harry Bluejay.[568]

"It is he that is in error, not me," said Chapman. "If he'd jes read the Swedenborg[569] I gave him he'd know that. It'd bring light into his life."

Harry Bluejay's car was missing its side mirrors, and its tires were the baldest Shadow had ever seen: perfectly smooth black rubber. Harry Bluejay told them the car drank oil, but as long as you kept pouring oil in, it would just keep running forever, unless it stopped.

Harry Bluejay filled a black garbage bag with shit from the car (said shit including several screw-top bottles of cheap beer, unfinished, a small packet of cannabis resin wrapped in silver foil and badly hidden in the car's ashtray, a skunk-tail, two dozen country and western cassettes and a battered, yellowing copy of *Stranger in a Strange Land*[570]). "Sorry I was jerking your chain before," said Harry Bluejay to Wednesday, passing him the car keys. "You know when I'll get the Winnebago?"

"Ask your uncle. He's the fucking used-car dealer," growled Wednesday.

"Wisakedjak is not my uncle," said Harry Bluejay. He took his black garbage bag and went into the nearest house, and closed the door behind him.

They dropped Johnny Chapman in Sioux Falls, outside a whole-food store.

Wednesday said nothing on the drive. He was brooding.

In a family restaurant just outside St. Paul Shadow picked

568. This paragraph and the next do not appear in the First Edition.

569. The writings of scientist and Swedish Lutheran theologian Emanuel Swedenborg (1688–1772) are the basis for what became known as the New Church (or Swedenborgianism), a religious movement for which Chapman proselytized.

570. The 1961 science-fiction novel by Robert A. Heinlein, in which young Valentine Michael Smith, the last survivor of a Martian colony and raised by Martians, comes to Earth and becomes the founder of a new religion, known as the Church of All Worlds.

up a newspaper someone else had put down. He looked at it once, then again, then he showed it to Wednesday. Wednesday was in a black sulk, as he had been since they left Whiskey Jack's place.

"Look at that," said Shadow.

Wednesday sighed, and looked down at the paper[571] with an expression of pain, as if lowering his head hurt more than he could put into words. "I am," he said, "delighted that the air-traffic controllers' dispute has been resolved without recourse to industrial action."

"Not that," said Shadow. "Look. It says it's the fourteenth of February."

"Happy Valentine's Day."

"So we set out January the what, twentieth, twenty-first? I wasn't keeping track of the dates, but it was the third week of January. We were three days on the road, all told. So how is it the fourteenth of February?"

"Because we walked for almost a month," said Wednesday. "In the Badlands. Backstage."

"Hell of a shortcut," said Shadow.

Wednesday pushed the paper away. "Fucking Johnny Appleseed, always going on about Paul Bunyan. In real life Chapman owned fourteen apple orchards. He farmed thousands of acres. Yes, he kept pace with the western frontier, but there's not a story out there about him with a word of truth in it, save that he went a little crazy once. But it doesn't matter. Like the newspapers used to say, if the truth isn't big enough, you print the legend.[572] This country needs its legends. And even the legends don't believe it any more."

"But you see it."

"I'm a has-been. Who the fuck cares about me?"[573]

Shadow said softly, "You're a god."

Wednesday looked at him sharply. He seemed to be about to say something, and then he slumped back in his seat, and looked down at the menu and said, "So?"

"It's a good thing to be a god," said Shadow.

"Is it?" asked Wednesday, and this time it was Shadow who looked away.

571. The balance of this sentence does not appear in the First Edition.

572. Wednesday paraphrases a line from the 1962 John Ford film *The Man Who Shot Liberty Valance*: "When the legend becomes fact, print the legend."

573. The Manuscript adds, "'I was king of America for a week, but I lost the title in a poker game in Little Rock."

In a gas station twenty-five miles outside Lakeside, on the wall by the restrooms, Shadow saw a homemade photo-copied notice: a black and white photo of Alison McGovern and the handwritten question *Have You Seen Me?* above it. Same yearbook photograph: smiling confidently, a girl with rubber-band braces on her top teeth who wants to work with animals when she grows up. *Have you seen me?*

Shadow bought a Snickers bar, a bottle of water, and a copy of the *Lakeside News*. The above-the-fold story, writ-ten by Marguerite Olsen, our Lakeside Reporter, showed a photograph of a boy and an older man, out on the fro-zen lake, standing by an outhouse-like ice-fishing shack, and between them they were holding a big fish. They were smiling. *Father and Son Catch Record Northern Pike. Full story inside.*

Wednesday was driving. He said, "Read me anything in-teresting you find in the paper."

Shadow looked carefully, and he turned the pages slowly, but he couldn't find anything.

Wednesday dropped him off in the driveway outside his apartment. A smoke-colored cat stared at him from the driveway, then fled when he bent to stroke it.

Shadow stopped on the wooden deck outside his apart-ment and looked out at the lake, dotted here and there with green and brown ice-fishing huts. Many of them had cars parked beside them. On the ice nearer the bridge sat the old green klunker, just as it had sat in the newspaper. "March the twenty-third," said Shadow, encouragingly. "Round nine fifteen in the morning. You can do it."

"Not a chance," said a woman's voice. "April third. Six P.M. That way the day warms up the ice." Shadow smiled. Mar-guerite Olsen was wearing a ski suit. She was at the far end of the deck, refilling the bird feeder with white blocks of suet.

"I read your article in the *Lakeside News* on the Town Record Northern Pike."

"Exciting, huh?"

"Well, educational, maybe."

"I thought you weren't coming back to us," she said. "You were gone for a while, huh?"

"My uncle needed me," said Shadow. "The time kind of got away from us."

She placed the last suet brick in its cage, and began to fill a net sock with thistle-seeds from a plastic milk-jug. Several goldfinches, olive in their winter coats, twitted impatiently from a nearby fir-tree.

"I didn't see anything in the paper about Alison Mc-Govern."

"There wasn't anything to report. She's still missing. There was a rumor that someone had seen her in Detroit, but it turned out to be a false alarm."

"Poor kid."

Marguerite Olsen screwed the top back onto the gallon jug. "I hope she's dead," she said, matter-of-factly.

Shadow was shocked. "Why?"

"Because the alternatives are worse."

The goldfinches hopped frantically from branch to branch of the fir-tree, impatient for the people to be gone. A downy woodpecker joined them.[574]

You aren't thinking about Alison, thought Shadow. *You're thinking of your son. You're thinking of Sandy.*

He remembered someone saying *I miss Sandy.* Who was that?

"Good talking to you," he said.

"Yeah," she said. "You, too."[575]

February passed in a succession of short, gray days. Some days the snow fell, most days it didn't. The weather warmed up, and on the good days it got above freezing. Shadow stayed in his apartment until it began to feel like a prison cell, and then, on the days that Wednesday did not need him, he began to walk.

He would walk for much of the day, long trudges out of the town. He walked, alone, until he reached the national forest to the north and the west, or the corn fields and cow pastures to the south. He walked the Lumber County Wilderness Trail, and he walked along the old railroad tracks,

574. This sentence does not appear in the First Edition.

575. Gaiman's note to himself in the Manuscript at this point is as follows: "The process of writing fiction is the process of moving from alternate to alternate, from possibility to possibility—things crystalise into realities, become certainties, become real. Meanwhile, writer's block, if such a beast exists, for me is the frozen moment of indecision. Is it better to send Shadow to dinner in Marguerite's—or to dinner at, say, Mabel's? I can do more naturalistic stuff at home, more strange stuff and cover more plot in the restaurant? And what about the storm? And Wednesday? I can see the end of the book faintly, as if walking a valley in mist, feeling my way. The way I have come is clear, the way I still have to go is strange and dark."

This note is followed by a scene in which Shadow discovers a visitor in his apartment: Low-Key, whom Shadow then recognizes as Loki. The scene now appears as a conversation outside the motel in the center of America with the limousine driver.

and he walked the back roads. A couple of times he even walked along the frozen lake, from north to south. Sometimes he'd see locals or winter tourists or joggers, and he'd wave and say hi. Mostly he saw nobody at all, just crows and finches and, a few times, he spotted a hawk feasting on a roadkill possum or raccoon. On one memorable occasion he watched an eagle snatch a silver fish from the middle of the White Pine River, the water frozen at the edges, but still rushing and flowing at the center. The fish wriggled and jerked in the eagle's talons, glittering in the midday sun; Shadow imagined the fish freeing itself and swimming off across the sky, and he smiled.

If he walked, he discovered, he did not have to think, and that was just the way he liked it; when he thought, his mind went to places he could not control, places that made him feel uncomfortable. Exhaustion was the best thing. When he was exhausted, his thoughts did not wander to Laura, or to the strange dreams, or to things that were not and could not be. He would return home from walking, and sleep without difficulty and without dreaming.

He ran into Police Chief Chad Mulligan in George's Barber Shop in the town square. Shadow always had high hopes for haircuts, but they never lived up to his expectations. After every haircut he looked more or less the same, only with shorter hair. Chad, seated in the barber's chair beside Shadow's, seemed surprisingly concerned about his own appearance. When his haircut was finished he gazed grimly at his reflection, as if he were preparing to give it a speeding ticket.

"It looks good," Shadow told him.

"Would it look good to you if you were a woman?"

"I guess."

They went across the square to Mabel's together, ordered mugs of hot chocolate. Chad said, "Hey. Mike. Have you ever thought about a career in law enforcement?"

Shadow shrugged. "I can't say I have," he said. "Seems like there's a whole lot of things you got to know."

Chad shook his head. "You know the main part of police work, somewhere like this? It's just keeping your head.

Something happens, somebody's screaming at you, scream-ing blue murder, you simply have to be able to say that you're sure that it's all a mistake, and you'll just sort it all out if they just step outside quietly. And you have to be able to mean it."

"And then you sort it out?"

"Mostly, that's when you put handcuffs on them. But yeah, you do what you can to sort it out. Let me know if you want a job. We're hiring. And you're the kind of guy we want."

"I'll keep that in mind, if the thing with my uncle falls through."

They sipped their hot chocolate. Mulligan said, "Say, Mike, what would you do if you had a cousin? Like a widow. And she started calling you?"

"Calling you how?"

"On the phone. Long distance. She lives out of state." His cheeks crimsoned. "I saw her last year at a family wed-ding, out in Oregon. She was married, back then, though, I mean, her husband was still alive, and she's family. Not a first cousin. Pretty distant."

"You got a thing for her?"

Blush. "I don't know about that."

"Well then, put it another way. Does she have a thing for you?"

"Well, she's said a few things when she called. She's a very fine-looking woman."

"So . . . what are you going to do about it?"

"I could ask her out here. I could do that, couldn't I? She's kind of said she'd like to come up here."

"You're both adults. I'd say go for it."

Chad nodded, and blushed, and nodded again.

The telephone in Shadow's apartment was silent and dead. He thought about getting it connected, but could think of no one he wanted to call. Late one night he picked it up and listened, and was convinced that he could hear a wind blowing and a distant conversation between a group of people whose voices were too faint to distinguish. He said, "Hello?" and "Who's there?" but there was no reply, only a sudden silence and then the faraway sound of laughter, so faint he was not certain he was not imagining it.

✦　✦　✦

SHADOW MADE MORE journeys with Wednesday in the weeks that followed.

He waited in the kitchen of a Rhode Island cottage, and listened while Wednesday sat in a darkened bedroom and argued with a woman who would not get out of bed, nor would she let Wednesday or Shadow look at her face. In the refrigerator was a plastic bag filled with crickets, and another filled with the corpses of baby mice.[576]

In a rock club in Seattle Shadow watched Wednesday shout his greeting, over the noise of the band, to a young woman with short red hair and blue-spiral tattoos. That talk must have gone well, for Wednesday came away from it grinning delightedly.

Five days later Shadow was waiting in the rental when Wednesday walked, scowling, from the lobby of an office building in Dallas. Wednesday slammed the car door when he got in, and sat there in silence, his face red with rage. He said, "Drive." Then he said, "Fucking Albanians.[577] Like anybody cares."

Three days after that they flew to Boulder, where they had a pleasant lunch with five young Japanese women.[578] It was a meal of pleasantries and politeness, and Shadow walked away from it unsure of whether anything had been agreed to or decided. Wednesday, though, seemed happy enough.

Shadow had begun to look forward to returning to Lakeside. There was a peace there, and a welcome, that he appreciated.

Each morning, when he was not away working for Wednesday, he would drive across the bridge to the town square. He would buy two pasties at Mabel's; he would eat one pasty then and there, and drink a coffee. If someone had left a newspaper out he would read it, although he was never interested enough in the news to purchase a newspaper himself.

576. This appears to be food for snakes—a suggestion that this recruit is Medusa, in Greek mythology a Gorgon, a winged human female with living venomous snakes in place of hair. We will see her, as well as the young woman from Seattle, at the final battle.

577. The Albanian gods were plentiful and reportedly unfriendly to humans. Ancient Albania was annexed by the Roman empire and later the Bulgarian (in the ninth century) and finally the Ottoman empire in the fifteenth century. Perhaps the ancient gods were squeezed out by successive deities and hence hostile to group efforts such as those proposed by Wednesday.

578. These are kitsune, Japanese fox spirits imbued with shapeshifting powers as well as long life and high intelligence. Later, one of the kitsune is killed and resumes her fox shape. See text accompanying note 829, below. A kitsune appears in Gaiman's *Sandman* novella "The Dream Hunters" (1999).

He would pocket the second pasty, wrapped in its paper bag, and eat it for his lunch.

He was reading *USA Today* one morning when Mabel said, "Hey, Mike. Where you going today?"

The sky was pale blue. The morning mist had left the trees covered with hoarfrost. "I don't know," said Shadow. "Maybe I'll walk the wilderness trail again."

She refilled his coffee. "You ever gone east on County Q? It's kind of pretty out thataway. That's the little road that starts acrost from the carpet store on Twentieth Avenue."

"No. Never have."

"Well," she said, "it's kind of pretty."

It was extremely pretty. Shadow parked his car at the edge of town, and walked along the side of the road, a winding, country road that curled around the hills to the east of the town. Each of the hills was covered with leafless maple trees, and bone-white birches, and dark firs and pines. There was no footpath, and Shadow walked along the middle of the road, making for the side whenever he heard a car.[579]

At one point a small dark cat kept pace with him beside the road. It was the color of dirt, with white forepaws. He walked over to it. It did not run away.

"Hey, cat," said Shadow, unselfconsciously.

The cat put its head on one side, looked up at him with emerald eyes. Then it hissed—not at him, but at something over on the side of the road, something he could not see.

"Easy," said Shadow. The cat stalked away across the road, and vanished into a field of old unharvested corn.

Around the next bend in the road Shadow came upon a tiny graveyard. The headstones were weathered, although several of them had sprays of fresh flowers resting against them. There was no wall about the graveyard, and no fence, only low mulberry trees, planted at the margins, bent over with ice and age. Shadow stepped over the piled-up ice and slush at the side of the road. There were two stone gateposts marking the entry to the graveyard, although there was no gate between them. He walked into the graveyard between the two posts.

Prince Hanzoku, terrorized by a nine-tailed fox (a kitsune)
Utagawa Kuniyoshi (ca. 1850)

579. This sentence does not appear in the First Edition.

He wandered around the graveyard, looking at the head-stones. There were no inscriptions later than 1969. He brushed the snow from a solid-looking granite angel, and he leaned against it.

He took the paper bag from his pocket, and removed the pasty from it. He broke off the top: it breathed a faint wisp of steam into the wintry air. It smelled really good, too. He bit into it.

Something rustled behind him. He thought for a moment it was the cat, but then he smelled perfume, and under the perfume, the scent of something rotten.

"Please don't look at me," she said, from behind him.

"Hello, Laura," said Shadow.

Her voice was hesitant, perhaps, he thought, even a little scared. She said, "Hello, puppy."

He broke off some pasty. "Would you like some?" he asked.

She was standing immediately behind him, now. "No," she said. "You eat it. I don't eat food any more."

He ate his pasty. It was good. "I want to look at you," he said.

"You won't like it," she told him.

"Please?"

She stepped around the stone angel. Shadow looked at her, in the daylight. Some things were different and some things were the same. Her eyes had not changed, nor had the crooked hopefulness of her smile. And she was, very obviously, very dead. Shadow finished his pasty. He stood up and tipped the crumbs out of the paper bag, then folded it up and put it back into his pocket.

The time he had spent in the funeral home in Cairo made it easier somehow for him to be in her presence. He did not know what to say to her.

Her cold hand sought his, and he squeezed it gently. He could feel his heart beating in his chest. He was scared, and what scared him was the normality of the moment. He felt so comfortable with her at his side that he would have been willing to stand there forever.

"I miss you," he admitted.

"I'm here," she said.

"That's when I miss you most. When you're here. When you aren't here, when you're just a ghost from the past or a dream from another life, it's easier then."

She squeezed his fingers.

"So," he asked. "How's death?"

"Hard," she said. "It just keeps going."

She rested her head on his shoulder, and it almost undid him. He said, "You want to walk for a bit?"

"Sure." She smiled up at him, a nervous, crooked smile in a dead face.

They walked out of the little graveyard, and made their way back down the road, toward the town, hand in hand. "Where have you been?" she asked.

"Here," he said. "Mostly."

"Since Christmas," she said, "I kind of lost you. Sometimes I would know where you were, for a few hours, for a few days. You'd be all over. Then you'd fade away again."

"I was in this town," he said. "Lakeside. It's a good little town."

"Oh," she said.

She no longer wore the blue dress in which she had been buried. Now she wore several sweaters, a long, dark, skirt, and burgundy boots. Shadow commented on them.

Laura ducked her head. She smiled. "Aren't they great boots? I found them in this great shoe store in Chicago."

"So what made you decide to come up from Chicago?"

"Oh, I've not been in Chicago for a while, puppy. I was heading south. The cold was bothering me. You'd think I'd welcome it. But it's something to do with being dead, I guess. You don't feel it as cold. You feel it as a sort of nothing, and when you're dead I guess the only thing that you're scared of is nothing. I was going to go to Texas. I planned to spend the winter in Galveston. I think I used to winter in Galveston, when I was a kid."

"I don't think you did," said Shadow. "You've never mentioned it before."

"No? Maybe it was someone else, then. I don't know. I remember seagulls—throwing bread in the air for seagulls, hundreds of them, the whole sky becoming nothing but seagulls as they flapped their wings and snatched the bread from the air." She paused. "If I didn't see it, I guess someone else did."

A car came around the corner. The driver waved them hello. Shadow waved back. It felt wonderfully normal to walk with his wife.

"This feels good," said Laura, as if she was reading his mind.

"Yes," said Shadow.

"I'm pleased it feels good for you, too.[580] When the call came I had to hurry back. I was barely into Texas."

"Call?"

She looked up at him. Around her neck the gold coin glinted. "It felt like a call," she said. "I started to think about you,[581] about how much more fun I would have with you than down in Galveston. About how much I needed to see you. It was like a hunger."

"You knew I was *here*, then?"

"Yes." She stopped. She frowned, and her upper teeth pressed into her blue lower lip, biting it gently. She put her head on one side and said, "I did. Suddenly, I did. I thought you were calling me, but it wasn't you, was it?"

"No."

"You didn't want to see me."

"It wasn't that." He hesitated. "No. I didn't want to see you. It hurts too much."

The snow crunched beneath their feet and it glittered diamonds as the sunlight caught it.

"It must be hard," said Laura, "not being alive."

"You mean it's hard for you to be dead? Look, I'm still going to figure out how to bring you back, properly. I think I'm on the right track—"

"No," she said. "I mean, I'm grateful. And I hope you really can do it. I did a lot of bad stuff . . ." She shook her head. "But I was talking about you."

"I'm alive," said Shadow. "I'm not dead. Remember?"

"You're not dead," she said. "But I'm not sure that you're alive, either. Not really."

580. This sentence does not appear in the First Edition.

581. The balance of this sentence does not appear in the First Edition.

This isn't the way this conversation goes, thought Shadow. *This isn't the way anything goes.*

"I love you," she said, dispassionately. "You're my puppy. But when you're really dead you get to see things clearer. It's like there isn't anyone there. You know? You're like this big, solid, man-shaped hole in the world." She frowned. "Even when we were together. I loved being with you because you adored me, and you would do anything for me. But sometimes I'd go into a room and I wouldn't think there was anybody in there. And I'd turn the light on, or I'd turn the light off, and I'd realize that you were in there, sitting on your own, not reading, not watching TV, not doing anything."

She hugged him then, as if to take the sting from her words, and she said, "The best thing about Robbie was that he was *somebody*. He was a jerk sometimes, and he could be a joke, and he loved to have mirrors around when we made love so he could watch himself fucking me, but he was alive, puppy. He *wanted* things. He filled the space." She stopped, looked up at him, tipped her head a little to one side. "I'm sorry. Did I hurt your feelings?"

He did not trust his voice not to betray him, so he simply shook his head.

"Good," she said. "That's good."

They were approaching the rest area where he had parked his car. Shadow felt that he needed to say something: *I love you*, or *please don't go*, or *I'm sorry*. The kind of words you use to patch a conversation that had lurched, without warning, into the dark places. Instead he said, "I'm not dead."

"Maybe not," she said. "But are you sure you're alive?"

"Look at me," he said.

"That's not an answer," said his dead wife. "You'll know it, when you are."

"What now?" he said.

"Well," she said, "I've seen you now. I'm going south again."

"Back to Texas?"

"Somewhere warm. I don't care."

"I have to wait here," said Shadow. "Until my boss needs me."

582. This and the next two paragraphs do not appear in the First Edition.

"That's not living," said Laura. She sighed; and then she smiled, the same smile that had been able to tug at his heart no matter how many times he saw it. Every time she smiled at him had been the first time all over again.

"Will I see you again?"[582]

She looked up at him and she stopped smiling. "I guess so," she said. "In the end. Nothing's finished, yet, is it?"

"No," he said. "It's not."

He went to put his arm around her, but she shook her head and pulled out of his reach. She sat down on the edge of a snow-covered picnic table, and she watched him drive away.

Interlude

The war had begun and nobody saw it. The storm was lowering and nobody knew it.

Wars are being fought all the time, with the world outside no more the wiser: the war on crime, the war on poverty, the war on drugs. This war was smaller than those, and huger, and more selective, but it was as real as any.[583]

A falling girder in Manhattan closed a street for two days. It killed two pedestrians, an Arabic taxi-driver and the taxi-driver's passenger.[584]

A trucker in Denver was found dead in his home. The murder instrument, a rubber-gripped claw-headed hammer, had been left on the floor beside his corpse. His face was untouched, but the back of his head was completely destroyed, and several words in a foreign alphabet were written on the bathroom mirror in brown lipstick.

In a postal sorting station in Phoenix, Arizona, a man went crazy, *went postal* as they said on the evening news, and shot Terry "The Troll" Evensen, a morbidly obese, awkward man who lived alone in a trailer.[585] Several other people in the sorting station were fired on, but only Evensen was killed. The man who fired the shots—first thought to be a disgruntled postal worker—was not caught, and was never identified.

"Frankly," said Terry "The Troll" Evensen's supervisor, on the *News at Five*, "if anyone around here was gonna go

583. This paragraph does not appear in the First Edition.

584. Is this Salim? If the attacks are on the old gods, then Salim could have been misidentified as an ifrit.

585. Presumably the "shell" of a real troll.

postal, we would have figured it was gonna be The Troll. Okay worker, but a weird guy. I mean, you never can tell, huh?"

That interview was cut when the segment was repeated, later that evening.

586. Religious hermits.

A community of nine anchorites[586] in Montana was found dead. Reporters speculated that it was a mass suicide, but soon the cause of death was reported as carbon monoxide poisoning from an elderly furnace.

A lobster tank was smashed in the lobby of an Atlanta seafood restaurant.[587]

587. This sentence does not appear in the First Edition.

A crypt was defiled in the Key West graveyard.

An Amtrak passenger train hit a UPS truck in Idaho, killing the driver of the truck. No passengers were seriously injured.

It was still a cold war at this stage, a phony war, nothing that could be truly won or lost.

The wind stirred the branches of the tree. Sparks flew from the fire. The storm was coming.

588. See note 95, above.

The Queen of Sheba,[588] half-demon, they said, on her father's side, witch-woman, wise-woman and queen, who ruled Sheba when Sheba was the richest land there ever was, when its spices and its gems and scented woods were taken by boat and camel-back to the corners of the earth, who was worshiped even when she was alive, worshiped as a living goddess by the wisest of kings, stands on the sidewalk of Sunset Boulevard at 2:00 A.M. staring blankly out at the traffic like a slutty plastic bride on a black and neon wedding cake. She stands as if she owns the sidewalk and the night that surrounds her.

When someone looks straight at her, her lips move, as if she is talking to herself. When men in cars drive past her she makes eye-contact and she smiles. She ignores the men who walk past her on the sidewalk (it happens, people walk everywhere, even in West Hollywood); she ignores them, does her best to pretend that they are not there.[589]

589. This sentence does not appear in the First Edition.

It's been a long night.

It's been a long week, and a long four thousand years.

She is proud that she owes nothing to anyone. The other girls on the street, they have pimps, they have habits, they have children, they have people who take what they make. Not her.

There is nothing holy left in her profession. Not any more.

A week ago the rains began in Los Angeles, slicking the streets into road accidents, crumbling the mud from the hillsides and toppling houses into canyons, washing the world into the gutters and storm drains, drowning the bums and the homeless camped down in the concrete channel of the river. When the rains come in Los Angeles they always take people by surprise.

Bilquis has spent the last week inside. Unable to stand on the sidewalk, she has curled up in her bed in the room the color of raw liver, listening to the rain pattering on the metal box of the window air conditioner and placing personals on the Internet. She has left her invitations on Adultfriendfinder.com, LA-escorts.com, Classyhollywood babes.com, has given herself an anonymous e-mail address. She was proud of herself for negotiating the new territories, but remains nervous—she has spent a long time avoiding anything that might resemble a paper trail. She has never even taken a small ad in the back pages of the *LA Weekly*, preferring to pick out her own customers, to find by eye and smell and touch the ones who will worship her as she needs to be worshiped, the ones who will let her take them all the way . . .

And it occurs to her now, standing and shivering on the street corner (for the late February rains have left off, but the chill they brought with them remains), that she has a habit as bad as that of the smack whores and the crack whores, and this distresses her, and her lips begin to move again. If you were close enough to her ruby-red lips you would hear her say,

"I will rise now and go about the city in the streets, and in the broad ways I will seek the one I love." She is whispering that, and she whispers, *"I am my beloved's, and my beloved is mine.*[590] *He said, this stature of mine is like to a*

590. This line is from the *Song of Songs*, 6:3 (King James Version). The rest is pieces of other sections of the book. The *Song of Songs*, also known as the *Song of Solomon*, is traditionally attributed to King Solomon and taken to describe his relationship with the Queen of Sheba. However, there is no textual evidence that the book was written during Solomon's time, and in fact the vocabulary, idiom, and syntax reflect a period centuries later.

palm tree, and my breasts like clusters of grapes. He said he would come to me then. I am my beloved's and his desire is only toward me."

Bilquis hopes that the break in the rains will bring the johns back. Most of the year she walks the two or three blocks on Sunset, enjoying the cool L.A. nights. Once a month she pays off a man named Sabbah,[591] an officer in the LAPD, who replaced another officer in the LAPD she used to pay off, who had vanished. That man's name was Jerry LeBec, and his disappearance had been a mystery to the LAPD. He had become obsessed with Bilquis, had taken to following her on foot, and one afternoon she woke, startled by a noise, and opened the door to her apartment, and found Jerry LeBec in civilian clothes kneeling and swaying on the worn carpet, his head bowed, waiting for her to come out. The noise she had heard was the noise of his head, thumping against her door as he rocked back and forth on his knees.

She stroked his hair and told him to come inside, and later she put his clothes into a black plastic garbage bag and tossed them into a Dumpster behind a hotel several blocks away. His gun and his wallet she put into a grocery store bag. She poured used coffee grounds and food waste on top of them, folded the top of the bag and dropped it into a trashcan at a bus-stop.

She kept no souvenirs.

The orange night-sky glimmers to the west with distant lightning, somewhere out to sea, and Bilquis knows that the rain will be starting soon. She sighs. She does not want to be caught in the rain. She will return to her apartment, she decides, and take a bath, and shave her legs, it seems to her she is always shaving her legs, and sleep.

"By night on my bed I sought him whom my soul loveth," she whispers. *"Let him kiss me with the kisses of his mouth. My beloved is mine and I am his."*[592]

She begins to walk up a side-street, walking up the hillside to where her car is parked.

Headlights come up behind her, slowing as they approach her, and she turns her face to the street and smiles.

591. The officer is unnamed in the First Edition.

592. This paragraph is not in the First Edition.

The smile freezes when she sees the car is a white stretch limo. Men in stretch limos want to fuck in stretch limos, not in the privacy of Bilquis's shrine. Still, it might be an investment. Something for the future.

A tinted window hums down and Bilquis walks over to the limo, smiling. "Hey, honey," she says. "You looking for something?"

"Sweet loving," says a voice from the back of the stretch. She peers inside, as much as she can through the open window: she knows a girl who got into a stretch with five drunk football players and got hurt real bad, but there's only one john in there that she can see, and he looks kind of on the young side. He doesn't feel like a worshiper, but money, good money that's passed from his hand to hers, that's an energy in its own right—*baraka*[593] they called it, once on a time—which she can use and frankly these days, every little helps.

"How much?" he asks.

"Depends on what you want and how long you want it for," she says. "And whether you can afford it." She can smell something smoky drifting out of the limo window. It smells like burning wires and overheating circuit boards. The door is pushed open from inside.

"I can pay for anything I want," says the john. She leans into the car and looks around. There's nobody else in there, just the john, a puffy-faced kid who doesn't even look old enough to drink. Nobody else, so she gets in.

"Rich kid, huh?" she says.

"Richer than rich," he tells her, edging along the leather seat towards her. He moves awkwardly. She smiles at him.

"Mm. Makes me hot, honey," she tells him. "You must be one of them dot-coms I read about?"

He preens then, puffs like a bullfrog. "Yeah. Among other things. I'm a technical boy." The car moves off.

"So," he says. "Tell me, Bilquis, how much just to suck my cock?"

"What you call me?"

"Bilquis," he says, again. And then he sings, in a voice not made for singing, "*You are an immaterial girl living in a*

> **593.** In Arabic, a blessing; in other tongues, good fortune.

594. The song "Material Girl," written by Peter Brown and Robert Rans and first recorded by Madonna, in 1985, has the lyrics "Cause we're living in a material world / And I am a material girl."

595. *The Love Bug* (1968) was the first of a series of Walt Disney Productions live-action comedies featuring Herbie, an anthropomorphosized 1963 Volkswagen racing Beetle. While Herbie does not speak and has a driver, he does repeatedly evidence a will of his own.

material world."[594] There is something rehearsed about his words, as if he's practiced this exchange in front of a mirror.

She stops smiling, and her face changes, becomes wiser, sharper, harder. "What do you want?"

"I told you. Sweet loving."

"I'll give you whatever you want," she says. She needs to get out of the limo. It's moving too fast for her to throw herself from the car, she figures, but she'll do it if she can't talk her way out of this. Whatever's happening here, she doesn't like it.

"What I want. Yes." He pauses. His tongue runs over his lips. "I want a clean world. I want to own tomorrow. I want evolution, devolution, and revolution. I want to move our kind from the fringes of the slipstream to the higher ground of the mainstream. You people are underground. That's wrong. We need to take the spotlight and shine. Front and center. You people have been so far underground for so long you've lost the use of your eyes."

"My name's Ayesha," she says. "I don't know what you're talking about. There's another girl on that corner, her name Bilquis. We could go back to Sunset, you could have both of us . . ."

"Oh, Bilquis," he says, and he sighs, theatrically. "There's only so much belief to go around. They're reaching the end of what they can give us. The credibility gap." And then he sings, once again, in his tuneless nasal voice, "You are an analog girl, living in a digital world." The limo takes a corner too fast, and he tumbles across the seat into her. The driver of the car is hidden behind tinted glass. An irrational conviction strikes her, that nobody is driving the car, that the white limo is driving through Beverly Hills like Herbie the Love Bug,[595] under its own power.

Then the john reaches out his hand and taps on the tinted glass.

The car slows, and before it has stopped moving Bilquis has pushed open the door and she half-jumps, half-falls out onto the blacktop. She's on a hillside road. To the left of her is a steep hill, to the right is a sheer drop. She starts to run down the road.

The limo sits there, unmoving.

It starts to rain, and her high heels slip and twist beneath her. She kicks them off and runs, soaked to the skin, looking for somewhere she can get off the road. She's scared. She has power, true, but it's hunger-magic, cunt-magic. It has kept her alive in this land for so long, true, but for everything else that's not simply living she uses her sharp eyes and her mind, her height and her presence.

There's a metal guard-rail at knee-height on her right, to stop cars from tumbling over the side of the hill, and now the rain is running down the hill-road turning it into a river, and the soles of her feet have started to bleed.

The lights of L.A. are spread out in front of her, a twinkling electrical map of an imaginary kingdom, the heavens laid out right here on earth, and she knows that all she needs to be safe is to get off the road.

I am black but comely, she mouths to the night and the rain. *I am the rose of Sharon, and the lily of the valleys. Stay me with flagons, comfort me with apples: for I am sick of love.*[596]

596. More lines from the *Song of Songs*.

A fork of lightning burns greenly across the night sky. She loses her footing, slides several feet, skinning her leg and elbow, and she is getting to her feet when she sees the lights of the car descending the hill toward her. It's coming down too fast for safety and she wonders whether to throw herself to the right, where it could crush her against the hillside, or the left, where she might tumble down the gully, and she runs across the road, intending to push herself up the wet earth, to climb, when the white stretch limo comes fishtailing down the slick hillside road, hell it must be doing eighty, maybe even aquaplaning on the surface of the road, and she's pushing her hands into a handful of weeds and earth, and she's going to get up and away, she knows, when the wet earth crumbles and she tumbles back down onto the road.

The car hits her with an impact that crumples the grille and tosses her into the air like a glove puppet. She lands on the road behind the limo, and the impact shatters her pelvis, fractures her skull. Cold rainwater runs over her face.

She begins to curse her killer: curse him silently, as

she cannot move her lips. She curses him in waking and in sleeping, in living and in death. She curses him as only someone who is half-demon on her father's side can curse.

A car door opens. Someone approaches her. "You were an analog girl," he sings again, tunelessly, "living in a digital world." And then he says, "You fucking madonnas. All you fucking madonnas." He walks away.

The car door slams.

The limo reverses, and runs back over her, slowly, for the first time. Her bones crunch beneath the wheels. Then the limo comes back down the hill toward her.

When, finally, it drives away, down the hill, all it leaves behind on the road is the smeared red meat of roadkill, barely recognizable as human, and soon even that will be washed away by the rain.

Interlude 2

"Hi, Samantha."

"Mags? Is that you?"

"Who else? Leon said that Auntie Sammy called when I was in the shower."

"We had a good talk. He's such a sweet kid."

"Yeah. I think I'll keep him."

A moment of discomfort for both of them, barely a crackle of a whisper over the telephone lines. Then, "Sammy, how's school?"

"They're giving us a week off. Problem with the furnaces. How are things in your neck of the Northwoods?"

"Well, I've got a new next-door neighbor. He does coin tricks. The *Lakeside News* letter column currently features a blistering debate on the potential rezoning of the town land down by the old cemetery on the southeast shore of the lake and yours truly has to write a strident editorial summarizing the paper's position on this without offending anybody or in fact giving anyone any idea what our position is."

"Sounds like fun."

"It's not. Alison McGovern vanished last week—Jilly and Stan McGovern's oldest. I don't think you met them.[597] Nice kid. She babysat for Leon a few times."

A mouth opens to say something, and it closes again, leaving whatever it was to say unsaid, and instead it says, "That's awful."

597. This sentence is not in the First Edition.

"Yes."

"So . . ." And there's nothing to follow that with that isn't going to hurt, so she says, "Is he cute?"

"Who?"

"The neighbor."

"His name's Ainsel. Mike Ainsel. He's okay. Too young for me. Big guy, looks . . . what's the word. Begins with an M."

"Mean? Moody? Magnificent? Married?"

A short laugh, then, "Yes, I guess he does look married. I mean, if there's a look that married men have, he kind of has it. But the word I was thinking of was melancholy. He looks melancholy."

"And mysterious?"

"Not particularly. When he moved in he seemed kinda helpless—he didn't even know to heat-seal the windows. These days he still looks like he doesn't know what he's doing here. When he's here—he's here, then he's gone again. I've seen him out walking from time to time. He's no trouble."[598]

"Maybe he's a bank robber."

"Uh-huh. Just what I was thinking."

"You were not. That was my idea. Listen, Mags, how are you? Are you okay?"

"Yeah."

"Really?"

"No."

A long pause then. "I'm coming up to see you."

"Sammy, no."

"It'll be after the weekend before the furnaces are working and school starts again. It'll be fun. You can make up a bed on the couch for me. And invite the mysterious neighbor over for dinner one night."

"Sam, you're matchmaking."

"Who's matchmaking? After Claudine-the-bitch-from-hell, maybe I'm ready to go back to boys for a while. I met a nice strange boy when I hitchhiked down to El Paso for Christmas."

"Oh. Look, Sam, you've got to stop hitchhiking."

"How do you think I'm going to get to Lakeside?"

598. The last sentence does not appear in the First Edition.

"Alison McGovern was hitchhiking. Even in a town like this, it's not safe. I'll wire you the money. You can take the bus."

"I'll be fine."

"Sammy."

"Okay, Mags. Wire me the money if it'll let you sleep easier."

"You know it will."

"Okay, bossy big sister. Give Leon a hug and tell him Auntie Sammy's coming up and he's not to hide his toys in her bed this time."

"I'll tell him. I don't promise it'll do any good. So when should I expect you?"

"Tomorrow night. You don't have to meet me at the bus station—I'll ask Hinzelmann to run me over in Tessie."

"Too late. Tessie's in mothballs for the winter. But Hinzelmann will give you a ride anyway. He likes you. You listen to his stories."

"Maybe you should get Hinzelmann to write your editorial for you. Let's see. *On the Rezoning of the Land by the Old Cemetery, it so happens that in the winter of ought three my grampaw shot a stag down by the old cemetery by the lake. He was out of bullets, so he used a cherrystone from the lunch my grandmama had packed for him. Creased the skull of the stag and it shot off like a bat out of heck. Two years later he was down that way and he sees this mighty buck with a spreading cherry tree growing between its antlers. Well, he shot it, and grandmama made cherry pies enough that they were still eating them come the next Fourth of July . . .*"[599]

And they both laughed, then.

Baron Munchausen meets the cherry stag.
Illustration by Gustave Doré, 1862

599. This is another tale told by the Baron Munchausen. See note 521, above.

Interlude 3

JACKSONVILLE, FLORIDA. 2:00 A.M.

The sign says 'help wanted.'"

"We're always hiring."

"I can only work the night shift. Is that going to be a problem?"

"Shouldn't be. I can get you an application to fill out. You ever worked in a gas station before?"

"No. I figure, how hard can it be?"

"Well, it ain't rocket science, that's for sure."

"I'm new here. I don't have a telephone. Waiting for them to put it in."**600**

"I surely know that one. I surely do. They just make you wait because they can. You know, ma'am, you don't mind my saying this, but you do not look well."

"I know. It's a medical condition. Looks worse than it is. Nothing life-threatening."

"Okay. You leave that application with me. We are really shorthanded on the late shift right now. Round here we call it the zombie shift. You do it too long, that's how you feel. Well now . . . is that Larna?"

"Laura."

"Laura. Okay. Well, I hope you don't mind dealing with weirdos. Because they come out at night."

"I'm sure they do. I can cope."

600. This paragraph and the next two sentences do not appear in the First Edition.

CHAPTER THIRTEEN

Hey, old friend.
What do you say, old friend?
Make it okay, old friend,
Give an old friendship a break.
Why so grim? We're going on forever.
You, me, him—too many lives are at stake . . .

—STEPHEN SONDHEIM,
"Old Friends"[601]

601. From the 1981 Broadway musical *Merrily We Roll Along.*

IT WAS SATURDAY morning. Shadow answered the door.

Marguerite Olsen was there. She did not come in, just stood there in the sunlight, looking serious. "Mister Ainsel . . . ?"

"Mike, please," said Shadow.

"Mike, yes. Would you like to come over for dinner tonight? About six-ish? It won't be anything exciting, just spaghetti and meatballs."

"Not a problem.[602] I like spaghetti and meatballs."

"Obviously, if you have any other plans . . ."

"I have no other plans."

"Six o'clock."

"Should I bring flowers?"

"If you must. But this is a social gesture. Not a romantic one." She closed the door behind her.[603]

602. This sentence does not appear in the First Edition.

603. This sentence does not appear in the First Edition.

604. The second half of this sentence does not appear in the First Edition.

605. The bumper sticker paraphrases the line "Life is a cabaret, old chum" from the title song of the 1966 Broadway musical and 1972 film *Cabaret*, lyrics by Fred Kander. The origin of the pun is unknown.

606. This sentence does not appear in the First Edition.

He showered. He went for a short walk, down to the bridge and back. The sun was up, a tarnished quarter in the sky, and he was sweating in his coat by the time he got home. It had to be above freezing. He drove the 4Runner down to Dave's Finest Foods and bought a bottle of wine. It was a twenty-dollar bottle, which seemed to Shadow like some kind of guarantee of quality. He didn't know wines, but he figured that for twenty bucks it ought to taste good.[604] He bought a Californian Cabernet, because Shadow had once seen a bumper sticker, back when he was younger and people still had bumper stickers on their cars, which said LIFE IS A CABERNET and it had made him laugh.[605]

He bought a plant in a pot as a gift. Green leaves, no flowers. Nothing remotely romantic about that.

He bought a carton of milk, which he would never drink, and a selection of fruit, which he would never eat.

Then he drove over to Mabel's and bought a single lunchtime pasty. Mabel's face lit up when she saw him. "Did Hinzelmann catch up with you?"

"I didn't know he was looking for me."

"Yup. Wants to take you ice-fishing. And Chad Mulligan wanted to know if I'd seen you around. His cousin's here from out of state. She's a widow.[606] His second cousin, what we used to call kissing cousins. Such a sweetheart. You'll love her." And she dropped the pasty into a brown paper bag, twisted the top of the bag over to keep the pasty warm.

Shadow drove the long way home, eating one-handed, the steaming pasty's pastry-crumbs tumbling onto his jeans and onto the floor of the 4Runner. He passed the library on the south shore of the lake. It was a black and white town in the ice and the snow. Spring seemed unimaginably far away: the klunker would always sit on the ice, with the ice-fishing shelters and the pickup trucks and the snowmobile tracks.

He reached his apartment, parked, walked up the drive, up the wooden steps to his apartment. The goldfinches and nuthatches on the bird feeder hardly gave him a glance. He went inside. He watered the plant, wondered whether or not to put the wine into the refrigerator.

There was a lot of time to kill until six.

Shadow wished he could comfortably watch television once more. He wanted to be entertained, not to have to think, just to sit and let the sounds and the light wash over him. *Do you want to see Lucy's tits?* something with a Lucy voice whispered in his memory, and he shook his head, although there was no one there to see him.

He was nervous, he realized. This would be his first real social interaction with other people—normal people, not people in jail, not gods or culture heroes or dreams—since he was first arrested, over three years ago. He would have to make conversation, as Mike Ainsel.

He checked his watch. It was two-thirty. Marguerite Olsen had told him to be there at six. Did she mean six exactly? Should he be there a little early? A little late? He decided, eventually, to walk next door at five past six.

Shadow's telephone rang.

"Yeah?" he said.

"That's no way to answer the phone," growled Wednesday.

"When I get my telephone connected I'll answer it politely," said Shadow. "Can I help you?"

"I don't know," said Wednesday. There was a pause. Then he said, "Organizing gods is like herding cats into straight lines. They don't take naturally to it." There was a deadness, and an exhaustion, in Wednesday's voice that Shadow had never heard before.

"What's wrong?"

"It's hard. It's too fucking hard. I don't know if this is going to work. We might as well cut our throats. Just cut our own throats."

"You mustn't talk like that."

"Yeah. Right."

"Well, if you do cut your throat," said Shadow, trying to jolly Wednesday out of his darkness, "maybe it wouldn't even hurt."

"It would hurt. Even for my kind, pain still hurts. If you move and act in the material world, then the material world acts on you. Pain hurts, just as greed intoxicates and lust burns. We may not die easy and we sure as hell don't die well, but we can die. If we're still loved and remembered, something else a whole lot like us comes along and takes our place and the whole damn thing starts all over again. And if we're forgotten, we're done."

Shadow did not know what to say. He said, "So where are you calling from?"

"None of your goddamn business."

"Are you drunk?"

"Not yet. I just keep thinking about Thor. You never knew him. Big guy, like you. Good hearted. Not bright, but he'd give you the goddamned shirt off his back if you asked him. And he killed himself. He put a gun in his mouth and blew his head off in Philadelphia in 1932. What kind of a way is that for a god to die?"

"I'm sorry."

"You don't give two fucking cents, son. He was a whole lot like you. Big and dumb." Wednesday stopped talking. He coughed.

"What's wrong?" said Shadow, for the second time.

"They got in touch."

"Who did?"

"The opposition."

"And?"

"They want to discuss a truce. Peace talks. Live and let fucking live."

"So what happens now?"

"Now I go and drink bad coffee with the modern assholes in a Kansas City Masonic hall."

"Okay. You going to pick me up, or shall I meet you somewhere?"

"You stay there and you keep your head down. Don't get into any trouble. You hear me?"

"But—"

There was a click, and the line went dead and stayed dead. There was no dial tone, but then, there never was.

Nothing but time to kill. The conversation with Wednesday had left Shadow with a sense of disquiet. He got up, intending to go for a walk, but already the light was fading, and he sat back down again.

Shadow picked up the *Minutes of the Lakeside City Council 1872–1884* and turned the pages, his eyes scanning the tiny print, not actually reading it, occasionally stopping to scan something that caught his eye.

In July of 1874, Shadow learned, the city council was concerned about the number of itinerant foreign loggers arriving in the town. An opera house was to be built on the corner of Third Street and Broadway. It was to be expected that the nuisances attendant to the damming of Mill Creek would abate once the mill-pond had become a lake. The council authorized the payment of seventy dollars to Mr. Samuel Samuels, and of eighty-five dollars to Mr. Heikki Salminen, in compensation for their land and for the expenses incurred in moving their domiciles out of the area to be flooded.

It had never occurred to Shadow before that the lake was man-made. Why call a town Lakeside, when the lake had begun as a dammed mill-pond? He read on, to discover that a Mr. Hinzelmann, originally of Hüdemuhlen in Brunswick,[607] was in charge of the lake-building project, and that the city council had granted him the sum of $370 toward the project, any shortfall to be made up by public subscription. Shadow tore off a strip of a paper towel and placed it into the book as a bookmark. He could imagine Hinzelmann's pleasure in seeing the reference to his grandfather. He wondered if the old man knew that his family had been instrumental in building the lake. Shadow flipped forward through the book, scanning for more references to the lake-building project.

They had dedicated the lake in a ceremony in the spring of 1876, as a precursor to the town's centennial celebrations. A vote of thanks to Mr. Hinzelmann was taken by the council.

Shadow checked his watch. It was five thirty. He went into the bathroom, shaved, combed his hair. He changed his clothes. Somehow the final fifteen minutes passed. He got the wine and the plant, and he walked next door.

The door opened as he knocked. Marguerite Olsen looked almost as nervous as he felt. She took the wine bottle

607. That is, the duchy of Brunswick in Germany, about 185 miles from Cologne, where the *heinselmännchen* were reported. See note 454, above.

and the potted plant, and said thank you. The television was on, *The Wizard of Oz* on video. It was still in sepia, and Dorothy was still in Kansas, sitting with her eyes closed in Professor Marvel's wagon as the old fraud pretended to read her mind, and the twister-wind that would tear her away from her life was approaching. Leon sat in front of the screen, playing with a toy fire truck. When he saw Shadow an expression of delight touched his face; he stood up and ran, tripping over his feet in his excitement, into a back bedroom, from which he emerged a moment later, triumphantly waving a quarter.

"Watch, Mike Ainsel!" he shouted. Then he closed both his hands and he pretended to take the coin into his right hand, which he opened wide. "I made it disappear, Mike Ainsel!"

"You did," agreed Shadow. "After we've eaten, if it's okay with your mom, I'll show you how to do it even smoother than that."

"Do it now if you want," said Marguerite. "We're still waiting for Samantha. I sent her out for sour cream. I don't know what's taking her so long."

And, as if that was her cue, footsteps sounded on the wooden deck, and somebody shouldered open the front door. Shadow did not recognize her at first, then she said, "I didn't know if you wanted the kind with calories or the kind that tastes like wallpaper paste so I went for the kind with calories," and he knew her then: the girl from the road to Cairo.

"That's fine," said Marguerite. "Sam, this is my neighbor, Mike Ainsel. Mike, this is Samantha Black Crow, my sister."

I don't know you, thought Shadow desperately. *You've never met me before. We're total strangers.* He tried to remember how he had thought snow, how easy and light that had been: this was desperate. He put out his hand and said, "Pleased to meetcha."

She blinked, looked up at his face. A moment of puzzlement, then recognition entered her eyes and curved the corners of her mouth into a grin. "Hello," she said.

"I'll see how the food is doing," said Marguerite, in the

taut voice of someone who burns things in kitchens if they leave them alone and unwatched even for a moment.

Sam took off her puffy coat and her hat. "So you're the melancholy but mysterious neighbor," she said. "Who'da thunk it?" She kept her voice down.

"And you," he said, "are girl Sam. Can we talk about this later?"

"If you promise to tell me what's going on."

"Deal."

Leon tugged at the leg of Shadow's pants. "Will you show me now?" he asked, and held out his quarter.

"Okay," said Shadow. "But if I show you, you have to remember that a master magician never tells anyone how it's done."

"I promise," said Leon, gravely.

Shadow took the coin in his left hand, then moved Leon's right hand in, cupping it in his own hand, huge by comparison, showing him how to appear to take the coin in his right hand while actually leaving it in Shadow's left hand. Then he put the coin into Leon's left hand and made him repeat the movements on his own.[608]

After several attempts the boy mastered the move. "Now you know half of it," said Shadow. "Because the moves are only half of it.[609] The other half is this: put your attention on the place where the coin ought to be. Look at the place it's meant to be. Follow it with your eyes. If you act like it's in your right hand, no one will even look at your left hand, no matter how clumsy you are."

Sam watched all this with her head tipped slightly on one side, saying nothing.

"Dinner!" called Marguerite, pushing her way in from the kitchen with a steaming bowl of spaghetti in her hands. "Leon, go wash your hands."

The food was good: crusty garlic bread, thick red sauce, good spicy meatballs. Shadow complimented Marguerite on it.

"Old family recipe," she told him, "from the Corsican side of the family."

"I thought you were Native American."

608. The explanation of the prestidigitation is less detailed in the First Edition.

609. This sentence and the sentence "Follow it with your eyes" do not appear in the First Edition.

409

610. This phrase does not appear in the First Edition.

611. A Navajo dish, a flat dough fried in oil or lard. Fry bread is also made into Navajo tacos. Traditionally, the bread originated on the "Long Walk" in 1864, when the Navajo were forced by the government to walk from Arizona to New Mexico and were given flour, sugar, salt, and lard as rations.

612. During the 1820s and up to 1832, there were violent conflicts between the Aborigine peoples and British colonists in Tasmania. In late 1830, Lieutenant-Governor George Arthur ordered formation of the "Black Line," consisting of about 550 soldiers, 738 convict servants, and 912 free settlers or civilians. Aided by Aboriginal guides, the Line formed a staggered front more than 300 km long that began pushing south and east across the island, intending to trap four of the nine Aboriginal nations in front of the line and drive them into a newly created "Aboriginal Reserve." Weather, terrain, and poor organization caused the cordon to break down, leaving many opportunities for the Aboriginal people to evade the line. At the same time, many of the men on the line deserted. The campaign's only success was the capture and killing, on October 25, of two Aboriginal people. The Black Line was officially disbanded on November 26, 1830.

613. The thylacine was a carnivorous marsupial, commonly known as the Tasmanian tiger or Tasmanian wolf. Actually, the Tasmanian Advisory Committee for Native Fauna recommended in 1928 that a reserve be established for the thylacine, but the last thylacine killed in the wild died in 1930, and the last in captivity died in 1936.

"Dad's Cherokee," said Sam. "Mag's mom's father came from Corsica." Sam was the only person in the room who was actually drinking the Cabernet. "Dad left her when Mags was ten and he moved across town. Six months after that, I was born. Mom and Dad got married when the divorce came through and I think they tried to make it work for a while,[610] and when I was ten he went away. I think he has a ten-year attention span."

"Well, he's been out in Oklahoma for ten years," said Marguerite.

"Now, my mom's family were European Jewish," continued Sam, "from one of those places that used to be communist and now are just chaos. I think she liked the idea of being married to a Cherokee. Fry bread[611] and chopped liver." Sam took another sip of the red wine.

"Her mom's a wild woman," said Marguerite, semi-approvingly.

"You know where she is now?" asked Sam. Shadow shook his head. "She's in Australia. She met a guy on the Internet, who lived in Hobart. When they met in the flesh she decided he was actually kind of icky. But she really liked Tasmania. So she's living down there, with a woman's group, teaching them to batik cloth and things like that. Isn't that cool? At her age?"

Shadow agreed that it was, and helped himself to more meatballs. Sam told them how all the aboriginal natives of Tasmania had been wiped out by the British, and about the human chain they made across the island to catch them which trapped only an old man and a sick boy.[612] She told him how the Tasmanian tigers, the thylacines, had been killed by farmers, scared for their sheep, how the politicians in the 1930s noticed that the thylacines should be protected only after the last of them was dead.[613] She finished her second glass of wine, poured her third.

"So, Mike," said Sam, suddenly, her cheeks reddening, "tell us about your family. What are the Ainsels like?" She was smiling, and there was mischief in that smile.

"We're real dull," said Shadow. "None of us ever got as

far as Tasmania. So you're at school in Madison. What's that like?"

"*You* know," she said. "I'm studying art history, women's studies, and casting my own bronzes."

"When I grow up," said Leon, "I'm going to do magic. Poof. Will you teach me, Mike Ainsel?"

"Sure," said Shadow. "If your mom doesn't mind."

Marguerite shrugged.[614]

Sam said, "After we've eaten, while you're putting Leon to bed, Mags, I think I'm going to get Mike to take me to the Buck Stops Here for an hour or so."

Marguerite did not shrug. Her head moved, an eyebrow raised slightly.

"I think he's interesting," said Sam. "And we have lots to talk about."

Marguerite looked at Shadow, who busied himself in dabbing an imaginary blob of red sauce from his chin with a paper napkin. "Well, you're grown-ups," she said, in a tone of voice that did its best to imply that they weren't, and that even if they were they shouldn't be.

After dinner Shadow helped Sam with the washing up—he dried—and then he did a trick for Leon, counting pennies into Leon's palm: each time Leon opened his hand and counted them there was one less coin than he had counted in. And as for the final penny—"Are you squeezing it? Tightly?"—when Leon opened his hand, he found it had transformed into a dime. Leon's plaintive cries of "How'd you *do* that? Momma, how'd he *do* that?" followed him out into the hall.

Sam handed him his coat. "Come on," she said. Her cheeks were flushed from the wine.

Outside it was cold.

Shadow stopped in his apartment, tossed the *Minutes of the Lakeside City Council* into a plastic grocery bag and brought it along. Hinzelmann might be down at the Buck, and he wanted to show him the mention of his grandfather.

They walked down the drive side by side.

He opened the garage door, and she started to laugh.

614. This sentence does not appear in the First Edition.

"Omigod," she said, when she saw the 4Runner. "Paul Gunther's car. You bought Paul Gunther's car. Omigod."

Shadow opened the door for her. Then he went around and got in. "You know the car?"

"When I came up here two or three years ago to stay with Mags. It was me that persuaded him to paint it purple."

"Oh," said Shadow. "It's good to have someone to blame."

He drove the car out onto the street. Got out and closed the garage door. Got back into the car. Sam was looking at him oddly as he got in, as if the confidence had begun to leak out of her. He put on his seatbelt, and she said, "I'm scared. This was a stupid thing to do, wasn't it? Getting into a car with a psycho-killer."

"I got you safe home last time," said Shadow.

"You killed two men," she said. "You're wanted by the Feds. And now I find out you're living under an assumed name next door to my sister. Unless Mike Ainsel is your real name?"

"No," said Shadow, and he sighed. "It's not." He hated saying it. It was if he was letting go of something important, abandoning Mike Ainsel by denying him, as if he were taking his leave of a friend.

"Did you kill those men?"

"No."

"They came to my house, and said we'd been seen together. And this guy showed me photographs of you. What was his name—Mister Hat? No. Mister Town. That was him. It was like *The Fugitive*.[615] But I said I hadn't seen you."

"Thank you."

"So," she said. "Tell me what's going on. I'll keep your secrets if you keep mine."

"I don't know any of yours," said Shadow.

"Well, you know that it was my idea to paint this thing purple, thus forcing Paul Gunther to become such an object of scorn and derision for several counties around that he was forced to leave town entirely. We were kind of stoned," she admitted.

"I doubt that bit of it's much of a secret," said Shadow.

615. Sam likely refers to the 1993 film starring Harrison Ford and Tommy Lee Jones, about Dr. Richard Kimble, an innocent man convicted of murdering his wife and, after his escape from prison, relentlessly pursued by an agent convinced of his guilt. Loosely based on Dumas's *Les Miserables* and the real-life case of Dr. Sam Sheppard, the film capsulized the successful television series of the same name which ran from 1963 to 1967 and featured David Janssen as Kimble and many well-known guest stars.

"Everyone in Lakeside must have known. It's a stoner sort of purple."

And then she said, very quiet, very fast, "If you're going to kill me please don't hurt me. I shouldn't have come here with you. I am so dumb. I am so fucking fucking dumb. I should have run away or called the cops when I first saw you.[616] I can identify you. Jesus. I am so dumb."

Shadow sighed. "I've never killed anybody. Really. Now I'm going to take you to the Buck," he said. "Or if you give the word, I'll turn this car around and take you home. I'll buy you a drink, if you're actually old enough to drink, and I'll buy you a soda if you're not.[617] Then I'll take you back to Marguerite, deliver you safe and sound, and hope you aren't going to call the cops."

There was silence as they crossed the bridge.

"Who did kill those men?" she asked.

"You wouldn't believe me if I told you."

"I *would*." She sounded angry now. He wondered if bringing the wine to the dinner had been a wise idea. Life was certainly not a Cabernet right now.

"It's not easy to believe."

"I," she told him, "can believe anything. You have no idea what I can believe."

"Really?"

"I can believe things that are true and I can believe things that aren't true and I can believe things where nobody knows if they're true or not. I can believe in Santa Claus and the Easter Bunny and Marilyn Monroe and the Beatles and Elvis and Mister Ed.[618] Listen—I believe that people are perfectible, that knowledge is infinite, that the world is run by secret banking cartels and is visited by aliens on a regular basis, nice ones that look like wrinkledy lemurs and bad ones who mutilate cattle and want our water and our women. I believe that the future sucks and I believe that the future rocks and I believe that one day White Buffalo Woman[619] is going to come back and kick everyone's ass. I believe that all men are just overgrown boys with deep problems communicating and that the decline in good sex in America is coincident with the decline in drive-in movie

616. This sentence does not appear in the First Edition.

617. This and the following sentence do not appear in the First Edition.

618. The talking horse who appeared in the eponymous television series from 1961 to 1966.

619. A sacred woman of supernatural origin, a prophet central to the religion of the Lakota people. Some say she had the power to turn into a white buffalo.

620. *War of the Worlds* is the 1897 novel by Herbert George (H. G.) Wells, in which an invasion of Earth by a militarily superior force of Martians is fortuitously halted when the Martians are felled by Earth's germs. The book was made into a famous 1938 radio broadcast by Orson Welles and several successful films. Sam may well have seen the popular 1953 film starring Gene Barry—or she may have read the book!

621. Dame Edith Sitwell (1887–1964) was a British poet and critic who was a strong proponent of her contemporaries, including Dylan Thomas. Her celebrity obscured the quality of her work, which was ultimately well-regarded.

622. Marquis (1878–1937) was a humorist and journalist, best remembered today for his newspaper columns featuring poetry written by a cockroach named Archy, who had been a free-verse poet in a previous life, jumping on Marquis's typewriter keyboard. Because Archy could not work the shift key, the poems were entirely in lowercase letters. The poems described Archy's adventures and often told of his friend Mehitabel, a stray cat. The first collection, *archy and mehitabel*, was published in 1927, and the entire oeuvre has been frequently reprinted.

623. It is widely reported—on the internet, for example, on the *Scientific American* blog (https://blogs.scientificamerican.com/cocktail-party-physics/every-sperm-is-sacred/) that ancient Chinese legends held jade to be dried semen of celestial dragons.

624. Atsula, whose story is told in the "Coming to America—14,000 B.C." section, is a one-armed Siberian shaman—a prior life of Sam?

theatres from state to state. I believe that all politicians are unprincipled crooks and I still believe that they are better than the alternative. I believe that California is going to sink into the sea when the big one comes, while Florida is going to dissolve into madness and alligators and toxic waste. I believe that antibacterial soap is destroying our resistance to dirt and disease so that one day we'll all be wiped out by the common cold like the Martians in *War of the Worlds*.[620] I believe that the greatest poets of the last century were Edith Sitwell[621] and Don Marquis,[622] that jade is dried dragon sperm,[623] and that thousands of years ago in a former life I was a one-armed Siberian shaman.[624] I believe that mankind's destiny lies in the stars. I believe that candy really did taste better when I was a kid, that it's aerodynamically impossible for a bumblebee to fly,[625] that light is a wave and a particle,[626] that there's a cat in a box somewhere who's alive and dead at the same time (although if they don't ever open the box to feed it it'll eventually just be two different kinds of dead),[627] and that there are stars in the universe billions of years older than the universe itself.[628] I believe in a personal god who cares about me and worries and oversees everything I do. I believe in an impersonal god who set the universe in motion and went off to hang with her girlfriends and doesn't even know that I'm alive. I believe in an empty and godless universe of causal chaos, background noise and sheer blind luck. I believe that anyone who says that sex is overrated just hasn't done it properly. I believe that anyone who claims to know what's going on will lie about the little things too. I believe in absolute honesty and sensible social lies. I believe in a woman's right to choose, a baby's right to live, that while all human life is sacred there's nothing wrong with the death penalty if you can trust the legal system implicitly, and that no one but a moron would ever trust the legal system. I believe that life is a game, life is a cruel joke and that life is what happens when you're alive and that you might as well lie back and enjoy it." She stopped, out of breath.

Shadow almost took his hands off the wheel to applaud.

Instead he said, "Okay. So if I tell you what I've learned you won't think that I'm a nut."

"Maybe," she said. "Try me."

"Would you believe that all the gods that people have ever imagined are still with us today?"

". . . maybe."

"And that there are new gods out there, gods of computers and telephones and whatever, and that they all seem to think there isn't room for them both in the world. And that some kind of war is kind of likely."

"And these gods killed those two men?"

"No, my wife killed those two men."

"I thought you said your wife was dead."

"She is."

"She killed them before she died, then?"

"After. Don't ask."

She reached up a hand and flicked her hair from her forehead.

They pulled up on Main Street, outside the Buck Stops Here. The sign over the window showed a surprised-looking stag standing on its hind legs holding a glass of beer. Shadow got out. He grabbed the bag with the book in it, and got out.

"Why would they have a war?" asked Sam. "It seems kind of redundant. What is there to win?"

"I don't know," admitted Shadow.

"It's easier to believe in aliens than in gods," said Sam. "Maybe Mister Town and Mister Whatever were Men in Black,[629] only the alien kind."

"Maybe they were, at that," said Shadow.[630]

They were standing on the sidewalk outside the Buck Stops Here and Sam stopped. She looked up at Shadow, and her breath hung on the night air like a faint cloud. She said, "Just tell me you're one of the good guys."

"I can't," said Shadow. "I wish I could. But I'm doing my best."

She looked up at him, and bit her lower lip. Then she nodded. "Good enough," she said. "I won't turn you in. You can buy me a beer."

625. This myth was repeated on www.quora .com, from a source who purported to have a master's degree in physics: "According to all known laws of aviation, there is no way that a bee should be able to fly. Its wings are too small to get its fat little body off the ground. The bee, of course, flies anyways. Because bees don't care what humans think is impossible." Of course this is nonsense; the aerodynamics of bumblebees and other insects is well understood.

626. Einstein pointed out, in the so-called photoelectric experiment, that light sometimes behaves like a wave and sometimes like a particle. Recently, scientists were able to create an image showing *both* aspects of light by firing a stream of electrons at a nanowire and using an ultrafast microscope to image the process.

627. This is "Schrödinger's cat," the subject of a thought experiment proposed by physicist Erwin Schrödinger in 1935 to explain the interpretation of quantum mechanics by the so-called Copenhagen school of thought.

628. Previous research had estimated the age of the oldest (so-called Methuselah) star to be about 16 billion years, predating the "Big Bang," which is thought to have occurred about 13.8 billion years ago. However, more recent research has revised the estimate of the star's age to be about 14.5 billion years, which (with the quantity of uncertainty inherent in the calculations) is consistent with the dating of the "Big Bang."

629. Government agents who deal with aliens—the characters first appeared in eponymous comics published by Aircel in 1990 and 1991 and were later adapted into a highly successful series of films beginning with *Men in Black* (1997), starring Will Smith and Tommy Lee Jones.

630. This sentence does not appear in the First Edition.

631. The balance of this sentence does not appear in the First Edition.

632. The presence of the cat is not noted in the Manuscript.

Shadow pushed the door open for her, and they were hit by a blast of heat and music,[631] enveloped by a cloud of warmth that smelled of beer and hamburgers. They went inside.

Sam waved at some friends. Shadow nodded to a handful of people whose faces—although not their names—he remembered from the day he had spent searching for Alison McGovern, or who he had met in Mabel's in the morning. Chad Mulligan was standing at the bar, with his arm around the shoulders of a small red-haired woman—the kissing cousin, Shadow figured. He wondered what she looked like, but she had her back to him. Chad's hand raised in a mock salute when he saw Shadow. Shadow grinned, and waved back at him. Shadow looked around for Hinzelmann, but the old man did not seem to be there this evening. He spied a free table at the back and started walking toward it.

Then somebody began to scream.

It was a bad scream, a full-throated, seen-a-ghost hysterical scream, which silenced all conversation. Shadow looked around, certain somebody was being murdered, and then he realized that all the faces in the bar were turning toward him. Even the black cat, who slept in the window during the day, was standing up on top of the jukebox with its tail high and its back arched and was staring at Shadow.[632]

Time slowed.

"Get him!" shouted a woman's voice, parked on the verge of hysteria. "Oh for god's sake, somebody stop him! Don't let him get away! Please!" It was a voice he knew.

Nobody moved. They stared at Shadow. He stared back at them.

Chad Mulligan stepped forward, walking through the people. The small woman walked behind him warily, her eyes wide, as if she was preparing to start screaming once more. Shadow knew her. Of course he knew her.

Chad was still holding his beer, which he put down on a nearby table. He said, "Mike."

Shadow said "Chad."

Audrey Burton was a step behind Chad Mulligan. Her face was white, and there were tears in her eyes. She had been screaming.[633] "Shadow," she said. "You bastard. You murderous evil bastard."

"Are you sure that you know this man, hon?" said Chad. He looked uncomfortable. It was obvious that he hoped that whatever was happening here was all some kind of case of mistaken identity, something that one day they might be able to laugh about.[634]

Audrey Burton looked at him incredulously. "Are you crazy? He worked for Robbie for *years*. His slutty wife was my best *friend*. He's wanted for *murder*. I had to answer *questions*. He's an escaped *convict*." She was way over the top, her voice trembling with suppressed hysteria, sobbing out her words like a soap actress going for a daytime Emmy.[635] *Kissing cousins*, thought Shadow, unimpressed.

Nobody in the bar said a word. Chad Mulligan looked up at Shadow. "It's probably a mistake. I'm sure we can sort this all out," he said, sensibly. Then he said, to the bar, "It's all fine. Nothing to worry about. We can sort this out. Everything's fine." Then, to Shadow. "Let's step outside, Mike." Quiet competence. Shadow was impressed.

"Sure," said Shadow.

He felt a hand touch his hand, and he turned to see Sam staring at him. He smiled down at her as reassuringly as he could.

Sam looked at Shadow, then she looked around the bar at the faces staring at them. She said to Audrey Burton, "I don't know who you are. But. You. Are. Such. A cunt." Then she went up on tiptoes and pulled Shadow down to her, and kissed him hard on the lips, pushing her mouth against his for what felt to Shadow like several minutes, and might have been as long as five seconds in real, clock-ticking time.

It was a strange kiss, Shadow thought, as her lips pressed against his: it wasn't intended for him. It was for the other people in the bar, to let them know that she had picked sides. It was a flag-waving kiss. Even as she kissed him, he became certain that she didn't even like him—well, not like that.

Still, there was a tale he had read once, long ago, as a small boy: the story of a traveler who had slipped down a

633. This sentence does not appear in the First Edition.

634. This sentence does not appear in the First Edition.

635. The "Daytime Emmys" are a series of awards given out by the Los Angeles–based Academy of Television Arts & Sciences and the New York–based National Academy of Television Arts and Sciences for daytime programming, including the daily serial dramas known as "soap operas."

cliff, with man-eating tigers above him and a lethal fall below him, who managed to stop his fall halfway down the side of the cliff, holding on for dear life. There was a clump of strawberries beside him, and certain death above him and below. *What should he do?* went the question. And the reply was, *Eat the strawberries.*[636]

The story had never made any sense to him as a boy. It did now.

So he closed his eyes, threw himself into the kiss and experienced nothing but Sam's lips and the softness of her skin against his, sweet as a wild strawberry.

"C'mon, Mike," said Chad Mulligan, firmly. "Please. Let's take it outside."

Sam pulled back. She licked her lips, and smiled, a smile that nearly reached her eyes. "Not bad," she said. "You kiss good for a boy.[637] Okay, go play outside." Then she turned to Audrey Burton. "But you," she said, "are still a cunt."

Shadow tossed Sam his car keys. She caught them, one-handed. He walked through the bar, and stepped outside, followed by Chad Mulligan. A gentle snow had begun to fall, the flakes spinning down into the light of the neon bar sign. "You want to talk about this?" asked Chad.

"Am I under arrest?" asked Shadow.[638]

Audrey followed them out onto the sidewalk. She looked as if she were ready to start screaming again. She said, her voice trembling, "He killed two men, Chad. The FBI came to my door. He's a psycho. I'll come down to the station with you, if you want."

"You've caused enough trouble, ma'am," said Shadow. He sounded tired, even to himself. "Please go away."

"Chad? Did you hear that? He threatened me!" said Audrey.

"Get back inside, Audrey," said Chad Mulligan. She looked as if she were about to argue, then she pressed her lips together so hard they went white, and went back into the bar.

"Would you like to comment on anything she said?" asked Chad Mulligan.

"I've never killed anyone," said Shadow.

636. This Zen tale—usually embellished with the added element that the man is climbing down a vine that is being chewed through by mice—is generally interpreted as an admonition to enjoy each moment of life. Another view, however, suggests that this tale illustrates man's inherent foolishness—faced with a life-or-death decision, we are often distracted by momentary pleasure.

637. In the Manuscript, Sam says "for a white boy." As we have seen, Shadow's racial heritage is never made explicit in the text, though he is played by Ricky Whittle, a black actor, in the Starz production of *American Gods*.

638. This sentence does not appear in the First Edition.

Chad nodded. "I believe you," he said. "I'm sure we can deal with these allegations easily enough. It's probably nothing.[639] I have to do this. You won't give me any trouble, will you, Mike?"

"No trouble," said Shadow. "This is all a mistake."

"Exactly," said Chad. "So I figure we ought to head down to my office and sort it all out there?"

"Am I under arrest?" asked Shadow, for the second time.

"Nope," said Chad. "Not unless you want to be. I figure, we go down to my office together, you come with me out of a sense of civic duty, and we do whatever we can to straighten all this out."[640]

Chad patted Shadow down, found no weapons. They got into Mulligan's car. Again Shadow sat in the back, looking out through the metal cage. He thought, *SOS. Mayday. Help.* He tried to push Mulligan with his mind, as he'd once pushed a cop in Chicago—*This is your old friend Mike Ainsel. You saved his life. Don't you know how silly this is? Why don't you just drop the whole thing?*

"I figure it was good to get you out of there," said Chad. "All you needed was some loudmouth deciding that you were Alison McGovern's killer and we'd've had a lynch mob on our hands."

"Point."

"So you sure there's nothing you want to tell me?"[641]

"Nope. Nothing to say."

They were silent for the rest of the drive to the Lakeside police offices. The building, Chad said, as they pulled up outside it, actually belonged to the county sheriff's department. The local police had a few rooms in there. Pretty soon the county would build something modern. For now they had to make do with what they had.

They walked inside.

"Should I call a lawyer?" asked Shadow.

"You aren't accused of anything," said Mulligan. "Up to you." They pushed through some swing doors. "Take a seat over there."

Shadow took a seat on the wooden chair with cigarette burns on the side. He felt stupid and numb. There was a

639. This sentence and the next do not appear in the First Edition.

640. In the First Edition, this sentence reads, "I figure, you come with me out of a sense of civic duty, and we'll straighten this all out."

641. This and the next sentence do not appear in the First Edition.

small poster on the notice board, beside a large NO SMOK-ING sign: ENDANGERED MISSING it said. The photograph was Alison McGovern's.

There was a wooden table, with old copies of *Sports Illustrated* and *Newsweek* on it,[642] with the place on the cover where an address label had been pasted cut neatly away. The light was bad. The paint on the wall was yellow, but it might once have been white.

After ten minutes Chad brought him a watery cup of vending machine hot chocolate. "What's in the bag?" he asked. And it was only then that Shadow realized he was still holding the plastic bag containing the *Minutes of the Lakeside City Council*.

"Old book," said Shadow. "Your grandfather's picture's in here. Or great-grandfather maybe."

"Yeah?"

Shadow flipped through the book until he found the portrait of the town council, and he pointed to the man called Mulligan. Chad chuckled. "If that don't beat all," he said.

Minutes passed, and hours, in that room. Shadow read two of the *Sports Illustrated*s and he started the *Newsweek*. From time to time Chad would come through, checking to see if Shadow needed to use the restroom, once to offer him a ham roll and a small packet of potato chips.

"Thanks," said Shadow, taking them. "Am I under arrest?"

Chad sucked the air between his teeth. "Well," he said, "we'll know pretty soon. It doesn't look like you came by the name Mike Ainsel legally. On the other hand, you can call yourself whatever you want in this state, if it's not for fraudulent purposes. You just hang loose."

"Can I make a phone call?"

"Is it a local call?"

"Long-distance."

"It'll save money if I put it on my calling card, otherwise you'll just be feeding ten bucks' worth of quarters into that thing in the hall."

Sure, thought Shadow. *And this way you'll know the*

---

642. The balance of this sentence does not appear in the First Edition.

number I dialed, and you'll probably be listening in on an extension.

"That would be great," said Shadow. They went into an empty office, next to Chad's. The light was slightly better in there.[643] The number Shadow gave Chad to dial for him was that of a funeral home in Cairo, Illinois. Chad dialed it, handed Shadow the receiver. "I'll leave you in here," he said, and went out.

The telephone rang several times, then it was picked up.

"Jacquel and Ibis. Can I help you?"

"Hi. Mister Ibis, this is Mike Ainsel. I helped out there for a few days over Christmas."

A moment's hesitation, then, "Of course. Mike. How are you?"

"Not great, Mister Ibis. In a patch of trouble. About to be arrested. Hoping you'd seen my uncle about, or maybe you could get a message to him."

"I can certainly ask around. Hold on, uh, Mike. There's someone here who wishes a word with you."

The phone was passed to somebody, and then a smoky female voice said, "Hi, honey. I miss you."

He was certain he'd never heard that voice before. But he knew her. He was sure that he knew her . . .

Let it go, the smoky voice whispered in his mind, in a dream. *Let it all go.*

"Who's that girl you were kissing, hon? You trying to make me jealous?"

"We're just friends," said Shadow. "I think she was trying to prove a point. How did you know she kissed me?"

"I got eyes wherever my folk walk," she said.[644] "You take care now, hon . . ." There was a moment of silence, then Mr. Ibis came back on the line and said, "Mike?"

"Yes."

"There's a problem getting hold of your uncle. He seems to be kind of tied up. But I'll try and get a message to your aunt Nancy. Best of luck." The line went dead.

Shadow sat down, expecting Chad to return. He sat in the empty office, wishing he had something to distract

643. This sentence does not appear in the First Edition.

644. Note that there was a black cat on top of the jukebox in the Buck Stops Here. In the Manuscript, Gaiman makes a note to himself to add the cat to the scene.

him. Reluctantly, he picked up the *Minutes* once more, opened it to somewhere in the middle of the book, and began to read.

An ordinance prohibiting expectoration on sidewalks and on the floors of public buildings, or throwing thereon tobacco in any form, was introduced and passed, eight to four, in December of 1876.

Lemmi Hautala was twelve years old and had, "it was feared, wandered away in a fit of delirium" on December the thirteenth, 1876. "A search being immediately effected, but impeded by the snows, which are blinding." The council had voted unanimously to send the Hautala family their condolences.

The fire at Olsen's livery stables the following week was extinguished without any injury or loss of life, human or equine.

Shadow scanned the closely printed columns. He found no further mention of Lemmi Hautala.

And then, on something slightly more than a whim, he flipped the pages forward to the winter of 1877. He found what he was looking for mentioned as an aside in the January minutes: Jessie Lovat, age not given, "a Negro child," had vanished on the night of the twenty-eighth of December. It was believed that she might have been "abducted by traveling so-called pedlars,[645] who were run out of town the previous week, having been discovered to be engaged in certain larcenous acts. They were said to be making for St. Paul." Telegrams had been sent to St. Paul, but no results were reported. Condolences were not sent to the Lovat family.

Shadow was scanning the minutes of winter 1878 when Chad Mulligan knocked and entered, looking shamefaced, like a child bringing home a bad report card.

"Mister Ainsel," he said. "Mike. I'm truly sorry about this. I appreciate how easy you've been about all this.[646] Personally, I like you. But that don't change anything, you know?"

Shadow said he knew.

"I got no choice in the matter," said Chad, "but to place you under arrest for violating your parole." Then Police

645. This and the next two sentences do not appear in the First Edition.

646. This sentence does not appear in the First Edition.

Chief Chad Mulligan read Shadow his rights. He filled out some paperwork. He took Shadow's prints. He walked him down the hall to the county jail, on the other side of the building.

There was a long counter and several doorways on one side of the room, two holding cells and a doorway on the other. One of the cells was occupied—a man slept on a cement bed under a thin blanket. The other was empty.

There was a sleepy-looking woman in a brown uniform behind the counter, watching Jay Leno on a small white portable television.[647] She took the papers from Chad, and signed for Shadow. Chad hung around, filled in more papers. The woman came around the counter, patted Shadow down, took all his possessions—wallet, coins, front door key, book, watch—and put them on the counter, then gave him a plastic bag with orange clothes in it and told him to go into the open cell and change into them. He could keep his own underwear and socks. He went in and changed into the orange clothes and the shower footwear. It stank evilly in there. The orange top he pulled over his head had LUMBER COUNTY JAIL written on the back, in large black letters.

The metal toilet in the cell had backed up, and was filled to the brim with a brown stew of liquid feces and sour, beerish urine.

Shadow came back out, gave the woman his clothes, which she put into the plastic bag with the rest of his possessions. She had him sign for them.[648] Shadow signed for them as Mike Ainsel, although he found that he was already thinking of Mike Ainsel as someone he had liked well enough in the past but would no longer be seeing in the future. He had thumbed through the wallet before he handed it over. "You take care of this," he had said to the woman. "My whole life is in here." The woman took the wallet from him, and assured him that it would be safe with them. She asked Chad if that wasn't true, and Chad, looking up from the last of his paperwork, said Liz was telling the truth, they'd never lost a prisoner's possessions yet.

Shadow had slipped the four hundred-dollar bills that he had palmed from the wallet into his socks, when he had

647. The comic Jay Leno was the host of the late-night talk show *Tonight* from 1992 to 2009; he succeeded Johnny Carson as the host.

648. This sentence and the next do not appear in the First Edition.

changed, along with the silver Liberty dollar he had palmed as he had emptied his pockets.

"Say," Shadow asked, when he came out. "Would it be okay if I finished reading the book?"

"Sorry, Mike. Rules are rules," said Chad.

Liz put Shadow's possessions in a bag in the back room. Chad said he'd leave Shadow in Officer Bute's capable hands. Liz looked tired and unimpressed. Chad left. The telephone rang, and Liz—Officer Bute—answered it. "Okay," she said. "Okay. No problem. Okay. No problem. Okay." She put down the phone and made a face.

"Problem?" asked Shadow.

"Yes. Not really. Kinda. They're sending someone up from Milwaukee to collect you. Okay, do you have any history of medical problems, diabetes, anything like that?"[649]

"No," said Shadow. "Nothing like that. Why is that a problem?"

"Because I got to keep you in here with me for three hours," she said. "And the cell over there"—she pointed to the cell by the door, with the sleeping man in it—"that's occupied. He's on suicide watch. I shouldn't put you in with him. But it's not worth the trouble to sign you in to the county and then sign you out again." She shook her head. "And you don't want to go in there"—she pointed to the empty cell in which he'd changed his clothes—"because the can is shot. It stinks in there, doesn't it?"

"Yes. It was gross."

"It's common humanity, that's what it is. The sooner we get into the new facilities, it can't be too soon for me. One of the women we had in yesterday must've flushed a tampon away. I tell 'em not to. We got bins for that. They clog the pipes. Every damn tampon down that john costs the county a hundred bucks in plumbers' fees. So, I can keep you out here, if I cuff you. Or you can go in the cell." She looked at him. "Your call," she said.

"I'm not crazy about them," he said. "But I'll take the cuffs."

She took a pair from her utility belt, then patted the

649. This sentence and the next two do not appear in the First Edition.

semi-automatic in its holster, as if to remind him that it was there. "Hands behind your back," she said.

The cuffs were a tight fit: he had big wrists. Then she put hobbles on his ankles, and sat him down on a bench on the far side of the counter, against the wall. "Now," she said. "You don't bother me, and I won't bother you." She tilted the television so that he could see it.

"Thanks," he said.

"When we get our new offices," she said, "there won't be none of this nonsense."

The Tonight Show finished. Jay and his guests grinned the world good night.[650] An episode of *Cheers* began. Shadow had never really watched *Cheers*. He had only ever seen one episode of it—the one where Coach's daughter comes to the bar—although he had seen that several times.[651] Shadow had noticed that you only ever catch one episode of shows you don't watch, over and over, years apart; he thought it must be some kind of cosmic law.

Officer Liz Bute sat back in her chair. She was not obviously dozing, but she was by no means awake, so she did not notice when the gang at *Cheers* stopped talking and getting off one-liners and just started staring out of the screen at Shadow.

Diane, the blonde barmaid who fancied herself an intellectual, was the first to talk. "Shadow," she said. "We were so worried about you. You'd fallen off the world. It's so good to see you again—albeit in bondage and orange couture."

"What I figure, is, the thing to do," pontificated bar-bore Cliff, "is to escape in hunting season, when everybody's wearing orange anyway."

Shadow said nothing.

"Ah, cat got your tongue, I see," said Diane. "Well, you've led us a merry chase!"

Shadow looked away. Officer Liz had begun, gently, to snore. Carla, the little waitress, snapped, "Hey, jerk-wad! We interrupt this broadcast to show you something that's going to make you piss in your friggin' pants. You ready?"

The screen flickered and went black. The words "LIVE

650. This sentence does not appear in the First Edition.

651. *Cheers* was a long-running television situation comedy that appeared from 1982 to 1993, telling stories about the regulars at a bar in Boston. 275 episodes were aired. The show originally starred Shelley Long and Ted Danson, along with Rhea Perlman, George Wendt, and other series regulars; later stars included Kirstie Alley and Kelsey Grammer. (Only Danson, Wendt, and Perlman appeared in all of the 11 seasons.) "The Coach's Daughter" is the fifth episode of Season 1 of *Cheers* and originally aired on NBC on October 28, 1982. As in the case of several other shows mentioned in *American Gods*, the show has had a long life after its original airing, still running on various stations around the world.

FEED" pulsated in white at the bottom left of the screen. A subdued female voice said, in voice-over, "It's certainly not too late to change to the winning side. But you know, you also have the freedom to stay just where you are. That's what it means to be an American. That's the miracle of America. Freedom to believe means the freedom to believe the wrong thing, after all. Just as freedom of speech gives you the right to stay silent."

The picture now showed a street scene. The camera lurched forward, in the manner of hand-held video cameras in real-life documentaries.

A man with thinning hair, a tan, and a faintly hangdog expression filled the frame. He was standing by a wall sipping a cup of coffee from a plastic cup. He looked into the camera and said, "Terrorism is too easy a word to bandy about.[652] It means that the real terrorists hide behind weasel-words, like freedom fighter, when they are murdering scum, pure and simple. It doesn't make our job any easier, but at least we know we're making a difference.[653] We're risking our lives to make a difference."

Shadow recognized the voice. He had been inside the man's head once. Mr. Town sounded different from inside—his voice was deeper, more resonant—but there was no mistaking it.

The cameras pulled back to show that Mr. Town was standing outside a brick building on an American street. Above the door was a set-square and compass framing the letter G.[654]

"In position," said somebody off-screen.

"Let's see if the cameras inside the hall are working," said the female voice-over voice. It was the kind of reassuring voice they use on commercials to try to sell you things only people as smart as you are going to take this opportunity to buy.[655]

The words LIVE FEED continued to blink at the bottom left of the screen. Now the picture showed the interior of a small hall: the room was underlit. Two men sat at a table at the far end of the room. One of them had his back to the camera. The camera zoomed in to them awkwardly, in

---

652. This sentence does not appear in the First Edition.

653. This sentence does not appear in the First Edition.

654. The symbol of the Masons fraternal order—hence, a Masonic hall.

655. This sentence does not appear in the First Edition.

a series of jagged movements. For a moment they were out of focus, and then they became sharp once more. The man facing the camera got up and began to pace, like a bear on a chain. It was Wednesday. He looked as if, on some level, he was enjoying this. As they came into focus the sound came on with a pop.

The man with his back to the screen was saying, "—we are offering is the chance to end this, here and now, with no more bloodshed, no more aggression, no more pain, no more loss of life. Isn't that worth giving up a little?"

Wednesday stopped pacing and turned. His nostrils flared. "First," he growled, "you have to understand that you are asking me to speak for all of us,[656] for each and every individual in my position across this country. Which is manifestly nonsensical. They will do what they will do, and I have no say in it.[657] Secondly, what on earth makes you think that I believe that you people are going to keep your word?"

The man with his back to the camera moved his head. "You do yourself an injustice," he said. "Obviously you people have no leaders. But you're the one they listen to. They pay attention to you, Mister Cargo. And as for keeping my word, well, these preliminary talks are being filmed and broadcast live," and he gestured back toward the camera. "Some of your people are watching as we speak. Others will see videotapes. Others will be told, by those they trust.[658] The camera does not lie."

"Everybody lies," said Wednesday.

Shadow recognized the voice of the man with his back to the camera. It was Mr. World, the one who had spoken to Town on the cell phone while Shadow was in Town's head.

"You don't believe," said Mr. World, "that we will keep our word?"

"I think your promises were made to be broken and your oaths to be forsworn. But I will keep *my* word."

"Safe conduct is safe conduct," said Mr. World, "and a flag of truce is what we agreed. I should tell you, by the way, that your young protégé is once more in our custody."

656. The balance of this sentence does not appear in the First Edition.

657. This sentence does not appear in the First Edition.

658. This sentence does not appear in the First Edition.

659. This sentence does not appear in the First Edition.

Wednesday snorted. "No," he said. "He's not."

"We were discussing the ways to deal with the coming paradigm shift. We don't have to be enemies. Do we?"

Wednesday still seemed shaken. He said, "I will do whatever is in my power . . ."

Shadow noticed something strange about the image of Wednesday on the television screen. A red glint burned on his left eye, the glass one. The eye burned with a scarlet light.[659] The glint left a phosphor-dot after-image as he moved. Wednesday seemed unaware of it.

"It's a big country," said Wednesday, marshaling his thoughts. He moved his head and the scarlet glitter-blur slipped to his cheek, a red laser-pointer dot. Then it edged up to his glass eye once more. "There is room for—"

There was a bang, muted by the television speakers, and the side of Wednesday's head exploded. His body tumbled backward.

Mr. World stood up, his back still to the camera, and walked out of shot.

"Let's see that again, in slow motion this time," said the announcer's voice, reassuringly.

The words LIVE FEED became REPLAY. Slowly now the red laser pointer traced its bead onto Wednesday's glass eye, and once again the side of his face dissolved into a cloud of blood. Freeze frame.

"Yes, it's still God's Own Country," said the announcer, a news reporter pronouncing the final tag line. "The only question is, which gods?"

Another voice—Shadow thought that it was Mr. World's, it had that same half-familiar quality—said, "We now return you to your regularly scheduled programming."

On *Cheers* Coach assured his daughter that she was truly beautiful, just like her mother.

The telephone rang, and Officer Liz sat up with a start. She picked it up. Said, "Okay. Okay. Yes. Okay, I'll be over there," put the phone down and got up from behind the counter. She said to Shadow, "Sorry. I'm going to have to put you in the cell. Don't use the can. If you need to go, press the buzzer by the door, and I'll come down as soon as I can and escort you to the restrooms out back.**660** The Lafayette sheriff's department should be here to collect you soon."

She removed the cuffs and the hobble, locked him into the holding cell. The smell was worse, now that the door was closed.

Shadow sat down on the concrete bed, slipped the Liberty dollar from his sock and began moving it from finger to palm, from position to position, from hand to hand, his only aim to keep the coin from being seen by anyone who might look in. He was passing the time. He was numb.

He missed Wednesday, then, sudden and deep. He missed the man's confidence, his attitude. His conviction.

He opened his hand, looked down at Lady Liberty, a silver profile. He closed his fingers over the coin, held it tightly. He wondered if he'd get to be one of those guys who got life for something they didn't do. If he even made it that far. From what he'd seen of Mr. World and Mr. Town, they would have little trouble pulling him out of the system. Perhaps he'd suffer an unfortunate accident on the way to the next holding facility. He could be shot while making a break for it. It did not seem at all unlikely.

There was a stir of activity in the room on the other side of the glass. Officer Liz came back in. She pressed a button, a door that Shadow could not see opened, and a black deputy in a brown sheriff's uniform entered and walked briskly over to the desk.

Shadow slipped the dollar coin back into his sock, pushing it down toward his ankle.

The new deputy handed over some papers, Liz scanned them and signed. Chad Mulligan came in, said a few words to the new man, then he unlocked the cell door and walked inside.

"It stinks in here."**661**

"Tell me about it."

"Okay. Folk are here to pick you up. Seems you're a matter of national security. You know that?"

"It'll make a great front-page story for the *Lakeside News*," said Shadow.

660. This sentence does not appear in the First Edition.

661. This sentence and the next do not appear in the First Edition.

Chad looked at him without expression. "That a drifter got picked up for parole violations? Not much of a story."

"So that's the way it is?"

"That's what they tell me," said Chad Mulligan. Shadow put his hands in front of him this time, and Chad cuffed him. Chad locked on the ankle hobbles, and a rod from the cuffs to the hobbles.

Shadow thought, *They'll take me outside. Maybe I can make a break for it, some kind of break for it, in hobbles and cuffs and lightweight orange clothes, out into the snow,* and even as he thought it he knew how stupid and hopeless it was.

Chad walked him out into the office. Liz had turned the TV off now. The black deputy looked him over. "He's a big guy," he said to Chad. Liz passed the new deputy the paper bag with Shadow's possessions in it, and he signed for it.

Chad looked at Shadow, then at the deputy. He said to the deputy, quietly, but loudly enough for Shadow to hear, "Look. I just want to say, I'm not comfortable with the way this is happening."

The deputy nodded. His voice was deep, and cultured: the voice of a man who could as easily organize a press briefing as a massacre.[662] "You'll have to take it up with the appropriate authorities, sir. Our job is simply to bring him in."

Chad made a sour face. He turned to Shadow. "Okay," said Chad. "Through that door and into the sally port."[663]

"What?"

"Out there. Where the car is."

Liz unlocked the doors. "You make sure that orange uniform comes right back here," she said to the deputy. "The last felon we sent down to Lafayette, we never saw the uniform again. They cost the county money." They walked Shadow out to the sally port, where a car was waiting. It wasn't a sheriff's-department car. It was a black town car. Another deputy, a grizzled white guy with a mustache, stood by the car, smoking a cigarette. He crushed it out underfoot as they came close, and opened the back door for Shadow.

Shadow sat down, awkwardly, his movements hampered

662. This sentence does not appear in the First Edition.

663. A small, controlled entryway to a fortification or prison.

by the cuffs and the hobble. There was no grille between the back and the front of the car.

The two deputies climbed into the front of the car. The black deputy started the motor. They waited for the sally port door to open.

"Come on, come on," said the black deputy, his fingers drumming against the steering wheel.

Chad Mulligan tapped on the side window. The white deputy glanced at the driver, then he lowered the window. "This is wrong," said Chad. "I just wanted to say that."

"Your comments have been noted, and will be conveyed to the appropriate authorities," said the driver.

The doors to the outside world opened. The snow was still falling, dizzying into the car's headlights. The driver put his foot on the gas, and they were heading back down the street and onto Main Street.

"You heard about Wednesday?" said the driver. His voice sounded different, now, older, and familiar. "He's dead."

"Yeah. I know," said Shadow. "I saw it on TV."

"Those fuckers," said the white officer. It was the first thing he had said, and his voice was rough and accented and, like the driver's, it was a voice that Shadow knew. "I tell you, they are fuckers, those fuckers."

"Thanks for coming to get me," said Shadow.

"Don't mention it," said the driver. In the light of an oncoming car his face already looked older. He looked smaller, too. The last time Shadow had seen him he had been wearing lemon-yellow gloves and a check jacket. "We were in Milwaukee. Still had to drive like demons when Ibis called."

"You think we let them lock you up and send you to the chair, when I'm still waiting to break your head with my hammer?" asked the white deputy gloomily, fumbling in his pocket for a pack of cigarettes. His accent was east European.

"The real shit will hit the fan in an hour or less," said Mr. Nancy, looking more like himself with each moment, "when they really turn up to collect you. We'll pull over before we get to Highway 53 and get you out of those shackles and back into your own clothes." Czernobog held up a handcuff key and smiled.

"I like the mustache," said Shadow. "Suits you."

Czernobog stroked it with a yellowed finger. "Thank you."

"Wednesday," said Shadow. "Is he really dead? This isn't some kind of trick is it?"

He realized that he had been holding on to some kind of hope, foolish though it was. But the expression on Nancy's face told him all he needed to know, and the hope was gone.

Coming to America
14,000 B.C.

Cold it was, and dark, when the vision came to her, for in the far north daylight was a gray dim time in the middle of the day that came, and went, and came again: an interlude between darknesses.

They were not a large tribe as these things were counted then: nomads of the Northern Plains. They had a god, who was the skull of a mammoth, and the hide of a mammoth fashioned into a rough cloak. Nunyunnini they called him. When they were not traveling, he rested on a wooden frame, at man height.

She was the holy woman of the tribe, the keeper of its secrets, and her name was Atsula, the fox. Atsula walked before the two tribesmen who carried their god on long poles, draped with bearskins, that it should not be seen by profane eyes, nor at times when it was not holy.

They roamed the tundra, with their tents. The finest of the tents was made of caribou-hide, and it was the holy tent, and there were four of them inside it: Atsula, the priestess, Gugwei, the tribal elder, Yanu, the war leader, and Kalanu, the scout. She called them there, the day after she had her vision.

Atsula scraped some lichen into the fire, then she threw in dried leaves with her withered left hand [664]: they smoked, with an eye-stinging gray smoke, and gave off an odor that was sharp and strange. Then she took a wooden cup from

664. A statue of Atsula appears in a dream of Shadow's. See text accompanying note 172, above.

the wooden platform, and she passed it to Gugwei. The cup was half-filled with a dark yellow liquid.

Atsula had found the pungh mushrooms—each with seven spots, only a true holy woman could find a seven-spotted mushroom—and had picked them at the dark of the moon, and dried them on a string of deer-cartilage.

Yesterday, before she slept, she had eaten the three dried mushroom caps. Her dreams had been confused and fearful things, of bright lights moving fast, of rock mountains filled with lights spearing upward like icicles. In the night she had woken, sweating, and needing to make water. She squatted over the wooden cup and filled it with her urine. Then she placed the cup outside the tent, in the snow, and returned to sleep.

When she woke, she picked the lumps of ice out from the wooden cup, as her mother had taught her,[665] leaving a darker, more concentrated liquid behind.

It was this liquid she passed around the skin tent, first to Gugwei, then to Yanu and to Kalanu. Each of them took a large gulp of the liquid, then Atsula took the final draught. She swallowed it, and poured what was left on the ground in front of their god, a libation to Nunyunnini.

They sat in the smoky tent, waiting for their god to speak. Outside, in the darkness, the wind wailed and breathed.

Kalanu, the scout, was a woman who dressed and walked as a man: she had even taken Dalani, a fourteen-year-old maiden, to be her wife. Kalanu blinked her eyes tightly, then she got up and walked over to the mammoth-skull. She pulled the mammoth-hide cloak over herself, and stood so her head was inside the mammoth-skull.

"There is evil in the land," said Nunyunnini.[666] "Evil, such that if you stay here, in the land of your mothers and your mother's mothers, you shall all perish."

The three listeners grunted.

"Is it the slavers? Or the great wolves?" asked Gugwei, whose hair was long and white, and whose face was as wrinkled as the gray skin of a thorn tree.

"It is not the slavers," said Nunyunnini, old stone-hide. "It is not the great wolves."

665. This phrase does not appear in the First Edition.

666. In the First Edition, the phrase "in Kalanu's voice" is added here.

"Is it a famine? Is a famine coming?" asked Gugwei.

Nunyunnini was silent. Kalanu came out of the skull and waited with the rest of them.

Gugwei put on the mammoth-hide cloak and put his head inside the skull. "It is not a famine as you know it," said Nunyunnini, through Gugwei's mouth, "although a famine will follow."

"Then what is it?" asked Yanu. "I am not afraid. I will stand against it. We have spears, and we have throwing rocks. Let a hundred mighty warriors come against us, still we shall prevail. We shall lead them into the marshes, and split their skulls with our rocks."

"It is not a man thing," said Nunyunnini, in Gugwei's old voice. "It will come from the skies, and none of your spears or your rocks will protect you."

"How can we protect ourselves?" asked Atsula. "I have seen flames in the skies. I have heard a noise louder than ten thunderbolts. I have seen forests flattened and rivers boil."

"Ai . . . ," said Nunyunnini, but he said no more. Gugwei came out of the skull, bending stiffly, for he was an old man, and his knuckles were swollen and knotted.

There was silence. Atsula threw more leaves on the fire, and the smoke made their eyes tear.

Then Yanu strode to the mammoth-head, put the cloak about his broad shoulders, put his head inside the skull. His voice boomed. "You must journey," said Nunyunnini. "You must travel to sun-ward. Where the sun rises, there you will find a new land, where you will be safe.[667] It will be a long journey: the moon will swell and empty, die and live, twice, and there will be slavers and beasts, but I shall guide you and keep you safe, if you travel toward the sunrise."

Atsula spat on the mud of the floor, and said, "No." She could feel the god staring at her. "No," she said. "You are a bad god to tell us this. We will die. We will all die, and then who will be left to carry you from high place to high place, to raise your tent, to oil your great tusks with fat?"

The god said nothing. Atsula and Yanu exchanged places. Atsula's face stared out through the yellowed mammoth-bone.

667. Some theorize the existence of a land bridge across the Bering Straits (that is, from Siberia to North America), resulting from a lowering of sea levels from about 30,000 to 11,000 years ago. This lowering would have occurred as a result of global cooling, resulting in the expansion of glaciers.

"Atsula has no faith," said Nunyunnini in Atsula's voice. "Atsula shall die before the rest of you enter the new land, but the rest of you shall live. Trust me: there is a land to the east that is manless. This land shall be your land and the land of your children and your children's children, for seven generations, and seven sevens. But for Atsula's faithlessness, you would have kept it forever. In the morning, pack your tents and your possessions, and walk toward the sunrise."

And Gugwei and Yanu and Kalanu bowed their heads and exclaimed at the power and wisdom of Nunyunnini.

The moon swelled and waned and swelled and waned once more. The people of the tribe walked east, toward the sunrise, struggling through the icy winds, which numbed their exposed skin. Nunyunnini had promised them truly: they lost no one from the tribe on the journey, save for a woman in childbirth, and women in childbirth belong to the moon, not to Nunyunnini.

They crossed the land-bridge.

Kalanu had left them at first light to scout the way. Now the sky was dark, and Kalanu had not returned, but the night sky was alive with lights, knotting and flickering and winding, flux and pulse, white and green and violet and red. Atsula and her people had seen the northern lights before, but they were still frightened by them, and this was a display like they had never seen before.

Kalanu returned to them, as the lights in the sky formed and flowed.

"Sometimes," she said to Atsula, "I feel that I could simply spread my arms and fall into the sky."

"That is because you are a scout," said Atsula, the priestess. "When you die, you shall fall into the sky and become a star, to guide us as you guide us in life."

"There are cliffs of ice to the east, high cliffs," said Kalanu, her raven-black hair worn long, as a man would wear it. "We can climb them, but it will take many days."

"You shall lead us safely," said Atsula. "I shall die at the foot of the cliff, and that shall be the sacrifice that takes you into the new lands."

To the west of them, back in the lands from which they had come, where the sun had set hours before, there was a flash of sickly yellow light, brighter than lightning, brighter than daylight: a burst of pure brilliance that forced the folk on the land bridge to cover their eyes and spit and exclaim.[668] Children began to wail.

"That is the doom that Nunyunnini warned us of," said Gugwei the old. "Surely he is a wise god and a mighty one."

"He is the best of all gods," said Kalanu. "In our new land we shall raise him up on high, and we shall polish his tusks and skull with fish oil and animal fat, and we shall tell our children, and our children's children, and our seventh children's children, that Nunyunnini is the mightiest of all gods, and shall never be forgotten."

"Gods are great," said Atsula, slowly, as if she were comprehending[669] a great secret. "But the heart is greater. For it is from our hearts they come, and to our hearts they shall return . . ."

And there is no telling how long she might have continued in this blasphemy, had it not been interrupted in a manner that brooked no argument.

The roar that erupted from the west was so loud that ears bled, that they could hear nothing for some time, temporarily blinded and deafened but alive, knowing that they were luckier than the tribes to the west of them.

"It is good," said Atsula, but she could not hear the words inside her head.

Atsula died at the foot of the cliffs when the spring sun was at its zenith. She did not live to see the New World, and the tribe walked into those lands with no holy woman.

They scaled the cliffs, and they went south and west, until they found a valley with fresh water, and rivers that teemed with silver fish, and deer that had never seen man before, and were so tame it was necessary to spit and to apologize to their spirits before killing them.

Dalani gave birth to three boys, and some said that Kalanu had performed the final magic and could do the man-thing with her bride; while others said that old Gug-

668. This would have been an unidentified impact with a meteor or another body from space. The Popigai crater in Siberia, Russia, more than 60 miles across, is tied for the title of the fourth-largest verified impact crater on Earth. It was the result of a large bolide impact approximately 35 million years ago during the late Eocene epoch (Priabonian stage), far earlier than the events recorded here. Another major Siberian meteor impact occurred in 1908, the so-called Tunguska event, which flattened more than 770 square miles of forest.

669. The word is "imparting" in the First Edition.

wei was not too old to keep a young bride company when her husband was away; and certainly once Gugwei died, Dalani had no more children.

And the ice times came and the ice times went, and the people spread out across the land, and formed new tribes and chose new totems for themselves: ravens and foxes and ground sloths and great cats and buffalo, each a taboo beast that marked a tribe's identity, each beast a god.

The mammoths of the new lands were bigger, and slower, and more foolish than the mammoths of the Siberian plains, and the pungh mushrooms, with their seven spots, were not to be found in the new lands, and Nunyunnini did not speak to the tribe any longer.

And in the days of the grandchildren of Dalani and Kalanu's grandchildren, a band of warriors, members of a big and prosperous tribe, returning from a slaving expedition in the north to their home in the south, found the valley of the First People: they killed most of the men, and they took the women and many of the children captive.

One of the children, hoping for clemency, took them to a cave in the hills, in which they found a mammoth-skull, the tattered remnants of a mammoth-skin cloak, a wooden cup, and the preserved head of Atsula the oracle.

While some of the warriors of the new tribe were for taking the sacred objects away with them, stealing the gods of the First People and owning their power, others counseled against it, saying that they would bring nothing but ill luck, and the malice of their own god (for these were the people of a raven tribe, and ravens are jealous gods).

So they threw the objects down the side of the hill, into a deep ravine, and took the survivors of the First People with them on their long journey south. And the raven tribes, and the fox tribes, grew more powerful in the land, and soon Nunyunnini was entirely forgot.

PART THREE

THE MOMENT OF THE STORM

CHAPTER FOURTEEN

―❧―

People are in the dark, they don't know what to do
I had a little lantern, oh but it got blown out too.
I'm reaching out my hand. I hope you are too.
I just want to be in the dark with you.

—GREG BROWN,
"*In the Dark with You*"**670**

670. Greg Brown is an Iowa-born folksinger, and he recorded this song in 1985 and released it on an album with the same name.

HEY CHANGED CARS at five in the morning, in Minneapolis, in the airport's long-term parking lot. They drove to the top floor, where the parking building was open to the sky.

Shadow took the orange uniform and the handcuffs and leg hobbles, put them in the brown paper bag that had briefly held his possessions, folded the whole thing up and dropped it into a parking lot garbage can. They had been waiting for ten minutes when a barrel-chested young man came out of an airport door and walked over to them. He was eating a packet of Burger King french fries. Shadow recognized him immediately: he had sat in the back of the car when they had left the House on the Rock, and hummed so deeply the car had vibrated. He now sported a white-streaked winter beard he had not had when they had met at the House on the Rock. It made him look older.

The man wiped the grease from his hands onto his sweater, extended one huge hand to Shadow. "I heard of the all-father's death," he said. "They will pay, and they will pay dearly."

"Wednesday was your father?" asked Shadow.

"He was the all-father," said the man. His deep voice caught in his throat. "You tell them, tell them all, that when we are needed my people will be there."

Czernobog picked at a flake of tobacco between his teeth and spat it out onto the frozen slush. "And how many of you is that? Ten? Twenty?"

The barrel-chested man's beard bristled. "And aren't ten of us worth a hundred of them? Who would stand against even one of my folk, in a battle? But there are more of us than that, at the edges of the cities. There are a few in the mountains. Some in the Catskills, a few living in the carny towns in Florida. They keep their axes sharp. They will come if I call them."

"You do that, Elvis," said Mr. Nancy. Shadow thought he said Elvis, anyway, but he couldn't be sure. Nancy had exchanged the deputy's uniform for a thick brown cardigan, corduroy trousers, and brown loafers. "You call them. It's what the old bastard would have wanted."

"They betrayed him. They killed him. I laughed at Wednesday, but I was wrong. None of us are safe any longer," said the man who might have been named Elvis. "But you can rely on us." He gently patted Shadow on the back and almost sent him sprawling. It was like being gently patted on the back by a wrecking ball.

Czernobog had been looking around the parking lot. Now he said, "You will pardon me asking, but our new vehicle is which?"

The barrel-chested man pointed. "There she is," he said.

Czernobog snorted. "That?"

It was a 1970 VW bus. There was a rainbow decal in the rear window.

"It's a fine vehicle. And it's the last thing that they'll be expecting you to be driving. The last thing they'll be looking for."[671]

Czernobog walked around the vehicle. Then he started to cough, a lung-rumbling, old-man, five-in-the-morning,

671. This sentence does not appear in the First Edition.

1970 Volkswagen bus in full hippie regalia

smoker's cough. He hawked, and spat, and put his hand to his chest, massaging away the pain. "Yes. The last car they will suspect. So what happens when the police pull us over, looking for the hippies, and the dope? Eh? We are not here to ride the magic bus. We are to blend in."

The bearded man unlocked the door of the bus. "So they take a look at you, they see you aren't hippies, they wave you goodbye. It's the perfect disguise. And it's all I could find at no notice."

Czernobog seemed to be ready to argue it further, but Mr. Nancy intervened smoothly. "Elvis, you come through for us. We are very grateful. Now, that car needs to get back to Chicago."

"We'll leave it in Bloomington," said the bearded man. "The wolves will take care of it. Don't give it another thought." He turned back to Shadow. "Again, you have my sympathy and I share your pain. Good luck. And if the vigil falls to you, my admiration, and my sympathy." He squeezed Shadow's hand in sympathy and in friendship[672] with his own catcher's-mitt fist. It hurt. "You tell his corpse when you see it. Tell him that Alviss son of Vindalf will keep the faith."[673]

The VW bus smelled of patchouli, of old incense and rolling tobacco. There was a faded pink carpet glued to the floor and to the walls.

"Who was that?" asked Shadow, as he drove them down the ramp, grinding the gears.

672. The phrase "in sympathy and in friendship" does not appear in the First Edition.

673. Alviss ("All-wise") is another of the creatures of Norse mythology, a dwarf known for his wisdom and his skills as a master smith. His tale is principally told in the Alvíssmál ("Ballad of the All-wise"): Alviss comes to Thor's home to claim his daughter in marriage. Thor wishes his daughter to wed only a god and so puts Alviss to a test, a battery of questions about the names of the earth, sea, sun, moon, etc. Alviss demonstrates his wisdom amply but fails the test, when he discovers that Thor has tricked him into talking all night, so that the rays of the dawning sun turn the dwarf to stone. See note 315, above, for his first appearance.

"Just like he said, Alviss son of Vindalf. He's the king of the dwarfs. The biggest, mightiest, greatest of all the dwarf folk."

"But he's not a dwarf," pointed out Shadow. "He's what, five eight? Five nine?"

"Which makes him a giant among dwarfs," said Czernobog from behind him. "Tallest dwarf in America."

"What was that about the vigil?" asked Shadow.

The two old men said nothing. Shadow glanced to his right. Mr. Nancy was staring out of the window.

"Well? He was talking about a vigil. You heard him."

Czernobog spoke up from the back seat. "You will not have to do it," he said.

"Do what?"

674. The balance of this sentence and the next two sentences do not appear in the First Edition.

"The vigil. He talks too much. All the dwarfs talk[674] and talk and talk. And sing. All the time, sing, sing, sing. Is nothing to think of. Better you put it out of your mind."

✢   ✢   ✢

675. The paragraph begins here in the First Edition.

THEY DROVE SOUTH, keeping off the freeways ("We must assume," said Mr. Nancy, "that they are in enemy hands. Or that they are perhaps enemy hands in their own right").[675] Driving south was like driving forward in time. The snows erased, slowly, and were completely gone by the following morning when the bus reached Kentucky. Winter was already over in Kentucky, and spring was on its way. Shadow began to wonder if there were some kind of equation to explain it—perhaps every fifty miles he drove south he was driving a day into the future.

He would have mentioned his idea to his passengers, but Mr. Nancy was asleep in the passenger seat in the front, while Czernobog snored unceasingly in the back.

Time seemed a flexible construct at that moment, an illusion he was imagining as he drove. He found himself becoming painfully aware of birds and animals: he saw the crows on the side of the road, or in the bus's path, picking at roadkill; flights of birds wheeled across the skies in patterns that almost made sense; cats stared at them from front lawns and fence-posts.

Czernobog snorted and woke, sitting up slowly. "I dreamed a strange dream," he said. "I dreamed that I am truly Bielebog. That forever the world imagines that there are two of us, the light god and the dark, but that now we are both old, I find it was only me all the time, giving them gifts, taking my gifts away." He broke the filter from a Lucky Strike, put it between his lips and lit it with his lighter.

Shadow wound down his window.

"Aren't you worried about lung cancer?" he said.

"I *am* cancer," said Czernobog. "I do not frighten myself." He chuckled, and then the chuckle became a wheeze and the wheeze turned into a cough.[676]

Nancy spoke. "Folk like us don't get cancer. We don't get arteriosclerosis or Parkinson's disease or syphilis. We're kind of hard to kill."

"They killed Wednesday," said Shadow.

He pulled over for gas, and then parked next door at a restaurant, for an early breakfast. As they entered, the payphone in the entrance began to jangle. They walked past it without answering it, and it stopped ringing.[677]

They gave their orders to an elderly woman with a worried smile, who had been sitting reading a paperback copy of *What My Heart Meant* by Jenny Kerton.[678] The telephone began to ring once more.[679] The woman sighed, then walked back and over to the phone, picked it up, said, "Yes." Then she looked back at the room, said, "Yep. Looks like they are. You just hold the line now," and walked over to Mr. Nancy.

"It's for you," she said.

"Okay," said Mr. Nancy. "Now, ma'am, you make sure those fries are real *crisp* now. Think burnt." He walked over to the payphone.

"This is he," he said.

"And what makes you think I'm dumb enough to trust you?" he said.

"I can find it," he said. "I know where it is."

"Yes," he said. "We want it. You know we want it. And I know you want to get rid of it. So don't give me any shit."

He put down the telephone, came back to the table.

676. This sentence does not appear in the First Edition.

677. This sentence does not appear in the First Edition.

678. See note 499, above.

679. This sentence does not appear in the First Edition.

"Who was it?" asked Shadow.

"Didn't say."

"What did they want?"

"They were offerin' us a truce, while they hand over the body."

"They lie," said Czernobog. "They want to lure us in, and then they will kill us. What they did to Wednesday. Is what I always used to do," he added, with gloomy pride. "Promise them anything, but do what you will."[680]

"It's on neutral territory," said Nancy. "Truly neutral."

Czernobog chuckled. It sounded like a metal ball rattling in a dry skull. "I used to say *that* also. Come to a neutral place, I would say, and then in the night we would rise up and kill them all. Those were the good days."

Mr. Nancy shrugged. He crunched down on his dark brown french fries, grinned his approval. "Mm-mm. These are fine fries," he said.

"We can't trust those people," said Shadow.

"Listen, I'm older than you and I'm smarter than you and I'm better lookin' than you," said Mr. Nancy, thumping the bottom of the ketchup bottle, blobbing ketchup over his burnt fries. "I can get more pussy in an afternoon than you'll get in a year. I can dance like an angel, fight like a cornered bear, plan better than a fox, sing like a nightingale . . ."

"And your point here is . . . ?"

Nancy's brown eyes gazed into Shadow's. "And they need to get rid of the body as much as we need to take it."

Czernobog said, "There is no such neutral place."

"There's one," said Mr. Nancy. "It's the center."

Czernobog shook his head abruptly.[681] "No. They would not meet us there. They can do nothing to us, there. It is a bad place for all of us."

"That's just why they've proposed to make the handover at the center."

Czernobog seemed to think about this for a while. And then he said, "Perhaps."

"When we get back on the road," said Shadow, "you can drive. I need to sleep."

680. This sentence does not appear in the First Edition.

681. This paragraph and the next three paragraphs do not appear in the First Edition.

* * *

DETERMINING THE EXACT center of anything can be problematic at best. With living things—people, for example, or continents—the problem becomes one of intangibles: What is the center of a man? What is the center of a dream? And in the case of the continental United States, should one count Alaska when one attempts to find the center? Or Hawaii?

As the twentieth century began, they made a huge model of the USA, the lower forty-eight states, out of cardboard, and to find the center they balanced it on a pin, until they found the single place it balanced.

Near as anyone could figure it out, the exact center of the continental United States was several miles from Lebanon, in Smith County, Kansas, on Johnny Grib's hog farm.[682] By the 1930s, the people of Lebanon were all ready to put a monument up in the middle of the hog farm, but Johnny Grib said that he didn't want millions of tourists coming in and tramping all over and upsetting the hogs, and the locals figured he had a point,[683] so they put the monument to the geographical center of the United States two miles north of the town. They built a park, and a stone monument to put in the park, and put a brass plaque to go on the monument[684] to tell you that you were indeed looking at the exact geographic center of the United States of America. They blacktopped the road from the town to the little park, and, certain of the influx of tourists just waiting to come to Lebanon, they even built a motel by the monument. They brought in a little mobile chapel as well, and took off the wheels.[685] Then they waited for the tourists and the holidaymakers to come: all the people who wanted to tell the world they'd been at the center of America, and marveled, and prayed.

The tourists did not come. Nobody came.

It's a sad little park, now, with a mobile chapel in it a little bigger than an ice-fishing hut that wouldn't fit a small funeral party, and a motel whose windows look like dead eyes.

682. According to the Center for Land Use Interpretation, a nonprofit organization "interested in understanding the nature and extent of human interaction with the surface of the earth," the story about the methodology used for the Lebanon marker is true. The Center also reports: "Forty-two miles south of Lebanon, a sign and plaque announce another center: the 'Geodetic Center of North America.' This sign makes no claims at being the geodetic center itself, rather it indicates that the actual geodetic center lies on private property eight miles away, in the fields of Smiths Ranch, where it is marked with a small bronze geodetic survey marker. Neither of these monuments should be confused with the Geographic Center of the United States (when you include Alaska and Hawaii), which sits seventeen miles west of Castle Rock, South Dakota, or the Geographic Center of North America, fifteen miles south west of Rugby, North Dakota." (http://www.clui.org/news letter/spring-1999/geographical-center -lower-48-united-states-lebanon-kansas) In an early essay considering the urge to find "centers," Oscar S. Adams, senior mathematician for the U.S. Coast and Geodetic Survey wrote, "Since there is no definite way to locate such a point, it would be best to ignore it entirely . . . the conclusion is forced upon us that there is no such thing as the geographical center of any state, country, or continent." Nonetheless, the continuing search for the "center" makes clear the validity of Mr. Nancy's assertion of the need of humans for something in which to believe.

683. This phrase does not appear in the First Edition.

684. The balance of this sentence does not appear in the First Edition.

685. This sentence and most of the next do not appear in the First Edition.

686. Located in the far northwest corner of Missouri, as of the 2010 census, the town had 1,048 people.

687. A breakfast cereal introduced in 1963 and still sold today. The box depicts Horatio Magellan Crunch, a late-eighteenth-century officer of an indeterminate navy whose rank seems to change over the years.

688. This sentence and most of the next do not appear in the First Edition.

689. Gwydion is a Celtic god, the son of Don the Enchanter and the brother of Gilfaethwy; he is the god of civilization and arts, magic and wisdom. Some place him as the Celtic equivalent of Odin. April Fool's Day is said to commemorate his trickery to rescue his companion Llew from a curse.

"Gwydion conquers Pryderi,"
by Ernest Wallcousins
Charles Squire's Celtic Myth, Legend, Poetry, and Romance *(1905)*

"Which is why," concluded Mr. Nancy, as they drove into Humansville, Missouri (pop. 1,084),[686] "the exact center of America is a tiny run-down park, an empty church, a pile of stones, and a derelict motel."

"Hog farm," said Czernobog. "You just said that the real center of America was a hog farm."

"This isn't about what is," said Mr. Nancy. "It's about what people *think* is. It's all imaginary anyway. That's why it's important. People only fight over imaginary things."

"My kind of people?" asked Shadow. "Or your kind of people?"

Nancy said nothing. Czernobog made a noise that might have been a chuckle, might have been a snort.

Shadow tried to get comfortable in the back of the bus. He had slept a little, but only a little. He had a bad feeling in the pit of his stomach. Worse than the feeling he had had in prison, worse than the feeling he had had back when Laura had come to him and told him about the robbery. This was bad. The back of his neck prickled, he felt sick and, several times, in waves, he felt scared.

Mr. Nancy pulled over in Humansville, parked outside a supermarket. Mr. Nancy went inside, and Shadow followed him in. Czernobog waited in the parking lot, stretching his legs, smoking his cigarette.

There was a young fair-haired man, little more than a boy, restocking the breakfast cereal shelves.

"Hey," said Mr. Nancy.

"Hey," said the young man. "It's true, isn't it? They killed him?"

"Yes," said Mr. Nancy. "They killed him."

The young man banged several boxes of Cap'n Crunch[687] down on the shelf. "They think they can crush us like cockroaches," he said. He had an eruption of acne across one cheek and over his forehead.[688] He had a silver bracelet high on one forearm. "We don't crush that easy, do we?"

"No," said Mr. Nancy. "We don't."

"I'll be there, sir," said the young man, his pale blue eyes blazing.

"I know you will, Gwydion,"[689] said Mr. Nancy.

Mr. Nancy bought several large bottles of RC Cola,[690] a six-pack of toilet paper, a pack of evil-looking black cigarillos, a bunch of bananas and a pack of Doublemint chewing gum.[691] "He's a good boy. Came over in the seventh century. Welsh."

The bus meandered first to the west and then to the north. Spring faded back into the dead end of winter. Kansas was the cheerless gray of lonesome clouds, empty windows and lost hearts. Shadow had become adept at hunting for radio stations, negotiating between Mr. Nancy, who liked talk radio and dance music, and Czernobog, who favored classical music, the gloomier the better, leavened with the more extreme evangelical religious stations. For himself, Shadow liked oldies stations.

Toward the end of the afternoon they stopped, at Czernobog's request, on the outskirts of Cherryvale, Kansas (pop. 2,464).[692] Czernobog led them to a meadow outside the town. There were still traces of snow in the shadows of the trees, and the grass was the color of dirt.

"Wait here," said Czernobog.

He walked, alone, to the center of the meadow. He stood there, in the winds of the end of February, for some time. At first he hung his head, then he began gesticulating.

"He looks like he's talking to someone," said Shadow.

"Ghosts," said Mr. Nancy. "They worshiped him here, over a hundred years ago. They made blood-sacrifice to him, libations spilled with the hammer. After a time, the townsfolk figured out why so many of the strangers who passed through the town didn't ever come back. This was where they hid some of the bodies."[693]

Czernobog came back from the middle of the field. His mustache seemed darker now, and there were streaks of black in his gray hair. He smiled, showing his iron tooth. "I feel good, now. Ahh. Some things linger, and blood lingers longest."

They walked back across the meadow to where they had parked the VW bus. Czernobog lit a cigarette, but did not cough. "They did it with the hammer," he said. "Grimnir, he would talk of the gallows and the spear, but for me, it is

690. Short for "Royal Crown Cola," this small competitor of Pepsi-Cola and Coca-Cola was introduced in 1905 and is today part of the Dr Pepper Snapple Group.

691. A variety introduced by the Wrigley company in 1914, supposedly with a "double-strength" mint flavor. Beginning in 1939, the product was advertised with illustrations of identical twins and in 1959, the company began using real identical twins as models in its advertising.

692. A town near the eastern border of Kansas, it had a population of 2,367 as of 2010. Vivian Vance, who played Ethel Mertz on *I Love Lucy*, was born there.

693. Between 1871 and 1873, eleven persons mysteriously vanished from the town. After investigation, it was determined that the Bender family, who maintained a small inn there, were serial killers. Between eight and eleven bodies were found buried in a cellar of the inn. Investigators later determined that guests at the inn were urged to sit against a separating curtain, and while dining, a family member behind the curtain hit the victim on the head with a hammer (perhaps inspired by Czernobog). The stunned (or deceased) victim was then dropped into the cellar, where the victim's throat was cut and the body stripped of valuables. The Benders were never caught. For more information on the Benders, see Rick Geary's *The Saga of the Bloody Benders* (New York: NBM Publishing, 2008) and Nile Cappello's essay "The Blood Benders: America's First Family of Serial Killers" (https://crimereads.com/the-bloody-benders-americas-first-family-of-serial-killers/).

Louise Brooks, ca. 1929

694. Louise Brooks (1906–1985), who became an icon of the flapper style and a sex symbol in the 1920s and 1930s, was born in Cherryvale.

695. The two preceding phrases do not appear in the First Edition.

one thing . . ." He reached out a nicotine-colored finger and tapped it, hard, in the center of Shadow's forehead.

"Please don't do that," said Shadow, politely.

"Please don't do that," mimicked Czernobog. "One day I will take my hammer and do much worse than that to you, my friend, remember?"

"Yes," said Shadow. "But if you tap my head again, I'll break your hand."

Czernobog snorted. Then he said, "They should be grateful, the people here. There was such power raised. Even thirty years after they forced my people into hiding, this land, this very land, gave us the greatest movie star of all time. She was the greatest there ever was."

"Judy Garland?" asked Shadow.

Czernobog shook his head curtly.

"He's talking about Louise Brooks," said Mr. Nancy.

Shadow decided not to ask who Louise Brooks was.[694] Instead he said, "So, look, when Wednesday went to talk to them, he did it under a truce."

"Yes."

"And now we're going to get Wednesday's body from them, as a truce."

"Yes."

"And we know that they want me dead or out of the way."

"They want all of us dead," said Nancy.

"So what I don't get is, why do we think they'll play fair this time, when they didn't for Wednesday?"

"That," said Czernobog, overenunciating each word, as he would for a deaf foreign idiot child,[695] "is why we are meeting at the center. Is . . ." He frowned. "What is the word for it? The opposite of sacred?"

"Profane," said Shadow, without thinking.

"No," said Czernobog. "I mean, when a place is less sacred than any other place. Of negative sacredness. Places where they can build no temples. Places where people will not come, and will leave as soon as they can. Places where gods only walk if they are forced to."

"I don't know," said Shadow. "I don't think there is a word for it."

"All of America has it, a little," said Czernobog. "That is why we are not welcome here. But the center," said Czernobog. "The center is worst. Is like a minefield. We all tread too carefully there to dare break the truce."

"I told you all this already," said Mr. Nancy.[696]

"Whatever," said Shadow.

They had reached the bus. Czernobog patted Shadow's upper arm. "You don't worry," he said, with gloomy reassurance. "Nobody else is going to kill you. Nobody but me."

✢   ✢   ✢

SHADOW FOUND THE center of America at evening that same day, before it was fully dark. It was on a slight hill to the northwest of Lebanon. He drove around the little hillside park, past the tiny mobile chapel and the stone monument, and when Shadow saw the one-story 1950s motel at the edge of the park his heart sank. There was a huge black car parked in front of it—a Humvee,[697] which looked like a jeep reflected in a fun-house mirror, as squat and pointless and ugly as an armored car. There were no lights on in the building.

They parked beside the motel, and as they did so, a man in a chauffeur's uniform and cap walked out of the motel and was illuminated by the headlights of the bus. He touched his cap to them, politely, got into the Humvee, and drove off.

"Big car, tiny dick," said Mr. Nancy.

"Do you think they'll even have beds here?" asked Shadow. "It's been days since I slept in a bed. This place looks like it's just waiting to be demolished."

"It's owned by hunters from Texas," said Mr. Nancy. "Come up here once a year. Damned if I know what they're huntin'. It stops the place being condemned and destroyed."

They climbed out of the bus. Waiting for them in front of the motel was a woman Shadow did not recognize. She was perfectly made-up, perfectly coiffed. She reminded him of every newscaster he'd ever seen on morning television sitting in a studio that didn't really resemble a living room, smiling at the good morning crowd.

696. This sentence and the next do not appear in the First Edition.

697. A High Mobility Multipurpose Wheeled Vehicle (HMMWV; colloquial: Humvee) is a four-wheel-drive utility vehicle produced by AM General and first used by the U.S. military in 1989. Subsequently, the Humvee became the utility vehicle of choice of military and paramilitary organizations throughout the world. In 1992, AM General began to produce a *civilian* vehicle known as the Hummer, an equally ugly but high-cachet transport aimed at the sports-utility vehicle market.

451

"Lovely to see you," she said. "Now, *you* must be Czernobog. I've heard a lot about you. And *you're* Anansi, always up to mischief, eh? You *jolly* old man. And you, you *must* be Shadow. You've certainly led us a merry chase, haven't *you*?" A hand took his, pressed it firmly; she looked him straight in the eye. "I'm Media. Good to meet you. I hope we can get this evening's business done as *pleasantly* as possible."

The main doors opened. "Somehow, Toto," said the fat kid Shadow had last seen sitting in a limo, "I don't believe we're in Kansas any more."

"We're in Kansas," said Mr. Nancy. "I think we must have driven through most of it today. Damn but this country is flat."

"This place has no lights, no power, and no hot water," said the fat kid. "And, no offense, you people really need the hot water. You just smell like you've been in that bus for a week."

"I don't think there's *any* need to go there," said the woman, smoothly. "We're all friends here. Come on in. We'll show you to your rooms. *We* took the first four rooms. Your late friend is in the fifth. All the ones beyond room five are empty—you can take your pick. I'm afraid it's *not* the Four Seasons, but then, what *is*?"

She opened the door to the motel lobby for them. It smelled of mildew, of damp and dust and of decay.

There was a man sitting in the lobby, in the near darkness. "You people hungry?" he asked.

"I can always eat," said Mr. Nancy.

"Driver's gone out for a sack of hamburgers," said the man. "He'll be back soon." He looked up. It was too dark to see faces, but he said, "Big guy. You're Shadow, huh? The asshole who killed Woody and Stone?"

"No," said Shadow. "That was someone else. And I know who you are." He did. He had been inside the man's head. "You're Town. Have you slept with Wood's widow yet?"

Mr. Town fell off his chair. In a movie, it would have been funny; in real life it was simply clumsy. He stood up quickly, came toward Shadow. Shadow looked down at him, and said, "Don't start anything you're not prepared to finish."

Mr. Nancy rested his hand on Shadow's upper arm. "Truce, remember?" he said. "We're at the center."

Mr. Town turned away, leaned over to the counter and picked up three keys. "You're down at the end of the hall," he said. "Here."

He handed the keys to Mr. Nancy and walked away, into the shadows of the corridor. They heard a motel room door open, and they heard it slam.

Mr. Nancy passed a key to Shadow, another to Czernobog. "Is there a flashlight on the bus?" asked Shadow.

"No," said Mr. Nancy. "But it's just dark. You mustn't be afraid of the dark."

"I'm not," said Shadow. "I'm afraid of the people in the dark."

"Dark is good," said Czernobog. He seemed to have no difficulty seeing where he was going, leading them down the darkened corridor, putting the keys into the locks without fumbling. "I will be in room ten," he told them. And then he said, "Media. I think I have heard of her. Isn't she the one who killed her children?"

"Different woman," said Mr. Nancy. "Same deal."[698]

Mr. Nancy was in room eight, and Shadow opposite the two of them, in room nine. The room smelled damp, and dusty, and deserted. There was a bed-frame in there, with a mattress on it, but no sheets. A little light entered the room from the gloaming outside the window. Shadow sat down on the mattress, pulled off his shoes, and stretched out at full length. He had driven too much in the last few days.

Perhaps he slept.

✢   ✢   ✢

He was walking.

A cold wind tugged at his clothes. The tiny snowflakes were little more than a crystalline dust which gusted and flurried in the wind.

There were trees, bare of leaves in the winter. There were high hills on each side of him. It was late on a winter's afternoon: the sky and the snow had attained the same deep shade of purple. Somewhere ahead of him—in this light,

698. Czernobog is recalling Medea, the daughter of King Aeëtes of Colchis, a niece of Circe and the granddaughter of the sun god Helios. According to the play *Medea* by Euripides, first produced in 431 B.C.E., Medea—spurned by her husband Jason—took her revenge by sending his new lover, Glauce, a dress and golden coronet covered in poison. This resulted in the deaths of both the princess and the king, Creon, when he tried to save his daughter Glauce. Medea then murdered two of her children by Jason. Afterward, she left Corinth and flew to Athens in a golden chariot driven by dragons sent by her grandfather. Many historians believe that the killing of her own children was the invention of Euripides, but Medea has since become synonymous with filicide.

distances were impossible to judge—the flames of a bonfire flickered, yellow and orange.

A gray wolf padded through the snow before him.

Shadow stopped. The wolf stopped also, and turned, and waited. One of its eyes glinted yellowish-green. Shadow shrugged and walked toward the flames and the wolf ambled ahead of him.

The bonfire burned in the middle of a grove of trees. There must have been a hundred trees, planted in two rows. There were shapes hanging from the trees. At the end of the rows was a building that looked a little like an overturned boat. It was carved of wood, and it crawled with wooden creatures and wooden faces—dragons, gryphons, trolls and boars—all of them dancing in the flickering light of the fire.

The bonfire was so high, and burning so hard, that Shadow could barely approach it. The wolf seemed unfazed, and it padded around the crackling fire.

He waited for it to return, but in place of the wolf a man walked back around the fire. He was leaning on a tall stick.

"You are in Uppsala, in Sweden," said the man, in a familiar, gravelly voice. "About a thousand years ago."[699]

"Wednesday?" said Shadow.

The man who might have been Wednesday continued to talk, as if Shadow was not there. "First every year, then, later, when the rot set in, and they became lax, every nine years, they would sacrifice here. A sacrifice of nines. Each day, for nine days, they would hang nine animals from trees in the grove. One of those animals was always a man."[700]

He strode away from the firelight, toward the trees, and Shadow followed him. As he approached the trees the shapes that hung from them resolved: legs and eyes and tongues and heads. Shadow shook his head: there was something about seeing a bull hanging by its neck from a tree that was darkly sad, and at the same time surreal enough almost to be funny. Shadow passed a hanging stag, a wolfhound, a brown bear, and a chestnut horse with a white mane, little bigger than a pony. The dog was still alive: every few seconds it would kick spasmodically, and

699. According to the medieval writer Adam of Bremen, Uppsala was the main pagan center of Sweden, and the Temple there held magnificent statues of Thor, Odin, and Frey. This information is confirmed in the thirteenth-century *Heimskringla* (roughly, "The Circle of the World"), by Snorri Sturluson.

700. In Norse traditions, nines abound in the stories and rituals of Odin. He hung on the world tree for nine days, learned nine names, nine runes, and twice-nine charms—hence, nine sacrifices. See text accompanying note 189, above.

it was making a strained whimpering noise, as it dangled from the rope.

The man he was following took his long stick, which Shadow realized now, as it moved, was actually a spear, and he slashed at the dog's stomach with it, in one knife-like cut downward. Steaming entrails tumbled onto the snow. "I dedicate this death to Odin," said the man, formally.

"It is only a gesture," he said, turning back to Shadow. "But gestures mean everything. The death of one dog symbolizes the death of all dogs. Nine men they gave to me, but they stood for all the men, all the blood, all the power. It just wasn't enough. One day, the blood stopped flowing. Belief without blood only takes us so far. The blood must flow."

"I saw you die," said Shadow.

"In the god business," said the figure—and now Shadow was certain it was Wednesday, nobody else had that rasp, that deep cynical joy in words, "it's not the death that matters. It's the opportunity for resurrection. And when the blood flows . . ." He gestured at the animals, at the people, hanging from the trees.

Shadow could not decide whether the dead humans they walked past were more or less horrifying than the animals: at least the humans had known the fate they were going to. There was a deep, boozy smell about the men that suggested that they had been allowed to anaesthetize themselves on their way to the gallows, while the animals would simply have been lynched, hauled up alive and terrified. The faces of the men looked so young: none of them was older than twenty.

"Who am I?" asked Shadow.

"You are a diversion," said the man. "You were an opportunity. You gave the whole affair an air of credibility I would have been hard put to deliver solo.[701] *Although both of us are committed enough to the affair to die for it. Eh?"*

"Who are you?" asked Shadow.

"The hardest part is simply surviving," said the man. The bonfire—and Shadow realized with a strange horror that it truly was a bone-fire: ribcages and fire-eyed skulls

701. In the First Edition, the phrase "are a diversion" does not appear, and this sentence reads "You were part of a grand tradition."

stared and stuck and jutted from the flames, sputtering trace-element colors into the night, greens and yellows and blues—was flaring and crackling and burning hotly. "Three days on the tree, three days in the underworld, three days to find my way back."

The flames sputtered and flared too brightly for Shadow to look at directly. He looked down into the darkness beneath the trees.

There was no fire, no snow. There were no trees, no hanged bodies, no bloody spear.[702]

702. This paragraph does not appear in the First Edition.

✦   ✦   ✦

A KNOCK ON the door—and now there was moonlight coming in the window. Shadow sat up with a start. "Dinner's served," said Media's voice.

Shadow put his shoes back on, walked over to the door, went out into the corridor. Someone had found some candles, and a dim yellow light illuminated the reception hall. The driver of the Humvee came in through the swing doors holding a cardboard tray and a paper sack. He wore a long black coat and a peaked chauffeur's cap.

"Sorry about the delay," he said, hoarsely. "I got everybody the same: a couple of burgers, large fries, large Coke, and apple pie. I'll eat mine out in the car." He put the food down, then walked back outside. The smell of fast food filled the lobby. Shadow took the paper bag and passed out the food, the napkins, the packets of ketchup.

They ate in silence while the candles flickered and the burning wax hissed.

Shadow noticed that Town was glaring at him. He turned his chair a little, so his back was to the wall. Media ate her burger with a napkin poised by her lips to remove crumbs.

"Oh. Great. These burgers are nearly cold," said the fat kid. He was still wearing his shades, which Shadow thought pointless and foolish, given the darkness of the room.

703. This sentence does not appear in the First Edition.

"Sorry about that. The guy had to drive a way to find them,"[703] said Town. "The nearest McDonald's is in Nebraska."

They finished their lukewarm hamburgers and cold fries. The fat kid bit into his single-person apple pie, and the filling spurted down his chin. Unexpectedly, the filling was still hot. "Ow," he said. He wiped at it with his hand, licking his fingers to get them clean. "That stuff burns!" he said. "Those pies are a class action suit waiting to fucking happen."[704]

Shadow realized he wanted to hit the kid. He'd wanted to hit him since the kid had his goons hurt him in the limo, after Laura's funeral. He knew it was not a wise thing to be thinking, not here, not now.[705] "Can't we just take Wednesday's body and get out of here?" he asked.

"Midnight," said Mr. Nancy and the fat kid, at the same time.

"These things must be done according to the rules," said Czernobog. "All things have rules."[706]

"Yeah," said Shadow. "But nobody tells me what they are. You keep talking about the goddamn rules, I don't even know what game you people are playing."

"It's like breaking the street date," said Media, brightly. "You know. When things are allowed to be on sale."

Town said, "I think the whole thing's a crock of shit. But if their rules make them happy, then my agency is happy and everybody's happy." He slurped his Coke. "Roll on midnight. You take the body, you go away. We're all lovey-fucking-dovey and we wave you goodbye. And then we can get on with hunting you down like the rats you are."

"Hey," said the fat kid to Shadow. "Reminds me. I told you to tell your boss he was history. Did you ever tell him?"

"I told him," said Shadow. "And you know what he said to me? He said to tell the little snot, if ever I saw him again, to remember that today's future is tomorrow's yesterday." Wednesday had never said any such thing,[707] but Shadow delivered it as Wednesday would have done. These people seemed to like clichés. The black sunglasses reflected the flickering candle-flames back at him, like eyes.

The fat kid said, "This place is such a fucking dump. No power. Out of wireless range. I mean, when you got to be wired, you're already back in the Stone Age." He sucked the

704. According to the Consumer Attorneys of California, "In 1992, 79-year-old Stella Liebeck bought a cup of takeout coffee at a McDonald's drive-thru in Albuquerque and spilled it on her lap. She sued McDonald's and a jury awarded her nearly $3 million in punitive damages for the burns she suffered." One of the jurors stated that the evidence of numerous claims over a long period of time proved that McDonald's had "callous disregard for the safety of the people."

705. In the First Edition, the sentence reads, "He pushed the thought away."

706. This sentence does not appear in the First Edition.

707. The balance of this sentence does not appear in the First Edition.

last of his Coke through the straw, dropped the cup on the table and walked away down the corridor.

Shadow reached over and placed the fat kid's garbage back into the paper sack. "I'm going to see the center of America," he announced. He got up and walked outside, into the night. Mr. Nancy followed him. They strolled together, across the little park, saying nothing until they reached the stone monument. The wind gusted at them, fitfully, first from one direction, then from another. "So," he said. "Now what?"

The half-moon hung pale in the dark sky.

"Now," said Nancy, "you should go back to your room. Lock the door. You try to get some more sleep. At midnight they give us the body. And then we get the hell out of here. The center is not a stable place for anybody."

"If you say so."

Mr. Nancy inhaled on his cigarillo. "This should never have happened," he said. "None of this should have happened. Our kind of people, we are . . ." he waved the cigarillo about, as if using it to hunt for a word, then stabbing forward with it, ". . . *exclusive*. We're not social. Not even me. Not even Bacchus. Not for long. We walk by ourselves or we stay in our own little groups. We do not play well with others. We like to be adored and respected and worshiped—me, I like them to be tellin' tales about me, tales showing my cleverness. It's a fault, I know, but it's the way I am. We like to be big. Now, in these shabby days, we are small. The new gods rise and fall and rise again. But this is not a country that tolerates gods for long. Brahma creates, Vishnu preserves, Shiva destroys, and the ground is clear for Brahma to create once more."

"So what are you saying?" asked Shadow. "The fighting's over, now? The battle's done?"

Mr. Nancy snorted. "Are you out of your mind? They killed Wednesday. They killed him and they bragged about it. They spread the word. They've showed it on every channel to those with eyes to see it. No, Shadow. It's only just begun."

He bent down at the foot of the stone monument,

stubbed out his cigarillo on the earth, and left it there, like an offering.

"You used to make jokes," said Shadow. "You don't any more."

"It's hard to find the jokes these days. Wednesday's dead. Are you comin' inside?"

"Soon."

Nancy walked away, toward the motel. Shadow reached out his hand and touched the monument's stones. He dragged his big fingers across the cold brass plate. Then he turned and walked over to the tiny white church, walked through the open doorway, into the darkness. He sat down in the nearest pew and closed his eyes and lowered his head, and thought about Laura, and about Wednesday, and about being alive.

There was a click from behind him, and a scuff of shoe against earth. Shadow sat up, and turned. Someone stood just outside the open doorway, a dark shape against the stars. Moonlight glinted from something metal.

"You going to shoot me?" asked Shadow.

"Jesus—I wish," said Mr. Town. "It's only for self-defense. So, you're praying? Have they got you thinking that they're gods? They aren't gods."

"I wasn't praying," said Shadow. "Just thinking."

"The way I figure it," said Town, "they're mutations. Evolutionary experiments. A little hypnotic ability, a little hocus-pocus, and they can make people believe anything. Nothing to write home about. That's all. They die like men, after all."

"They always did," said Shadow. He got up, and Town took a step back. Shadow walked out of the little chapel, and Mr. Town kept his distance. "Hey," Shadow said. "Do you know who Louise Brooks was?"

"Friend of yours?"

"Nope. She was a movie star from south of here."

Town paused. "Maybe she changed her name, and became Liz Taylor or Sharon Stone or someone,"[708] he suggested, helpfully.

708. Elizabeth Taylor (1932–2011) was one of the most popular actresses of the glamorous 1950s and regarded as one of the most beautiful women in the world. The actress Sharon Stone, who continues to work regularly, came to stardom as a result of a near-pornographic scene in the 1992 film *Basic Instinct* and is in some ways the opposite of the ever-classy Taylor.

"Maybe." Shadow started to walk back to the motel. Town kept pace with him.

"You should be back in prison," said Mr. Town. "You should be on fucking death row."

"I didn't kill your associates," said Shadow. "But I'll tell you something a guy once told me, back when I was in prison. Something I've never forgotten."

"And that is?"

"There was only one guy in the whole Bible Jesus ever personally promised a place with him in Paradise. Not Peter, not Paul, not any of those guys. He was a convicted thief, being executed.[709] So don't knock the guys on death row. Maybe they know something you don't."

The driver stood by the Humvee. "G'night, gentlemen," he said, as they passed.

"Night," said Mr. Town. And then he said, to Shadow, "I personally don't give a fuck about any of this. What I do, is what Mister World says. It's easier that way."

Shadow walked down the corridor to room nine.

He unlocked the door, went inside. He said, "Sorry. I thought this was my room."

"It is," said Media. "I was waiting for you." He could see her hair in the moonlight, and her pale face. She was sitting on his bed, primly.

"I'll find another room."

"I won't be here for long," she said. "I just thought it might be an appropriate time to make you an *offer*."

"Okay. Make the offer."

"Relax," she said. There was a smile in her voice. "You have *such* a stick up your butt. Look, Wednesday's *dead*. You don't owe anyone anything. Throw in with us. Time to Come Over to the Winning Team."

Shadow said nothing.

"We can make you *famous*, Shadow. We can give you power over what people believe and say and wear and dream. You want to be the next Cary Grant? We can make that *happen*. We can make you the next Beatles."[710]

"I think I preferred it when you were offering to show me Lucy's tits," said Shadow. "If that was you."

709. The thief, who died on the cross beside Jesus, is mentioned in Luke 23. The thief knew that only Jesus could forgive his sins and begged, "Jesus, remember me when you come into your kingdom." Jesus promised him, "Today you will be with me in paradise." (Luke 23:42–43)

710. Note that Media is already behind the times with her proffers: Cary Grant and the Beatles were performers whose time in the spotlight had already ended. Grant made his last film in 1966, twenty years before his death, and the Beatles recorded nothing after 1969.

"Ah," she said.

"I need my room back. Good night."

"And then of course," she said, not moving, as if he had not spoken, "we can turn it all around. We can make it *bad* for you. You could be a bad joke forever, Shadow. Or you could be remembered as a monster. You could be remembered forever, but as a Manson, a Hitler . . . how would you *like* that?"

"I'm sorry, ma'am, but I'm kind of tired," said Shadow. "I'd be grateful if you'd leave now."

"I offered you the world," she said. "When you're dying in a gutter, you re*mem*ber that."

"I'll make a point of it," he said.

After she had gone her perfume lingered. He lay on the bare mattress and thought about Laura, but whatever he thought about—Laura playing Frisbee, Laura eating a root-beer float without a spoon, Laura giggling, showing off the exotic underwear she had bought when she attended a travel agents' convention in Anaheim—always morphed, in his mind, into Laura sucking Robbie's cock as a truck slammed them off the road and into oblivion. And then he heard her words, and they hurt every time.

You're not dead, said Laura in her quiet voice, in his head. *But I'm not sure that you're alive, either.*

There was a knock. Shadow got up and opened the door. It was the fat kid. "Those hamburgers," he said. "They were just icky. Can you believe it? Fifty miles from McDonald's. I didn't think there was anywhere in the *world* that was fifty miles from McDonald's."[711]

"This place is turning into Grand Central Station," said Shadow. "Okay, so I guess you're here to offer me the freedom of the Internet if I come over to your side of the fence. Right?"

The fat kid was shivering. "No. You're already dead meat," he said. "You-you're a fucking illuminated gothic black-letter manuscript. You couldn't be hypertext if you tried. I'm . . . I'm synaptic, while, while you're synoptic . . ." He smelled strange, Shadow realized. There was a guy in the cell across the way, whose name Shadow had never known.

711. It may be hard for contemporary readers to recall that in the pre-smartphone days described here, people had to rely on billboards or personal communication to obtain directions to restaurants and other points of interest.

He had taken off all his clothes in the middle of the day and told everyone that he had been sent to take them away, the truly good ones, like him, in a silver spaceship to a perfect place. That had been the last time Shadow had seen him. The fat kid smelled like that guy.

"Are you here for a reason?"

"Just wanted to talk," said the fat kid. There was a whine in his voice. "It's creepy in my room. That's all. It's *creepy* in there. Fifty miles to a McDonald's, can you believe that? Maybe I could stay in here with you."

"What about your friends from the limo? The ones who hit me? Shouldn't you ask them to stay with you?"

"The children wouldn't operate out here. We're in a dead zone."

Shadow said, "It's a while until midnight, and it's longer to dawn. I think maybe you need rest. I know I do."

The fat kid said nothing for a moment, then he nodded, and walked out of the room.

Shadow closed his door, and locked it with the key. He lay back on the mattress.

After a few moments the noise began. It took him a few moments to figure out what it had to be, then he unlocked his door and walked out into the hallway. It was the fat kid, now back in his own room. It sounded like he was throwing something huge against the walls of the room. From the sounds, Shadow guessed that what he was throwing was himself. "It's just me!" he was sobbing. Or perhaps, "It's just meat." Shadow could not tell.

"Quiet!" came a bellow from Czernobog's room, down the hall.

Shadow walked down to the lobby and out of the motel. He was tired.

The driver still stood beside the Humvee, a dark shape in a peaked cap.

"Couldn't sleep, sir?" he asked.

"No," said Shadow.

"Cigarette, sir?"

"No, thank you."

"You don't mind if I do?"

"Go right ahead."

The driver used a Bic disposable lighter, and it was in the yellow light of the flame that Shadow saw the man's face, actually saw it for the first time, and recognized him, and began to understand.

Shadow knew that thin face. He knew that there would be close-cropped orange hair beneath the black driver's cap, cut close to the scalp[712] like the embers of a fire. He knew that when the man's lips smiled they would crease into a network of rough scars.

"You're looking good, big guy," said the driver.

"Low Key?" Shadow stared at his old cellmate warily.

Prison friendships are good things: they get you through bad places and through dark times. But a prison friendship ends at the prison gates, and a prison friend who reappears in your life is at best a mixed blessing.

"Jesus. Low Key Lyesmith," said Shadow, and then he heard what he was saying[713] and he understood. "Loki," he said. "Loki Lie-Smith."

"You're slow," said Loki, "but you get there in the end." And his lips twisted into a crooked smile and embers danced in the shadows of his eyes.

✳   ✳   ✳

THEY SAT IN Shadow's room in the abandoned motel, sitting on the bed, at opposite ends of the mattress. The sounds from the fat kid's room had pretty much stopped.

"You lied to me," said Shadow.[714]

"It's one of the things I'm good at," said Loki. "But you were lucky we were inside together. You would never have survived your first year without me."

"You couldn't have walked out if you wanted?"

"It's easier just to do the time. You got to understand the god thing. It's not magic. Not exactly. It's about focus.[715] It's about being you, but the *you* that people believe in. It's about being the concentrated, magnified essence of you. It's about becoming thunder, or the power of a running horse, or wisdom. You take all the belief, all the prayers, and they become a kind of certainty, something that lets you become

712. The balance of this sentence does not appear in the First Edition.

713. According to scholars, the name is properly pronounced "Lock-key" but it has been highly conventionalized as "Low-key."

714. This sentence and the next do not appear in the First Edition.

715. This and the previous sentence do not appear in the First Edition.

716. In the First Edition, this sentence reads, "You take all the belief, and you become bigger, cooler, more than human."

717. This sentence does not appear in the First Edition.

718. The balance of this sentence and the next sentence do not appear in the First Edition.

719. This sentence does not appear in the First Edition.

bigger, cooler, more than human.[716] You crystallize." He paused. "And then one day they forget about you, and they don't believe in you, and they don't sacrifice, and they don't care, and the next thing you know you're running a three-card monte game on the corner of Broadway and Forty-third."

"Why were you in my cell?"

"Coincidence. Pure and simple. That was where they put me.[717] You don't believe me? It's true."

"And now you're[718] a driver?"

"I do other stuff too."

"Driving for the opposition."

"If you want to call them that. It depends where you're standing. The way I figure it, I'm driving for the winning team."

"But you and Wednesday, you were from the same, you're both—"

"Norse pantheon. We're both from the Norse pantheon. Is that what you're trying to say?"

"Yeah."

"So?"

Shadow hesitated. "You must have been friends. Once."

"No. We were never friends. I'm not sorry he's dead. He was just holding the rest of us back. With him gone, the rest of them are going to have to face up to the facts: it's change or die, evolve or perish. I'm all for evolution—it's the old change-or-die game.[719] He's dead. War's over."

Shadow looked at him, puzzled. "You aren't that stupid," he said. "You were always so sharp. Wednesday's death isn't going to end anything. It's just pushed all of the ones who were on the fence over the edge."

"Mixing metaphors, Shadow. Bad habit."

"Whatever," said Shadow. "It's still true. Jesus. His death did in an instant what he'd spent the last few months trying to do. It united them. It gave them something to believe in."

"Perhaps." Loki shrugged. "As far as I know, the thinking on this side of the fence was that with the troublemaker out of the way, the trouble would also be gone. It's not any of my business, though. I just drive."

"So tell me," said Shadow, "why does everyone care about me? They act like I'm important. Why does it matter what I do."

"You're an investment," said Loki.[720] "You were important to us because you were important to Wednesday. As for the why of it[721] . . . I don't think any of us know. He did. He's dead. Just another one of life's little mysteries."

"I'm tired of mysteries."

"Yeah? I think they add a kind of zest to the world. Like salt in a stew."

"So you're their driver. You drive for all of them?"

"Whoever needs me," said Loki. "It's a living."

He raised his wristwatch to his face, pressed a button: the dial glowed a gentle blue, which illuminated his face, giving it a haunting, haunted appearance. "Five to midnight. Time," said Loki. "Time to light the candles.[722] Say a few words about the dearly departed. Do the formalities. You coming?"

Shadow took a deep breath. "I'm coming," he said.

They walked down the dark motel corridor.[723] "I bought some candles for this, but there were plenty of old ones around too," said Loki. "Old stumps and stubs and candle-ends in the rooms, and in a box in a closet. I don't think I missed any. And I got a box of matches. You start lighting candles with a lighter, the end gets too hot."

They reached room five.[724]

"You want to come in?" asked Loki.

Shadow didn't want to enter that room. "Okay," he said. They went in.

Loki took a box of matches from his pocket, and thumbnailed a match into flame. The momentary flare hurt Shadow's eyes. A candlewick flickered and caught. And another. Loki lit a new match, and continued to light candles: they were on the windowsills and on the headboard of the bed and on the sink in the corner of the room. They showed him the room by candlelight.[725]

The bed had been hauled from its position against the wall into the middle of the motel room, leaving a few feet of space between the bed and the wall on each side. There

720. This sentence does not appear in the First Edition.

721. The balance of this sentence and the next two sentences do not appear in the First Edition.

722. This sentence and the next two do not appear in the First Edition.

723. The balance of this paragraph does not appear in the First Edition.

724. The next two sentences do not appear in the First Edition.

725. This sentence does not appear in the First Edition.

465

726. The balance of this sentence does not appear in the First Edition.

727. This phrase does not appear in the First Edition.

were sheets draped over the bed, old motel sheets, moth-holed and stained,[726] which Loki must have found in a closet somewhere. On top of the sheets lay Wednesday, perfectly still.

He was fully dressed, in the pale suit he had been wearing when he was shot. The right side of his face was untouched, perfect, unmarred by blood. The left side of his face was a ragged mess, and the left shoulder and front of the suit was spattered with dark spots, a pointillist mess.[727] His hands were at his sides. The expression on that wreck of a face was far from peaceful: it looked hurt—a soul-hurt, a real down deep hurt, filled with hatred and anger and raw craziness. And, on some level, it looked satisfied.

Shadow imagined Mr. Jacquel's practiced hands smoothing that hatred and pain away, rebuilding a face for Wednesday with mortician's wax and make-up, giving him a final peace and dignity that even death had denied him.

Still, the body seemed no smaller in death. It had not shrunk. And it still smelled faintly of Jack Daniel's.

The wind from the plains was rising: he could hear it howling around the old motel at the exact imaginary center of America. The candles on the windowsill guttered and flickered.

He could hear footsteps in the hallway. Someone knocked on a door, called, "Hurry up please, it's time," and they began to shuffle in, heads lowered.

Town came in first, followed by Media and Mr. Nancy and Czernobog. Last of all came the fat kid: he had fresh red bruises on his face, and his lips were moving all the time, as if he were reciting some words to himself, but he was making no sound. Shadow found himself feeling sorry for him.

Informally, without a word being spoken, they ranged themselves about the body, each an arm's length away from the next. The atmosphere in the room was religious—deeply religious, in a way that Shadow had never previously experienced. There was no sound but the howling of the wind and the crackling of the candles.

"We are come together, here in this godless place," said

Loki, "to pass on the body of this individual to those who will dispose of it properly according to the rites. If anyone would like to say something, say it now."

"Not me," said Town. "I never properly met the guy. And this whole thing makes me feel uncomfortable."

Czernobog said, "These actions will have consequences. You know that? This can only be the start of it all."

The fat kid started to giggle, a high-pitched, girlish noise. He said, "Okay. Okay I've got it." And then, all on one note, he recited:

> "Turning and turning in the widening gyre
> The falcon cannot hear the falconer;
> Things fall apart; the center cannot hold . . ."[728]

and then he broke off, his brow creasing. He said, "Shit. I used to know the whole thing," and he rubbed his temples and made a face and was quiet.

And then they were all looking at Shadow. The wind was screaming now. He didn't know what to say. He said, "This whole thing is pitiful. Half of you killed him or had a hand in his death. Now you're giving us his body. Great. He was an irascible old fuck but I drank his mead and I'm still working for him. That's all."

Media said, "In a world where people die every day, I think the *important* thing to remember is that for each moment of sorrow we get when people *leave* this world there's a corresponding moment of *joy* when a new baby comes into this world. That first wail is—well, it's *magic*, isn't it? Perhaps it's a *hard* thing to say, but joy and sorrow are like milk and cookies. *That's* how well they go together. I think we should all take a moment to meditate on that."

And Mr. Nancy cleared his throat and said, "So. I got to say it, because nobody else here will. We are at the center of this place: a land that has no time for gods, and here at the center it has less time for us than anywhere. It is a no-man's land, a place of truce, and we observe our truces, here. We have no choice. So. You give us the body of our friend. We accept it. You will pay for this, murder for murder, blood for blood."

728. The poem is "The Second Coming," by William Butler Yeats, written in 1919 on the eve of the Irish War of Independence.

> Turning and turning in the widening
> gyre
> The falcon cannot hear the falconer;
> Things fall apart; the centre cannot hold;
> Mere anarchy is loosed upon the world,
> The blood-dimmed tide is loosed, and
> everywhere
> The ceremony of innocence is drowned;
> The best lack all conviction, while the
> worst
> Are full of passionate intensity.
>
> Surely some revelation is at hand;
> Surely the Second Coming is at hand.
> The Second Coming! Hardly are those
> words out
> When a vast image out of Spiritus
> Mundi
> Troubles my sight: somewhere in sands
> of the desert
> A shape with lion body and the head of
> a man,
> A gaze blank and pitiless as the sun,
> Is moving its slow thighs, while all
> about it
> Reel shadows of the indignant desert
> birds.
> The darkness drops again; but now I
> know
> That twenty centuries of stony sleep
> Were vexed to nightmare by a rocking
> cradle,
> And what rough beast, its hour come
> round at last,
> Slouches towards Bethlehem to be born?

729. As we will see, all of Czernobog's curses come to pass.

730. This sentence does not appear in the First Edition.

Town said, "Whatever. You could save yourselves a lot of time and effort by going back to your homes and shooting yourselves in the heads. Cut out the middleman."

"Fuck you," said Czernobog. "Fuck you and fuck your mother and fuck the fucking horse you fucking rode in on. You will not even die in battle. No warrior will taste your blood. No one alive will take your life. You will die a soft, poor death. You will die with a kiss on your lips and a lie in your heart." [729]

"Leave it, old man," said Town.

"The blood-dimmed tide is loose," said the fat kid. "I think that comes next."

The wind howled.

"Okay," said Loki. "He's yours. We're done. Take the old bastard away."

He made a gesture with his fingers, and Town, Media and the fat kid left the room. He smiled at Shadow. "Call no man happy, huh, kid?" he said. And then he, too, walked away.

"What happens now?" asked Shadow.

"Now we wrap him up," said Anansi. "And we take him away from here."

They wrapped the body in the motel sheets, wrapped it well in its impromptu shroud, so there was no body to be seen, and they could carry it. The two old men walked to each end of the body, but Shadow said, "Let me see something," and he bent his knees and slipped his arms around the white-sheeted figure, pushed him up and over his shoulder. He straightened his knees, until he was standing, more or less easily. "Okay," he said. "I've got him. Let's put him into the back of the car."

Czernobog looked as if he were about to argue, but he closed his mouth. He spat on his forefinger and thumb and began to snuff the candles between his fingertips. Shadow could hear them fizz as he walked from the darkening room.

Wednesday was heavy, but Shadow could cope, if he walked steadily. He had no choice. Wednesday's words were in his head with every step he took along the corridor, and he could taste the sour-sweetness of mead in the back of his throat. *You work for me.* [730] *You protect me. You help me.*[731] *You transport me from place to place. You investigate, from time to time—go places and ask questions for me.*[732] *You run errands. In an emergency, but only in an emergency, you hurt people who need to be hurt. In the unlikely event of my death, you will hold my vigil . . .*

A deal was a deal, and this one was in his blood and in his bones.[733]

Mr. Nancy opened the motel lobby door for him, then hurried over and opened the back of the bus. The other four were already standing by their Humvee, watching them as if they could not wait to be off. Loki had put his driver's cap back on. The cold wind whipped at the sheets, tugged at Shadow as he walked.

He placed Wednesday down as gently as he could in the back of the bus.

Someone tapped him on the shoulder. He turned. Town stood there with his hand out. He was holding something.

"Here," said Mr. Town, "Mister World wanted you to have this." It was a glass eye. There was a hairline crack down the middle of it, and a tiny chip gone from the front. "We found it in the Masonic hall, when we were cleaning up. Keep it for luck. God knows you'll need it."

Shadow closed his hand around the eye. He wished he could come back with something smart and sharp and clever, but Town was already back at the Humvee, and climbing up into the car; and Shadow still couldn't think of anything clever to say.

*   *   *

CZERNOBOG WAS THE last person out of the motel. As he locked the building he watched the Humvee pull out of the park and head off down the blacktop. He put the key to the motel beneath a rock by the lobby door, and he shook his head. "I should have eaten his heart," he said to Shadow, conversationally. "Not just cursed his death. He needs to be taught respect." He climbed into the back of the bus.[734]

"You ride shotgun," said Mr. Nancy to Shadow. "I'll drive a while."

He drove east.

731. This sentence does not appear in the First Edition.

732. This sentence does not appear in the First Edition.

733. This sentence does not appear in the First Edition.

734. This paragraph and the next do not appear in the First Edition.

✦   ✦   ✦

735. A town of 1,166 people in 2010, on the upper edge of the state of Missouri, Princeton was the birthplace of "Calamity Jane," whose real name was Martha Jane Cannary (or Canary) Burke (1852–1903), a frontierswoman who appeared in "Buffalo" Bill Cody's Wild West show. Calamity Jane wrote a pamphlet about her life that was distributed at the show, and she became a popular figure in literature and drama, though it is very difficult to find much about her that is verifiable.

736. This sentence does not appear in the First Edition.

737. This sentence does not appear in the First Edition.

DAWN FOUND THEM in Princeton, Missouri.[735] Shadow had not slept yet.

Nancy said, "Anywhere you want us to drop you? If I were you, I'd rustle up some ID and head for Canada. Or Mexico."

"I'm sticking with you guys," said Shadow. "It's what Wednesday would have wanted."

"You aren't working for him any more. He's dead. Once we drop his body off, you are free to go."

"And do what?"

"Keep out of the way, while the war is on. Like I say, you should leave the country,"[736] said Nancy. He flipped his turn signal, and took a left.

"Hide yourself, for a little time," said Czernobog. "Then, when this is over, you will come back to me, and I will finish the whole thing. With my hammer."[737]

Shadow said, "Where are we taking the body?"

"Virginia. There's a tree," said Nancy.

"A world tree," said Czernobog with gloomy satisfaction. "We had one in my part of the world. But ours grew under the world, not above it."

"We put him at the foot of the tree," said Nancy. "We leave him there. We let you go. We drive south. There's a battle. Blood is shed. Many die. The world changes, a little."

"You don't want me at your battle? I'm pretty big. I'm good in a fight."

Nancy turned his head to Shadow and smiled—the first real smile Shadow had seen on Mr. Nancy's face since he had rescued Shadow from the Lumber County Jail. "Most of this battle will be fought in a place you cannot go, and you cannot touch."

"In the hearts and the minds of the people," said Czernobog. "Like at the big roundabout."

"Huh?"

"The carousel," said Mr. Nancy.

"Oh," said Shadow. "Backstage. I got it. Like the desert with all the bones in it."

Mr. Nancy raised his head. "Backstage. Yes. Every time I figure you don't have enough sense to bring guts to a bear, you surprise me. That's right. Backstage.[738] That's where the real battle will happen. Everything else will just be flash and thunder."

"Tell me about the vigil," said Shadow.

"Someone has to stay with the body. It's a tradition. One of our people will do it."[739]

"He wanted me to do it."

"No," said Czernobog. "It will kill you. Bad, bad, bad idea."

"Yeah? It'll kill me? To stay with his body?"

"It's what happens when the all-father dies," said Mr. Nancy. "It wouldn't be true for me.[740] When I die, I just want them to plant me somewhere warm. And then when pretty women walk over my grave I would grab their ankles, like in that movie."

"I never saw that movie," said Czernobog.

"Of course you did. It's right at the end. It's the high school movie. All the children going to the prom."

Czernobog shook his head.

Shadow said, "The film's called *Carrie*,[741] Mister Czernobog. Okay, one of you tell me about the vigil."

Nancy said, "You tell him. I'm drivin'."

"I never heard of no film called *Carrie*. You tell him."

Nancy said, "The person on the vigil—gets tied to the tree. Just like Wednesday was. And then they hang there for nine days and nine nights. No food, no water. All alone. At the end they cut the person down, and if they lived . . . well, it could happen. And Wednesday will have had his vigil."

Czernobog said, "Maybe Alviss will send us one of his people. A dwarf could survive it."

"I'll do it," said Shadow.

"No," said Mr. Nancy.

"Yes," said Shadow.

The two old men were silent. Then Nancy said, "Why?"

"Because it's the kind of thing a living person would do," said Shadow.

"You are crazy," said Czernobog.

738. The discussion of "backstage" is omitted from this paragraph.

739. In the First Edition, this sentence reads, "We'll find somebody."

740. In place of these two sentences, the First Edition reads, "It's not what I'd want at my funeral."

741. A 1976 horror film starring Sissy Spacek, based on the 1974 Stephen King novel of the same name. *Carrie* is a high-school student who is bullied by her fellow students, none of whom know that she has telekinetic powers. Carrie is humiliated at the prom but destroys the gymnasium where the prom is held, killing the bullies as well as many bystanders. The scene mentioned by Mr. Nancy takes place as a kind of coda after Carrie and an attacker have been immolated by a fire at Carrie's house that she has ignited with her mind. As her friend Sue places a wreath on the remains of the house, Carrie reaches up from under the ground to grab Sue's ankle. However, this is a dream from which Sue awakens screaming.

742. The balance of this sentence does not appear in the First Edition.

"Maybe. But I'm going to hold Wednesday's vigil."

When they stopped for gas Czernobog announced he felt sick, and wanted to ride in the front. Shadow didn't mind moving to the back of the bus. He could stretch out more, and sleep.

They drove on in silence. Shadow felt that he'd done something very big and very strange,**742** and he wasn't certain exactly what it was.

"Hey. Czernobog," said Mr. Nancy, after a while. "You check out the technical boy back at the motel? He was not happy. He's been screwin' with something that screwed him right back. That's the biggest trouble with the new kids—they figure they know everythin', and you can't teach them nothin' but the hard way."

"Good," said Czernobog.

Shadow was stretched out full length on the seat in the back. He felt like two people, or more than two. There was part of him that felt gently exhilarated: he had *done* something. He had moved. It wouldn't have mattered if he hadn't wanted to live, but he did want to live, and that made all the difference. He hoped he would live through this, but he was willing to die, if that was what it took to be alive. And, for a moment he thought that the whole thing was funny, just the funniest thing in the world; and he wondered if Laura would appreciate the joke.

There was another part of him—maybe it was Mike Ainsel, he thought, vanished off into nothing at the press of a button in the Lakeside Police Department—who was still trying to figure it all out, trying to see the big picture.

"Hidden Indians," he said out loud.

"What?" came Czernobog's irritated croak from the front seat.

"The pictures you'd get to color in as kids. 'Can you see the hidden Indians in this picture? There are ten Indians in this picture, can you find them all?' And at first glance you could only see the waterfall and the rocks and the trees, then you see that if you just tip the picture on its side that shadow is an Indian . . ." He yawned.

"Sleep," suggested Czernobog.

"But the big picture," said Shadow. Then he slept, and dreamed of hidden Indians.

✧   ✧   ✧

THE TREE WAS in Virginia. It was a long way away from anywhere, on the back of an old farm. To get to the farm they had to drive for almost an hour south from Blacksburg,[743] to drive roads with names like Pennywinkle Branch and Rooster Spur. They got turned around twice and Mr. Nancy and Czernobog both lost their tempers with Shadow and with each other.

They stopped to get directions at a tiny general store, set at the bottom of the hill in the place where the road forked. An old man came out of the back of the store and stared at them: he wore OshKosh B'gosh denim overalls and nothing else, not even shoes. Czernobog bought a pickled hog's foot from the huge jar of hogs' feet on the counter, and went outside to eat it on the deck, while Nancy and the man in the overalls took turns drawing each other maps on the back of napkins, marking off turnings and local landmarks.

They set off once more, with Mr. Nancy driving, and they were there in ten minutes. A sign on the gate said ASH.

Shadow got out of the bus, and opened the gate. The bus drove through, jolting through the meadowland. Shadow closed the gate. He walked a little behind the bus, stretching his legs, jogging when the bus got too far in front of him. Enjoying the sensation of moving his body.

He had lost all sense of time on the drive from Kansas. Had they been driving for two days? Three days? He did not know.

The body in the back of the bus did not seem to be rotting. He could smell it—a faint odor of Jack Daniel's, overlaid with something that might have been sour honey. But the smell was not unpleasant. From time to time he would take out the glass eye from his pocket and look at it: it was shattered deep inside, fractured from what he imagined was the impact of a bullet, but apart from a chip to one side of the iris the surface was unmarred. Shadow would run it through his hands, palming it, rolling it, pushing it

743. A town of about 42,000 people in the Shenandoah Valley of Virginia. Founded in 1798 by Samuel Black, the town thrived, and it is currently the home of Virginia Tech and various high-technology employers. Blacksburg was also the birthplace of Henry Lee Lucas, a serial killer who confessed to over 3,000 killings between 1960 and 1983. Lucas was convicted of 11 homicides, including that of his mother, but researchers are very dubious about how many additional killings he actually committed.

744. The World Tree, Yggdrasil, is said to overshadow the whole world, its roots and branches binding heaven and hell. There are many creatures associated with the tree. Vithofnir, a golden cock, sits on its peak; an eagle sits on the highest branch, with the falcon Vedfolnir atop its head. The dragon/serpent Nidhogg or Nidhoggr gnaws on its roots, and the squirrel Ratatosk runs between the eagle and the serpent, sowing discord. Four stags, Dain, Dvalin, Duneyr, and Durathor, feed on twigs; dew drops from their antlers to the world below. Odin's goat Hedrun or Heidrun eats the branches and supplies mead from her teats to the gods (and, according to Gaiman's *Norse Mythology*, to the dead in Valhalla). Odin's spear Gungnir was made from a branch of the tree. Ratatosk is part of a funny story told by Loki about Thor in *Sandman*.

745. The balance of this sentence does not appear in the First Edition.

746. This parenthetical phrase does not appear in the First Edition.

747. These are of course the Norns, mentioned earlier (see note 277, above).

along with his fingers. It was a ghastly souvenir, but oddly comforting: and he suspected that it would have amused Wednesday to know that his eye had wound up in Shadow's pocket.

The farmhouse was dark and shut up. The meadows were overgrown and seemed abandoned. The building's roof was crumbling at the back; it was covered in black plastic sheeting. They jolted over a ridge and Shadow saw the tree.[744]

It was silver-gray and it was higher than the farmhouse. It was the most beautiful tree Shadow had ever seen: spectral and yet utterly real and almost perfectly symmetrical. It also looked instantly familiar: he wondered if he had dreamed it, then realized that no, he had seen it before, or a representation of it, many times. It was Wednesday's silver tiepin.

The VW bus jolted and bumped across the meadow, and came to a stop about twenty feet from the trunk of the tree.

There were three women standing by the tree. At first glance Shadow thought that they were the Zorya, but[745] he realized in moments that he was mistaken. They were three women he did not know. They looked tired and bored, as if they had been standing there for a long time. Each of them held a wooden ladder. The biggest one of them also carried a brown sack. They looked like a set of Russian dolls: a tall one—she was Shadow's height, or even taller—a middle-sized one, and a woman so short and hunched that at first glance Shadow wrongly supposed her to be a child. Still, they looked so much alike—something in the forehead, or the eyes, or the set of the chin[746]—that Shadow was certain that the women must be sisters.[747]

The smallest of the women dropped to a curtsy when the bus drew up. The other two just stared. They were sharing a cigarette, and they smoked it down to the filter before one of them stubbed it out against a root.

Czernobog opened the back of the bus and the biggest of the women pushed past him, and, easily as if it were a sack of flour, she lifted Wednesday's body out of the back and carried it to the tree. She laid it in front of the tree, put it down about ten feet from the trunk. She and her sisters unwrapped Wednesday's body. He looked worse by daylight than he had by candlelight in the motel room, and after one quick glance Shadow looked away. The women arranged his clothes, tidied his suit, then placed him at the corner of the sheet, and wound it around him once more.

Then the women came over to Shadow.

—*You are the one?* the biggest of them asked.

—*The one who will mourn the all-father?* asked the middle-sized one.

—*You have chosen to take the vigil?* asked the smallest.

Shadow nodded. Afterward, he was unable to remember whether he had actually heard their voices. Perhaps he had simply understood what they had meant from their looks and their eyes.

Mr. Nancy, who had gone back to the house to use the bathroom, came walking back to the tree. He was smoking a cigarillo. He looked thoughtful.

"Shadow," he called. "You really don't have to do this. We can find somebody more suited. You ain't ready for this." [748]

"I'm doing it," said Shadow, simply.

"You don't have to," said Mr. Nancy. "You don't know what you're lettin' yourself in for." [749]

"It doesn't matter," said Shadow.

"And if you die?" asked Mr. Nancy. "If it kills you?"

"Then," said Shadow, "it kills me."

Mr. Nancy flicked his cigarillo into the meadow, angrily. "I said you had shit for brains, and you still have shit for brains. Can't see when somebody's tryin' to give you an out?"

"I'm sorry," said Shadow. He didn't say anything else. Nancy walked back to the bus.

Czernobog walked over to Shadow. He did not look pleased. "You must come through this alive," he said. "Come through this safely for me." And then he tapped his knuckle gently against Shadow's forehead and said, *"Bam!"* He squeezed Shadow's shoulder, patted his arm, and walked back to the bus.

The biggest woman, whose name seemed to be Urtha or Urder—Shadow could not repeat it back to her to her satisfaction—told him, in pantomime, to take off his clothes.

"All of them?"

"The Ash Yggdrasil"
By Friedrich Wilhelm Heine, from Asgard and the Gods *by Wilhelm Wagner, 1886*

748. This sentence does not appear in the First Edition.

749. This paragraph and the next do not appear in the First Edition.

The big woman shrugged. Shadow stripped to his briefs and T-shirt. The women propped the ladders against the tree. One of the ladders—it was painted by hand, with little flowers and leaves twining up the struts—they pointed out to him.

He climbed the nine steps. Then, at their urging, he stepped onto a low branch.

The middle woman tipped out the contents of the sack onto the meadow-grass. It was filled with a tangle of thin ropes, brown with age and dirt, and the woman began to sort them out into lengths, and to lay them carefully on the ground beside Wednesday's body.

They climbed their own ladders now, and they began to knot the ropes, intricate and elegant knots, and they wrapped the ropes first about the tree, and then about Shadow. Unembarrassed, like midwives or nurses or those who lay out corpses, they removed his T-shirt and briefs, then they bound him, never tightly, but firmly and finally. He was amazed at how comfortably the ropes and the knots bore his weight. The ropes went under his arms, between his legs, around his waist, his ankles, his chest, binding him to the tree.

The final rope was tied, loosely, about his neck. It was initially uncomfortable, but his weight was well distributed and none of the ropes cut his flesh.

His feet were five feet above the ground. The tree was leafless and huge, its branches black against the gray sky, its bark a smooth silvery gray.

They took the ladders away. There was a moment of panic as he dropped a few inches, as all his weight was taken by the ropes. He made no sound.

He was entirely naked by that point.[750]

The women placed the body, wrapped in its motel-sheet shroud, at the foot of the tree, and they left him there.

They left him there alone.

750. This sentence does not appear in the First Edition.

CHAPTER FIFTEEN

Hang me, O hang me, and I'll be dead and gone,
Hang me, O hang me, and I'll be dead and gone,
I wouldn't mind the hangin', it's bein' gone so long,
It's lyin' in the grave so long.

—OLD SONG **751**

HE FIRST DAY that Shadow hung from the tree he experienced only discomfort, that edged slowly into pain and fear and, occasionally, an emotion that was somewhere between boredom and apathy: a gray acceptance, a waiting.

He hung.

The wind was still.

After several hours fleeting bursts of color started to explode across his vision in blossoms of crimson and gold, throbbing and pulsing with a life of their own.

The pain in his arms and legs became, by degrees, intolerable. If he relaxed them, let his body go slack and dangle, if he flopped forward, then the rope around his neck would take up the slack and the world would shimmer and swim. So he pushed himself back against the trunk of the tree. He could feel his heart laboring in his chest, a pounding arrhythmic tattoo as it pumped the blood through his body . . .

Emeralds and sapphires and rubies crystallized and

751. The song is usually described as "traditional," meaning no composer can be identified. Here is one set of the lyrics, from Dave Von Ronk:

> *Hang me oh hang me and I'll be dead*
> *and gone.*
> *Hang me oh hang me, and I'll be dead*
> *and gone.*
> *I wouldn't mind the hangin', just laying*
> *in this grave so long.*
> *Poor boy I've been all around the*
> *world.*
>
> *Been all round cape Jordan, and parts*
> *of Arkansas,*
> *been around cape Jordan and parts of*
> *Arkansas.*
> *I got so god damn hungry, I could hide*
> *behind a straw.*
> *Poor boy I've been all around the world.*
>
> *So I went up on the mountain, there I*
> *made my stand.*
> *Went up on the mountain, there I made*
> *my stand.*
> *Rifle on my shoulder, a dagger swinging*
> *in my hand.*
> *Poor boy I've been all around the world.*
>
> *Hang me oh hang me and I'll be dead*
> *and gone.*

*Hang me oh hang me, and I'll be dead
and gone.*
*I wouldn't mind the hangin', just laying
in this grave so long.*
Poor boy I've been all around the world.

*So put the rope around my neck, and
hung me up so high.*
*He put the rope around my neck and
hung me up so high.*
*What's worse I heard him saying was, it
won't be long before you die.*

*Oh hang me oh hang me and I'll be
dead and gone.*
*Hang me oh hang me, and I'll be dead
and gone.*
*I wouldn't mind the hangin', just laying
in this grave so long.*
Poor boy I've been all around the world.

The Library of Congress states that the first known recording of the song, "I've Been All Around This World" (AFS 1531), is by Justis Begley. Alan and Elizabeth Lomax recorded Begley singing the song at Hazard, Kentucky, in October 1937. *Outlaw Ballads, Legends & Lore,* by Wayne Erbsen (Asheville, NC: Native Ground Music, 2008) claims that the song was inspired by a man hanged in Fort Smith, Arkansas. Note that the lyrics that begin the second stanza are similar to the Kingston Trio's 1958 hit "Tom Dooley."

752. This sentence does not appear in the First Edition.

burst in front of his eyes. His breath came in shallow gulps. The bark of the tree was rough against his back. The chill of the afternoon on his naked skin made him shiver, made his flesh prickle and goose.

It's easy, said someone in the back of his head. *There's a trick to it. Either you do it, or you die.*

It was a wise thing to have thought, he decided.[752] He was pleased with it, and repeated it over and over in the back of his head, part mantra, part nursery rhyme, rattling along to the drumbeat of his heart.

It's easy, there's a trick to it, you do it or you die.
It's easy, there's a trick to it, you do it or you die.
It's easy, there's a trick to it, you do it or you die.
It's easy, there's a trick to it, you do it or you die.

Time passed. The chanting continued. He could hear it. Someone was repeating the words, only stopping when Shadow's mouth began to dry out, when his tongue turned dry and skin-like in his mouth. He pushed himself up and away from the tree with his feet, trying to support his weight in a way that would still allow him to fill his lungs.

He breathed until he could hold himself up no more, and then he fell back into the bonds, and hung from the tree.

When the chattering started—an angry, laughing chattering noise—he closed his mouth, concerned that it was he himself making it; but the noise continued. *It's the world laughing at me, then,* thought Shadow. His head lolled to one side. Something ran down the tree-trunk beside him, stopping beside his head. It chittered loudly in his ear, one word, which sounded a lot like "ratatosk." Shadow tried to repeat it, but his tongue stuck to the roof of his mouth. He turned, slowly, and stared into the gray-brown face and pointed ears of a squirrel.

In close-up, he learned, a squirrel looks a lot less cute than it does from a distance. The creature was rat-like, and dangerous, not sweet or charming. And its teeth looked sharp. He hoped that it would not perceive him as a threat, or as a food source. He did not think that squirrels were carnivorous . . . but then, so many things he had not thought had turned out to be so . . .

He slept.

The pain woke him several times in the next few hours. It pulled him from a dark dream in which dead children rose and came to him, their eyes peeling, swollen pearls, and they reproached him for failing them[753] and it pulled him from another dream, in which he was staring up at a mammoth, hairy and dark, as it lumbered toward him from the mist, but—*awake for a moment, a spider edging across his face, and he shook his head, dislodging or frightening it*—now the mammoth was an elephant-headed man, pot-bellied, one tusk broken, and he was riding toward Shadow on the back of a huge mouse. The elephant-headed man curled his trunk towards Shadow and said, "If you had invoked me before you began this journey, perhaps some of your troubles might have been avoided." Then the elephant took the mouse, which had, by some means that Shadow could not perceive, become tiny while not changing in size at all, and passed it from hand to hand to hand, fingers curling about it as the little brown creature scampered from palm to palm, and Shadow was not at all surprised when the elephant-headed god[754] finally opened all four of his hands to reveal them perfectly empty. He shrugged arm after arm after arm in a peculiar fluid motion, and looked at Shadow, his face unreadable.

"It's in the trunk," Shadow told the elephant man, who had seen the flickering tail vanish.

The elephant man nodded his huge head, and said, "Yes. In the trunk. You will forget many things. You will give many things away. You will lose many things. But do not lose this." And then the rains began, and Shadow was awake once more. He tumbled, shivering and wet, from deep sleep to wakefulness in moments. The shivering intensified, until it scared Shadow: he was shivering more violently than he had ever imagined possible, a series of convulsive shudders which built upon each other. He willed himself to stop shaking, but still he shivered, his teeth banging together, his limbs twitching and jerking beyond his control. There

753. The First Edition omits the portion of the sentence up to "a spider."

754. Ganesh or Ganesha is the Hindu god of wisdom, eloquence, science, and skills, the first scribe. Ganesh was born with human form but Shiva cut off or burnt off his head; to appease his mother (or because Brahma took pity), his head was replaced with the nearest head at hand, that of an elephant. Ganesh either lost a tusk in a fight with Parasuraman, an avatar of Vishnu, or broke it off to use it as a writing implement to record the *Mahabharata*. He is usually depicted with four arms and a fat belly and travels on a mouse or a shrew.

Ganesha (artist unknown, 1730)

was real pain there, too, a deep, knife-like pain that covered his body with tiny, invisible wounds, intimate and unbearable.

✤　✤　✤

HE OPENED HIS mouth to catch the rain as it fell, moistening his cracked lips and his dry tongue, wetting the ropes that bound him to the trunk of the tree. There was a flash of lightning so bright it felt like a blow to his eyes, transforming the world into an intense panorama of image and after-image. Then the thunder, a crack and a boom and a rumble, and, as the thunder echoed, the rain redoubled. In the rain and the night the shivering abated; the knife-blades were put away. Shadow no longer felt the cold, or rather, he felt only the cold, but the cold had now become part of himself, it belonged to him and he belonged to it.

Shadow hung from the tree while the lightning flickered and forked across the sky, and the thunder subsided into an omnipresent rumbling, with occasional bangs and roars like distant bombs exploding in the night, and the wind tugged at Shadow, trying to pull him from the tree, flaying his skin, cutting to the bone; and at the height of the storm—and Shadow knew in his soul that the real storm had truly begun,[755] the true storm, and that now it was here there was nothing any of them could do but ride it out: none of them, old gods or new, spirits, powers, women or men . . .

A strange joy rose within Shadow then, and he started laughing, as the rain washed his naked skin and the lightning flashed and thunder rumbled so loudly that he could barely hear himself. He laughed and exulted.

He was alive. He had never felt like this. Ever.

If he did die, he thought, if he died right now, here on the tree, it would be worth it to have had this one, perfect, mad moment.

"Hey!" he shouted, at the storm. "Hey! It's me! I'm here!"

He trapped some water between his bare shoulder and the trunk of the tree, and he twisted his head over and drank the trapped rainwater, sucking and slurping at it, and he drank more and he laughed, laughed with joy and

755. The balance of this sentence does not appear in the First Edition.

delight, not madness, until he could laugh no more, until he hung there, too exhausted to move.

At the foot of the tree, on the ground, the rain had made the sheet partly transparent, and had lifted it and pushed it forward so that Shadow could see Wednesday's dead hand, waxy and pale, and the shape of his head, and he thought of the shroud of Turin [756] and he remembered the open girl on Jacquel's slab in Cairo, and then, as if to spite the cold, he observed that he was feeling warm and comfortable, and the bark of the tree felt soft, and he slept once more, and if he dreamed any dreams in the darkness this time he could not remember them.

✲　✲　✲

BY THE FOLLOWING morning the pain was omnipresent. It was no longer local, not confined to the places where the ropes cut into his flesh, or where the bark scraped his skin. Now the pain was everywhere.

And he was hungry, with empty pangs down in the pit of him. His head was pounding. Sometimes he imagined that he had stopped breathing, that his heart had ceased to beat. Then he would hold his breath until he could hear his heart pounding an ocean in his ears and he was forced to suck air like a diver surfacing from the depths.

It seemed to him that the tree reached from hell to heaven, and that he had been hanging there forever. A brown hawk circled the tree, landed on a broken branch near to him, and then took to the wing, flying west.

The storm, which had abated at dawn, began to return as the day passed. Gray, roiling clouds stretched from horizon to horizon; a slow drizzle began to fall. The body at the base of the tree seemed to have become less, in its stained motel winding sheet, crumbling into itself like a sugar cake left in the rain.

Sometimes Shadow burned, sometimes he froze.

When the thunder started once more he imagined that he heard drums beating, kettledrums in the thunder and the thump of his heart, inside his head or outside, it did not matter.

756. The "shroud of Turin" is a linen cloth with a negative image of a man's body imprinted on it. It is on display at the Cathedral of Saint John the Baptist in Turin, Italy. Said to be the winding-cloth of Jesus, used after his crucifixion, and therefore the image to be that of Jesus, it is venerated by believers. The Catholic Church has not taken a position on the authenticity of the shroud, and scientific testing, while suggesting that it dates from the Middle Ages and not the Common Era, has been controversial and indefinite.

757. Dadaism was a short-lived art movement beginning around 1916 that sought to ridicule the meaninglessness of contemporary society. Key figures were Marcel Duchamp, Georges Grosz, and Max Ernst, though Dada influenced surrealism, pop art, and eventually punk rock.

758. Scooby-Doo, a dog, is the central character in an American television and film franchise that began in 1969 and continues today, with stories about a gang of teenagers who solve mysteries.

He perceived the pain in colors: the red of a neon bar-sign, the green of a traffic light on a wet night, the blue of an empty video screen.

The squirrel dropped from the bark of the trunk onto Shadow's shoulder, sharp claws digging into his skin. "Ratatosk!" it chattered. The tip of its nose touched his lips. "Ratatosk." It sprang back onto the tree.

His skin was on fire with pins and needles, a pricking covering his whole body. The sensation was intolerable.

His life was laid out below him, on the motel sheet shroud, literally laid out, like the items at some Dada picnic,[757] a surrealist tableau: he could see his mother's puzzled stare, the American embassy in Norway, Laura's eyes on their wedding day . . .

He chuckled through dry lips.

"What's so funny, puppy?" asked Laura.

"Our wedding day," he said. "You bribed the organist to change from playing the 'Wedding March' to the theme-song from *Scooby-Doo*[758] as you walked toward me down the aisle. Do you remember?"

"Of course I remember, darling. I would have made it too, if it wasn't for those meddling kids."

"I loved you so much," said Shadow.

He could feel her lips on his, and they were warm and wet and living, not cold and dead, so he knew that this was another hallucination. "You aren't here, are you?" he asked.

"No," she said. "But you are calling me, for the last time. And I am coming."

Breathing was harder now. The ropes cutting his flesh were an abstract concept, like free will or eternity.

"Sleep, puppy," she said, although he thought it might have been his own voice he heard, and he slept.

✦   ✦   ✦

THE SUN WAS a pewter coin in a leaden sky. Shadow was, he realized slowly, awake, and he was cold. But the part of him that understood that seemed very far away from the rest of him. Somewhere in the distance he was aware that his mouth and throat were burning, painful and cracked.

Sometimes, in the daylight, he would see stars fall; other times he saw huge birds, the size of delivery trucks, flying toward him. Nothing reached him; nothing touched him.

"Ratatosk. Ratatosk." The chattering had become a scolding.

The squirrel landed, heavily, with sharp claws, on his shoulder and stared into his face. He wondered if he were hallucinating: the animal was holding a walnut-shell, like a doll's-house cup, in its front paws. The animal pressed the shell to Shadow's lips. Shadow felt the water, and, involuntarily, he sucked it into his mouth, drinking from the tiny cup. He ran the water around his cracked lips, his dry tongue. He wet his mouth with it, and swallowed what was left, which was not much.

The squirrel leapt back to the tree, and ran down it, towards the roots, and then, in seconds, or minutes, or hours, Shadow could not tell which (all the clocks in his mind were broken, he thought, and their gears and cogs and springs were simply a jumble down there in the writhing grass), the squirrel returned with its walnut-shell cup, climbing carefully, and Shadow drank the water it brought to him.

The muddy-iron taste of the water filled his mouth, cooled his parched throat. It eased his fatigue and his madness.

By the third walnut-shell, he was no longer thirsty.

He began to struggle, then, pulling at the ropes, flailing his body, trying to get down, to get free, to get away. He moaned.

The knots were good. The ropes were strong, and they held, and soon he exhausted himself once more.

✳   ✳   ✳

IN HIS DELIRIUM, Shadow became the tree. Its roots went deep into the loam of the earth, deep down into time, into the hidden springs. He felt the spring of the woman called Urd, which is to say, *Past*. She was huge, a giantess, an underground mountain of a woman, and the waters she guarded were the waters of time. Other roots went to other places. Some of them were secret. Now, when he

483

was thirsty, he pulled water from his roots, pulled them up into the body of his being.

He had a hundred arms which broke into a hundred thousand fingers, and all of his fingers reached up into the sky. The weight of the sky was heavy on his shoulders.

It was not that the discomfort was lessened, but the pain belonged to the figure hanging from the tree, rather than to the tree itself, and Shadow in his madness was now so much more than the man on the tree. He was the tree, and he was the wind rattling the bare branches of the world tree; he was the gray sky and the tumbling clouds; he was Ratatosk the squirrel running from the deepest roots to the highest branches; he was the mad-eyed hawk who sat on a broken branch at the top of the tree surveying the world; he was the worm in the heart of the tree.

The stars wheeled, and he passed his hundred hands over the glittering stars, palming them, switching them, vanishing them . . .

⁜   ⁜   ⁜

A MOMENT OF clarity, in the pain and the madness: Shadow felt himself surfacing. He knew it would not be for long. The morning sun was dazzling him. He closed his eyes, wishing he could shade them.

There was not long to go. He knew that, too.

When he opened his eyes, Shadow noticed that there was a young man in the tree with him.

His skin was dark brown. His forehead was high and his dark hair was tightly curled. He was sitting on a branch high above Shadow's head. Shadow could see him clearly by craning his head. And the man was mad. Shadow could see that at a glance.

"You're naked," confided the madman, in a cracked voice. "I'm naked, too."

"I see that," croaked Shadow.

The madman looked at him, then he nodded and twisted his head down and around, as if he were trying to remove a crick from his neck. Eventually he said, "Do you know me?"

"No," said Shadow.

"I know you. I watched you in Cairo. I watched you after. My sister likes you."

"You are . . ." The name escaped him. *Eats roadkill. Yes.* "You are Horus."

The madman nodded. "Horus," he said. "I am the falcon of the morning, the hawk of the afternoon. I am the sun. As you are the sun.[759] And I know the true name of Ra. My mother told me."[760]

"That's great," said Shadow, politely.

The madman stared at the ground below them intently, saying nothing. Then he dropped from the tree.

A hawk fell like a stone to the ground, pulled out of its plummet into a swoop, beat its wings heavily and flew back to the tree, a baby rabbit in its talons. It landed on a branch closer to Shadow.

"Are you hungry?" asked the madman.

"No," said Shadow. "I guess I should be, but I'm not."

"I'm hungry," said the madman. He ate the rabbit rapidly, pulling it apart, sucking, tearing, rending. As he finished with them, he dropped the gnawed bones and the fur to the ground. He walked further down the branch until he was only an arm's length from Shadow. Then he peered at Shadow unselfconsciously, inspecting him with care and caution, from his feet to his head. There was rabbit-blood on the man's chin and his chest, and he wiped it off with the back of his hand.

Shadow felt he had to say something. "Hey," he said.

"Hey," said the madman. He stood up on the branch, turned away from Shadow and let a stream of dark urine arc out into the meadow below. It went on for a long time. When he had finished he crouched down again on the branch.

"What do they call you?" asked Horus.

"Shadow," said Shadow.

The madman nodded. "You are the shadow. I am the light," he said. "Everything that is, casts a shadow." Then he said, "They will fight soon. I was watching them as they started to arrive. I was high in the sky, and none of them saw me, although some of them have keen eyes."[761]

And then the madman said, "You are dying. Aren't you?"

Baldur
Johannes Gehrts, 1901

759. Baldur was the Norse god of light and sun.

760. Horus's mother is Isis, the spouse of Osiris. Some would say that the true name of Ra is Horus; both were sun-gods, and worship of Ra eventually displaced worship of Horus. Both were depicted as falcon-headed men.

761. This sentence does not appear in the First Edition.

762. This sentence does not appear in the First Edition.

But Shadow could no longer speak. Everything was very far away.[762] A hawk took wing, and circled slowly upward, riding the updrafts into the morning.

✦   ✦   ✦

MOONLIGHT.

A cough shook Shadow's frame, a racking painful cough that stabbed his chest and his throat. He gagged for breath.

"Hey, puppy," called a voice that he knew.

He looked down.

The moonlight burned whitely through the branches of the tree, bright as day, and there was a woman standing in the moonlight on the ground below him, her face a pale oval. The wind rattled in the branches of the tree.

"Hi, puppy," she said.

He tried to speak, but he coughed instead, deep in his chest, for a long time.

"You know," she said, helpfully, "that doesn't sound good."

He croaked, "Hello, Laura."

She looked up at him with dead eyes, and she smiled.

"How did you find me?" he asked.

She was silent, for a while, in the moonlight. Then she said, "You are the nearest thing I have to life. You are the only thing I have left, the only thing that isn't bleak and flat and gray. I could be blindfolded and dropped into the deepest ocean and I would know where to find you. I could be buried a hundred miles underground and I would know where you are."

He looked down at the woman in the moonlight, and his eyes stung with tears.

"I'll cut you down," she said, after a while. "I spend too much time rescuing you, don't I?"

He coughed again. Then, "No, leave me. I have to do this."

She looked up at him, and shook her head. "You're crazy," she said. "You're dying up there. Or you'll be crippled, if you aren't already."

"Maybe," he said. "But I'm alive."

"Yes," she said, after a moment. "I guess you are."

"You told me," he said. "In the graveyard."

"It seems like such a long time ago, puppy," she said. Then she said, "I feel better, here. It doesn't hurt as much. You know what I mean? But I'm so dry."

The wind let up, and he could smell her now: a stink of rotten meat and sickness and decay, pervasive and unpleasant.

"I lost my job," she said. "It was a night job, but they said people had complained. I told them I was sick, and they said they didn't care. I'm so thirsty."

"The women," he told her. "They have water. The house."

"Puppy . . ." She sounded scared.

"Tell them . . . tell them I said to give you water . . ."

The white face stared up at him. "I should go," she told him. Then she hacked, and made a face, and spat a mass of something white onto the grass. It broke up when it hit the ground and wriggled away.

It was almost impossible to breathe. His chest felt heavy, and his head was swaying.

"Stay," he said, in a breath that was almost a whisper, unsure whether or not she could hear him. "Please don't go." He started to cough. "Stay the night."

"I'll stop a while," she said. And then, like a mother to a child she said, "Nothing's gonna hurt you when I'm here. You know that?"

Shadow coughed once more. He closed his eyes—only for a moment, he thought, but when he opened them again the moon had set and he was alone.

✤   ✤   ✤

A CRASHING AND a pounding in his head, beyond the pain of migraine, beyond all pain. Everything dissolved into tiny butterflies which circled him like a multicolored dust storm and then evaporated into the night.

The white sheet wrapped about the body at the base of the tree flapped noisily in the morning wind.

The pounding eased. Everything slowed. There was nothing left to make him keep breathing. His heart ceased to beat in his chest.

The darkness that he entered this time was deep, and lit by a single star, and it was final.

CHAPTER SIXTEEN

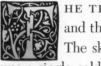

763. This sentence does not appear in the First Edition.

I know it's crooked. But it's the only game in town.
—CANADA BILL JONES [763]

HE TREE WAS gone, and the world was gone, and the morning-gray sky above him was gone. The sky was now the color of midnight. There was a single cold star shining high above him, a blazing, twinkling light, and nothing else. He took a single step and almost tripped.

Shadow looked down. There were steps cut into the rock, going down, steps so huge that he could only imagine that giants had cut them and descended them a long time ago.

He clambered downward, half jumping, half vaulting from step to step. His body ached, but it was the ache of lack of use, not the tortured ache of a body that has hung on a tree until it was dead.

He observed, without surprise, that he was now fully dressed, in jeans and a white T-shirt. He was barefoot. He experienced a profound moment of déjà vu: this was what he had been wearing when he stood in Czernobog's apartment the night when Zorya Polunochnaya had come to him and told him about the constellation called Odin's Wain. She had taken the moon down from the sky for him.

He knew, suddenly, what would happen next. Zorya Polunochnaya would be there.

She was waiting for him at the bottom of the steps. There was no moon in the sky, but she was bathed in moonlight nonetheless: her white hair was moon-pale, and she wore the same lace-and-linen nightdress she had worn that night in Chicago.

She smiled when she saw him, and looked down, as if momentarily embarrassed. "Hello," she said.

"Hi," said Shadow.

"How are you?"

"I don't know," he said. "I think this is maybe another strange dream on the tree. I've been having crazy dreams since I got out of prison."

Her face was silvered by the moonlight (but no moon hung in that plum-black sky, and now, at the foot of the steps, even the single star was lost to view) and she looked both solemn and vulnerable. She said, "All your questions can be answered, if that is what you want. But once you learn your answers, you can never unlearn them. You have to understand that."[764]

"I got it," he said.

Beyond her, the path forked. He would have to decide which path to take, he knew that. But there was one thing he had to do first. He reached into the pocket of his jeans and was relieved when he felt the familiar weight of the coin at the bottom of the pocket. He eased it out, held it between finger and thumb: a 1922 Liberty dollar. "This is yours," he said.

He remembered then that his clothes were really at the foot of the tree. The women had placed his clothes in the canvas sack from which they had taken the ropes, and tied the end of the sack, and the biggest of the women had placed a heavy rock on it to stop it from blowing away. And so he knew that, in reality, the Liberty dollar was in a pocket in that sack, beneath the rock. But still, it was heavy in his hand, at the entrance to the underworld.

She took it from his palm with her slim fingers.

"Thank you. It bought you your liberty twice," she said. "And now it will light your way into dark places."

She closed her hand around the dollar, then she reached

764. This sentence and the next do not appear in the First Edition.

765. The preceding words of this sentence do not appear in the First Edition.

766. The balance of this sentence does not appear in the First Edition.

767. This sentence does not appear in the First Edition.

up and placed it in the air, as high as she could reach. She let go of it. Shadow knew, then, that this was another dream, for[765] instead of falling, the coin floated upward until it was a foot or so above Shadow's head. It was no longer a silver coin, though. Lady Liberty and her crown of spikes were gone. The face he saw on the coin was the indeterminate face of the moon in the summer sky,[766] the face that was only visible until you stared at it, whereupon it would become dark seas and shapes on the moon's cratered surface, the pattern and the face replaced by shadows of pure randomness and chance.

Shadow could not decide whether he was looking at a moon the size of a dollar, a foot above his head; or whether he was looking at a moon the size of the Pacific Ocean, many thousands of miles away. Nor whether there was any difference between the two ideas. Perhaps it was all a matter of perspective. Perhaps it was all a matter of point of view.

He looked at the forking path ahead of him.

"Which path should I take?" he asked. "Which one is safe?"

"Take one, and you cannot take the other," she said. "But neither path is safe. Which way would you walk—the way of hard truths or the way of fine lies?"

Shadow hesitated.[767] "Truths," he said. "I've come too far for more lies."

She looked sad. "There will be a price," she said.

"I'll pay it. What's the price?"

"Your name," she said. "Your real name. You will have to give it to me."

"How?"

"Like this," she said. She reached a perfect hand toward his head. He felt her fingers brush his skin, then he felt them penetrate his skin, his skull, felt them push deep into his head. Something tickled, in his skull and all down his spine. She pulled her hand out of his head. A flame, like a candle-flame but burning with a clear magnesium-white luminance, was flickering on the tip of her forefinger.

"Is that my name?" he asked.

She closed her hand, and the light was gone. "It was," she said. She extended her hand, and pointed to the right-hand path. "That way," she said. "For now."

Nameless, Shadow walked down the right-hand path in the moonlight. When he turned around to thank her, he saw nothing but darkness. It seemed to him that he was deep under the ground, but when he looked up into the darkness above him he still saw the tiny moon.

He turned a corner.

If this was the afterlife, he thought, it was a lot like the House on the Rock: part diorama, part nightmare.

He was looking at himself in prison blues, in the warden's office, as the warden told him that Laura had died in a car crash. He saw the expression on his own face—he looked like a man who had been abandoned by the world. It hurt him to see it, the nakedness and the fear. He hurried on, pushed through the warden's gray office, and found himself looking at the VCR repair store on the outskirts of Eagle Point. Three years ago. Yes.

Inside the store, he knew, he was beating the living crap out of Larry Powers and B. J. West, bruising his knuckles in the process: pretty soon he would walk out of there, carrying a brown supermarket bag filled with twenty-dollar bills. The money they could never prove he had taken: his share of the proceeds, and a little more, for they shouldn't have tried to rip him and Laura off like that. He was only the driver, but he had done his part, done everything that she had asked of him . . .

At the trial, nobody mentioned the bank robbery, although he was certain everybody wanted to. They couldn't prove a thing, as long as nobody was talking. And nobody was. The prosecutor was forced instead to stick to the bodily damage that Shadow had inflicted on Powers and West. He showed photographs of the two men on their arrival in the local hospital. Shadow barely defended himself in court; it was easier that way. Neither Powers nor West seemed able to remember what the fight had been about, but they each admitted that Shadow had been their assailant.

Nobody talked about the money.

Nobody even mentioned Laura, and that was all that Shadow had wanted.

Shadow wondered whether the path of comforting lies would have been a better one to walk. He walked away from that place, and followed the rock path down into what looked like a hospital room, a public hospital in Chicago, and he felt the bile rise in his throat. He stopped. He did not want to look. He did not want to keep walking.

In the hospital bed his mother was dying again, as she'd died when he was sixteen, and, yes, here he was, a large, clumsy sixteen-year-old with acne pocking his cream-and-coffee skin, sitting at her bedside, unable to look at her, reading a thick paperback book. Shadow wondered what the book was, and he walked around the hospital bed to inspect it more closely. He stood between the bed and the chair looking from the one to the other, the big boy hunched into his chair, his nose buried in *Gravity's Rainbow*,[768] trying to escape from his mother's death into London during the blitz, the fictional madness of the book no escape and no excuse.

His mother's eyes were closed in a morphine peace: what she had thought was just another sickle-cell crisis, another bout of pain to be endured, had turned out, they had discovered, too late, to be lymphoma. There was a lemonish-gray tinge to her skin. She was in her early thirties, but she looked much older.

Shadow wanted to shake himself, the awkward boy that he once was, get him to hold her hand, talk to her, do *something* before she slipped away, as he knew that she would. But he could not touch himself, and he continued to read; and so his mother died while he sat in the chair next to her, reading a fat book.

After that he had more or less stopped reading. You could not trust fiction. What good were books, if they couldn't protect you from something like that?

Shadow walked away from the hospital room, down the winding corridor, deep into the bowels of the earth.

He sees his mother first and he cannot believe how young she is, not yet twenty-five he guesses, before her medical discharge and they're in their apartment, another embassy

768. A 1973 novel by Thomas Pynchon, with over 750 pages and an expansive cast of characters. Largely set in Europe during World War II, it principally focuses on the V-2 rockets manufactured by the German military. However, it explores metaphysics, sexuality, human history, and science; broadly funny, mad, scatological in places, and deeply moving, it is regarded by some as one of the greatest American novels. In an early Manuscript, the book was *Dhalgren* by Samuel R. Delany, another really long book.

rental somewhere in Northern Europe, he looks around for something to give him a clue, and he's just a shrimp of a kid now, big pale-gray eyes and straight dark hair. They are arguing. Shadow knows without hearing the words what they're arguing about: it was the only thing they quarreled about, after all.

—*Tell me about my father.*

—*He's dead. Don't ask about him.*

—*But who was he?*

—*Forget him. Dead and gone and you ain't missed nothing.*

—*I want to see a picture of him.*

—*I ain't got a picture,* she'd say, and her voice would get quiet and fierce, and he knew that if he kept asking her questions she would shout, or even hit him, and he knew that he could not stop asking questions, so he turned away and walked on down the tunnel.

The path he followed twisted and wound and curled back on itself, and it put him in mind of snakeskins and intestines and of deep, deep tree roots. There was a pool to his left; he heard the *drip, drip* of water into it somewhere at the back of the tunnel, the falling water barely ruffling the mirrored surface of the pool. He dropped to his knees and drank, using his hand to bring the water to his lips. Then he walked on until he was standing in the floating disco-glitter patterns of a mirror-ball. It was like being in the exact center of the universe with all the stars and planets circling him, and he could not hear anything, not the music, nor the shouted conversations over the music, and now Shadow was staring at a woman who looked just like his mother never looked in all the years he knew her, she's little more than a child, after all . . .

And she is dancing.

Shadow found that he was completely unsurprised when he recognized the man who dances with her. He had not changed that much in thirty-three years.

She is drunk: Shadow could see that at a glance. She is not very drunk, but she is unused to drink, and in a week or so she will take a ship to Norway. They have been drinking

769. In Gaiman's story "Monarch of the Glen," set about two years after the events of *American Gods*, we learn that "the name on Shadow's birth certificate was Balder Moon" and that he was born in Norway. However, Shadow makes clear his identity as ancient spirits call to him to release them: "'Hail sun-bringer! Hail Baldur!'" they shout. But Shadow replies, "'I am not him . . . I am not the one you are waiting for.'" Shadow is not a god, but he is a demi-god, half-human, half-deity. A further adventure, in which his semi-deity status brings him to the attention of certain spirits, is Gaiman's "Black Dog," apparently set shortly before the events of "Monarch of the Glen."

In Norse mythology, Balder (Baldur) was a son born to Odin by Frigg, though Odin is said to have had many wives and many sons, including Thor. According to the *Prose Edda* (Anderson translation, 1901): "Odin's second son is Balder, and of him good things are to be told. He is the best, and all praise him. He is so fair of face and so bright that rays of light issue from him; and there is a plant so white that it is likened unto Balder's brow, and it is the whitest of all plants. From this you can judge of the beauty both of his hair and of his body. He is the wisest, mildest, and most eloquent of all the asas; and such is his nature that none can alter the judgment he has pronounced. He inhabits the place in heaven called Breidablik, and there nothing unclean can enter." *Gylfaginning* (The Tricking of King Gylfi), 22.

Balder was reportedly loved by all but Loki, and Loki plotted his death (see note 838, below) and connived to keep him in the underworld. For a detailed account of Balder's death and Loki's plotting, see "The Death of Balder" in Gaiman's *Norse Mythology*, pp. 229–48.

margaritas, and she has salt on her lips and salt clinging to the back of her hand.

Wednesday is not wearing a suit and tie, but the pin in the shape of a silver tree he wears over the pocket of his shirt glitters and glints when the mirror-ball light catches it. He does not dance badly; they make a fine-looking couple, considering the difference in their ages. There is a lupine grace to his movements.

A slow dance. He pulls her close to him, and his paw-like hand curves around the seat of her skirt possessively, moving her closer to him. His other hand takes her chin, pushes it upward into his face, and the two of them kiss, there on the floor, as the glitter-ball lights circle them into the center of the universe.

Soon after, they leave. She sways against him, and he leads her from the dance hall. Shadow buries his head in his hands, and does not follow them, unable or unwilling to witness his own conception.[769]

The mirror lights were gone, and now the only illumination came from the tiny moon that burned high above his head.

He walked on. At a bend in the path he stopped for a moment, to catch his breath.

He felt a hand run gently up his back, and gentle fingers ruffle the hair on the back of his head.

"Hello, hon," whispered a smoky female voice, over his shoulder.

"Hello," he said, turning to face her.

She had brown hair and brown skin and her eyes were the deep golden-amber of good honey. Her pupils were vertical slits. "Do I know you?" he asked, puzzled.

"Intimately," she said, and she smiled. "I used to sleep on your bed. And my people have been keeping their eyes on you, for me." She turned to the path ahead of him, pointed to the three ways he could go. "Okay," she said. "One way will make you wise. One way will make you whole. And one way will kill you."

"I'm already dead, I think," said Shadow. "I died on the tree."

She made a moue. "There's dead," she said, "and there's dead, and there's dead. It's a relative thing." Then she smiled again. "I could make a joke about that, you know. Something about dead relatives."

"No," said Shadow. "It's okay."

"So," she said. "Which way do you want to go?"

"I don't know," he admitted.

She tipped her head on one side, a perfectly feline gesture. Suddenly,[770] Shadow knew exactly who she was, and where he knew her from. He felt himself beginning to blush. "If you trust me," said Bast, "I can choose for you."

"I trust you," he said, without hesitation.

"Do you want to know what it's going to cost you?"

"I've already lost my name," he told her.

"Names come and names go. Was it worth it?"

"Yes. Maybe. It wasn't easy. As revelations go, it was kind of personal."

"All revelations are personal," she said. "That's why all revelations are suspect."

"I don't understand."

"No," she said, "you don't. I'll take your heart. We'll need it later," and she reached her hand deep inside his chest, and she pulled it out with something ruby and pulsing held between her sharp fingernails. It was the color of pigeon's blood, and it was made of pure light. Rhythmically it expanded and contracted.

She closed her hand, and it was gone.

"Take the middle way," she said.[771]

Shadow hesitated. "Are you really here?" he asked.

She tipped her head on one side, regarded him gravely, said nothing at all.

"What are you?" he asked. "What *are* you people?"

She yawned, showing a perfect, dark-pink tongue. "Think of us as symbols—we're the dream that humanity creates to make sense of the shadows on the cave wall. Now go on, keep moving. Your body is already growing cold. The fools are gathering on the mountain. The clock is ticking."

Shadow nodded, and walked on.

The path was becoming slippery now. There was ice on

770. In the First Edition, the balance of the sentence reads, "remembered the claw marks on his shoulder."

771. The next four paragraphs do not appear in the First Edition.

772. The next two sentences do not appear in the First Edition.

773. This sentence does not appear in the First Edition.

774. This sentence and the next do not appear in the First Edition.

the rock.[772] Shadow stumbled and skidded as he walked down the rock path, toward the place where it divided, scraping his knuckles on a jut of rock at chest height. He edged forward as slowly as he could. The moon above him glittered through the ice-crystals in the air: there was a ring about the moon, a moonbow, diffusing the light. It was beautiful, but it made walking harder. The path was unreliable.

He reached the place where the path divided.

He looked at the first path with a feeling of recognition. It opened into a vast chamber, or a set of chambers, like a dark museum. He knew it already. He had been there once, although for several moments he was unable to remember where or when.[773] He could hear the long echoes of tiny noises. He could hear the noise that the dust makes as it settles.

It was the place that he had dreamed of, that first night that Laura had come to him, in the motel, so long ago; the endless memorial hall to the gods that were forgotten, and the ones whose very existence had been lost.

He took a step backward.

He walked to the path on the far side, and looked ahead. There was a Disneyland quality to the corridor: black Plexiglas walls with lights set in them. The colored lights blinked and flashed in the illusion of order, for no particular reason, like the console lights on a television starship.

He could hear something there as well: a deep vibrating bass drone which Shadow could feel in the pit of his stomach.

He stopped and looked around. Neither way seemed right. Not any longer. He was done with paths. The middle way, the way the cat-woman had told him to walk, that was his way. He moved toward it.

The moon above him was beginning to fade: the edge of it was pinking and going into eclipse. The path was framed by a huge doorway.

There were no deals to make any more, no more bargains.[774] There was nothing to do but enter. So Shadow walked through the doorway, in darkness. The air was warm, and it smelled of wet dust, like a city street after the summer's first rain.

He was not afraid.

Not any more. Fear had died on the tree, as Shadow had died. There was no fear left, no hatred, no pain. Nothing left but essence.

Something big splashed, quietly, in the distance, and the splash echoed into the vastness. He squinted, but could see nothing. It was too dark. And then, from the direction of the splashes, a ghost-light glimmered and the world took form: he was in a cavern, and in front of him, mirror-smooth, was water.

The splashing noises came closer and the light became brighter, and Shadow waited on the shore. Soon enough a low, flat boat came into sight, a flickering white lantern burning at its raised prow, another reflected in the glassy black water several feet below it. The boat was being poled by a tall figure, and the splashing noise Shadow had heard was the sound of the pole being lifted and moved as it pushed the craft across the waters of the underground lake.

"Hello there!" called Shadow. Echoes of his words suddenly surrounded him: he could imagine that a whole chorus of people were welcoming him, and calling to him, and each of them had his voice.

The person poling the boat made no reply.

The boat's pilot was tall, and very thin. He—if it was a he—wore an unadorned white robe, and the pale head that topped it was so utterly inhuman that Shadow was certain that it had to be a mask of some sort: it was a bird's head, small on a long neck, its beak long and high. Shadow was certain he had seen it before, this ghostly, bird-like figure. He grasped at the memory and then, disappointed, realized that he was picturing the clockwork penny-in-the-slot machine in the House on the Rock, and the pale, bird-like, half-glimpsed figure that glided out from behind the crypt for the drunkard's soul.

Water dripped and echoed from the pole and the prow, and the ship's wake rippled the glassy waters. The boat was made of reeds, bound and tied.

The boat came close to the shore. The pilot leaned on its pole. Its head turned slowly, until it was facing Shadow. "Hello," it said, without moving its long beak. The voice was male, and, like everything else in Shadow's afterlife so far, familiar. "Come on board. You'll get your feet wet, I'm afraid, but there's not a thing can be done about that. These are old boats, and if I come in closer I could rip out the bottom."

Shadow took off the shoes he had not been aware he was wearing, and stepped out into the water. It came halfway up his calves, and was, after the initial shock of wetness, surprisingly warm. He reached the boat, and the pilot put down a hand, and pulled him aboard. The reed boat rocked a little, and water splashed over the low sides of it, and then it steadied.

The pilot poled off away from the shore. Shadow stood there and watched, his pants-legs dripping.

"I know you," he said to the creature at the prow.

"You do indeed," said the boatman. The oil lamp which hung at the front of the boat burned more fitfully, and the smoke from the lamp made Shadow cough. "You worked for me. I'm afraid we had to inter Lila Goodchild without you." The voice was fussy and precise.

The smoke stung Shadow's eyes. He wiped the tears away with his hand, and, through the smoke, he thought he saw a tall man, in a suit, with gold-rimmed spectacles. The smoke cleared and the boatman was once more a half-human creature with the head of a river-bird.

"Mister Ibis?"

"Good to see you, Shadow," said the creature, with Mr. Ibis's voice. "Do you know what a *psychopomp* is?"

Shadow thought he knew the word, but it had been a long time. He shook his head.

"It's a fancy term for an escort," said Mr. Ibis. "We all have so many functions, so many ways of existing. In my own vision of myself, I am a scholar who lives quietly, and pens his little tales, and dreams about a past that may or may not ever have existed. And that is true, as far as it goes. But I am also, in one of my capacities, like so many of the people you have chosen to associate with, a psychopomp. I escort the living to the world of the dead."

"I thought this was the world of the dead," said Shadow.

"No. Not per se. It's more of a preliminary."

The boat slipped and slid across the mirror-surface of the underground pool. The bird-head of the creature at the prow stared ahead.[775] And then Mr. Ibis said, without moving its beak, "You people talk about the living and the dead as if they were two mutually exclusive categories. As if you cannot have a river that is also a road, or a song that is also a color."

"You can't," said Shadow. "Can you?" The echoes whispered his words back at him from across the pool.

"What you have to remember," said Mr. Ibis, testily, "is that life and death are different sides of the same coin. Like the heads and tails of a quarter."

"And if I had a double-headed quarter?"

"You don't.[776] They only belong to fools, and gods."

Shadow had a frisson, then, as they crossed the dark water. He imagined he could see the faces of children staring up at him reproachfully from beneath the water's glassy surface: their faces were waterlogged and softened, their blind eyes clouded. There was no wind in that underground cavern to disturb the black surface of the lake.

"So I'm dead," said Shadow. He was getting used to the idea. "Or I'm going to be dead."

"We are on our way to the Hall of the Dead. I requested that I be the one to come for you."

"Why?"

"I'm a psychopomp.[777] I like you. You were a hard worker. Why not?"

"Because . . ." Shadow marshaled his thoughts. "Because I never believed in you. Because I don't know much about Egyptian mythology. Because I didn't expect this. What happened to Saint Peter and the Pearly Gates?"

The long-beaked white head shook from side to side, gravely. "It doesn't matter that you didn't believe in us," said Mr. Ibis. "We believed in you."

The boat touched bottom. Mr. Ibis stepped off the side,

775. This sentence does not appear in the First Edition.

776. The balance of this paragraph does not appear in the First Edition.

777. This sentence and the next do not appear in the First Edition.

into the pool, and told Shadow to do the same. Mr. Ibis took a line from the prow of the boat, and passed Shadow the lantern to carry. It was in the shape of a crescent moon. They walked ashore, and Mr. Ibis tied the boat to a metal ring set in the rock floor. Then he took the lamp from Shadow and walked swiftly forward, holding the lamp high as he walked, throwing vast shadows across the rock floor and the high rock walls.

"Are you scared?" asked Mr. Ibis.

"Not really."

"Well, try to cultivate the emotions of true awe and spiritual terror, as we walk. They are the appropriate feelings for the situation at hand."

Shadow was not scared. He was interested, and apprehensive, but no more. He was not scared of the shifting darkness, nor of being dead, nor even of the dog-headed creature the size of a grain silo who stared at them as they approached. It growled, deep in its throat, and Shadow felt his neck-hairs prickle.

"Shadow," it said. "Now is the time of judgment."

Shadow looked up at the creature. "Mister Jacquel?" he said.

The hands of Anubis came down, huge dark hands, and they picked Shadow up and brought him close.

The jackal head examined him with bright and glittering eyes; examined him as dispassionately as Mr. Jacquel had examined the dead girl on the slab. Shadow knew that all his faults, all his failings, all his weaknesses were being taken out and weighed and measured; that he was, in some way, being dissected, and sliced, and tasted.

We do not always remember the things that do no credit to us. We justify them, cover them in bright lies or with the thick dust of forgetfulness. All of the things that Shadow had done in his life of which he was not proud, all the things he wished he had done otherwise or left undone, came at him then in a swirling storm of guilt and regret and shame, and he had nowhere to hide from them. He was as naked and as open as a corpse on a table, and dark Anubis the jackal god was his prosector and his prosecutor and his persecutor.

"Please," said Shadow. "Please stop."

But the examination did not stop. Every lie he had ever told, every object he had stolen, every hurt he had inflicted on another person, all the little crimes and the tiny murders that make up the day, each of these things and more were extracted and held up to the light by the jackal-headed judge of the dead.

Shadow began to weep, painfully, in the palm of the dark god's hand. He was a tiny child again, as helpless and as powerless as he had ever been.

And then, without warning, it was over. Shadow panted, and sobbed, and snot streamed from his nose; he still felt helpless, but the hands placed him, carefully, almost tenderly, down on the rock floor.

"Who has his heart?" growled Anubis.

"I do," purred a woman's voice. Shadow looked up. Bast was standing there beside the thing that was no longer Mr. Ibis, and she held Shadow's heart in her right hand. It lit her face with a ruby light.

"Give it to me," said Thoth, the ibis-headed god, and he took the heart in his hands, which were not human hands, and he glided forward.

Anubis placed a pair of golden scales in front of him.

"So is this where we find out what I get?" whispered Shadow to Bast. "Heaven? Hell? Purgatory?"

"If the feather balances," she said, "you get to choose your own destination."

"And if not?"

She shrugged, as if the subject made her uncomfortable. Then she said, "Then we feed your heart and your soul to Ammet, the Eater of Souls . . ."

"Maybe," he said. "Maybe I can get some kind of a happy ending."

"Not only are there no happy endings," she told him. "There aren't even any endings."

On one of the pans of the scales, carefully, reverently, Anubis placed a feather.

Anubis put Shadow's heart on the other pan of the scales. Something moved in the shadows under the scale, something it made Shadow uncomfortable to examine too closely.

It was a heavy feather, but Shadow had a heavy heart, and the scales tipped and swung worryingly.

But they balanced, in the end, and the creature in the shadows skulked away, unsatisfied.[778]

778. See the image on p. 197.

"So that's that," said Bast, wistfully. "Just another skull for the pile. It's a pity. I had hoped that you would do some good, in the current troubles. It's like watching a slow-motion car crash and being powerless to prevent it."

"You won't be there?"

She shook her head. "I don't like other people picking my battles for me," she said.

There was silence then, in the vasty hall of death, where it echoed of water and the dark.

Shadow said, "So now I get to choose where I go next?"

"Choose," said Thoth. "Or we can choose for you."

"No," said Shadow. "It's okay. It's my choice."

"Well?" roared Anubis.

"I want to rest now," said Shadow. "That's what I want. I want nothing. No heaven, no hell, no anything. Just let it end."

"You're certain?" asked Thoth.

"Yes," said Shadow.

Mr. Jacquel opened the last door for Shadow, and behind that door there was nothing. Not darkness. Not even oblivion. Only nothing.

Shadow accepted it, completely and without reservation, and he walked through the door into nothing with a strange fierce joy.

CHAPTER SEVENTEEN

Everything is upon a great scale upon this continent. The rivers are immense, the climate violent in heat and cold, the prospects magnificent, the thunder and lightning tremendous. The disorders incident to the country make every constitution tremble. Our own blunders here, our misconduct, our losses, our disgraces, our ruin, are on a great scale.

—LORD CARLISLE, TO GEORGE SELWYN, 1778 [779]

HE MOST IMPORTANT place in the southeastern United States is advertised on hundreds of aging barn-roofs across Georgia and Tennessee and up into Kentucky. On a winding road through a forest a driver will pass a rotting red barn, and see, painted on its roof

SEE ROCK CITY
THE EIGHTH WONDER OF THE WORLD

and on the roof of a tumbledown milking shed nearby, painted in white block letters,

SEE SEVEN STATES FROM ROCK CITY
THE WORLD'S WONDER

The driver is led by this to believe that Rock City is surely just around the nearest corner instead of being a day's drive

779. On October 23, 1778, the Earl of Carlisle wrote to George Selwyn, "Everything is upon a great scale upon this continent. The rivers are immense, the climate violent in heat and cold, the prospects magnificent, the thunder and lightning tremendous. The disorders incident to the country make every constitution tremble. We have nothing on a great scale with us but our blunders, our misconduct, our ruin, our losses, our disgraces and misfortunes that will mark the reign of a prince, who deserves better treatment and kinder fortunes. Whatever may be our reception at home I think I have strength of mind enough to stem the torrent, let it set against me with all its fury. I have served my King with zeal and attachment for his government and person. If I had succeeded my country would have reaped the benefit of my labours; as I have not, I only hope the approbation of the attempt will not be refused me." Quoted in *Life and Correspondence of Joseph Reed: Military Secretary of Washington*, by William B. Reed (Philadelphia: Lindsay and Blakiston, 1847), vol. I, pp. 393–94.

780. In fact, it is only six miles from downtown Chattanooga.

781. The balance of this sentence does not appear in the First Edition.

782. The "Indian Removal Act," passed in 1830 and signed into law by President Andrew Jackson, was couched as a benevolent swap of land, territory in what would become Oklahoma to be exchanged for traditional tribal lands. In a statement to Congress, Jackson reported, "It gives me pleasure to announce to Congress that the benevolent policy of the Government, steadily pursued for nearly thirty years, in relation to the removal of the Indians beyond the white settlements is approaching to a happy consummation. Two important tribes have acceded the provision made for their removal at the last session of Congress, and it is believed that their example will induce the remaining tribes also to seek the same obvious advantages." In fact, several tribes did accede to the policy, but most fought it bitterly. The government signed "treaties" with factions in various tribes, in which relocation was agreed, but the Cherokee resisted, and only in 1838 were they forcibly removed by the military from their lands in Georgia and made to walk the so-called Trail of Tears to Oklahoma.

783. The "Battle Above the Clouds," as Brigadier General Montgomery C. Meigs termed the Battle of Lookout Mountain, was fought November 24, 1863, as part of the Chattanooga campaign of the American Civil War. Union forces under Maj. Gen. Joseph Hooker assaulted Lookout Mountain and defeated the Confederate forces commanded by Maj. Gen. Carter L. Stevenson. The battle was instrumental in allowing Union forces to lift the siege of Chattanooga and led to a sweep of the Deep South.

away, on Lookout Mountain, a hair over the state line, in Georgia, just southwest of Chattanooga, Tennessee.[780]

Lookout Mountain is not much of a mountain. It resembles an impossibly high and commanding hill,[781] brown from a distance, green with trees and houses from up close. The Chickamauga, a branch of the Cherokee, lived there when the white men came; they called the mountain Chattotonoogee, which has been translated as *the mountain that rises to a point.*

In the 1830s Andrew Jackson's Indian Removal Act[782] forced them all from their land—all the Choctaw and Chickamauga and Cherokee and Chickasaw—and U.S. troops forced every one of them they could find and catch to walk over a thousand miles to the new Indian Territories in what would one day be Oklahoma, down the Trail of Tears: a cheerful gesture of casual genocide. Thousands of men, women, and children died on the way. When you've won, you've won, and nobody can argue with that.

For whoever controlled Lookout Mountain controlled the land; that was the legend. It was a sacred site, after all, and it was a high place. In the Civil War, the War Between the States, there was a battle there: the Battle Above the Clouds, that was the first day's fighting, and then the Union forces did the impossible, and, without orders, swept up Missionary Ridge and took it.[783] The troops of General Grant won the day, and the North took Lookout Mountain and the North took the war.

Ruby Falls (before construction of lighting)

Entrance to Rock City

The point of Rock City

There are tunnels and caves, some very old, beneath Lookout Mountain. For the most part they are blocked off now, although a local businessman excavated an underground waterfall, which he called Ruby Falls.[784]

It can be reached by elevator. It's a tourist attraction, although the biggest tourist attraction of all is at the top of Lookout Mountain. That is Rock City.

Rock City begins as an ornamental garden on a mountainside: its visitors walk a path that takes them through rocks, over rocks, between rocks. They throw corn into a deer enclosure, cross a hanging bridge and peer out through a-quarter-a-throw binoculars at a view that promises them

784. Ruby Falls is 1,120 feet below the surface of Lookout Mountain, according to its publicity, and claims to be the tallest underground waterfall in America, at 144 feet. Leo Lambert, who developed the attraction, did not create the falls, though he took the liberty of naming it after his wife—he merely excavated the entrance to what he named Ruby Falls Cave.

Viewing station atop Lookout Mountain

seven states on the rare sunny days when the air is perfectly clear.

And from there, like a drop into some strange hell, the path takes the visitors, millions upon millions of them every year, down into caverns, where they stare at black-lit dolls arranged into nursery-rhyme and fairy-tale dioramas. When they leave, they leave bemused, uncertain of why they came, of what they have seen, of whether they had a good time or not.

✧   ✧   ✧

THEY CAME TO Lookout Mountain from all across the United States. They were not tourists. They came by car and they came by plane and by bus and by railroad and on foot. Some of them flew—they flew low, and they flew only in the dark of the night, but still, they flew. Several of them traveled their own ways beneath the earth. Many of them hitchhiked, cadging rides from nervous motorists or from truck drivers. Those who had cars or trucks would see the ones who had not walking beside the roads or at rest stations and in diners on the way, and, recognizing them for what they were, would offer them rides.

They arrived dust-stained and weary at the foot of Lookout Mountain. Looking up to the heights of the tree-covered slope they could see, or imagine that they could see, the paths and gardens and streams of Rock City.

They started arriving early in the morning. A second wave of them arrived at dusk. And for several days they simply kept coming.

A battered U-Haul truck pulled up, disgorging several travel-weary *vila*[785] and *rusalka,*[786] their make-up smudged, runs in their stockings, their expressions heavy-lidded and tired.

In a clump of trees at the bottom of the hill, an elderly *wampyr*[787] offered a Marlboro to a huge naked ape-like creature covered with a tangle of orange fur. It accepted graciously, and they smoked in silence, side by side.

A Toyota Previa pulled up by the side of the road, and seven Chinese men and women got out of it. They looked, above all, clean, and they wore the kind of dark suits that, in some countries, are worn by minor government officials. One of them carried a clipboard, and he checked the inventory as they unloaded large golf-bags from the back of the car: the bags contained ornate swords with lacquer handles, and carved sticks, and mirrors. The weapons were distributed, checked off, signed for.

A once-famous comedian, believed to have died in the 1920s, climbed out of his rusting car, and proceeded to remove his clothing: his legs were goat-legs, and his tail was short and goatish.[788]

Four Mexicans arrived, all smiles, their hair black and very shiny: they passed among themselves a beer bottle which they kept out of sight in a brown paper bag, its contents a bitter mixture of powdered chocolate, liquor, and blood.

A small, dark-bearded man with a dusty black derby on

The Rusalki
Ivan Kramskoi (1871)

785. Nymphs in Slavic folklore.

786. Slavic spirits or fairies, usually female, though not necessarily evil.

787. The German word for "vampire"—in German, "W" is pronounced "vee." Bram Stoker originally thought to name the eponymous lead of *Dracula* "Count Wampyr."

788. Lawrence "Larry" Semon (1889–1928) was a writer, producer, director, and star of well over 100 silent comedies, probably best remembered today as having appeared with both Oliver Hardy and Stan Laurel before they teamed up. Semon often appeared as a bumbling fool in white-face, wearing a derby hat. His father was the stage magician Zera the Great, and his mother was Zera's assistant; it was from them that Semon learned early in life about the stage. What if Zera came by his magical talents naturally?

789. In Jewish folklore, a golem is an inanimate creature, usually made of clay, brought to life by rituals and incantations. The most famous legend of a golem is that of the so-called Golem of Prague, brought to life by Rabbi Judah Loew to protect the residents of the Prague ghetto in the sixteenth century. The story is the basis for Gustav Meyrink's 1914 novel *Der Golem* and a trilogy of films in the 1920s, two of which are lost, by Paul Wegener. In most versions, the creature is activated by a name of God ("shem") being inscribed on the creature's forehead or written on a paper placed in the golem's mouth; the inscription or paper could be removed to deactivate the creature. The word "truth" (*emet*, אמת) is the *shem* used in most versions of the legend; when the first letter, aleph (א), is removed, the word remaining (*met*, מת) means "death."

790. Usually depicted with fangs and sharp claws.

791. Also known as Legua, Leba, or Liba, Legba is the trickster-god of Dahomey and later Haiti, the son of the creator-god.

Rabbi Loew and the Golem
Mikoláš Aleš (1899)

his head, curling *payess* at his temples, and a ragged fringed prayer shawl came to them walking across the fields. He was several feet in front of his companion, who was twice his height and was the blank gray color of good Polish clay: the word inscribed on his forehead meant *truth*.[789]

They kept coming. A cab drew up and several *rakshasas*, the demons of the Indian subcontinent,[790] climbed out and milled around, staring at the people at the bottom of the hill without speaking, until they found Mama-ji, her eyes closed, her lips moving in prayer. She was the only thing here that was familiar to them, but still, they hesitated to approach her, remembering old battles. Her hands rubbed the necklace of skulls about her neck. Her brown skin became slowly black, the glassy black of jet, of obsidian: her lips curled and her long white teeth were very sharp. She opened all her eyes, and beckoned the *rakshasas* to her, and greeted them as she would have greeted her own children.

The storms of the last few days, to the north and the east, had done nothing to ease the feeling of pressure and discomfort in the air. Local weather forecasters had begun to warn of cells that might spawn tornados, of high-pressure areas that did not move. It was warm by day there, but the nights were cold.

They clumped together in informal companies, banding together sometimes by nationality, by race, by temperament, even by species. They looked apprehensive. They looked tired.

Some of them were talking. There was laughter, on occasion, but it was muted and sporadic. Six-packs of beer were handed around.

Several local men and women came walking over the meadows, their bodies moving in unfamiliar ways: their voices, when they spoke, were the voices of the *loa* who rode them: a tall, black man spoke in the voice of Papa Legba who opens the gates;[791] while Baron Samedi, the *voudon* lord of death, had taken over the body of a teenage Goth girl from Chattanooga, possibly because she possessed her own black silk top hat, which sat on her dark hair at a jaunty angle. She spoke in the baron's own deep voice, smoked a cigar of enormous size, and commanded three of the Gédé, the *Loa* of the dead.[792] The Gédé inhabited the bodies of three middle-aged brothers. They carried shotguns and told continual jokes of such astounding filthiness that only they were willing to laugh at them, which they did, raucously and repeatedly.

Two ageless Chickamauga women, in oil-stained blue jeans and battered leather jackets, walked around, watching the people and the preparations for battle. Sometimes they pointed and laughed; they did not intend to take part in the coming conflict.

The moon swelled and rose in the east, a day away from full. It seemed half as big as the sky as it rose, a deep reddish-orange, immediately above the hills. As it crossed the sky it seemed to shrink and pale until it hung high in the sky like a lantern.

There were so many of them waiting there, in the moonlight, at the foot of Lookout Mountain.

✢ ✢ ✢

LAURA WAS THIRSTY.

Sometimes living people burned steadily in her mind like candles and sometimes they flamed like torches. It made them easy to avoid, and it made them easy, on occasion, to find. Shadow had burned so strangely, with his own light, up on that tree.

She had chided him once, on that day when they had walked and held hands, for not being alive. She had hoped, perhaps, to see a spark of raw emotion,[793] something that would show her that the man she had once been married to was a real man, a live one. And she had seen nothing at all.

She remembered walking beside him, wishing that he could understand what she was trying to say.

Now, dying on the tree, Shadow was utterly alive. She had watched him as the life had faded, and he had been focused and real. And he had asked her to stay with him, to stay the whole night. He had forgiven her . . . perhaps he had forgiven her. It did not matter. He had changed; that was all she knew.

Vèvè for Papa Legba

792. The *loa* are the spirits of *voudon*, and the Ghede or Gédé, are the family of spirits associated with the dead and fertility. Among the incarnations of the *loa* are Baron Samedi, Baron Cimetiere, Baron La Croix, and Baron Piquant. Samedi is worshipped as the god of the dead and has healing powers. He is usually depicted wearing a black coat, top hat, dark glasses, and smoking a cigar or cigarette. Of course, this girl very much resembles Death, one of the Endless in Gaiman's *Sandman*.

793. In the First Edition, the balance of the paragraph reads "To have seen anything."

Vèvè (religious symbol) for Baron Samedi

Shadow had told her to go to the farmhouse, that they would give her water to drink there. There were no lights burning in the farm building, and she could feel nobody at home. But he had told her that they would care for her. She pushed against the door of the farmhouse and it opened, rusty hinges protesting the whole while.

Something moved in her left lung, something that pushed and squirmed and made her cough.

She found herself in a narrow hallway, her way almost blocked by a tall and dusty piano. The inside of the building smelled of old damp. She squeezed past the piano, pushed open a door and found herself in a dilapidated drawing room, filled with ramshackle furniture. An oil lamp burned on the mantelpiece. There was a coal fire burning in the fireplace beneath it, although she had neither seen nor smelled smoke outside the house. The coal fire did nothing to lift the chill she felt in that room, although, Laura was willing to concede, that might not be the fault of the room.

Death hurt Laura, although the hurt consisted mostly of absences, of things that were not there: a parching thirst that drained every cell of her, a cold in her bones that no heat could lift. Sometimes she would catch herself wondering whether the crisp and crackling flames of a pyre would warm her, or the soft brown blanket of the earth; whether the cold sea would quench her thirst . . .

The room, she realized, was not empty.

Three women sat on an elderly couch, as if they had come as a matched set in some outlandish artistic exhibition. The couch was upholstered in threadbare velvet, a faded brown that might, once, a hundred years ago, have been a bright canary yellow.[794] The women were dressed in identical fog-gray skirts and sweaters. Their eyes were too deeply set, their skin the white of fresh bone. The one on the left of the sofa was a giantess, or almost, the one on the right was little more than a dwarf, and, between them, was a woman Laura was certain would be her own height. They followed her with their eyes as she entered the room, and they said nothing.

794. The next three sentences do not appear in the First Edition.

Laura had not known they would be there.

Something wriggled and fell in her nasal cavity. Laura fumbled in her sleeve for a tissue, and she blew her nose into it. She crumpled the tissue and flung it and its contents onto the coals of the fire, watched it crumple and blacken and become orange lace. She watched the maggots shrivel and brown and burn.

This done, she turned back to the women on the couch. They had not moved since she had entered, not a muscle, not a hair. They stared at her.

"Hello. Is this your farm?" she asked.

The largest of the women nodded. Her hands were very red, and her expression was impassive.

"Shadow—that's the guy hanging on the tree. He's my husband. He said I should tell you that he wants you to give me water." Something large shifted in her bowels. It squirmed, and then was still.

The smallest woman nodded. She clambered off the couch. Her feet had not previously touched the floor. She scurried from the room.

Laura could hear doors opening and closing, through the farmhouse. Then, from outside, she could hear a series of loud creaks. Each was followed by a splash of water.

Soon enough, the small woman returned. She was carrying a brown earthenware jug of water. She put it down, carefully, on the table, and retreated to the couch. She pulled herself up, with a wriggle and a shiver, and was seated beside her sisters once again.

"Thank you." Laura walked over to the table, looked around for a cup or a glass, but there was nothing like that to be seen. She picked up the jug. It was heavier than it looked. The water in it was perfectly clear.

She raised the jug to her lips and began to drink.

The water was colder than she had ever imagined liquid water could be. It froze her tongue and her teeth and her gullet. Still, she drank, unable to stop drinking, feeling the water freezing its way into her stomach, her bowels, her heart, her veins.

The water flowed into her. It was like drinking liquid ice.

She realized that the jug was empty and, surprised, she put it down on the table.

The women were observing her, dispassionately. Since her death, Laura had not thought in metaphors: things were, or they were not. But now, as she looked at the women on the sofa, she found herself thinking of juries, of scientists observing a laboratory animal.

She shook, suddenly and convulsively. She reached out a hand to the table to steady herself, but the table was slipping and lurching, and it almost avoided her grasp. As she put her hand on the table she began to vomit. She brought up bile and formalin, centipedes, and maggots. And then she felt herself starting to void, and to piss: stuff was being pushed violently, wetly, from her body. She would have screamed if she could; but then the dusty floorboards came up to meet her so fast and so hard that, had she been breathing, they would have knocked the breath from her body.

Time rushed over her and into her, swirling like a dust-devil. A thousand memories began to play at once: she was wet and stinking on the floor of the farmhouse;[795] and she was lost in a department store the week before Christmas and her father was nowhere to be seen; and now she was sitting in the bar at Chi-Chi's, ordering a strawberry daiquiri and checking out her blind date, the big, grave man-child, and wondering how he kissed; and she was in the car as, sickeningly, it rolled and jolted, and Robbie was screaming at her until the metal post finally stopped the car, but not its contents, from moving . . .

The water of time, which comes from the spring of fate, Urd's Well,[796] is not the water of life. Not quite. It feeds the roots of the world tree, though. And there is no other water like it.

When Laura woke in the empty farmhouse room, she was shivering, and her breath actually steamed in the morning air. There was a scrape on the back of her hand, and a wet smear on the scrape, the red-orange of fresh blood.

And she knew where she had to go. She had drunk from

795. This phrase does not appear in the First Edition.

796. See note 277, above.

the water of time, which comes from the spring of fate. She could see the mountain in her mind. She licked the blood from the back of her hand, marveling at the film of saliva, and she began to walk.

*   *   *

IT WAS A wet March day, and it was unseasonably cold, and the storms of the previous few days had lashed their way across the southern states, which meant that there were very few real tourists at Rock City on Lookout Mountain. The Christmas lights had been taken down, the summer visitors were yet to start arriving.

Still, there were a number of people there. There was even a tour bus that drew up that morning, releasing a dozen men and women with perfect tans and gleaming, re-assuring smiles. They looked like news anchors, and one could almost imagine there was a phosphor-dot quality to them: they seemed to blur gently as they moved. A black Humvee was parked in the front lot of Rock City, near to Rocky the animatronic gnome.

The TV people walked intently through Rock City, sta-tioning themselves near the balancing rock, where they talked to each other in pleasant, reasonable voices.

They were not the only visitors. If you had walked the paths of Rock City that day, you might have noticed people who looked like movie stars, and people who looked like aliens and a number of people who looked most of all like the idea of a person and nothing like the reality. You might have seen them, but most likely you would never have no-ticed them at all.

They came to Rock City in long limousines and in small sports cars and in oversized SUVs. Many of them wore the sunglasses of those who habitually wear sunglasses indoors and out, and do not willingly or comfortably remove them. There were suntans and suits and shades and smiles and scowls. They came in all sizes and shapes, all ages and styles.

All they had in common was a look, a very specific look.

It said, *You know me;* or perhaps, *You ought to know me.* An instant familiarity that was also a distance, a look, or an attitude—the confidence that the world existed for them, and that it welcomed them, and that they were adored.

The fat kid moved among them with the shuffling walk of one who, despite having no social skills, has still become successful beyond his dreams. His black coat flapped in the wind.

Something that stood beside the soft drink stand in Mother Goose Court coughed to attract his attention. It was massive, and scalpel-blades jutted from its face and its fingers. Its face was cancerous. "It will be a mighty battle," it told him, in a glutinous voice.

"It's not going to be a battle," said the fat kid. "All we're facing here is a fucking paradigm shift. It's a shakedown. Modalities like *battle* are so fucking Lao Tzu."[797]

The cancerous thing blinked at him. "Waiting," is all it said in reply.

"Whatever," said the fat kid. Then, "I'm looking for Mister World. You seen him?"

The thing scratched itself with a scalpel-blade, a tumorous lower lip pushed out in concentration. Then it nodded. "Over there," it said.

The fat kid walked away, without a thank-you, in the direction indicated. The cancerous thing waited, saying nothing, until the kid was out of sight.

"It *will* be a battle," said the cancerous thing to a woman whose face was smudged with phosphor-dots.

She nodded, and leaned closer to it. "So how does that make you *feel*?" she asked, in a sympathetic voice.[798]

It blinked, and then it began to tell her.

* * *

TOWN'S FORD EXPLORER had a global positioning system, a little silver box that listened to the satellites and whispered back to the car its location, but he still got lost once he got south of Blacksburg and onto the country roads: the roads he drove seemed to bear little relationship to the tangle of lines on the map on the screen. Eventually he

---

797. A Chinese philosopher, probably the contemporary of Confucius in the sixth century B.C.E., regarded as the founder of Taoism. Taoism emphasizes living in harmony with "the Way" (*Tao*), the source, pattern, and substance of everything.

798. A common complaint about the media's coverage of disasters is that newscasters unhesitatingly thrust their microphones and cameras into the faces of victims, making this inquiry. The ultimate parody is Woody Allen's 1971 film *Bananas*, in which Howard Cosell, the well-known sportscaster who achieved his own celebrity, playing himself, buttonholes an assassinated South American dictator and asks, "Sir, you've been shot. When did you know it was all over? I guess now you'll have to announce your retirement. The dead man does not answer. Well, good luck to you, sir, good luck to you."

stopped the car in a country lane, wound down the window and asked a fat white woman being pulled by a wolfhound on its early morning walk for directions to Ashtree farm.

She nodded, and pointed and said something to him. He could not understand what she had said, but he said thanks a million and wound up the window and drove off in the general direction she had indicated.

He kept going for another forty minutes, down country road after country road, each of them promising, none of them the road he sought. Town began to chew his lower lip.

"I'm too old for this shit," he said aloud, relishing the movie-star world-weariness of the line.

He was pushing fifty. Most of his working life had been spent in a branch of government which went only by its initials, and whether or not he had left his government job a dozen years ago for employment by the private sector was a matter of opinion: some days he thought one way, some days another. Anyway, it was only when you got down to the joes on the street that anyone seemed to assume there was a difference.

He was on the verge of giving up on the farm when he drove up a hill and saw the sign, hand painted, on the gate. It said simply, as he had been told it would, ASH. He pulled up the Ford Explorer, climbed out and untwisted the wire that held the gate closed. He got back in the car and drove through.

It was like cooking a frog, he thought. You put the frog in the water, and then you turn on the heat. And by the time the frog notices that there's anything wrong, it's already been cooked. The world in which he worked was all too weird. There was no solid ground beneath his feet; the water in the pot was bubbling fiercely.

When he'd been transferred to the Agency it had all seemed so simple. Now it was all so—not complex, he decided; merely bizarre. He had been sitting in Mr. World's office at two that morning, and he had been told what he was to do. "You got it?" said Mr. World, handing him the knife in its dark leather sheath. "Cut me a stick. It doesn't have to be longer than a couple of feet."

"Affirmative," he said. And then he said, "Why do I have to do this, sir?"

"Because I tell you to," said Mr. World, flatly. "Find the tree. Do the job. Meet me down in Chattanooga. Don't waste any time."

"And what about the asshole?"

"Shadow? If you see him, just avoid him. Don't touch him. Don't even mess with him. I don't want you turning him into a martyr. There's no room for martyrs in the current game-plan." He smiled then, his scarred smile. Mr. World was easily amused. Mr. Town had noticed this on several occasions. It had amused him to play chauffeur, in Kansas, after all.**799**

"Look—"

"No martyrs, Town."

And Town had nodded, and taken the knife in its sheath, and pushed the rage that welled up inside him down deep and away.

Mr. Town's hatred of Shadow had become a part of him. As he was falling asleep he would see Shadow's solemn face, see that smile that wasn't a smile, the way Shadow had of smiling without smiling that made Town want to sink his fist into the man's gut, and even as he fell asleep he could feel his jaws squeeze together, his temples tense, his gullet burn.

He drove the Ford Explorer across the meadow, past an abandoned farmhouse. He crested a ridge and saw the tree. He parked the car a little way past it, and turned off the engine. The clock on the dashboard said it was 6:38 A.M. He left the keys in the car, and walked toward the tree.

The tree was large; it seemed to exist on its own sense of scale. Town could not have said if it was fifty feet high or two hundred. Its bark was the gray of a fine silk scarf.

There was a naked man tied to the trunk a little way above the ground by a webwork of ropes, and there was something wrapped in a sheet at the foot of the tree. Town realized what it was as he passed it. He pushed at the sheet with his foot. Wednesday's ruined half-a-face stared out at him.**800** He would have expected it to be alive with maggots

799. The loop finally closes: Mr. World was the chauffeur; the chauffeur was Low-Key; Low-Key is Loki; Loki is Mr. World. Why would Loki, Odin's former partner, kill Odin?

800. The balance of this paragraph does not appear in the First Edition.

and flies, but it was untouched by insects. It didn't even smell bad. It looked just as it had when he had taken it to the motel.

Town reached the tree. He walked a little way around the thick trunk, away from the sightless eyes of the farmhouse, then he unzipped his fly and pissed against the trunk of the tree. He did up his fly. He walked back over to the house, found a wooden extension ladder, carried it back to the tree. He leaned it carefully against the trunk. Then he climbed up it.

Shadow hung, limply, from the ropes that tied him to the tree. Town wondered if the man were still alive: his chest did not rise or fall. Dead or almost dead, it did not matter.

"Hello, asshole," Town said, aloud. Shadow did not move.

Town reached the top of the ladder, and he pulled out the knife. He found a small branch which seemed to meet Mr. World's specifications, and hacked at the base of it with the knife-blade, cutting it half-through, then breaking it off with his hand. It was about thirty inches long.

He put the knife back in its sheath. Then he started to climb back down the ladder. When he was opposite Shadow, he paused. "God, I hate you," he said. He wished he could just have taken out a gun and shot him, and he knew that he could not. And then he jabbed the stick in the air toward the hanging man, in a stabbing motion. It was an instinctive gesture, containing all the frustration and rage inside Town. He imagined that he was holding a spear and twisting it into Shadow's guts.[801]

"Come on," he said, aloud. "Time to get moving." Then he thought, *First sign of madness. Talking to yourself.* He climbed down a few more steps, then jumped the rest of the way to the ground. He looked at the stick he was holding, and felt like a small boy, holding his stick as a sword or a spear. *I could have cut a stick from any tree, he thought. It didn't have to be this tree. Who the fuck would have known?*

And he thought, *Mr. World would have known.*

He carried the ladder back to the farmhouse. From the corner of his eye he thought he saw something move, and

801. As noted earlier, Odin mutilated himself with his spear Gungnir.

he looked in through the window, into the dark room filled with broken furniture, with the plaster peeling from the walls, and for a moment, in a half-dream, he imagined that he saw three women sitting in the dark parlor.

One of them was knitting. One of them was staring directly at him. One of them appeared to be asleep. The woman who was staring at him began to smile, a huge smile that seemed to split her face lengthwise, a smile that crossed from ear to ear. Then she raised a finger and touched it to her neck, and ran it gently from one side of her neck to the other.

That was what he thought he saw, all in a moment, in that empty room, which contained, he saw at a second glance, nothing more than old rotting furniture and fly-spotted prints and dry rot. There was nobody there at all.

He rubbed his eyes.

Town walked back to the brown Ford Explorer and climbed in. He tossed the stick onto the white leather of the passenger seat. He turned the key in the ignition. The dashboard clock said 6:37 A.M. Town frowned, and checked his wristwatch, which blinked that it was 13:58.

Great, he thought. *I was either up on that tree for eight hours, or for minus a minute.* That was what he thought, but what he believed was that both timepieces had, coincidentally, begun to misbehave.

On the tree, Shadow's body began to bleed. The wound was in his side. The blood that came from it was slow and thick and molasses-black.

He did not move. If he was sleeping, he did not wake.[802]

* * *

CLOUDS COVERED THE top of Lookout Mountain.

Easter sat some distance away from the crowd at the bottom of the mountain, watching the dawn over the hills to the east. She had a chain of blue forget-me-nots tattooed around her left wrist, and she rubbed them, absently, with her right thumb.

Another night had come and gone, and nothing. The folk were still coming, by ones and twos. The last night had

802. This paragraph does not appear in the First Edition.

brought several creatures from the southwest, including two young boys each the size of an apple tree,[803] and something which she had only glimpsed, but which had looked like a disembodied head the size of a VW Bug. They had disappeared into the trees at the base of the mountain.

Nobody bothered them. Nobody from the outside world even seemed to have noticed they were there: she imagined the tourists at Rock City staring down at them through their insert-a-quarter binoculars, staring straight at a ramshackle encampment of things and people at the foot of the mountain, and seeing nothing but trees and bushes and rocks.

She could smell the smoke from a cooking fire, a smell of burning bacon on the chilly dawn wind. Someone at the far end of the encampment began to play the harmonica, which made her, involuntarily, smile and shiver. She had a paperback book in her backpack, and she waited for the sky to become light enough for her to read.

There were two dots in the sky, immediately below the clouds: a small one and a larger one. A spatter of rain brushed her face in the morning wind.

A barefoot girl came out from the encampment, walking toward her. She stopped beside a tree, hitched up her skirts, and squatted. When she had finished, Easter hailed her. The girl walked over.

"Good morning, lady," she said. "The battle will start soon now." The tip of her pink tongue touched her scarlet lips. She had a black crow's wing tied with leather onto her shoulder, a crow's foot on a chain around her neck. Her arms were blue-tattooed with lines and patterns and intricate knots.

"How do you know?"

The girl grinned. "I am Macha, of the Morrigan.[804] When war comes, I can smell it in the air. I am a war goddess, and I say, blood shall be spilled this day."

"Oh," said Easter. "Well. There you go." She was watching the smaller dot in the sky as it tumbled down toward them, dropping like a rock.

"And we shall fight them, and we shall kill them, every one," said the girl. "And we shall take their heads as trophies,

803. Warrior twins appear in mythology of the Pueblo Indians, sometimes called Masewi (Brother Elder) and Oyoyewi (Brother Younger). Among the Zunis, they are collectively known as the Ahayuta, with the elder named Ahayuta also and the younger Matsilema. The Zuni name them as the guides who led them out of the interior of the earth (see note 372, above, for a discussion of other Southwest emergence myths). Their father was the Sun; their mother was impregnated by a ray of light. The twins travelled the land searching for their father and hunting for magical weapons. Though twins appear in many pantheons, Masewi and Oyoyewi are literally "creatures from the southwest."

804. The triple-goddesses of war of the Irish, the word means "great queen." The Morrigan are usually named as Ana, Badb, and Macha (the last meaning "raven"—see, e.g., Robert Graves's *The White Goddess* New York: Farrar, Straus, and Giroux, amended and enlarged edition, 1966, p. 370) but the names vary. The Morrigan had a prominent role in many stories of Cuchulain, the hero of the Ulster cycle of Old Irish epic poetry; most variations tell that Cuchulain repulsed the Morrigan's romantic advances, with the result that the Morrigan repeatedly opposed him in battle. Eventually, the Morrigan, by means of signs and portents, tried unsuccessfully to save Cuchulain from death. The Morrigan appear as one of many triple-goddesses in *Sandman*.

and the crows shall have their eyes and their corpses." The dot had become a bird, its wings outstretched, riding the gusty morning winds above them.

Easter cocked her head on one side. "Is that some hidden war goddess knowledge?" she asked. "The whole 'who's going to win' thing? Who gets whose head?"

"No," said the girl. "I can smell the battle, but that's all. But we'll win. Won't we? We *have* to. I saw what they did to the all-father. It's them or us."

"Yeah," said Easter. "I suppose it is."

The girl smiled again, in the half-light, and made her way back to the camp. Easter put her hand down and touched a green shoot which stabbed up from the earth like a knife blade. As she touched it it grew, and opened, and twisted, and changed, until she was resting her hand on a green tulip head. When the sun was high the flower would open.

Easter looked up at the hawk. "Can I help you?" she said.

The hawk circled about fifteen feet above Easter's head, slowly, then it glided down to her, and landed on the ground nearby. It looked up at her with mad eyes.

"Hello, cutie," she said. "Now, what do you really look like, eh?"

The hawk hopped toward her, uncertainly, and then it was no longer a hawk, but a young man. He looked at her, and then looked down at the grass. "You?" he said. His glance went everywhere, to the grass, to the sky, to the bushes. Not to her.

"Me," she said. "What about me?"

"You." He stopped. He seemed to be trying to muster his thoughts; strange expressions flitted and swam across his face. *He spent too long a bird,* she thought. *He has forgotten how to be a man.* She waited patiently. Eventually, he said, "Will you come with me?"

"Maybe. Where do you want me to go?"

"The man on the tree. He needs you. A ghost hurt, in his side. The blood came, then it stopped. I think he is dead."

"There's a war on. I can't just go running away."

The naked man said nothing, just moved from one foot to

another as if he were uncertain of his weight, as if he were used to resting on the air or on a swaying branch, not on the solid and unchanging earth. Then he said, "If he is gone forever, it is all over."

"But the battle—"

"If he is lost, it will not matter who wins." He looked like he needed a blanket, and a cup of sweet coffee, and someone to take him somewhere he could shiver and babble until he got his mind back. He held his arms stiffly against his sides.

"Where is this? Nearby?"

He stared at the tulip plant, and shook his head. "Way away."

"Well," she said, "I'm needed here. And I can't just leave. How do you expect me to get there? I can't fly, like you, you know."

"No," said Horus. "You can't." Then he looked up, gravely, and pointed to the other dot that circled them, as it dropped from the darkening clouds, growing in size. "*He* can."

✢   ✢   ✢

ANOTHER SEVERAL HOURS' pointless driving, and by now Town hated the GPS almost as much as he hated Shadow. There was no passion in the hate, though. He had thought finding his way to the farm, to the great silver ash tree, had been hard; finding his way *away* from the farm was much harder. It did not seem to matter which road he took, which direction he drove down the narrow country lanes— the twisting Virginia back roads which must have begun, he was sure, as deer trails and cow paths—eventually he would find himself passing the farm once more, and the hand-painted sign, ASH.

This was crazy, wasn't it? He simply had to retrace his way, take a left turn for every right he had taken on his way here, a right turn for every left.

Only that was what he had done last time, and now here he was, back at the farm once more. There were heavy storm clouds coming in, it was getting dark fast, it felt like night, not morning, and he had a long drive ahead of him: he would never get to Chattanooga before afternoon at this rate.

His cell phone gave him only a *No Service* message. The fold-out map in the car's glove compartment showed the main roads, all the interstates and the real highways, but as far as it was concerned nothing else existed.

Nor was there anyone around that he could ask. The houses were set back from the roads; there were no welcoming lights. Now the fuel gauge was nudging Empty. He heard a rumble of distant thunder, and a single drop of rain splashed heavily onto his windshield.

So when Town saw the woman walking along the side of the road, he found himself smiling, involuntarily. "Thank God," he said, aloud, and he drew up beside her. He thumbed down her window. "Ma'am? I'm sorry. I'm kind of lost. Can you tell me how to get to Highway 81 from here?"

She looked at him through the open passenger-side window and said, "You know, I don't think I can explain it. But I can show you, if you like." She was pale and her wet hair was long and dark.

"Climb in," said Town. He didn't even hesitate. "First thing, we need to buy some gas."

"Thanks," she said. "I needed a ride." She got in. Her eyes were astonishingly blue. "There's a stick here, on the seat," she said, puzzled.

"Just throw it in the back. Where are you heading?" he asked. "Lady, if you can get me to a gas station, and back to a freeway, I'll take you all the way to your own front door."

She said, "Thank you. But I think I'm going further than you are. If you can get me to the freeway, that will be fine. Maybe a trucker will give me a ride." And she smiled, a crooked, determined smile. It was the smile that did it.

"Ma'am," he said, "I can give you a finer ride than any trucker." He could smell her perfume. It was heady and heavy, a cloying scent, like magnolias or lilacs, but he did not mind.

"I'm going to Georgia," she said. "It's a long way."

"I'm going to Chattanooga. I'll take you as far as I can."

"Mmm," she said. "What's your name?"

"They call me Mack," said Mr. Town. When he was talking to women in bars, he would sometimes follow that up with "And the ones that know me really well call me Big Mack." That could wait. They would have many hours in each other's company to get to know each other, after all. "What's yours?"

"Laura," she told him.

"Well, Laura," he said, "I'm sure we're going to be great friends."

＊　　＊　　＊

THE FAT KID found Mr. World in the Rainbow Room—a walled section of the path, its window glass covered in clear plastic sheets of green and red and yellow film. He was walking impatiently from window to window, staring out, in turn, at a golden world, a red world, a green world. His hair was reddish-orange and close-cropped to his skull. He wore a Burberry raincoat.

The fat kid coughed. Mr. World looked up.

"Excuse me? Mister World?"

"Yes? Is everything on schedule?"

The fat kid's mouth was dry. He licked his lips, and said, "I've set up everything. I don't have confirmation on the choppers."

"The helicopters will be here when we need them."

"Good," said the fat kid. "Good." He stood there, not saying anything, not going away. There was a bruise on his forehead.

After a while Mr. World said, "Is there anything else I can do for you?"

A pause. The boy swallowed and nodded. "Something else," he said. "Yes."

"Would you feel more comfortable discussing it in private?"

The boy nodded again.

Mr. World walked with the kid back to his operations center: a damp cave containing a diorama of drunken pixies making moonshine with a still. A sign outside warned

805. The passenger pigeon or wild pigeon once densely populated the North American continent. In 1831, John James Audubon reported a flock that took 3 days to pass out of view. "The air was literally filled with Pigeons; the light of noon-day was obscured as by an eclipse; the dung fell in spots, not unlike melting flakes of snow, and the continued buzz of wings had a tendency to lull my senses to repose . . ." Although hunted by Native Americans for food before the arrival of Europeans, widespread commercial hunting between 1800 and 1870 reduced the population slowly but steadily; after 1870, it declined rapidly. The last confirmed wild bird is thought to have been shot in 1901, and the last in captivity died in 1914.

806. This sentence does not appear in the First Edition.

807. A story in the *Prose Edda* tells of a wager Loki made with the dwarf Brok, the subject of which was a gold ring. If Loki lost the wager, the dwarf was to take Loki's head. Loki lost, but when the dwarf came to collect, "Loki said that the head was his, but not the neck. Then the dwarf took thread and a knife and wanted to pierce holes in Loki's lips, so as to sew his mouth together, but the knife would not cut. Then said he, it would be better if he had his brother's awl, and as soon as he named it the awl was there and it pierced Loki's lips. Now Brok sewed Loki's mouth together, and broke off the thread at the end of the sewing. The thread with which the mouth of Loke was sewed together is called Vartare (a strap)." (Translation by Rasmus Björn Anderson, 1901)

808. "Omerta" means a code of silence practiced by the Mafia, non-cooperation with authorities. Lip-sewing could be used to enforce such a code, though there is no record of such use, and it is almost always temporary. Rather, lip-sewing is usually a form of protest, a symbolic expression of silence or, in some cases, fasting.

tourists away during renovations. The two men sat down on plastic chairs.

"How can I help you?" asked Mr. World.

"Yes. Okay. Right, two things, Okay. One. What are we waiting for? And two. Two is harder. Look. We have the guns. Right. We have the firepower. They have fucking swords and knives and fucking hammers and stone axes. And like, tire irons. We have fucking *smart* bombs."

"Which we will not be using," pointed out the other man.

"I know that. You said that already. I know that. And that's doable. But. Look, ever since I did the job on that bitch in L.A. I've been . . ." He stopped, made a face, seemed unwilling to go on.

"You've been troubled?"

"Yes. Good word. *Troubled.* Yes. Like a home for troubled teens. Funny. Yes."

"And what exactly is troubling you?"

"Well, we fight, we win."

"And that is a source of trouble? I find it a matter of triumph and delight, myself."

"But. They'll die out anyway. They are passenger pigeons and thylacines.[805] Yes? Who cares? This way, it's going to be a bloodbath. If we just wait them out, we get the whole thing."[806]

"Ah." Mr. World nodded.

He was following. That was good. The fat kid said, "Look, I'm not the only one who feels this way. I've checked with the crew at Radio Modern, and they're all for settling this peacefully; and the Intangibles are pretty much in favor of letting market forces take care of it. I'm being. You know. The voice of reason here."

"You are indeed. Unfortunately, there is information you do not have." The smile that followed was twisted and scarred.

The boy blinked. He said, "Mister World? What happened to your lips?"

World sighed. "The truth of the matter," he said, "is that somebody sewed them together. A long time ago."[807]

"Whoa," said the fat kid. "Serious *omertà* shit."[808]

"Yes. You want to know what we're waiting for? Why we didn't strike last night?"

The fat kid nodded. He was sweating, but it was a cold sweat.

"We didn't strike yet, because I'm waiting for a stick."

"A stick?"

"That's right. A stick. And do you know what I'm going to do with the stick?"

A head shake. "Okay. I'll bite. What?"

"I could tell you," said Mr. World, soberly. "But then I'd have to kill you." He winked, and the tension in the room evaporated.

The fat kid began to giggle, a low, snuffling laugh in the back of his throat and in his nose. "Okay," he said. "*Hee. Hee.* Okay. *Hee.* Got it. Message received on Planet Technical. Loud and clear. Ixnay on the estionsquay."[809]

Mr. World shook his head. He rested a hand on the fat kid's shoulder. "Hey," he said. "You really want to know?"

"Sure."

"Well," said Mr. World, "seeing that we're friends, here's the answer: I'm going to take the stick, and I'm going to throw it over the armies as they come together. As I throw it, it will become a spear. And then, as the spear arcs over the battle, I'm going to shout, 'I dedicate this battle to Odin.'"

"Huh?" said the fat kid. "Why?"

"Power," said Mr. World. He scratched his chin. "And food. A combination of the two. You see, the outcome of the battle is unimportant. What matters is the chaos, and the slaughter."

"I don't get it."

"Let me show you. It'll be just like this," said Mr. World. "Watch!" He took the wooden-bladed hunter's knife from the pocket of his Burberry and, in one fluid movement, he slipped the blade of it into the soft flesh beneath the fat kid's chin, and pushed hard upward, toward the brain. "I dedicate this death to Odin," he said, as the knife sank in.

There was a leakage onto his hand of something that was not actually blood, and a sputtering sparking noise behind

809. "No more questions," says the Technical Boy in "Pig Latin," a simple encrypted language in which the initial consonant of a word is moved to the end and "ay" is appended. Thus he states here: "Nix on the questions." Although "dog Latin" or "hog Latin" is referred to as early as Shakespeare, the modern version seems to have been promulgated by a 1919 song, "Pig Latin Love," recorded by Arthur Fields, which is subtitled "I-Yay Ove-Lay oo-yay earie-day"

the fat kid's eyes. The smell on the air was that of burning insulation wire, as if somewhere a plug was overloading.

The fat kid's hand twitched spastically, and then he fell. The expression on his face was one of puzzlement, and misery. "Look at him," said Mr. World, conversationally, to the air. "He looks as if he just saw a sequence of zeroes and ones turn into a cluster of brightly colored birds, and then just fly away."

There was no reply from the empty rock corridor.

Mr. World shouldered the body as if it weighed very little, and he opened the pixie diorama and dropped the body beside the still, covering it with its long black raincoat. He would dispose of it that evening, he decided, and he grinned his scarred grin: hiding a body on a battlefield would almost be too easy. Nobody would ever notice. Nobody would care.

For a little while there was silence in that place. And then a gruff voice which was not Mr. World's cleared its throat in the shadows, and said, "Good start."

CHAPTER EIGHTEEN

They tried to stand off the soldiers, but the men fired and killed them both. So the song's wrong about the jail, but that's put in for poetry. You can't allus have things like they are in poetry. Poetry ain't what you'd call truth. There ain't room enough in the verses.

—A SINGER'S COMMENTARY
on "The Ballad of Sam Bass,"
A Treasury of American Folklore[810]

ONE OF THIS can actually be happening. If it makes you more comfortable, you could simply think of it as metaphor. Religions are, by definition, metaphors, after all: God is a dream, a hope, a woman, an ironist, a father, a city, a house of many rooms, a watchmaker who left his prize chronometer in the desert, someone who loves you—even, perhaps, against all evidence, a celestial being whose only interest is to make sure your football team, army, business, or marriage thrives, prospers and triumphs over all opposition.

Religions are places to stand and look and act, vantage points from which to view the world.

So, none of this is happening. Such things could not occur in this day and age. Never a word of it is literally true, although it all happened, and the next thing that happened, happened like this:

At the foot of Lookout Mountain, which is scarcely more

810. The verse of "The Ballad of Sam Bass" reports:

> *A-ridin' back to Texas they robbed the*
> *U. P. train,*
> *For safety split in couples and started*
> *out again*
> *The sheriff took Jo Collins who had a*
> *sack of mail*
> *And with his partner landed him inside*
> *the county jail*

The singer comments, "Sam Leech, done give information and the posse caught up with Collins and his partner Bill Heffridge in Kansas right where was some U.S. army men who lit out after the outlaws." He continues as quoted above. *A Treasury of American Folklore*, edited by B. A. Botkin (New York: Crown Publishers, 1944), p. 120.

811. This phrase does not appear in the First Edition.

812. Russian for "grandfather"—thus a reference to Czernobog's age.

813. Isten is the chief god of the Hungarian pantheon, the creator of the world—the word simply means "God" in Hungarian.

814. This is the third and final appearance of the "nameless god." In a private conversation with this editor, Gaiman promised that the identity of the "nameless god" will be revealed in the sequel to *American Gods* when it is written—if he can remember it!

815. This and the next two sentences do not appear in the First Edition.

than a very high hill,[811] men and women were gathered around a small bonfire in the rain. They stood beneath the trees, which provided poor cover, and they were arguing.

The lady Kali, with her ink-black skin and white, sharp teeth, said, "It is time."

Anansi, with lemon-yellow gloves and silvering hair, shook his head. "We can wait," he said. "While we *can* wait, we *should* wait."

There was a murmur of disagreement from the crowd.

"No, listen. He's right," said an old man with iron-gray hair: Czernobog. He was holding a small sledgehammer, resting the head of it on his shoulder. "They have the high ground. The weather is against us. This is madness, to begin this now."

Something that looked a little like a wolf and a little more like a man grunted and spat on the forest floor. "When better to attack them, *dedushka*?[812] Shall we wait until the weather clears, when they expect it? I say we go now. I say we move."

"There are clouds, between us and them," pointed out Isten of the Hungarians.[813] He had a fine black mustache, a large, dusty black hat, and the grin of a man who makes his living selling aluminum siding and new roofs and gutters to senior citizens but who always leaves town the day after the checks clear whether the work is done or not.

A man in an elegant suit, who had until now said nothing, put his hands together, stepped into the firelight, and made his point succinctly and clearly. There were nods and mutters of agreement.[814]

A voice came from one of three warrior-women who comprised the Morrigan, standing so close together in the shadows that they had become an arrangement of blue-tattooed limbs and dangling crow's wings. She said, "It doesn't matter whether this is a good time or a bad time. This is *the* time. They have been killing us. They will continue to kill us, whether we fight or not.[815] Perhaps we will triumph. Perhaps we will die. Better to die together, on the attack, like gods, than to die fleeing and singly, like rats in a cellar."

Another murmur, this time one of deep agreement. She had said it for all of them. Now was the time.

"The first head is mine," said a very tall Chinese man, with a rope of tiny skulls around his neck.[816] He began to walk, slowly and intently, up the mountain, shouldering a staff with a curved blade at the end of it, like a silver moon.

*   *   *

EVEN NOTHING CANNOT last forever.

He might have been there, been Nowhere, for ten minutes or for ten thousand years. It made no difference. Time was an idea for which he no longer had any need.

He could no longer remember his real name. He felt empty and cleansed, in that place that was not a place.

He was without form, and void.

He was nothing.

And into that nothing a voice said, "Ho-hoka, cousin. We got to talk."

And something that might once have been Shadow said, "Whiskey Jack?"

"Yeah," said Whiskey Jack, in the darkness. "You are a hard man to hunt down, when you're dead. You didn't go to any of the places I figured. I had to look all over before I thought of checking here. Say, you ever find your tribe?"

Shadow remembered the man and the girl in the disco beneath the spinning mirror-ball. "I guess I found my family. But no, I never found my tribe."

"Sorry to have to disturb you."

"No. You aren't sorry.[817] Let me be. I got what I wanted. I'm done."

"They are coming for you," said Whiskey Jack. "They are going to revive you."

"But I'm done," said Shadow. "It was all over and done."

"No such thing," said Whiskey Jack. "Never any such thing. We'll go to my place. You want a beer?"

He guessed he *would* like a beer, at that. "Sure."

"Get me one too. There's a cooler outside the door," said Whiskey Jack, and he pointed. They were in his shack.

Shadow opened the door to the shack with hands it

Sha Wujing, in traditional Chinese literature (note the necklace of skulls)

816. This may be Sha Wujing, a Buddhist monk who figures in the Ming Dynasty novel *Journey to the West*, by Wing Cheng'en. He was originally a general in Heaven but was exiled to the Earth by the Jade Emperor. There he was obedient to his master, the Buddhist pilgrim Tang Sanzang. Known as "Sand" or "Sandy," a name derived from his river-home, he wore a distinctive necklace of skulls. The character in the novel is clearly a version of earlier folkloric figures, and the necklace itself appears around the neck of several predecessors, including Tang Sanzang's own incarnation.

817. In the First Edition, this paragraph begins with, "Let me be."

seemed to him he had not possessed moments before. There was a plastic cooler filled with chunks of river-ice out there, and, in the ice, a dozen cans of Budweiser. He pulled out a couple of cans of beer and then sat in the doorway and looked out over the valley.

They were at the top of a hill, near a waterfall, swollen with melting snow and runoff. It fell, in stages, maybe seventy feet below them, maybe a hundred. The sun reflected from the ice which sheathed the trees that overhung the waterfall basin. The churning noise as the water crashed and fell filled the air.

"Where are we?" asked Shadow.

"Where you were last time," said Whiskey Jack. "My place. You planning on holding on to my Bud till it warms up? They aren't good like that."[818]

Shadow stood up and passed him the can of beer. "You didn't have a waterfall outside your place last time I was here," he said.

Whiskey Jack said nothing. He popped the top of the Bud, and drank half the can in one long slow swallow. Then he said, "You remember my nephew? Harry Bluejay? The poet? He traded his Buick for your Winnebago. Remember?"

"Sure. I didn't know he was a poet."

Whiskey Jack raised his chin and looked proud. "Best damn poet in America," he said.

He drained the rest of his can of beer, belched, and got another can, while Shadow popped open his own can of beer, and the two men sat outside on a rock, by the pale green ferns, in the morning sun, and they watched the falling water and they drank their beer. There was still snow on the ground, in the places where the shadows never lifted.

The earth was muddy and wet.

"Harry was diabetic," continued Whiskey Jack. "It happens. Too much. You people came to America, you take our sugar cane, potatoes and corn, then you sell us potato chips and caramel popcorn, and we're the ones who get sick." He sipped his beer, reflecting. "He'd won a couple of prizes for his poetry. There were people in Minnesota who wanted to

818. This sentence does not appear in the First Edition.

put his poems into a book. He was driving to Minnesota in a sports car to talk to them. He had traded your 'Bago for a yellow Miata. The doctors said they think he went into a coma while he was driving, went off the road, ran the car into one of your road signs. Too lazy to look at where you are, to read the mountains and the clouds, you people need road signs everywhere. And so Harry Bluejay went away forever, went to live with brother Wolf. So I said, nothing keeping me there any longer. I came north. Good fishing up here."

"I'm sorry about your nephew."

"Me too. So now I'm living here in the north. Long way from white man's diseases. White man's roads. White man's road signs. White man's yellow Miatas. White man's caramel popcorn."

"White man's beer?"

Whiskey Jack looked at the can. "When you people finally give up and go home, you can leave us the Budweiser breweries," he said.

"Where are we?" asked Shadow. "Am I on the tree? Am I dead? Am I here? I thought everything was finished. What's real?"

"Yes," said Whiskey Jack.

"*Yes?* What kind of an answer is *Yes?*"

"It's a good answer. True answer, too."

Shadow said, "Are you a god as well?"

Whiskey Jack shook his head. "I'm a culture hero," he said. "We do the same shit gods do, we just screw up more and nobody worships us. They tell stories about us, but they tell the ones which make us look bad along with the ones where we came out fairly okay."

"I see," said Shadow. And he did see, more or less.

"Look," said Whiskey Jack. "This is not a good country for gods. My people figured that out early on. There are creator spirits who found the earth or made it or shit it out, but you think about it: who's going to worship Coyote? He made love to Porcupine Woman and got his dick shot through with more needles than a pincushion. He'd argue with rocks and the rocks would win.[819]

819. This was a popular story told about Coyote, the trickster figure of many Native American religions.

"So, yeah, my people figured that maybe there's something at the back of it all, a creator, a great spirit, and so we say thank you to it, because it's always good to say thank you. But we never built churches. We didn't need to. The land was the church. The land was the religion. The land was older and wiser than the people who walked on it. It gave us salmon and corn and buffalo and passenger pigeons. It gave us wild rice and walleye. It gave us melon and squash and turkey. And we were the children of the land, just like the porcupine and the skunk and the blue jay."

He finished his second beer and gestured toward the river at the bottom of the waterfall. "You follow that river for a way, you'll get to the lakes where the wild rice grows. In wild rice time, you go out in your canoe with a friend, and you knock the wild rice into your canoe, and cook it, and store it, and it will keep you for a long time. Different places grow different foods. Go far enough south there are orange trees, lemon trees, and those squashy green guys, look like pears—"

"Avocados."

"Avocados," agreed Whiskey Jack. "That's them. They don't grow up this way. This is wild rice country. Moose country. What I'm trying to say is that America is like that. It's not good growing country for gods. They don't grow well here. They're like avocados trying to grow in wild rice country."

"They may not grow well," said Shadow, remembering, "but they're going to war."

That was the only time he ever saw Whiskey Jack laugh. It was almost a bark, and it had little humor in it. "Hey, Shadow," said Whiskey Jack. "If all your friends jumped off a cliff, would you jump off too?"

"Maybe." Shadow felt good. He didn't think it was just the beer. He couldn't remember the last time he had felt so alive, and so together.

"It's not going to be a war."

"Then what is it?"

Whiskey Jack crushed the beer can between his hands, pressing it until it was flat. "Look," he said, and pointed to the waterfall. The sun was high enough that it caught the waterfall spray: a rainbow nimbus hung in the air. Shadow thought it was the most beautiful thing he had ever seen.

"It's going to be a bloodbath," said Whiskey Jack, flatly.

Shadow saw it then. He saw it all, stark in its simplicity. He shook his head, then he began to chuckle, and he shook his head some more, and the chuckle became a full-throated laugh.

"You okay?"

"I'm fine," said Shadow. "I just saw the hidden Indians. Not all of them. But I saw them anyhow."

"Probably Ho Chunk, then. Those guys never could hide worth a damn." He looked up at the sun. "Time to go back," he said. He stood up.

"It's a two-man con," said Shadow. "It's not a war at all, is it?"

Whiskey Jack patted Shadow's arm. "You're not so dumb," he said.

They walked back to Whiskey Jack's shack. He opened the door. Shadow hesitated. "I wish I could stay here with you," he said. "This seems like a good place."

"There are a lot of good places," said Whiskey Jack. "That's kind of the point. Listen, gods die when they are forgotten. People too. But the land's still here. The good places, and the bad. The land isn't going anywhere. And neither am I."

Shadow closed the door. Something was pulling at him. He was alone in the darkness once more, but the darkness became brighter and brighter until it was burning like the sun.

And then the pain began.

✣   ✣   ✣

THERE WAS A woman who walked through a meadow, and spring flowers blossomed where she had passed. In this place and at this time, she called herself Easter.

She passed a place where, long ago, a farmhouse had stood. Even today several walls were still standing, jutting out of the weeds and the meadow-grass like rotten teeth. A thin rain was falling. The clouds were dark and low, and it was cold.

A little way beyond the place where the farmhouse had been there was a tree, a huge silver-gray tree, winter-dead to all appearances, and leafless, and in front of the tree, on the grass, were frayed clumps of colorless fabric. The woman stopped at the fabric, and bent down, and picked up something brownish-white: it was a much-gnawed fragment of bone which might, once, have been a part of a human skull. She tossed it back down onto the grass.

Then she looked at the man on the tree and she smiled wryly. "They just aren't as interesting naked," she said. "It's the unwrapping that's half the fun. Like with gifts, and eggs."

The hawk-headed man who walked beside her looked down at his penis and seemed, for the first time, to become aware of his own nakedness. He said, "I can look at the sun without even blinking."

"That's very clever of you," Easter told him, reassuringly. "Now, let's get him down from there."

The wet ropes that held Shadow to the tree had long ago weathered and rotted, and they parted easily as the two people pulled on them. The body on the tree slipped and slid down toward the roots. They caught him as he fell, and they took him up, carrying him easily, although he was a very big man, and they put him down in the gray meadow.

The body on the grass was cold, and it did not breathe. There was a patch of dried black blood on its side, as if it had been stabbed with a spear.

"What now?"

"Now," she said, "we warm him. You know what you have to do."

"I know. I cannot."

"If you are not willing to help, then you should not have called me here."

"But it has been too long."[820]

"It has been too long for all of us."

"And I am quite mad."

"I know." She reached out a white hand to Horus, and she

820. This sentence and the next three do not appear in the First Edition.

touched his black hair. He blinked at her, intently. Then he shimmered, as if in a heat haze.

The hawk eye that faced her glinted orange, as if a flame had just been kindled inside it; a flame that had been long extinguished.[821]

The hawk took to the air, and it swung upward, circling and ascending in a rising gyre, circling the place in the gray clouds where the sun might conceivably be, and as the hawk rose it became first a dot and then a speck, and then, to the naked eye, nothing at all, something that could only be imagined. The clouds began to thin and to evaporate, creating a patch of blue sky through which the sun glared. The single bright sunbeam penetrating the clouds and bathing the meadow was beautiful, but the image faded as more clouds vanished. Soon the morning sun was blazing down on that meadow like a summer sun at noon, burning the water vapor from the morning's rain into mists and burning the mist off into nothing at all.

The golden sun bathed the body on the floor of the meadow with its radiance and its heat. Shades of pink and of warm brown touched the dead thing.

The woman dragged the fingers of her right hand lightly across the body's chest. She imagined she could feel a shiver in his breast—something that was not a heartbeat, but still . . . She let her hand remain there, on his chest, just above his heart.

She lowered her lips to Shadow's lips, and she breathed into his lungs, a gentle in and out, and then the breath became a kiss. Her kiss was gentle, and it tasted of spring rains and meadow flowers.

The wound in his side began to flow with liquid blood once more—a scarlet blood, which oozed like liquid rubies in the sunlight, and then the bleeding stopped.

She kissed his cheek and his forehead. "Come on," she said. "Time to get up. It's all happening. You don't want to miss it."

His eyes fluttered, and then they opened, two eyes of a gray so deep it was colorless, the gray of evening, and he looked at her.

821. Horus was of course the sun-god of Egypt.

She smiled, and then she removed her hand from his chest.

He said, "You called me back." He said it slowly, as if he had forgotten how to speak English. There was hurt in his voice, and puzzlement.

"Yes."

"I was done. I was judged. It was over. You called me back. You dared."

"I'm sorry."

"Yes."

He sat up, slowly. He winced, and touched his side. Then he looked puzzled: there was a beading of wet blood there, but there was no wound beneath it.

He reached out a hand, and she put her arm around him and helped him to his feet. He looked across the meadow as if he was trying to remember the names of the things he was looking at: the flowers in the long grass, the ruins of the farmhouse, the haze of green buds that fogged the branches of the huge silver tree.

"Do you remember?" she asked. "Do you remember what you learned?"

"Yes. It will fade though. Like a dream. I know that.[822] I lost my name, and I lost my heart. And you brought me back."

"I'm sorry," she said, for the second time. "They are going to fight, soon. The old gods and the new ones."

"You want me to fight for you? You wasted your time."

"I brought you back because that was what I had to do," she said. "It's what I can do. It's what I'm best at.[823] What you do now is whatever you have to do. Your call. I did my part." Suddenly, she became aware of his nakedness, and she blushed a burning scarlet flush, and she looked down and away.

✢   ✢   ✢

IN THE RAIN and the cloud, shadows moved up the side of the mountain, up to the rock pathways.

White foxes padded up the hill in company with red-haired men in green jackets. There was a bull-headed mi-

822. The preceding sentences of this paragraph do not appear in the First Edition.

823. This and the preceding sentence do not appear in the First Edition.

notaur walking beside an iron-fingered dactyl.[824] A pig, a monkey, and a sharp-toothed ghoul clambered up the hillside,[825] in company with a blue-skinned man holding a flaming bow,[826] a bear with flowers twined into its fur, and a man in golden chain mail holding his sword of eyes.[827]

Beautiful Antinous, who was the lover of Hadrian, walked up the hillside at the head of a company of leather queens, their arms and chests steroid-swollen and sculpted into perfect shapes.[828]

A gray-skinned man, his one cyclopean eye a huge cabochon emerald, walked stiffly up the hill, ahead of several squat and swarthy men, their impassive faces as regular as Aztec carvings: they knew the secrets that the jungles had swallowed.

A sniper at the top of the hill took careful aim at a white fox, and fired. There was an explosion, and a puff of cordite, gunpowder scent on the wet air. The corpse was a young Japanese woman with her stomach blown away, and her face all bloody. Slowly, the corpse began to fade.[829]

The people continued up the hill, on two legs, on four legs, on no legs at all.

✦　✦　✦

THE DRIVE THROUGH the Tennessee mountain country had been startlingly beautiful whenever the storm had eased, and nerve-wracking whenever the rain had pelted down. Town and Laura had talked and talked and talked the whole way. He was so glad he had met her. It was like meeting an old friend, a really good old friend you'd simply never met before. They talked history and movies and music, and she turned out to be the only person, and I mean the *only* other person, he had ever met who had seen a foreign film (Mr. Town was sure it was Spanish, while Laura was just as certain it was Polish) from the sixties called *The Manuscript Found in Saragossa*, a film he had been starting to believe he had hallucinated.[830]

When Laura pointed out the first SEE ROCK CITY barn to him he chuckled and admitted that that was where he was headed. She said that was so cool. She always wanted

824. A mythical race of male beings, offspring of Cybele or Rhea, the mothergoddess. The dactyls were smiths, and Ovid tells of one who was made diamond-hard by Zeus because he offended Rhea.

825. These are the three companions of Xuanzang, the Buddhist pilgrim who is the protagonist of the seventeenth-century Chinese novel *Journey to the West* (*Xiyou Ji*).

826. This is likely Rama, an avatar of the Hindu god Vishnu, commonly depicted in this manner.

827. Gaiman could not, in private conversation with this editor, identify this figure.

828. Antinous, a Greek youth and lover of the emperor Hadrian, probably lived between 111 and 130 C.E. Hadrian deified Antinous after his death, naming a city after him and commissioning games in his name. "Leather queens" here means gay men with a fetish for leather.

829. This is one of the kitsune. See note 578, above.

Dactyls

830. *The Manuscript Found in Saragossa* is a novel by the Polish count Jan Potocki at the end of the eighteenth century. The novel was adapted into a 1965 Polish-language film, *The Saragossa Manuscript*, set and shot in Spain (perhaps affecting Town's recollection), and is a collection of erotic and supernatural tales. The film was greatly admired by Martin Scorsese and Francis Ford Coppola, who, together with the Grateful Dead's Jerry Garcia, financed its restoration in the 1990s.

831. Laura paraphrases Blanche Dubois, from Tennessee Williams's 1947 play *A Streetcar Named Desire*, who expresses, "I have always depended on the kindness of strangers." Jessica Tandy originated the role on Broadway. The line is repeated in the 1951 film adaptation starring Vivian Leigh. The balance of this paragraph does not appear in the First Edition.

to visit those kinds of places, but she never made the time, and always regretted it later. That was why she was on the road right now. She was having an adventure.

She was a travel agent, she told him. Separated from her husband. She admitted that she didn't think they could ever get back together, and said it was her fault.

"I can't believe that."

She sighed. "It's true, Mack. I'm just not the woman he married anymore."

Well, he told her, people change, and before he could think he was telling her everything he *could* tell her about his life, he was even telling her about Woody and Stoner, how the three of them were the three musketeers, and the two of them were killed, you think you'd get hardened to that kind of thing in government work, but you never did. It never happened.

And she reached out one hand—it was cold enough that he turned up the car's heating—and squeezed his hand tightly in hers.

Lunchtime, they ate bad Japanese food while a thunderstorm lowered on Knoxville, and Town didn't care that the food was late, that the miso soup was cold, or that the sushi was warm.

He loved the fact that she was out, with him, having an adventure.

"Well," confided Laura, "I hated the idea of getting stale. I was just rotting away where I was. So I set off without my car and without my credit cards. I'm just relying on the kindness of strangers.[831] And I've had the best time. People have been so good to me."

"Aren't you scared?" he asked. "I mean, you could be stranded, you could be mugged, you could starve."

She shook her head. Then she said, with a hesitant smile, "I met you, didn't I?" and he couldn't find anything to say.

When the meal was over they ran through the storm to his car holding Japanese-language newspapers to cover their heads, and they laughed as they ran, like schoolchildren in the rain.

"How far can I take you?" he asked, when they made it

back into the car. "I'll go as far as you're going, Mack," she told him, shyly.

He was glad he hadn't used the Big Mack line. This woman wasn't a bar-room one-nighter, Mr. Town knew that in his soul. It might have taken him fifty years to find her, but this was finally it, this was the one, this wild, magical woman with the long dark hair.

This was love.

"Look," he said, as they approached Chattanooga. The wipers slooshed the rain across the windshield, blurring the gray of the city. "How about I find a motel for you tonight? I'll pay for it. And once I make my delivery, we can. Well, we can take a hot bath together, for a start. Warm you up."

"That sounds wonderful," said Laura. "What are you delivering?"

"That stick," he told her, and chuckled. "The one on the back seat."

"Okay," she said, humoring him. "Then don't tell me, Mister Mysterious."

He told her it would be best if she waited in the car in the Rock City parking lot while he made his delivery. He drove up the side of Lookout Mountain in the gusting rain, never breaking thirty miles per hour, with his headlights burning.

They parked at the back of the parking lot. He turned off the engine.

"Hey. Mack. Before you get out of the car, don't I get a hug?" asked Laura with a smile.

"You surely do," said Mr. Town, and he put his arms around her, and she snuggled close to him while the rain pattered a tattoo on the roof of the Ford Explorer. He could smell her hair. There was a faintly unpleasant scent beneath the perfume. Travel would do it, every time. That bath, he decided, was a real must for both of them. He wondered if there was anyplace in Chattanooga where he could get those scented bath bombs his first wife had loved so much. Laura raised her head against his, and her hand stroked the line of his neck, absently.

"Mack . . . I keep thinking. You must really want to know

what happened to those friends of yours," she said. "Woody and Stone. Do you?"

"Yeah," he said, moving his lips down to hers, for their first kiss. "Sure I do."

So she showed him.

✦   ✦   ✦

SHADOW WALKED THE meadow, making his own slow circles around the trunk of the tree, gradually widening his circle. Sometimes he would stop and pick something up: a flower, or a leaf, or a pebble, or a twig, or a blade of grass. He would examine it minutely, as if concentrating entirely on the *twigness* of the twig, the *leafness* of the leaf, as if he were seeing it for the first time.

Easter found herself reminded of the gaze of a baby, at the point where it learns to focus.

She did not dare to talk to him. At that moment, it would have been sacrilegious. She watched him, exhausted as she was, and she wondered.

About twenty feet out from the base of the tree, half-overgrown with long meadow-grass and dead creepers, he found a canvas bag. Shadow picked it up, untied the knots at the top of the bag, loosened the draw-string.

The clothes he pulled out were his own. They were old, but still serviceable. He turned the shoes over in his hands. He stroked the fabric of the shirt, the wool of the sweater, stared at them as if he were looking at them across a million years.

For some time he looked at them, then, one by one, he put them on.

He put his hands into his pockets, and looked puzzled as he pulled one hand out holding what looked to Easter like a white and gray marble.

He said, "No coins." It was the first thing he had said in several hours.

"No coins?" echoed Easter.

He shook his head. "It was good to have the coins," he said.[832] "They gave me something to do with my hands." He bent down to pull on his shoes.

832. This sentence does not appear in the First Edition.

Once he was dressed, he looked more normal. Grave, though. She wondered how far he had traveled, and what it had cost him to return. He was not the first whose return she had initiated, and she knew that, soon enough, the million-year stare would fade, and the memories and the dreams that he had brought back from the tree would be elided by the world of things you could touch. That was the way it always went.

She led their way to the rear of the meadow. Her mount waited in the trees.

"It can't carry both of us," she told him. "I'll make my own way home."

Shadow nodded. He seemed to be trying to remember something. Then he opened his mouth, and he screeched a cry of welcome and of joy.

The thunderbird opened its cruel beak, and it screeched a welcome back at him.

Superficially, at least, it resembled a condor. Its feathers were black, with a purplish sheen, and its neck was banded with white. Its beak was black and cruel: a raptor's beak, made for tearing. At rest, on the ground, with its wings folded away, it was the size of a black bear, and its head was on a level with Shadow's own.

Horus said, proudly, "I brought him. They live in the mountains."

Shadow nodded. "I had a dream of thunderbirds once," he said. "Damnedest dream I ever had."

The thunderbird opened its beak and made a surprisingly gentle noise, *Crawroo?* "You heard my dream too?" asked Shadow.

He reached out a hand and rubbed it gently against the bird's head. The thunderbird pushed up against him like an affectionate pony. He scratched it behind where the ears must have been.

Shadow turned to Easter. "You rode him here?"

"Yes," she said. "You can ride him back, if he lets you."

"How do you ride him?"

"It's easy," she said. "If you don't fall. Like riding the lightning."

833. This sentence and the next two do not appear in the First Edition.

834. In the Manuscript, Shadow asks Easter whether she can bring Laura back from the dead, but Easter states that she cannot.

"Will I see you back there?"

She shook her head. "I'm done, honey," she told him. "You go do what you need to do. I'm tired. Bringing you back like that . . . it took a lot out of me.[833] I need to rest, to save up my energies until my festival begins. I'm sorry. Good luck."

Shadow nodded. "Whiskey Jack. I saw him. After I passed on. He came and found me. We drank beer together."

"Yes," she said. "I'm sure you did."

"Will I ever see you again?" asked Shadow.

She looked at him with eyes the green of ripening corn. She said nothing. Then, abruptly, she shook her head. "I doubt it," she said.

Shadow clambered awkwardly onto the thunderbird's back. He felt like a mouse on the back of a hawk. There was an ozone taste in his mouth, metallic and blue. Something crackled. The thunderbird extended its wings, and began to flap them, hard.[834]

As the ground fell away beneath them, Shadow clung on, his heart pounding in his chest like a wild thing.

It was exactly like riding the lightning.

✳   ✳   ✳

LAURA TOOK THE stick from the back seat of the car. She left Mr. Town in the front seat of the Ford Explorer, and climbed out of the car, and walked through the rain to Rock City. The ticket office was closed. The door to the gift shop was not locked and she walked through it, past the rock candy and the display of SEE ROCK CITY birdhouses, into the Eighth Wonder of the World.

Nobody challenged her, although she passed several men and women on the path, in the rain. Many of them looked faintly artificial; several of them were translucent. She walked across a swinging rope bridge. She passed the white deer gardens, and pushed herself through the Fat Man's Squeeze, where the path ran between two rock walls.

And, in the end, she stepped over a chain, with a sign on it telling her that this part of the attraction was closed, and she went into a cavern, and she saw a man sitting on a plastic chair, in front of a diorama of drunken gnomes. He was reading the *Washington Post* by the light of a small electric lantern. When he saw her he folded the paper and placed it beneath his chair. He stood up, a tall man with close-cropped orange hair in an expensive raincoat, and he gave her a small bow.

"I shall assume that Mister Town is dead," he said. "Welcome, spear-carrier."

"Thank you. I'm sorry about Mack," she said. "Were you friends?"

"Not at all. He should have kept himself alive, if he wanted to keep his job. But you brought his stick." He looked her up and down with eyes that glimmered like the orange embers of a dying fire. "I am afraid you have the advantage of me. They call me Mister World, here at the top of the hill."

"I'm Shadow's wife."

"Of course. The lovely Laura," he said. "I should have recognized you. He had several photographs of you up above his bed, in the cell that once we shared. And, if you don't mind my saying so, you are looking lovelier than you have any right to look. Shouldn't you be further along on the whole road-to-rot-and-ruin business by now?"

"I was," she said simply. "I was much further along.[835] I'm not sure what changed. I know when I started feeling better. It was this morning. Those women, in the farm, they gave me water from their well."

An eyebrow raised. "Urd's Well? Surely not."

She pointed to herself. Her skin was pale, and her eye-sockets were dark, but she was manifestly whole: if she was indeed a walking corpse, she was freshly dead.

"It won't last," said Mr. World. "The Norns gave you a little taste of the past. It will dissolve into the present soon enough, and then those pretty blue eyes will roll out of their sockets and ooze down those pretty cheeks, which will, by then, of course, no longer be so pretty. By the way, you have my stick. Can I have it, please?"

He pulled out a pack of Lucky Strikes, took a cigarette, lit it with a disposable black Bic.

She said, "Can I have one of those?"

"Sure. I'll give you a cigarette if you give me my stick."

835. This sentence and the next three do not appear in the First Edition.

836. This sentence and the next do not appear in the First Edition.

837. The balance of this paragraph does not appear in the First Edition.

838. Mr. World, it will be seen, has a history with mistletoe. According to the *Dictionary of Ancient Deities*, Loki "caused the death of Balder by convincing the blind Hoth to throw mistletoe at him, the only thing said to have been able to kill him. Balder would have been allowed to leave Hel if every living thing would weep for him. When Loki heard of this edict, he took on the form of a woman and became the one exception and would not weep for him." (p. 294)

839. This sentence does not appear in the First Edition.

840. This sentence does not appear in the First Edition. In the First Draft, at this point, Laura asks about Wednesday's involvement. Loki explains that the original plan was to fake Odin's death, with a blood-bladder, an off-screen shot, and appropriate dying exhortations by Odin. However, Loki decided that it was easier just to really kill him.

"No," she said. "If you want it, it's worth more than just a cigarette."

He said nothing.

She said, "I want answers. I want to know things."

He lit a cigarette and passed it to her. She took it and inhaled. Then she blinked. "I can almost taste this one," she said. "I think maybe I can." She smiled. "Mm. Nicotine."

"Yes," he said. "Why did you go to the women in the farmhouse?"

"Shadow told me to go to them," she said. "He said to ask them for water."

"I wonder if he knew what it would do. Probably not. Still, that's the good thing about having him dead on his tree. I know where he is at all times, now. He's off the board."

"You set up my husband," she said. "You set him up all the way, you people. He has a good heart, you know that?"

"Yes," said Mr. World. "I know."

"Why did you want him?"[836]

"Patterns, and distraction," said Mr. World. "When this is all done with, I guess I'll sharpen a stick of mistletoe and go down to the ash tree, and ram it through his eye.[837] That's what those morons fighting out there have never been able to grasp. It's never a matter of old and new. It's only about patterns. Now. My stick, please."

"Why do you want it?"

"It's a souvenir of this whole sorry mess," said Mr. World. "Don't worry, it's not mistletoe."[838] He flashed a grin. "It symbolizes a spear, and in this sorry world, the symbol *is* the thing."

The noises from outside grew louder.

"Which side are you on?" she asked.

"It's not about sides," he told her. "But since you asked, I'm on the winning side. Always. That's what I do best."[839]

She nodded, and she did not let go of the stick. "I can see that," she said.[840]

She turned away from him, and looked out of the cavern door. Far below her, in the rocks, she could see something that glowed and pulsed. It wrapped itself around a thin, mauve-faced bearded man, who was beating at it with a squeegee stick, the kind of squeegee that people like him use to smear across car windshields at traffic lights. There was a scream, and they both disappeared from view.

"Okay. I'll give you the stick," she said.

Mr. World's voice came from behind her. "Good girl," he said reassuringly, in a way that struck her as being both patronizing and indefinably male. It made her skin crawl.

She waited in the rock doorway until she could hear his breath in her ear. She had to wait until he got close enough. She had that much figured out.

✳ ✳ ✳

THE RIDE WAS more than exhilarating; it was electric.

They swept through the storm like jagged bolts of lightning, flashing from cloud to cloud; they moved like the thunder's roar, like the swell and rip of the hurricane. It was a crackling, impossible journey,[841] and Shadow forgot to be scared almost immediately. You cannot be afraid when you ride the thunderbird. There is no fear: only the power of the storm, unstoppable and all-consuming, and the joy of the flight.

Shadow dug his fingers into the thunderbird's feathers, feeling the static prickle on his skin. Blue sparks writhed across his hands like tiny snakes. Rain washed his face.

"This is the best," he shouted, over the roar of the storm.

As if it understood him, the bird began to rise higher, every wing-beat a clap of thunder, and it swooped and dove and tumbled through the dark clouds.

"In my dream, I was hunting you," said Shadow, his words ripped away by the wind. "In my dream. I had to bring back a feather."

Yes. The word was a static crackle in the radio of his mind. *They came to us for feathers, to prove that they were men; and they came to us to cut the stones from our heads, to give their dead our lives.*

An image filled his mind then: of a thunderbird—a female, he assumed, for her plumage was brown, not black—lying freshly dead on the side of a mountain. Beside it was a woman. She was breaking open its skull with a knob of flint.

841. The balance of this sentence and the next do not appear in the First Edition.

She picked through the wet shards of bone and the brains until she found a smooth clear stone the tawny color of garnet, opalescent fires flickering in its depths. *Eagle stones,* thought Shadow. She was going to take it to her infant son, dead these last three nights, and she would lay it on his cold breast. By the next sunrise the boy would be alive and laughing, and the jewel would be gray and clouded and, like the bird it had been stolen from, quite dead.

"I understand," he said to the bird.

The bird threw back its head and crowed, and its cry was the thunder.

The world beneath them flashed past in one strange dream.

✤ ✤ ✤

LAURA ADJUSTED HER grip on the stick, and she waited for the man she knew as Mr. World to come to her. She was facing away from him, looking out at the storm, and the dark green hills below.

In this sorry world, she thought, *the symbol is the thing. Yes.*

She felt his hand close softly onto her right shoulder.

Good, she thought. *He does not want to alarm me. He is scared that I will throw his stick out into the storm, that it will tumble down the mountainside, and he will lose it.*

She leaned back, just a little, until she was touching his chest with her back. His left arm curved around her. It was an intimate gesture. His left hand was open in front of her. She closed both of her hands around the top of the stick, exhaled, concentrated.

"Please. My stick," he said, in her ears.

"Yes," she said. "It's yours." And then, not knowing if it would mean anything, she said, "I dedicate this death to Shadow," and she stabbed the stick into her chest, just below the breastbone, felt it writhe and change in her hands as the stick became a spear.

The boundary between sensation and pain had diffused since she had died. She felt the spear head penetrate her chest, felt it push out through her back. A moment's resistance—she pushed harder—and the spear thrust into Mr. World. She could feel the warm breath of him on the cool skin of her neck, as he wailed in hurt and surprise, impaled on the spear.

She did not recognize the words he spoke, nor the language he said them in. She pushed the shaft of the spear further in, forcing it through her body, into and through his.

She could feel his hot blood spurting onto her back.

"Bitch," he said, in English. "You fucking bitch." There was a wet gurgling quality to his voice. She guessed that the blade of the spear must have sliced a lung. Mr. World was moving now, or trying to move, and every move he made rocked her too: they were joined by the pole, impaled together like two fish on a single spear. He now had a knife in one hand, she saw, and he stabbed her chest and breasts randomly and wildly with the knife, unable to see what he was doing.

She did not care. What are knife-cuts to a corpse?

She brought her fist down, hard, on his waving wrist, and the knife went flying to the floor of the cavern. She kicked it away.

And now he was crying and wailing. She could feel him pushing against her, his hands fumbling at her back, his hot tears on her neck. His blood was soaking her back, spurting down the back of her legs.

"This must look so undignified," she said, in a dead whisper which was not without a certain dark amusement.

She felt Mr. World stumble behind her, and she stumbled too, and then she slipped in the blood—all of it his—that was puddling on the floor of the cave, and they both went down.

✦   ✦   ✦

THE THUNDERBIRD LANDED in the Rock City parking lot. Rain was falling in sheets. Shadow could barely see a dozen feet in front of his face. He let go of the thunderbird's feathers and half-slipped, half-tumbled to the wet tarmac.

The bird looked at him.[842] Lightning flashed, and the bird was gone.

842. This sentence does not appear in the First Edition.

Shadow climbed to his feet.

The parking lot was three-quarters empty. Shadow started toward the entrance. He passed a brown Ford Explorer, parked against a rock wall. There was something deeply familiar about the car, and he glanced up at it curiously, noticing the man inside the car, slumped over the steering wheel as if asleep.

Shadow pulled open the driver's door.

He had last seen Mr. Town standing outside the motel in the center of America. The expression on his face was one of surprise. His neck had been expertly broken. Shadow touched the man's face. Still warm.

Shadow could smell a scent on the air in the car; it was faint, like the perfume of someone who left a room years before, but Shadow would have known it anywhere. He slammed the door of the Explorer and made his way across the parking lot.

As he walked he felt a twinge in his side, a sharp, jabbing pain that must have only existed in his head, as it lasted for only a second, or less, and then it was gone.

There was nobody in the gift shop, nobody selling tickets. He walked through the building and out into the gardens of Rock City.

Thunder rumbled, and it rattled the branches of the trees and shook deep inside the huge rocks, and the rain fell with cold violence. It was late afternoon, but it was dark as night.

A trail of lightning speared across the clouds, and Shadow wondered if that was the thunderbird returning to its high crags, or just an atmospheric discharge, or whether the two ideas were, on some level, the same thing.

And of course they were. That was the point, after all.

Somewhere a man's voice called out. Shadow heard it. The only words he recognized or thought he recognized were "... *to Odin!*"

Shadow hurried across Seven States Flag Court, the flagstones now running fast with a dangerous amount of rainwater. Once he slipped on the slick stone. There was a thick layer of cloud surrounding the mountain, and in the gloom and the storm beyond the courtyard he could see no states at all.

There was no sound. The place seemed utterly abandoned.

He called out, and imagined he heard something answering. He walked toward the place from which he thought the sound had come.

Nobody. Nothing. Just a chain marking the entrance to a cave as off-limits to guests.

Shadow stepped over the chain.

He looked around, peering into the darkness.

His skin prickled.

A voice from behind him, in the shadows, said, very quietly, "You have never disappointed me."

Shadow did not turn. "That's weird," he said. "I disappointed myself all the way. Every time."

"Not at all," chuckled the voice. "You did everything you were meant to do, and more. You took everybody's attention, so they never looked at the hand with the coin in it. It's called misdirection. And there's power in the sacrifice of a son—power enough, and more than enough, to get the whole ball rolling. To tell the truth, I'm proud of you."

"It was crooked," said Shadow. "All of it. None of it was for real. It was just a set-up for a massacre."

"Exactly," said Wednesday's voice from the shadows. "It was crooked. But it was the only game in town."

"I want Laura," said Shadow. "I want Loki. Where are they?"

There was only silence. A spray of rain gusted at him. Thunder rumbled somewhere close at hand.

He walked further in.

Loki Lie-Smith sat on the ground with his back to a metal cage. Inside the cage, drunken pixies tended their still. He was covered with a blanket. Only his face showed, and his hands, white and long, came around the blanket. An electric lantern sat on a chair beside him. The lantern's batteries were close to failing, and the light it cast was faint and yellow.

He looked pale, and he looked rough.

His eyes, though. His eyes were still fiery, and they glared at Shadow as he walked through the cavern.

When Shadow was several paces from Loki, he stopped.

"You are too late," said Loki. His voice was raspy and wet. "I have thrown the spear. I have dedicated the battle. It has begun."

"No shit," said Shadow.

"No shit," said Loki. "It does not matter what you do any more. It is too late."[843]

"Okay," said Shadow. He stopped and thought. Then he said, "You say there's some spear you had to throw to kick off the battle. Like the whole Uppsala thing.[844] This is the battle you'll be feeding on. Am I right?"

Silence. He could hear Loki breathing, a ghastly rattling inhalation.

"I figured it out," said Shadow. "Kind of. I'm not sure when I figured it out. Maybe when I was hanging on the tree. Maybe before. It was from something Wednesday said to me, at Christmas."

Loki just stared at him, saying nothing.

"It's just a two-man con," said Shadow. "Like the bishop and the diamond necklace and the cop. Like the guy with the fiddle, and the guy who wants to buy the fiddle, and the poor sap in between them who pays for the fiddle. Two men, who appear to be on opposite sides, playing the same game."

Loki whispered, "You are ridiculous."

"Why? I liked what you did at the motel. That was smart. You needed to be there, to make sure that everything went according to plan. I saw you. I even realized who you were. And I still never twigged that you were their Mister World. Or maybe I did, somewhere down deep.[845] I knew I knew your voice, anyway."

Shadow raised his voice. "You can come out," he said, to the cavern. "Wherever you are. Show yourself."

The wind howled in the opening of the cavern, and it drove a spray of rainwater in toward them. Shadow shivered.

843. This sentence does not appear in the First Edition.

844. See note 699, above.

845. This sentence and the next do not appear in the First Edition.

"I'm tired of being played for a sucker," said Shadow. "Show yourself. Let me see you."

There was a change in the shadows at the back of the cave. Something became more solid; something shifted. "You know too damned much, m'boy," said Wednesday's familiar rumble.

"So they didn't kill you."

"They killed me," said Wednesday, from the shadows. "None of this would have worked if they hadn't." His voice was faint—not actually quiet, but there was a quality to it that made Shadow think of an old radio not quite tuned in to a distant station. "If I hadn't died for real, we could never have got them here," said Wednesday. "Kali and the Morrigan and the *Loa* and the fucking Albanians and—well, you've seen them all. It was my death that drew them all together. I was the sacrificial lamb."

"No," said Shadow. "You were the Judas Goat."

The wraith-shape in the shadows swirled and shifted. "Not at all. That implies that I was betraying the old gods for the new. Which was not what we were doing."

"Not at all," whispered Loki.

"I can see that," said Shadow. "You two weren't betraying either side. You were betraying both sides."

"I guess we were at that," said Wednesday. He sounded pleased with himself.

"You wanted a massacre. You needed a blood sacrifice. A sacrifice of gods."

The wind grew stronger; the howl across the cave door became a screech, as if of something immeasurably huge in pain.

"And why the hell not? I've been trapped in this damned land for almost twelve hundred years. My blood is thin. I'm hungry."

"And you two feed on death," said Shadow.

He thought he could see Wednesday, now,[846] standing in the shadows. Behind him—through him—were the bars of a cage which held what looked like plastic leprechauns. He was a shape made of darkness, who became more real the

846. The balance of this sentence and the next do not appear in the First Edition.

more Shadow looked away from him, allowed him to take shape in his peripheral vision.

"I feed on death that is dedicated to me," said Wednesday.

"Like my death on the tree," said Shadow.

"That," said Wednesday, "was special."

"And do you also feed on death?" asked Shadow, looking at Loki.

Loki shook his head, wearily.

"No, of course not," said Shadow. "*You* feed on chaos."

Loki smiled at that, a brief pained smile, and orange flames danced in his eyes, and flickered like burning lace beneath his pale skin.

"We couldn't have done it without you," said Wednesday, from the corner of Shadow's eye. "I'd been with so many women . . ."

"You needed a son," said Shadow.

Wednesday's ghost-voice echoed. "I needed *you*, my boy. Yes. My own boy. I knew that you had been conceived, but your mother left the country.[847] It took us so long to find you. And when we did find you, you were in prison. We needed to find out what made you tick. What buttons we could press to make you move. Who you were." Loki looked, momentarily, pleased with himself. Shadow wanted to hit him.[848] "And you had a wife to go back home to. It was unfortunate. Not insurmountable."

"She was no good for you," whispered Loki. "You were better off without her."

"If it could have been any other way," said Wednesday, and this time Shadow knew what he meant.

"And if she'd had—the grace—to stay dead," panted Loki. "Wood and Stone—were good men. You were going—to be allowed to escape—when the train crossed the Dakotas . . ."

"Where is she?" asked Shadow.

Loki reached a pale arm, and pointed to the back of the cavern.

"She went that-a-way," he said. Then, without warning, he tipped forward, his body collapsing onto the rock floor.

847. It remains unclear whether the impregnation of Shadow's mother was intentional. It sounds like Odin was simply impregnating as many women as possible, hoping one of them would produce a son who might be pliable.

848. This sentence does not appear in the First Edition.

Shadow saw what the blanket had hidden from him; the pool of blood, the hole through Loki's back, the fawn raincoat soaked black with blood. "What happened?" he said.

Loki said nothing.

Shadow did not think he would be saying anything any more.

"Your wife happened to him, m'boy," said Wednesday's distant voice. He had become harder to see, as if he was fading back into the ether. "But the battle will bring him back. As the battle will bring me back for good. I'm a ghost, and he's a corpse, but we've still won. The game was rigged."

"Rigged games," said Shadow, remembering, "are the easiest to beat."

There was no answer. Nothing moved in the shadows.

Shadow said, "Goodbye," and then he said, "Father." But by then there was no trace of anybody else in the cavern. Nobody at all.

Shadow walked back up to the Seven States Flag Court, but saw nobody, and heard nothing but the crack and whip of the flags in the storm-wind. There were no people with swords at the Thousand-Ton Balanced Rock, no defenders of the Swing-A-Long Bridge. He was alone.

There was nothing to see. The place was deserted. It was an empty battlefield.

No. Not deserted. Not exactly.

He was just in the wrong place.[849]

This was Rock City. It had been a place of awe and worship for thousands of years; today the millions of tourists who walked through the gardens and swung their way across the Swing-A-Long Bridge had the same effect as water turning a million prayer wheels. Reality was thin here. And Shadow knew where the battle must be taking place.

With that, he began to walk. He remembered how he had felt on the Carousel, tried to feel like that, but in a new moment of time . . .

He remembered turning the Winnebago, shifting it at right angles to *everything*. He tried to capture that sensation—

And then, easily and perfectly, it happened.

849. This sentence does not appear in the First Edition.

It was like pushing through a membrane, like plunging up from deep water into air. With one step he had moved from the tourist path on the mountain to . . .

To somewhere real. He was Backstage.

He was still on the top of a mountain. That much remained the same. But it was so much more than that. This mountaintop was the quintessence of place, the heart of things as they were. Compared to it, the Lookout Mountain he had left was a painting on a backdrop, or a papier-mâché model seen on a TV screen—merely a representation of the thing, not the thing itself.

This was the true place.

The rock walls formed a natural amphitheater. Paths of stone wound around and across it, forming twisty natural bridges that Eschered through and across the rock walls.

And the sky . . .

The sky was dark. It was lit, and the world beneath it was illuminated, by a burning greenish-white streak, brighter than the sun, which forked crazily across the sky from end to end, like a white rip in the darkened sky.

It was lightning, Shadow realized. Lightning held in one frozen moment that stretched into forever. The light it cast was harsh and unforgiving: it washed out faces, hollowed eyes into dark pits.

This was the moment of the storm.

The paradigms were shifting. He could feel it. The old world, a world of infinite vastness and illimitable resources and future, was being confronted by something else—a web of energy, of opinions, of gulfs.

People believe, thought Shadow. It's what people do. They believe. And then they will not take responsibility for their beliefs; they conjure things, and do not trust the conjurations. People populate the darkness; with ghosts, with gods, with electrons, with tales. People imagine, and people believe: and it is that belief, that rock-solid belief, that makes things happen.

The mountaintop was an arena; he saw that immediately. And on each side of the arena he could see them arrayed.

They were too big. Everything was too big in that place.

There were old gods in that place: gods with skins the brown of old mushrooms, the pink of chicken-flesh, the yellow of autumn leaves. Some were crazy and some were sane. Shadow recognized the old gods. He'd met them already, or he'd met others like them. There were ifrits and piskies, giants and dwarfs. He saw the woman he had met in the darkened bedroom in Rhode Island, saw the writhing green snake-coils of her hair.[850] He saw Mama-ji, from the Carousel, and there was blood on her hands and a smile on her face. He knew them all.

He recognized the new ones, too.

There was somebody who had to be a railroad baron, in an antique suit, his watch-chain stretched across his vest. He had the air of one who had seen better days. His forehead twitched.

There were the great gray gods of the airplanes, heirs to all the dreams of heavier-than-air travel.

There were car gods there: a powerful, serious-faced contingent, with blood on their black gloves and on their chrome teeth: recipients of human sacrifice on a scale undreamed-of since the Aztecs. Even they looked uncomfortable. Worlds change.

Others had faces of smudged phosphors; they glowed gently, as if they existed in their own light.

Shadow felt sorry for them all.

There was an arrogance to the new ones. Shadow could see that. But there was also a fear.

They were afraid that unless they kept pace with a changing world, unless they remade and redrew and rebuilt the world in their image, their time would already be over.

Each side faced the other with bravery. To each side, the opposition were the demons, the monsters, the damned.

Shadow could see an initial skirmish had taken place. There was already blood on the rocks.

They were readying themselves for the real battle; for the real war. It was now or never, he thought. If he did not move now, it would be too late.

850. This is Medusa, last seen in the text accompanying note 576, above.

In America everything goes on forever, said a voice in the back of his head. The 1950s lasted for a thousand years. You have all the time in the world.

Shadow walked in something that was half a stroll, half a controlled stumble, into the center of the arena.

He could feel eyes on him, eyes and things that were not eyes. He shivered.

The buffalo voice said, *You are doing just fine.*

Shadow thought, *Damn right. I came back from the dead this morning. After that, everything else should be a piece of cake.*

"You know," said Shadow, to the air, in a conversational voice, "this is not a war. This was never intended to be a war. And if any of you think this is a war, you are deluding yourselves." He heard grumbling noises from both sides. He had impressed nobody.

"We are fighting for our survival," lowed a minotaur from one side of the arena.

"We are fighting for our existence," shouted a mouth in a pillar of glittering smoke, from the other.

"This is a bad land for gods," said Shadow. As an opening statement it wasn't *Friends, Romans, Countrymen*, but it would do. "You've probably all learned that, in your own way. The old gods are ignored. The new gods are as quickly taken up as they are abandoned, cast aside for the next big thing. Either you've been forgotten, or you're scared you're going to be rendered obsolete, or maybe you're just getting tired of existing on the whim of people."

The grumbles were fewer now. He had said something they agreed with. Now, while they were listening, he had to tell them the story.

"There was a god who came here from a far land, and whose power and influence waned as belief in him faded. He was a god who took his power from sacrifice, and from death, and especially from war. He would have deaths of those who fell in war dedicated to him—whole battlefields which, in the old country, gave him power and sustenance.

"Now he was old. He made his living as a grifter, working with another god from his pantheon, a god of chaos and deceit. Together they rooked the gullible. Together they took people for all they'd got.

"Somewhere in there—maybe fifty years ago, maybe a hundred—they put a plan into motion, a plan to create a reserve of power they could both tap into. Something that would make them stronger than they had ever been. After all, what could be more powerful than a battlefield covered with dead gods? The game they played was called 'Let's You and Him Fight.'

"Do you see?

"The battle you're here to fight isn't something that any of you can win or lose. The winning and the losing are unimportant to him, to them. What matters is that enough of you die. Each of you that falls in battle gives him power. Every one of you that dies, feeds him. Do you understand?"

The roaring, whoompfing sound of something catching on fire echoed across the arena. Shadow looked to the place the noise came from. An enormous man, his skin the deep brown of mahogany, his chest naked, wearing a top hat, cigar sticking rakishly from his mouth, spoke in a voice as deep as the grave. Baron Samedi said, "Okay. But Odin. He *died*. At the peace talks. Motherfuckers killed him. He died. I *know* death. Nobody goin' to fool me about death."

Shadow said, "Obviously. He had to die for real. He sacrificed his physical body to make this war happen. After the battle he would have been more powerful than he had ever been."

Somebody called, "Who are you?"

"I am—I was—I am his son."

One of the new gods—Shadow suspected it was a drug from the way it smiled and spangled and shivered—said, "But Mister World said—"

"There *was* no Mister World. There never was. He was just another one of you bastards trying to feed on the chaos he created." He could see that they believed him, and he could see the hurt in their eyes.

Shadow shook his head. "You know," he said, "I think I would rather be a man than a god. We don't need anyone to believe in us. We just keep going anyhow. It's what we do."

There was silence, in the high place.

And then, with a shocking crack, the lightning bolt frozen in the sky crashed to the mountaintop, and the arena went entirely dark.

They glowed, many of those presences, in the darkness.

Shadow wondered if they were going to argue with him, to attack him, to try to kill him. He waited for some kind of response.

And then Shadow realized that the lights were going out. The gods were leaving that place, first in handfuls, and then by scores, and finally in their hundreds.

A spider the size of a rottweiler scuttled heavily toward him, on seven legs; its cluster of eyes glowed faintly.

Shadow held his ground, although he felt slightly sick.

When the spider got close enough, it said, in Mr. Nancy's voice, "That was a good job. Proud of you. You done good, kid."

"Thank you," said Shadow.

"We should get you back. Too long in this place is goin' to mess you up." It rested one brown-haired spider-leg on Shadow's shoulder . . .

. . . and, back on Seven States Flag Court, Mr. Nancy coughed. His right hand rested on Shadow's shoulder. The rain had stopped. Mr. Nancy held his left hand across his side, as if it hurt. Shadow asked if he was okay.

"I'm tough as old nails," said Mr. Nancy. "Tougher." He did not sound happy. He sounded like an old man in pain.

There were dozens of them, standing or sitting on the ground or on the benches. Some of them looked badly injured.

Shadow could hear a rattling noise in the sky, approaching from the south. He looked at Mr. Nancy. "Helicopters?"

Mr. Nancy nodded. "Don't you worry about them. Not any more. They'll just clean up the mess, and leave. They're good at it."

"Got it."

Shadow knew that there was one part of the mess he wanted to see for himself, before it was cleaned up. He borrowed a flashlight from a gray-haired man who looked like a retired news anchor and began to hunt.

He found Laura stretched out on the ground in a side-cavern, beside a diorama of mining gnomes straight out of *Snow White*. The floor beneath her was sticky with blood. She was on her side, where Loki must have dropped her after he had pulled the spear out of them both.

One of Laura's hands clutched her chest. She looked dreadfully vulnerable. She also looked dead, but then Shadow was almost used to that by now.

Shadow squatted beside her, and he touched her cheek with his hand, and he said her name. Her eyes opened, and she lifted her head and turned it until she was looking at him.

"Hello, puppy," she said. Her voice was thin.

"Hi, Laura. What happened here?"

"Nothing," she said. "Just stuff. Did they win?"

"I don't know," said Shadow.[851] "I think these things are kind of relative. But I stopped the battle they were trying to start."

"My clever puppy," she said. "That man, Mister World, he said he was going to put a stick through your eye. I didn't like him at all."

"He's dead. You killed him, hon."

She nodded. She said, "That's good."

Her eyes closed. Shadow's hand found her cold hand, and he held it in his. In time she opened her eyes again.

"Did you ever figure out how to bring me back from the dead?" she asked.

"I guess," he said. "I know one way, anyway."

"That's good," she said. She squeezed his hand with her cold hand. And then she said, "And the opposite? What about that?"

"The opposite?"

"Yes," she whispered. "I think I must have earned it."

"I don't want to do that."

She said nothing. She simply waited.

Shadow said, "Okay." Then he took his hand from hers and put it to her neck.

851. This sentence and the next do not appear in the First Edition.

She said, "That's my husband." She said it proudly.

"I love you, babes," said Shadow.

"Love you, puppy," she whispered.

He closed his hand around the golden coin that hung around her neck. He tugged, hard, at the chain, which snapped easily. Then he took the gold coin between his finger and thumb, and blew on it, and opened his hand wide.

The coin was gone.

Her eyes were still open, but they did not move.

He bent down then, and kissed her, gently, on her cold cheek, but she did not respond. He did not expect her to. Then he got up and walked out of the cavern, to stare into the night.

The storms had cleared. The air felt fresh and clean and new once more.

Tomorrow, he had no doubt, would be one hell of a beautiful day.

PART FOUR

EPILOGUE

Something That the
Dead Are Keeping Back

CHAPTER NINETEEN

*One describes a tale best by telling the tale. You see? The way
one describes a story, to oneself or to the world, is by telling
the story. It is a balancing act and it is a dream. The more
accurate the map, the more it resembles the territory. The most
accurate map possible would be the territory, and thus would
be perfectly accurate and perfectly useless. The tale is the map
which is the territory. You must remember this.*

—FROM THE NOTEBOOKS OF MR. IBIS

HE TWO OF them were driving the VW bus
down to Florida on I-75. They'd been driving
since dawn, or rather, Shadow had driven, and
Mr. Nancy had sat up front in the passenger seat and, from
time to time, and with a pained expression on his face, offered to drive. Shadow always said no.

"Are you happy?" asked Mr. Nancy, suddenly. He had
been staring at Shadow for several hours. Whenever
Shadow glanced over to his right, Mr. Nancy was looking at
him with his earth-brown eyes.

"Not really," said Shadow. "But I'm not dead yet."

"Huh?"

"*Call no man happy until he is dead.* Herodotus."

Mr. Nancy raised a white eyebrow, and he said, "*I'm* not
dead yet, and, mostly *because* I'm not dead yet, I'm happy
as a clamboy."

"The Herodotus thing. It doesn't mean that the dead

are happy," said Shadow. "It means that you can't judge the shape of someone's life until it's over and done."

"I don't even judge then," said Mr. Nancy. "And as for happiness, there's a lot of different kinds of happiness, just as there's a hell of a lot of different kinds of dead. Me, I'll just take what I can get when I can get it."

Shadow changed the subject. "Those helicopters," he said. "The ones that took away the bodies, and the injured."

"What about them?"

"Who sent them? Where did they come from?"

"You shouldn't worry yourself about that. They're like valkyries or buzzards. They come because they have to come."

"If you say so."

"The dead and the wounded will be taken care of. You ask me, old Jacquel's going to be very busy for the next month or so. Tell me somethin', Shadow-boy."

"Okay."

"You learn anythin' from all this?"

Shadow shrugged. "I don't know. Most of what I learned on the tree I've already forgotten," he said. "I think I met some people. But I'm not certain of anything any more. It's like one of those dreams that changes you. You keep some of the dream forever, and you know things down deep inside yourself, because it happened to you, but when you go looking for details they kind of just slip out of your head."

"Yeah," said Mr. Nancy. And then he said, grudgingly, "You're not so dumb."

"Maybe not," said Shadow. "But I wish I could have kept more of what passed through my hands, since I got out of prison. I was given so many things, and I lost them again."

"Maybe," said Mr. Nancy, "you kept more than you think."

"No," said Shadow.

They crossed the border into Florida, and Shadow saw his first palm tree. He wondered if they'd planted it there on purpose, at the border, just so that you knew you were in Florida now.

Mr. Nancy began to snore, and Shadow glanced over at him. The old man still looked very gray, and his breath was rasping. Shadow wondered, not for the first time, if he had sustained some kind of chest or lung injury in the fight. Nancy had refused any medical attention.

Florida went on for longer than Shadow had imagined, and it was late by the time he pulled up outside a small, one-story wooden house, its windows tightly shuttered, on the outskirts of Fort Pierce. Nancy, who had directed him through the last five miles, invited him to stay the night.

"I can get a room in a motel," said Shadow. "It's not a problem."

"You *could* do that, and I'd be hurt. Obviously I wouldn't say anythin'. But I'd be real hurt, real bad," said Mr. Nancy. "So you better stay here, and I'll make you a bed up on the couch."

Mr. Nancy unlocked the hurricane shutters, and pulled open the windows. The house smelled musty and damp, and a little sweet, as if it were haunted by the ghosts of long-dead cookies.

Shadow agreed, reluctantly, to stay the night there, just as he agreed, even more reluctantly, to walk with Mr. Nancy to the bar at the end of the road, for just one late-night drink while the house aired out.

"Did you see Czernobog?" asked Nancy, as they strolled through the muggy Floridian night. The air was alive with whirring palmetto bugs and the ground crawled with creatures that scuttled and clicked. Mr. Nancy lit a cigarillo, and coughed and choked on it. Still, he kept right on smoking.

"He was gone when I came out of the cave."

"He will have headed home. He'll be waitin' for you there, you know."

"Yes."

They walked in silence to the end of the road. It wasn't much of a bar, but it was open.

"I'll buy the first beers," said Mr. Nancy.

"We're only having one beer, remember," said Shadow.

"What are you?" asked Mr. Nancy. "Some kind of cheapskate?"

Mr. Nancy bought them their first beers, and Shadow bought the second round. He stared in horror as Mr. Nancy

852. A popular tune recorded by Tom Jones in 1966, written by Burt Bacharach and Hal David, the title tune for the eponymous film written by Woody Allen, his first produced screenplay.

853. Probably the 1936 tune first performed by Fred Astaire and written by Dorothy Fields and Jerome Kern for the film *Swing Time*.

854. Written by Bennie Benjamin, Gloria Caldwell, and Sol Marcus, it was first recorded by Nina Simone in 1964 and later that year by The Animals, for whom it was a major hit.

talked the barman into turning on the karaoke machine, and then watched in fascinated embarrassment as the old man belted his way through "What's New Pussycat?"[852] before crooning out a moving, tuneful version of "The Way You Look Tonight."[853] He had a fine voice, and by the end the handful of people still in the bar were cheering and applauding him.

When he came back to Shadow at the bar he was looking brighter. The whites of his eyes were clear, and the gray pallor that had touched his skin was gone. "Your turn," he said.

"Absolutely not," said Shadow.

But Mr. Nancy had ordered more beers and was handing Shadow a stained printout of songs from which to choose. "Just pick a song you know the words to."

"This is not funny," said Shadow. The world was beginning to swim, a little, but he couldn't muster the energy to argue, and then Mr. Nancy was putting on the backing tape to "Don't Let Me Be Misunderstood,"[854] and pushing—literally *pushing*—Shadow up onto the tiny makeshift stage at the end of the bar.

Shadow held the mike as if it was probably live, and then the backing music started and he croaked out the initial "*Baby . . .*" Nobody in the bar threw anything in his direction. And it felt good. "*Can you understand me now?*" His voice was rough but melodic, and rough suited the song just fine. "*Sometimes I feel a little mad. Don't you know that no one alive can always be an angel . . .*"

And he was still singing it as they walked home through the busy Florida night, the old man and the young, stumbling and happy.

"*I'm just a soul whose intentions are good,*" he sang to the crabs and the spiders and the palmetto beetles and the lizards and the night. "*Oh lord, please don't let me be misunderstood.*"

Mr. Nancy showed him to the couch. It was much smaller than Shadow, who decided to sleep on the floor, but by the time he had finished deciding to sleep on the floor he was already fast asleep, half-sitting, half-lying, on the tiny sofa.

At first, he did not dream. There was just the comforting

darkness. And then he saw a fire burning in the darkness and he walked toward it.

"You did well," whispered the buffalo man without moving his lips.

"I don't know what I did," said Shadow.

"You made peace," said the buffalo man. "You took our words and made them your own. They never understood that *they* were here—and the people who worshiped them were here—because it suits us that they are here. But we can change our minds. And perhaps we will."

"Are you a god?" asked Shadow.

The buffalo-headed man shook his head. Shadow thought, for a moment, that the creature was amused. "I am the land," he said.

And if there was more to that dream then Shadow did not remember it.

He heard something sizzling. His head was aching, and there was a pounding behind his eyes.

Mr. Nancy was already cooking breakfast: a pile of pancakes, sizzling bacon, perfect eggs, and coffee. He looked in the peak of health.

"My head hurts," said Shadow.

"You get a good breakfast inside you, you'll feel like a new man."

"I'd rather feel like the same man, just with a different head," said Shadow.

"Eat," said Mr. Nancy.

Shadow ate.

"How do you feel now?"

"Like I've got a headache, only now I've got some food in my stomach and I think I'm going to throw up."

"Come with me." Beside the sofa, on which Shadow had spent the night, covered with an African blanket, was a trunk, made of some dark wood, which looked like an undersized pirate chest. Mr. Nancy undid the padlock, and opened the lid. Inside the trunk there were a number of boxes. Nancy rummaged among the boxes. "It's an ancient African herbal remedy," he said. "It's made of ground willow bark, things like that."

"Like aspirin?"

"Yup," said Mr. Nancy. "Just like that." From the bottom of the trunk he produced a giant economy-sized bottle of generic aspirin. He unscrewed the top, and shook out a couple of white pills. "Here."

"Nice trunk," said Shadow. He took the bitter pills, swallowed them with a glass of water.

"My son sent it to me," said Mr. Nancy. "He's a good boy. I don't see him as much as I'd like."[855]

"I miss Wednesday," said Shadow. "Despite everything he did. I keep expecting to see him. But I look up and he's not there." He kept staring at the pirate trunk, trying to figure out what it reminded him of.

You will lose many things. Do not lose this. Who said that?

"You miss him? After what he put you through? Put us all through?"

"Yes," said Shadow. "I guess I do. Do you think he'll be back?"

"I think," said Mr. Nancy, "that wherever two men are gathered together to sell a third man a twenty-dollar violin for ten thousand dollars, he will be there in spirit."

"Yes, but—"

"We should get back into the kitchen," said Mr. Nancy, his expression becoming stony. "Those pans won't wash themselves."

Mr. Nancy washed the pans and the dishes. Shadow dried them, and put them away. Somewhere in there the headache began to ease. They went back into the sitting room.

Shadow stared at the old trunk some more, willing himself to remember. "If I don't go to see Czernobog," he said, "what would happen?"

"You'll see him," said Mr. Nancy flatly. "Maybe he'll find you. Or maybe he'll bring you to him. But one way or another, you'll see him."

Shadow nodded. Something started to fall into place.[856] "Hey," he said. "Is there a god with an elephant's head?"

855. We will learn in *Anansi Boys* that his son Spider gave the trunk to his father.

856. The sentence "A dream, on the tree." appears here in the First Edition.

"Ganesh? He's a Hindu god. He removes obstacles and makes journeys easier. Good cook, too."

Shadow looked up. ". . . *it's in the trunk*," he said. "I knew it was important, but I didn't know why. I thought maybe it meant the trunk of the tree. But he wasn't talking about that at all, was he?"

Mr. Nancy frowned. "You lost me."

"It's in the trunk," said Shadow. He knew it was true. He did not know why it should be true, not quite. But of that he was completely certain.

He got to his feet. "I got to go," he said. "I'm sorry."

Mr. Nancy raised an eyebrow. "Why the hurry?"

"Because," said Shadow, "the ice is melting."

CHAPTER TWENTY

857. Cummings (1894–1962) was a great experimentalist with language and form, single-handedly reshaping poetry into a form that would later be embraced by the Beats and other poets. This poem, given the title "in Just-" from its first line, is part of his cycle titled "Chansons Innocente" and was first published in 1920:

> it's
> spring
> and
>   the
>   goat-footed
> balloonMan   whistles
> far
> and
> wee
>
> —E.E. CUMMINGS [857]

 HADOW WAS DRIVING a rental, and he came out of the forest slowly, about 8:30 in the morning, drove down the hill doing under forty-five miles per hour, and entered the town of Lakeside three weeks after he was certain he had left it for good.

He drove through the city, surprised at how little it had changed in the last few weeks, which were a lifetime, and he parked halfway down the driveway that led to the lake. Then he got out of the car.

There were no more ice-fishing huts on the frozen lake any longer, no SUVs, nobody sitting at a fishing hole with a line and a twelve-pack. The lake was dark: no longer covered with a blind white layer of snow, now there were reflective patches of water on the surface of the ice, and the water beneath the ice was dark, and the ice itself was clear enough that the darkness beneath showed through. The sky was gray, but the icy lake was bleak and empty.

Almost empty.

There was one car remaining on the ice, parked out on the frozen lake almost beneath the bridge, so that anyone driving through the town, anyone crossing the town, could not help but see it. It was a dirty green in color; the sort of car that people abandon in parking lots,[858] the kind that they just park and leave because it's just not worth coming back for. It had no engine. It was a symbol of a wager, waiting for the ice to become rotten enough, and soft enough, and dangerous enough to allow the lake to take it forever.

There was a chain across the short driveway that led down to the lake, and a warning sign forbidding entrance to people or to vehicles. THIN ICE, it said. Beneath it was a hand-painted sequence of pictograms with lines through them: no cars, no pedestrians, no snowmobiles. *Danger.*

Shadow ignored the warnings and scrambled down the bank. It was slippery—the snow had already melted, turning the earth to mud under his feet, and the brown grass barely offered traction. He skidded and slid down to the lake and walked, carefully, out onto a short wooden jetty, and from there he stepped down onto the ice.

The layer of water on the ice, made up of melted ice and melted snow, was deeper than it had looked from above, and the ice beneath the water was slicker and more slippery than any skating rink, so that Shadow was forced to fight to keep his footing. He splashed through the water, as it covered his boots to the laces and seeped inside. Ice water. It numbed where it touched. He felt strangely distant as he trudged across the frozen lake, as if he were watching himself on a movie screen—a movie in which he was the hero, a detective, perhaps:[859] there was a feeling of inevitability, now, as if everything that was going to happen would play itself out, and there was nothing he could have done to change a moment of it.

He walked toward the klunker, painfully aware that the ice was too rotten for this, and that the water beneath the ice was as cold as water could be without freezing. He felt

in Just-
spring   when the world is mud-
luscious the little
lame balloonman

whistles   far   and wee

and eddieandbill come
running from marbles and
piracies and it's
spring

when the world is puddle-wonderful

the queer
old balloonman whistles
far   and   wee
and bettyandisbel come dancing

from hop-scotch and jump-rope and

it's
spring
and
*   the*

*   goat-footed*

balloonMan   whistles
far
and
wee

858. The balance of this sentence does not appear in the First Edition.

859. The balance of this sentence does not appear in the First Edition.

very exposed, out on the ice alone.[860] He kept walking, and
he slipped and slid. Several times he fell.

He passed empty beer bottles and cans left to litter the
ice, and he passed circular holes cut into the ice, for fishing,
holes that had not frozen again, each hole filled with black
water.

The klunker seemed further away than it had looked
from the road. He heard a loud crack from the south of the
lake, like a stick breaking, followed by the sound of something huge thrumming, as if a bass string the size of a lake
was vibrating. Massively, the ice creaked and groaned, like
an old door protesting being opened. Shadow kept walking,
as steadily as he could.

This is suicide, whispered a sane voice in the back of his
mind. *Can't you just let it go?*

"No," he said, aloud. "I have to *know.*" And he kept right
on walking.

He arrived at the klunker, and even before he reached it
he knew that he had been right. There was a miasma that
hung about the car, something that was at the same time a
faint, foul smell and was also a bad taste in the back of his
throat. He walked around the car, looking inside. The seats
were stained, and ripped. The car was obviously empty. He
tried the doors. They were locked. He tried the trunk. Also
locked.

He wished that he had brought a crowbar.

He made a fist of his hand inside his glove. He counted
to three, then smashed his hand, hard, against the driver's-
side window-glass.

His hand hurt. The side-window was undamaged.

He thought about running at it—he could kick the window in, he was certain, if he didn't skid and fall on the wet
ice. But the last thing he wanted to do was to disturb the
klunker enough that the ice beneath it would crack.

He looked at the car. Then he reached for the radio
antenna—it was the kind which was meant to go up and
down, but which had stopped going down a decade ago,

and had remained in the up position ever since—and, with a little waggling, he broke it off at the base. He took the thin end of the antenna—it had once had a metal button on the end, but that was lost in time, and, with strong fingers, he bent it back up into a makeshift hook.

Then he rammed the extended metal antenna down between the rubber and the glass of the front window, deep into the mechanism of the door. He fished in the mechanism, twisting, moving, pushing the metal antenna about until it caught: and then he pulled up.

He felt the improvised hook sliding from the lock, uselessly.

He sighed. Fished again, slower, more carefully. He could imagine the ice grumbling beneath his feet as he shifted his weight. And slow . . . and . . .

He *had* it. He pulled up on the aerial and the front door locking mechanism popped up. Shadow reached down one gloved hand and took the door handle, pressed the button, and pulled. The door did not open.

It's stuck, he thought, *iced up. That's all.*

He tugged, sliding on the ice, and suddenly the door of the klunker flew open, ice scattering everywhere.

The miasma was worse inside the car, a stench of rot and illness. Shadow felt sick.

He reached under the dashboard, found the black plastic handle that opened the trunk, and tugged on it, hard.

There was a thunk from behind him as the trunk door released.

Shadow walked out onto the ice, slipped and splashed around the car, holding on to the side of it as he went.

It's in the trunk, he thought.

The trunk was open an inch. He reached down and opened it the rest of the way, pulling it up.

The smell was bad, but it could have been much worse: the bottom of the trunk was filled with an inch or so of half-melted ice. There was a girl in the trunk. She wore a scarlet snowsuit, now stained, and her mousy hair was long and her mouth was closed, so Shadow could not see the blue

861. This sentence does not appear in the First Edition.

862. This sentence and the next do not appear in the First Edition.

rubber-band braces, but he knew that they were there. The cold had preserved her, kept her as fresh as if she had been in a freezer.

Her eyes were wide open, and she looked as if she had been crying when she died, and the tears that had frozen on her cheeks had still not melted. Her gloves were bright green.[861]

"You were here all the time," said Shadow to Alison Mc-Govern's corpse. "Every single person who drove over that bridge saw you. Everyone who drove through the town saw you. The ice fishermen walked past you every day. And nobody knew." And then he realized how foolish that was.

Somebody knew.

Somebody had put her here.

He reached into the trunk—to see if he could pull her out. He had found her, after all.[862] Now he had to get her out. He put his weight on the car, as he leaned in. Perhaps that was what did it.

The ice beneath the front wheels went at that moment, perhaps from his movements, perhaps not. The front of the car lurched downward several feet into the dark water of the lake. Water began to pour into the car through the open driver's door. Water splashed about Shadow's ankles, although the ice he stood on was still solid. He looked around urgently, wondering how to get away—and then it was too late, and the ice tipped precipitously, throwing him against the car and the dead girl in the trunk; and the back of the car went down, and Shadow went down with it, into the cold waters of the lake. It was ten past nine in the morning, on March the twenty-third.

He took a deep breath before he went under, closing his eyes, but the cold of the lake water hit him like a wall, knocking the breath from his body.

He tumbled downward, into the murky ice water, pulled down by the car.

He was under the lake, down in the darkness and the cold, weighed down by his clothes and his gloves and his boots, trapped and swathed in his coat, which seemed to have become heavier and bulkier than he could have imagined.

He was falling, still. He tried to push away from the car, but it was pulling him with it, and then there was a bang which he could hear with his whole body, not his ears, and his left foot was wrenched at the ankle, the foot twisted and trapped beneath the car as it settled on the lake bottom, and panic took him.

He opened his eyes.

He knew it was dark down there: rationally, he knew it was too dark to see anything, but still, he could see; he could see everything. He could see Alison McGovern's white face staring at him from the open trunk. He could see other cars as well—the klunkers of bygone years, rotten hulk shapes in the darkness, half-buried in the lake mud. *And what else would they have dragged out onto the lake,* thought Shadow, *before there were cars?*

Each one, he knew, without any question, had a dead child in the trunk. There were scores of them down there. Each had sat out on the ice, in front of the eyes of the world, all through the cold winter. Each had tumbled into the cold waters of the lake, when the winter was done.

This was where they rested: Lemmi Hautala and Jessie Lovat and Sandy Olsen and Jo Ming and Sarah Lindquist and all the rest of them. Down where it was silent and cold . . .

He pulled at his foot. It was stuck fast, and the pressure in his lungs was becoming unbearable. There was a sharp, terrible hurt in his ears. He exhaled slowly, and the air bubbled around his face.

Soon, he thought, *soon I'll have to breathe. Or I'll choke.*

He reached down, put both hands around the bumper of the klunker, and pushed, with everything he had, leaning into it. Nothing happened.

It's only the shell of a car, he told himself. *They took out the engine. That's the heaviest part of the car. You can do it. Just keep pushing.*

He pushed.

Agonizingly slowly, a fraction of an inch at a time, the car slipped forward in the mud, and Shadow pulled his foot from the mud beneath the car, and kicked, and tried to push himself out into the cold lake water. He didn't move. *The coat,* he told himself. *It's the coat. It's stuck, or caught on something.* He pulled his arms from his coat, fumbled with numb fingers at the frozen zipper. Then he pulled both hands on each side of the zipper, felt the coat give and rend. Hastily, he freed himself from its embrace, and pushed upward, away from the car.

There was a rushing sensation but no sense of up, no sense of down, and he was choking and the pain in his chest and in his head was too much to bear, so that he was certain that he was going to have to inhale, to breathe in the cold water, to die. And then his head hit something solid.

Ice. He was pushing against the ice on the top of the lake. He hammered at it with his fists, but there was no strength left in his arms, nothing to hold on to, nothing to push against. The world had dissolved into the chill blackness beneath the lake. There was nothing left but cold.

This is ridiculous, he thought. And he thought, remembering some old Tony Curtis film he'd seen as a kid, *I should roll onto my back and push the ice upward and press my face to it, and find some air, I could breathe again, there's air there somewhere,* but he was just floating and freezing and he could no longer move a muscle, not if his life depended on it, which it did.[863]

The cold became bearable. Became warm. And he thought, *I'm dying.* There was anger there this time, a deep fury, and he took the pain and the anger and reached with it, flailed, forced muscles to move that were resigned never to move again.

He pushed up with his hand, and felt it scrape the edge of the ice and move up into the air. He flailed for a grip, and felt another hand take his own, and pull.

His head banged against the ice, his face scraped the underneath of the ice, and then his head was up in the air, and he could see that he was coming up through a hole in the ice, and for a moment all he could do was breathe, and let the black lake water run from his nose and his mouth, and blink his eyes, which could see nothing more than a blinding daylight, and shapes, and someone was pulling

863. Shadow is recalling the 1953 film *Houdini*, in which Curtis starred as the legendary escape artist and used this technique to save himself.

him, now, forcing him out of the water, saying something about how he'd freeze to death, so come on, man, *pull*, and Shadow wriggled and shook like a bull seal coming ashore, shaking and coughing and shuddering.

He breathed deep gasps of air, stretched flat out on the creaking ice, and even that would not hold for long, he knew, but it was no good. His thoughts were coming with difficulty, treacle-slow.

"Just leave me," he tried to say. "I'll be fine." His words were a slur, and everything was drawing to a halt.

He just needed to rest for a moment, that was all, just rest, and then he would get up and move on, for obviously he could not just lie there forever.

There was a jerk; water splashed his face. His head was lifted up. Shadow felt himself being hauled across the ice, sliding on his back across the slick surface, and he wanted to protest, to explain that he just needed a little rest—maybe a little sleep, was that asking for so much?—and he would be just fine. If they just left him alone.

He did not believe that he had fallen asleep, but he was standing on a vast plain, and there was a man there with the head and shoulders of a buffalo, and a woman with the head of an enormous condor, and there was Whiskey Jack standing between them, looking at him sadly, shaking his head.

Whiskey Jack turned and walked slowly away from Shadow. The Buffalo man walked away beside him. The thunderbird woman also walked, and then she ducked and kicked and she was gliding out into the skies.

Shadow felt a sense of loss. He wanted to call to them, to plead with them to come back, not to give up on him, but everything was becoming formless and devoid of shape: they were gone, and the plains were fading, and everything became void.

✳   ✳   ✳

THE PAIN WAS intense: it was as if every cell in his body, every nerve, was melting and waking and advertising its presence by burning him and hurting him.

There was a hand at the back of his head, gripping it by

the hair, and another hand beneath his chin. He opened his eyes, expecting to find himself in some kind of hospital.

His feet were bare. He was wearing jeans. He was naked from the waist up. There was steam in the air. He could see a shaving mirror on the wall facing him, and a small basin, and a blue toothbrush in a toothpaste-stained glass.

Information was processed slowly, one datum at a time.

His fingers burned. His toes burned.

He began to whimper from the pain.

"Easy now, Mike. Easy there," said a voice he knew.

"What?" he said, or tried to say. "What's happening?" It sounded strained and strange to his ears.

He was in a bathtub. The water was hot. He thought the water was hot, although he could not be certain. The water was up to his neck.

"Dumbest thing you can do with a fellow freezing to death is to put him in front of a fire. The second-dumbest thing you can do is to wrap him in blankets—especially if he's in cold wet clothes already. Blankets insulate him— keep the cold in. The third-dumbest thing—and this is my private opinion—is to take the fellow's blood out, warm it up, and put it back. That's what doctors do these days. Complicated, expensive. Dumb." The voice was coming from above and behind his head.

"The smartest, quickest thing you can do is what sailors have done to men overboard for hundreds of years. You put the fellow in hot water. Not *too* hot. Just hot.[864] Now, just so you know, you were basically dead, when I found you on the ice back there. How are you feeling now, Houdini?"[865]

"It hurts," said Shadow. "Everything hurts. You saved my life."

"I guess maybe I did, at that. Can you hold your head up on your own now?"

"Maybe."

"I'm going to let you go. If you start sinking below the water I'll pull you back up again."

The hands released their grip on his head.

He felt himself sliding forward in the bathtub. He put out his hands, pressed them against the sides of the tub, and

864. A well-known technique. See, e.g., http://www.basecampmd.com/expguide /frostbite.shtml.

865. A coincidental reference? See note 863, above. Or does Hinzelmann read minds?

leaned back. The bathroom was small. The tub was metal, and the enamel was stained and scratched.

An old man moved into his field of vision. He looked concerned.

"Feeling better?" asked Hinzelmann. "You just lay back and relax. I've got the den nice and warm. You tell me when you're ready, I got a robe you can wear, and I can throw your jeans into the dryer with the rest of your clothes. Sound good, Mike?"

"That's not my name."

"If you say so." The old man's goblin face twisted into an expression of discomfort.

Shadow had no real sense of time: he lay in the bath until the burning stopped and his toes and fingers flexed without real discomfort. Hinzelmann helped Shadow to his feet and let out the warm water. Shadow sat on the side of the bath and together they pulled off his jeans.

He squeezed, without much difficulty, into a terrycloth robe too small for him, and, leaning on the old man, he went through to the den, and flopped down on an ancient sofa. He was tired and weak: deeply fatigued, but alive. A log fire burned in the fireplace. A handful of surprised-looking deer heads peered down dustily from around the walls, where they jostled for space with several large varnished fish.

Hinzelmann went away with Shadow's jeans, and from the room next door Shadow could hear a brief pause in the rattle of a clothes dryer, before it resumed. The old man returned with a steaming mug.

"It's coffee," he said, "which is a stimulant. And I splashed a little schnapps into it. Just a little. That's what we always did in the old days. A doctor wouldn't recommend it."

Shadow took the coffee with both hands. On the side of the mug was a picture of a mosquito and the message, GIVE BLOOD—VISIT WISCONSIN!!

"Thanks," he said.

"It's what friends are for," said Hinzelmann. "One day, you can save my life. For now, forget about it."

Shadow sipped the coffee. "I thought I was dead."

"You were lucky. I was up on the bridge—I'd pretty much figured that today was going to be the big day, you get a feel for it, when you get to my age—so I was up there with my old pocket watch, and I saw you heading out onto the lake. I shouted, but I sure as heck don't think you coulda heard me. I saw the car go down, and I saw you go down with it, and I thought I'd lost you, so I went out onto the ice. Gave me the heebie-jeebies. You must have been under the water for the best part of two minutes. Then I saw your hand come up through the place where the car went down—it was like seeing a ghost, seeing you there . . ." He trailed off. "We were both damn lucky that the ice took our weight as I dragged you back to the shore."

Shadow nodded.

"You did a good thing," he told Hinzelmann, and the old man beamed all over his goblin face.

Somewhere in the house, Shadow heard a door close. He sipped at his coffee.

Now that he was able to think clearly, he was starting to ask himself questions.

He wondered how an old man, a man half his height and perhaps a third his weight, had been able to drag him, unconscious, across the ice, or get him up the bank to a car. He wondered how Hinzelmann had gotten Shadow into the house and the bath.

Hinzelmann walked over to the fire, picked up the tongs and placed a thin log, carefully, onto the blazing fire.

"Do you want to know what I was doing out on the ice?"

Hinzelmann shrugged. "None of my business."

"You know what I don't understand . . . ," said Shadow. He hesitated, putting his thoughts in order. "I don't understand why you saved my life."

"Well," said Hinzelmann, "the way I was brought up, if you see another fellow in trouble—"

"No," said Shadow. "That's not what I mean. I mean, you killed all those kids. Every winter. I was the only one to have figured it out. You must have seen me open the trunk. Why didn't you just let me drown?"

Hinzelmann tipped his head on one side. He scratched

his nose, thoughtfully, rocked back and forth as if he were thinking. "Well," he said. "That's a good question. I guess it's because I owed a certain party a debt. And I'm good for my debts."

"Wednesday?"

"That's the fellow."

"There was a reason he hid me in Lakeside, wasn't there? There was a reason nobody should have been able to find me here."

Hinzelmann said nothing. He unhooked a heavy black poker from its place on the wall, and he prodded at the fire with it, sending up a cloud of orange sparks and smoke. "This is my home," he said, petulantly. "It's a *good* town."

Shadow finished his coffee. He put the cup down on the floor. The effort was exhausting. "How long have you been here?"

"Long enough."

"And you made the lake?"

Hinzelmann peered at him, surprised. "Yes," he said. "I made the lake. They were calling it a lake when I got here, but it weren't nothing more than a spring and a mill-pond and a creek." He paused. "I figured that this country is hell on my kind of folk. It eats us. I didn't want to be eaten. So I made a deal. I gave them a lake, and I gave them prosperity . . ."

"And all it cost them was one child every winter."

"Good kids," said Hinzelmann, shaking his old head, slowly. "They were all good kids. I'd only pick ones I liked. Except for Charlie Nelligan. He was a bad seed, that one. He was, what, 1924? 1925? Yeah. That was the deal."

"The people of the town," said Shadow. "Mabel. Marguerite. Chad Mulligan. Do they *know*?"

Hinzelmann said nothing. He pulled the poker from the fire: the first six inches at the tip glowed a dull orange. Shadow knew that the handle of the poker must be too hot to hold, but it did not seem to bother Hinzelmann, and he prodded the fire again. He put the poker back into the fire, tip first, and left it there. Then he said, "They know that they live in a good place. While every other town and city in this county, heck, in this part of the state, is crumbling into nothing. They know that."

"And that's your doing?"

"This town," said Hinzelmann. "I care for it. Nothing happens here that I don't want to happen. You understand that? Nobody comes here that I don't want to come here. That was why your father sent you here. He didn't want you out there in the world, attracting attention. That's all."

"And you betrayed him."

"I did no such thing. He was a crook. But I always pay my debts."

"I don't believe you," said Shadow.

Hinzelmann looked offended. One hand tugged at the clump of white hair at his temple. "I keep my word."

"No. You don't. Laura came here. She said something was calling her here. And what about the coincidence that brought Sam Black Crow and Audrey Burton here, on the same night? I don't believe in coincidence any more.

"Sam Black Crow and Audrey Burton. Two people who both knew who I really was, and that there were people out there looking for me. I guess if one of them failed, there was always the other. And if all of them had failed, who else was on their way to Lakeside, Hinzelmann? My old prison warden, up here for a weekend's ice-fishing? Laura's mother?" Shadow realized that he was angry. "You wanted me out of your town. You just didn't want to have to tell Wednesday that was what you were doing."

In the firelight, Hinzelmann seemed more like a gargoyle than an imp. "This is a good town," he said. "Without his smile he looked waxen and corpse-like. "You could have attracted too much attention. Not good for the town."

"You should have left me back there on the ice," said Shadow. "You should have left me in the lake. I opened the trunk of the klunker. Right now Alison is still iced into the trunk. But the ice will melt, and her body'll float out and up to the surface. And then they'll go down and look and see what else they can find down there. Find your whole stash of kids. I guess some of those bodies are pretty well preserved."

Hinzelmann reached down and picked up the poker. He made no pretense of stirring the fire with it any longer; he held it like a sword, or a baton, the glowing orange-white tip of it waving in the air. It smoked. Shadow was very aware that he was next-to-naked, and he was still tired, and clumsy, and far from able to defend himself.

"You want to kill me?" said Shadow. "Go ahead. Do it. I'm a dead man anyway. I know you own this town—it's your little world. But if you think no one's going to come looking for me, you're living in a dream world. It's over, Hinzelmann. One way or another, it's done."

Hinzelmann pushed himself to his feet, using the poker as a walking stick. The carpet charred and smoked where he rested the red-hot tip as he got up. He looked at Shadow and there were tears in his pale blue eyes. "I love this town," he said. "I really like being a cranky old man, and telling my stories and driving Tessie and ice-fishing. Remember what I told you, it's not the fish you bring home from a day's fishing. It's the peace of mind."

He extended the tip of the poker in Shadow's direction: Shadow could feel the heat of it from a foot away.

"I could kill you," said Hinzelmann, "I could fix it. I've done it before. You're not the first to figure it out. Chad Mulligan's father, he figured it out. I fixed him. I can fix you."

"Maybe," said Shadow. "But for how long, Hinzelmann? Another year? Another decade? They have computers. They aren't stupid. They pick up on patterns. Every year a kid's going to vanish. They'll come sniffing about here. Just like they'll come looking for me. Tell me—how old *are* you?" He curled his fingers around a sofa cushion, and prepared to pull it over his head: it would deflect a first blow.

Hinzelmann's face was expressionless. "They were giving their children to me before the Romans came to the Black Forest," he said. "I was a god before ever I was a kobold."

"Maybe it's time to move on," said Shadow. He wondered what a kobold was.[866]

Hinzelmann stared at him. Then he took the poker, and pushed the tip of it back into the burning embers. "Maybe it is, at that," he said.[867] "But it's not that simple. What makes

866. A kobold is a household fairy or spirit in German folklore, equivalent to a brownie. The hinzelmann was the specific name given to a kobold who reportedly occupied the castle at Hudemuhlen. The Pastor Feldmann, in 1704, wrote a book about the spirit, titled (from the German): *The multi-faceted Hintzelmann or circumstantial and strange haunting of a spirit, which can be seen on the house Hudemühlen and afterwards to Estrup in the land Lüneburg under varied forms and surprising change.* The Brothers Grimm also wrote of the hinzelmann, based on Feldmann's book, in their *German Legends* (Berlin: Nicolai, 1816) and described the spirit as spiteful and malicious, inflicting punishment and torture, if the spirit disapproved of one's conduct. Kobolds often took the form of young children, accompanied by the knives that killed them. No previous folklorist, however, has suggested that the hinzelmann was once a god.

867. This sentence does not appear in the First Edition.

you think I can leave this town, even if I want to, Shadow? I'm part of this town. You going to make me go, Shadow? You ready to kill me? So I can leave?"

Shadow looked down at the floor. There were still glimmers and sparks in the carpet, where the poker-tip had rested. Hinzelmann followed the look with his own, and crushed the embers out with his foot, twisting. In Shadow's mind came, unbidden, children, hundreds of them, staring at him with bone-blind eyes, the hair twisting slowly around their faces like fronds of seaweed. They were looking at him reproachfully.

He knew that he was letting them down. He just didn't know what else to do.

Shadow said, "I can't kill you. You saved my life."

He shook his head. He felt like crap, in every way he could feel like crap. He didn't feel like a hero or a detective any more—just another fucking sell-out, waving a stern finger at the darkness before turning his back on it.

"You want to know a secret?" asked Hinzelmann.

"Sure," said Shadow, with a heavy heart. He was ready to be done with secrets.

"Watch this."

Where Hinzelmann had been standing stood a male child, no more than five years old. His hair was dark brown, and long. He was perfectly naked, save for a worn leather band around his neck. He was pierced with two swords, one of them going through his chest, the other entering at his shoulder, with the point coming out beneath the ribcage. Blood flowed through the wounds without stopping and ran down the child's body to pool and puddle on the floor. The swords looked unimaginably old.

The little boy stared up at Shadow with eyes that held only pain.

And Shadow thought to himself, *Of course*. That's as good a way as any other of making a tribal god. He did not have to be told. He knew.

You take a baby and you bring it up in the darkness, letting it see no one, touch no one, and you feed it well as the years pass, feed it better than any of the village's other children, and then, five winters on, when the night is at its longest, you drag the terrified child out of its hut and into the circle of bonfires, and you pierce it with blades of iron and of bronze. Then you smoke the small body over charcoal fires until it is properly dried, and you wrap it in furs and carry it with you from encampment to encampment, deep in the Black Forest, sacrificing animals and children to it, making it the luck of the tribe. When, eventually, the thing falls apart from age, you place its fragile bones in a box, and you worship the box; until one day the bones are scattered and forgotten, and the tribes who worshiped the child-god of the box are long gone; and the child-god, the luck of the village, will be barely remembered, save as a ghost or a brownie, a kobold.

Shadow wondered which of the people who had come to northern Wisconsin a hundred and fifty years ago, a woodcutter, perhaps, or a mapmaker, had crossed the Atlantic with Hinzelmann living in his head.

And then the bloody child was gone, and the blood, and there was only an old man with a fluff of white hair and a goblin smile, his sweater-sleeves still soaked from putting Shadow into the bath that had saved his life.

"Hinzelmann?" The voice came from the doorway of the den.

Hinzelmann turned. Shadow turned too.

"I came over to tell you," said Chad Mulligan, and his voice was strained, "that the klunker went through the ice. I saw it had gone down when I drove over that way, and thought I'd come over and let you know, in case you'd missed it."

He was holding his gun. It was pointed at the floor.

"Hey, Chad," said Shadow.

"Hey, pal," said Chad Mulligan. "They sent me a note said you'd died in custody. Heart attack."

"How about that?" said Shadow. "Seems like I'm dying all over the place."

"He came down here, Chad," said Hinzelmann. "He threatened me."

"No," said Chad Mulligan. "He didn't. I've been here for

the last ten minutes, Hinzelmann. I heard everything you said. About my old man. About the lake." He walked further into the den. He did not raise the gun. "I mean, Jesus, Hinzelmann. You can't drive through this town without seeing that goddamned lake. It's at the center of everything. So what the hell am I supposed to do?"

"You got to arrest him. He said he was going to kill me," said Hinzelmann, a scared old man in a dusty den. "Chad, I'm pleased you're here."

"No," said Chad Mulligan. "You're not."

Hinzelmann sighed. He bent down, as if resigned, and he pulled the poker out from the fire. The tip of it was burning bright orange.

"Put that down, Hinzelmann. Just put it down slowly, keep your hands in the air where I can see them, and turn and face the wall."

There was an expression of pure fear on the old man's face, and Shadow would have felt sorry for him, but he remembered the frozen tears on the cheeks of Alison McGovern,[868] and could not feel anything. Hinzelmann did not move. He did not put down the poker. He did not turn to the wall. Shadow was about to reach for Hinzelmann, to try to take the poker away from him, when the old man threw the burning poker at Chad Mulligan.

Hinzelmann threw it awkwardly, lobbing it across the room as if for form's sake, and as he threw it he was already hurrying for the door.

The poker glanced off Chad's left arm.

The noise of the shot, in the close quarters of the old man's room, was deafening.

One shot to the head, and that was all.

Mulligan said, "Better get your clothes on." His voice was dull and dead.

Shadow nodded. He walked to the room next door, opened the door of the clothes dryer and pulled out his clothes. The jeans were still damp. He put them on anyway. By the time he got back to the den, fully dressed—except for his coat, which was somewhere deep in the freezing mud of the lake, and his boots, which he could not find—

868. The balance of this sentence does not appear in the First Edition.

Mulligan had already hauled several smoldering logs out from the fireplace.

Mulligan said, "It's a bad day for a cop when he has to commit arson, just to cover up a murder." Then he looked up at Shadow. "You need boots," he said.

"I don't know where he put them," said Shadow.

"Hell," said Mulligan. Then he said, "Sorry about this, Hinzelmann," and he picked the old man up by the collar and by the belt buckle, and he swung him forward, dropped the body with its head resting in the open fireplace. The white hair crackled and flared, and the room began to fill with the smell of charring flesh.

"It wasn't murder. It was self-defense," said Shadow.

"I know what it was," said Mulligan, flatly. He had already turned his attention to the smoking logs he had scattered about the room. He pushed one of them to the edge of the sofa, picked up an old copy of the *Lakeside News* and pulled it into its component pages, which he crumpled up and dropped onto the log. The newspaper pages browned and then burst into flame.

"Get outside," said Chad Mulligan.

He opened the windows as they walked out of the house, and he sprang the lock on the front door to lock it before he closed it.

Shadow followed him out to the police car in his bare feet. Mulligan opened the front passenger door for him, and Shadow got in and wiped his feet off on the mat. Then he put on his socks, which were pretty much dry by now.

"We can get you some boots at Henning's Farm and Home," said Chad Mulligan.

"How much did you hear in there?" asked Shadow.

"Enough," said Mulligan. Then he said, "Too much."

They drove to Henning's Farm and Home in silence. When they got there the police chief said, "What size feet?"

Shadow told him.

Mulligan walked into the store. He returned with a pair of thick woolen socks, and a pair of leather farm boots. "All they had left in your size," he said. "Unless you wanted gumboots. I figured you didn't."

Shadow pulled on the socks and the boots. They fitted fine. "Thanks," he said.

"You got a car?" asked Mulligan.

"It's parked by the road down to the lake. Near the bridge."

Mulligan started the car and pulled out of the Henning's parking lot.

"What happened to Audrey?" asked Shadow.

"Day after they took you away, she said she liked me as a friend, but it would never work out between us, us being family and all, and she went back to Eagle Point. Broke my gosh-darn heart."

"Makes sense," said Shadow. "And it wasn't personal. Hinzelmann didn't need her here any more."

They drove back past Hinzelmann's house. A thick plume of white smoke was coming up from the chimney.

"She only came to town because he wanted her here. She was something to help him to get me out of town. I was bringing attention he didn't need."

"I thought she liked me."

They pulled up beside Shadow's rental car. "What are you going to do now?" asked Shadow.

"I don't know," said Mulligan. His normally harassed face was starting to look more alive than it had at any point since Hinzelmann's den. It also looked more troubled. "I figure, I got a couple of choices. Either I'll . . ." And he made a gun of his first two fingers, and put the fingertips into his open mouth, and removed them. ". . . put a bullet through my brain. Or I'll wait another couple of days until the ice is mostly gone, and tie a concrete block to my leg and jump off the bridge. Or pills. Sheesh. Maybe I should just drive a while, out to one of the forests. Take pills out there. I don't want to make one of my guys have to do the clean-up. Leave it for the county, huh?" He sighed, and shook his head.

"You didn't kill Hinzelmann, Chad. He died a long time ago, a long way from here."

"Thanks for saying that, Mike. But I killed him. I shot a man in cold blood, and I covered it up. And if you asked me why I did it, why I really did it, I'm darned if I could tell you."

Shadow put out a hand, touched Mulligan on the arm. "Hinzelmann owned this town," he said. "I don't think you had a lot of choice about what happened back there. I think he brought you there. He wanted you to hear what you heard. He set you up. I guess it was the only way he could leave."

Mulligan's miserable expression did not change. Shadow could see that the police chief had barely heard anything that he had said. He had killed Hinzelmann and built him a pyre, and now, obeying the last of Hinzelmann's desires, or simply because it was the only thing he could do to live with himself,[869] he would commit suicide.

Shadow closed his eyes, remembering the place in his head that he had gone when Wednesday had told him to make snow: that place that pushed, mind to mind, and he smiled a smile he did not feel and he said, "Chad. Let it go." There was a cloud in the man's mind, a dark, oppressive cloud, and Shadow could almost see it and, concentrating on it, imagined it fading away like a fog in the morning. "Chad," he said, fiercely, trying to penetrate the cloud, "this town is going to change now. It's not going to be the only good town in a depressed region any more. It's going to be a lot more like the rest of this part of the world. There's going to be a lot more trouble. People out of work. People out of their heads. More people getting hurt. More bad shit going down. They are going to need a police chief with experience. The town needs you." And then he said, "Marguerite needs you."

Something shifted in the storm cloud that filled the man's head. Shadow could feel it change. He *pushed* then, envisioning Marguerite Olsen's practical brown hands and her dark eyes, and her long, long black hair. He pictured the way she tipped her head on one side and half-smiled when she was amused. "She's waiting for you," said Shadow, and he knew it was true as he said it.

"Margie?" said Chad Mulligan.

869. This phrase does not appear in the First Edition.

And at that moment, although he could never tell you how he had done it, and he doubted that he could ever do it again, Shadow reached in to Chad Mulligan's mind, easy as anything, and he plucked the events of that afternoon from it as precisely and dispassionately as a raven picking an eye from roadkill.

The creases in Chad's forehead smoothed, and he blinked, sleepily.

"Go see Margie," said Shadow. "It's been good seeing you, Chad. Take care of yourself."

"Sure," yawned Chad Mulligan.

A message crackled over the police radio, and Chad reached out for the handset. Shadow got out of the car.

Shadow walked over to his rental car. He could see the gray flatness of the lake at the center of the town. He thought of the dead children who waited at the bottom of the water.

Soon, Alison would float to the surface . . .

As Shadow drove past Hinzelmann's place he could see the plume of smoke had already turned into a blaze. He could hear a siren wail.

He drove south, heading for Highway 51. He was on his way to keep his final appointment. But before that, he thought, he would stop off in Madison, for one last goodbye.

✢ ✢ ✢

BEST OF EVERYTHING, Samantha Black Crow liked closing up the Coffee House at night. It was a perfectly calming thing to do: it gave her a feeling that she was putting order back into the world. She would put on an Indigo Girls CD, and she would do her final chores of the night at her own pace and in her own way. First, she would clean the espresso machine. Then she would do the final rounds, ensuring that any missed cups or plates were deposited back in the kitchen, and that the newspapers that were always scattered around the Coffee House by the end of each day were collected together and piled neatly by the front door, all ready for recycling.

She loved the Coffee House. She'd gone there as a customer for six months before she talked Jeff, the manager, into giving her a job.[870] It was a long, winding series of rooms filled with armchairs and sofas and low tables, on a street lined with second-hand bookstores.

She covered the leftover slices of cheesecake and put them into the large refrigerator for the night, then she took a cloth and wiped the last of the crumbs away. She enjoyed being alone.

As she worked she would sing along with the Indigo Girls. Sometimes she would break into a dance for a step or two, before catching herself, and stopping, smiling wryly at herself.[871]

A tapping on the window jerked her attention from her chores back to the real world. She went to the door, opened it, to admit a woman of about Sam's age, with pigtailed magenta hair. Her name was Natalie.

"Hello," said Natalie. She went up on tiptoes and kissed Sam, depositing the kiss snugly between Sam's cheek and the corner of her mouth. You can say a lot of things with a kiss like that. "You done?"

"Nearly."

"You want to see a movie?"

"Sure. Love to. I've got a good five minutes left here, though. Why don't you sit and read the *Onion*?"[872]

"I saw this week's already." She sat on a chair near the door, ruffled through the pile of newspapers put aside for recycling until she found something, and she read it, while Sam bagged up the last of the money in the till and put it in the safe.

They had been sleeping together for a week now. Sam wondered if this was it, the relationship she'd been waiting for all her life. She told herself that it was just brain chemicals and pheromones that made her happy when she saw Natalie, and perhaps that was what it was; still, all she knew for sure was that she smiled when she saw Natalie, and that when they were together she felt comfortable and comforted.

"This paper," said Natalie, "has another one of those articles in it. 'Is America Changing?'"

870. This sentence does not appear in the First Edition.

871. This paragraph does not appear in the First Edition.

872. The satirical newspaper began weekly print publication in 1988 in Madison, Wisconsin; it is now wholly published online but includes audio and video articles.

"Well, is it?"

"They don't say. They say that maybe it is, but they don't know how and they don't know why, and maybe it isn't happening at all."

Sam smiled broadly. "Well," she said, "that covers every option, doesn't it?"

"I guess." Natalie's brow creased and she went back to her newspaper.

Sam washed the dishcloth and folded it. "I think it's just that, despite the government and whatever, everything just feels suddenly good right now. Maybe it's just spring coming a little early. It was a long winter, and I'm glad it's over."

"Me, too." A pause. "It says in the article that lots of people have been reporting weird dreams. I haven't really had any weird dreams. Nothing weirder than normal."

Sam looked around to see if there was anything she had missed. Nope. It was a good job well done. She took off her apron, hung it back in the kitchen. Then she came back and started to turn off the lights. "I've had some weird dreams recently," she said. "They got weird enough that I actually started keeping a dream journal. They seem to mean so much while I'm dreaming them.[873] I write them down when I wake up. And then when I read them, they don't mean anything at all."

She put on her street coat, and her one-size-fits-all gloves.

"I did some dream work," said Natalie. Natalie had done a little of everything, from arcane self-defense disciplines and sweat lodges to feng shui and jazz dancing. "Tell me. I'll tell you what they mean."

"Okay." Sam unlocked the door and turned the last of the lights off. She let Natalie out, and she walked out onto the street and locked the door to the Coffee House firmly behind her. "Sometimes I have been dreaming of people who fell from the sky. Sometimes I'm underground, talking to a woman with a buffalo head. And sometimes I dream about this guy I kissed once in a bar."

Natalie made a noise. "Something you should have told me about?"

873. This sentence does not appear in the First Edition.

"Maybe. But not like that. It was a Fuck-Off Kiss."

"You were telling him to fuck off?"

"No, I was telling everyone else they could fuck off. You had to be there, I guess."

Natalie's shoes clicked down the sidewalk. Sam padded on next to her. "He owns my car," said Sam.

"That purple thing you got at your sister's?"

"Yup."

"What happened to him? Why doesn't he want his car?"

"I don't know. Maybe he's in prison. Maybe he's dead."

"Dead?"

"I guess." Sam hesitated. "A few weeks back, I was certain he was dead. ESP. Or whatever. Like, I knew. But then, I started to think maybe he wasn't. I don't know. I guess my ESP isn't that hot."

"How long are you going to keep his car?"

"Until someone comes for it. I think it's what he would have wanted."

Natalie looked at Sam, then she looked again. Then she said, "Where did you get *those* from?"

"What?"

"The flowers. The ones you're *holding*, Sam. Where did they come from? Did you have them when we left the Coffee House? I would have seen them."

Sam looked down. Then she grinned. "You are so sweet. I should have said something when you gave them to me, shouldn't I?" she said. "They are lovely. Thank you so much. But wouldn't red have been more appropriate?"

They were roses, their stems wrapped in paper. Six of them, and white.

"I didn't give them to you," said Natalie, her lips firming.

And neither of them said another word until they reached the movie theater.

When she got home that night Sam put the roses in an improvised vase. Later, she cast them in bronze, and she kept to herself the tale of how she got them, although she told Caroline, who came after Natalie, the story of the ghost-roses one night when they were both very drunk, and

Caroline agreed with Sam that it was a really, really strange and a spooky story, and, deep down, did not actually believe a word of it, so that was all right.

✦   ✦   ✦

SHADOW HAD PARKED near the capitol building, and walked slowly around the square, stretching his legs after the long drive. His clothes were uncomfortable, although they had dried on his body, and the new boots were still tight. He passed a payphone. He called information, and they gave him the number.

No, he was told. She isn't here. She's not back yet. She's probably still at the Coffee House.

He stopped on the way to the Coffee House to buy flowers.

He found the Coffee House, then he crossed the road and stood in the doorway of a used bookstore, and waited, and watched.

The place closed at eight, and at ten past eight Shadow saw Sam Black Crow walk out of the Coffee House in the company of a smaller woman whose pigtailed hair was a peculiar shade of red. They were holding hands tightly, as if simply holding hands could keep the world at bay, and they were talking—or rather, Sam was doing most of the talking while her friend listened. Shadow wondered what Sam was saying. She smiled as she talked.

The two women crossed the road, and they walked past the place where Shadow was standing. The pigtailed girl passed within a foot of him; he could have reached out and touched her, and they didn't see him at all.

He watched them walking away from him down the street, and felt a pang, like a minor chord being played inside him.

It had been a good kiss, Shadow reflected, but Sam had never looked at him the way she was looking at the pigtailed girl, and she never would.

"What the hell. We'll always have Peru," he said, under his breath, as Sam walked away from him. "And El Paso. We'll always have that."

Then he ran after her, and put the flowers into Sam's hands. He hurried away, so she could not give them back.

Then he walked up the hill back to his car, and he took Highway 90 south to Chicago. He drove at or slightly under the speed limit.

It was the last thing he had to do.

He was in no hurry.

*   *   *

HE SPENT THE night in a Motel 6. He got up the next morning, and realized his clothes still smelled like the bottom of the lake. He put them on anyway. He figured he wouldn't need them much longer.

Shadow paid his bill. He drove to the brownstone apartment building. He found it without any difficulty. It was smaller than he remembered.

He walked up the stairs steadily, not fast, that would have meant he was eager to go to his death, and not slow, that would have meant he was afraid. Someone had cleaned the stairwell: the black garbage bags had gone. The place smelled of the chlorine-smell of bleach, no longer of rotting vegetables.

The red-painted door at the top of the stairs was wide open: the smell of old meals hung in the air. Shadow hesitated, then he pressed the doorbell.

"I come!" called a woman's voice, and, dwarf-small and dazzlingly blonde, Zorya Utrennyaya came out of the kitchen and bustled towards him, wiping her hands on her apron. She looked different, Shadow realized. She looked happy. Her cheeks were rouged red, and there was a sparkle in her old eyes. When she saw him her mouth became an O and she called out, "Shadow? You came back to us?" and she hurried toward him with her arms outstretched. He bent down and embraced her, and she kissed his cheek. "So good to see you!" she said. "Now you must go away."

Shadow stepped into the apartment. All the doors in the apartment (except, unsurprisingly, Zorya Polunochnaya's) were wide open, and all the windows he could see were open as well. A gentle breeze blew fitfully through the corridor.

"You're spring cleaning," he said to Zorya Utrennyaya.

874. Czernobog will be gone because he will *become* Bielebog.

"We have a guest coming," she told him. "Now, you must go away. First, you want coffee?"

"I came to see Czernobog," said Shadow. "It's time."

Zorya Utrennyaya shook her head violently. "No, no," she said. "You *don't* want to see him. Not a good idea."

"I know," said Shadow. "But you know, the only thing I've really learned about dealing with gods is that if you make a deal, you keep it. They get to break all the rules they want. We don't. Even if I tried to walk out of here, my feet would just bring me back."

She pushed up her bottom lip, then said, "Is true. But go today. Come back tomorrow. He will be gone then."[874]

"Who is it?" called a woman's voice, from further down the corridor. "Zorya Utrennyaya, to who are you talking? This mattress, I cannot turn on my own, you know."

Shadow walked down the corridor, and said, "Good morning, Zorya Vechernyaya. Can I help?" which made the woman in the room squeak with surprise and drop her corner of the mattress.

The bedroom was thick with dust: it covered every surface, the wood and the glass, and motes of it floated and danced through the beams of sunshine coming through the open window, disturbed by occasional breezes and the lazy flapping of the yellowed lace curtains.

He remembered this room. This was the room they had given to Wednesday, that night. Bielebog's room.

Zorya Vechernyaya eyed him uncertainly. "The mattress," she said. "It needs to be turned."

"Not a problem," said Shadow. He reached out and took the mattress, lifted it with ease and turned it over. It was an old wooden bed, and the feather mattress weighed almost as much as a man. Dust flew and swirled as the mattress went down.

"Why are you here?" asked Zorya Vechernyaya. It was not a friendly question, the way she asked it.

"I'm here," said Shadow, "because back in December a young man played a game of checkers with an old god, and he lost."

The old woman's gray hair was up on the top of her head

in a tight bun. She pursed her lips. "Come back tomorrow," said Zorya Vechernyaya.

"I can't," he said, simply.

"Is your funeral. Now, you go and sit down. Zorya Utrennyaya will bring you coffee. Czernobog will be back soon."

Shadow walked along the corridor to the sitting room. It was just as he remembered, although now the window was open. The gray cat slept on the arm of the sofa. It opened an eye as Shadow came in and then, unimpressed, it went back to sleep.

This was where he had played checkers with Czernobog; this was where he had wagered his life to get the old man to join them on Wednesday's last doomed grift. The fresh air came in through the open window, blowing the stale air away.

Zorya Utrennyaya came in with a red wooden tray. A small enameled cup of steaming black coffee sat on the tray, beside a saucer filled with small chocolate-chip cookies. She put it down on the table in front of him.

"I saw Zorya Polunochnaya again," he said. "She came to me under the world, and she gave me the moon to light my way. And she took something from me. But I don't remember what."

"She likes you," said Zorya Utrennyaya. "She dreams so much. And she guards us all. She is so brave."

"Where's Czernobog?"

"He says the spring-cleaning makes him uncomfortable. He goes out to buy newspaper, sit in the park. Buy cigarettes. Perhaps he will not come back today. You do not have to wait. Why don't you go? Come back tomorrow."

"I'll wait," said Shadow. This was no *geas*,[875] forcing him to wait, he knew that. This was *him*. It was one last thing that needed to happen, and if it was *the* last thing that happened, well, he was going there of his own volition. After this there would be no more obligations, no more mysteries, no more ghosts.

He sipped the hot coffee, as black and as sweet as he remembered.

He heard a deep male voice in the corridor, and he sat

875. In Irish folklore, an obligation or inhibition placed on a person, by magical means—similar in many respects to a curse. Conflicting *geasa* can lead to disaster: For example, in Irish myth, Cuchulain is subject to a *geas* that requires him to abstain from eating dog meat. He is also under a *geas* that he must eat any food offered to him by a woman. The story tells that when a hag offers him dog meat, he is caught on the horns of the dilemma, and events lead to his death.

In the First Edition, the word is "magic."

up straighter. He was pleased to see that his hand was not trembling. The door opened.

"Shadow?"

"Hi," said Shadow. He stayed sitting down.

Czernobog walked into the room. He was carrying a folded copy of the *Chicago Sun-Times,* which he put down on the coffee table. He stared at Shadow, then he put his hand out, tentatively. The two men shook hands.

"I came," said Shadow. "Our deal. You came through with your part of it. This is my part."

Czernobog nodded. His brow creased. The sunlight glinted on his gray hair and mustache, making them appear almost golden. "Is . . ." He frowned. "Is not . . ." He broke off. "Maybe you should go. Is not a good time."

"Take as long as you need," said Shadow. "I'm ready."

Czernobog sighed. "You are a very stupid boy. You know that?"

"I guess."

"You are a stupid boy. And on the mountaintop, you did a very good thing."

"I did what I had to do."

"Perhaps."

Czernobog walked to the old wooden sideboard, and, bending down, pulled an attaché case from underneath it. He flipped the catches on the case. Each one sprang back with a satisfying thump. He opened the case. He took a hammer out, and hefted it, experimentally. The hammer looked like a scaled-down sledgehammer; its wooden haft was stained.

Then he stood up. He said, "I owe you much. More than you know. Because of you, things are changing. This is spring time. The true spring."

"I know what I did," said Shadow. "I didn't have a lot of choice."

Czernobog nodded. There was a look in his eyes that Shadow did not remember seeing before. "Did I ever tell you about my brother?"

"Bielebog?" Shadow walked to the center of the ash-stained carpet. He went down on his knees. "You said you hadn't seen him in a long time."

"Yes," said the old man, raising the hammer. "It has been a long winter, boy. A very long winter. But the winter is ending, now." And he shook his head, slowly, as if he were remembering something. And he said, "Close your eyes."

Shadow closed his eyes and raised his head, and he waited.

The head of the sledgehammer was cold, icy cold, and it touched his forehead as gently as a kiss.

"*Pock!* There," said Czernobog. "Is done." There was a smile on his face that Shadow had never seen before, an easy, comfortable smile, like sunshine on a summer's day. The old man walked over to the case, and he put the hammer away, and closed the bag, and pushed it back under the sideboard.

"Czernobog?" asked Shadow. Then, "*Are* you Czernobog?"

"Yes. For today," said the old man. "By tomorrow, it will all be Bielebog. But today, is still Czernobog."

"Then why? Why didn't you kill me when you could?"

The old man took out an unfiltered cigarette from a pack in his pocket. He took a large box of matches from the mantelpiece and lit the cigarette with a match. He seemed deep in thought. "Because," said the old man, after some time, "there is blood. But there is also gratitude. And it has been a long, long winter."

Shadow got to his feet. There were dusty patches on the knees of his jeans, where he had knelt, and he brushed the dust away.

"Thanks," he said.

"You're welcome," said the old man. "Next time you want to play checkers, you know where to find me. *This* time, I play white."[876]

"Thanks. Maybe I will," said Shadow. "But not for a while." He looked into the old man's twinkling eyes, and he wondered if they had always been that cornflower shade of blue. They shook hands, and neither of them said goodbye.

Shadow kissed Zorya Utrennyaya on the cheek on his way out, and he kissed Zorya Vechernyaya on the back of her hand, and he took the stairs out of that place two at a time.

876. White is of course characteristic of Bielobog.

POSTSCRIPT

EYKJAVÍK IN ICELAND is a strange city, even for those who have seen many strange cities. It is a volcanic city—the heat for the city comes from deep underground.

There are tourists, but not as many of them as you might expect, not even in early July. The sun was shining, as it had shone for weeks now: it ceased shining for an hour or so in the small hours. There would be a dusky dawn of sorts between two and three in the morning, and then the day would begin once more.

The big tourist had walked most of Reykjavík that morning, listening to people talk in a language that had changed little in a thousand years. The natives here could read the ancient sagas as easily as they could read a newspaper. There was a sense of continuity on this island that scared him, and that he found desperately reassuring. He was very tired: the unending daylight had made sleep almost impossible, and he had sat in his hotel room through the whole long nightless night alternately reading a guidebook and *Bleak House,* a novel he had bought in an airport in the last few weeks, but which airport he could no longer remember. Sometimes, he had stared out of the window.

Finally the clock as well as the sun proclaimed it morning.

He bought a bar of chocolate at one of the many candy stores, walked the sidewalk, occasionally finding himself reminded of the volcanic nature of Iceland: he would turn a corner and notice, for a moment, a sulphurous quality to the air. It put him in mind not of Hades but of rotten eggs.

Many of the women he passed were very beautiful: slender and pale. The kind of women that Wednesday had liked. Shadow wondered what could have attracted Wednesday to Shadow's mother, who had been beautiful but had been neither of those things.

Shadow smiled at the pretty women, because they made him feel pleasantly male, and he smiled at the other women too, because he was having a good time.

He was not sure when he became aware that he was being observed. Somewhere on his walk through Reykjavík he became certain that someone was watching him. He would turn, from time to time, trying to get a glimpse of who it was, and he would stare into store windows and out at the reflected street behind him, but he saw no one out of the ordinary, no one who seemed to be observing him.

He went into a small restaurant, where he ate smoked puffin and cloudberries and arctic char and boiled potatoes, and he drank Coca-Cola, which tasted sweeter, more sugary than he remembered it tasting back in the States.

The waiter brought his bill—the meal was more expensive than Shadow had expected, but that seemed to be true of meals in every place on Shadow's wandering.[877] As the waiter put the bill down on the table, he said, "Excuse me. You are American?"

"Yes."

"Then, happy Fourth of July," said the waiter. He looked pleased with himself.

Shadow had not realized that it was the Fourth. Independence Day. Yes. He liked the idea of independence. He left the money and a tip on the table, and walked outside. There was a cool breeze coming in off the Atlantic, and he buttoned up his coat.

He sat down on a grassy bank and looked at the city that surrounded him, and thought, one day he would have to go home. And one day he would have to make a home to go back to. He wondered whether home was a thing that hap-

877. This sentence does not appear in the First Edition.

878. This sentence does not appear in the First Edition.

879. "How is it going? Do you remember me?"

880. The Aesir, the race of the Norse gods to which Odin belongs.

pened to a place after a while, or if it was something that you found in the end, if you simply walked and waited and willed it long enough.

He pulled out his book.[878]

An old man came striding across the hillside toward him: he wore a dark gray cloak, ragged at the bottom, as if he had done a lot of traveling, and he wore a broad-brimmed blue hat, with a seagull feather tucked into the band, at a jaunty angle. He looked like an aging hippie, thought Shadow. Or a long-retired gunfighter. The old man was ridiculously tall.

The man squatted beside Shadow on the hillside. He nodded, curtly, to Shadow. He had a piratical black eye patch over one eye, and a jutting white chin-beard. Shadow wondered if the man was going to hit him up for a cigarette.

"*Hvernig gengur? Manst Þú eftir mér?*" said the old man.[879]

"I'm sorry," said Shadow. "I don't speak Icelandic." Then he said, awkwardly, the phrase he had learned from his phrase book in the daylight of the small hours of that morning: "*Ég tala bara ensku.* I speak only English. "American."

The old man nodded slowly. He said, "My people went from here to America a long time ago. They went there, and then they returned to Iceland. They said it was a good place for men, but a bad place for gods. And without their gods they felt too . . . alone." His English was fluent, but the pauses and the beats of the sentence were strange. Shadow looked at him: close-up, the man seemed older than Shadow had imagined possible. His skin was lined with tiny wrinkles and cracks, like the cracks in granite.

The old man said, "I do know you, boy."

"You do?"

"You and I, we have walked the same path. I also hung on the tree for nine days, a sacrifice of myself to myself. I am the lord of the Aes.[880] I am the god of the gallows."

"You are Odin," said Shadow.

The man nodded thoughtfully, as if weighing up the name. "They call me many things, but, yes, I am Odin, Bor's son," he said.

"I saw you die," said Shadow. "I stood vigil for your body.

You tried to destroy so much, for power. You would have sacrificed so much for yourself. You did that."

"I did not do that."

"Wednesday did. He was you."

"He was me, yes. But I am not him." The man scratched the side of his nose. His gull-feather bobbed.

"Will you go back?" asked the Lord of the Gallows. "To America?"

"Nothing to go back for," said Shadow, and as he said it he knew it was a lie.

"Things wait for you there," said the old man. "But they will wait until you return."

A white butterfly flew crookedly past them. Shadow said nothing. He had had enough of gods and their ways to last him several lifetimes. He would take the bus to the airport, he decided, and change his ticket. Get a plane to some- where he had never been. He would keep moving.

"Hey," said Shadow. "I have something for you." His hand dipped into his pocket, and palmed the object he needed. "Hold your hand out," he said.

Odin looked at him strangely and seriously. Then he shrugged, and extended his right hand, palm down. Shadow reached over and turned it so the palm was upward.

He opened his own hands, showed them, one after the other, to be completely empty. Then he pushed the glass eye into the leathery palm of the old man's hand and left it there.

"How did you do that?"

"Magic," said Shadow, without smiling.

The old man grinned and laughed and clapped his hands together. He looked at the eye, holding it between finger and thumb, and nodded, as if he knew exactly what it was, and then he slipped it into a leather bag that hung by his waist. "*Takk kærlega*.[881] I shall take care of this."

"You're welcome," said Shadow. He stood up, brushed the grass from his jeans. He closed the book, put it back into the side-pocket of his backpack.[882]

"Again," said the Lord of Asgard, with an imperious mo- tion of his head, his voice deep and commanding. "More. Do again."

881. "Thanks a lot."

882. This sentence does not appear in the First Edition.

"You people," said Shadow. "You're never satisfied. Okay. This is one I learned from a guy who's dead now."

He reached into nowhere, and took a gold coin from the air. It was a normal sort of gold coin. It couldn't bring back the dead or heal the sick, but it was a gold coin sure enough. "And that's all there is," he said, displaying it between finger and thumb. "That's all she wrote."[883]

He tossed the coin into the air with a flick of his thumb. It spun golden at the top of its arc, in the sunlight, and it glittered and glinted and hung there in the mid-summer sky as if it was never going to come down. Maybe it never would. Shadow didn't wait to see. He walked away and he kept on walking.

883. In a journal, Gaiman made a note to himself: "I need the Icelandic for 'goodbye Baldur, my son,'" which likely would have appeared here. Another note to himself was "Can I get the eighteenth charm into the final scene?" (See note 491, above, for an explanation of the 18th charm.)

ACKNOWLEDGMENTS TO THE
TENTH ANNIVERSARY EDITION

IT'S BEEN A long book, and a long journey, and I owe many people a great deal.

Mrs. Hawley lent me her Florida house to write in, and all I had to do in return was scare away the vultures. She lent me her Irish house to finish it in and cautioned me not to scare away the ghosts. My thanks to her and Mr. Hawley for all their kindness and generosity. Jonathan and Jane lent me their house and hammock to write in, and all I had to do was fish the occasional peculiar Floridian beastie out of the lizard pool. I'm very grateful to them all.

Dan Johnson, MD, gave me medical information whenever I needed it, pointed out stray and unintentional anglicisms (everybody else did this as well), answered the oddest questions, and, on one July day, even flew me around northern Wisconsin in a tiny plane. In addition to keeping my life going by proxy while I wrote this book, my assistant, the fabulous Lorraine Garland, became very blasé about finding out the population of small American towns for me; I'm still not sure quite how she did it. (She's part of a band called the Flash Girls: buy their new record, *Play Each Morning, Wild Queen,* and make her happy.) Terry Pratchett helped unlock a knotty plot point for me on the train to Gothenburg. Eric Edelman answered my diplomatic questions. Anna Sunshine Ison unearthed a bunch of stuff for me on the West Coast Japanese internment camps, which will have to wait for another book to be written for it never quite fitted into this one. I stole the best line of dialogue in the epilogue from Gene Wolfe, to whom, my thanks. Sergeant Kathy Ertz graciously answered even my weirdest police procedural questions and Deputy Sheriff Marshall Multhauf took me on a drive-along. Pete Clark submitted to some ridiculously personal questioning with grace and good humor. Dale Robertson was the book's consulting hydrologist. I appreciated Dr. Jim Miller's comments about people, language and fish, as I did the linguistic help of Margret Rodas. Jamy Ian Swiss made sure that the coin magic was magical. Any mistakes in the book are mine, not theirs.

Many good people read the manuscript and offered valuable suggestions, corrections, encouragement, and information. I am especially grateful to Colin Greenland and Susanna Clarke, John Clute and Samuel R. Delany. I'd also like to thank Owl Goingback (who really does have the world's coolest name), Iselin Røsjø Evensen, Peter Straub, Jonathan Carroll, Kelli Bickman, Dianna Graf, Lenny Henry, Pete Atkins, Chris Ewen, Teller, Kelly Link, Barb Gilly, Will Shetterly, Connie Zastoupil, Rantz Hoseley, Diana Schutz, Steve Brust, Kelly Sue DeConnick, Roz Kaveney, Ian McDowell, Karen Berger, Wendy Japhet, Terje Nordberg, Gwenda Bond, Therese Littleton, Lou Aronica, Hy Bender, Mark Askwith, Alan Moore (who also graciously lent me "Litvinoff's Book"), and the original Joe Sanders. Thanks also to Rebecca Wilson; and particular thanks to Stacy Weiss, for her insight. After she read the first draft, Diana Wynne Jones warned me what kind of book this was, and the perils I risked writing it, and she's been right on every count so far.

I wish Professor Frank McConnell were still with us. I think he would have enjoyed this one.

Once I'd written the first draft I realized that a number of other people had tackled these themes before ever I got to them: in particular my favorite unfashionable author, James Branch Cabell, the late Roger Zelazny, and, of course, the inimitable Harlan Ellison, whose collection *Deathbird Stories* burned itself onto the back of my head when I was still of an age where a book could change me forever.

I can never quite see the point of noting down for posterity the music you listened to while writing a book, and there was an awful lot of music listened to while I was writing this. Still, without Greg Brown's *Dream Café* and the Magnetic Fields' *69 Love Songs* it would have been a different book, so thanks to Greg and to Stephin. And I feel it my duty to tell you that you can experience the music of the House on the Rock on tape or CD, including that of the Mikado machine and of the World's Largest Carousel. It's unlike, although certainly not better than, anything else you've heard. Write to: The House on the Rock, Spring Green, WI 53588 USA, or call 1-608-935-3639.

My agents—Merrilee Heifetz at Writers House, Jon Levin and Erin Culley La Chapelle at CAA—were invaluable as sounding boards and pillars of wisdom.

Many people, who were waiting for things I had promised them just as soon as I finished writing this book, were astonishingly patient. I'd like to thank the good folk at Warner Bros. pictures (particularly Kevin McCormick and Lorenzo di Bonaventura), at Village Roadshow, at Sunbow, and at Miramax; and Shelly Bond, who put up with a lot.

The two people without whom: Jennifer Hershey at HarperCollins in the U.S. and Doug Young at Hodder Headline in the UK. I'm lucky to have good editors, and these are two of the best editors I've known. Not to mention two of the most uncomplaining, patient, and, as the deadlines whirled past us like dry leaves in a gust of wind, positively stoic.

Bill Massey came in at the end, at Headline, and lent the book his editorial eagle eye. Kelly Notaras helped shepherd it through production with grace and polish.

Lastly, I want to thank my family, Mary, Mike, Holly, and Maddy, who were the most patient of all, who loved me, and who, for long periods during the writing of this book, put up with my going away both to write and to find America—which turned out, when I eventually found it, to have been in America all along.

NEIL GAIMAN
near Kinsale, County Cork
15 January 2001

ACKNOWLEDGMENTS TO THE
ANNOTATED EDITION

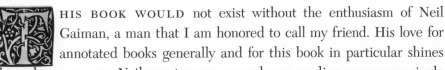

THIS BOOK WOULD not exist without the enthusiasm of Neil Gaiman, a man that I am honored to call my friend. His love for annotated books generally and for this book in particular shines through every page. Neil spent many, many hours reading over every single note, talking me through his journals and manuscripts, expanding the information presented, and suggesting additional notes. He also kindly lodged me at his lovely home so that I could study the materials in depth. His assistant Mary Edgeberg went out of her way to feed me, make me comfortable, and guide me through the baskets-full of papers. Special thanks also to Gigi Stevens of Fremantle North America and Nancy Schaaf of The House on the Rock, who were immensely helpful with images. Finally, much gratitude to our editor Jennifer Brehl, who worked tirelessly to get the project approved and then, with her ace team including Nate Lanman, Andrea Molitor, Jessica Rozler, Fritz Metsch, Aryana Hendrawan, Pamela Barricklow, Elizabeth Blaise, Tavia Kowalchuk, Heidi Richter, and Liate Stehlik, made such a beautiful volume.

I couldn't immerse myself in these projects without the support of my agent Don Maass, my attorney Jonathan Kirsch, and my publicity guru Megan Beatie; great writing pals like Laurie R. King and Cornelia Funke; my forgiving law partners; my embracing family; and of course *the* woman, advisor, proofreader, wisest critic, and closest friend, my wife, Sharon. I pray that the Gods—all of them—shed blessings upon them!

LESLIE S. KLINGER
Malibu, September 2019

APPENDIX A

’d been looking forward to writing the meeting of Shadow and Jesus for most of the book: I couldn't write about America without mentioning Jesus, after all. He's part of the warp and the weft of the country.

And then I wrote their first scene together in chapter fifteen, and it didn't work for me; I felt like I was alluding to something that I couldn't simply mention in passing and then move on from. It was too big.

So I took it out again.

I nearly put it back in, assembling this author's preferred text. Actually, I did put it back in. And then I took it out again, and put it here. You can read it. I'm just not sure that it's necessarily part of American Gods.

Consider it an apocryphal scene, perhaps.

One day, Shadow will come back to America.

There are some extremely interesting conversations awaiting him . . .

❖   ❖   ❖

PEOPLE WERE WALKING around beside him, in his mind or out of it.[884] Some of the people he seemed to recognize, others were strangers.

"And what's a stranger but a friend you haven't met yet?" said someone to him, passing him a drink.

He took the drink, walked with the person down a light brown corridor. They were in a Spanish-style building, and they moved from adobe corridor to

884. The scene is in the Manuscript, and it occurs while Shadow is carrying out Odin's vigil on the Tree.

open courtyard to corridor once more, while the sun beat down on the water gardens and the fountains.

"It might be an enemy you've not met yet too," said Shadow.

"Bleak, Shadow, very bleak," said the man. Shadow sipped his drink. It was a brackish red wine.

"It's been a bleak few months," said Shadow. "It's been a bleak few years."

The man was slender, tanned, of medium height, and he looked up at Shadow with a gentle, empathetic smile. "How's the vigil going, Shadow?"

"The tree?" Shadow had forgotten that he was hanging from the silver tree. He wondered what else he had forgotten. "It hurts."

"Suffering is sometimes cleansing," said the man. His clothes were casual, but expensive. "It can purify."

"It can also fuck you up," said Shadow.

The man led Shadow into a vast office. There was no desk in there, though. "Have you thought about what it means to be a god?" asked the man. He had a beard and a baseball cap. "It means you give up your mortal existence to become a meme: something that lives forever in people's minds, like the tune of a nursery rhyme. It means that everyone gets to re-create you in their own minds. You barely have your own identity any more. Instead, you're a thousand aspects of what people need you to be. And everyone wants something different from you. Nothing is fixed, nothing is stable."

Shadow sat in a comfortable leather chair, by the window. The man sat on the enormous sofa. "Great place you've got here," said Shadow.

"Thanks. Be honest now, how's the wine?"

Shadow hesitated. "Kind of sour, I'm afraid."

"Sorry. That's the trouble with wine. Okay wine I can do easily, but *good* wine, let alone *great* wine . . . well, you've got weather, soil acidity, rainfall, even which side of a hill the grapes are grown on. Don't get me started on vintages . . ."

"It's fine, really," said Shadow, and he swallowed the rest of the wine in one long gulp. He could feel it burning in his empty stomach, feel the bubbles of drunkenness rising at the back of his head.

"And then this whole deal of new gods, old gods," said his friend. "You ask me, I welcome new gods. Bring them on. The god of the guns. The god of bombs. All the gods of ignorance and intolerance, of self-righteousness, idiocy and blame. All the stuff they try and land me with. Take a lot of the weight off my shoulders." He sighed.

"But you're so successful," said Shadow. "Look at this place." He gestured, indicating the paintings on the walls, the hardwood floor, the fountain in the courtyard below them.

His friend nodded. "It has a cost," he said. "Like I said. You have to be all things to all people. Pretty soon, you're spread so thin you're hardly there at all. It's not good."

He reached out one callused hand—the fingers were etched with old chisel scars[885]—and squeezed Shadow's hand. "I know, I know. I should count my blessings. And one of those blessings is getting time just to meet you like this, and to talk. It's great that you were able to make it," he said. "Really great. Don't be a stranger now."

"No. I'll just be a friend you've not met yet," said Shadow.

"Funny guy," said the man with the beard.

"Ratatosk, ratatosk," chattered the squirrel in Shadow's ear. He could taste the bitter wine still, in his mouth and the back of his throat, and it was almost dark.

885. Jesus was of course a carpenter by trade.

APPENDIX B

OVERALL STORY[886]

1. Meet Shadow—he gets out of prison—meets Wednesday
2. Wednesday offers him job—he flees—but accepts. Fight with leprechaun.
3. Goes to wife's funeral—throws in coin.
4. Wife back from the dead.
5. They leave town Wednesday is expecting a *lot* of people at the House on the Rock . . . only Czernobog, Anansi are there . . . and Easter?

---

6. Odin been going up and down the land making sure the gods are okay, pulling strings, getting team work, doing all he can . . . he's hurt that more of them aren't there—
7. Still, he and Shadow have things to do—and he has things to do too.
8. Low-key working for both sides—need to meet him soon.
9. To Florida—retired circus people? Computers, etc. seem aware of Shadow
10. Seeing into everywhere . . .
11. The kids in the ice story . . . —wife

---

12. He tells someone his life story. Or narrator tells it.
13. Set piece in location. —wife

886. From the journals of Neil Gaiman, written ca. Spring 2000.

14. Wednesday's death—
15. Shadow's vigil and ordeal
16. Making love to Easter—strange, beautiful—fertility incarnate
17. Wife vs. Easter—Life vs. Death

When Odin dies things get very bad. Lots of things think Shadow has the secret and they will worse-than-kill him to get it

SPOOKS—CIA FBI ETC. keeping tabs on Wednesday

Idea—tie in things and people from other books names from Wall, Mr. Alice, something from Neverwhere

QUESTIONS

A. Is what happens to Shadow going to change America? . . . Does Shadow go on trial for America?
B. How do we resolve the Shadow/Laura relationship?
C. How do you have a war going on while no-one notices?

———

What is the arc of this? If it were a TV series for example what would the arc be?

Idea—make Czernobog become Bielebog

Go back—why is it worth it to you?

Carousel Room: only about ten people—or more—are there—disappointed— ambush—people blame Wednesday for attack—get to the Carousel

SHADOW IS INTERROGATED by spooks

Moonlight . . . stars

—bed made up from them on the sofa . . . sleep

Wakes up:—the night? Or he can't sleep . . . standing in the kitchen

—woman moves, for a moment he thinks it's Laura—but no, it's Zorya

Midnight—sister Midnight . . .

They talk:

He tells her about Laura—

She says yes . . .

She is pale as moonlight and stars

—talks about Czernobog having the right to bash in his brains

. . . keep the giant in the stars a prisoner

Okay—next to go are:

1. Wrap the House on the Rock
    —Meet Easter.
    —end of House on the Rock—attack by spook team?

———————

Specific objectives?
plot coupons
Or simply rounds people up for war

———————

Need Czernobog, Nancy and Odin and Easter and Shadow.
—Do I send them . . . somewhere?
Or does Shadow do one journey with each of them?

OKAY: SHAPE

1. The gods are attacked in the Carousel Room
2. Wednesday makes his speech
3. The round-up—spook attack. Shadow is caught—most of the others escape.
4. Interrogation (?)—Low Key tells him they're going to ruin him
5. Wife frees him—kills the guards.

END OF BOOK ONE
BOOK SHAPE
BOOK 2.

A. Predict Shadow die 3 times. Mad Sweeney? Ibis? At Mad Sweeney's wake.
    BAST?
        Odin, pickup—needs to take—go round—things happen
        MEANWHILE
        Out on the Lake.
        Learns—Sam's sister—kids—death on the ice
        —Funny old tall-tale man
        (Freezing) walk in winter—deer jump out of its skin—)
        —BACK & FORTH—
        A picture builds up
        If Odin marshalling his forces—meanwhile Mr. World & Co. are
            closing in . . .

Then . . .
Everything comes together—

OKAY—BOOK THREE
"THE TREE AND THE STORM"
SO, THINGS TO INSERT ON THE WAY

1. Cats . . .
2. Shadow
   Hallucination on tree—the spear in his side—Uppsala sacrifice . . . the
      death of the Vikas guy on the tree by Sutter Starkadder
   The tree—three deaths of Shadow. This is the first . . .
   (Lake is the second).
   Shadow—whose shadow is he? His own? Or Odin's?
3. Don't forget—underworld and all-seeing . . .
   . . . spear throw across opposing army

From a journal:

Writing is, in every sense, a confidence trick: the trick of it is confidence. We write like the cartoon animals run across chasms and canyons, only falling when our confidence parts us. Of course, a novel like this is like building a path across the canyon—or from mountain-top to mountain-top.

APPENDIX C
GOD ATLAS

Name	Description	First Appearance
Shadow Moon, aka Baldur	Demi-god, son of Odin and mortal woman (Norse mythology)	13
Low Key Lyesmith, aka Loki	Norse trickster god, occasional partner of Odin, destined to fight against the gods at Ragnarok	14
Iceman, aka Ull	Norse god of winter, skiing, and archery	16
Sam Fetisher	Undifferentiated totem god	20
Buffalo man	The land	28
Mr. Wednesday, aka Odin, aka Grimnir	The All-Father of Norse mythology	31
Bilquis, aka the Queen of Sheba	A Biblical figure, but not a god	39
Mad Sweeney, aka Suibhne Geiltm	A mad Irish king, perhaps a leprechaun	47
Technical Boy	One of the "New Gods"	66
Coatlicue	An Aztec god	73
Leucotios	A war god of many names	73
Hubur	River of the underworld, goddess of the sea	73
Hershef	An Egyptian, later Greek fertility god	73
Three-headed goddess	Possibly Hecate, possibly Qudshu-Astarte-Anat	73
Bird-headed god	Possibly Horus or Thoth (Egyptian)	74
Tyr	Son of Odin (Norse mythology)	86
Thor	Norse god of thunder and lightning	86
Freya	Odin's ex-wife	87
Zorya Vechernyaya	The Evening Star (Slavic mythology)	90

Name	Description	First Appearance
Zorya Utrennyaya	The Morning Star (Slavic mythology)	92
Czernobog	The Black God (Slavic mythology)—perhaps an aspect of Bielobog	92
Bielobog	The Light God (Slavic mythology)—perhaps an aspect of Czernobog	92
Zorya Polunochnya	The Midnight Star (perhaps invented, perhaps Slavic mythology)	104
Piskies	Pixies or fairies of the West Country	110
Spriggans	Malicious fairies	110
Black dogs of the moor	Creatures found in the British Isles	110
Seal-women	Selkies, mer-creatures	110
Knockers	Mine-spirits	113
Blue-caps	Mine-spirits	113
Bucca	Storm spirits	113
Apple-tree men	Creatures of English folklore	114
Raw-Head and Bloody-Bones	An English boogeyman	116
Norns	Urd, Verdandi, and Skuld, the Norse goddesses of destiny	137
Mr. Nancy	Anansi, a West African trickster-god	142
Lion-God	Son of Ra and Bast, an Egyptian god of protection	156
Banshees	Irish death spirit	156
Kubera	Hindu god of wealth	156
Frau Holle	Teutonic god of weather	156
Ashtaroth	Ishtar or Astarte, Near Eastern goddess of love	156
Credit-card	New god	157
Freeway	New god	157
Internet	New god	157
Telephone	New god	157
Radio	New god	157
Hospital	New god	157
Television	New god	157
Plastic	New god	157
Beeper	New god	157
Neon	New god	157
Mama-ji	Kali, a Hindu goddess, destroyer of evil forces	157
Nameless god	Mythology unknown; a god of money and fortune. His existence is always quickly forgotten by those mortals who meet him.	160
Alviss	King of the dwarves	161
Anubis	Egyptian god of mummification and funerals	196

Name	Description	First Appearance
Bast	Egyptian cat-goddess of love	196
Thoth	Egyptian god of knowledge	197
Ifrit	Arabian spirit	206
Set	Egyptian god of evil	219
Horus	Egyptian falcon-headed sun-god	219
Ammet	Egyptian soul-eater, part hippopotamus, part crocodile, part lion	224
Mithras	Babylonian sun-god	224
Jesus	The Christian son of God	224
Bran	Celtic deity	243
Brigid	Early Irish goddess	243
Finn	Leader of the Fenians	243
Oisín	Ireland's greatest poet	243
Conan the Bald	Another member of the Fenians	243
Hinzelmann	A kobold, a spirit of Cologne	268
Thunderbirds	Creatures of Native American legend, bringers of lightning and thunder, which lay "eagle stones"	309
Easter	Eastre, a Germanic goddess of spring and rebirth	326
Elegba	Messenger of Mawu and other West African gods	346
Mawu	A West African deity	347
Damballa-Weda	Patron of rain, a Haitian god probably brought from West Africa	350
Ogu	West African god of warriors	350
Shango	West African god of thunder and lightning	350
Zaka	West African god of the harvest	350
Whiskey Jack	Wisagatcak, the creator-god of the Cree People	369
Apple Johnny	John Chapman, also known as "Johnny Appleseed"	370
Paul Bunyan	A fictional creature of lumberjack mythology	371
Kitsune	Japanese fox spirits	384
Nunyunnini	A primitive god	433
Gwydion	A Celtic god of civilization and knowledge	448
Media	A new god	452
Ratatosk	A squirrel	478
Ganesha	The Hindu elephant-headed god of wisdom	479
Vila	Slavic spirits	507
Rusalka	Slavic spirits	507
Wampyr	A vampire	507
Apelike being with orange fur	A yeti?	507
Chinese men with swords	Unknown	507

Name	Description	First Appearance
Mexican men with dark hair	Unknown	507
Golem with rabbi	The Golem of Prague, with Rabbi Loew	507
Satyr	Described as a famous comedian	507
Rakshasas	Hindu demons	508
Legba	Trickster-god of Haiti	508
Baron Samedi	Haitian lord of death	508
Gédé	Spirits of other Haitian gods	509
Cancerous thing	Unknown	514
Young boys the size of apple trees	Warrior-twins of the Pueblo Indians	519
Macha	One of the Morrigan, Irish war-goddesses	519
Wolf-man	Perhaps a werewolf	528
Isten	Chief of the Hungarian gods	528
Man in elegant suit	Perhaps the forgotten god?	528
Chinese man with necklace of skulls	Perhaps Sha Wujing, a Buddhist monk of legend	529
Coyote	Native American trickster-god	531
Porcupine Woman	A Native American spirit	531
Minotaur	A bull-headed creature	536
Dactyl	A race of beings	537
Ghoul	An undead	537
Bear with flowers in fur	Unidentified	537
Blue-skinned man with flaming bow	Unidentified	537
Man in golden armor with sword of eyes	Unidentified	537
Antinous	Lover of the Emperor Hadrian	537
Cyclops	A one-eyed creature	537
Squat and swarthy men	Aztecs?	537
Railroad god	A new god	555
Car gods	New gods	555
Airplane gods	New gods	555

BIBLIOGRAPHY[887]

Allen, Richard Hinckley. *Star Names and Their Meanings.* New York and London: G. E. Stechert (1899).

Bane, Theresa. *Encyclopedia of Spirits and Ghosts in World Mythology.* Jefferson, North Carolina, and London: McFarland Publishing Co., Inc. (2016).

Barth, Jack, Doug Kirby, Ken Smith, and Mike Wilkins. *Roadside America.* New York: Fireside/Simon and Schuster (1986). (NG)

Battle, Kemp. *Great American Folklore.* New York: Doubleday (1986). (NG)

Bealer, Tracy L., Rachel Luria, and Wayne Yuen, eds. *Neil Gaiman and Philosophy: Gods Gone Wild.* Chicago and LaSalle, Illinois: Open Court Publishing Co. (2012).

Bedi, Anjula. *Gods and Goddesses of India.* Eeshwar (1998). (NG)

Bierhorst, John. *The Mythology of North America.* Oxford: Oxford University Press (2002). (earlier edition, NG)

Blomqvist, Rut, "The Road of Our Senses: Search for Personal Meaning and the Limitations of Myth in Neil Gaiman's *American Gods,*" *Mythlore,* 4th ser. 30.3 (2012).

Bobo, J. B. *Modern Coin Magic.* Minneapolis: Carl W. Jones (1952).

Botkin, B. A., ed. *A Treasury of American Folklore.* New York: Crown Publishers (1944).

Briggs, Katharine. *The Fairies in Tradition and Literature* (Routledge Classics). London and Routledge (2002).

_____. *An Encyclopedia of Fairies: Hobgoblins; Brownies; Bogies; & Other Supernatural Creatures.* New York: Pantheon Books (1978).

_____. *Folktales of England.* Chicago: University of Chicago Press (1998).

Brunvand, Jan Harald, ed. *American Folklore: An Encyclopedia.* New York: Garland Publishing (1996). (NG)

887. The following bibliography combines the "astonishingly incomplete bibliography" published by Gaiman on his blog (http://www.neilgaiman.com/works/Books/American+Gods/in/183/) and the books consulted by this editor in compiled *Annotated American Gods.* Books on Gaiman's list are indicated by (NG).

Burdge, Anthony S., Jessica Burke, and Kristine Larsen, eds. *The Mythological Dimensions of Neil Gaiman*. Crawfordville, Florida: Kitsune Books (2012).

Campbell, Hayley. *The Art of Neil Gaiman*. New York: Harper Design (2014).

Campbell, Joseph. *The Hero with a Thousand Faces*. Novato, California: New World Library (2008).

_____. *The Masks of God; Vol. 1: Primitive Mythology*. New York: Penguin (1991).

_____. *The Masks of God; Vol. 2: Oriental Mythology*. New York: Penguin (1991).

_____. *The Masks of God; Vol. 3: Occidental Mythology*. New York: Penguin (1991).

Camus, Cyril, "Fantasy and Landscape: Mountain as Myth in Neil Gaiman's Stories," in *Mountains Figured and Disfigured in the English-speaking World*. Edited by Françoise Besson. Newcastle: Cambridge Scholars (2010), 379–91.

Carroll, Siobhan, "Imagined Nation: Place and National Identity in Neil Gaiman's 'American Gods,'" *Extrapolation* 53.3 (2009), 307–26.

Clune, Anne, "Mythologising Sweeney," *Irish University Review*, 26, No. 1 (1996), 48–60.

Coleman, Loren, and Jerome Clark. *Cryptozoology A to Z*. New York: Fireside/Simon and Schuster (1999). (NG)

Cotterell, Arthur. *A Dictionary of World Mythology*. New York: G. P. Putnam's Sons (1980). (NG)

Courlander, Harold. *A Treasury of African Folklore*. New York: Crown Publishing Group (1988). (NG)

_____. *A Treasury of Afro-American Folklore*. New York: Da Capo Press (2002). (earlier edition, NG)

Crossley-Holland, Kevin. *The Norse Myths*. New York: Pantheon Fairytale and Folklore Library (1981). (NG)

Davidson, Basil. *The African Slave Trade*. New York: Back Bay Books (1980). (NG)

Davidson, Gustav. *Dictionary of Angels: Including the Fallen Angels*. Free Press (1994).

Deloria, Jr., Vine. *God Is Red: A Native View of Religion*. Golden, CO: Fulcrum Publishing (1994). (NG)

Devol, George. *Forty Years a Gambler on the Mississippi*. Cincinnati: Devol & Haynes (1887).

Dorson, Richard M. *American Folklore*. Chicago: University of Chicago Press (1959). (NG)

_____. *American Folklore and the Historian*. Chicago: University of Chicago Press (1971). (NG)

_____. *Bloodstoppers and Bearwalkers: Folk Traditions of the Upper Peninsula*. Cambridge, Massachusetts, and London: Harvard University Press (1952). (NG)

_____. *Buying the Wind: Regional Folklore in the United States*. Chicago: University of Chicago Press (1972). (NG)

Erbsen, Wayne. *Outlaw Ballads, Legends & Lore*. Asheville, North Carolina: Native Ground Music (2008).

Erdoes, Richard. *American Indian Myths and Legends*. New York: Pantheon Fairytale and Folklore Library (1984). (NG)

Evans, Timothy H., "Folklore, Intertextuality, and the Folkloresque in the Works of Neil Gaiman," in *The Folkloresque: Reframing Folklore in a Popular Culture World*. Edited by Michael Dylan Foster and Jeffrey A. Tolbert. Logan: Utah State University Press (2016), 64–80.

Farmer, J. S., and W. E. Henley. *Historical Dictionary of Slang.* Ware, Herefordshire: Wordsworth Editions Ltd. (1987). (Originally published as *Slang and Its Analogues*, 1890).

Frazier, Ian. *On the Rez.* New York: Farrar Straus and Giroux (2000). (NG)

Gaiman, Neil. *Anansi Boys.* New York: William Morrow (2005).

_____. "Black Dog," *Trigger Warnings.* New York: William Morrow (2015), pp. 265–308.

_____. *Norse Mythology.* New York: W. W. Norton & Co. (2017).

_____. "Monarch of the Glen," *Fragile Things.* New York: William Morrow (2006), pp. 301–55. First appeared in *Legends II* (2004).

_____. "Wall: A Prologue," *A Fall of Stardust.* Edited by Charles Vess. Privately printed (1999).

Gates, Henry Louis, Jr., and Maria Tatar, eds. *The Annotated African American Folktales.* New York: Liveright Publishing Corp. (2017).

Geary, Rick. *The Saga of the Bloody Benders.* New York: NBM Publishing (2008).

Gill, Sam D., and Irene F. Sullivan. *Dictionary of Native American Mythology.* New York and Oxford: Oxford University Press (1992).

Gonzalez-Crussi, Frank. *The Day of the Dead and Other Mortal Reflections.* San Diego: Harcourt (1993). (NG)

Graves, Robert. *The Greek Myths.* London: Folio Society (2002).

_____. *The White Goddess.* Amended and enlarged edition. New York: Farrar Straus Giroux (1966).

Graves, Robert, and Raphael Patai. *Hebrew Myths: The Book of Genesis.* McGraw Hill Paperbacks (1966).

Green, Roger Lancelyn. *Myths of the Norsemen: Retold from the Old Norse Poems and Tales.* Harmondsworth, Eng.: Puffin Books (1994). (earlier edition, NG)

Hill, Mark, "Neil Gaiman's *American Gods*: An Outsider's Critique of American Culture" (2005). University of New Orleans Theses and Dissertations. 282. https://scholarworks.uno.edu/td/282

Horwitz, Tony. *Confederates in the Attic: Despatches from the Unfinished Civil War.* New York: Vintage Books (1999). (NG)

Hultkrantz, Ake. *The Religions of the American Indians.* Translated by Monica Setterwall. Berkeley: University of California Press (1967, 1979). (NG)

Jeunesse, Jake La, "Locating Lakeside, Wisconsin: Neil Gaiman's American Gods and the American Small-town Utopia," *Mythlore: A Journal of J.R.R. Tolkien, C.S. Lewis, Charles Williams, and Mythopoeic Literature*: Vol. 35: No. 1 (2016), Article 4. Available at: https://dc.swosu.edu/mythlore/vol35/iss1/4.

Jones, Terry L., Alice A. Storey, Elizabeth A. Matisoo-Smith, and José Miguel Ramírez-Aliaga, eds. *Polynesians in America: Pre-Columbian Contacts with the New World.* Lanham, Pennsylvania: AltaMira Press (2011).

Jordan, Michael. *Encyclopedia of Gods.* New York: Facts on File (1993). (NG)

Karras, Ruth Mazo. *Sexuality in Medieval Europe: Doing unto Others.* London and New York: Routledge (2017).

Kempt, Robert, compiler. *The American Joe Miller: A Collection of Yankee Wit and Humour.* London: Adams and Francis (1865).

Klapcsik, Sándor, "Neil Gaiman's Irony, Liminal Fantasies, and Fairy Tale Adaptations," *Hungarian Journal of English and American Studies* (HJEAS) 14.2 (2008), 317–34.

Leach, Maria, ed. *Dictionary of Folklore, Mythology and Legend.* New York: Funk & Wagnalls (1949).

Leeming, David, and Jake Page. *Myths, Legends and Folktales of America: An Anthology.* Oxford: Oxford University Press (1999). (NG)

Lesy, Michael. *The Forbidden Zone.* New York: Farrar Straus and Giroux (1987). (NG)

Loewen, James W. *Lies Across America: What Our Historic Sites Get Wrong.* New York: Touchstone/Simon and Schuster (1999). (NG)

_____. *Lies My Teacher Told Me: Everything Your American History Textbook Got Wrong.* New York: The New Press (1995). (NG)

Mellon, James, ed. *Bullwhip Days: The Slaves Remember—An Oral History.* New York: Grove Press (1988). (NG)

Metraux, Alfred. *Voodoo in Haiti.* New York: Schocken Books (1959). (NG)

Philip, Neil. *Penguin Book of English Folk Tales.* New York: Penguin Books Ltd. (1992).

Prescott, Tara, ed. *Neil Gaiman in the 21st Century: Essays on the Novels, Children's Stories, Online Writings, Comics and Other Works.* Jefferson, North Carolina, and London: McFarland & Company, Inc. (2015).

Prescott, Tara, and Aaron Drucker, eds. *Feminism in the Worlds of Neil Gaiman.* Jefferson, North Carolina, and London: McFarland & Company, Inc. (2012).

Proulx, Jean-Pierre. *Basque Whaling in Labrador in the 16th Century.* Silver Spring, Maryland: Accents Publications Service (1993).

Radford, E., and M. A. *Encylcopedia of Superstitions.* New York: Greenwood Press (1969).

Roberts, Alison. *Hathor Rising: The Power of the Goddess in Ancient Egypt.* Rochester, VT: Inner Traditions/Bear & Company (1997). (NG)

Robinson, Herbert Spencer, and Knox Wilson. *Myths and Legends of All Nations.* New York: Bantam Books (1961). (earlier edition, NG)

Rodman, Gilbert B. *Elvis After Elvis: The Posthumous Career of a Living Legend.* New York: Routledge (1996).

Rowsome, Frank, and Carl Rose. *The Verse by the Side of the Road: The Story of the Burma-Shave Signs and Jingles.* Brattleboro, Vermont: Stephen Greene Press (1965).

The Sagas of the Icelanders. Various translators. New York: Viking (2000). (NG)

Saxon, Dreyer and Robert Tallant. *Gumbo Ya-Ya: A Collection of Louisiana Folktales.* Gretna, LA: Pelican Publishing Company (1945). (NG)

Schweitzer, Darrell. *The Neil Gaiman Reader.* Cabinjohn, Maryland: Wildside Press (2006).

Simek, Rudolf. *Dictionary of Northern Myth.* Translated by Angela Hall. Martlesham, Suffolk: Boydell and Brewer Ltd. (1992). (NG)

Simpson, Jacqueline, and Steve Roud. *A Dictionary of English Folklore* (Oxford Paperback Reference). Oxford: Oxford University Press (2001).

Slabbert, Mathilda, "Inventions and Transformations: An Exploration of Mythification and Remythification in Four Contemporary Novels." University of South Africa, 2006. 15 Feb 2012. http://uir.unisa.ac.za/bitstream/handle/10500/2267/thesis.pdf.

_____ and Leonie Viljoen, "Sustaining the Imaginative Life: Mythology and Fantasy in Neil Gaiman's *American Gods,*" *Literator: Journal of Literary Criticism, Comparative Linguistics and Literary Studies* 27, No. 3 (Dec. 2006): 135–155. https://literator.org.za/index.php/literator/article/view/204/177.

Snurlusson, Snorri. *Prose Edda*. Translated by Rasmus B. Anderson. Chicago: Scott, Foresman and Company (1901). https://www.gutenberg.org/files/18947/18947-h/18947-h.htm.

Spence, Lewis. *Encyclopedia of the Occult*. London: Bracken Books (1994).

Swanstrom, Elizabeth, "Mr. Wednesday's Game of Chance," *Neil Gaiman and Philosophy: Gods Gone Wild*. Edited by Tracy L. Bealer, Rachel Luria, and Wayne Yuen. Chicago and LaSalle, Illinois: Open Court Publishing Co. (2012), pp. 3–19.

Swierczynski, Duane. *The complete idiot's guide to frauds, scams, and cons*. Indianapolis: Alpha Books (2002).

Sykes, Egerton. *Who's Who in Non-Classical Mythology*. Revised by Alan Kendall. Oxford: Oxford University Press (1993). (NG)

Takaki, Ronald. *Stranger from a Distant Shore: A History of Asian Americans*. New York: Back Bay Books (1998). (NG)

Tallant, Robert. *Voodoo in New Orleans*. Gretna, LA: Pelican Publishing Company (1946). (NG)

Taylor, Nelson. *American Bizarro*. New York: St. Martin's Griffin (2000). (NG)

Thomas, Hugh. *The Slave Trade: The Story of the African Slave Trade 1440–1870*. New York: Touchstone/Simon and Schuster (1997). (NG)

Turner, Patricia, and Charles Russell Coulter. *Dictionary of Ancient Deities*. Oxford: Oxford University Press (2001).

Vries, Merel J. de. "Mythological Melting Pot: A Study of the Use of Simulacra and Myth in Neil Gaiman's *American Gods*." (2014) Utrecht University Faculty of Humanities Theses (Bachelor thesis) https://dspace.library.uu.nl/handle/1874/295658.

Wagner, Hank, Christopher Golden, and Stephen R. Bissette. *Prince of Stories: The Many Worlds of Neil Gaiman*. New York: St. Martin's Press (2008).

Wearring, Andrew, "Changing, Out-of-Work, Dead, and Reborn Gods in the Fiction of Neil Gaiman," *Literature & Aesthetics* 19, No. 2 (December 2009), 236–46.

Westwood, Jennifer, and Jacqueline Simpson. *The Lore of the Land: A Guide to England's Legends; From Spring-Heeled Jack to the Witches of Warboys*. New York: Penguin Books Ltd. (2006).

Wilkins, Mike, Ken Smith, and Doug Kirby. *The New Roadside America*. New York: Fireside/Simon and Schuster (1992). (NG)

ABOUT THE AUTHOR

NEIL GAIMAN is the #1 *New York Times* bestselling author of more than twenty books, including *Norse Mythology*, *Neverwhere*, and *The Graveyard Book*. Among his numerous literary awards are the Newbery and Carnegie medals, and the Hugo, Nebula, World Fantasy, and Will Eisner awards. Originally from England, he now lives in America.

ABOUT THE EDITOR

LESLIE S. KLINGER is the *New York Times* bestselling editor of numerous other works and anthologies of mystery, fantasy, and horror. He is the two-time winner of the Edgar Award for Best Critical/Biographical and has been nominated for many other literary awards, including the Bram Stoker, Agatha, Macavity, World Fantasy, and Silver Falchion awards. He lives in Malibu with his wife, dog, and cat.